MORE STORIES TO REMEMBER

VOLUME I

MORE STORIES TO REMEMBER

SELECTED BY

Thomas B. Costain *and* John Beecroft

ILLUSTRATIONS BY FREDERICK E. BANBERY

Doubleday & Company, Inc., Garden City, New York

BOOKS BY THOMAS B. COSTAIN

The Three Edwards: *The Pageant of England*

Below the Salt

Stories to Remember [*with John Beecroft*]

The Tontine

The Mississippi Bubble

The White and the Gold: *The French Regime in Canada*

The Silver Chalice

The Magnificent Century: *The Pageant of England*

Son of a Hundred Kings

The Conquerors: *The Pageant of England*

High Towers

The Moneyman

The Black Rose

Ride with Me

Joshua: A Biography [*with Rogers MacVeagh*]

For My Great Folly

BOOKS BY JOHN BEECROFT

Plain and Fancy Cats

The Gentleman from Indianapolis

Stories to Remember [*with Thomas B. Costain*]

A Treasury of Great Mysteries [*with Howard Haycraft*]

The Best Stories of W. Somerset Maugham

Kipling: A *Selection of His Stories and Poems*

Mr. Maugham Himself

The Modern Reader

INTRODUCTION

The first reason for issuing *More Stories to Remember* is that the original two volumes had an astonishingly successful acceptance, which is always a pleasant thing for all concerned, for the publishers, for the authors whose work has been used, and for the hard-working editors who selected and assembled the contents. A still more valid reason is that a most gratifying number of people who read *Stories to Remember* have expressed a desire for more.

In the course of a review of the first volumes, one critic declared, "What we have here is extended proof that entertaining writing can also be distinguished writing." This phrase summed up clearly and succinctly the purpose with which we had begun. We quote it here because our objective remains the same: to offer only stories which can be read with pleasure and which at the same time bear the hallmark of masterly technique. It follows that the names which make up our new contents page are most exceptional names. We are proud to present such a list, particularly as we may honestly assure our readers that they will encounter these masters of storytelling in the most beguiling of moods.

Sometimes there is little to be told about the genesis of a great story or novel. It is written with much labor and absorption in the seclusion of the author's study and later is published with the customary rites; and, if it deserves a long life and a sustained popularity, it achieves both without owing anything to attendant circumstances. However, in the essential scrutiny of pedigrees, which is part of the task of compiling anthologies, it has developed that circumstances most interesting in themselves surrounded the launching of some of our selections. In telling of these briefly we wish to make it clear that we are not expressing thereby any preference for them over the equally great stories offered without such reference. In fact, most of the others stand up ruggedly against the horizon of time on the foundations of long acceptance. Some few, moreover, are in a sense "discoveries," and in not speaking of them in advance we are allowing our readers to experience the same pleasure we felt in first reading them.

It is seldom that an author takes the whole public completely and spontaneously by storm with his first work. This happened in 1836 when a very young man named Charles Dickens, an exuberantly gifted young man who had been acting as a shorthand reporter in the House of Commons and publishing little sketches about life in London, suddenly threw all England into delighted laughter with the first numbers of *The Posthumous Papers of the Pickwick Club*. It was not until Number V appeared that a definite success was turned into a positive explosion of popularity with the appearance in the story of one Samuel Weller. Sam Weller was new. He was fairly bursting with the racy and slightly vulgar humor of the lower middle class (a departure indeed for strait-laced Victorian England) and he has remained one of the deservedly best loved and remembered characters in English literature.

To the unfortunates who may never have read *Pickwick*, no better service could be rendered than to offer them the chapter from the book in which the busy "boots" of a London inn, the inimitable Samuel, makes his bow.

In his introduction to Robert Louis Stevenson's *New Arabian Nights*, Edmund Gosse said: "Never was a book composed in a truer spirit of glory and joy. But the impact of the world was rude upon it." The sober readers of the *London*, where "The Young Man with the Cream Tarts" appeared, were wooden of face as they turned down their supposedly sophisticated thumbs. Stevenson's publishers rejected it. In deep chagrin R.L.S. wrote to Gosse with a suggestion as to what might be done with publishers in general. "In choirs and places where they sing," he said, "here shall a publisher be shot out of a gun." Four years later, however, it was demonstrated that the stolid subscribers of the *London* and the timorous publishers had been wrong about these rather fantastic stories. The *New Arabian Nights* was brought out in two thin volumes and, as Gosse puts it, "the success of the work was then instant and decisive."

In 1935 Grace George appeared in a most successful play on Broadway called *Kind Lady* which succeeded in the first few minutes in projecting out over the footlights, until every spectator tingled with it, a sense of horror and dismay. The play was based on a short story, "The Silver Mask," by the novelist Hugh Walpole, published in England two years earlier. Theatergoers who saw the play (it was revived in the forties) will not be disappointed in the story, which is included in this selection, for the same sense of almost unbearable suspense can be absorbed from the printed page. For those who did not see *Kind Lady*, as well as for those who did, the story will be a thrilling experience.

"Clerical Error" by James Gould Cozzens is an interesting study in technique. Here is an idea, which would have served for a full-bodied story, even a novelette, which nevertheless is told clearly and adequately in a few hundred words. It is pure supposition on the part of the editors that Mr. Cozzens was striving to find how short a story might be made without diminishing the impact of an original idea. This little gem, at any rate, might well be studied as an example of perfect compression.

The same might be said for the other very short tales which have been included, particularly "Old Man at the Bridge" by Ernest Hemingway and "Anty Bligh" by the English poet laureate, John Masefield.

"The Murder of Roger Ackroyd" by Agatha Christie is, in every sense a classic in the mystery field, based on the most original idea evolved by an author famous for the ingenuity of her plots. "Roger Ackroyd" should be kept to the fore. For those who have not read it, the story will always come as a great event in a reading lifetime. To those who have read it and so are familiar with its remarkable denouement, it is still a story to remember and savor again and again.

In the nineteen-twenties, when Brian Donn-Byrne was writing his charming tales of Destiny Bay, the political feeling in Ireland was running bitter and high. As he was dealing with a locality in Ulster and with Ulster people, he came in for some manifestations of hostility. As we are including the pleasantest of the Destiny Bay annals, "The Tale of My Aunt Jenepher's Wooing," in which some of this feeling may perhaps be detected, it will be interesting to quote two sentences from the introduction he wrote for the book. "If any phrases in this book of Destiny Bay show a predilection toward one or the other way of politics, the author prays that they may not be taken as serious. He has never yet seen a government that brought heavier apples to the trees or heavier salmon in the rivers or a more purple heather, and for this reason politics mean nothing to him."

It could not have been said better; and the editors take this opportunity to express their deep regret that Donn-Byrne did not live long enough to write more about this corner of Ireland where the salmon were always heavy and the heather always very purple and the people high-hearted and with a lilt on their tongues.

"The Rollicking God" was Nunnally Johnson's first magazine story. One of the editors, who was with *The Saturday Evening Post* at the time, can remember the delight felt in the offices of that publication over the appearance of a writer who held the promise of being a very great humorist indeed. He continued to turn out stories for a few years and then was taken up on a high mountain in Hollywood and shown such financial prospects that he turned away from his typewriter. For the last thirty years or so he has been a most successful producer of motion pictures. On re-reading "The Rollicking God" (it seems certain he drew on Babe Ruth and even perchance, in a very small way, on the late Heywood Broun) one realizes how sad it has been (but not for Nunnally Johnson himself) that he was lured away and that ever since the main outlets for his abundant humor have been as letter-writer and raconteur.

The writer of these notes had the privilege many years ago of riding through Virginia with John P. Marquand and Erdmann Brandt, who was the former's literary agent at the time. We made the trip in an open roadster and it was a particularly hot week in late August. None of us felt any discomfort, however. Mr. Marquand was planning to write a series of connected short stories about the great cavalry leader of the Confederacy, "Jeb" Stuart, and the object of the trip was to visit the battlegrounds where that colorful, banjo-twanging leader had appeared. The talk was all about the Civil War and the business of writing, two of the most engrossing of subjects, and not even the glare of the sun on that open car could diminish our interest.

The stories, five of them, were duly written and published. The best of them carried the title of "Jack Still" and we are happy to include it in this collection.

And now, last but decidedly not least: Arthur Machen in "The Bowmen." Mr. Machen, who had won for himself a wide critical as well as popular recognition as the author of rather macabre stories, was sent to the front as a newspaper correspondent at the start of World War I. He was with the British Expeditionary Force—"that contemptible little army," as the Kaiser called it—when the task of holding the left of the French line, to prevent encirclement, fell to the relatively few and lightly equipped British regiments. Feeling the heavy pounding of the German artillery and watching the seemingly endless waves of gray-uniformed Teutonic soldiers hurling themselves against the fast-diminishing battalions in khaki, Machen conceived an idea for a story. He wrote it down in frantic haste and sent it on to his newspaper. The editor thought so well of it that he published it on the front page the day it arrived. The readers of the paper, fearing a catastrophic defeat and ready to clutch eagerly at any straw, not only thought well of it but more than half believed it. Out of this grew a strange rumor which passed from mouth to mouth and which the people believed for some time at least, the Legend of the Angels of Mons.

"The Bowmen" is offered here because of the uplifting effect it had at a moment of dire apprehension, and also because it is as fine an example of etching with words on the clear copper of illusion as can be found in any language.

THOMAS B. COSTAIN

CONTENTS

VOLUME II

LOST HORIZON

JAMES HILTON

PROLOGUE

CIGARS had burned low, and we were beginning to sample the disillusionment that usually afflicts old school friends who have met again as men and found themselves with less in common than they had believed they had. Rutherford wrote novels; Wyland was one of the Embassy secretaries; he had just given us dinner at Tempelhof—not very cheerfully, I fancied, but with the equanimity which a diplomat must always keep on tap for such occasions. It seemed likely that nothing but the fact of being three celibate Englishmen in a foreign capital could have brought us together, and I had already reached the conclusion that the slight touch of priggishness which I remembered in Wyland Tertius had not diminished with years and an M.V.O. Rutherford I liked more; he had ripened well out of the skinny, precocious infant whom I had once alternately bullied and patronized. The probability that he was making much more money and having a more interesting life than either of us, gave Wyland and me our one mutual emotion—a touch of envy.

The evening, however, was far from dull. We had a good view of the big Luft-Hansa machines as they arrived at the aerodrome from all parts of Central Europe, and towards dusk, when arc-flares were lighted, the scene took on a rich, theatrical brilliance. One of the planes was English, and its pilot, in full flying-kit, strolled past our table and saluted Wyland, who did not at first recognize him. When he did so there were introductions all around, and the stranger was invited to join us. He was a pleasant, jolly youth named Sanders. Wyland made some apologetic remark about the difficulty of identifying people when they were all dressed up in Sibleys and flying-helmets; at which Sanders laughed and answered: "Oh, rather, I know that well enough. Don't forget I was at Baskul." Wyland laughed also, but less spontaneously, and the conversation then took other directions.

Sanders made an attractive addition to our small company, and we all drank a great deal of beer together. About ten o'clock Wyland left us for a moment to speak to some one at a table near by, and Rutherford, into the sudden hiatus of talk, remarked: "Oh, by the way, you mentioned Baskul just now. I know the place slightly. What was it you were referring to that happened there?"

Sanders smiled rather shyly. "Oh, just a bit of excitement we had once when I was in the Service." But he was a youth who could not long refrain from being confidential. "Fact is, an Afghan or an Afridi or somebody ran off with one of our buses, and there was the very devil to pay afterwards, as you can imagine. Most impudent thing I ever heard of. The blighter waylaid the pilot, knocked him out, pinched his kit, and climbed into the cockpit without a soul spotting him. Gave the mechanics the proper signals, too, and was up and away in fine style. The trouble was, he never came back."

Rutherford looked interested. "When did this happen?"

"Oh—must have been about a year ago. May, 'thirty-one. We were evacuating civilians from Baskul to Peshawar owing to the revolution—perhaps you remember the business. The place was in a bit of an upset, or I don't suppose the thing could have happened. Still, it *did* happen—and it goes some way to show that clothes make the man, doesn't it?"

Rutherford was still interested. "I should have thought you'd have had more than one fellow in charge of a plane on an occasion like that?"

"We did, on all the ordinary troop-carriers, but this machine was a special one, built for some maharajah originally—quite a stunt kind of outfit. The Indian Survey people had been using it for high-altitude flights in Kashmir."

"And you say it never reached Peshawar?"

"Never reached there, and never came down anywhere else, so far as we could discover. That was the queer part about it. Of course, if the fellow was a tribesman he might have made for the hills, thinking to hold the passengers for ransom. I suppose they all got killed, somehow. There are heaps of places on the frontier where you might crash and not be heard of afterwards."

"Yes, I know the sort of country. How many passengers were there?"

"Four, I think. Three men and some woman missionary."

"Was one of the men, by any chance, named Conway?"

Sanders looked surprised. "Why, yes, as a matter of fact. 'Glory' Conway —did you know him?"

"He and I were at the same school," said Rutherford a little self-consciously, for it was true enough, yet a remark which he was aware did not suit him.

"He was a jolly fine chap, by all accounts of what he did at Baskul," went on Sanders.

Rutherford nodded. "Yes, undoubtedly . . . but how extraordinary . . . extraordinary . . ." He appeared to collect himself after a spell of mind-wandering. Then he said: "It was never in the papers, or I think I should have read about it. How was that?"

Sanders looked suddenly rather uncomfortable, and even, I imagined, was on the point of blushing. "To tell you the truth," he replied, "I seem to have let out more than I should have. Or perhaps it doesn't matter now—it must be stale news in every mess, let alone in the bazaars. It was hushed up, you see—I mean, about the way the thing happened. Wouldn't have sounded well. The Government people merely gave out that one of their machines was missing, and mentioned the names. Sort of thing that didn't attract an awful lot of attention among outsiders."

At this point Wyland rejoined us, and Sanders turned to him half apologetically. "I say, Wyland, these chaps have been talking about 'Glory' Conway. I'm afraid I spilled the Baskul yarn—I hope you don't think it matters?"

Wyland was severely silent for a moment. It was plain that he was reconciling the claims of compatriot courtesy and official rectitude. "I can't help feeling," he said at length, "that it's a pity to make a mere anecdote of it. I always thought you air fellows were put on your honor not to tell tales out of school." Having thus snubbed the youth, he turned, rather more graciously, to Rutherford. "Of course, it's all right in your case, but I'm sure you realize that it's sometimes necessary for events up on the Frontier to be shrouded in a little mystery."

"On the other hand," replied Rutherford dryly, "one has a curious itch to know the truth."

"It was never concealed from any one who had any real reason for wanting to know it. I was at Peshawar at the time, and I can assure you of that. Did you know Conway well—since schooldays, I mean?"

"Just a little at Oxford, and a few chance meetings since. Did *you* come across him much?"

"At Angora, when I was stationed there, we met once or twice."

"Did you like him?"

"I thought he was clever, but rather slack."

Rutherford smiled. "He was certainly clever. He had a most exciting university career—until war broke out. Rowing Blue and a leading light at the Union and prizeman for this, that, and the other—also I reckon him the best amateur pianist I ever heard. Amazingly many-sided fellow, the kind, one feels, that Jowett would have tipped for a future premier. Yet, in point of fact, one never heard much about him after those Oxford days. Of course the War cut into his career. He was very young and I gather he went through most of it."

"He was blown up or something," responded Wyland, "but nothing very serious. Didn't do at all badly, got a D.S.O. in France. Then I believe he went back to Oxford for a spell as a sort of don. I know he went East in 'twenty-one. His Oriental languages got him the job without any of the usual preliminaries. He had several posts."

Rutherford smiled more broadly. "Then, of course, that accounts for everything. History will never disclose the amount of sheer brilliance wasted in the routine of decoding F.O. chits and handing round tea at Legation bun-fights."

"He was in the Consular Service, not the Diplomatic," said Wyland loftily. It was evident that he did not care for chaff, and he made no protest when, after a little more badinage of a similar kind, Rutherford rose to go. In any case it was getting late, and I said I would go, too. Wyland's attitude as we made our farewells was still one of official propriety suffering in silence, but Sanders was very cordial and said he hoped to meet us again sometime.

I was catching a transcontinental train at a very dismal hour of the early morning, and, as we waited for a taxi, Rutherford asked me if I would care to spend the interval at his hotel. He had a sitting-room, he said, and we could talk. I said it would suit me excellently, and he answered: "Good. We can talk about Conway, if you like, unless you're completely bored with his affairs."

I said that I wasn't, at all, though I had scarcely known him. "He left at the end of my first term, and I never met him afterwards. But he was extraordinarily kind to me on one occasion. I was a new boy and there was no earthly reason why he should have done what he did. It was only a trivial thing, but I've always remembered it."

Rutherford assented. "Yes, I liked him a good deal too, though I also saw surprisingly little of him, if you measure it in time."

And then there was a somewhat odd silence, during which it was evident that we were both thinking of some one who had mattered to us far more than might have been judged from such casual contacts. I have often found since then that others who met Conway, even quite formally and for a moment, remembered him afterwards with great vividness. He was certainly remarkable as a youth, and to me, who had known him at the hero-worshiping age, his memory is still quite romantically distinct. He was tall and extremely good looking, and not only excelled at games but walked off with every conceivable kind of school prize. A rather sentimental headmaster once referred to his exploits as "glorious," and from that arose his nickname. Perhaps only he could have survived it. He gave a Speech Day oration in Greek, I recollect, and was outstandingly first-rate in school theatricals. There was something rather Elizabethan about him—his casual versatility, his good looks, that effervescent combination of mental with physical activities. Something a bit Philip-Sidneyish. Our civilization doesn't often breed people like that nowadays. I made a remark of this kind to Rutherford, and he replied: "Yes, that's true, and we have a special word of disparagement for them—we call them dilettanti. I suppose some people must have called Conway that, people like Wyland, for instance. I don't much care for Wyland. I can't stand his type—all that primness and mountainous self-importance. And the complete head-prefectorial mind, did you notice it? Little phrases about 'putting people on their honor' and 'telling tales out of school'—as though the bally Empire were the Fifth Form at St. Dominic's! But, then, I always fall foul of these sahib diplomats."

We drove a few blocks in silence, and then he continued: "Still, I wouldn't have missed this evening. It was a peculiar experience for me, hearing Sanders tell that story about the affair at Baskul. You see, I'd heard it before, and hadn't properly believed it. It was part of a much more fantastic story, which I saw no reason to believe at all, or well, only one very slight reason, anyway. *Now* there are *two* very slight reasons. I dare say you can guess that I'm not a particularly gullible person. I've spent a good deal of my life traveling about, and I know there are queer things in the world—if you see them yourself, that is, but not so often if you hear of them second-hand. And yet . . ."

He seemed suddenly to realize that what he was saying could not mean very much to me, and broke off with a laugh. "Well, there's one thing certain —I'm not likely to take Wyland into my confidence. It would be like trying to sell an epic poem to *Tit-Bits*. I'd rather try my luck with you."

"Perhaps you flatter me," I suggested.

"Your book doesn't lead me to think so."

I had not mentioned my authorship of that rather technical work (after all, a neurologist's is not everybody's "shop"), and I was agreeably surprised that Rutherford had even heard of it. I said as much, and he answered: "Well, you see, I was interested, because amnesia was Conway's trouble at one time."

We had reached the hotel and he had to get his key at the bureau. As we went up to the fifth floor he said: "All this is mere beating about the bush. The fact is, Conway isn't dead. At least he wasn't a few months ago."

This seemed beyond comment in the narrow space and time of an elevator ascent. In the corridor a few seconds later I responded: "Are you sure of that? How do you know?"

And he answered, unlocking his door: "Because I traveled with him from Shanghai to Honolulu in a Jap liner last November." He did not speak again till we were settled in armchairs and had fixed ourselves with drinks and cigars. "You see, I was in China in the autumn on a holiday. I'm always wandering about. I hadn't seen Conway for years. We never corresponded, and I can't say he was often in my thoughts, though his was one of the few faces that have always come to me quite effortlessly if I tried to picture it. I had been visiting a friend in Hankow and was returning by the Pekin express. On the train I chanced to get into conversation with a very charming Mother Superior of some French sisters of charity. She was traveling to Chung-Kiang, where her convent was, and, because I knew a little French, she seemed to enjoy chattering to me about her work and affairs in general. As a matter of fact, I haven't much sympathy with ordinary missionary enterprise, but I'm prepared to admit, as many people are nowadays, that the Romans stand in a class by themselves, since at least they work hard and don't pose as commissioned officers in a world full of other ranks. Still, that's by the by. The point is that this lady, talking to me about the mission hospital at Chung-Kiang, mentioned a fever case that had been brought in some weeks back, a man who they thought must be a European, though he could give no account of himself and had no papers. His clothes were native, and of the poorest kind, and when taken in by the nuns he had been very ill indeed. He spoke fluent Chinese, as well as pretty good French, and my train companion assured me that before he realized the nationality of the nuns, he had also addressed them in English with a refined accent. I said I couldn't imagine such a phenomenon, and chaffed her gently about being able to detect a refined accent in a language she didn't know. We joked about these and other matters, and it ended by her inviting me to visit the mission if ever I happened to be thereabouts. This, of course, seemed then as unlikely as that I should climb Everest, and when the train reached Chung-Kiang I shook hands with genuine regret that our chance contact had come to an end. As it happened, though, I was back in Chung-Kiang within a few hours. The train broke down a mile or two further on, and with much difficulty pushed us back to the station, where we learned that a relief engine could not possibly arrive for twelve hours. That's the sort of thing that often happens on Chinese railways. So there was half a day to be lived through in Chung-Kiang—which made me decide to take the good lady at her word and call at the mission.

"I did so, and received a cordial, though naturally a somewhat astonished, welcome. I suppose one of the hardest things for a non-Catholic to realize is how easily a Catholic can combine official rigidity with non-official broad-mindedness. Is that too complicated? Anyhow, never mind, those mission people made quite delightful company. Before I'd been there an hour I found that a meal had been prepared, and a young Chinese Christian doctor sat down with me to it and kept up a conversation in a jolly mixture of French and English. Afterwards, he and the Mother Superior took me to see the hospital, of which they were very proud. I had told them I was a writer, and they were simple-minded enough to be a-flutter at the thought that I might put them all into a book. We walked past the beds while the doctor explained the cases. The place was spotlessly clean and looked to be very competently run. I had forgotten all about the mysterious patient with the refined English accent till the Mother Superior reminded me that we were just coming to him. All I could see was the back of the man's head; he was apparently asleep. It was suggested that I should address him in English, so I said 'Good afternoon,' which was the first and not very original thing I could think of. The man looked up suddenly and said 'Good afternoon' in answer. It was true; his accent was educated. But I hadn't time. to be surprised at that, for I had already recognized him, despite his beard and altogether changed appearance and the fact that we hadn't met for so long. He was Conway. I was certain he was, and yet, if I'd paused to think about it, I might well have come to the conclusion that he couldn't possibly be. Fortunately I acted on the impulse of the moment. I called out his name and my own, and though he looked at me without any definite sign of recognition, I was positive I hadn't made any mistake. There was an odd little twitching of the facial muscles that I had noticed in him before, and he had the same eyes that at Balliol we used to say were so much more of a Cambridge blue than an Oxford. But besides all that, he was a man one simply didn't make mistakes about—to see him once was to know him always. Of course the doctor and the Mother Superior were greatly excited. I told them that I knew the man, that he was English, and a friend of mine, and that if he didn't recognize me, it could only be because he had completely lost his memory. They agreed, in a rather amazed way, and we had a long consultation about the case. They weren't able to make any suggestions as to how Conway could possibly have arrived at Chung-Kiang in his condition.

"To make the story brief, I stayed there over a fortnight, hoping that somehow or other I might induce him to remember things. I didn't succeed, but he regained his physical health, and we talked a good deal. When I told him quite frankly who I was and who he was, he was docile enough not to argue about it. He was quite cheerful, even, in a vague sort of way, and seemed glad enough to have my company. To my suggestion that I should take him home, he simply said that he didn't mind. It was a little unnerving, that apparent lack of any personal desire. As soon as I could I arranged for our departure. I made a confidant of an acquaintance in the consular office at Hankow, and thus the necessary passport and so on were made out without the fuss there might otherwise have been. Indeed, it seemed to me that for Conway's sake the whole business had better be kept free from publicity and newspaper headlines, and I'm glad to say I succeeded in that. It would have been jam, of course, for the press.

"Well, we made our exit from China in quite a normal way. We sailed down the Yang-tse to Nanking, and then took train for Shanghai. There was a Jap liner leaving for 'Frisco that same night, so we made a great rush and got on board."

"You did a tremendous lot for him," I said.

Rutherford did not deny it. "I don't think I should have done quite as much for any one else," he answered. "But there was something about the fellow, and always had been—it's hard to explain, but it made one enjoy doing what one could."

"Yes," I agreed. "He had a peculiar charm, a sort of winsomeness that's pleasant to remember even now when I picture it, though, of course, I think of him still as a schoolboy in cricket flannels."

"A pity you didn't know him at Oxford. He was just brilliant—there's no other word. After the War people said he was different. I, myself, think he was. But I can't help feeling that with all his gifts he ought to have been doing bigger work. All that Britannic Majesty stuff isn't my idea of a great man's career. And Conway was—or should have been—*great*. You and I have both known him, and I don't think I'm exaggerating when I say it's an experience we shan't ever forget. And even when he and I met in the middle of China, with his mind a blank and his past a mystery, there was still that queer core of attractiveness in him."

Rutherford paused reminiscently and then continued: "As you can imagine, we renewed our old friendship on the ship. I told him as much as I knew about himself, and he listened with an attention that might almost have seemed a little absurd. He remembered everything quite clearly since his arrival at Chung-Kiang, and another point that may interest you is that he hadn't forgotten languages. He told me, for instance, that he knew he must have had something to do with India, because he could speak Hindostani.

"At Yokohama the ship filled up, and among the new passengers was Sieveking, the pianist, *en route* for a concert tour in the States. He was at our dining table and sometimes talked with Conway in German. That will show you how outwardly normal Conway was. Apart from his loss of memory, which didn't show in ordinary intercourse, there couldn't have seemed much wrong with him.

"A few nights after leaving Japan, Sieveking was prevailed upon to give a piano recital on board, and Conway and I went to hear him. He played well, of course, some Brahms and Scarlatti, and a lot of Chopin. Once or twice I glanced at Conway and judged that he was enjoying it all, which appeared very natural, in view of his own musical past. At the end of the program the show lengthened out into an informal series of encores which Sieveking bestowed, very amiably, I thought, upon a few enthusiasts grouped round the piano. Again he played mostly Chopin; he rather specializes in it, you know. At last he left the piano and moved towards the door, still followed by admirers, but evidently feeling that he had done enough for them. In the meantime a rather odd thing was beginning to happen. Conway had sat down at the keyboard and was playing some rapid, lively piece that I didn't recognize, but which drew Sieveking back in great excitement to ask what it was. Conway, after a long and rather strange silence, could only reply that he didn't know. Sieveking exclaimed that that was incredible, and grew more excited still. Conway then made what appeared to be a tremendous physical and mental effort to remember, and said at last that the thing was a Chopin study. I didn't think myself it could be, and I wasn't surprised when Sieveking denied it absolutely. Conway, however, grew suddenly quite indignant about the matter—which startled me, because up to then he had shown so little emotion about anything. 'My dear fellow,' Sieveking remonstrated, 'I know everything of Chopin's that exists, and I can assure you that he never wrote what you have just played. He might well have done so, because it's utterly in his style, but he just didn't. I challenge you to show me the score in any of the editions.' To which Conway replied at length: 'Oh, yes, I remember now, it was never printed. I only know it myself from meeting a man who used to be one of Chopin's pupils. . . . Here's another unpublished thing I learned from him.' "

Rutherford steadied me with his eyes as he went on: "I don't know if you're a musician, but even if you're not, I dare say you'll be able to imagine something of Sieveking's excitement, and mine, too, as Conway continued to play. To me, of course, it was a sudden and quite mystifying glimpse into his past, the first clew of any kind that had escaped. Sieveking was naturally engrossed in the musical problem, which was perplexing enough, as you'll realize when I remind you that Chopin died in 1849.

"The whole incident was so unfathomable, in a sense, that perhaps I should add that there were at least a dozen witnesses of it, including a Californian university professor of some repute. Of course, it was easy to say that Conway's explanation was chronologically impossible, or almost so; but there was still the music itself to be explained. If it wasn't what Conway said it was, then what *was* it? Sieveking assured me that if those two pieces were published, they would be in every virtuoso's repertoire within six months. Even if this is an exaggeration, it shows Sieveking's opinion of them. After much argument at the time, we weren't able to settle anything, for Conway stuck to his story, and as he was beginning to look fatigued, I was anxious to get him away from the crowd and off to bed. The last episode was about making some phonograph records. Sieveking said he would fix up all arrangements as soon as he reached America, and Conway gave his promise to play before the microphone. I often feel it was a great pity, from every point of view, that he wasn't able to keep his word."

Rutherford glanced at his watch and impressed on me that I should have plenty of time to catch my train, since his story was practically finished. "Because that night—the night after the recital—he got back his memory. We had both gone to bed and I was lying awake, when he came into my cabin and told me. His face had stiffened into what I can only describe as an expression of overwhelming sadness—a sort of universal sadness, if you know what I mean—something remote or impersonal, a *Wehmut* or *Weltschmerz*, or whatever the Germans call it. He said he could call to mind everything, that it had begun to come back to him during Sieveking's playing, though only in patches at first. He sat for a long while on the edge of my bed, and I let him take his own time and make his own method of telling me. I said that I was glad his memory had returned, but sorry if he already wished that it hadn't. He looked up then and paid me what I shall always regard as a marvelously high compliment. 'Thank God, Rutherford,' he said, 'you are capable of imagining things.' After a while I dressed and persuaded him to do the same, and we walked up and down the boat deck. It was a calm night, starry and very warm, and the sea had a pale, sticky look, like condensed milk. Except for the vibration of the engines, we might have been pacing an esplanade. I let Conway go on in his own way, without questions at first. Somewhere about dawn he began to talk consecutively, and it was break-fast-time and hot sunshine when he had finished. When I say 'finished' I don't mean that there was nothing more to tell me after that first confession. He filled in a good many important gaps during the next twenty-four hours. He was very unhappy, and couldn't have slept, so we talked almost constantly. About the middle of the following night the ship was due to reach Honolulu. We had drinks in my cabin the evening before; he left me about ten o'clock, and I never saw him again."

"You don't mean—" I had a picture in mind of a very calm, deliberate suicide I once saw on the mailboat from Holyhead to Kingstown.

Rutherford laughed. "Oh, Lord, no—he wasn't that sort. He just gave me the slip. It was easy enough to get ashore, but he must have found it hard to avoid being traced when I set people searching for him, as of course I did. Afterwards I learned that he'd managed to join the crew of a banana-boat going south to Fiji."

"How did you get to know that?"

"Quite straightforwardly. He wrote to me, three months later, from Bangkok, enclosing a draft to pay the expenses I'd been put to on his account,

He thanked me and said he was very fit. He also said he was about to set out on a long journey—to the northwest. That was all."

"Where did he mean?"

"Yes, it's pretty vague, isn't it? A good many places must lie to the northwest of Bangkok. Even Berlin does, for that matter."

Rutherford paused and filled up my glass and his own. It had been a queer story—or else he had made it seem so; I hardly knew which. The music part of it, though puzzling, did not interest me so much as the mystery of Conway's arrival at that Chinese mission hospital; and I made this comment. Rutherford answered that in point of fact they were both parts of the same problem. "Well, how *did* he get to Chung-Kiang?" I asked. "I suppose he told you all about it that night on the ship?"

"He told me something about it, and it would be absurd of me, after letting you know so much, to be secretive about the rest. Only, to begin with, it's a longish sort of tale, and there wouldn't be time even to outline it before you'd have to be off for your train. And besides, as it happens, there's a more convenient way. I'm a little diffident about revealing the tricks of my dishonorable calling, but the truth is, Conway's story, as I pondered over it afterwards, appealed to me enormously. I had begun by making simple notes after our various conversations on the ship, so that I shouldn't forget details; later, as certain aspects of the thing began to grip me, I had the urge to do more, to fashion the written and recollected fragments into a single narrative. By that I don't mean that I invented or altered anything. There was quite enough material in what he told me: he was a fluent talker and had a natural gift for communicating an atmosphere. Also, I suppose, I felt I was beginning to understand the man himself." He went to an attaché-case and took out a bundle of typed manuscript. "Well, here it is, anyhow, and you can make what you like of it."

"By which I suppose you mean that I'm not expected to believe it?"

"Oh, hardly so definite a warning as that. But mind, if you *do* believe, it will be for Tertullian's famous reason—you remember?—*quia impossibile est.* Not a bad argument, maybe. Let me know what you think, at all events."

I took the manuscript away with me and read most of it on the Ostend express. I intended returning it with a long letter when I reached England, but there were delays, and before I could post it I got a short note from Rutherford to say that he was off on his wanderings again and would have no settled address for some months. He was going to Kashmir, he wrote, and thence "east." I was not surprised.

CHAPTER ONE

During that third week of May the situation in Baskul had become much worse and, on the 20th, Air Force machines arrived by arrangement from Peshawar to evacuate the white residents. These numbered about eighty, and most were safely transported across the mountains in troop-carriers. A few miscellaneous aircraft were also employed, among them being a cabin machine lent by the Maharajah of Chandapore. In this, about 10 A.M., four passengers embarked: Miss Roberta Brinklow, of the Eastern Mission; Henry D. Barnard, an American; Hugh Conway, H.M. Consul; and Captain Charles Mallinson, H.M. Vice-Consul.

These names are as they appeared later in Indian and British newspapers.

Conway was thirty-seven. He had been at Baskul for two years, in a job which now, in the light of events, could be regarded as a persistent backing of the wrong horse. A stage of his life was finished; in a few weeks' time, or perhaps after a few months' leave in England, he would be sent somewhere else. Tokio or Teheran, Manila or Muscat; people in his profession never knew what was coming. He had been ten years in the Consular Service, long enough to assess his own chances as shrewdly as he was apt to do those of others. He knew that the plums were not for him; but it was genuinely consoling, and not merely sour grapes, to reflect that he had no taste for plums. He preferred the less formal and more picturesque jobs that were on offer, and as these were often not good ones, it had doubtless seemed to others that he was playing his cards rather badly. Actually, he felt he had played them rather well; he had had a varied and moderately enjoyable decade.

He was tall, deeply bronzed, with brown, short cropped hair and slate-blue eyes. He was inclined to look severe and brooding until he laughed, and then (but it happened not so very often) he looked boyish. There was a slight nervous twitch near the left eye which was usually noticeable when he worked too hard or drank too much, and as he had been packing and destroying documents throughout the whole of the day and night preceding the evacuation, the twitch was very conspicuous when he climbed into the aeroplane. He was tired out, and overwhelmingly glad that he had contrived to be sent in the maharajah's luxurious air liner instead of in one of the crowded troop-carriers. He spread himself indulgently in the basket seat as the plane soared aloft. He was the sort of man who, being used to major hardships, expects minor comforts by way of compensation. Cheerfully he might endure the rigors of the road to Samarkand, but from London to Paris he would spend his last tenner on the Golden Arrow.

It was after the flight had lasted more than an hour that Mallinson said he thought the pilot wasn't keeping a straight course. Mallinson sat immediately in front. He was a youngster in his middle twenties, pink-cheeked, intelligent without being intellectual, beset with public school limitations, but also with their excellences. Failure to pass an examination was the chief cause of his being sent to Baskul, where Conway had had six months of his company and had grown to like him.

But Conway did not want to make the effort that an aeroplane conversation demands. He opened his eyes drowsily and replied that whatever the course taken, the pilot presumably knew best.

Half an hour later, when weariness and the drone of the engine had lulled him nearly to sleep, Mallinson disturbed him again. "I say, Conway, I thought Fenner was piloting us?"

"Well, isn't he?"

"The chap turned his head just now and I'll swear it wasn't he."

"It's hard to tell, through that glass panel."

"I'd know Fenner's face anywhere."

"Well, then, it must be some one else. I don't see that it matters."

"But Fenner told me definitely that he was taking this machine."

"They must have changed their minds and given him one of the others."

"Well, who is this man, then?"

"My dear boy, how should I know? You don't suppose I've memorized the face of every flight-lieutenant in the Air Force, do you?"

"I know a good many of them, anyway, but I don't recognize this fellow."

"Then he must belong to the minority whom you don't know." Conway smiled and added: "When we arrive in Peshawar very soon you can make his acquaintance and ask him all about himself."

"At this rate we shan't get to Peshawar at all. The man's right off his course. And I'm not surprised, either—flying so damned high he can't see where he is."

Conway was not bothering. He was used to air travel, and took things for granted. Besides, there was nothing particular he was eager to do when he got to Peshawar, and no one particular he was eager to see; so it was a matter of complete indifference to him whether the journey took four hours or six. He was unmarried; there would be no tender greetings on arrival. He had friends, and a few of them would probably take him to the club and stand him drinks; it was a pleasant prospect, but not one to sigh for in anticipation.

Nor did he sigh retrospectively, when he viewed the equally pleasant, but not wholly satisfying vista of the past decade. Changeable, fair intervals, becoming rather unsettled; it had been his own meteorological summary during that time, as well as the world's. He thought of Baskul, Pekin, Macao, and the other places—he had moved about pretty often. Remotest of all was Oxford, where he had had a couple of years of donhood after the War, lecturing on Oriental History, breathing dust in sunny libraries, cruising down the High on a push-bicycle. The vision attracted, but did not stir him; there was a sense in which he felt that he was still a part of all that he might have been.

A familiar gastric lurch informed him that the plane was beginning to descend. He felt tempted to rag Mallinson about his fidgets, and would perhaps have done so had not the youth risen abruptly, bumping his head against the roof, and waking Barnard, the American, who had been dozing in his seat at the other side of the narrow gangway. "My God!" Mallinson cried, peering through the window. "Look down there!"

Conway looked. The view was certainly not what he had expected, if, indeed, he had expected anything. Instead of the trim, geometrically laid-out cantonments and the larger oblongs of the hangars, nothing was visible but an opaque mist veiling an immense, sun-brown desolation. The plane, though descending rapidly, was still at a height unusual for ordinary flying. Long, corrugated mountain-ridges could be picked out, perhaps a mile or so closer than the cloudier smudge of the valleys. It was typical Frontier scenery, though Conway had never viewed it before from such an altitude. It was also, which struck him as odd, nowhere that he could imagine near Peshawar. "I don't recognize this part of the world," he commented. Then, more privately, for he did not wish to alarm the others, he added into Mallinson's ear: "Looks as if you're right. The man's lost his way."

The plane was swooping down at a tremendous speed, and as it did so, the air grew hotter; the scorched earth below was like an oven with the door suddenly opened. One mountain top after another lifted itself above the horizon in craggy silhouette; now the flight was along a curving valley, the base of which was strewn with rocks and the débris of dried-up watercourses. It looked like a floor littered with nut-shells. The plane bumped and tossed in air-pockets as uncomfortably as a row-boat in a swell. All four passengers had to hold on to their seats.

"Looks like he wants to land!" shouted the American hoarsely.

"He can't!" Mallinson retorted. "He'd be simply mad if he tried to! He'll crash and then—"

But the pilot did land. A small cleared space opened by the side of a gully, and with considerable skill the machine was jolted and heaved to a standstill. What happened after that, however, was more puzzling and less reassuring. A swarm of bearded and turbanned tribesmen came forward from all directions, surrounding the machine and effectively preventing any one from getting out of it except the pilot. The latter clambered to earth and held excited colloquy with them, during which proceeding it became clear that, so far from being Fenner, he was not an Englishman at all, and possibly not even a European. Meanwhile cans of gasoline were fetched from a dump close by, and emptied into the exceptionally capacious tanks. Grins and disregarding silence met the shouts of the four imprisoned passengers, while the slightest attempt to alight provoked a menacing movement from a score of rifles. Conway, who knew a little Pushtu, harangued the tribesmen as well as he could in that language, but without effect; while the pilot's sole retort to remarks addressed to him in any language was a significant flourish of his revolver. Midday sunlight, blazing on the roof of the cabin, grilled the air inside till the occupants were almost fainting with the heat and with the exertion of their protests. They were quite powerless; it had been a condition of the evacuation that they should carry no arms.

When the tanks were at last screwed up, a gasoline can filled with tepid water was handed through one of the cabin windows. No questions were answered, though it did not appear that the men were personally hostile. After a further parley the pilot climbed back into the cockpit, a Pathan clumsily swung the propeller, and the flight was resumed. The take-off, in that confined space and with the extra gasoline load, was even more skillful than the landing. The plane rose high into the hazy vapors; then turned east, as if setting a course. It was midafternoon.

A most extraordinary and bewildering business! As the cooler air refreshed them, the passengers could hardly believe that it had really happened; it was an outrage to which none could recall any parallel, or suggest any precedent, in all the turbulent records of the Frontier. It would have been incredible, indeed, had they not been victims of it themselves. It was quite natural that high indignation should follow incredulity, and anxious speculation only when indignation had worn itself out. Mallinson then developed the theory which, in the absence of any other, they found easiest to accept. They were being kidnaped for ransom. The trick was by no means new in itself, though this particular technique must be regarded as original. It was a little more comforting to feel that they were not making entirely virgin history; after all, there had been kidnapings before, and a good many of them had ended up all right. The tribesmen kept you in some lair in the mountains till the Government paid up and you were released. You were treated quite decently, and as the money that had to be paid wasn't your own, the whole business was only unpleasant while it lasted. Afterwards, of course, the Air people sent a bombing squadron, and you were left with one good story to tell for the rest of your life. Mallinson enunciated the proposition a shade nervously; but Barnard, the American, chose to be heavily facetious. "Well, gentlemen, I dare say this is a cute idea on somebody's part, but I can't exactly see that your Air Force has covered itself with glory. You Britishers make jokes about the hold-ups in Chicago and all that, but I don't recollect any instance of a gunman running off with one of Uncle Sam's aeroplanes. And I should like to know, by the way, what this fellow did with the real pilot. Sandbagged him, I bet." He yawned. He was a large, fleshy man, with a hard-bitten face in which good-humored wrinkles were not quite offset by pessimistic pouches. Nobody in Baskul had known much about him except that he had arrived from Persia, where it was presumed he had something to do with oil.

Conway meanwhile was busying himself with a very practical task. He had collected every scrap of paper that they all had, and was composing messages in various native languages to be dropped to earth at intervals. It was a slender chance, in such sparsely populated country, but worth taking.

The fourth occupant, Miss Brinklow, sat tight-lipped and straight-backed, with few comments and no complaints. She was a small, rather leathery woman, with an air of having been compelled to attend a party at which there were goings-on that she could not wholly approve.

Conway had talked less than the two other men, for translating SOS messages into dialects was a mental exercise requiring concentration. He had, however, answered questions when asked, and had agreed, tentatively, with Mallinson's kidnaping theory. He had also agreed, to some extent, with Barnard's strictures on the Air Force. "Though one can see, of course, how it may have happened. With the place in commotion as it was, one man in flying-kit would look very much like another. No one would think of doubting the *bona fides* of any man in the proper clothes who looked as if he knew his job. And this fellow *must* have known it—the signals, and so forth.

Pretty obvious, too, that he knows how to fly . . . still, I agree with you that it's the sort of thing that some one ought to get into hot water about. And somebody will, you may be sure, though I suspect he won't deserve it."

"Well, sir," responded Barnard, "I certainly do admire the way you manage to see both sides of the question. It's the right spirit to have, no doubt, even when you're being taken for a ride."

Americans, Conway reflected, had the knack of being able to say patronizing things without being offensive. He smiled tolerantly, but did not continue the conversation. His tiredness was of a kind that no amount of possible peril could stave off. Towards late afternoon, when Barnard and Mallinson, who had been arguing, appealed to him on some point, it appeared that he had fallen asleep.

"Dead beat," Mallinson commented. "And I don't wonder at it, after these last few weeks."

"You're his friend?" queried Barnard.

"I've worked with him at the Consulate. I happen to know that he hasn't been in bed for the last four nights. As a matter of fact, we're damned lucky in having him with us in a tight corner like this. Apart from knowing the languages, he's got a sort of way with him in dealing with people. If any one can get us out of the mess, he'll do it. He's pretty cool about most things."

"Well, let him have his sleep, then," agreed Barnard.

Miss Brinklow made one of her rare remarks. "I think he *looks* like a very brave man," she said.

Conway was far less certain that he *was* a very brave man. He had closed his eyes in sheer physical fatigue, but without actually sleeping. He could hear and feel every movement of the plane, and he heard also, with mixed feelings, Mallinson's eulogy of himself. It was then that he had his doubts, recognizing a tight sensation in his stomach which was his own bodily reaction to a disquieting mental survey. He was not, as he knew well from experience, one of those persons who love danger for its own sake. There was an aspect of it which he sometimes enjoyed, an excitement, a purgative effect upon sluggish emotions, but he was far from fond of risking his life. Twelve years earlier he had grown to hate the perils of trench warfare in France, and had several times avoided death by declining to attempt valorous impossibilities. Even his D.S.O. had been won, not so much by physical courage, as by a certain hardly developed technique of endurance. And since the War, whenever there had been danger again, he had faced it with increasing lack of relish unless it promised extravagant dividends in thrills.

He still kept his eyes closed. He was touched, and a little dismayed, by what he had heard Mallinson say. It was his fate in life to have his equanimity always mistaken for pluck, whereas it was actually something much more dispassionate and much less virile. They were all in a damnably awkward situation, it seemed to him, and so far from being full of bravery about it, he felt chiefly an enormous distaste for whatever trouble might be in store. There was Miss Brinklow, for instance. He foresaw that in certain circumstances he would have to act on the supposition that because she was a woman she mattered far more than the rest of them put together, and he shrank from a situation in which such disproportionate behavior might be unavoidable.

Nevertheless, when he showed signs of wakefulness, it was to Miss Brinklow that he spoke first. He realized that she was neither young nor pretty—negative virtues, but immensely helpful ones in such difficulties as those in which they might soon find themselves. He was also rather sorry for her, because he suspected that neither Mallinson nor the American liked missionaries, especially female ones. He himself was unprejudiced, but he was afraid she would find his open mind a less familiar and therefore an even more disconcerting phenomenon. "We seem to be in a queer fix," he said, leaning forward to her ear, "but I'm glad you're taking it calmly. I don't really think anything dreadful is going to happen to us."

"I'm certain it won't if you can prevent it," she answered; which did not console him.

"You must let me know if there is anything we can do to make you more comfortable."

Barnard caught the word. "Comfortable?" he echoed raucously. "Why, of course we're comfortable. We're just enjoying the trip. Pity we haven't a pack of cards—we could play a rubber of bridge."

Conway welcomed the spirit of the remark, though he disliked bridge. "I don't suppose Miss Brinklow plays," he said, smiling.

But the missionary turned round briskly to retort: "Indeed I do, and I could never see any harm in cards at all. There's nothing against them in the Bible."

They all laughed, and seemed obliged to her for providing an excuse. At any rate, Conway thought, she wasn't hysterical.

All afternoon the plane had soared through the thin mists of the upper atmosphere, far too high to give clear sight of what lay beneath. Sometimes, at longish intervals, the veil was torn for a moment, to display the jagged outline of a peak, or the glint of some unknown stream. The direction could be determined roughly from the sun; it was still east, with occasional twists to the north; but where it had led depended on the speed of travel, which Conway could not judge with any accuracy. It seemed likely, though, that the flight must already have exhausted a good deal of the gasoline; though that again depended on uncertain factors. Conway had no technical knowledge of aircraft, but he was sure that the pilot, whoever he might be, was altogether an expert. That halt in the rock-strewn valley had demonstrated it, and also other incidents since. And Conway could not repress a feeling that was always his in the presence of any superb and indisputable competence. He was so used to being appealed to for help that mere awareness of some one who would neither ask nor need it was slightly tranquilizing, even amidst the greater perplexities of the future. But he did not expect his companions to share such a tenuous emotion. He recognized that they were likely to have far more personal reasons for anxiety than he had himself. Mallinson, for instance, was engaged to a girl in England; Barnard might be married; Miss Brinklow had her work, vocation, or however she might regard it. Mallinson, incidentally, was by far the least composed; as the hours passed he showed himself increasingly excitable—apt, also, to resent to Conway's face the very coolness which he had praised behind his back. Once, above the roar of the engine, a sharp storm of argument arose. "Look here," Mallinson shouted angrily, "are we bound to sit here twiddling our thumbs while this maniac does everything he damn well wants? What's to prevent us from smashing that panel and having it out with him?"

"Nothing at all," replied Conway, "except that he's armed and we're not, and that in any case, none of us would know how to bring the machine to earth afterwards."

"It can't be very hard, surely. I dare say you could do it."

"My dear Mallinson, why is it always *me* you expect to perform these miracles?"

"Well, anyway, this business is getting hellishly on my nerves. Can't we *make* the fellow come down?"

"How do you suggest it should be done?"

Mallinson was becoming more and more agitated. "Well, he's *there*, isn't he? About six feet away from us, and we're three men to one! Have we got to stare at his damned back all the time? At least we might force him to tell us what the game is."

"Very well, we'll see." Conway took a few paces forward to the partition between the cabin and the pilot's cockpit, which was situated in front and somewhat above. There was a pane of glass, about six inches square and made to slide open, through which the pilot, by turning his head and stooping slightly, could communicate with his passengers. Conway tapped on this with his knuckles. The response was almost comically as he had expected. The glass panel slid sideways and the barrel of a revolver obtruded. Not a word; just that. Conway retreated without arguing the point, and the panel slid back again.

Mallinson, who had watched the incident, was only partly satisfied. "I don't suppose he'd have dared to shoot," he commented. "It's probably bluff."

"Quite," agreed Conway, "but I'd rather leave you to make sure."

"Well, I do feel we ought to put up some sort of a fight before giving in tamely like this."

Conway was sympathetic. He recognized the convention, with all its associations of red-coated soldiers and school history books, that Englishmen fear nothing, never surrender, and are never defeated. He said: "Putting up a fight without a decent chance of winning is a poor game, and I'm not that sort of hero."

"Good for you, sir," interposed Barnard heartily. "When somebody's got you by the short hairs you may as well give in pleasantly and admit it. For my part I'm going to enjoy life while it lasts and have a cigar. I hope you don't think a little bit of extra danger matters to us?"

"Not so far as I'm concerned, but it might bother Miss Brinklow."

Barnard was quick to make amends. "Pardon me, madam, but do you mind if I smoke?"

"Not at all," she answered graciously. "I don't do so myself, but I just love the smell of a cigar."

Conway felt that of all the women who could possibly have made such a remark, she was easily the most typical. Anyhow, Mallinson's excitement had calmed a little, and to show friendliness he offered him a cigarette, though he did not light one himself. "I know how you feel," he said gently. "It's a bad outlook, and it's all the worse, in some ways, because there isn't much we can do about it."

"And all the better, too, in other ways," he could not help adding to himself. For he was still immensely fatigued. There was also in his nature a trait which some people might have called laziness, though it was not quite that. No one was capable of harder work, when it had to be done, and few could better shoulder responsibility; but the facts remained that he was not passionately fond of activity, and did not enjoy responsibility at all. Both were included in his job, and he made the best of them, but he was always ready to give way to any one else who could function as well or better. It was partly this, no doubt, that had made his success in the Service less striking than it might have been. He was not ambitious enough to shove his way past others, or to make an important parade of doing nothing when there was really nothing doing. His despatches were sometimes laconic to the point of curtness, and his calm in emergencies, though admired, was often suspected of being too sincere. Authority likes to feel that a man is imposing some effort on himself, and that his apparent nonchalance is only a cloak to disguise an outfit of well-bred emotions. With Conway the dark suspicion had sometimes been current that he really was as unruffled as he looked, and that whatever happened, he did not give a damn. But this, too, like the laziness, was an imperfect interpretation. What most observers failed to perceive in him was something quite bafflingly simple—a love of quietness, contemplation, and being alone.

Now, since he was so inclined and there was nothing else to do, he leaned back in the basket chair and went definitely to sleep. When he woke he noticed that the others, despite their various anxieties, had likewise succumbed. Miss Brinklow was sitting bolt upright with her eyes closed, like some rather dingy and outmoded idol; Mallinson had lolled forward in his place with his chin in the palm of a hand. The American was even snoring. Very sensible of them all, Conway thought; there was no point in wearying themselves with shouting. But immediately he was aware of certain physical sensations in himself, slight dizziness and heart-thumping and a tendency to inhale sharply and with effort. He remembered similar symptoms once before—in the Swiss Alps.

Then he turned to the window and gazed out. The surrounding sky had cleared completely, and in the light of late afternoon there came to him a vision which, for the instant, snatched the remaining breath out of his lungs. Far away, at the very limit of distance, lay range upon range of snow-peaks, festooned with glaciers, and floating, in appearance, upon vast levels of cloud. They compassed the whole arc of the circle, merging towards the west in a horizon that was fierce, almost garish in coloring, like an impressionist back-drop done by some half-mad genius. And meanwhile, the plane, on that stupendous stage, was droning over an abyss in face of a sheer white wall that seemed part of the sky itself until the sun caught it. Then, like a dozen piled-up Jungfraus seen from Mürren, it flamed into superb and dazzling incandescence.

Conway was not apt to be easily impressed, and as a rule he did not care for "views," especially the more famous ones for which thoughtful municipal-ities provide garden seats. Once, on being taken to Tiger Hill, near Dar-jeeling, to watch the sunrise upon Everest, he had found the highest moun-tain in the world a definite disappointment. But this fearsome spectacle beyond the windowpane was of different caliber; it had no air of posing to be admired. There was something raw and monstrous about those uncom-promising ice-cliffs, and a certain sublime impertinence in approaching them thus. He pondered, envisaging maps, calculating distances, estimating times and speeds. Then he became aware that Mallinson had wakened also. He touched the youth on the arm.

CHAPTER TWO

It was typical of Conway that he let the others waken for themselves, and made small response to their exclamations of astonishment; yet later, when Barnard sought his opinion, gave it with something of the detached fluency of a university professor elucidating a problem. He thought it likely, he said, that they were still in India; they had been flying east for several hours, too high to see much, but probably the course had been along some river valley, one stretching roughly east and west. "I wish I hadn't to rely on memory, but my impression is that the valley of the upper Indus fits in well enough. That would have brought us by now to a very spectacular part of the world, and, as you see, so it has."

"You know where we are, then?" Barnard interrupted.

"Well, no—I've never been anywhere near here before, but I wouldn't be surprised if that mountain is Nanga Parbat, the one Mummery lost his life on. In structure and general lay-out it seems in accord with all I've heard about it."

"You are a mountaineer yourself?"

"In my younger days I was keen. Only the usual Swiss climbs, of course."

Mallinson intervened peevishly: "There'd be more point in discussing where we're going to. I wish to God somebody could tell us."

"Well, it looks to me as if we're heading for that range yonder," said Bar-

nard. "Don't you think so, Conway? You'll excuse me calling you that, but
if we're all going to have a little adventure together, it's a pity to stand on
ceremony."

Conway thought it very natural that any one should call him by his own
name, and found Barnard's apologies for so doing a trifle needless. "Oh, certainly," he agreed, and added: "I think that range must be the Karakorams.
There are several passes if our man intends to cross them."

"Our man?" exclaimed Mallinson. "You mean our maniac! I reckon it's
time we dropped the kidnaping theory. We're far past the Frontier country
by now, there aren't any tribes living around here. The only explanation I
can think of is that the fellow's a raving lunatic. Would anybody except a
lunatic fly into this sort of country?"

"I know that nobody except a damn fine airman *could*," retorted Barnard.
"I never was great at geography, but I understand that these are reputed to
be the highest mountains in the world, and if that's so, it'll be a pretty
first-class performance to cross them."

"And also the will of God," put in Miss Brinklow unexpectedly.

Conway did not offer his opinion. The will of God or the lunacy of man
—it seemed to him that you could take your choice, if you wanted a good
enough reason for most things. Or, alternatively (and he thought of it as he
contemplated the small orderliness of the cabin against the window background of such frantic natural scenery), the will of man and the lunacy of
God. It must be satisfying to be quite certain which way to look at it. Then,
while he watched and pondered, a strange transformation took place. The
light turned to bluish over the whole mountain, with the lower slopes dark-
ening to violet. Something deeper than his usual aloofness rose in him—not
quite excitement, still less fear, but a sharp intensity of expectation. He said:
"You're quite right, Barnard, this affair grows more and more remarkable."

"Remarkable or not, I don't feel inclined to propose a vote of thanks about
it," Mallinson persisted. "We didn't ask to be brought here, and Heaven
knows what we shall do when we get *there*, wherever *there* is. And I don't
see that it's any less of an outrage because the fellow happens to be a stunt
flyer. Even if he is, he can be just as much a lunatic. I once heard of a pilot
going mad in mid-air. This fellow must have been mad from the beginning.
That's my theory, Conway."

Conway was silent. He found it irksome to be continually shouting above
the roar of the machine, and after all, there was little point in arguing possibilities. But when Mallinson pressed for an opinion, he said: "Very well-
organized lunacy, you know. Don't forget the landing for gasoline, and also
that this was the only machine that could climb to such a height."

"That doesn't prove he isn't mad. He may have been mad enough to plan
everything."

"Yes, of course, that's possible."

"Well, then, we've got to decide on a plan of action. What are we going
to do when he comes to earth? If he doesn't crash and kill us all, that is.

What are we going to *do?* Rush forward and congratulate him on his marvelous flight, I suppose."

"Not on your life," answered Barnard. "I'll leave you to do all the rushing forward."

Again Conway was loth to prolong the argument, especially since the American, with his level-headed banter, seemed quite capable of handling it himself. Already Conway found himself reflecting that the party might have been far less fortunately constituted. Only Mallinson was inclined to be cantankerous, and that might partly be due to the altitude. Rarefied air had different effects on people; Conway, for instance, derived from it a combination of mental clarity and physical apathy that was not unpleasant. Indeed, he breathed the clear cold air in little spasms of content. The whole situation, no doubt, was appalling, but he had no power at the moment to resent anything that proceeded so purposefully and with such captivating interest.

And there came over him, too, as he stared at that superb mountain, a glow of satisfaction that there were such places still left on earth, distant, inaccessible, as yet unhumanized. The icy rampart of the Karakorams was now more striking than ever against the northern sky, which had become mouse-colored and sinister; the peaks had a chill gleam; utterly majestic and remote, their very namelessness had dignity. Those few thousand feet by which they fell short of the known giants might save them eternally from the climbing expedition; they offered a less tempting lure to the record-breaker. Conway was the antithesis of such a type; he was inclined to see vulgarity in the Western ideal of superlatives, and "the utmost for the highest" seemed to him a less reasonable and perhaps more commonplace proposition than "the much for the high." He did not, in fact, care for excessive striving, and he was bored by mere exploits.

While he was still contemplating the scene, twilight fell, steeping the depths in a rich, velvet gloom that spread upwards like a dye. Then the whole range, much nearer now, paled into fresh splendor; a full moon rose, touching each peak in succession like some celestial lamp-lighter, until the long horizon glittered against a blue-black sky. The air grew cold and a wind sprang up, tossing the machine uncomfortably. These new distresses lowered the spirits of the passengers; it had not been reckoned that the flight could go on after dusk, and now the last hope lay in the exhaustion of gasoline. That, however, was bound to come soon. Mallinson began to argue about it, and Conway, with some reluctance, for he really did not know, gave as his estimate that the utmost distance might be anything up to a thousand miles, of which they must already have covered most. "Well, where would that bring us?" queried the youth miserably.

"It's not easy to judge, but probably some part of Tibet. If these are the Karakorams, Tibet lies beyond. One of the crests, by the way, must be K2, which is generally counted the second highest mountain in the world."

"Next on the list after Everest," commented Barnard. "Gee, this is some scenery."

"And from a climber's point of view much stiffer than Everest. The Duke of Abruzzi gave it up as an absolutely impossible peak."

"*Oh, God!*" muttered Mallinson testily, but Barnard laughed. "I guess you must be the official guide on this trip, Conway, and I'll admit that if I only had a flask of café cognac I wouldn't care if it's Tibet or Tennessee."

"But what are we going to do about it?" urged Mallinson again. "Why are we here? What can be the point of it all? I don't see how you can make jokes about it."

"Well, it's as good as making a scene about it, young fellow. Besides, if the man *is* off his nut, as you've suggested, there probably *isn't* any point."

"He *must* be mad. I can't think of any other explanation. Can you, Conway?"

Conway shook his head.

Miss Brinklow turned round as she might have done during the interval of a play. "As you haven't asked my opinion, perhaps I oughtn't to give it," she began, with shrill modesty, "but I should like to say that I agree with Mr. Mallinson. I'm sure the poor man can't be quite right in his head. The pilot, I mean, of course. There would be no excuse for him, anyhow, if he were *not* mad." She added, shouting confidentially above the din: "And do you know, this is my first trip in the air! My very first! Nothing would ever induce me to do it before, though a friend of mine tried her very best to persuade me to fly from London to Paris."

"And now you're flying from India to Tibet instead," said Barnard. "That's the way things happen."

She went on: "I once knew a missionary who had been to Tibet. He said the Tibetans were very odd people. They believe we are descended from monkeys."

"Real smart of 'em."

"Oh, dear, no, I don't mean in the modern way. They've had the belief for hundreds of years, it's only one of their superstitions. Of course I'm against all of it myself, and I think Darwin was far worse than any Tibetan. I take my stand on the Bible."

"Fundamentalist, I suppose?"

But Miss Brinklow did not appear to understand the term. "I used to belong to the L.M.S.," she shrieked, "but I disagreed with them about infant baptism."

Conway continued to feel that this was a rather comic remark long after it had occurred to him that the initials were those of the London Missionary Society. Still picturing the inconveniences of holding a theological argument at Euston Station, he began to think that there was something slightly fascinating about Miss Brinklow. He even wondered if he could offer her any article of his clothing for the night, but decided at length that her constitution was probably wirier than his. So he huddled up, closed his eyes, and went quite easily and peacefully to sleep.

And the flight proceeded.

Suddenly they were all wakened by a lurch of the machine. Conway's head struck the window, dazing him for the moment; a returning lurch sent him floundering between the two tiers of seats. It was much colder. The first thing he did, automatically, was to glance at his watch; it showed half-past one, he must have been asleep for some time. His ears were full of a loud, flapping sound, which he took to be imaginary until he realized that the engine had been shut off and that the plane was rushing against a gale. Then he stared through the window and could see the earth quite close, vague and snail-gray, scampering underneath. "He's going to land!" Mallinson shouted; and Barnard, who had also been flung out of his seat, responded with a saturnine: "If he's lucky." Miss Brinklow, whom the entire commotion seemed to have disturbed least of all, was adjusting her hat as calmly as if Dover Harbor were just in sight.

Presently the plane touched ground. But it was a bad landing this time —"Oh, my God, damned bad, *damned* bad!" Mallinson groaned as he clutched at his seat during ten seconds of crashing and swaying. Something was heard to strain and snap, and one of the tires exploded. "That's done it," he added in tones of anguished pessimism. "A broken tail-skid, we'll have to stay where we are now, that's certain."

Conway, never talkative at times of crisis, stretched his stiffened legs and felt his head where it had banged against the window. A bruise, nothing much. He must do something to help these people. But he was the last of the four to stand up when the plane came to rest. "Steady," he called out as Mallinson wrenched open the door of the cabin and prepared to make the jump to earth; and eerily, in the comparative silence, the youth's answer came: "No need to be steady—this looks like the end of the world— there's not a soul about, anyhow."

A moment later, chilled and shivering, they were all aware that this was so. With no sound in their ears save the fierce gusts of wind and their own crunching footsteps, they felt themselves at the mercy of something dour and savagely melancholy—a mood in which both earth and air were saturated. The moon looked to have disappeared behind clouds, and starlight illumined a tremendous emptiness heaving with wind. Without thought or knowledge, one could have guessed that this bleak world was mountain-high, and that the mountains rising from it were mountains on top of mountains. A range of them gleamed on a far horizon like a row of dog-teeth.

Mallinson, feverishly active, was already making for the cockpit. "I'm not scared of the fellow on land, whoever he is," he cried. "I'm going to tackle him right away. . . ."

The others watched apprehensively, hypnotized by the spectacle of such energy. Conway sprang after him, but too late to prevent the investigation. After a few seconds, however, the youth dropped down again, gripping his arm and muttering in a hoarse, sobered staccato: "I say, Conway, it's queer. . . . I think the fellow's ill or dead or something. . . . I can't get a word out of him. Come up and look. . . . I took his revolver, at any rate."

"Better give it to me," said Conway, and though still rather dazed by the recent blow on his head, he nerved himself for action. Of all times and places and situations on earth, this seemed to him to combine the most hideous discomforts. He hoisted himself stiffly into a position from which he could see, not very well, into the enclosed cockpit. There was a strong smell of gasoline, so he did not risk striking a match. He could just discern the pilot, huddled forward, his head sprawling over the controls. He shook him, unfastened his helmet, and loosened the clothes round his neck. A moment later he turned round to report: "Yes, there's something happened to him. We must get him out." But an observer might have added that something had happened to Conway as well. His voice was sharper, more incisive; no longer did he sound to be hovering on the brink of some profound doubtfulness. The time, the place, the cold, his fatigue, were now of less account; there was a job that simply had to be done, and the more conventional part of him was uppermost and preparing to do it.

With Barnard and Mallinson assisting, the pilot was extracted from his seat and lifted to the ground. He was unconscious, not dead. Conway had no particular medical knowledge, but, as to most men who have lived in outlandish places, the phenomena of illness were mostly familiar. "Possibly a heart attack brought on by the high altitude," he diagnosed, stooping over the unknown man. "We can do very little for him out here—there's no shelter from this infernal wind. Better get him inside the cabin, and ourselves too. We haven't an idea where we are, and it's hopeless to make a move until daylight."

The verdict and the suggestion were both accepted without dispute. Even Mallinson concurred. They carried the man into the cabin and laid him full-length along the gangway between the seats. The interior was no warmer than outside, but offered a screen to the flurries of wind. It was the wind, before much time had passed, that became the central preoccupation of them all—the *leit-motif*, as it were, of the whole mournful night. It was not an ordinary wind. It was not merely a strong wind or a cold wind. It was somehow a frenzy that lived all around them, a master stamping and ranting over his own domain. It tilted the loaded machine and shook it viciously, and when Conway glanced through the windows it seemed as if the same wind were whirling splinters of light out of the stars.

The stranger lay inert, while Conway, with difficulty in the dimness and confined space, made what examination he could by the light of matches. But it did not reveal much. "His heart's faint," he said at last, and then Miss Brinklow, after groping in her handbag, created a small sensation. "I wonder if this would be any use to the poor man," she proffered condescendingly. "I never touch a drop myself, but I always carry it with me in case of accidents. And this *is* a sort of accident, isn't it?"

"I should say it was," replied Conway with grimness. He unscrewed the bottle, smelt it, and poured some of the brandy into the man's mouth. "Just the stuff for him. Thanks." After an interval the slightest movement of eyelids was visible. Mallinson suddenly became hysterical. "I can't help it," he cried, laughing wildly. "We all look such a lot of damn fools striking matches over a corpse. . . . And he isn't much of a beauty, is he? Chink, I should say, if he's anything at all."

"Possibly." Conway's voice was level and rather severe. "But he's not a corpse yet. With a bit of luck we may bring him round."

"Luck? It'll be his luck, not ours."

"Don't be too sure. And shut up for the time being, anyhow."

There was enough of the schoolboy still in Mallinson to make him respond to the curt command of a senior, though he was obviously in poor control of himself. Conway, though sorry for him, was more concerned with the immediate problem of the pilot, since he, alone of them all, might be able to give some explanation of their plight. Conway had no desire to discuss the matter further in a merely speculative way; there had been enough of that during the journey. He was uneasy now beyond his continuing mental curiosity, for he was aware that the whole situation had ceased to be excitingly perilous and was threatening to become a trial of endurance ending in catastrophe. Keeping vigil throughout that gale-tormented night, he faced facts none the less frankly because he did not trouble to enunciate them to the others. He guessed that the flight had progressed far beyond the western range of the Himalaya towards the less known heights of the Kuen-Lun. In that event they would by now have reached the loftiest and least hospitable part of the earth's surface, the Tibetan plateau, two miles high even in its lowest valleys, a vast, uninhabited, and largely unexplored region of wind-swept upland. Somewhere they were, in that forlorn country, marooned in far less comfort than on most desert islands. Then abruptly, as if to answer his curiosity by increasing it, a rather awe-inspiring change took place. The moon, which he had thought to be hidden by clouds, swung over the lip of some shadowy eminence and, whilst still not showing itself directly, unveiled the darkness ahead. Conway could see the outline of a long valley, with rounded, sad-looking low hills on either side, jet-black against the deep electric blue of the night-sky. But it was to the head of the valley that his eyes were led irresistibly, for there, soaring into the gap, and magnificent in the full shimmer of moonlight, appeared what he took to be the loveliest mountain on earth. It was an almost perfect cone of snow, simple in outline as if a child had drawn it, and impossible to classify as to size, height, or nearness. It was so radiant, so serenely poised, that he wondered for a moment if it were real at all. Then, while he gazed, a tiny puff clouded the edge of the pyramid, giving life to the vision before the faint rumble of the avalanche confirmed it.

He had an impulse to rouse the others to share the spectacle, but decided after consideration that its effect might not be tranquilizing. Nor was it so, from a common sense viewpoint; such virgin splendors merely emphasized the facts of isolation and danger. There was quite a probability that the nearest human settlement was hundreds of miles away. And they had no food; they were unarmed except for one revolver; the aeroplane was damaged and almost fuel-less, even if any one had known how to fly. They had no clothes suited to the terrific chills and winds; Mallinson's motoring coat and his own ulster were quite inadequate, and even Miss Brinklow, woolied and mufflered as for a polar expedition (ridiculous, he had thought, on first beholding her), could not be feeling happy. They were all, too, except himself, affected by the altitude. Even Barnard had sunk into melancholy under the strain. Mallinson was muttering to himself; it was clear what would happen to him if these hardships went on for long. In face of such distressful prospects Conway found himself quite unable to restrain an admiring glance at Miss Brinklow. She was not, he reflected, a normal person; no woman who taught Afghans to sing hymns could be considered so. But she was, after every calamity, still normally abnormal, and he was deeply obliged to her for it. "I hope you're not feeling too bad?" he said sympathetically, when he caught her eye.

"The soldiers during the War had to suffer worse things than this," she replied.

The comparison did not seem to Conway a very valuable one. In point of fact, he had never spent a night in the trenches quite so thoroughly unpleasant, though doubtless many others had. He concentrated his attention on the pilot, now breathing fitfully and sometimes slightly stirring. Probably Mallinson was right in guessing the man Chinese. He had the typical Mongol nose and cheekbones, despite his successful impersonation of a British flight-lieutenant. Mallinson had called him ugly, but Conway, who had lived in China, thought him a fairly passable specimen, though now, in the burnished circle of match-flame, his pallid skin and gaping mouth were not pretty.

The night dragged on, as if each minute were something heavy and tangible that had to be pushed to make way for the next. Moonlight faded after a time, and with it that distant specter of the mountain; then the triple mischiefs of darkness, cold, and wind increased until dawn. As though at its signal, the wind dropped, leaving the world in compassionate quietude. Framed in the pale triangle ahead, the mountain showed again, gray at first, then silver, then pink as the earliest sun rays caught the summit. In the lessening gloom the valley itself took shape, revealing a floor of rock and shingle sloping upwards. It was not a friendly picture, but to Conway, as he surveyed, there came a queer perception of fineness in it, of something that had no romantic appeal at all, but a steely, almost an intellectual quality. The white pyramid in the distance compelled the mind's assent as passionlessly as a Euclidean theorem, and when at last the sun rose into a sky of deep delphinium blue, he felt only a little less than comfortable again.

As the air grew warmer the others wakened, and he suggested carrying the pilot into the open, where the sharp dry air and the sunlight might help to revive him. This was done, and they began a second and pleasanter vigil. Eventually the man opened his eyes and began to speak convulsively. His four passengers stooped over him, listening intently to sounds that were meaningless except to Conway, who occasionally made answers. After some time the man became weaker, talked with increasing difficulty, and finally died. That was about mid-morning.

Conway then turned to his companions. "I'm sorry to say he told me very little—little, I mean, compared with what we should like to know. Merely that we are in Tibet, which is obvious. He didn't give any coherent account of why he had brought us here, but he seemed to know the locality. He spoke a kind of Chinese that I don't understand very well, but I think he said something about a lamasery near here, along the valley, I gathered, where we could get food and shelter. Shangri-La, he called it. *La* is Tibetan for mountain pass. He was most emphatic that we should go there."

"Which doesn't seem to me any reason at all why we should," said Mallinson. "After all, he was probably off his head. Wasn't he?"

"You know as much about that as I do. But if we don't go to this place, where else are we to go?"

"Anywhere you like, I don't care. All I'm certain of is that this Shangri-La, if it's in that direction, must be a few extra miles from civilization. I should feel happier if we were lessening the distance, not increasing it. Damnation, man, aren't you going to get us back?"

Conway replied patiently: "I don't think you properly understand the position, Mallinson. We're in a part of the world that no one knows very much about, except that it's difficult and dangerous, even for a fully equipped expedition. Considering that hundreds of miles of this sort of country probably surround us on all sides, the notion of walking back to Peshawar doesn't strike me as very hopeful."

"I don't think I could possibly manage it," said Miss Brinklow seriously.

Barnard nodded. "It looks as if we're darned lucky, then, if this lamasery *is* round the corner."

"Comparatively lucky, maybe," agreed Conway. "After all, we've no food, and as you can see for yourselves, the country isn't the kind it would be easy to live on. In a few hours we shall all be famished. And then to-night, if we were to stay here, we should have to face the wind and the cold again. It's not a pleasant prospect. Our only chance, it seems to me, is to find some other human beings, and where else should we begin looking for them except where we've been told they exist?"

"And what if it's a trap?" asked Mallinson, but Barnard supplied an answer. "A nice warm trap," he said, "with a piece of cheese in it, would suit me down to the ground."

They laughed, except Mallinson, who looked distraught and nerve-racked. Finally Conway went on: "I take it, then, that we're all more or less agreed? There's an obvious way along the valley; it doesn't look too steep, though we shall have to take it slowly. In any case, we could do nothing here. We couldn't even bury this man without dynamite. Besides, the lamasery people may be able to supply us with porters for the journey back. We shall need them. I suggest we start at once, so that if we don't locate the place by late afternoon we shall have time to return for another night in the cabin."

"And supposing we *do* locate it?" queried Mallinson, still intransigent. "Have we any guarantee that we shan't be murdered?"

"None at all. But I think it is a less, and perhaps also a preferable risk

to being starved or frozen to death." He added, feeling that such chilly logic might not be entirely suited for the occasion: "As a matter of fact, murder is the very last thing one would expect in a Buddhist monastery. It would be rather less likely than being killed in an English cathedral."

"Like Saint Thomas of Canterbury," said Miss Brinklow, nodding an emphatic agreement, but completely spoiling his point. Mallinson shrugged his shoulders and responded with melancholy irritation: "Very well, then, we'll be off to Shangri-La. Wherever and whatever it is, we'll try it. But let's hope it's not half-way up that mountain."

The remark served to fix their glances on the glittering cone towards which the valley pointed. Sheerly magnificent it looked in the full light of day; and then their gaze turned to a stare, for they could see, far away and approaching them down the slope, the figures of men. "Providence!" whispered Miss Brinklow.

CHAPTER THREE

Part of Conway was always an onlooker, however active might be the rest. Just now, while waiting for the strangers to come nearer, he refused to be fussed into deciding what he might or mightn't do in any number of possible contingencies. And this was not bravery, or coolness, or any especially sublime confidence in his own power to make decisions on the spur of the moment. It was, if the worst view be taken, a form of indolence, an unwillingness to interrupt his mere spectator's interest in what was happening.

As the figures moved down the valley they revealed themselves to be a party of a dozen or more, carrying with them a hooded chair. In this, a little later, could be discerned a person robed in blue. Conway could not imagine where they were all going, but it certainly seemed providential, as Miss Brinklow had said, that such a detachment should chance to be passing just there and then. As soon as he was within hailing distance he left his own party and walked ahead, though not hurriedly, for he knew that Orientals enjoy the ritual of meeting and like to take their time over it. Halting when a few yards off, he bowed with due courtesy. Much to his surprise the robed figure stepped from the chair, came forward with dignified deliberation, and held out his hand. Conway responded, and observed an old or elderly Chinese, gray-haired, clean-shaven, and rather pallidly decorative in a silk embroidered gown. He in his turn appeared to be submitting Conway to the same kind of ready reckoning. Then, in precise and perhaps too accurate English, he said: "I am from the lamasery of Shangri-La."

Conway bowed again, and after a suitable pause began to explain briefly the circumstances that had brought him and his three companions to such an unfrequented part of the world. At the end of the recital the Chinese made a gesture of understanding. "It is indeed remarkable," he said, and gazed reflectively at the damaged aeroplane. Then he added: "My name is Chang, if you would be so good as to present me to your friends."

Conway managed to smile urbanely. He was rather taken with this latest phenomenon, a Chinese who spoke perfect English and observed the social formalities of Bond Street amidst the wilds of Tibet. He turned to the others, who had by this time caught up and were regarding the encounter with varying degrees of astonishment. "Miss Brinklow . . . Mr. Barnard, who is an American . . . Mr. Mallinson . . . and my own name is Conway. We are all glad to see you, though the meeting is almost as puzzling as the fact of our being here at all. Indeed, we were just about to make our way to your lamasery, so it is doubly fortunate. If you could give us directions for the journey—"

"There is no need for that. I shall be delighted to act as your guide."

"But I could not think of putting you to such trouble. It is exceedingly kind of you, but if the distance is not far—"

"It is not far, but it is not easy, either. I shall esteem it an honor to accompany you and your friends."

"But really—"

" "I must insist."

Conway thought that the argument, in its context of place and circumstance, was in some danger of becoming ludicrous. "Very well," he responded. "I'm sure we are all most obliged."

Mallinson, who had been somberly enduring these pleasantries, now interposed with something of the shrill acerbity of the barrack-square. "Our stay won't be long," he announced curtly. "We shall pay for anything we have, and we should like to hire some of your men to help us on our journey back. We want to return to civilization as soon as possible."

"And are you so very certain that you are away from it?"

The query, delivered with much suavity, only stung the youth to further sharpness. "I'm quite sure I'm far away from where I want to be, and so are we all. We shall be grateful for temporary shelter, but we shall be more grateful still if you'll provide means for us to return. How long do you suppose the journey to India will take?"

"I really could not say at all."

"Well, I hope we're not going to have any trouble about it. I've had some experience of hiring native porters, and we shall expect you to use your influence to get us a square deal."

Conway felt that most of all this was rather needlessly truculent, and he was just about to intervene when the reply came, still with immense dignity: "I can only assure you, Mr. Mallinson, that you will be honorably treated and that ultimately you will have no regrets."

"*Ultimately?*" Mallinson exclaimed, pouncing on the word, but there was greater ease in avoiding a scene since wine and fruit were now on offer, having been unpacked by the marching party, stocky Tibetans in sheepskins, fur hats, and yak-skin boots. The wine had a pleasant flavor, not unlike a good hock, while the fruit included mangoes, perfectly ripened and almost painfully delicious after so many hours of fasting. Mallinson ate and drank with incurious relish; but Conway, relieved of immediate worries and reluctant to cherish distant ones, was wondering how mangoes could be cultivated at such an altitude. He was also interested in the mountain beyond the valley; it was a sensational peak, by any standards, and he was surprised that some traveler had not made much of it in the kind of book that a journey in Tibet invariably elicits. He climbed it in mind as he gazed, choosing a route by *col* and *couloir* until an exclamation from Mallinson drew his attention back to earth; he looked round then and saw that the Chinese had been earnestly regarding him. "You were contemplating the mountain, Mr. Conway?" came the enquiry.

"Yes. It's a fine sight. It has a name, I suppose?"

"It is called Karakal."

"I don't think I ever heard of it. Is it very high?"

"Over twenty-eight thousand feet."

"Indeed? I didn't realize there would be anything on that scale outside the Himalaya. Has it been properly surveyed? Whose are the measurements?"

"Whose would you expect, my dear sir? Is there anything incompatible between monasticism and trigonometry?"

Conway savored the phrase and replied: "Oh, not at all—not at all." Then he laughed politely. He thought it a poorish joke, but one perhaps worth making the most of. Soon after that the journey to Shangri-La was begun.

All morning the climb proceeded, slowly and by easy gradients; but at such height the physical effort was considerable, and none had energy to spare for talk. The Chinese traveled luxuriously in his chair, which might have seemed unchivalrous had it not been absurd to picture Miss Brinklow in such a regal setting. Conway, whom the rarefied air troubled less than the rest, was at pains to catch the occasional chatter of the chair-bearers. He knew a very little Tibetan, just enough to gather that the men were glad to be returning to the lamasery. He could not, even had he wished, have continued converse with their leader, since the latter, with eyes closed and face half hidden behind curtains, appeared to have the knack of instant and well-timed sleep.

Meanwhile the sun was warm; hunger and thirst had been appeased, if not satisfied; and the air, clean as from another planet, was more precious with every intake. One had to breathe consciously and deliberately, which, though disconcerting at first, induced after a time an almost ecstatic tranquillity of mind. The whole body moved in a single rhythm of breathing, walking, and thinking; the lungs, no longer discreet and automatic, were disciplined to harmony with mind and limb. Conway, in whom a mystical strain ran in curious consort with skepticism, found himself not unhappily puzzled over the sensation. Once or twice he spoke a cheerful word to Mallinson, but the youth was laboring under the strain of the ascent. Barnard also gasped asthmatically, while Miss Brinklow was engaged in some grim pulmonary warfare which for some reason she made efforts to conceal. "We're nearly at the top," Conway said encouragingly.

"I once ran for a train and felt just like this," she answered.

So also, Conway reflected, there were people who considered cider was just like champagne. It was a matter of palate.

He was surprised to find that beyond his puzzlement he had few misgivings, and none at all on his own behalf. There were moments in life when one opened wide one's soul just as one might open wide one's purse if an evening's entertainment were proving unexpectedly costly but also unexpectedly novel. Conway, on that breathless morning in sight of Karakal, made just such a willing, relieved, yet not excited response to the offer of new experience. After ten years in various parts of Asia he had attained to a somewhat fastidious valuation of places and happenings; and this, he was bound to admit, promised unusually.

About a couple of miles along the valley the ascent grew steeper, but by this time the sun was overclouded and a silvery mist obscured the view. Thunder and avalanches resounded from the snow-fields above; the air took chill, and then, with the sudden changefulness of mountain regions, became bitterly cold. A flurry of wind and sleet drove up, drenching the party and adding immeasurably to their discomfort; even Conway felt at one moment that it would be impossible to go much further. But shortly afterwards it seemed that the summit of the ridge had been reached, for the chair-bearers halted to readjust their burden. The condition of Barnard and Mallinson, who were both suffering severely, led to continued delay; but the Tibetans were clearly anxious to press on, and made signs that the rest of the journey would be less fatiguing.

After these assurances it was disappointing to see them uncoiling ropes. "Do they mean to hang us already?" Barnard managed to exclaim, with desperate facetiousness; but the guides soon showed that their less sinister intention was merely to link the party together in ordinary mountaineering fashion. When they observed that Conway was familiar with rope-craft, they became much more respectful and allowed him to dispose the party in his own way. He put himself next to Mallinson, with Tibetans ahead and to the rear, and with Barnard and Miss Brinklow and more Tibetans further back still. He was prompt to notice that the men, during their leader's continuing sleep, were inclined to let him deputize. He felt a familiar quickening of authority; if there were to be any difficult business he would give what he knew was his to give—confidence and command. He had been a first-class mountaineer in his time, and was still, no doubt, pretty good. "You've got to look after Barnard," he told Miss Brinklow, half jocularly, half meaning it; and she answered, with the coyness of an eagle: "I'll do my best, but you know, I've never been roped before."

But the next stage, though occasionally exciting, was less arduous than he had been prepared for, and a relief from the lung-bursting strain of the ascent. The track consisted of a traverse cut along the flank of a rock wall whose height above them the mist obscured. Perhaps mercifully it also obscured the abyss on the other side, though Conway, who had a good eye for heights, would have liked to see where he was. The path was scarcely more than two feet wide in places, and the manner in which the bearers maneuvered the chair at such points drew his admiration almost as strongly as did the nerves of the occupant who could manage to sleep through it all. The Tibetans were reliable enough, but they seemed happier when the path widened and became slightly downhill. Then they began to sing amongst themselves, lilting barbaric tunes that Conway could imagine orchestrated by Massenet for some Tibetan ballet. The rain ceased and the air grew warmer. "Well, it's quite certain we could never have found our way here by ourselves," said Conway, intending to be cheerful, but Mallinson did not find the remark very comforting. He was, in fact, acutely terrified, and in more danger of showing it now that the worst was over. "Should we be missing much?" he retorted bitterly. The track went on, more sharply downhill, and at one spot Conway found some edelweiss, the first welcome sign of more hospitable levels. But this, when he announced it, consoled Mallinson even less. "Good God, Conway, d'you fancy you're pottering about the Alps? What sort of hell's kitchen are we making for, that's what I'd like to know? And what's our plan of action when we get to it? *What are we going to do?*"

Conway said quietly: "If you'd had all the experiences I've had, you'd know that there are times in life when the most comfortable thing is to do nothing at all. Things happen to you and you just let them happen. The War was rather like that. One is fortunate if, as on this occasion, a touch of novelty seasons the unpleasantness."

"You're too confoundedly philosophic for me. That wasn't your mood during the trouble at Baskul."

"Of course not, because then there was a chance that I could alter events by my own actions. But now, for the moment at least, there's no such chance. We're here because we're here, if you want a reason. I've usually found it a soothing one."

"I suppose you realize the appalling job we shall have to get back by the way we've come. We've been slithering along the face of a perpendicular mountain for the last hour—I've been taking notice."

"So have I."

"Have you?" Mallinson coughed excitedly. "I dare say I'm being a nuisance, but I can't help it. I'm suspicious about all this. I feel we're doing far too much what these fellows want us to. They're getting us into a corner."

"Even if they are, the only alternative was to stay out of it and perish."

"I know that's logical, but it doesn't seem to help. I'm afraid I don't find it as easy as you do to accept the situation. I can't forget that two days ago we were in the consulate at Baskul. To think of all that has happened since is a bit overwhelming to me. I'm sorry. I'm overwrought. It makes me realize how lucky I was to miss the War; I suppose I should have got hysterical about things. The whole world seems to have gone completely mad all round me. I must be pretty wild myself to be talking to you like this."

Conway shook his head. "My dear boy, not at all. You're twenty-four years old, and you're somewhere about two and a half miles up in the air: those are reasons enough for anything you may happen to feel at the moment. I think you've come through a trying ordeal extraordinarily well, better than I should at your age."

"But don't *you* feel the madness of it all? The way we flew over those mountains and that awful waiting in the wind and the pilot dying and then meeting these fellows, doesn't it all seem nightmarish and incredible when you look back on it?"

"It does, of course."

"Then I wish I knew how you manage to keep so cool about everything."

"Do you really wish that? I'll tell you if you like, though you'll perhaps think me cynical. It's because so much else that I can look back on seems nightmarish too. This isn't the only mad part of the world, Mallinson. After all, if you *must* think of Baskul, do you remember just before we left how the revolutionaries were torturing their captives to get information? An ordinary washing-mangle, quite effective, of course, but I don't think I ever saw anything more comically dreadful. And do you recollect the last message that came through before we were cut off? It was a circular from a Manchester textile firm asking if we knew of any trade openings in Baskul for the sale of corsets! Isn't that mad enough for you? Believe me, in arriving here the worst that can have happened is that we've exchanged one form of lunacy for another. And as for the War, if you'd been in it you'd have done the same as I did, learned how to funk with a stiff lip."

They were still conversing when a sharp but brief ascent robbed them of breath, inducing in a few paces all their earlier strain. Presently the ground leveled, and they stepped out of the mist into clear, sunny air. Ahead, and only a short distance away, lay the lamasery of Shangri-La.

To Conway, seeing it first, it might have been a vision fluttering out of that solitary rhythm in which lack of oxygen had encompassed all his faculties. It was, indeed, a strange and half-incredible sight. A group of colored

pavilions clung to the mountainside with none of the grim deliberation of a Rhineland castle, but rather with the chance delicacy of flower-petals impaled upon a crag. It was superb and exquisite. An austere emotion carried the eye upward from milk-blue roofs to the gray rock bastion above, tremendous as the Wetterhorn above Grindelwald. Beyond that, in a dazzling pyramid, soared the snow slopes of Karakal. It might well be, Conway thought, the most terrifying mountainscape in the world, and he imagined the immense stress of snow and glacier against which the rock functioned as a gigantic retaining wall. Someday, perhaps, the whole mountain would split, and a half of Karakal's icy splendor come toppling into the valley. He wondered if the slightness of the risk combined with its fearfulness might even be found agreeably stimulating.

Hardly less an enticement was the downward prospect, for the mountain wall continued to drop, nearly perpendicularly, into a cleft that could only have been the result of some cataclysm in the far past. The floor of the valley, hazily distant, welcomed the eye with greenness; sheltered from winds,

and surveyed rather than dominated by the lamasery, it looked to Conway a
delightfully favored place, though if it were inhabited its community must be
completely isolated by the lofty and sheerly unscalable ranges on the further
side. Only to the lamasery did there appear to be any climbable egress at
all. Conway experienced, as he gazed, a slight tightening of apprehension;
Mallinson's misgivings were not, perhaps, to be wholly disregarded. But the
feeling was only momentary, and soon merged in the deeper sensation, half
mystical, half visual, of having reached at last some place that was an end, a
finality.

He never exactly remembered how he and the others arrived at the lamasery, or with what formalities they were received, unroped, and ushered
into the precincts. That thin air had a dream-like texture, matching the
porcelain-blue of the sky; with every breath and every glance he took in a
deep anesthetizing tranquillity that made him impervious alike to Mallinson's uneasiness, Barnard's witticisms, and Miss Brinklow's coy portrayal of a
lady well prepared for the worst. He vaguely recollected surprise at finding
the interior spacious, well warmed, and quite clean; but there was no time to
do more than notice these qualities, for the Chinese had left his hooded
chair and was already leading the way through various antechambers. He
was quite affable now. "I must apologize," he said, "for leaving you to yourselves on the way, but the truth is, journeys of that kind don't suit me, and I
have to take care of myself. I trust you were not too fatigued?"

"We managed," replied Conway with a wry smile.

"Excellent. And now, if you will come with me, I will show you to your
apartments. No doubt you would like baths. Our accommodation is simple,
but I hope adequate."

At this point Barnard, who was still affected by shortness of breath, gave
vent to an asthmatic chuckle. "Well," he gasped, "I can't say I like your
climate yet—the air seems to stick on my chest a bit—but you've certainly got
a darned fine view out of your front windows. Do we all have to line up for
the bathroom, or is this an American hotel?"

"I think you will find everything quite satisfactory, Mr. Barnard."

Miss Brinklow nodded primly. "I should hope so, indeed."

"And afterwards," continued the Chinese, "I should be greatly honored if
you will all join me at dinner."

Conway replied courteously. Only Mallinson had given no sign of his attitude in the face of these unlooked-for amenities. Like Barnard, he had been
suffering from the altitude, but now, with an effort, he found breath to
exclaim: "And afterwards also, if you don't mind, we'll make our plans for
getting away. The sooner the better, so far as I'm concerned."

CHAPTER FOUR

"So you see," Chang was saying, "we are less barbarian than you expected. . . ."

Conway, later that evening, was not disposed to deny it. He was enjoying that pleasant mingling of physical ease and mental alertness which seemed to him, of all sensations, the most truly civilized. So far, the appointments of Shangri-La had been all that he could have wished, certainly more than he could ever have expected. That a Tibetan monastery should possess a system of central heating was not, perhaps, so very remarkable in an age that supplied even Lhasa with telephones; but that it should combine the mechanics of Western hygiene with so much else that was Eastern and traditional, struck him as exceedingly singular. The bath, for instance, in which he had recently luxuriated, had been of a delicate green porcelain, a product, according to inscription, of Akron, Ohio. Yet the native attendant had valeted him in Chinese fashion, cleansing his ears and nostrils, and passing a thin, silk swab under his lower eyelids. He had wondered at the time if and how his three companions were receiving similar attentions.

Conway had lived for nearly a decade in China, not wholly in the bigger cities; and he counted it, all things considered, the happiest part of his life. He liked the Chinese, and felt at home with Chinese ways. In particular he liked Chinese cooking, with its subtle undertones of taste; and his first meal at Shangri-La had therefore conveyed a welcome familiarity. He suspected, too, that it might have contained some herb or drug to relieve respiration, for he not only felt a difference himself, but could observe a greater ease among his fellow guests. Chang, he noticed, ate nothing but a small portion of green salad, and took no wine. "You will excuse me," he had explained at the outset, "but my diet is very restricted; I am obliged to take care of myself."

It was the reason he had given before, and Conway wondered by what form of invalidism he was afflicted. Regarding him now more closely, he found it difficult to guess his age; his smallish and somehow undetailed features, together with the moist clay texture of his skin, gave him a look that might either have been that of a young man prematurely old or of an old man remarkably well preserved. He was by no means without attractiveness of a kind; a certain stylized courtesy hung about him in a fragrance too delicate to be detected till one had ceased to think about it. In his embroidered gown of blue silk, with the usual side-slashed skirt and tight-ankled trousers, all the hue of water color skies, he had a cold metallic charm which Conway found pleasing, though he knew it was not everybody's taste.

The atmosphere, in fact, was Chinese rather than specifically Tibetan; and this in itself gave Conway an agreeable sensation of being at home, though again it was one that he could not expect the others to share. The room, too, pleased him; it was admirably proportioned, and sparingly adorned with tapestries and one or two fine pieces of lacquer. Light was from paper lanterns, motionless in the still air. He felt a soothing comfort of mind and body, and his renewed speculations as to some possible drug were hardly apprehensive. Whatever it was, if it existed at all, it had relieved Barnard's breathlessness and Mallinson's truculence; both had dined well, finding satisfaction in eating rather than talk. Conway also had been hungry enough, and was not sorry that etiquette demanded gradualness in approaching matters of importance. He had never cared for hurrying a situation that was itself enjoyable, so that the technique well suited him. Not, indeed, until he had begun a cigarette did he give a gentle lead to his curiosity; he remarked then, addressing Chang: "You seem a very fortunate community, and most hospitable to strangers. I don't imagine, though, that you receive them often."

"Seldom indeed," replied the Chinese, with measured stateliness. "It is not a traveled part of the world."

Conway smiled at that. "You put the matter mildly. It looked to me, as I came, the most isolated spot I ever set eyes on. A separate culture might flourish here without contamination from the outside world."

"Contamination, would you say?"

"I use the word in reference to dance bands, cinemas, electric signs, and so on. Your plumbing is quite rightly as modern as you can get it, the only certain boon, to my mind, that the East can take from the West. I often think that the Romans were fortunate; their civilization reached as far as hot baths without touching the fatal knowledge of machinery."

Conway paused. He had been talking with an impromptu fluency which, though not insincere, was chiefly designed to create and control an atmosphere. He was rather good at that sort of thing. Only a willingness to respond to the superfine courtesy of the occasion prevented him from being more openly curious.

Miss Brinklow, however, had no such scruples. "Please," she said, though the word was by no means submissive, "will you tell us about the monastery?"

Chang raised his eyebrows in very gentle deprecation of such immediacy. "It will give me the greatest of pleasure, madam, so far as I am able. What exactly do you wish to know?"

"First of all, how many are there of you here, and what nationality do you belong to?" It was clear that her orderly mind was functioning no less professionally than at the Baskul mission-house.

Chang replied: "Those of us in full lamahood number about fifty, and there are a few others, like myself, who have not yet attained to complete initiation. We shall do so in due course, it is to be hoped. Till then we are half-lamas, postulants, you might say. As for our racial origins, there are representatives of a great many nations among us, though it is perhaps natural that Tibetans and Chinese make up the majority."

Miss Brinklow would never shirk a conclusion, even a wrong one. "I see.

It's really a native monastery, then. Is your head lama a Tibetan or a Chinese?"

"No."

"Are there any English?"

"Several."

"Dear me, that seems very remarkable." Miss Brinklow paused only for breath before continuing: "And now, tell me what you all believe in."

Conway leaned back with somewhat amused expectancy. He had always found pleasure in observing the impact of opposite mentalities; and Miss Brinklow's girl-guide forthrightness applied to lamaistic philosophy promised to be entertaining. On the other hand, he did not wish his host to take fright. "That's rather a big question," he said, temporizingly.

But Miss Brinklow was in no mood to temporize. The wine, which had made the others more reposeful, seemed to have given her an extra liveliness. "Of course," she said with a gesture of magnanimity, "I believe in the true religion, but I'm broadminded enough to admit that other people, foreigners, I mean, are quite often sincere in their views. And naturally in a monastery I wouldn't expect to be agreed with."

Her concession evoked a formal bow from Chang. "But why not, madam?" he replied in his precise and flavored English. "Must we hold that because one religion is true, all others are bound to be false?"

"Well, of course, that's rather obvious, isn't it?"

Conway again interposed. "Really, I think we had better not argue. But Miss Brinklow shares my own curiosity about the motive of this unique establishment."

Chang answered rather slowly and in scarcely more than a whisper: "If I were to put it into a very few words, my dear sir, I should say that our prevalent belief is in moderation. We inculcate the virtue of avoiding excess of all kinds—even including, if you will pardon the paradox, excess of virtue itself. In the valley which you have seen, and in which there are several thousand inhabitants living under the control of our order, we have found that the principle makes for a considerable degree of happiness. We rule with moderate strictness, and in return we are satisfied with moderate obedience. And I think I can claim that our people are moderately sober, moderately chaste, and moderately honest."

Conway smiled. He thought it well expressed, besides which it made some appeal to his own temperament. "I think I understand. And I suppose the fellows who met us this morning belonged to your valley people?"

"Yes. I hope you had no fault to find with them during the journey?"

"Oh, no, none at all. I'm glad they were more than moderately sure-footed, anyhow. You were careful, by the way, to say that the rule of moderation applied to *them*—am I to take it that it does not apply to your priesthood also?"

But at that Chang could only shake his head. "I regret, sir, that you have touched upon a matter which I may not discuss. I can only add that our community has various faiths and usages, but we are most of us moderately heretical about them. I am deeply grieved that at the moment I cannot say more."

"Please don't apologize. I am left with the pleasantest of speculations." Something in his own voice, as well as in his bodily sensations, gave Conway a renewed impression that he had been very slightly doped. Mallinson appeared to have been similarly affected, though he seized the present chance to remark: "All this has been very interesting, but I really think it's time we began to discuss our plans for getting away. We want to return to India as soon as possible. How many porters can we be supplied with?"

The question, so practical and uncompromising, broke through the crust of suavity to find no sure foothold beneath. Only after a longish interval came Chang's reply: "Unfortunately, Mr. Mallinson, I am not the proper person to approach. But in any case, I hardly think the matter could be arranged immediately."

"But something has *got* to be arranged! We've all got our work to return to, and our friends and relatives will be worrying about us. We simply *must* return. We're obliged to you for receiving us like this, but we really can't slack about here doing nothing. If it's at all feasible, we should like to set out not later than to-morrow. I expect there are a good many of your people who would volunteer to escort us—we should make it well worth their while, of course."

Mallinson ended nervously, as if he had hoped to be answered before saying so much; but he could extract from Chang no more than a quiet and almost reproachful: "But all this, you know, is scarcely in my province."

"Isn't it? Well, perhaps you can do *something*, at any rate. If you could get us a large scale map of the country, it would help. It looks as if we shall have a long journey, and that's all the more reason for making an early start. You have maps, I suppose?"

"Yes, we have a great many."

"We'll borrow some of them, then, if you don't mind. We can return them to you afterwards, I suppose you must have communications with the outer world from time to time. And it would be a good idea to send messages ahead, also, to reassure our friends. How far away is the nearest telegraph line?"

Chang's wrinkled face seemed to have acquired a look of infinite patience, but he did not reply.

Mallinson waited a moment and then continued: "Well, where do you send to when you want anything? Anything civilized, I mean." A touch of scaredness began to appear in his eyes and voice. Suddenly he thrust back his chair and stood up. He was pale, and passed his hand wearily across his forehead. "I'm so tired," he stammered, glancing round the room. "I don't feel that any of you are really trying to help me. I'm only asking a simple question. It's obvious you must know the answer to it. When you had all these modern baths installed, how did they get here?"

There followed another silence.

"You won't tell me, then? It's part of the mystery of everything else, I suppose. Conway, I must say I think you're damned slack. Why don't *you* get at the truth? I'm all in, for the time being—but—to-morrow, mind—we *must* get away to-morrow—it's essential—"

He would have slid to the floor had not Conway caught him and helped him to a chair. Then he recovered a little, but did not speak.

"To-morrow he will be much better," said Chang gently. "The air here is difficult for the stranger at first, but one soon becomes acclimatized."

Conway felt himself waking from a trance. "Things have been a little trying for him," he commented with rather rueful mildness. He added, more briskly: "I expect we're all feeling it somewhat. I think we'd better adjourn this discussion and go to bed. Barnard, will you look after Mallinson? And I'm sure *you're* in need of sleep too, Miss Brinklow." There had been some signal given, for at that moment a servant appeared. "Yes, we'll get along—good night—good night—I shall soon follow." He almost pushed them out of the room, and then, with a scantness of ceremony that was in marked contrast with his earlier manner, turned to his host. Mallinson's reproach had spurred him.

"Now, sir, I don't want to detain you long, so I'd better come to the point. My friend is impetuous, but I don't blame him, he's quite right to make things clear. Our return journey has to be arranged, and we can't do it without help from you or from others in this place. Of course, I realize that leaving to-morrow is impossible, and for my own part I hope to find a minimum stay quite interesting. But that, perhaps, is not the attitude of my companions. So if it's true, as you say, that you can do nothing for us yourself, please put us in touch with some one else who can."

The Chinese answered: "You are wiser than your friends, my dear sir, and therefore you are less impatient. I am glad."

"That's not an answer."

Chang began to laugh, a jerky, high pitched chuckle so obviously forced that Conway recognized in it the polite pretense of seeing an imaginary joke with which the Chinese "saves face" at awkward moments. "I feel sure you have no cause to worry about the matter," came the reply, after an interval. "No doubt in due course we shall be able to give you all the help you need. There are difficulties, as you can imagine, but if we all approach the problem sensibly, and without undue haste—"

"I'm not suggesting haste. I'm merely seeking information about porters."

"Well, my dear sir, that raises another point. I very much doubt whether you will easily find men willing to undertake such a journey. They have their homes in the valley, and they don't care for leaving them to make long and arduous trips outside."

"They can be prevailed upon to do so, though, or else why and where were they escorting you this morning?"

"This morning? Oh, that was quite a different matter."

"In what way? Weren't you setting out on a journey when I and my friends chanced to come across you?"

There was no response to this, and presently Conway continued in a

quieter voice: "I understand. Then it was *not* a chance meeting. I had wondered all along, in fact. So you came there deliberately to intercept us. That
suggests you must have known of our arrival beforehand. And the interesting
question is, *How?*"

His words laid a note of stress amidst the exquisite quietude of the scene.
The lantern light showed up the face of the Chinese; it was calm and
statuesque. Suddenly, with a small gesture of the hand, Chang broke the
strain; pulling aside a silken tapestry he undraped a window leading to a
balcony. Then, with a touch upon Conway's arm, he led him into the cold
crystal air. "You are clever," he said dreamily, "but not entirely correct. For
that reason I should counsel you not to worry your friends by these abstract discussions. Believe me, neither you nor they are in any danger at
Shangri-La."

"But it isn't danger we're bothering about. It's delay."

"I realize that. And of course there *may* be a certain delay, quite un-
avoidably."

"If it's only for a short time, and genuinely unavoidable, then naturally
we shall have to put up with it as best we can."

"How very sensible, for we desire nothing more than that you and your
companions should enjoy every moment of your stay here."

"That's all very well, and as I told you, in a personal sense I can't say
I shall mind a great deal. It's a new and interesting experience, and in any
case, we need some rest."

He was gazing upward to the gleaming pyramid of Karakal. At that moment, in bright moonlight, it seemed as if a hand reached high might just
touch it; it was so brittle-clear against the blue immensity beyond.

"To-morrow," said Chang, "you may find it even more interesting. And as
for rest, if you are fatigued, there are not many better places in the world."

Indeed, as Conway continued to gaze, a deeper repose overspread him, as
if the spectacle were as much for the mind as for the eye. There was hardly
any stir of wind, in contrast to the upland gales that had raged the night
before; the whole valley, he perceived, was a land-locked harbor, with
Karakal brooding over it, lighthouse-fashion. The simile grew as he considered it, for there was actually light on the summit, an ice blue gleam that
matched the splendor it reflected. Something prompted him then to enquire
the literal interpretation of the name, and Chang's answer came as a whispered echo of his own musing. "Karakal, in the valley patois, means Blue
Moon," said the Chinese.

Conway did not pass on his conclusion that the arrival of himself and
party at Shangri-La had been in some way expected by its inhabitants. He
had had it in mind that he must do so, and he was aware that the matter
was important; but when morning came his awareness troubled him so little, in any but a theoretical sense, that he shrank from being the cause of
greater concern in others. One part of him insisted that there was something
distinctly queer about the place, that the attitude of Chang on the previous

evening had been far from reassuring, and that the party were virtually prisoners unless and until the authorities chose to do more for them. And it was clearly his duty to compel them to do this. After all, he was a representative of the British Government, if nothing else; it was iniquitous that the inmates of a Tibetan monastery should refuse him any proper request. . . . That, no doubt, was the normal official view that would be taken; and part of Conway was both normal and official. No one could better play the strong man on occasion; during those final difficult days before the evacuation he had behaved in a manner which (he reflected wryly) should earn him nothing less than a knighthood and a Henty school prize novel entitled *With Conway at Baskul*. To have taken on himself the leadership of some scores of mixed civilians, including women and children, to have sheltered them all in a small consulate during a hot-blooded revolution led by antiforeign agitators, and to have bullied and cajoled the revolutionaries into permitting a wholesale evacuation by air, it was not, he felt, a bad achievement. Perhaps by pulling wires and writing interminable reports, he could wangle something out of it in the next New Year Honors. At any rate it had won him Mallinson's fervent admiration. Unfortunately, the youth must now be finding him so much more of a disappointment. It was a pity, of course, but Conway had grown used to people liking him only because they misunderstood him. He was not genuinely one of those resolute, strong-jawed, hammer-and-tongs empire builders; the semblance he had given was merely a little one act play, repeated from time to time by arrangement with fate and the Foreign Office, and for a salary which any one could turn up in the pages of Whitaker.

The truth was, the puzzle of Shangri-La, and of his own arrival there, was beginning to exercise over him a rather charming fascination. In any case he found it hard to feel any personal misgivings. His official job was always liable to take him into odd parts of the world, and the odder they were, the less, as a rule, he suffered from boredom; why, then, grumble because accident, instead of a chit from Whitehall, had sent him to this oddest place of all?

He was, in fact, very far from grumbling. When he rose in the morning and saw the soft lapis blue of the sky through his window, he would not have chosen to be elsewhere on earth either in Peshawar or Piccadilly. He was glad to find that on the others, also, a night's repose had had a heartening effect. Barnard was able to joke quite cheerfully about beds, baths, breakfasts, and other hospitable amenities. Miss Brinklow admitted that the most strenuous search of her apartment had failed to reveal any of the drawbacks she had been well prepared for. Even Mallinson had acquired a touch of half sulky complacency. "I suppose we shan't get away to-day after all," he muttered, "unless somebody looks pretty sharp about it. These fellows are typically Oriental, you can't get them to do anything quickly and efficiently."

Conway accepted the remark. Mallinson had been out of England just under a year; long enough, no doubt, to justify a generalization which he would probably still repeat when he had been out for twenty. And it was true, of course, in some degree. Yet to Conway it did not appear that the Eastern races were abnormally dilatory, but rather that Englishmen and

Americans charged about the world in a state of continual and rather preposterous fever-heat. It was a point of view that he hardly expected any fellow Westerner to share, but he was more faithful to it as he grew older in
years and experience. On the other hand, it was true enough that Chang
was a subtle quibbler and that there was much justification for Mallinson's
impatience. Conway had a slight wish that he could feel impatient too; it
would have been so much easier for the boy.

He said: "I think we'd better wait and see what to-day brings. It was
perhaps too optimistic to expect them to do anything last night."

Mallinson looked up sharply. "I suppose you think I made a fool of myself, being so urgent? I couldn't help it; I thought that Chinese fellow was
damned fishy, and I do still. Did you succeed in getting any sense out of
him after I'd gone to bed?"

"We didn't stay talking long. He was rather vague and noncommittal
about most things."

"We shall jolly well have to keep him up to scratch to-day."

"No doubt," agreed Conway, without marked enthusiasm for the prospect.
"Meanwhile this is an excellent breakfast." It consisted of pomelo, tea, and
chupatties, perfectly prepared and served. Towards the finish of the meal
Chang entered and with a little bow began the exchange of politely conventional greetings which, in the English language, sounded just a trifle unwieldy. Conway would have preferred to talk in Chinese, but so far he had
not let it be known that he spoke any Eastern tongue; he felt it might be a
useful card up his sleeve. He listened gravely to Chang's courtesies, and gave
assurances that he had slept well and felt much better. Chang expressed his
pleasure at that, and added: "Truly, as your national poet says, 'Sleep knits
up the raveled sleeve of care.'"

This display of erudition was not too well received. Mallinson answered
with that touch of scorn which any healthy-minded young Englishman must
feel at the mention of poetry. "I suppose you mean Shakespeare, though I
don't recognize the quotation. But I know another one that says 'Stand not
upon the order of your going, but go at once.' Without being impolite, that's
rather what we should all like to do. And I want to hunt round for those
porters right away, this morning, if you've no objection."

The Chinese received the ultimatum impassively, replying at length: "I
am sorry to tell you that it would be of little use. I fear we have no men
available who would be willing to accompany you so far from their homes."

"But good God, man, you don't suppose we're going to take that for an
answer, do you?"

"I am sincerely regretful, but I can suggest no other."

"You seem to have figgered it all out since last night," put in Barnard.
"You weren't nearly so dead sure of things then."

"I did not wish to disappoint you when you were so tired from your journey. Now, after a refreshing night, I am in hope that you will see matters
in a more reasonable light."

"Look here," intervened Conway briskly, "this sort of vagueness and prevarication won't do. You know we can't stay here indefinitely. It's equally obvious that we can't get away by ourselves. What, then, do you propose?"

Chang smiled with a radiance that was clearly for Conway alone. "My dear sir, it is a pleasure to make the suggestion that is in my mind. To your friend's attitude there was no answer, but to the demand of a wise man there is always a response. You may recollect that it was remarked yesterday, again by your friend, I believe, that we are bound to have occasional communication with the outside world. That is quite true. From time to time we require certain things from distant *entrepôts*, and it is our habit to obtain them in due course, by what methods and with what formalities I need not trouble you. The point of importance is that such a consignment is expected to arrive shortly, and as the men who make delivery will afterwards return, it seems to me that you might manage to come to some arrangement with them. Indeed I cannot think of a better plan, and I hope, when they arrive—"

"When *do* they arrive?" interrupted Mallinson bluntly.

"The exact date is, of course, impossible to forecast. You have yourself had experience of the difficulty of movement in this part of the world. A hundred things may happen to cause uncertainty, hazards of weather—"

Conway again intervened. "Let's get this clear. You're suggesting that we should employ as porters the men who are shortly due here with some goods. That's not a bad idea as far as it goes, but we must know a little more about it. First, as you've already been asked, when are these people expected? And second, where will they take us?"

"That is a question you would have to put to them."

"Would they take us to India?"

"It is hardly possible for me to say."

"Well, let's have an answer to the other question. When will they be here? I don't ask for a date, I just want some idea whether it's likely to be next week or next year."

"It might be about a month from now. Probably not more than two months."

"Or three, four, or five months," broke in Mallinson hotly. "And you think we're going to wait here for this convoy or caravan or whatever it is to take us God knows where at some completely vague time in the distant future?"

"I think, sir, the phrase 'distant future' is hardly appropriate. Unless something unforeseen occurs, the period of waiting should not be longer than I have said."

"But *two months!* Two months in this place! It's preposterous! Conway, you surely can't contemplate it! Why, two weeks would be the limit!"

Chang gathered his gown about him in a little gesture of finality. "I am sorry. I did not wish to offend. The lamasery continues to offer all of you its utmost hospitality for as long as you have the misfortune to remain. I can say no more."

"You don't need to," retorted Mallinson furiously. "And if you think you've got the whip hand over us, you'll soon find you're damn well mistaken! We'll get all the porters we want, don't worry. You can bow and scrape and say what you like—"

Conway laid a restraining hand on his arm. Mallinson in a temper presented a child-like spectacle; he was apt to say anything that came into his head, regardless alike of point and decorum. Conway thought it readily forgivable in one so constituted and circumstanced, but he feared it might affront the more delicate susceptibilities of a Chinese. Fortunately Chang had ushered himself out, with admirable tact, in good time to escape the worst.

CHAPTER FIVE

They spent the rest of the morning discussing the matter. It was certainly a shock for four persons who in the ordinary course should have been luxuriating in the clubs and mission houses of Peshawar, to find themselves faced instead with the prospect of two months in a Tibetan monastery. But it was in the nature of things that the initial shock of their arrival should have left them with slender reserves either of indignation or astonishment; even Mallinson, after his first outburst, subsided into a mood of half-bewildered fatalism. "I'm past arguing about it, Conway," he said, puffing at a cigarette with nervous irritability. "You know how I feel. I've said all along that there's something queer about this business. It's crooked. I'd like to be out of it this minute."

"I don't blame you for that," replied Conway. "Unfortunately, it's not a question of what any of us would like, but of what we've all got to put up with. Frankly, if these people say they won't or can't supply us with the necessary porters, there's nothing for it but to wait till the other fellows come. I'm sorry to admit that we're so helpless in the matter, but I'm afraid it's the truth."

"You mean we've got to stay here for two months?"

"I don't see what else we can do."

Mallinson flicked his cigarette ash with a gesture of forced nonchalance. "All right, then. Two months it is. And now let's all shout hooray about it."

Conway went on: "I don't see why it should be much worse than two months in any other isolated part of the world. People in our jobs are used to being sent to odd places, I think I can say that of us all. Of course, it's bad for those of us who have friends and relatives. Personally, I'm fortunate in that respect, I can't think of any one who'll worry over me acutely, and my work, whatever it might have been, can easily be done by somebody else."

He turned to the others as if inviting them to state their own cases. Mallinson proffered no information, but Conway knew roughly how he was situated. He had parents and a girl in England; it made things hard.

Barnard, on the other hand, accepted the position with what Conway had learned to regard as an habitual good humor. "Well, I guess I'm pretty lucky, for that matter, two months in the penitentiary won't kill me. As for the folks in my home town, they won't bat an eye. I've always been a bad letter writer."

"You forget that our names will be in the papers," Conway reminded him. "We shall all be posted missing, and people will naturally assume the worst."

Barnard looked startled for the moment; then he replied, with a slight grin: "Oh, yes, that's true, but it don't affect me, I assure you."

Conway was glad it didn't, though the matter remained a little puzzling. He turned to Miss Brinklow, who till then had been remarkably silent; she had not offered any opinion during the interview with Chang. He imagined that she too might have comparatively few personal worries. She said brightly: "As Mr. Barnard says, two months here is nothing to make a fuss about. It's all the same, wherever one is, when one's in the Lord's service. Providence has sent me here. I regard it as a call."

Conway thought the attitude a very convenient one, in the circumstances. "I'm sure," he said encouragingly, "you'll find your mission society pleased with you when you *do* return. You'll be able to give much useful information. We'll all of us have had an experience, for that matter. That should be a small consolation."

The talk then became general. Conway was rather surprised at the ease with which Barnard and Miss Brinklow had accommodated themselves to the new prospect. He was relieved, however, as well; it left him with only one disgruntled person to deal with. Yet even Mallinson, after the strain of all the arguing, was experiencing a reaction; he was still perturbed, but more willing to look at the brighter side of things. "Heaven knows what we shall find to do with ourselves," he exclaimed, but the mere fact of making such a remark showed that he was trying to reconcile himself.

"The first rule must be to avoid getting on each other's nerves," replied Conway. "Happily, the place seems big enough, and by no means overpopulated. Except for servants, we've only seen one of its inhabitants so far."

Barnard could find another reason for optimism. "We won't starve, at any rate, if our meals up to now are a fair sample. You know, Conway, this place isn't run without plenty of hard cash. Those baths, for instance, they cost real money. And I can't see that anybody earns anything here, unless those chaps in the valley have jobs, and even then, they wouldn't produce enough for export. I'd like to know if they work any minerals."

"The whole place is a confounded mystery," responded Mallinson. "I dare say they've got pots of money hidden away, like the Jesuits. As for the baths, probably some millionaire supporter presented them. Anyhow, it won't worry me, once I get away. I must say, though, the view *is* rather good, in its way. Fine winter sport center if it were in the right spot. I wonder if one could get any skiing on some of those slopes up yonder?"

Conway gave him a searching and slightly amused glance. "Yesterday, when I found some edelweiss, you reminded me that I wasn't in the Alps. I think it's my turn to say the same thing now. I wouldn't advise you to try any of your Wengen-Scheidegg tricks in this part of the world."

"I don't suppose anybody here has ever seen a ski-jump."

"Or even an ice-hockey match," responded Conway banteringly. "You might try to raise some teams. What about 'Gentlemen *v.* Lamas'?"

"It would certainly teach them to play the game," Miss Brinklow put in with sparkling seriousness.

Adequate comment upon this might have been difficult, but there was no necessity, since lunch was about to be served, and its character and promptness combined to make an agreeable impression. Afterwards, when Chang entered, there was small disposition to continue the squabble. With great tactfulness the Chinese assumed that he was still on good terms with everybody, and the four exiles allowed the assumption to stand. Indeed, when he suggested that they might care to be shown a little more of the lamasery buildings, and that if so, he would be pleased to act as guide, the offer was readily accepted. "Why, surely," said Barnard. "We may as well give the place the once-over while we're here. I reckon it'll be a long time before any of us pay a second visit."

Miss Brinklow struck a more thought-giving note. "When we left Baskul in that aeroplane I'm sure I never dreamed we should ever get to a place like this," she murmured as they all moved off under Chang's escort.

"And we don't know yet why we have," answered Mallinson unforgetfully.

Conway had no race or color prejudice, and it was an affectation for him to pretend, as he sometimes did in clubs and first-class railway carriages, that he set any particular store on the "whiteness" of a lobster-red face under a topee. It saved trouble to let it be so assumed, especially in India, and Conway was a conscientious trouble-saver. But in China it had been less necessary; he had had many Chinese friends, and it had never occurred to him to treat them as inferiors. Hence, in his intercourse with Chang, he was sufficiently unpreoccupied to see in him a mannered old gentleman who might not be entirely trustworthy, but who was certainly of high intelligence. Mallinson, on the other hand, tended to regard him through the bars of an imaginary cage; Miss Brinklow was sharp and sprightly, as with the heathen in his blindness; while Barnard's wise-cracking *bonhomie* was of the kind he would have cultivated with a butler.

Meanwhile the grand tour of Shangri-La was interesting enough to transcend these attitudes. It was not the first monastic institution Conway had inspected, but it was easily the largest and, apart from its situation, the most remarkable. The mere procession through rooms and courtyards was an afternoon's exercise, though he was aware of many apartments passed by, indeed, of whole buildings into which Chang did not offer admission. The party were shown enough, however, to confirm the impressions each one of them had formed already. Barnard was more certain than ever that the lamas were rich; Miss Brinklow discovered abundant evidence that they were immoral. Mallinson, after the first novelty had worn off, found himself no less fatigued than on many sight-seeing excursions at lower altitudes; the lamas, he feared, were not likely to be his heroes.

Conway alone submitted to a rich and growing enchantment. It was not so much any individual thing that attracted him as the gradual revelation of elegance, of modest and impeccable taste, of harmony so fragrant that it seemed to gratify the eye without arresting it. Only indeed by a conscious effort did he recall himself from the artist's mood to the connoisseur's, and then he recognized treasures that museums and millionaires alike would have bargained for, exquisite pearl blue Sung ceramics, paintings in tinted inks preserved for more than a thousand years, lacquers in which the cold and lovely detail of fairyland was not so much depicted as orchestrated. A world of incomparable refinements still lingered tremulously in porcelain and varnish, yielding an instant of emotion before its dissolution into purest thought. There was no boastfulness, no striving after effect, no concentrated attack upon the feelings of the beholder. These delicate perfections had an air of having fluttered into existence like petals from a flower. They would have maddened a collector, but Conway did not collect; he lacked both money and the acquisitive instinct. His liking for Chinese art was an affair of the mind; in a world of increasing noise and hugeness, he turned in private to gentle, precise, and miniature things. And as he passed through room after room, a certain pathos touched him remotely at the thought of Karakal's piled immensity over against such fragile charms.

The lamasery, however, had more to offer than a display of Chinoiserie. One of its features, for instance, was a very delightful library, lofty and spacious, and containing a multitude of books so retiringly housed in bays and alcoves that the whole atmosphere was more of wisdom than of learning, of good manners rather than seriousness. Conway, during a rapid glance at some of the shelves, found much to astonish him; the world's best literature was there, it seemed, as well as a great deal of abstruse and curious stuff that he could not appraise. Volumes in English, French, German, and Russian abounded, and there were vast quantities of Chinese and other Eastern scripts. A section which interested him particularly was devoted to Tibetiana, if it might be so called; he noticed several rarities, among them the *Novo Descubrimento de grao catayo ou dos Regos de Tibet*, by Antonio de Andrada (Lisbon, 1626); Athanasius Kircher's *China* (Antwerp, 1667); Thevenot's *Voyage à la Chine des Pères Grueber et d'Orville*; and Beligatti's *Relazione Inedita di un Viaggio al Tibet*. He was examining the last named when he noticed Chang's eyes fixed on him in suave curiosity. "You are a scholar, perhaps?" came the enquiry.

Conway found it hard to reply. His period of donhood at Oxford gave him some right to assent, but he knew that the word, though the highest of compliments from a Chinese, had yet a faintly priggish sound for English ears, and chiefly out of consideration for his companions he demurred to it. He said: "I enjoy reading, of course, but my work during recent years hasn't supplied many opportunities for the studious life."

"Yet you wish for it?"

"Oh, I wouldn't say all that, but I'm certainly aware of its attractions."

Mallinson, who had picked up a book, interrupted: "Here's something for your studious life, Conway. It's a map of the country."

"We have a collection of several hundreds," said Chang. "They are all open to your inspection, but perhaps I can save you trouble in one respect. You will not find Shangri-La marked on any."

"Curious," Conway made comment. "I wonder why?"

"There is a very good reason, but I am afraid that is all I can say."

Conway smiled, but Mallinson looked peevish again. "Still piling up the mystery," he said. "So far we haven't seen much that any one need bother to conceal."

Suddenly Miss Brinklow came to life out of a mute preoccupation. "Aren't you going to show us the lamas at work?" she fluted, in the tone which one felt had intimidated many a Cook's man. One felt, too, that her mind was probably full of hazy visions of native handicrafts, prayer-mat weaving, or something picturesquely primitive that she could talk about when she got home. She had an extraordinary knack of never seeming very much surprised, yet of always seeming very slightly indignant, a combination of fixities which was not in the least disturbed by Chang's response: "I am sorry to say it is impossible. The lamas are never, or perhaps I should say only very rarely, seen by those outside the lamahood."

"I guess we'll have to miss 'em then," agreed Barnard. "But I do think it's a real pity. You've no notion how much I'd like to have shaken the hand of your head-man."

Chang acknowledged the remark with benign seriousness. Miss Brinklow, however, was not yet to be side-tracked. "What do the lamas do?" she continued.

"They devote themselves, madam, to contemplation and to the pursuit of wisdom."

"But that isn't *doing* anything."

"Then, madam, they do nothing."

"I thought as much." She found occasion to sum up. "Well, Mr. Chang, it's a pleasure being shown all these things, I'm sure, but you won't convince me that a place like this does any real good. I prefer something more practical."

"Perhaps you would like to take tea?"

Conway wondered at first if this were intended ironically, but it soon appeared not; the afternoon had passed swiftly, and Chang, though frugal in eating, had the typical Chinese fondness for tea-drinking at frequent intervals. Miss Brinklow, too, confessed that visiting art galleries and museums always gave her a touch of headache. The party, therefore, fell in with the suggestion, and followed Chang through several courtyards to a scene of quite sudden and unmatched loveliness. From a colonnade steps descended to a garden, in which a lotus pool lay entrapped, the leaves so closely set that they gave an impression of a floor of moist green tiles. Fringing the pool were posed a brazen menagerie of lions, dragons, and unicorns, each offering a stylized ferocity that emphasized rather than offended the surrounding peace. The whole picture was so perfectly proportioned that the eye was entirely unhastened from one part to another; there was no vying or vanity, and even the summit of Karakal, peerless above the blue tiled roofs, seemed to have surrendered within the framework of an exquisite artistry. "Pretty little place," commented Barnard, as Chang led the way into an open pavilion which, to Conway's further delight, contained a harpsichord and a modern grand piano. He found this in some ways the crowning astonishment of a rather astonishing afternoon. Chang answered all his questions with complete candor up to a point; the lamas, he explained, held Western music in high esteem, particularly that of Mozart; they had a collection of all the great European compositions, and some were skilled performers on various instruments.

Barnard was chiefly impressed by the transport problem. "D'you mean to tell me that this pi-anno was brought here by the route we came along yesterday?"

"There is no other."

"Well, that certainly beats everything! Why, with a phonograph and a radio you'd be all fixed complete! Perhaps, though, you aren't yet acquainted with up-to-date music?"

"Oh, yes, we have had reports, but we are advised that the mountains would make wireless reception impossible, and as for a phonograph, the suggestion has already come before the authorities, but they have felt no need to hurry in the matter."

"I'd believe that even if you hadn't told me," Barnard retorted. "I guess that must be the slogan of your society, 'No hurry.'" He laughed loudly and then went on: "Well, to come down to details, suppose in due course your bosses decide that they *do* want a phonograph, what's the procedure? The makers wouldn't deliver here, that's a sure thing. You must have an agent in Pekin or Shanghai or somewhere, and I'll bet everything costs plenty by the time you handle it."

But Chang was no more to be drawn than on a previous occasion. "Your surmises are intelligent, Mr. Barnard, but I fear I cannot discuss them."

So there they were again, Conway reflected, edging the invisible borderline between what might and might not be revealed. He thought he could soon begin to map out that line in imagination, though the impact of a new surprise deferred the matter. For servants were already bringing in the shallow bowls of scented tea, and along with the agile, lithe-limbed Tibetans there had also entered, quite inconspicuously, a girl in Chinese dress. She went directly to the harpsichord and began to play a gavotte by Rameau. The first bewitching twang stirred in Conway a pleasure that was beyond amazement; those silvery airs of eighteenth century France seemed to match in elegance the Sun vases and exquisite lacquers and the lotus pool beyond; the same death-defying fragrance hung about them, lending immortality through an age to which their spirit was alien. Then he noticed the player. She had the long, slender nose, high cheekbones, and egg-shell pallor of the Manchu; her black hair was drawn tightly back and braided; she looked very finished and miniature. Her mouth was like a little pink convolvulus, and she was quite still, except for her long-fingered hands. As soon as the gavotte was ended, she made a little obeisance and went out.

Chang smiled after her and then, with a touch of personal triumph, upon Conway. "You are pleased?" he queried.

"Who is she?" asked Mallinson, before Conway could reply.

"Her name is Lo-Tsen. She has much skill with Western keyboard music. Like myself, she has not yet attained the full initiation."

"I should think not, indeed!" exclaimed Miss Brinklow. "She looks hardly more than a child. So you have women lamas, then?"

"There are no sex distinctions among us."

"Extraordinary business, this lamahood of yours," Mallinson commented loftily, after a pause. The rest of the tea-drinking proceeded without conversation; echoes of the harpsichord seemed still in the air, imposing a strange spell. Presently, leading the departure from the pavilion, Chang ventured to hope that the tour had been enjoyable. Conway, replying for the others, see-sawed with the customary courtesies. Chang then assured them of his own equal enjoyment, and hoped they would consider the resources of the music room and library wholly at their disposal throughout their stay. Conway, with some sincerity, thanked him again. "But what about the lamas?" he added. "Don't they ever want to use them?"

"They yield place with much gladness to their honored guests."

"Well, that's what I call real handsome," said Barnard. "And what's more, it shows that the lamas do really know we exist. That's a step forward, anyhow, makes me feel much more at home. You've certainly got a swell outfit here, Chang, and that little girl of yours plays the pi-anno very nicely. How old would she be, I wonder?"

"I am afraid I cannot tell you."

Barnard laughed. "You don't give away secrets about a lady's age, is that it?"

"Precisely," answered Chang with a faintly shadowing smile.

That evening, after dinner, Conway made occasion to leave the others and stroll out into the calm, moon-washed courtyards. Shangri-La was lovely then, touched with the mystery that lies at the core of all loveliness. The air was cold and still; the mighty spire of Karakal looked nearer, much nearer than by daylight. Conway was physically happy, emotionally satisfied, and mentally at ease; but in his intellect, which was not quite the same thing as mind, there was a little stir. He was puzzled. The line of secrecy that he had begun to map out grew sharper, but only to reveal an inscrutable background. The whole amazing series of events that had happened to him and his three chance companions swung now into a sort of focus; he could not yet understand them, but he believed they were somehow to be understood.

Passing along a cloister, he reached the terrace leaning over the valley. The scent of tuberose assailed him, full of delicate associations; in China it was called "the smell of moonlight." He thought whimsically that if moonlight had a sound also, it might well be the Rameau gavotte he had heard so

recently; and that set him thinking of the little Manchu. It had not occurred
to him to picture women at Shangri-La; one did not associate their presence
with the general practice of monasticism. Still, he reflected, it might not be
a disagreeable innovation; indeed, a female harpsichordist might be an asset
to any community that permitted itself to be (in Chang's words) "moderately heretical."

He gazed over the edge into the blue-black emptiness. The drop was
phantasmal; perhaps as much as a mile. He wondered if he would be allowed
to descend it and inspect the valley civilization that had been talked of.
The notion of this strange culture-pocket, hidden amongst unknown ranges,
and ruled over by some vague kind of theocracy, interested him as a student
of history, apart from the curious though perhaps related secrets of the
lamasery.

Suddenly, on a flutter of air, came sounds from far below. Listening intently, he could hear gongs and trumpets and also (though perhaps only in
imagination) the massed wail of voices. The sounds faded on a veer of the
wind, then returned to fade again. But the hint of life and liveliness in those
veiled depths served only to emphasize the austere serenity of Shangri-La.
Its forsaken courts and pale pavilions simmered in repose from which all the
fret of existence had ebbed away, leaving a hush as if moments hardly dared
to pass. Then, from a window high above the terrace, he caught the rose-gold
of lantern light; was it there that the lamas devoted themselves to contemplation and the pursuit of wisdom, and were those devotions now in
progress? The problem seemed one that he could solve merely by entering

at the nearest door and exploring through gallery and corridor until the truth were his; but he knew that such freedom was illusory, and that in fact his movements were watched. Two Tibetans had padded across the terrace and were idling near the parapet. Good-humored fellows they looked, shrugging their colored cloaks negligently over naked shoulders. The whisper of gongs and trumpets uprose again, and Conway heard one of the men question his companion. The answer came: "They have buried Talu." Conway, whose knowledge of Tibetan was very slight, hoped they would continue talking; he could not gather much from a single remark. After a pause the questioner, who was inaudible, resumed the conversation, and obtained answers which Conway overheard and loosely understood as follows:

"He died outside."

"He obeyed the high ones of Shangri-La."

"He came through the air over the great mountains with a bird to hold him."

"Strangers he brought, also."

"Talu was not afraid of the outside wind, nor of the outside cold."

"Though he went outside long ago, the valley of Blue Moon remembers him still."

Nothing more was said that Conway could interpret, and after waiting for some time he went back to his own quarters. He had heard enough to turn another key in the locked mystery, and it fitted so well that he wondered he had failed to supply it by his own deductions. It had, of course, crossed his mind, but a certain initial and fantastic unreasonableness about it had been too much for him. Now he perceived that the unreasonableness, however fantastic, was to be swallowed. That flight from Baskul had *not* been the meaningless exploit of a madman. It had been something planned, prepared, and carried out at the instigation of Shangri-La. The dead pilot was known by name to those who lived there; he had been one of them, in some sense; his death was mourned. Everything pointed to a high directing intelligence bent upon its own purposes; there had been, as it were, a single arch of intention spanning the inexplicable hours and miles. But what *was* that intention? For what possible reason could four chance passengers in a British Government aeroplane be whisked away to these trans-Himalayan solitudes?

Conway was somewhat aghast at the problem, but by no means wholly displeased with it. It challenged him in the only way in which he was readily amenable to challenge—by touching a certain clarity of brain that only demanded a sufficient task. One thing he decided instantly; the cold thrill of discovery must not yet be communicated, neither to his companions, who could not help him, nor to his hosts, who doubtless would not.

CHAPTER SIX

"I reckon some folks have to get used to worse places," Barnard remarked towards the close of his first week at Shangri-La, and it was doubtless one of the many lessons to be drawn. By that time the party had settled themselves into something like a daily routine, and with Chang's assistance the boredom was no more acute than on many a planned holiday. They had all become acclimatized to the atmosphere, finding it quite invigorating so long as heavy exertion was avoided. They had learned that the days were warm and the nights cold, that the lamasery was almost completely sheltered from winds, that avalanches on Karakal were most frequent about midday, that the valley grew a good brand of tobacco, that some foods and drinks were more pleasant than others, and that each one of themselves had personal tastes and peculiarities. They had, in fact, discovered as much about each other as four new pupils of a school from which every one else was mysteriously absent. Chang was tireless in his efforts to make smooth the rough places. He conducted excursions, suggested occupations, recommended books, talked with his slow, careful fluency whenever there was an awkward pause at meals, and was on every occasion benign, courteous, and resourceful. The line of demarcation was so marked between information willingly supplied and politely declined that the latter ceased to stir resentment, except fitfully from Mallinson. Conway was content to take note of it, adding another fragment to his constantly accumulating data. Barnard even "jollied" the Chinese after the manner and traditions of a Middle West Rotary convention. "You know, Chang, this is a damned bad hotel. Don't you have any newspapers sent here ever? I'd give all the books in your library for this morning's *Herald-Tribune*." Chang's replies were always serious, though it did not necessarily follow that he took every question seriously. "We have the files of *The Times*, Mr. Barnard, up to a few years ago. But only, I regret to say, the London *Times*."

Conway was glad to find that the valley was not to be "out of bounds," though the difficulties of the descent made unescorted visits impossible. In company with Chang they all spent a whole day inspecting the green floor that was so pleasantly visible from the cliff-edge, and to Conway, at any rate, the trip was of absorbing interest. They traveled in bamboo sedan chairs, swinging perilously over precipices while their bearers in front and to the rear picked a way nonchalantly down the steep track. It was not a route for the squeamish, but when at last they reached the lower levels of forest and foothill the supreme good fortune of the lamasery was everywhere to be realized. For the valley was nothing less than an enclosed paradise of amazing fertility, in which the vertical difference of a few thousand feet spanned the whole gulf between temperate and tropical. Crops of unusual diversity grew in profusion and contiguity, with not an inch of ground untended. The whole cultivated area stretched for perhaps a dozen miles,

varying in width from one to five, and though narrow, it had the luck to take
sunlight at the hottest part of the day. The atmosphere, indeed, was pleasantly warm even out of the sun, though the little rivulets that watered the
soil were ice-cold from the snows. Conway felt again, as he gazed up at the
stupendous mountain wall, that there was a superb and exquisite peril in
the scene; but for some chance-placed barrier, the whole valley would clearly
have been a lake, nourished continually from the glacial heights around it.
Instead of which, a few streams dribbled through to fill reservoirs and irrigate
fields and plantations with a disciplined conscientiousness worthy of a
sanitary engineer. The whole design was almost uncannily fortunate, so long
as the structure of the frame remained unmoved by earthquake or landslide.

But even such vaguely future fears could only enhance the total loveliness
of the present. Once again Conway was captivated, and by the same qualities
of charm and ingenuity that had made his years in China happier than others. The vast encircling *massif* made perfect contrast with the tiny lawns and
weedless gardens, the painted tea-houses by the stream, and the frivolously
toy-like houses. The inhabitants seemed to him a very successful blend of
Chinese and Tibetan; they were cleaner and handsomer than the average of
either race, and seemed to have suffered little from the inevitable inbreeding
of such a small society. They smiled and laughed as they passed the chaired
strangers, and had a friendly word for Chang; they were good-humored and
mildly inquisitive, courteous and carefree, busy at innumerable jobs but not
in any apparent hurry over them. Altogether Conway thought it one of the
pleasantest communities he had ever seen, and even Miss Brinklow, who had
been watching for symptoms of pagan degradation, had to admit that everything looked very well "on the surface." She was relieved to find the natives
"completely" clothed, even though the women did wear ankle-tight Chinese
trousers; and her most imaginative scrutiny of a Buddhist temple revealed
only a few items that could be regarded as somewhat doubtfully phallic.
Chang explained that the temple had its own lamas, who were under loose
control from Shangri-La, though not of the same order. There were also, it
appeared, a Taoist and a Confucian temple further along the valley. "The
jewel has facets," said the Chinese, "and it is possible that many religions
are moderately true."

"I agree with that," said Barnard heartily. "I never did believe in sectarian
jealousies. Chang, you're a philosopher. I must remember that remark of
yours. 'Many religions are moderately true.' You fellows up on the mountain
must be a lot of wise guys to have thought that out. You're right, too, I'm
dead certain of it."

"But we," responded Chang dreamily, "are only *moderately* certain."

Miss Brinklow could not be bothered with all that, which seemed to her
a sign of mere laziness. In any case she was preoccupied with an idea of her
own. "When I get back," she said with tightening lips, "I shall ask my society
to send a missionary here. And if they grumble at the expense, I shall just
bully them until they agree."

That, clearly, was a much healthier spirit, and even Mallinson, little as he sympathized with foreign missions, could not forbear his admiration. "They ought to send *you*," he said. "That is, of course, if you'd like a place like this."

"It's hardly a question of *liking* it," Miss Brinklow retorted. "One wouldn't like it, naturally—how could one? It's a matter of what one feels one ought to do."

"I think," said Conway, "if I were a missionary I'd choose this rather than quite a lot of other places."

"In that case," snapped Miss Brinklow, "there would be no merit in it, obviously."

"But I wasn't thinking of merit."

"More's the pity, then. There's no good in doing a thing because you like doing it. Look at these people here!"

"They all seem very happy."

"*Exactly*," she answered with a touch of fierceness. She added: "Anyhow, I don't see why I shouldn't make a beginning by studying the language. Can you lend me a book about it, Mr. Chang?"

Chang was at his most mellifluous. "Most certainly, madam, with the greatest of pleasure. And, if I may say so, I think the idea an excellent one."

When they ascended to Shangri-La that evening he treated the matter as one of immediate importance. Miss Brinklow was at first a little daunted by the massive volume compiled by an industrious nineteenth century German (she had more probably imagined some slighter work of a "Brush up your Tibetan" type), but with help from the Chinese and encouragement from Conway she made a good beginning and was soon observed to be extracting grim satisfaction from her task.

Conway, too, found much to interest him, apart from the engrossing problem he had set himself. During the warm, sunlit days he made full use of the library and music room, and was confirmed in his impression that the lamas were of quite exceptional culture. Their taste in books was catholic, at any rate; Plato in Greek touched Omar in English; Nietzsche partnered Newton; Thomas More was there, and also Hannah More, Thomas Moore, George Moore, and even Old Moore. Altogether Conway estimated the number of volumes at between twenty and thirty thousand; and it was tempting to speculate upon the method of selection and acquisition. He sought also to discover how recently there had been additions, but he did not come across anything later than a cheap reprint of *Im Westen Nichts Neues*. During a subsequent visit, however, Chang told him that there were other books published up to about the middle of 1930 which would doubtless be added to the shelves eventually; they had already arrived at the lamasery. "We keep ourselves fairly up-to-date, you see," he commented.

"There are people who would hardly agree with you," replied Conway with a smile. "Quite a lot of things have happened in the world since last year, you know."

"Nothing of importance, my dear sir, that could not have been foreseen in 1920, or that will not be better understood in 1940."

"You're not interested, then, in the latest developments of the world crisis?"

"I shall be very deeply interested—in due course."

"You know, Chang, I believe I'm beginning to understand you. You're geared differently, that's what it is. Time means less to you than it does to most people. If I were in London I wouldn't always be eager to see the latest hour-old newspaper, and you at Shangri-La are no more eager to see a year-old one. Both attitudes seem to me quite sensible. By the way, how long is it since you last had visitors here?"

"That, Mr. Conway, I am unfortunately unable to say."

It was the usual ending to a conversation, and one that Conway found less irritating than the opposite phenomenon from which he had suffered much in his time—the conversation which, try as he would, seemed never to end. He began to like Chang rather more as their meetings multiplied, though it still puzzled him that he met so few of the lamasery personnel; even assuming that the lamas themselves were unapproachable, were there not other postulants besides Chang?

There was, of course, the little Manchu. He saw her sometimes when he visited the music room; but she knew no English, and he was still unwilling to disclose his own Chinese. He could not quite determine whether she played merely for pleasure, or was in some way a student. Her playing, as indeed her whole behavior, was exquisitely formal, and her choice lay always among the more patterned compositions—those of Bach, Corelli, Scarlatti, and occasionally Mozart. She preferred the harpsichord to the piano, but when Conway went to the latter she would listen with grave and almost dutiful appreciation. It was impossible to know what was in her mind; it was difficult even to guess her age. He would have doubted her being over thirty or under thirteen; and yet, in a curious way, such manifest unlikelihoods could neither of them be ruled out as wholly impossible.

Mallinson, who sometimes came to listen to the music for want of anything better to do, found her a very baffling proposition. "I can't think what she's doing here," he said to Conway more than once. "This lama business may be all right for an old fellow like Chang, but what's the attraction in it for a girl? How long has she been here, I wonder?"

"I wonder too, but it's one of those things we're not likely to be told."

"Do you suppose she *likes* being here?"

"I'm bound to say she doesn't appear to *dis*like it."

"She doesn't appear to have feelings at all, for that matter. She's like a little ivory doll more than a human being."

"A charming thing to be like, anyhow."

"As far as it goes."

Conway smiled. "And it goes pretty far, Mallinson, when you come to think about it. After all, the ivory doll has manners, good taste in dress, attractive looks, a pretty touch on the harpsichord, and she doesn't move about a room as if she were playing hockey. Western Europe, so far as I recollect it, contains an exceptionally large number of females who lack those virtues."

"You're an awful cynic about women, Conway."

Conway was used to the charge. He had not actually had a great deal to do with the other sex, and during occasional leaves in Indian hill-stations the reputation of cynic had been as easy to sustain as any other. In truth he had had several delightful friendships with women who would have been pleased to marry him if he had asked them—but he had not asked them. He had once got nearly as far as an announcement in the *Morning Post*, but the girl did not want to live in Pekin and he did not want to live at Tunbridge Wells, mutual reluctances which proved impossible to dislodge. So far as he had had experience of women at all, it had been tentative, intermittent, and somewhat inconclusive. But he was not, for all that, a cynic about them.

He said with a laugh: "I'm thirty-seven—you're twenty-four. That's all it amounts to."

After a pause Mallinson asked suddenly: "Oh, by the way, how old should you say Chang is?"

"Anything," replied Conway lightly, "between forty-nine and a hundred and forty-nine."

Such information, however, was less trustworthy than much else that was available to the new arrivals. The fact that their curiosities were sometimes unsatisfied tended to obscure the really vast quantity of data which Chang was always willing to outpour. There were no secrecies, for instance, about the customs and habits of the valley population, and Conway, who was interested, had talks which might have been worked up into a quite serviceable degree thesis. He was particularly interested, as a student of affairs, in the way the valley population was governed; it appeared, on examination, to be a rather loose and elastic autocracy, operated from the lamasery with a benevolence that was almost casual. It was certainly an established success, as every descent into that fertile paradise made more evident. Conway was puzzled as to the ultimate basis of law and order; there appeared to be neither soldiers nor police, yet surely some provision must be made for the incorrigible? Chang replied that crime was very rare, partly because only serious things were considered crimes, and partly because every one enjoyed a sufficiency of everything he could reasonably desire. In the last resort the personal servants of the lamasery had power to expel an offender from the valley—though this, which was considered an extreme and dreadful punishment, had only very occasionally to be imposed. But the chief factor in the government of Blue Moon, Chang went on to say, was the inculcation of good manners, which made men feel that certain things were "not done," and that they lost caste by doing them. "You English inculcate the same feeling," said Chang, "in your public schools, but not, I fear, in regard to the same things. The inhabitants of our valley, for instance, feel that it is 'not done' to be inhospitable to strangers, to dispute acrimoniously, or to strive for priority amongst one another. The idea of enjoying what your English headmasters call the mimic warfare of the playing-field would seem to them entirely barbarous—indeed, a sheerly wanton stimulation of all the lower instincts."

Conway asked if there were never disputes about women.

"Only very rarely, because it would not be considered good manners to take a woman that another man wanted."

"Supposing somebody wanted her so badly that he didn't care a damn whether it was good manners or not?"

"Then, my dear sir, it would be good manners on the part of the other man to let him have her, and also on the part of the woman to be equally agreeable. You would be surprised, Conway, how the application of a little courtesy all round helps to smooth out these problems."

Certainly during visits to the valley Conway found a spirit of good will and contentment that pleased him all the more because he knew that of all the arts that of government has been brought least to perfection. When he made some complimentary remark, however, Chang responded: "Ah, but you see, we believe that to govern perfectly it is necessary to avoid governing too much."

"Yet you don't have any democratic machinery—voting, and so on?"

"Oh, no. Our people would be quite shocked by having to declare that one policy was completely right and another completely wrong."

Conway smiled. He found the attitude a curiously sympathetic one.

Meanwhile, Miss Brinklow derived her own kind of satisfaction from a study of Tibetan; meanwhile, also, Mallinson fretted and groused, and Barnard persisted in an equanimity which seemed almost equally remarkable, whether it were real or simulated.

"To tell you the truth," said Mallinson, "the fellow's cheerfulness is just about getting on my nerves. I can understand him trying to keep a stiff lip, but that continual joking of his begins to upset me. He'll be the life and soul of the party if we don't watch him."

Conway too had once or twice wondered at the ease with which the American had managed to settle down. He replied: "Isn't it rather lucky for us he *does* take things so well?"

"Personally, I think it's damned peculiar. What do you *know* about him, Conway? I mean who he is, and so on."

"Not much more than you do. I understood he came from Persia and was supposed to have been oil-prospecting. It's his way to take things easily—when the air evacuation was arranged I had quite a job to persuade him to join us at all. He only agreed when I told him that an American passport wouldn't stop a bullet."

"By the way, did you ever see his passport?"

"Probably I did, but I don't remember. Why?"

Mallinson laughed. "I'm afraid you'll think I haven't exactly been minding my own business. Why should I, anyhow? Two months in this place ought to reveal all our secrets, if we have any. Mind you, it was a sheer accident, in the way it happened, and I haven't let slip a word to any one else, of course. I didn't think I'd tell even you, but now we've got on to the subject I may as well."

"Yes, of course, but I wish you'd let me know what you're talking about."

"Just this. Barnard was traveling on a forged passport and he isn't Barnard at all."

Conway raised his eyebrows with an interest that was very much less than concern. He liked Barnard, so far as the man stirred him to any emotion at all; but it was quite impossible for him to care intensely who he really was or wasn't. He said: "Well, who do you think he is, then?"

"He's Chalmers Bryant."

"The deuce he is! What makes you think so?"

"He dropped a pocketbook this morning and Chang picked it up and gave it to me, thinking it was mine. I couldn't help seeing it was stuffed with newspaper clippings—some of them fell out as I was handling the thing, and I don't mind admitting that I looked at them. After all, newspaper clippings aren't private, or shouldn't be. They were all about Bryant and the search for him, and one of them had a photograph which was absolutely like Barnard except for a mustache."

"Did you mention your discovery to Barnard himself?"

"No, I just handed him his property without any comment."

"So the whole thing rests on your identification of a newspaper photograph?"

"Well, so far, yes."

"I don't think I'd care to convict any one on that. Of course you might be right—I don't say he couldn't *possibly* be Bryant. If he were, it would account for a good deal of his contentment at being here—he could hardly have found a better place to hide."

Mallinson seemed a trifle disappointed by this casual reception of news which he evidently thought highly sensational. "Well, what are you going to do about it?" he asked.

Conway pondered a moment and then answered: "I haven't much of an idea. Probably nothing at all. What *can* one do, in any case?"

"But dash it all, if the man *is* Bryant—"

"My dear Mallinson, if the man were Nero it wouldn't have to matter to us for the time being! Saint or crook, we've got to make what we can of each other's company as long as we're here, and I can't see that we shall help matters by striking any attitudes. If I'd suspected who he was at Baskul, of course, I'd have tried to get in touch with Delhi about him—it would have been merely a public duty. But now I think I can claim to be *off* duty."

"Don't you think that's rather a slack way of looking at it?"

"I don't care if it's slack so long as it's sensible."

"I suppose that means your advice to me is to forget what I've found out?"

"You probably can't do that, but I certainly think we might both of us keep our own counsel about it. Not in consideration for Barnard or Bryant or whoever he is, but to save ourselves the deuce of an awkward situation when we get away."

"You mean we ought to let him go?"

"Well, I'll put it a bit differently and say we ought to give somebody else the pleasure of catching him. When you've lived quite sociably with a man for a few months, it seems a little out of place to call for the handcuffs."

"I don't think I agree. The man's nothing but a large-scale thief—I know plenty of people who've lost their money through him."

Conway shrugged his shoulders. He admired the simple black-and-white of Mallinson's code; the public school ethic might be crude, but at least it was downright. If a man broke the law, it was every one's duty to hand him over to justice—always provided that it was the kind of law one was not allowed to break. And the law pertaining to checks and shares and balance-sheets was decidedly that kind. Bryant had transgressed it, and though Conway had not taken much interest in the case, he had an impression that it was a fairly bad one of its kind. All he knew was that the failure of the giant Bryant group in New York had resulted in losses of about a hundred million dollars—a record crash, even in a world that exuded records. In some way or other (Conway was not a financial expert) Bryant had been monkeying on Wall Street, and the result had been a warrant for his arrest, his escape to Europe, and extradition orders against him in half a dozen countries.

Conway said finally: "Well, if you take my tip you'll say nothing about it —not for his sake but for ours. Please yourself, of course, so long as you don't forget the possibility that he mayn't be the fellow at all."

But he was, and the revelation came that evening after dinner. Chang had left them; Miss Brinklow had turned to her Tibetan grammar; the three male exiles faced each other over coffee and cigars. Conversation during the meal would have languished more than once but for the tact and affability of the Chinese; now, in his absence, a rather unhappy silence supervened. Barnard was for once without jokes. It was clear to Conway that it lay beyond Mallinson's power to treat the American as if nothing had happened, and it was equally clear that Barnard was shrewdly aware that something *had* happened.

Suddenly the American threw away his cigar. "I guess you all know who I am," he said.

Mallinson colored like a girl, but Conway replied in the same quiet key: "Yes, Mallinson and I think we do."

"Darned careless of me to leave those clippings lying about."

"We're all apt to be careless at times."

"Well, you're mighty calm about it, that's something."

There was another silence, broken at length by Miss Brinklow's shrill voice: "I'm sure *I* don't know who you are, Mr. Barnard, though I must say I guessed all along you were traveling *incognito*." They all looked at her enquiringly and she went on: "I remember when Mr. Conway said we should all have our names in the papers, you said it didn't affect you. I thought then that Barnard probably wasn't your real name."

The culprit gave a slow smile as he lit himself another cigar. "Madam," he said eventually, "you're not only a smart detective, but you've hit on a really polite name for my present position. I'm traveling *incognito*. You've said it, and you're dead right. As for you boys, I'm not sorry in a way that you've found me out. So long as none of you had an inkling, we could all have managed, but considering how we're fixed it wouldn't seem very neighborly to play the high hat with you now. You folks have been so darned nice to me that I don't want to make a lot of trouble. It looks as if we were all going to be joined together for better or worse for some little time ahead, and it's up to us to help one another out as far as we can. As for what happens afterwards, I reckon we can leave that to settle itself."

All this appeared to Conway so eminently reasonable that he gazed at Barnard with considerably greater interest, and even—though it was perhaps odd at such a moment—a touch of genuine appreciation. It was curious to think of that heavy, fleshy, good-humored, rather paternal looking man as the world's hugest swindler. He looked far more the type that, with a little extra education, would have made a popular headmaster of a prep school. Behind his joviality there were signs of recent strains and worries, but that did not mean that the joviality was forced. He obviously was what he looked —a "good fellow" in the world's sense, by nature a lamb and only by profession a shark.

Conway said: "Yes, that's very much the best thing, I'm certain."

Then Barnard laughed. It was as if he possessed even deeper reserves of good humor which he could only now draw upon. "Gosh, but it's mighty queer," he exclaimed, spreading himself in his chair. "The whole darned business, I mean. Right across Europe, and on through Turkey and Persia to that little one-horse burg! Police after me all the time, mind you—they nearly got me in Vienna! It's pretty exciting at first, being chased, but it gets on your nerves after a bit. I got a good rest at Baskul, though—I thought I'd be safe in the midst of a revolution."

"And so you were," said Conway with a slight smile, "except from bullets."

"Yeah, and that's what bothered me at the finish. I can tell you it was a mighty hard choice—whether to stay in Baskul and get plugged, or accept a trip in your Government's aeroplane and find the bracelets waiting at the other end. I wasn't exactly keen to do either."

"I remember you weren't."

Barnard laughed again. "Well, that's how it was, and you can figger it out for yourself that the change of plan which brought me here, don't worry me an awful lot. It's a first-class mystery, but, speaking personally, there couldn't have been a better one. It isn't my way to grumble as long as I'm satisfied."

Conway's smile became more definitely cordial. "A very sensible attitude, though I think you rather overdid it. We were all beginning to wonder how you managed to be so contented."

"Well, I *was* contented. This ain't a bad place, when you get used to it. The air's a bit snappy at first, but you can't have everything. And it's nice and quiet for a change. Every fall I go down to Palm Beach for a rest cure, but they don't give it you, those places—you're in the racket just the same. But here I guess I'm having just what the doctor ordered, and it certainly feels grand to me. I'm on a different diet, I can't look at the tape, and my broker can't get me on the telephone."

"I dare say he wishes he could."

"Sure. There'll be a tidy-sized mess to clear up, and I know it."

He said this with such simplicity that Conway could not help responding: "I'm not much of an authority on what people call high finance."

It was a lead, and the American accepted it without the slightest reluctance. "High finance," he said, "is mostly a lot of bunk."

"So I've often suspected."

"Look here, Conway, I'll put it like this. A feller does what he's been doing for years, and what lots of other fellers have been doing, and suddenly the market goes against him. He can't help it, but he braces up and waits for the turn. But somehow the turn don't come as it always used to, and when he's lost ten million dollars or so he reads in some paper that a Swede professor thinks it's the end of the world. Now I ask you, does that sort of thing help markets? Of course, it gives him a bit of a shock, but he still can't help it. And there he is till the cops come—if he waits for 'em. I didn't."

"You claim it was all just a run of bad luck, then?"

"Well, I certainly had a large packet."

"You also had other people's money," put in Mallinson sharply.

"Yeah, I did. And why? Because they all wanted something for nothing and hadn't the brains to get it for themselves."

"I don't agree. It was because they trusted you and thought their money was safe."

"Well, it wasn't safe. It couldn't be. There isn't safety anywhere, and those who thought there was were like a lot of saps trying to hide under an umbrella in a typhoon."

Conway said pacifyingly: "Well, we'll all admit you couldn't help the typhoon."

"I couldn't even pretend to help it—any more than you could help what happened after we left Baskul. The same thing struck me then as I watched you in the aeroplane keeping dead calm while Mallinson here had the fidgets. You knew you couldn't do anything about it, and you weren't caring two hoots. Just like I felt myself when the crash came."

"That's nonsense!" cried Mallinson. "Any one can help swindling. It's a matter of playing the game according to the rules."

"Which is a darned difficult thing to do when the whole game's going to pieces. Besides, there isn't a soul in the world who knows what the rules are. All the professors of Harvard and Yale couldn't tell you 'em."

Mallinson replied rather scornfully: "I'm referring to a few quite simple rules of everyday conduct."

"Then I guess your everyday conduct doesn't include managing trust companies."

Conway made haste to intervene. "We'd better not argue. I don't object in the least to the comparison between your affairs and mine. No doubt we've all been flying blind lately, both literally and in other ways. But we're here now, that's the important thing, and I agree with you that we could easily have had more to grumble about. It's curious, when you come to think about it, that out of four people picked up by chance and kidnaped a thousand miles, three should be able to find some consolation in the business. You want a rest-cure and a hiding place; Miss Brinklow feels a call to evangelize the heathen Tibetan."

"Who's the third person you're counting?" Mallinson interrupted. "Not me, I hope?"

"I was including myself," answered Conway. "And my own reason is perhaps the simplest of all—I just rather like being here."

Indeed, a short time later, when he took what had come to be his usual solitary evening stroll along the terrace or beside the lotus pool, he felt an extraordinary sense of physical and mental settlement. It was perfectly true; he just rather liked being at Shangri-La. Its atmosphere soothed while its mystery stimulated, and the total sensation was agreeable. For some days now he had been reaching, gradually and tentatively, a curious conclusion about the lamasery and its inhabitants; his brain was still busy with it, though in a deeper sense he was unperturbed. He was like a mathematician with an abstruse problem—worrying over it, but worrying very calmly and impersonally.

As for Bryant, whom he decided he would still think of and address as Barnard, the question of his exploits and identity faded instantly into the background, save for a single phrase of his—"the whole game's going to pieces." Conway found himself remembering and echoing it with a wider significance than the American had probably intended; he felt it to be true of more than American banking and trust company management. It fitted Baskul and Delhi and London, war making and empire building, consulates and trade concessions and dinner parties at Government House; there was a reek of dissolution over all that recollected world, and Barnard's cropper had only, perhaps, been better dramatized than his own. The whole game *was* doubtless going to pieces, but fortunately the players were not as a rule put on trial for the pieces they failed to save. In that respect financiers were unlucky.

But here, at Shangri-La, all was in deep calm. In a moonless sky the stars were lit to the full, and a pale blue sheen lay upon the dome of Karakal. Conway realized then that if by some change of plan the porters from the outside world were to arrive immediately, he would not be completely overjoyed at being spared the interval of waiting. And neither would Barnard, he reflected with an inward smile. It was amusing, really; and then suddenly he knew that he still liked Barnard, or he wouldn't have found it amusing. Somehow the loss of a hundred million dollars was too much to bar a man for; it would have been easier if he had only stolen one's watch. And after all, how *could* any one lose a hundred millions? Perhaps only in the sense in which a cabinet minister might airily announce that he had been "given India."

And then again he thought of the time when he would leave Shangri-La with the returning porters. He pictured the long, arduous journey, and that eventual moment of arrival at some planter's bungalow in Sikkim or Baltistan —a moment which ought, he felt, to be deliriously cheerful, but which would probably be slightly disappointing. Then the first hand-shakings and self-introductions; the first drinks on clubhouse verandas; sun-bronzed faces staring at him in barely concealed incredulity. At Delhi, no doubt, interviews with the Viceroy and the C.I.C.; salaams of turbanned menials; endless reports to be prepared and sent off. Perhaps even a return to England and Whitehall; deck games on the P. & O.; the flaccid palm of an under-secretary; newspaper interviews; hard, mocking, sex-thirsty voices of women—"And is it really true, Mr. Conway, that when you were in Tibet . . . ?" There was no doubt of one thing; he would be able to dine out on his yarn for at least a season. But would he enjoy it? He recalled a sentence penned by Gordon during the last days at Khartoum—"I would sooner live like a Dervish with the Mahdi than go out to dinner every night in London." Conway's aversion was less definite—a mere anticipation that to tell his story in the past tense would bore him a great deal as well as sadden him a little.

Abruptly, in the midst of his reflections, he was aware of Chang's approach. "Sir," began the Chinese, his slow whisper slightly quickening as he spoke, "I am proud to be the bearer of important news. . . ."

So the porters *had* come before their time, was Conway's first thought; it was odd that he should have been thinking of it so recently. And he felt the pang that he was half prepared for. "Well?" he queried.

Chang's condition was as nearly that of excitement as seemed physically possible for him. "My dear sir, I congratulate you," he continued. "And I am happy to think that I am in some measure responsible—it was after my own strong and repeated recommendations that the High Lama made his decision. He wishes to see you immediately."

Conway's glance was quizzical. "You're being less coherent than usual, Chang. What has happened?"

"The High Lama has sent for you."

"So I gather. But why all the fuss?"

"Because it is extraordinary and unprecedented—even I who urged it did not expect it to happen yet. A fortnight ago you had not arrived, and now you are about to be received by *him!* Never before has it occurred so soon!"

"I'm still rather fogged, you know. I'm to see your High Lama—I realize that all right. But is there anything else?"

"Is it not enough?"

Conway laughed. "Absolutely, I assure you—don't imagine I'm being discourteous. As a matter of fact, something quite different was in my head at first. However, never mind about that now. Of course, I shall be both honored and delighted to meet the gentleman. When is the appointment?"

"Now. I have been sent to bring you to him."

"Isn't it rather late?"

"That is of no consequence. My dear sir, you will understand many things very soon. And may I add my own personal pleasure that this interval—always an awkward one—is now at an end. Believe me, it has been irksome to me to have to refuse you information on so many occasions—extremely irksome. I am joyful in the knowledge that such unpleasantness will never again be necessary."

"You're a queer fellow, Chang," Conway responded. "But let's be going, don't bother to explain any more. I'm perfectly ready and I appreciate your nice remarks. Lead the way."

CHAPTER SEVEN

Conway was quite unruffled, but his demeanor covered an eagerness that grew in intensity as he accompanied Chang across the empty courtyards. If the words of the Chinese meant anything, he was on the threshold of discovery; soon he would know whether his theory, still half formed, were less impossible than it appeared.

Apart from this, it would doubtless be an interesting interview. He had met many peculiar potentates in his time; he took a detached interest in them, and was shrewd as a rule in his assessments. Without self-consciousness he had also the valuable knack of being able to say polite things in languages of which he knew very little indeed. Perhaps, however, he would be chiefly a listener on this occasion. He noticed that Chang was taking him through rooms he had not seen before, all of them rather dim and lovely in lantern light. Then a spiral staircase climbed to a door at which the Chinese knocked, and which was opened by a Tibetan servant with such promptness that Conway suspected he had been stationed behind it. This part of the lamasery, on a higher storey, was no less tastefully embellished than the rest, but its most immediately striking feature was a dry, tingling warmth, as if all the windows were tightly closed and some kind of steam heating plant were working at full pressure. The airlessness increased as he passed on, until at last Chang paused before a door which, if bodily sensation could have been trusted, might well have admitted to a Turkish bath.

"The High Lama," whispered Chang, "will receive you alone." Having opened the door for Conway's entrance, he closed it afterwards so silently that his own departure was almost imperceptible. Conway stood hesitant, breathing an atmosphere that was not only sultry, but full of dusk, so that it was several seconds before he could accustom his eyes to the gloom. Then he slowly built up an impression of a dark-curtained, low-roofed apartment, simply furnished with table and chairs. On one of these sat a small, pale, and wrinkled person, motionlessly shadowed, and yielding an effect as of some fading, antique portrait in chiaroscuro. If there were such a thing as presence divorced from actuality, here it was, adorned with a classic dignity that was more an emanation than an attribute. Conway was curious about his own intense perception of all this, and wondered if it were dependable or merely his reaction to the rich, crepuscular warmth; he felt dizzy under the gaze of those ancient eyes, took a few forward paces, and then halted. The occupant of the chair grew now less vague in outline, but scarcely more corporeal; he was a little old man in Chinese dress, its folds and flounces loose against a flat, emaciated frame. "You are Mr. Conway?" he whispered in excellent English.

The voice was pleasantly soothing, and touched with a very gentle melancholy that fell upon Conway with strange beatitude; though once again the skeptic in him was inclined to hold the temperature responsible.

"I am," he answered.

The voice went on. "It is a pleasure to see you, Mr. Conway. I sent for you because I thought we should do well to have a talk together. Please sit down beside me and have no fear. I am an old man and can do no one any harm."

Conway answered: "I feel it a signal honor to be received by you."

"I thank you, my dear Conway—I shall call you that, according to your English fashion. It is, as I said, a moment of great pleasure for me. My sight is poor, but believe me, I am able to see you in my mind, as well as with my eyes. I trust you have been comfortable at Shangri-La since your arrival?"

"Extremely so."

"I am glad. Chang has done his best for you, no doubt. It has been a great pleasure to him also. He tells me you have been asking many questions about our community and its affairs?"

"I am certainly interested in them."

"Then if you can spare me a little time, I shall be pleased to give you a brief account of our foundation."

"There is nothing I should appreciate more."

"That is what I had thought—and hoped. . . . But first of all, before our discourse . . ."

He made the slightest stir of a hand, and immediately, by what technique of summons Conway could not detect, a servant entered to prepare the elegant ritual of tea-drinking. The little egg-shell bowls of almost colorless fluid were placed on a lacquered tray; Conway, who knew the ceremony, was by no means contemptuous of it. The voice resumed: "Our ways are familiar to you, then?"

Obeying an impulse which he could neither analyze nor find desire to control, Conway answered: "I lived in China for some years."

"You did not tell Chang."

"No."

"Then why am I so honored?"

Conway was rarely at a loss to explain his own motives, but on this occasion he could not think of any reason at all. At length he replied: "To be quite candid, I haven't the slightest idea, except that I must have wanted to tell you."

"The best of all reasons, I am sure, between those who are to become friends. . . . Now tell me, is this not a delicate aroma? The teas of China are many and fragrant, but this, which is a special product of our own valley, is in my opinion their equal."

Conway lifted the bowl to his lips and tasted. The savor was slender, elusive, and recondite, a ghostly bouquet that haunted rather than lived on the tongue. He said: "It is very delightful, and also quite new to me."

"Yes, like a great many of our valley herbs, it is both unique and precious. It should be tasted, of course, very slowly—not only in reverence and affection, but to extract the fullest degree of pleasure. This is a famous lesson that we may learn from Kou Kai Tchou, who lived some fifteen centuries ago. He would always hesitate to reach the succulent marrow when he was eating a piece of sugar-cane, for, as he explained—'I introduce myself gradually into the region of delights.' Have you studied any of the great Chinese classics?"

Conway replied that he was slightly acquainted with a few of them. He knew that the allusive conversation would, according to etiquette, continue until the tea-bowls were taken away; but he found it far from irritating, despite his keenness to hear the history of Shangri-La. Doubtless there was a certain amount of Kou Kai Tchou's reluctant sensibility in himself.

At length the signal was given, again mysteriously, the servant padded in and out, and with no more preamble the High Lama of Shangri-La began:

"Probably you are familiar, my dear Conway, with the general outline of Tibetan history. I am informed by Chang that you have made ample use of our library here, and I doubt not that you have studied the scanty but exceedingly interesting annals of these regions. You will be aware, anyhow, that Nestorian Christianity was widespread throughout Asia during the Middle Ages, and that its memory lingered long after its actual decay. In the seventeenth century a Christian revival was impelled directly from Rome through the agency of those heroic Jesuit missionaries whose journeys, if I may permit myself the remark, are so much more interesting to read of than those of St. Paul. Gradually the Church established itself over an immense area, and it is a remarkable fact, not realized by many Europeans to-day, that for thirty-eight years there existed a Christian mission in Lhasa itself. It was not, however, from Lhasa but from Pekin, in the year 1719, that four Capuchin friars set out in search of any remnants of the Nestorian faith that might still be surviving in the hinterland.

"They traveled southwest for many months, by Lanchow and the Koko-Nor, facing hardships which you will well imagine. Three died on the way, and the fourth was not far from death when by accident he stumbled into the rocky defile that remains to-day the only practical approach to the valley of Blue Moon. There, to his joy and surprise, he found a friendly and prosperous population who made haste to display what I have always regarded as our oldest tradition—that of hospitality to strangers. Quickly he recovered health and began to preach his mission. The people were Buddhists, but willing to hear him, and he had considerable success. There was an ancient lamasery existing then on this same mountain-shelf, but it was in a state of decay both physical and spiritual, and as the Capuchin's harvest increased, he conceived the idea of setting up on the same magnificent site a Christian monastery. Under his surveillance the old buildings were repaired and largely reconstructed, and he himself began to live here in the year 1734, when he was fifty-three years of age.

"Now let me tell you more about this man. His name was Perrault, and he was by birth a Luxembourger. Before devoting himself to Far Eastern missions he had studied at Paris, Bologna, and other universities; he was something of a scholar. There are few existing records of his early life, but it was not in any way unusual for one of his age and profession. He was fond of music and the arts, had a special aptitude for languages, and before he was sure of his vocation he had tasted all the familiar pleasures of the world. Malplaquet was fought when he was a youth, and he knew from personal contact the horrors of war and invasion. He was physically sturdy; during his first years here he labored with his hands like any other man, tilling his own garden, and learning from the inhabitants as well as teaching them. He found gold deposits along the valley, but they did not tempt him; he was more deeply interested in local plants and herbs. He was humble and by no means bigoted. He deprecated polygamy, but he saw no reason to inveigh against the prevalent fondness for the *tangatse* berry, to which were ascribed medicinal properties, but which was chiefly popular because its effects were those of a mild narcotic. Perrault, in fact, became somewhat of an addict himself; it was his way to accept from native life all that it offered which he found harmless and pleasant, and to give in return the spiritual treasure of the West. He was not an ascetic; he enjoyed the good things of the world, and was careful to teach his converts cooking as well as catechism. I want you to have an impression of a very earnest, busy, learned, simple, and enthusiastic person who, along with his priestly functions, did not disdain to put on a mason's overall and help in the actual building of these very rooms. That was, of course, a work of immense difficulty, and one which nothing but his pride and steadfastness could have overcome. Pride, I say, because it was undoubtedly a dominant motive at the beginning—the pride in his own Faith that made him decide that if Gautama could inspire men to build a temple on the ledge of Shangri-La, Rome was capable of no less.

"But time passed, and it was not unnatural that this motive should yield place gradually to more tranquil ones. Emulation is, after all, a young man's spirit, and Perrault, by the time his monastery was well established, was already full of years. You must bear in mind that he had not, from a strict point of view, been acting very regularly; though some latitude must surely be extended to one whose ecclesiastical superiors are located at a distance measurable in years rather than miles. But the folk of the valley and the monks themselves had no misgivings; they loved and obeyed him, and as years went on, came to venerate him also. At intervals it was his custom to send reports to the Bishop of Pekin, but often they never reached him, and as it was to be presumed that the bearers had succumbed to the perils of the journey, Perrault grew more and more unwilling to hazard their lives, and after about the middle of the century he gave up the practice. Some of his earlier messages, however, must have got through, and a doubt of his activities have been aroused, for in the year 1769 a stranger brought a letter written twelve years before, summoning Perrault to Rome.

"He would have been over seventy had the command been received without delay; as it was, he had turned eighty-nine. The long trek over mountain and plateau was unthinkable; he could never have endured the scouring gales and fierce chills of the wilderness outside. He sent, therefore, a courteous reply explaining the situation, but there is no record that his message ever passed the barrier of the great ranges.

"So Perrault remained at Shangri-La, not exactly in defiance of superior orders, but because it was physically impossible for him to fulfill them. In any case he was an old man, and death would probably soon put an end both to him and his irregularity. By this time the institution he had founded had begun to undergo a subtle change. It might be deplorable, but it was not really very astonishing; for it could hardly be expected that one man unaided should uproot permanently the habits and traditions of an epoch. He had no Western colleagues to hold firm when his own grip relaxed; and it had perhaps been a mistake to build on a site that held such older and differing memories. It was asking too much; but was it not asking even more to expect a white-haired veteran, just entering the nineties, to realize the mistake that he had made? Perrault, at any rate, did not then realize it. He was far too old and happy. His followers were devoted even when they forgot his teaching, while the people of the valley held him in such reverent affection that he forgave with ever-increasing ease their lapse into former customs. He was still active, and his faculties had remained exceptionally keen. At the age of ninety-eight he began to study the Buddhist writings that had been left at Shangri-La by its previous occupants, and his intention was then to devote the rest of his life to the composition of a book attacking Buddhism from the standpoint of orthodoxy. He actually finished this task (we have his manuscript complete), but the attack was very gentle, for he had by that time reached the round figure of a century—an age at which even the keenest acrimonies are apt to fade.

"Meanwhile, as you may suppose, many of his early disciples had died, and as there were few replacements, the number resident under the rule of the old Capuchin steadily diminished. From over eighty at one time, it dwindled to a score, and then to a mere dozen, most of them very aged themselves. Perrault's life at this time grew to be a very calm and placid waiting for the end. He was far too old for disease and discontent; only the everlasting sleep could claim him now, and he was not afraid. The valley people, out of kindness, supplied food and clothing; his library gave him work. He had become rather frail, but still kept energy to fulfill the major ceremonial of his office; the rest of the tranquil days he spent with his books, his memories, and the mild ecstasies of the narcotic. His mind remained so extraordinarily clear that he even embarked upon a study of certain mystic practices that the Indians call *yoga*, and which are based upon various special methods of breathing. For a man of such an age the enterprise might well have seemed hazardous, and it was certainly true that soon afterwards, in that memorable year 1789, news descended to the valley that Perrault was dying at last.

"He lay in this room, my dear Conway, where he could see from the window the white blurr that was all his failing eyesight gave him of Karakal; but he could see with his mind also; he could picture the clear and matchless outline that he had first glimpsed half a century before. And there came to him, too, the strange parade of all his many experiences, the years of travel across desert and upland, the great crowds in Western cities, the clang and glitter of Marlborough's troops. His mind had straitened to a snow-white calm; he was ready, willing, and glad to die. He gathered his friends and servants round him and bade them all farewell; then he asked to be left alone awhile. It was during such a solitude, with his body sinking and his mind lifted to beatitude, that he had hoped to give up his soul . . . but it did not happen so. He lay for many weeks without speech or movement, and then he began to recover. He was a hundred and eight."

The whispering ceased for a moment, and to Conway, stirring slightly, it appeared that the High Lama had been translating, with fluency, out of a remote and private dream. At length he went on:

"Like others who have waited long on the threshold of death, Perrault had been granted a vision of some significance to take back with him into the world; and of this vision more must be said later. Here I will confine myself to his actions and behavior, which were indeed remarkable. For instead of convalescing idly, as might have been expected, he plunged forthwith into rigorous self-discipline somewhat curiously combined with narcotic indulgence. Drug-taking and deep-breathing exercises—it could not have seemed a very death-defying regimen; yet the fact remains that when the last of the old monks died, in 1794, Perrault himself was still living.

"It would almost have brought a smile had there been any one at Shangri-La with a sufficiently distorted sense of humor. The wrinkled Capuchin, no more decrepit than he had been for a dozen years, persevered in a secret ritual he had evolved, while to the folk of the valley he soon became veiled in mystery, a hermit of uncanny powers who lived alone on that formidable cliff. But there was still a tradition of affection for him, and it came to be regarded as meritorious and luck-bringing to climb to Shangri-La and leave a simple gift, or perform some manual task that was needed there. On all such pilgrims Perrault bestowed his blessing—forgetful, it might be, that they were lost and straying sheep. For 'Te Deum Laudamus' and 'Om Mane Padme Hum' were now heard equally in the temples of the valley.

"As the new century approached, the legend grew into a rich and fantastic folk-lore—it was said that Perrault had become a god, that he worked miracles, and that on certain nights he flew to the summit of Karakal to hold a candle to the sky. There is a paleness always on the mountain at full moon; but I need not assure you that neither Perrault nor any other man has ever climbed there. I mention it, even though it may seem unnecessary, because there is a mass of unreliable testimony that Perrault did and could do all kinds of impossible things. It was supposed, for instance, that he practiced the art of self-levitation, of which so much appears in accounts of Buddhist mysticism; but the more sober truth is that he made many experiments to that end, but entirely without success. He did, however, discover that the impairment of ordinary senses could be somewhat offset by a development of others; he acquired skill in telepathy which was perhaps remarkable, and though he made no claim to any specific powers of healing, there was a quality in his mere presence that was helpful in certain cases.

"You will wish to know how he spent his time during these unprecedented years. His attitude may be summed up by saying that, as he had not died at a normal age, he began to feel that there was no discoverable reason why he either should or should not do so at any definite time in the future. Having already proved himself abnormal, it was as easy to believe that the abnormality might continue as to expect it to end at any moment. And that being so, he began to behave without care for the imminence with which he had been so long preoccupied; he began to live the kind of life that he had always desired, but had so rarely found possible; for he had kept at heart and throughout all vicissitudes the tranquil tastes of a scholar. His memory was astonishing; it appeared to have escaped the trammels of the physical into some upper region of immense clarity; it almost seemed that he could now learn *everything* with far greater ease than during his student days he had been able to learn *anything*. He was soon, of course, brought up against a need for books, but there were a few he had had with him from the first, and they included, you may be interested to hear, an English grammar and dictionary and Florio's translation of Montaigne. With these to work on he contrived to master the intricacies of your language, and we still possess in our library the manuscript of one of his first linguistic exercises —a translation of Montaigne's essay on Vanity into Tibetan—surely a unique production."

Conway smiled. "I should be interested to see it sometime, if I might."

"With the greatest of pleasure. It was, you may think, a singularly unpractical accomplishment, but recollect that Perrault had reached a singularly unpractical age. He would have been lonely without some such occupation—at any rate until the fourth year of the nineteenth century, which marks an important event in the history of our foundation. For it was then that a second stranger from Europe arrived in the valley of Blue Moon. He was a young Austrian named Henschell who had soldiered against Napoleon in Italy—a youth of noble birth, high culture, and much charm of manner. The wars had ruined his fortunes, and he had wandered across Russia into Asia with some vague intention of retrieving them. It would be interesting to know how exactly he reached the plateau, but he had no very clear idea himself; indeed, he was as near death when he arrived here as Perrault himself had once been. Again the hospitality of Shangri-La was extended, and the stranger recovered—but there the parallel breaks down. For Perrault had come to preach and proselytize, whereas Henschell took a more immediate interest in the gold deposits. His first ambition was to enrich himself and return to Europe as soon as possible.

"But he did not return. An odd thing happened—though one that has happened so often since that perhaps we must now agree that it cannot be very odd after all. The valley, with its peacefulness and its utter freedom from worldly cares, tempted him again and again to delay his departure, and one day, having heard the local legend, he climbed to Shangri-La and had his first meeting with Perrault.

"That meeting was, in the truest sense, historic. Perrault, if a little beyond such human passions as friendship or affection, was yet endowed with a rich benignity of mind which touched the youth as water upon a parched soil. I will not try to describe the association that sprang up between the two; the one gave utmost adoration, while the other shared his knowledge, his ecstasies, and the wild dream that had now become the only reality left for him in the world."

There was a pause, and Conway said very quietly: "Pardon the interruption, but that is not quite clear to me."

"I know." The whispered reply was completely sympathetic. "It would be remarkable indeed if it were. It is a matter which I shall be pleased to explain before our talk is over, but for the present, if you will forgive me, I will confine myself to simpler things. A fact that will interest you is that Henschell began our collections of Chinese art, as well as our library and musical acquisitions. He made a remarkable journey to Pekin and brought back the first consignment in the year 1809. He did not leave the valley again, but it was his ingenuity which devised the complicated system by which the lamasery has ever since been able to obtain anything needful from the outer world."

"I suppose you found it easy to make payment in gold?"

"Yes, we have been fortunate in possessing supplies of a metal which is held in such high esteem in other parts of the world."

"Such high esteem that you must have been very lucky to escape a gold rush."

The High Lama inclined his head in the merest indication of agreement. "That, my dear Conway, was always Henschell's fear. He was careful that none of the porters bringing books and art treasures should ever approach too closely; he made them leave their burdens a day's journey outside, to be fetched afterwards by our valley folk themselves. He even arranged for sentries to keep constant watch on the entrance to the defile. But it soon occurred to him that there was an easier and more final safeguard."

"Yes?" Conway's voice was guardedly tense.

"You see there was no need to fear invasion by an army. That will never be possible, owing to the nature and distances of the country. The most ever to be expected was the arrival of a few half-lost wanderers who, even if they were armed, would probably be so weakened as to constitute no danger. It was decided, therefore, that henceforward strangers might come as freely as they chose—with but one important proviso.

"And, over a period of years, such strangers did come. Chinese merchants, tempted into the crossing of the plateau, chanced occasionally on this one traverse out of so many others possible to them. Nomad Tibetans, wandering from their tribes, strayed here sometimes like weary animals. All were made welcome, though some reached the shelter of the valley only to die. In the year of Waterloo two English missionaries, traveling overland to Pekin, crossed the ranges by an unnamed pass and had the extraordinary luck to arrive as calmly as if they were paying a call. In 1820 a Greek trader, accompanied by sick and famished servants, was found dying at the topmost ridge of the pass. In 1822 three Spaniards, having heard some vague story of gold, reached here after many wanderings and disappointments. Again, in 1830, there was a larger influx. Two Germans, a Russian, an Englishman, and a Swede made the dreaded crossing of the Tian-Shans, impelled by a motive that was to become increasingly common—scientific exploration. By the time of their approach a slight modification had taken place in the attitude of Shangri-La towards its visitors—not only were they now welcomed if they chanced to find their way into the valley, but it had become customary to meet them if they ever ventured within a certain radius. All this was for a reason I shall later discuss, but the point is of importance as showing that the lamasery was no longer hospitably indifferent; it had already both a need and a desire for new arrivals. And indeed in the years to follow it happened that more than one party of explorers, glorying in their first distant glimpse of Karakal, encountered messengers bearing a cordial invitation—and one that was rarely declined.

"Meanwhile the lamasery had begun to acquire many of its present characteristics. I must stress the fact that Henschell was exceedingly able and talented, and that the Shangri-La of to-day owes as much to him as to its founder. Yes, quite as much, I often think. For his was the firm yet kindly hand that every institution needs at a certain stage of its development, and his loss would have been altogether irreparable had he not completed more than a lifework before he died."

Conway looked up to echo rather than question those final words. "He died!"

"Yes. It was very sudden. He was killed. It was in the year of your Indian Mutiny. Just before his death a Chinese artist had sketched him, and I can show you that sketch now—it is in this room."

The slight gesture of the hand was repeated, and once again a servant entered. Conway, as a spectator in a trance, watched the man withdraw a small curtain at the far end of the room and leave a lantern swinging amongst the shadows. Then he heard the whisper inviting him to move, and it was extraordinary how hard it was to do so.

He stumbled to his feet and strode across to the trembling circle of light. The sketch was small, hardly more than a miniature in colored inks, but the artist had contrived to give the flesh-tones a waxwork delicacy of texture. The features were of great beauty, almost girlish in modeling, and Conway found in their winsomeness a curiously personal appeal, even across the barriers of time, death, and artifice. But the strangest thing of all was one that he realized only after his first gasp of admiration: the face was that of a young man.

He stammered as he moved away: "But—you said—this was done just before his death?"

"Yes. It is a very good likeness."

"Then if he died in the year you said—"

"He did."

"And he came here, you told me, in 1803, when he was a youth?"

"Yes."

Conway did not answer for a moment; presently, with an effort, he collected himself to say: "And he was killed, you were telling me?"

"Yes. An Englishman shot him. It was a few weeks after the Englishman had arrived at Shangri-La. He was another of those explorers."

"What was the cause of it?"

"There had been a quarrel—about some porters. Henschell had just told him of the important proviso that governs our reception of guests. It was a task of some difficulty, and ever since, despite my own enfeeblement, I have felt constrained to perform it myself."

The High Lama made another and longer pause, with just a hint of enquiry in his silence; when he continued, it was to add: "Perhaps you are wondering, my dear Conway, what that proviso may be?"

Conway answered slowly and in a low voice: "I think I can already guess."

"Can you, indeed! And can you guess anything else after this long and curious story of mine?"

Conway dizzied in brain as he sought to answer the question; the room was now a whorl of shadows with that ancient benignity at its center. Throughout the narrative he had listened with an intentness that had perhaps shielded him from realizing the fullest implications of it all; now, with the mere attempt at conscious expression, he was flooded over with amazement, and the gathering certainty in his mind was almost stifled as it sprang to words. "It seems impossible," he stammered. "And yet I can't help thinking of it—it's astonishing—and extraordinary—and quite incredible—and yet not *absolutely* beyond my powers of belief—"

"What is, my *son?*"

And Conway answered, shaken with an emotion for which he knew no reason and which he did not seek to conceal: "*That you are still alive, Father Perrault.*"

CHAPTER EIGHT

There had been a pause, imposed by the High Lama's call for further refreshment; Conway did not wonder at it, for the strain of such a long recital must have been considerable. Nor was he himself ungrateful for the respite. He felt that the interval was as desirable from an artistic as from any other point of view, and that the bowls of tea, with their accompaniment of conventionally improvised courtesies, fulfilled the same function as a *cadenza* in music. This reflection brought out (unless it were mere coincidence) an odd example of the High Lama's telepathic powers, for he immediately began to talk about music and to express pleasure that Conway's taste in that direction had not been entirely unsatisfied at Shangri-La. Conway answered with suitable politeness and added that he had been surprised to find the lamasery in possession of such a complete library of European composers. The compliment was acknowledged between slow sips of tea. "Ah, my dear Conway, we are fortunate in that one of our number is a gifted musician—he was, indeed, a pupil of Chopin's—and we have been happy to place in his hands the entire management of our salon. You must certainly meet him."

"I should like to. Chang, by the way, was telling me that your favorite Western composer is Mozart."

"That is so," came the reply. "Mozart has an austere elegance which we find very satisfying. He builds a house which is neither too big nor too little, and he furnishes it in perfect taste."

The exchange of comments continued until the tea-bowls were taken away; by that time Conway was able to remark quite calmly: "So, to resume our earlier discussion, you intend to keep us? That, I take it, is the important and invariable proviso?"

"You have guessed correctly, my son."

"In other words, we are to stay here for ever?"

"I should greatly prefer to employ your excellent English idiom and say that we are all of us here 'for good.' "

"What puzzles me is why we four, out of all the rest of the world's inhabitants, should have been chosen."

Relapsing into his earlier and more consequential manner, the High Lama responded: "It is an intricate story, if you would care to hear it. You must know that we have always aimed, as far as possible, to keep our numbers in fairly constant recruitment—since, apart from any other reasons, it is pleasant to have with us people of various ages and representative of different periods. Unfortunately, since the recent European War and the Russian Revolution, travel and exploration in Tibet have been almost completely held up; in fact, our last visitor, a Japanese, arrived in 1912, and was not, to be candid, a very valuable acquisition. You see, my dear Conway, we are not quacks or charlatans; we do not and cannot guarantee success; some of our visitors derive no benefit at all from their stay here; others merely live to what might be called a normally advanced age and then die from some trifling ailment. In general we have found that Tibetans, owing to their being inured to both the altitude and other conditions, are much less sensitive than outside races; they are charming people, and we have admitted many of them, but I doubt if more than a few will pass their hundredth year. The Chinese are a little better, but even among them we have a high percentage of failures. Our best subjects, undoubtedly, are the Nordic and Latin races of Europe; perhaps the Americans would be equally adaptable, and I count it our great good fortune that we have at last, in the person of one of your companions, secured a citizen of that nation. But I must continue with the answer to your question. The position was, as I have been explaining, that for nearly two decades we had welcomed no new-comers, and as there had been several deaths during that period, a problem was beginning to arise. A few years ago, however, one of our number came to the rescue with a novel idea; he was a young fellow, a native of our valley, absolutely trustworthy and in fullest sympathy with our aims; but, like all the valley people, he was denied by nature the chance that comes more fortunately to those from a distance. It was he who suggested that he should leave us, make his way to some surrounding country, and bring us additional colleagues by a method which would have been impossible in an earlier age. It was in many respects a revolutionary proposal, but we gave our consent after due consideration. For we must move with the times, you know, even at Shangri-La."

"You mean that he was sent out deliberately to bring some one back by air?"

"Well, you see, he was an exceedingly gifted and resourceful youth, and we had great confidence in him. It was his own idea, and we allowed him a free hand in carrying it out. All we knew definitely was that the first stage of his plan included a period of tuition at an American flying-school."

"But how could he manage the rest of it? It was only by chance that there happened to be that aeroplane at Baskul—"

"True, my dear Conway—many things are by chance. But it happened, after all, to be just the chance that Talu was looking for. Had he not found it, there might have been another chance in a year or two—or perhaps, of course, none at all. I confess I was surprised when our sentinels gave news of his descent on the plateau. The progress of aviation is rapid, but it had seemed likely to me that much more time would elapse before an average machine could make such a crossing of the mountains."

"It wasn't an average machine. It was a rather special one, made for mountain-flying."

"Again by chance? Our young friend was indeed fortunate. It is a pity that we cannot discuss the matter with him—we were all grieved at his death. You would have liked him, Conway."

Conway nodded slightly; he felt it very possible. He said, after a silence: "But what's the idea behind it all?"

"My son, your way of asking that question gives me infinite pleasure. In the course of a somewhat long experience it has never before been put to me in tones of such calmness. My revelation has been greeted in almost every conceivable manner—with indignation, distress, fury, disbelief, and hysteria —but never until this night with mere interest. It is, however, an attitude that I most cordially welcome. To-day you are interested; to-morrow you will feel concern; eventually, it may be, I shall claim your devotion."

"That is more than I should care to promise."

"Your very doubt pleases me—it is the basis of profound and significant

faith. . . . But let us not argue. You are interested, and that, from you, is
much. All I ask in addition is that what I tell you now shall remain, for the
present, unknown to your three companions."

Conway was silent.

"The time will come when they will learn, like you, but that moment,
for their own sakes, had better not be hastened. I am so certain of your
wisdom in this matter that I do not ask for a promise; you will act, I know,
as we both think best. . . . Now let me begin by sketching for you a very
agreeable picture. You are still, I should say, a youngish man by the world's
standards; your life, as people say, lies ahead of you; in the normal course
you might expect twenty or thirty years of only slightly and gradually diminishing activity. By no means a cheerless prospect, and I can hardly expect
you to see it as I do—as a slender, breathless, and far too frantic interlude.
The first quarter-century of your life was doubtless lived under the cloud of
being too young for things, while the last quarter-century would normally
be shadowed by the still darker cloud of being too old for them; and between those two clouds, what small and narrow sunlight illumines a human
lifetime! But you, it may be, are destined to be more fortunate, since by
the standards of Shangri-La your sunlit years have scarcely yet begun. It will
happen, perhaps, that decades hence you will feel no older than you are today—you may preserve, as Henschell did, a long and wondrous youth. But
that, believe me, is only an early and superficial phase. There will come a
time when you will age like others, though far more slowly, and into a condition infinitely nobler; at eighty you may still climb to the pass with a
young man's gait, but at twice that age you must not expect the whole marvel
to have persisted. We are not workers of miracles; we have made no conquest of death or even of decay. All we have done and can sometimes do is
to slacken the *tempo* of this brief interval that is called life. We do this by
methods which are as simple here as they are impossible elsewhere; but make
no mistake; the end awaits us all.

"Yet it is, nevertheless, a prospect of much charm that I unfold for you
—long tranquillities during which you will observe a sunset as men in the
outer world hear the striking of a clock, and with far less care. The years
will come and go, and you will pass from fleshly enjoyments into austerer
but no less satisfying realms; you may lose the keenness of muscle and appetite, but there will be gain to match your loss; you will achieve calmness
and profundity, ripeness and wisdom, and the clear enchantment of memory.
And, most precious of all, you will have Time—that rare and lovely gift that
your Western countries have lost the more they have pursued it. Think for
a moment. You will have time to read—never again will you skim pages to
save minutes, or avoid some study lest it prove too engrossing. You have
also a taste for music—here, then, are your scores and instruments, with Time,
unruffled and unmeasured, to give you their richest savor. And you are also,
we will say, a man of good fellowship—does it not charm you to think of
wise and serene friendships, a long and kindly traffic of the mind from which
death may not call you away with his customary hurry? Or, if it is solitude

that you prefer, could you not employ our pavilions to enrich the gentleness of lonely thoughts?"

The voice made a pause which Conway did not seek to fill.

"You make no comment, my dear Conway. Forgive my eloquence—I belong to an age and a nation that never considered it bad form to be articulate. . . . But perhaps you are thinking of wife, parents, children, left behind in the world? Or maybe ambitions to do this or that? Believe me, though the pang may be keen at first, in a decade from now even its ghost will not haunt you. Though in point of fact, if I read your mind correctly, you have no such griefs."

Conway was startled by the accuracy of the judgment. "That's so," he replied. "I'm unmarried; I have few close friends and no ambitions."

"No ambitions? And how have you contrived to escape those widespread maladies?"

For the first time Conway felt that he was actually taking part in a conversation. He said: "It always seemed to me in my profession that a good deal of what passed for success would be rather disagreeable, apart from needing more effort than I felt called upon to make. I was in the Consular Service—quite a subordinate post, but it suited me well enough."

"Yet your soul was not in it?"

"Neither my soul nor my heart nor more than half my energies. I'm naturally rather lazy."

The wrinkles deepened and twisted till Conway realized that the High Lama was very probably smiling. "Laziness in doing stupid things can be a great virtue," resumed the whisper. "In any case, you will scarcely find us exacting in such a matter. Chang, I believe, explained to you our principle of moderation, and one of the things in which we are always moderate is activity. I myself, for instance, have been able to learn ten languages; the ten might have been twenty had I worked immoderately. But I did not. And it is the same in other directions; you will find us neither profligate nor ascetic. Until we reach an age when care is advisable, we gladly accept the pleasures of the table, while—for the benefit of our younger colleagues—the women of the valley have happily applied the principle of moderation to their own chastity. All things considered, I feel sure you will get used to our ways without much effort. Chang, indeed, was very optimistic—and so, after this meeting, am I. But there is, I admit, an odd quality in you that I have never met in any of our visitors hitherto. It is not quite cynicism, still less bitterness; perhaps it is partly disillusionment, but it is also a clarity of mind that I should not have expected in any one younger than—say, a century or so. It is, if I had to put a single word to it, passionlessness."

Conway answered: "As good a word as most, no doubt. I don't know whether you classify the people who come here, but if so, you can label me '1914–1918.' That makes me, I should think, a unique specimen in your museum of antiquities—the other three who arrived along with me don't enter the category. I used up most of my passions and energies during the years I've mentioned, and though I don't talk much about it, the chief thing

I've asked from the world since then is to leave me alone. I find in this place a certain charm and quietness that appeals to me, and no doubt, as you remark, I shall get used to things."

"Is that all, my son?"

"I hope I am keeping well to your own rule of moderation."

"You are clever—as Chang told me, you are very clever. But is there nothing in the prospect I have outlined that tempts you to any stronger feeling?"

Conway was silent for an interval and then replied: "I was deeply impressed by your story of the past, but to be candid, your sketch of the future interests me only in an abstract sense. I can't look so far ahead. I should certainly be sorry if I had to leave Shangri-La to-morrow, or next week, or perhaps even next year; but how I shall feel about it if I live to be a hundred isn't a matter to prophesy. I can face it, like any other future, but in order to make me keen it must have a point. I've sometimes doubted whether life itself has any; and if not, long life must be even more pointless."

"My friend, the traditions of this building, both Buddhist and Christian, are very reassuring."

"Maybe. But I'm afraid I still hanker after some more definite reason for envying the centenarian."

"There *is* a reason, and a very definite one indeed. It is the whole reason for this colony of chance-sought strangers living beyond their years. We do not follow an idle experiment, a mere whimsy. We have a dream and a vision. It is a vision that first appeared to old Perrault when he lay dying in this room in the year 1789. He looked back then on his long life, as I have already told you, and it seemed to him that all the loveliest things were transient and perishable, and that war, lust, and brutality might some day crush them until there were no more left in the world. He remembered sights he had seen with his own eyes, and with his mind he pictured others; he saw the nations strengthening, not in wisdom, but in vulgar passions and the will to destroy; he saw their machine power multiplying until a single-weaponed man might have matched a whole army of the Grand Monarque. And he perceived that when they had filled the land and sea with ruin, they would take to the air. . . . Can you say that his vision was untrue?"

"True indeed."

"But that was not all. He foresaw a time when men, exultant in the technique of homicide, would rage so hotly over the world that every precious thing would be in danger, every book and picture and harmony, every treasure garnered through two millenniums, the small, the delicate, the defenseless—all would be lost like the lost books of Livy, or wrecked as the English wrecked the Summer Palace in Pekin."

"I share your opinion of that."

"Of course. But what are the opinions of reasonable men against iron and steel? Believe me, that vision of old Perrault will come true. And that, my son, is why I am here, and why you are here, and why we may pray to outlive the doom that gathers around on every side."

"To outlive it?"

"There is a chance. It will all come to pass before you are as old as I am."

"And you think that Shangri-La will escape?"

"Perhaps. We may expect no mercy, but we may faintly hope for neglect. Here we shall stay with our books and our music and our meditations, conserving the frail elegancies of a dying age, and seeking such wisdom as men will need when their passions are all spent. We have a heritage to cherish and bequeath. Let us take what pleasure we may until that time comes."

"And then?"

"Then, my son, when the strong have devoured each other, the Christian ethic may at last be fulfilled, and the meek shall inherit the earth."

A shadow of emphasis had touched the whisper, and Conway surrendered to the beauty of it; again he felt the surge of darkness around, but now symbolically, as if the world outside were already brewing for the storm. And then he saw that the High Lama of Shangri-La was actually astir, rising from his chair, standing upright like the half-embodiment of a ghost. In mere politeness Conway made to assist; but suddenly a deeper impulse seized him, and he did what he had never done to any man before; he knelt, and hardly knew why he did.

"I understand you, Father," he said.

He was not perfectly aware of how at last he took his leave; he was in a dream from which he did not emerge till long afterwards. He remembered the night air icy after the heat of those upper rooms, and Chang's presence, a silent serenity, as they crossed the starlit courtyards together. Never had Shangri-La offered more concentrated loveliness to his eyes; the valley lay imaged over the edge of the cliff, and the image was of a deep unrippled pool that matched the peace of his own thoughts. For Conway had passed beyond astonishments. The long talk, with its varying phases, had left him empty of all save a satisfaction that was as much of the mind as of the emotions, and as much of the spirit as of either; even his doubts were now no longer harassing, but part of a subtle harmony. Chang did not speak, and neither did he. It was very late, and he was glad that all the others had gone to bed.

CHAPTER NINE

In the morning he wondered if all that he could call to mind were part of a waking or a sleeping vision.

He was soon reminded. A chorus of questions greeted him when he appeared at breakfast. "You certainly had a long talk with the boss last night," began the American. "We meant to wait up for you, but we got tired. What sort of guy is he?"

"Did he say anything about the porters?" asked Mallinson eagerly.

"I hope you mentioned to him about having a missionary stationed here," said Miss Brinklow.

The bombardment served to raise in Conway his usual defensive armament. "I'm afraid I'm probably going to disappoint you all," he replied, slipping easily into the mood. "I didn't discuss with him the question of missions; he didn't mention the porters to me at all; and as for his appearance, I can only say that he's a very old man who speaks excellent English and is quite intelligent."

Mallinson cut in with irritation: "The main thing to us is whether he's to be trusted or not. Do you think he means to let us down?"

"He didn't strike me as a dishonorable person."

"Why on earth didn't you worry him about the porters?"

"It didn't occur to me."

Mallinson stared at him incredulously. "I can't understand you, Conway. You were so damned good in that Baskul affair that I can hardly believe you're the same man. You seem to have gone all to pieces."

"I'm sorry."

"No good being sorry. You ought to buck up and look as if you cared what happens."

"You misunderstand me. I meant that I was sorry to have disappointed you."

Conway's voice was curt, an intended mask to his feelings, which were, indeed, so mixed that they could hardly have been guessed by others. He had slightly surprised himself by the ease with which he had prevaricated; it was clear that he intended to observe the High Lama's suggestion and keep the secret. He was also puzzled by the naturalness with which he was accepting a position which his companions would certainly and with some justification think traitorous; as Mallinson had said, it was hardly the sort of thing to be expected of a hero. Conway felt a sudden half-pitying fondness for the youth; then he steeled himself by reflecting that people who hero-worship must be prepared for disillusionments. Mallinson at Baskul had been far too much the new boy adoring the handsome games-captain, and now the games-captain was tottering if not already fallen from the pedestal. There was always something a little pathetic in the smashing of an ideal, however false; and Mallinson's admiration might have been at least a partial solace for the strain of pretending to be what he was not. But pretense was impossible anyway. There was a quality in the air of Shangri-La—perhaps due to its altitude—that forbade one the effort of counterfeit emotion.

He said: "Look here, Mallinson, it's no use harping continually on Baskul. Of course I was different then—it was a completely different situation."

"And a much healthier one in my opinion. At least we knew what we were up against."

"Murder and rape—to be precise. You can call that healthier if you like."

The youth's voice rose in pitch as he retorted: "Well, I *do* call it healthier—in one sense. It's something I'd rather face than all this mystery business." Suddenly he added: "That Chinese girl, for instance—how did *she* get here? Did the fellow tell you?"

"No. Why should he?"

"Well, why shouldn't he? And why shouldn't you ask, if you had any interest in the matter at all? Is it usual to find a young girl living with a lot of monks?"

That way of looking at it was one that had scarcely occurred to Conway before. "This isn't an ordinary monastery," was the best reply he could give after some thought.

"My God, it isn't!"

There was a silence, for the argument had evidently reached a dead-end. To Conway the history of Lo-Tsen seemed rather far from the point; the little Manchu lay so quietly in his mind that he hardly knew she was there. But at the mere mention of her Miss Brinklow had looked up suddenly from the Tibetan grammar which she was studying even over the breakfast table (just as if, thought Conway, with secret meaning, she hadn't all her life for it). Chatter of girls and monks reminded her of those stories of Indian temples that men missionaries told their wives, and that the wives passed on to their unmarried female colleagues. "Of course," she said between tightened lips, "the morals of this place are quite hideous—we might have expected that." She turned to Barnard as if inviting support, but the American only grinned. "I don't suppose you folks'd value my opinion on a matter of morals," he remarked dryly. "But I should say myself that quarrels are just as bad. Since we've gotter be here for some time yet, let's keep our tempers and make ourselves comfortable."

Conway thought this good advice, but Mallinson was still unplacated. "I can quite believe you find it more comfortable than Dartmoor," he said meaningly.

"Dartmoor? Oh, that's your big penitentiary?—I get you. Well, yes, I certainly never did envy the folks in them places. And there's another thing, too—it don't hurt when you chip me about it. Thick-skinned and tender-hearted, that's my mixture."

Conway glanced at him in appreciation, and at Mallinson with some hint of reproof; but then abruptly he had the feeling that they were all acting on a vast stage, of whose background only he himself was conscious; and such knowledge, so incommunicable, made him suddenly want to be alone. He nodded to them and went out into the courtyard. In sight of Karakal misgivings faded, and qualms about his three companions were lost in an uncanny acceptance of the new world that lay so far beyond their guesses. There came a time, he realized, when the strangeness of everything made it increasingly difficult to realize the strangeness of anything; when one took things for granted merely because astonishment would have been as tedious for oneself as for others. Thus far had he progressed at Shangri-La, and he remembered that he had attained a similar though far less pleasant equanimity during his years at the War.

He needed equanimity, if only to accommodate himself to the double life he was compelled to lead. Thenceforward, with his fellow exiles, he lived in a world conditioned by the arrival of porters and a return to India; at all other times the horizon lifted like a curtain; time expanded and space contracted, and the name Blue Moon took on a symbolic meaning, as if the future, so delicately plausible, were of a kind that might happen once in a blue moon only. Sometimes he wondered which of his two lives was the more real, but the problem was not pressing; and again he was reminded of the War, for during heavy bombardments he had had the same comforting sensation that he had many lives, only one of which could be claimed by death.

Chang, of course, now talked to him completely without reserve, and they had many conversations about the rule and routine of the lamasery. Conway learned that during his first five years he would live a normal life, without any special regimen; this was always done, as Chang said, "to enable the body to accustom itself to the altitude, and also to give time for the dispersal of mental and emotional regrets."

Conway remarked with a smile: "I suppose you're certain, then, that no human affection can outlast a five-year absence?"

"It can, undoubtedly," replied the Chinese, "but only as a fragrance whose melancholy we may enjoy."

After the probationary five years, Chang went on to explain, the process of retarding age would begin, and if successful, might give Conway half a century or so at the apparent age of forty—which was not a bad time of life at which to remain stationary.

"What about yourself?" Conway asked. "How did it work out in your case?"

"Ah, my dear sir, I was lucky enough to arrive when I was quite young only twenty-two. I was a soldier, though you might not have thought it; I had command of troops operating against brigand tribes in the year 1855. I was making what I should have called a reconnaissance if I had ever returned to my superior officers to tell the tale, but in plain truth I had lost my way in the mountains, and of my men only seven out of over a hundred survived the rigors of the climate. When at last I was rescued and brought to Shangri-La I was so ill that extreme youth and virility alone could have saved me."

"Twenty-two," echoed Conway, performing the calculation. "So you're now ninety-seven?"

"Yes. Very soon, if the lamas give their consent, I shall receive full initiation."

"I see. You have to wait for the round figure?"

"No, we are not restricted by any definite age limit, but a century is generally considered to be an age beyond which the passions and moods of ordinary life are likely to have disappeared."

"I should certainly think so. And what happens afterwards? How long do you expect to carry on?"

"There is reason to hope that I shall enter lamahood with such prospects as Shangri-La has made possible. In years, perhaps another century or more."

Conway nodded. "I don't know whether I ought to congratulate you—you seem to have been granted the best of both worlds, a long and pleasant youth behind you, and an equally long and pleasant old age ahead. When did you begin to grow old in appearance?"

"When I was over seventy. That is often the case, though I think I may still claim to look younger than my years."

"Decidedly. And suppose you were to leave the valley now, what would happen?"

"Death, if I remained away for more than a very few days."

"The atmosphere, then, is essential?"

"There is only one valley of Blue Moon, and those who expect to find another are asking too much of nature."

"Well, what would have happened if you had left the valley, say, thirty years ago, during your prolonged youth?"

Chang answered: "Probably I should have died even then. In any case, I should have acquired very quickly the full appearance of my actual age. We had a curious example of that some years ago, though there had been several others before. One of our number had left the valley to look out for a party of travelers whom we had heard might be approaching. This man, a Russian, had arrived here originally in the prime of life, and had taken to our ways so well that at nearly eighty he did not look more than half as old. He should have been absent no longer than a week (which would not have mattered), but unfortunately he was taken prisoner by nomad tribes and carried away some distance. We suspected an accident and gave him up for lost. Three months later, however, he returned to us, having made his escape. But he was a very different man. Every year of his age was in his face and behavior, and he died shortly afterwards, as an old man dies."

Conway made no remark for some time. They were talking in the library, and during most of the narrative he had been gazing through a window towards the pass that led to the outer world; a little wisp of cloud had drifted across the ridge. "A rather grim story, Chang," he commented at length. "It gives one the feeling that Time is like some balked monster, waiting outside the valley to pounce on the slackers who have managed to evade him longer than they should."

"*Slackers?*" queried Chang. His knowledge of English was extremely good, but sometimes a colloquialism proved unfamiliar.

" 'Slacker,' " explained Conway, "is a slang word meaning a lazy fellow, a good-for-nothing. I wasn't, of course, using it seriously."

Chang bowed his thanks for the information. He took a keen interest in languages, and liked to weigh a new word philosophically. "It is significant," he said after a pause, "that the English regard slackness as a vice. We, on the other hand, should vastly prefer it to tension. Is there not too much tension in the world at present, and might it not be better if more people were slackers?"

"I'm inclined to agree with you," Conway answered with solemn amusement.

During the course of a week or so after the interview with the High Lama, Conway met several others of his future colleagues. Chang was neither eager nor reluctant to make the introductions, and Conway sensed a new and to him rather attractive atmosphere in which urgency did not clamor nor postponement disappoint. "Indeed," as Chang explained, "some of the lamas may not meet you for a considerable time—perhaps years—but you must not be surprised at that. They are prepared to make your acquaintance when it may so happen, and their avoidance of hurry does not imply any degree of unwillingness." Conway, who had often had similar feelings when calling on new arrivals at foreign consulates, thought it a very intelligible attitude.

The meetings he did have, however, were quite successful, and conversation with men thrice his age held none of the social embarrassments that might have obtruded in London or Delhi. His first encounter was with a genial German named Meister, who had entered the lamasery during the 'eighties, as the survivor of an exploring party. He spoke English well, though with an accent. A day or two later a second introduction took place, and Conway enjoyed his first talk with the man whom the High Lama had particularly mentioned—Alphonse Briac, a wiry, small-statured Frenchman who did not look especially old, though he announced himself as a pupil of Chopin. Conway thought that both he and the German would prove agreeable company. Already he was subconsciously analyzing, and after a few further meetings he reached one or two general conclusions; he perceived that though the lamas he met had individual differences, they all possessed that quality for which agelessness was not an outstandingly good name, but the only one he could think of. Moreover, they were all endowed with a calm intelligence which pleasantly overflowed into measured and well balanced opinions. Con-

way could give an exact response to that kind of approach, and he was aware
that they realized it and were gratified. He found them quite as easy to get
on with as any other group of cultured people he might have met, though
there was often a sense of oddity in hearing reminiscences so distant and apparently so casual. One white-haired and benevolent-looking person, for instance, asked Conway, after a little conversation, if he were interested in the
Brontës. Conway said he was, to some extent, and the other replied: "You
see, when I was a curate in the West Riding during the 'forties, I once
visited Haworth and stayed at the Parsonage. Since coming here I've made
a study of the whole Brontë problem—indeed, I'm writing a book on the
subject. Perhaps you might care to go over it with me sometime?"

Conway responded cordially, and afterwards, when he and Chang were
left together, commented on the vividness with which the lamas appeared to
recollect their pre-Tibetan lives. Chang answered that it was all part of the
training. "You see, my dear sir, one of the first steps towards the clarifying
of the mind is to obtain a panorama of one's own past, and that, like any other
view, is more accurate in perspective. When you have been among us long
enough you will find your old life slipping gradually into focus as through
a telescope when the lens is adjusted. Everything will stand out still and
clear, duly proportioned and with its correct significance. Your new acquaintance, for instance, discerns that the really big moment of his entire life
occurred when he was a young man visiting a house in which there lived an
old parson and his three daughters."

"So I suppose I shall have to set to work to remember my own big moments?"

"It will not be an effort. They will come to you."

"I don't know that I shall give them much of a welcome," answered Conway moodily.

But whatever the past might yield, he was discovering happiness in the
present. When he sat reading in the library, or playing Mozart in the music
room, he often felt the invasion of a deep spiritual emotion, as if Shangri-La
were indeed a living essence, distilled from the magic of the ages and mirac-
ulously preserved against time and death. His talk with the High Lama
recurred memorably at such moments; he sensed a calm intelligence brooding
gently over every diversion, giving a thousand whispered reassurances to ear
and eye. Thus he would listen while Lo-Tsen marshaled some intricate fugue
rhythm, and wonder what lay behind the faint impersonal smile that stirred
her lips into the likeness of an opening flower. She talked very little, even
though she now knew that Conway could speak her language; to Mallinson,
who liked to visit the music room sometimes, she was almost dumb. But
Conway discerned a charm that was perfectly expressed by her silences.

Once he asked Chang her history, and learned that she came of royal
Manchu stock. "She was betrothed to a prince of Turkestan, and was traveling
to Kashgar to meet him when her carriers lost their way in the mountains.

The whole party would doubtless have perished but for the customary meeting with our emissaries."

"When did this happen?"

"In 1884. She was eighteen."

"Eighteen *then?*"

Chang bowed. "Yes, we are succeeding very well with her, as you may judge for yourself. Her progress has been consistently excellent."

"How did she take things when she first came?"

"She was, perhaps, a little more than averagely reluctant to accept the situation—she made no protest, but we were aware that she was troubled for a time. It was, of course, an unusual occurrence—to intercept a young girl on the way to her wedding. . . . We were all particularly anxious that she should be happy here." Chang smiled blandly. "I am afraid the excitement of love does not make for an easy surrender, though the first five years proved ample for their purpose."

"She was deeply attached, I suppose, to the man she was to have married?"

"Hardly that, my dear sir, since she had never seen him. It was the old custom, you know. The excitement of her affections was entirely impersonal."

Conway nodded, and thought a little tenderly of Lo-Tsen. He pictured her as she might have been half a century before, statuesque in her decorated chair as the carriers toiled over the plateau, her eyes searching the wind-swept horizons that must have seemed so harsh after the gardens and lotus pools of the East. "Poor child!" he said, thinking of such elegance held captive over the years. Knowledge of her past increased rather than lessened his content with her stillness and silence; she was like a lovely cold vase, unadorned save by an escaping ray.

He was also content, though less ecstatically, when Briac talked to him of Chopin, and played the familiar melodies with much brilliance. It appeared that the Frenchman knew several Chopin compositions that had never been published, and as he had written them down, Conway devoted pleasant hours to memorizing them himself. He found a certain piquancy in the reflection that neither Cortot nor Pachmann had been so fortunate. Nor were Briac's recollections at an end; his memory continually refreshed him with some little scrap of tune that the composer had thrown off or improvised on some occasion; he took them all down on paper as they came into his head, and some were very delightful fragments. "Briac," Chang explained, "has not long been initiated, so you must make allowances if he talks a great deal about Chopin. The younger lamas are naturally preoccupied with the past; it is a necessary step to envisaging the future."

"Which is, I take it, the job of the older ones?"

"Yes. The High Lama, for instance, spends almost his entire life in clairvoyant meditation."

Conway pondered a moment and then said: "By the way, when do you suppose I shall see him again?"

"Doubtless at the end of the first five years, my dear sir."

But in that confident prophecy Chang was wrong, for less than a month after his arrival at Shangri-La Conway received a second summons to that torrid upper room. Chang had told him that the High Lama never left his apartments, and that their heated atmosphere was necessary for his bodily existence; and Conway, being thus prepared, found the change less disconcerting than before. Indeed, he breathed easily as soon as he had made his bow and been granted the faintest answering liveliness of the sunken eyes. He felt kinship with the mind beyond them, and though he knew that this second interview following so soon upon the first was an unprecedented honor, he was not in the least nervous or weighed down with solemnity. Age was to him no more an obsessing factor than rank or color; he had never felt debarred from liking people because they were too young or too old. He held the High Lama in most cordial respect, but he did not see why their social relations should be anything less than urbane.

They exchanged the usual courtesies, and Conway answered many polite questions. He said he was finding the life very agreeable and had already made friendships.

"And you have kept our secrets from your three companions?"

"Yes, up to now. It has proved awkward for me at times, but probably less so than if I had told them."

"Just as I surmised; you have acted as you thought best. And the awkwardness, after all, is only temporary. Chang tells me he thinks that two of them will give little trouble."

"I dare say that is so."

"And the third?"

Conway replied: "Mallinson is an excitable youth—he's pretty keen to get back."

"You like him?"

"Yes, I like him very much."

At this point the tea-bowls were brought in, and talk became less serious between sips of the scented liquid. It was an apt convention, enabling the verbal flow to acquire a touch of that almost frivolous fragrance, and Conway was responsive. When the High Lama asked him whether Shangri-La was not unique in his experience, and if the Western world could offer anything in the least like it, he answered with a smile: "Well, yes—to be quite frank, it reminds me very slightly of Oxford, where I used to lecture. The scenery there is not so good, but the subjects of study are often just as impractical, and though even the oldest of the dons is not quite so old, they appear to age in a somewhat similar way."

"You have a sense of humor, my dear Conway," replied the High Lama, "for which we shall all be grateful during the years to come."

CHAPTER TEN

"Extraordinary," Chang said, when he heard that Conway had seen the High Lama again. And from one so reluctant to employ superlatives, the word was significant. It had never happened before, he emphasized, since the routine of the lamasery became established; never had the High Lama desired a second meeting until the five years' probation had effected a purge of all the exile's likely emotions. "Because, you see, it is a great strain on him to talk to the average new-comer. The mere presence of human passions is an unwelcome and, at his age, an almost unendurable unpleasantness. Not that I doubt his entire wisdom in the matter. It teaches us, I believe, a lesson of great value—that even the fixed rules of our community are only moderately fixed. But it is extraordinary, all the same."

To Conway, of course, it was no more extraordinary than anything else, and after he had visited the High Lama on a third and fourth occasion, he began to feel that it was not very extraordinary at all. There seemed, indeed, something almost preordained in the ease with which their two minds approached each other; it was as if in Conway all secret tensions were relaxed, giving him, when he came away, a sumptuous tranquillity. At times he had the sensation of being completely bewitched by the mastery of that central intelligence, and then, over the little pale blue tea-bowls, the cerebration would contract into a liveliness so gentle and miniature that he had an impression of a theorem dissolving limpidly into a sonnet.

Their talks ranged far and fearlessly; entire philosophies were unfolded; the long avenues of history surrendered themselves for inspection and were given new plausibility. To Conway it was an entrancing experience, but he did not suspend the critical attitude, and once, when he had argued a point, the High Lama replied: "My son, you are young in years, but I perceive that your wisdom has the ripeness of age. Surely some unusual thing has happened to you?"

Conway smiled. "No more unusual than has happened to many others of my generation."

"I have never met your like before."

Conway answered after an interval: "There's not a great deal of mystery about it. That part of me which seems old to you was worn out by intense and premature experience. My years from nineteen to twenty-two were a supreme education, no doubt, but rather exhausting."

"You were very unhappy at the War?"

"Not particularly so. I was excited and suicidal and scared and reckless and sometimes in a tearing rage—like a few million others, in fact. I got mad-drunk and killed and lechered in great style. It was the self-abuse of all one's emotions, and one came through it, if one did at all, with a sense of almighty boredom and fretfulness. That's what made the years afterwards so difficult. Don't think I'm posing myself too tragically—I've had pretty fair luck since, on the whole. But it's been rather like being in a school where there's a bad headmaster—plenty of fun to be got if you feel like it, but nerve-racking off and on, and not really very satisfactory. I think I found that out rather more than most people."

"And your education thus continued?"

Conway gave a shrug. "Perhaps the exhaustion of the passions is the beginning of wisdom, if you care to alter the proverb."

"That also, my son, is the doctrine of Shangri-La."

"I know. It makes me feel quite at home."

He had spoken no less than the truth. As the days and weeks passed he began to feel an ache of contentment uniting mind and body; like Perrault and Henschell and the others, he was falling under the spell. Blue Moon had taken him, and there was no escape. The mountains gleamed around in a hedge of inaccessible purity, from which his eyes fell dazzled to the green depths of the valley; the whole picture was incomparable, and when he heard the harpsichord's silver monotony across the lotus pool, he felt that it threaded the perfect pattern of sight and sound.

He was, and he knew it, very quietly in love with the little Manchu. His love demanded nothing, not even reply; it was a tribute of the mind, to which his senses added only a flavor. She stood for him as a symbol of all that was delicate and fragile; her stylized courtesies and the touch of her fingers on the keyboard yielded a completely satisfying intimacy. Sometimes he would address her in a way that might, if she had cared, have led to less formal conversation; but her replies never broke through the exquisite privacy of her thoughts, and in a sense he did not wish them to. He had suddenly come to realize a single facet of the promised jewel; he had Time, Time for everything that he wished to happen, such Time that desire itself was quenched in the certainty of fulfillment. A year, a decade hence, there would still be Time. The vision grew on him, and he was happy with it.

Then, at intervals, he stepped into the other life to encounter Mallinson's impatience, Barnard's heartiness, and Miss Brinklow's robust intention. He felt he would be glad when they all knew as much as he; and, like Chang, he could imagine that neither the American nor the missionary would prove difficult cases. He was even amused when Barnard once said: "You know, Conway, I'm not sure that this wouldn't be a nice little place to settle down in. I thought at first I'd miss the newspapers and the movies, but I guess one can get used to anything."

"I guess one can," agreed Conway.

He learned afterwards that Chang had taken Barnard down to the valley, at his own request, to enjoy everything in the way of a "night out" that the resources of the locality could provide. Mallinson, when he heard of this, was rather scornful. "Getting tight, I suppose," he remarked to Conway, and to Barnard himself he commented: "Of course it's none of my business, but you'll want to keep yourself pretty fit for the journey, you know. The porters are due in a fortnight's time, and from what I gather, the return trip won't be exactly a joy ride."

Barnard nodded equably. "I never figgered it would," he answered. "And as for keeping fit, I guess I'm fitter than I've been for years. I get exercise daily, I don't have any worries, and the speakeasies down in the valley don't let you go too far. Moderation, y'know—the motto of the firm."

"Yes, I've no doubt you've been managing to have a moderately good time," said Mallinson acidly.

"Certainly I have. This establishment caters for all tastes—some people like little Chink gels who play the pi-anno, isn't that so? You can't blame anybody for what they fancy."

Conway was not at all put out, but Mallinson flushed like a schoolboy. "You can send them to jail, though, when they fancy other people's property," he snapped, stung to fury that set a raw edge to his wits.

"Sure, if you can catch 'em." The American grinned affably. "And that leads me to something I may as well tell you folks right away, now we're on the subject. I've decided to give those porters a miss. They come here pretty regular, and I'll wait for the next trip, or maybe the next but one. That is, if the monks'll take my word that I'm still good for my hotel expenses."

"You mean you're not coming with us?"

"That's it. I've decided to stop over for a while. It's all very fine for you— you'll have the band playing when *you* get home, but all the welcome I'll get is from a row of cops. And the more I think about it, the more it don't seem good enough."

"In other words, you're just afraid to face the music?"

"Well, I never did like music, anyhow."

Mallinson said with cold scorn: "I suppose it's your own affair. Nobody can prevent you from stopping here all your life if you feel inclined." Nevertheless he looked round with a flash of appeal. "It's not what everybody would choose to do, but ideas differ. What do you say, Conway?"

"I agree. Ideas *do* differ."

Mallinson turned to Miss Brinklow, who suddenly put down her book and remarked: "As a matter of fact, I think I shall stay too."

"*What?*" they all cried together.

She continued, with a bright smile that seemed more an attachment to her face than an illumination of it: "You see, I've been thinking over the way things happened to bring us all here, and there's only one conclusion I can come to. There's a mysterious power working behind the scenes. Don't you think so, Mr. Conway?"

Conway might have found it hard to reply, but Miss Brinklow went on in a gathering hurry: "Who am I to question the dictates of Providence? I was sent here for a purpose, and I shall stay."

"Do you mean you're hoping to start a mission here?" Mallinson asked.

"Not only hoping, but fully intending. I know just how to deal with these people—I shall get my own way, never fear. There's no real grit in any of them."

"And you intend to introduce some?"

"Yes, I do, Mr. Mallinson. I'm strongly opposed to that idea of moderation that we hear so much about. You can call it broadmindedness if you like, but in my opinion it leads to the worst kinds of laxity. The whole trouble with the people here is their so-called broadmindedness, and I intend to fight it with all my powers."

"And they're so broadminded that they're going to let you?" said Conway, smiling.

"Or else she's so strong-minded that they can't stop her," put in Barnard. He added with a chuckle: "It's just what I said—this establishment caters for all tastes."

"Possibly, if you happen to *like* prison," Mallinson snapped.

"Well, there's two ways of looking even at that. My goodness, if you think of all the folks in the world who'd give all they've got to be out of the racket and in a place like this, only they can't *get* out! Are *we* in the prison or are *they?*"

"A comforting speculation for a monkey in a cage," retorted Mallinson; he was still furious.

Afterwards he spoke to Conway alone. "That man still gets on my nerves," he said, pacing the courtyard. "I'm not sorry we shan't have him with us when we go back. You may think me touchy, but being chipped about that Chinese girl didn't appeal to my sense of humor."

Conway took Mallinson's arm. It was becoming increasingly clear to him that he was very fond of the youth, and that their recent weeks in company had deepened the feeling, despite jarring moods. He answered: "I rather took it that *I* was being ragged about her, not you."

"No, I think he intended it for me. He knows I'm interested in her. I am, Conway. I can't make out why she's here, and whether she really likes being here. My God, if I spoke her language as you do, I'd soon have it out with her."

"I wonder if you would. She doesn't say a great deal to any one, you know."

"It puzzles me that you don't badger her with all sorts of questions."

"I don't know that I care for badgering people."

He wished he could have said more, and then suddenly the sense of pity and irony floated over him in a filmy haze; this youth, so eager and ardent, would take things very hardly. "I shouldn't worry about Lo-Tsen if I were you," he added. "She's happy enough."

The decision of Barnard and Miss Brinklow to remain behind seemed to Conway all to the good, though it threw Mallinson and himself into an apparently opposite camp for the time being. It was an extraordinary situation, and he had no definite plans for tackling it.

Fortunately there was no apparent need to tackle it at all. Until the two months were past, nothing much could happen; and afterwards there would be a crisis no less acute for his having tried to prepare himself for it. For this and other reasons he was disinclined to worry over the inevitable, though he did once say: "You know, Chang, I'm bothered about young Mallinson. I'm afraid he'll take things very badly when he finds out."

Chang nodded with some sympathy. "Yes, it will not be easy to persuade him of his good fortune. But the difficulty is, after all, only a temporary one. In twenty years from now our friend will be quite reconciled."

Conway felt that this was looking at the matter almost too philosophically. "I'm wondering," he said, "just how the truth's going to be broached to him. He's counting the days to the arrival of the porters, and if they don't come—"

"But they *will* come."

"Oh? I rather imagined that all your talk about them was just a pleasant fable to let us down lightly."

"By no means. Although we have no bigotry on the point, it is our custom at Shangri-La to be moderately truthful, and I can assure you that my statements about the porters were almost correct. At any rate, we are expecting the men at or about the time I said."

"Then you'll find it hard to stop Mallinson from joining them."

"But we should never attempt to do so. He will merely discover—no doubt by personal experiment—that the porters are reluctantly unable to take any one back with them."

"I see. So that's the method? And what do you expect to happen afterwards?"

"Then, my dear sir, after a period of disappointment, he will—since he is young and optimistic—begin to hope that the next convoy of porters, due in nine or ten months' time, will prove more amenable to his suggestions. And this is a hope which, if we are wise, we shall not at first discourage."

Conway said sharply: "I'm not so sure that he'll do that at all. I should think he's far more likely to try an escape on his own."

"*Escape?* Is that *really* the word that should be used? After all, the pass is open to any one at any time. We have no jailers, save those that Nature herself has provided."

Conway smiled. "Well, you must admit that she's done her job pretty well. But I don't suppose you rely on her in every case, all the same. What about the various exploring parties that have arrived here? Was the pass always equally open to *them* when they wanted to get away?"

It was Chang's turn now to smile. "Special circumstances, my dear sir, have sometimes required special consideration."

"Excellent. So you only allow people the chance of escape when you know they'd be fools to take it? Even so, I expect some of them do."

"Well, it has happened very occasionally, but as a rule the absentees are glad to return after the experience of a single night on the plateau."

"Without shelter and proper clothing? If so, I can quite understand that your mild methods are as effective as stern ones. But what about the less usual cases that don't return?"

"You have yourself answered the question," replied Chang. "They do *not* return." But he made haste to add: "I can assure you, however, that there are few indeed who have been so unfortunate, and I trust your friend will not be rash enough to increase the number."

Conway did not find these responses entirely reassuring, and Mallinson's future remained a preoccupation. He wished it were possible for the youth to return by consent, and this would not be unprecedented, for there was the recent case of Talu, the airman. Chang admitted that the authorities were fully empowered to do anything that they considered wise. "But *should* we be wise, my dear sir, in trusting ourselves and our future entirely to your friend's feelings of gratitude?"

Conway felt that the question was pertinent, for Mallinson's attitude left little doubt as to what he would do as soon as he reached India. It was his favorite theme, and he had often enlarged upon it.

But all that, of course, was in the mundane world that was gradually being pushed out of his mind by the rich, pervasive world of Shangri-La. Except when he thought about Mallinson he was extraordinarily content; the slowly revealed fabric of this new environment continued to astonish him by its intricate suitability to his own needs and tastes.

Once he said to Chang: "By the way, how do you people here fit love into your scheme of things? I suppose it does sometimes happen that those who come here develop attachments?"

"Quite often," replied Chang with a broad smile. "The lamas, of course, are immune, and so are most of us when we reach the riper years, but until then we are as other men, except that I think we can claim to behave more reasonably. And this gives me the opportunity, Mr. Conway, of assuring you that the hospitality of Shangri-La is of a comprehensive kind. Your friend Mr. Barnard has already availed himself of it."

Conway returned the smile. "Thanks," he answered dryly. "I've no doubt he has, but my own inclinations are not—at the moment—so assertive. It was the emotional more than the physical aspect that I was curious about."

"You find it easy to separate the two? Is it possible that you are falling in love with Lo-Tsen?"

Conway was somewhat taken aback, though he hoped he did not show it. "What makes you ask that?"

"Because, my dear sir, it would be quite suitable if you were to do so—always, of course, in moderation. Lo-Tsen would not respond with any degree of passion—that is more than you could expect—but the experience would be very delightful, I assure you. And I speak with some authority, for I was in love with her myself when I was much younger."

"Were you indeed? And did she respond then?"

"Only by the most charming appreciation of the compliment I paid her, and by a friendship which has grown more precious with the years."

"In other words, she didn't respond?"

"If you prefer it so." Chang added, a little sententiously: "It has always been her way to spare her lovers the moment of satiety that goes with all absolute attainment."

Conway laughed. "That's all very well in your case, and perhaps in mine too—but what about the attitude of a hot-blooded young fellow like Mallinson?"

"My dear sir, it would be the best possible thing that could happen! Not for the first time, I assure you, would Lo-Tsen comfort the sorrowful exile when he learned that there is to be no return."

"Comfort?"

"Yes, though you must not misunderstand my use of the term. Lo-Tsen gives no caresses, except such as touch the stricken heart from her very presence. What does your Shakespeare say of Cleopatra?—'She makes hungry where she most satisfies.' A popular type, doubtless, among the passion-driven races, but such a woman, I assure you, would be altogether out of place at Shangri-La. Lo-Tsen, if I might amend the quotation, *removes* hunger where she *least* satisfies. It is a more delicate and lasting accomplishment."

"And one, I assume, which she has much skill in performing?"

"Oh, decidedly—we have had many examples of it. It is her way to calm the throb of desire to a murmur that is no less pleasant when left unanswered."

"In that sense, then, you could regard her as a part of the training equipment of the establishment?"

"*You* could regard her as that, if you wished," replied Chang with deprecating blandness. "But it would be more graceful, and just as true, to liken her to the rainbow reflected in a glass bowl or to the dewdrops on the blossom of the fruit tree."

"I entirely agree with you, Chang. That would be *much* more graceful." Conway enjoyed the measured yet agile repartees which his good-humored ragging of the Chinese very often elicited.

But the next time he was alone with the little Manchu he felt that Chang's remarks had had a great deal of shrewdness in them. There was a fragrance about her that communicated itself to his own emotions, kindling the embers to a glow that did not burn, but merely warmed. And suddenly then he realized that Shangri-La and Lo-Tsen were quite perfect, and that he did not wish for more than to stir a faint and eventual response in all that stillness. For years his passions had been like a nerve that the world jarred on; now at last the aching was soothed, and he could yield himself to love that was neither a torment nor a bore. As he passed by the lotus pool at night he sometimes pictured her in his arms, but the sense of time washed over the vision, calming him to an infinite and tender reluctance.

He did not think he had ever been so happy, even in the years of his life before the great barrier of the War. He liked the serene world that Shangri-La offered him, pacified rather than dominated by its single tremendous idea. He liked the prevalent mood in which feelings were sheathed in thoughts, and thoughts softened into felicity by their transference into language. Conway, whom experience had taught that rudeness is by no means a guarantee of good faith, was even less inclined to regard a well-turned phrase as a proof of insincerity. He liked the mannered, leisurely atmosphere in which talk was an accomplishment, not a mere habit. And he liked to realize that the idlest things could now be freed from the curse of time-wasting, and the frailest dreams receive the welcome of the mind. Shangri-La was always tranquil, yet always a hive of unpursuing occupations; the lamas lived as if indeed they had time on their hands, but time that was scarcely a feather-weight. Conway met no more of them, but he came gradually to realize the extent and variety of their employments; besides their knowledge of languages, some, it appeared, took to the full seas of learning in a manner that would have yielded big surprises to the Western world. Many were engaged in writing manuscript books of various kinds; one (Chang said) had made valuable researches into pure mathematics; another was co-ordinating Gibbon and Spengler into a vast thesis on the history of European civilization. But this kind of thing was not for them all, nor for any of them always; there were many tideless channels in which they dived in mere waywardness, retrieving, like Briac, fragments of old tunes, or like the English ex-curate, a new theory about *Wuthering Heights*. And there were even fainter impracticalities than these. Once, when Conway made some remark in this connection, the High Lama replied with a story of a Chinese artist in the third century B.C. who, having spent many years in carving dragons, birds, and horses upon a cherry-stone, offered his finished work to a royal prince. The prince could see nothing in it at first except a mere stone, but the artist bade him "have a wall built, and make a window in it, and observe the stone through the window in the glory of the dawn." The prince did so, and then perceived that the stone was indeed very beautiful. "Is not that a charming story, my dear Conway, and do you not think it teaches a very valuable lesson?"

Conway agreed; he found it pleasant to realize that the serene purpose of Shangri-La could embrace an infinitude of odd and apparently trivial employments, for he had always had a taste for such things himself. In fact, when he regarded his past, he saw it strewn with images of tasks too vagrant or too taxing ever to have been accomplished; but now they were all possible, even in a mood of idleness. It was delightful to contemplate, and he was not disposed to sneer when Barnard confided in him that he too envisaged an interesting future at Shangri-La.

It seemed that Barnard's excursions to the valley, which had been growing more frequent of late, were not entirely devoted to drink and women. "You see, Conway, I'm telling you this because you're different from Mallinson—he's got his knife into me, as probably you've gathered. But I feel you'll be better at understanding the position. It's a funny thing—you British officials are so darned stiff and starchy at first, but you're the sort a fellow can put his trust in, when all's said and done."

"I wouldn't be too sure," replied Conway, smiling. "And anyhow, Mallinson's just as much a British official as I am."

"Yes, but he's a mere boy. He don't look at things reasonably. You and me are men of the world—we take things as we find them. This joint here, for instance—we still can't understand all the ins and outs of it, and why we've been landed here, but then, isn't that the usual way of things? Do we know why we're in the world at all, for that matter?"

"Perhaps some of us don't, but what's all this leading up to?"

Barnard dropped his voice to a rather husky whisper. "Gold, my lad," he answered with a certain ecstasy. "Just that, and nothing less. There's tons of it—literally—in the valley. I was a mining engineer in my young days and I haven't forgotten what a reef looks like. Believe me, it's as rich as the Rand, and ten times easier to get at. I guess you thought I was on the loose whenever I went down there in my little armchair. Not a bit of it. I knew what I was doing. I'd figgered it out all along, you know, that these guys here couldn't get all their stuff sent in from outside without paying mighty high for it, and what else could they pay with except gold or silver or diamonds or something? Only logic, after all. And when I began to scout round, it didn't take me long to discover the whole bag of tricks."

"You found it out on your own?" asked Conway.

"Well, I won't say that, but I made my guess, and then I put the matter to Chang—straight, mind you, as man to man. And believe me, Conway, that Chink's not as bad a fellow as we might have thought."

"Personally, I never thought him a bad fellow at all."

"Of course, I know you always took to him, so you won't be surprised at the way we got on together. We certainly did hit it famously. He showed me all over the workings, and it may interest you to know that I've got the full permission of the authorities to prospect in the valley as much as I like and make a comprehensive report. What d'you think of that, my lad? They seemed quite glad to have the services of an expert, especially when I said I could probably give 'em tips how to increase output."

"I can see you're going to be altogether at home here," said Conway.

"Well, I must say I've found a job, and that's something. And you never know how a thing'll turn out in the end. Maybe the folks at home won't be so keen to jail me when they know I can show 'em the way to a new gold mine. The only difficulty is—would they take my word about it?"

"They might. It's extraordinary what people *will* believe."

Barnard nodded with enthusiasm. "Glad you get the point, Conway. And that's where you and I can make a deal. We'll go fifty-fifty in everything, of course. All you've gotter do is to put your name to my report—British Consul, you know, and all that. It'll carry weight."

Conway laughed. "We'll have to see about it. Make your report first."

It amused him to contemplate a possibility so unlikely to happen, and at the same time he was glad that Barnard had found something that yielded such immediate comfort.

So also was the High Lama, whom Conway began to see more and more frequently. He often visited him in the late evening and stayed for many hours, long after the servants had taken away the last bowls of tea and had been dismissed for the night. The High Lama never failed to ask him about the progress and welfare of his three companions, and once he enquired particularly as to the kind of careers that their arrival at Shangri-La had so inevitably interrupted.

Conway answered reflectively: "Mallinson might have done quite well in his own line—he's energetic and has ambitions. The two others—" He shrugged his shoulders. "As a matter of fact, it happens to suit them both to stay here—for a while, at any rate."

He noticed a flicker of light at the curtained window; there had been mutterings of thunder as he crossed the courtyards on his way to the now familiar room. No sound could be heard, and the heavy tapestries subdued the lightning into mere sparks of pallor.

"Yes," came the reply, "we have done our best to make both of them feel at home. Miss Brinklow wishes to convert us, and Mr. Barnard would also like to convert us—into a limited liability company. Harmless projects—they will pass the time quite pleasantly for them. But your young friend, to whom neither gold nor religion can offer solace, how about *him?*"

"Yes, he's going to be the problem."

"I am afraid he is going to be *your* problem."

"Why mine?"

There was no immediate answer, for the tea-bowls were introduced at that moment, and with their appearance the High Lama rallied a faint and desiccated hospitality. "Karakal sends us storms at this time of the year," he remarked, feathering the conversation according to ritual. "The people of Blue Moon believe they are caused by demons raging in the great space beyond the pass. The 'outside,' they call it—perhaps you are aware that in their patois the word is used for the entire rest of the world. Of course they know nothing of such countries as France or England or even India—they imagine the dread altiplano stretching, as it almost does, illimitably. To them, so snug at their warm and windless levels, it appears unthinkable that any one inside the valley should ever wish to leave it; indeed, they picture all unfortunate 'outsiders' as passionately desiring to enter. It is just a question of viewpoint, is it not?"

Conway was reminded of Barnard's somewhat similar remarks, and quoted them. "How very sensible!" was the High Lama's comment. "And he is our first American, too—we are truly fortunate."

Conway found it piquant to reflect that the lamasery's fortune was to have acquired a man for whom the police of a dozen countries were actively searching; and he would have liked to share the piquancy but for feeling that Barnard had better be left to tell his own story in due course. He said: "Doubtless he's quite right, and there are many people in the world nowadays who would be glad enough to be here."

"*Too* many, my dear Conway. We are a single lifeboat riding the seas in a gale; we can take a few chance survivors, but if all the shipwrecked were to reach us and clamber aboard we should go down ourselves. . . . But let us not think of it just now. I hear that you have been associating with our excellent Briac. A delightful fellow countryman of mine, though I do not share his opinion that Chopin is the greatest of all composers. For myself, as you know, I prefer Mozart. . . ."

Not till the tea-bowls were removed and the servant had been finally dismissed, did Conway venture to recall the unanswered question. "We were discussing Mallinson, and you said he was going to be *my* problem. Why mine, particularly?"

Then the High Lama replied very simply: "Because, my son, I am going to die."

It seemed an extraordinary statement, and for a time Conway was speechless after it. Eventually the High Lama continued: "You are surprised? But surely, my friend, we are all mortal—even at Shangri-La. And it is possible that I may still have a few moments left to me—or even, for that matter, a few years. All I announce is the simple truth that already I see the end. It is charming of you to appear so concerned, and I will not pretend that there is not a touch of wistfulness, even at my age, in contemplating death. Fortunately little is left of me that can die physically, and as for the rest, all our religions display a pleasant unanimity of optimism. I am quite content, but I must accustom myself to a strange sensation during the hours that remain—I must realize that I have time for only one thing more. Can you imagine what that is?"

Conway was silent.

"It concerns you, my son."

"You do me a great honor."

"I have in mind to do much more than that."

Conway bowed slightly, but did not speak, and the High Lama, after waiting awhile, resumed: "You know, perhaps, that the frequency of these talks has been unusual here. But it is our tradition, if I may permit myself the paradox, that we are never slaves to tradition. We have no rigidities, no inexorable rules. We do as we think fit, guided a little by the example of the past, but still more by our present wisdom, and by our clairvoyance of the future. And thus it is that I am encouraged to do this final thing."

Conway was still silent.

"I place in your hands, my son, the heritage and destiny of Shangri-La."

At last the tension broke, and Conway felt beyond it the power of a bland and benign persuasion; the echoes swam into silence, till all that was left was his own heartbeat, pounding like a gong. And then, intercepting the rhythm, came the words:

"I have waited for you, my son, for quite a long time. I have sat in this room and seen the faces of new-comers, I have looked into their eyes and heard their voices, and always in hope that some day I might find you. My colleagues have grown old and wise, but you who are still young in years are as wise already. My friend, it is not an arduous task that I bequeath, for our order knows only silken bonds. To be gentle and patient, to care for the riches of the mind, to preside in wisdom and secrecy while the storm rages without—it will all be very pleasantly simple for you, and you will doubtless find great happiness."

Again Conway sought to reply, but could not, till at length a vivid lightning-flash paled the shadows and stirred him to exclaim: "The storm . . . this storm you talk of. . . ."

"It will be such a one, my son, as the world has not seen before. There will be no safety by arms, no help from authority, no answer in science. It will rage till every flower of culture is trampled, and all human things are leveled in a vast chaos. Such was my vision when Napoleon was still a name unknown; and I see it now, more clearly with each hour. Do you say I am mistaken?"

Conway answered: "No, I think you may be right. A similar crash came once before, and then there were the Dark Ages lasting five hundred years."

"The parallel is not quite exact. For those Dark Ages were not really so very dark—they were full of flickering lanterns, and even if the light had gone out of Europe altogether, there were other rays, literally from China to Peru, at which it could have been rekindled. But the Dark Ages that are to come will cover the whole world in a single pall; there will be neither escape nor sanctuary, save such as are too secret to be found or too humble to be noticed. And Shangri-La may hope to be both of these. The airman bearing loads of death to the great cities will not pass our way, and if by chance he should, he may not consider us worth a bomb."

"And you think all this will come in my time?"

"I believe that you will live through the storm. And after, through the long age of desolation, you may still live, growing older and wiser and more patient. You will conserve the fragrance of our history and add to it the touch of your own mind. You will welcome the stranger, and teach him the rule of age and wisdom; and one of these strangers, it may be, will succeed you when you are yourself very old. Beyond that, my vision weakens, but I see, at a great distance, a new world stirring in the ruins, stirring clumsily but in hopefulness, seeking its lost and legendary treasures. And they will all be here, my son, hidden behind the mountains in the valley of Blue Moon, preserved as by miracle for a new Renaissance. . . ."

The speaking finished, and Conway saw the face before him full of a remote and drenching beauty; then the glow faded and there was nothing left but a mask, dark-shadowed, and crumbling like old wood. It was quite motionless, and the eyes were closed. He watched for a while, and presently, as part of a dream, it came to him that the High Lama was dead.

It seemed necessary to rivet the situation to some kind of actuality, lest it become too strange to be believed in; and with instinctive mechanism of hand and eye, Conway glanced at his wrist-watch. It was a quarter past midnight. Suddenly, when he crossed the room to the door, it occurred to him that he did not in the least know how or whence to summon help. The Tibetans, he knew, had all been sent away for the night, and he had no idea where to find Chang or any one else. He stood uncertainly on the threshold of the dark corridor; through a window he could see that the sky was clear, though the mountains still blazed in lightning like a silver fresco. And then, in the midst of the still encompassing dream, he felt himself master of Shangri-La. These were his beloved things, all around him, the things of that inner mind in which he lived increasingly, away from the fret of the world. His eyes strayed into the shadows and were caught by golden pinpoints sparkling in rich, undulating lacquers; and the scent of tuberose, so faint that it expired on the very brink of sensation, lured him from room to room. At last he stumbled into the courtyards and by the fringe of the pool; a full moon sailed behind Karakal. It was twenty minutes to two.

Later, he was aware that Mallinson was near him, holding his arm and leading him away in a great hurry. He did not gather what it was all about, but he could hear that the boy was chattering excitedly.

CHAPTER ELEVEN

They reached the balconied room where they had meals, Mallinson still clutching his arm and half dragging him along. "Come on, Conway, we've till dawn to pack what we can and get away. Great news, man—I wonder what old Barnard and Miss Brinklow will think in the morning when they find us gone . . . still, it's their own choice to stay, and we'll probably get on far better without them. . . . The porters are about five miles beyond the pass—they came yesterday with loads of books and things . . . to-morrow they begin the journey back. . . . It just shows how these fellows here intended to let us down—they never told us—we should have been stranded here for God knows how much longer. . . . I say, what's the matter? Are you ill?"

Conway had sunk into a chair, and was leaning forward with elbows on the table. He passed his hand across his eyes. "Ill? No, I don't think so. Just —rather—tired."

"Probably the storm. Where were you all the while? I'd been waiting for you for hours."

"I—I was visiting the High Lama."

"Oh, him! Well, that's for the last time, anyhow, thank God."

"Yes, Mallinson, for the last time."

Something in Conway's voice, and still more in his succeeding silence, roused the youth to irascibility. "Well, I wish you wouldn't sound so deuced leisurely about it—we've got to get a considerable move on, you know."

Conway stiffened for the effort of emerging into keener consciousness. "I'm sorry," he said. Partly to test his nerve and the reality of his sensations he lit a cigarette. He found that both hands and lips were unsteady. "I'm afraid I don't quite follow . . . you say the porters . . ."

"Yes, the porters, man—do pull yourself together."

"You're thinking of going out to them?"

"Thinking of it? I'm damn well certain—they're only just over the ridge. And we've got to start immediately."

"Immediately?"

"Yes, yes—why not?"

Conway made a second attempt to transfer himself from the one world into the other. He said at length, having partly succeeded: "I suppose you realize that it mayn't be quite as simple as it sounds?"

Mallinson was lacing a pair of knee-high Tibetan mountain-boots as he answered jerkily: "I realize everything, but it's something we've got to do, and we shall do it, with luck, if we don't delay."

"I don't see how—"

"Oh, Lord, Conway, must you fight shy of everything? Haven't you any guts left in you at all?"

The appeal, half passionate and half derisive, helped Conway to collect himself. "Whether I have or haven't isn't the point, but if you want me to explain myself, I will. It's a question of a few rather important details. Suppose you *do* get beyond the pass and find the porters there, how do you know they'll take you with them? What inducement can you offer? Hasn't it struck you that they mayn't be quite so willing as you'd like them to be? You can't just present yourself and demand to be escorted. It all needs arrangement, negotiations beforehand—"

"Or anything else to cause a delay," exclaimed Mallinson bitterly. "God, what a fellow you are! Fortunately I haven't you to rely on for arranging things. Because they *have* been arranged—the porters have been paid in advance, and they've agreed to take us. And here are clothes and equipment for the journey, all ready. So your last excuse disappears. Come on, let's *do* something."

"But—I don't understand. . . ."

"I don't suppose you do, but it doesn't matter."

"Who's been making all these plans?"

Mallinson answered brusquely: "Lo-Tsen, if you're really keen to know. She's with the porters now. She's waiting."

"*Waiting?*"

"Yes. She's coming with us. I assume you've no objection?"

At the mention of Lo-Tsen the two worlds touched and fused suddenly in Conway's mind. He cried sharply, almost contemptuously: "That's nonsense. It's impossible."

Mallinson was equally on edge. "Why is it impossible?"

"Because . . . well, it is. There are all sorts of reasons. Take my word for it; it won't do. It's incredible enough that she should be out there now—I'm astonished at what you say has happened—but the idea of her going any further is just preposterous."

"I don't see that it's preposterous at all. It's as natural for her to want to leave here as for me."

"But she doesn't want to leave. That's where you make the mistake."

Mallinson smiled tensely. "You think you know a good deal more about her than I do, I dare say," he remarked. "But perhaps you don't, for all that."

"What do you mean?"

"There are other ways of getting to understand people without learning heaps of languages."

"For Heaven's sake, what *are* you driving at?" Then Conway added more quietly: "This is absurd. We mustn't wrangle. Tell me, Mallinson, what's it all about? I still don't understand."

"Then why are you making such an almighty fuss?"

"Tell me the truth, *please* tell me the truth."

"Well, it's simple enough. A kid of her age, shut up here with a lot of queer old men—naturally she'll get away if she's given a chance. She hasn't had one up to now."

"Don't you think you may be imagining her position in the light of your own? As I've always told you, she's perfectly happy."

"Then why did she say she'd come?"

"She said that? How could she? She doesn't speak English."

"I asked her—in Tibetan—Miss Brinklow worked out the words. It wasn't a very fluent conversation, but it was quite enough to—to lead to an understanding." Mallinson flushed a little. "Damn it, Conway, don't stare at me like that—any one would think I'd been poaching on *your* preserves."

Conway answered: "No one would think so at all, I hope, but the remark tells me more than you were perhaps intending me to know. I can only say that I'm very sorry."

"And why the devil should you be?"

Conway let the cigarette fall from his fingers. He felt tired, bothered, and full of deep conflicting tendernesses that he would rather not have had aroused. He said gently: "I wish we weren't always at such cross-purposes. Lo-Tsen is very charming, I know, but why should we quarrel about it?"

"*Charming?*" Mallinson echoed the word with scorn. "She's a good bit more than that. You mustn't think everybody's as cold-blooded about these things as you are yourself. Admiring her as if she were an exhibit in a museum may be your idea of what she deserves, but mine's more practical, and when I see some one I like in a rotten position I try and *do* something."

"But surely there's such a thing as being too impetuous? Where do you think she'll go to if she does leave?"

"I suppose she must have friends in China or somewhere. Anyhow, she'll be better off than here."

"How can you possibly be so sure of that?"

"Well, I'll see that she's looked after myself, if nobody else will. After all, if you're rescuing people from something quite hellish, you don't usually stop to enquire if they've anywhere else to go to."

"And you think Shangri-La is hellish?"

"Definitely, I do. There's something dark and evil about it. The whole business has been like that, from the beginning—the way we were brought here, without reason at all, by some madman—and the way we've been detained since, on one excuse or another. But the most frightful thing of all—to me—is the effect it's had on you."

"On *me?*"

"Yes, on you. You've just mooned about as if nothing mattered and you were content to stay here for ever. Why, you even admitted you liked the place. . . . Conway, what *has* happened to you? Can't you manage to be your real self again? We got on so well together at Baskul—you were absolutely different in those days."

"My *dear* boy!"

Conway reached his hand towards Mallinson's, and the answering grip was hot and eagerly affectionate. Mallinson went on: "I don't suppose you realize it, but I've been terribly alone these last few weeks. Nobody seemed to be caring a damn about the only thing that was really important—Barnard and Miss Brinklow had reasons of a kind, but it was pretty awful when I found *you* against me."

"I'm sorry."

"You keep on saying that, but it doesn't help."

Conway replied on sudden impulse: "Then let me help, if I can, by telling you something. When you've heard it, you'll understand, I hope, a great deal of what now seems very curious and difficult. At any rate, you'll realize why Lo-Tsen can't possibly go back with you."

"I don't think anything would make me see that. And do cut it as short as you can, because we really haven't time to spare."

Conway then gave, as briefly as he could, the whole story of Shangri-La, as told him by the High Lama, and as amplified by conversation both with the latter and with Chang. It was the last thing he had ever intended to do, but he felt that in the circumstances it was justified and even necessary; it was true enough that Mallinson *was* his problem, to solve as he thought fit. He narrated rapidly and easily, and in doing so came again under the spell of that strange, timeless world; its beauty overwhelmed him as he spoke of it, and more than once he felt himself reading from a page of memory, so clearly had ideas and phrases impressed themselves. Only one thing he withheld—and that to spare himself an emotion he could not yet grapple with—the fact of the High Lama's death that night and of his own succession.

When he approached the end he felt comforted; he was glad to have got it over, and it was the only solution, after all. He looked up calmly when he had finished, confident that he had done well.

But Mallinson merely tapped his fingers on the table-top and said, after a long wait: "I really don't know what to say, Conway . . . except that you must be completely mad. . . ."

There followed a long silence, during which the two men stared at each other in far differing moods—Conway withdrawn and disappointed, Mallinson in hot, fidgeting discomfort. "So you think I'm mad?" said Conway at length.

Mallinson broke into a nervous laugh. "Well, I should damn well say so, after a tale like that. I mean . . . well, really . . . such utter nonsense . . . it seems to me rather beyond arguing about."

Conway looked and sounded immensely astonished. "You think it's nonsense?"

"Well . . . how else can I look at it? I'm sorry, Conway—it's a pretty strong statement—but I don't see how any sane person could be in any doubt about it."

"So you still hold that we were brought here by blind accident—by some lunatic who made careful plans to run off with an aeroplane and fly it a thousand miles just for the fun of the thing?"

Conway offered a cigarette, and the other took it. The pause was one for which they both seemed grateful. Mallinson answered eventually: "Look here, it's no good arguing the thing point by point. As a matter of fact, your theory that the people here sent some one vaguely into the world to decoy strangers, and that this fellow deliberately learned flying and bided his time until it happened that a suitable machine was due to leave Baskul with four passengers . . . well, I won't say that it's literally impossible, though it does seem to me ridiculously far-fetched. If it stood by itself, it might just be worth considering, but when you tack it on to all sorts of other things that are *absolutely* impossible—all this about the lamas being hundreds of years old, and having discovered a sort of elixir of youth, or whatever you'd call it . . . well, it just makes me wonder what kind of microbe has bitten you, that's all."

Conway smiled. "Yes, I dare say you find it hard to believe. Perhaps I did myself at first—I scarcely remember. Of course it *is* an extraordinary story, but I should think your own eyes have had enough evidence that this is an extraordinary place. Think of all that we've actually seen, both of us—a lost valley in the midst of unexplored mountains, a monastery with a library of European books—"

"Oh, yes, and a central heating plant, and modern plumbing, and afternoon tea, and everything else—it's all very marvelous, I know."

"Well, then, what do you make of it?"

"Damn little, I admit. It's a complete mystery. But that's no reason for accepting tales that are physically impossible. Believing in hot baths because you've had them is different from believing in people hundreds of years old just because they've told you they are." He laughed again, still uneasily. "Look here, Conway, it's got on your nerves, this place, and I really don't wonder at it. Pack up your things and let's quit. We'll finish this argument a month or two hence after a jolly little dinner at Maiden's."

Conway answered quietly: "I've no desire to go back to that life at all."

"What life?"

"The life you're thinking of . . . dinners . . . dances . . . polo . . . all that. . . ."

"But I never said anything about dances and polo! Anyhow, what's wrong with them? D'you mean that you're not coming with me? You're going to stay here like the other two? Then at least you shan't stop *me* from clearing out of it!" Mallinson threw down his cigarette and sprang towards the door with eyes blazing. "You're off your head!" he cried wildly. "You're mad, Conway, that's what's the matter with you! I know you're always calm, and I'm always excited, but I'm sane, at any rate, and you're not! They warned me about it before I joined you at Baskul, and I thought they were wrong, but now I can see they weren't—"

"What did they warn you of?"

"They said you'd been blown up in the War, and you'd been queer at times ever since. I'm not reproaching you—I know it was nothing you could help—and Heaven knows I hate talking like this. . . . Oh, I'll go. It's all frightful and sickening, but I must go. I gave my word."

"To Lo-Tsen?"

"Yes, if you want to know."

Conway got up and held out his hand. "Good-by, Mallinson."

"For the last time, you're not coming?"

"I can't."

"Good-by, then."

They shook hands, and Mallinson left.

Conway sat alone in the lantern light. It seemed to him, in a phrase engraved on memory, that all the loveliest things were transient and perishable, that the two worlds were finally beyond reconciliation, and that one of them hung, as always, by a thread. After he had pondered for some time he looked at his watch; it was ten minutes to three.

He was still at the table, smoking the last of his cigarettes, when Mallinson returned. The youth entered with some commotion, and on seeing him, stood back in the shadows as if to gather his wits. He was silent, and Conway began, after waiting a moment: "Hullo, what's happened? Why are you back?"

The complete naturalness of the question fetched Mallinson forward; he pulled off his heavy sheepskins and sat down. His face was ashen and his whole body trembled. "I hadn't the nerve," he cried, half sobbing. "That place where we were all roped—you remember? I got as far as that. . . . I couldn't manage it. I've no head for heights, and in moonlight it looked fearful. Silly, isn't it?" He broke down completely and was hysterical until Conway pacified him. Then he added: "They needn't worry, these fellows here—nobody will ever threaten them by land. But, my God, I'd give a good deal to fly over with a load of bombs!"

"Why would you like to do that, Mallinson?"

"Because the place wants smashing up, whatever it is. It's unhealthy and unclean—and for that matter, if your impossible yarn were true, it would be more hateful still! A lot of wizened old men crouching here like spiders for any one who comes near . . . it's filthy . . . who'd want to live to an age like that, anyhow? And as for your precious High Lama, if he's half as old as you say he is, it's time some one put him out of his misery. . . . Oh, why *won't* you come away with me, Conway? I hate imploring you for my own sake, but damn it all, I'm young and we've been pretty good friends together—does my whole life mean nothing to you compared with the lies of these awful creatures? And Lo-Tsen, too—*she's* young—doesn't *she* count at all?"

"Lo-Tsen is not young," said Conway.

Mallinson looked up and began to titter hysterically. "Oh, no, not young—not young at all, of course. She looks about seventeen, but I suppose you'll tell me she's really a well-preserved ninety."

"Mallinson, she came here in 1884."

"You're raving, man!"

"Her beauty, Mallinson, like all other beauty in the world, lies at the mercy of those who do not know how to value it. It is a fragile thing that can only live where fragile things are loved. Take it away from this valley and you will see it fade like an echo."

Mallinson laughed harshly, as if his own thoughts gave him confidence. "I'm not afraid of that. It's here that she's only an echo, if she's one anywhere at all." He added after a pause: "Not that this sort of talk gets us anywhere. We'd better cut out all the poetic stuff and come down to realities. Conway, I want to help you—it's all the sheerest nonsense, I know, but I'll argue it out if it'll do you any good. I'll pretend it's something possible that you've told me, and that it really does need examining. Now tell me, seriously, what evidence have you for this story of yours?"

Conway was silent.

"Merely that some one spun you a fantastic rigmarole. Even from a thoroughly reliable person whom you'd known all your life, you wouldn't accept that sort of thing without proof. And what proofs have you in this case? None at all, so far as I can see. Has Lo-Tsen ever told you her history?"

"No, but—"

"Then why believe it from some one else? And all this longevity business—can you point to a single outside fact in support of it?"

Conway thought a moment and then mentioned the unknown Chopin works that Briac had played.

"Well, that's a matter that means nothing to me—I'm not a musician. But even if they're genuine, isn't it possible that he could have got hold of them in some way without his story being true?"

"Quite possible, no doubt."

"And then this method that you say exists—of preserving youth and so on. What is it? You say it's a sort of drug—well, I want to know *what* drug? Have you ever seen it or tried it? Did any one ever give you any positive facts about the thing at all?"

"Not in detail, I admit."

"And you never asked for details? It didn't strike you that such a story needed any confirmation at all? You just swallowed it whole?" Pressing his advantage, he continued: "How much do you actually know of this place, apart from what you've been told? You've seen a few old men—that's all it amounts to. Apart from that, we can only say that the place is well fitted up, and seems to be run on rather highbrow lines. How and why it came into existence we've no idea, and why they want to keep us here, if they do, is equally a mystery, but surely all that's hardly an excuse for believing any old legend that comes along! After all, man, you're a critical sort of person— you'd hesitate to believe all you were told even in an English monastery—I really can't see why you should jump at everything just because you're in Tibet!"

Conway nodded. Even in the midst of far keener perceptions he could not restrain approval of a point well made. "That's an acute remark, Mallinson. I suppose the truth is that when it comes to believing things without actual evidence, we all incline to what we find most attractive."

"Well, I'm dashed if I can see anything attractive about living till you're half dead. Give me a short life and a gay one, for choice. And this stuff about a future war—it all sounds pretty thin to me. How does any one know when the next war's going to be or what it'll be like? Weren't all the prophets wrong about the last war?" He added, when Conway did not reply: "Anyhow, I don't believe in saying things are inevitable. And even if they were, there's no need to get into a funk about them. Heaven knows I'd most likely be scared stiff if I had to fight in a war, but I'd rather face up to it than bury myself here."

Conway smiled. "Mallinson, you have a superb knack of misunderstanding me. When we were at Baskul you thought I was a hero—now you take me for a coward. In point of fact, I'm neither—though of course it doesn't matter. When you get back to India you can tell people, if you like, that I decided to stay in a Tibetan monastery because I was afraid there'd be another war. It isn't my reason at all, but I've no doubt it'll be believed by the people who already think me mad."

Mallinson answered rather sadly: "It's silly, you know, to talk like that. Whatever happens, I'd never say a word against you. You can count on that. I don't understand you—I admit that—but—but—I wish I did. Oh, I wish I did. Conway, can't I possibly help you? Isn't there anything I can say or do?"

There was a long silence after that, which Conway broke at last by saying: "There's just a question I'd like to ask—if you'll forgive me for being terribly personal."

"Yes?"

"Are you in love with Lo-Tsen?"

The youth's pallor changed quickly to a flush. "I dare say I am. I know you'll say it's absurd and unthinkable, and probably it is, but I can't help my feelings."

"I don't think it's absurd at all."

The argument seemed to have sailed into a harbor after many buffetings, and Conway added: "I can't help *my* feelings either. You and that girl happen to be the two people in the world I care most about . . . though you may think it odd of me." Abruptly he got up and paced the room. "We've said all we *can* say, haven't we?"

"Yes, I suppose we have." But Mallinson went on, in a sudden rush of eagerness: "Oh, what stupid nonsense it all is—about her not being young! And foul and horrible nonsense, too. Conway, you *can't* believe it! It's just too ridiculous. How can it really mean anything?"

"How can you really know that she's young?"

Mallinson half turned away, his face lit with a grave shyness. "Because I *do* know. . . . Perhaps you'll think less of me for it . . . but I *do* know. I'm afraid you never properly understood her, Conway. She was cold on the surface, but that was the result of living here—it had frozen all the warmth. But the warmth was there."

"To be unfrozen?"

"Yes . . . that would be one way of putting it."

"And she's *young*, Mallinson—you are so *sure* of that?"

LOST HORIZON

111

Mallinson answered softly: "God, yes—she's just a girl. I was terribly sorry for her, and we were both attracted, I suppose. I don't see that it's anything to be ashamed of. In fact in a place like this I should think it's about the decentest thing that's ever happened. . . ."

Conway went to the balcony and gazed at the dazzling plume of Karakal; the moon was riding high in a waveless ocean. It came to him that a dream had dissolved, like all too lovely things, at the first touch of reality; that the whole world's future, weighed in the balance against youth and love, would be light as air. And he knew, too, that his mind dwelt in a world of its own, Shangri-La in microcosm, and that this world also was in peril. For even as he nerved himself, he saw the corridors of his imagination twist and strain under impact; the pavilions were toppling; all was about to be in ruins. He was only partly unhappy, but he was infinitely and rather sadly perplexed. He did not know whether he had been mad and was now sane, or had been sane for a time and was now mad again.

When he turned, there was a difference in him; his voice was keener, almost brusque, and his face twitched a little; he looked much more the Conway who had been a hero at Baskul. Clenched for action, he faced Mallinson with a suddenly new alertness. "Do you think you could manage that tricky bit with a rope if I were with you?" he asked.

Mallinson sprang forward. "*Conway!*" he cried chokingly. "You mean you'll *come*? You've made up your mind at last?"

They left as soon as Conway had prepared himself for the journey. It was surprisingly simple to leave—a departure rather than an escape; there were no incidents as they crossed the bars of moonlight and shadow in the courtyards. One might have thought there was no one there at all, Conway reflected; and immediately the idea of such emptiness became an emptiness in himself; while all the time, though he hardly heard him, Mallinson was chattering about the journey. How strange that their long argument should have ended thus in action, that this secret sanctuary should be forsaken by one who had found in it such happiness! For indeed, less than an hour later, they halted breathlessly at a curve of the track and saw the last of Shangri-La. Deep below them the valley of Blue Moon was like a cloud, and to Conway the scattered roofs had a look of floating after him through the haze. Now, at that moment, it was farewell. Mallinson, whom the steep ascent had kept silent for a time, gasped out: "Good man, we're doing fine—carry on!"

Conway smiled, but did not reply; he was already preparing the rope for the knife-edge traverse. It was true, as the youth had said, that he had made up his mind; but it was only what was left of his mind. That small and active fragment now dominated; the rest comprised an absence hardly to be endured. He was a wanderer between two worlds and must ever wander; but for the present, in a deepening inward void, all he felt was that he liked Mallinson and must help him; he was doomed, like millions, to flee from wisdom and be a hero.

Mallinson was nervous at the precipice, but Conway got him over in tradi-

tional mountaineering fashion, and when the trial was past, they leaned together over Mallinson's cigarettes. "Conway, I must say it's damned good of you. . . . Perhaps you guess how I feel. . . . I can't tell you how glad I am. . . ."

"I wouldn't try, then, if I were you."

After a long pause, and before they resumed the journey, Mallinson added: "But I *am* glad—not only for my own sake, but for yours as well. . . . It's fine that you can realize now that all that stuff was sheer nonsense . . . it's just wonderful to see you your real self again. . . ."

"Not at all," responded Conway with a wryness that was for his own private comforting.

Towards dawn they crossed the divide, unchallenged by sentinels, even if there were any; though it occurred to Conway that the route, in the true spirit, might only be moderately well watched. Presently they reached the plateau, picked clean as a bone by roaring winds, and after a gradual descent the encampment of porters came in sight. Then all was as Mallinson had foretold; they found the men ready for them, sturdy fellows in furs and sheepskins, crouching under the gale and eager to begin the journey to Tatsien-Fu—eleven hundred miles eastward on the China border.

"He's coming with us!" Mallinson cried excitedly when they met Lo-Tsen. He forgot that she knew no English; but Conway translated.

It seemed to him that the little Manchu had never looked so radiant. She gave him a most charming smile, but her eyes were all for the boy.

EPILOGUE

It was in Delhi that I met Rutherford again. We had been guests at a Viceregal dinner-party, but distance and ceremonial kept us apart until the turbanned flunkeys handed us our hats afterwards. "Come back to my hotel and have a drink," he invited.

We shared a cab along the arid miles between the Lutyens still-life and the warm, palpitating motion picture of Old Delhi. I knew from the newspapers that he had just returned from Kashgar. His was one of those well-groomed reputations that get the most out of everything; any unusual holiday acquires the character of an exploration, and though the explorer takes care to do nothing really original, the public does not know this, and he capitalizes the full value of a hasty impression. It had not seemed to me, for instance, that Rutherford's journey, as reported in the press, had been particularly epoch-making; the buried cities of Khotan were old stuff, if any one remembered Stein and Sven Hedin. I knew Rutherford well enough to chaff him about this, and he laughed. "Yes, the truth would have made a better story," he admitted cryptically.

We went to his hotel room and drank whisky. "So you *did* search for Conway?" I suggested when the moment seemed propitious.

"Search is much too strong a word," he answered. "You can't search a country half as big as Europe for one man. All I can say is that I visited places where I was prepared to come across him or to get news of him. His last message, you remember, was that he had left Bangkok for the northwest. There were traces of him up-country for a little way, and my own opinion is that he probably made for the tribal districts on the Chinese border. I don't think he'd have cared to enter Burma, where he might have run up against British officials. Anyhow, the definite trail, you may say, peters out somewhere in Upper Siam, but of course I never expected to follow it far that end."

"You thought it might be easier to look for the valley of Blue Moon?"

"Well, it did seem as if it might be a more fixed proposition. I suppose you glanced at that manuscript of mine?"

"Much more than glanced at it. I should have returned it, by the way, but you left no address."

Rutherford nodded. "I wonder what you made of it?"

"I thought it very remarkable—assuming, of course, that it's all quite genuinely based on what Conway told you."

"I give you my solemn word for that. I invented nothing at all—indeed, there's even less of my own language in it than you might think. I've a good memory, and Conway always had a way of describing things. Don't forget that we had about twenty-four hours of practically continuous talk."

"Well, as I said, it's all very remarkable."

He leaned back and smiled. "If that's all you're going to say, I can see I shall have to speak for myself. I suppose you consider me a rather credulous person. I don't really think I am. People make mistakes in life through believing too much, but they have a damned dull time if they believe too little. I was certainly taken with Conway's story—in more ways than one—and that was why I felt interested enough to put as many tabs on it as I could—apart from the chance of running up against the man himself."

He went on, after lighting a cigar: "It meant a good deal of odd journeying, but I like that sort of thing, and my publishers can't object to a travel book once in a while. Altogether I must have done some thousands of miles—Baskul, Bangkok, Chung-Kiang, Kashgar—I visited them all, and somewhere inside the area between them the mystery lies. But it's a pretty big area, you know, and all my investigations didn't touch more than the fringe of it—or of the mystery either, for that matter. Indeed, if you want the actual downright facts about Conway's adventures, so far as I've been able to verify them, all I can tell you is that he left Baskul on the twentieth of May and arrived in Chung-Kiang on the fifth of October. And the last we know of him is that he left Bangkok again on the third of February. All the rest is probability, possibility, guesswork, myth, legend, whatever you like to call it."

"So you didn't find anything in Tibet?"

"My dear fellow, I never got into Tibet at all. The people up at Government House wouldn't hear of it; it's as much as they'll do to sanction an Everest expedition, and when I said I thought of wandering about the Kuen-Luns on my own, they looked at me rather as if I'd suggested writing a life of Gandhi. As a matter of fact, they knew more than I did. Strolling about Tibet isn't a one-man job; it needs an expedition properly fitted out and run by some one who knows at least a word or two of the language. I remember when Conway was telling me his story I kept wondering why there was all that fuss about waiting for porters—why didn't they all simply walk off? I wasn't very long in discovering. The Government people were quite right—all the passports in the world couldn't have got me over the Kuen-Luns. I actually went as far as seeing them in the distance, on a very clear day—perhaps fifty miles off. Not many Europeans can claim even that."

"Are they so very forbidding?"

"They looked just like a white frieze on the horizon, that was all. At Yarkand and Kashgar I questioned every one I met about them, but it was extraordinary how little I could discover. I should think they must be the least-explored range in the world. I had the luck to meet an American traveler who had once tried to cross them, but he'd been unable to find a pass. There *are* passes, he said, but they're terrifically high and unmapped. I asked him if he thought it possible for a valley to exist of the kind Conway described, and he said he wouldn't call it impossible, but he thought it not very likely—on geological grounds, at any rate. Then I asked if he had ever heard of a cone-shaped mountain almost as high as the highest of the Himalayas, and his answer to that was rather intriguing. There was a legend, he said, about such a mountain, but he thought himself there could be no foundation for it. There were even rumors, he added, about mountains actually higher than Everest, but he didn't himself give credit to them. 'I doubt if any peak in the Kuen-Luns is more than twenty-five thousand feet, if that,' he said. But he admitted that they had never been properly surveyed.

"Then I asked him what he knew about Tibetan lamaseries—he'd been in the country several times—and he gave me just the usual accounts that one can read in all the books. They weren't beautiful places, he assured me, and the monks in them were generally corrupt and dirty. 'Do they live long?' I asked, and he said, yes, they often did, if they didn't die of some filthy disease. Then I went boldly to the point and asked if he'd ever heard legends of extreme longevity among the lamas. 'Heaps of them,' he answered; 'it's one of the stock yarns you hear everywhere, but you can't verify them. You're told that some foul-looking creature has been walled up in a cell for a hundred years, and he certainly looks as if he might have been, but of course you can't demand his birth certificate.' I asked him if he thought they had any occult or medicinal way of prolonging life or preserving youth, and he said they were supposed to have a great deal of very curious knowledge about such things, but he suspected that if you came to look into it, it was rather like the Indian rope trick—always something that somebody else had seen. He did say, however, that the lamas appeared to have odd powers of bodily control. 'I've watched them,' he said, 'sitting by the edge of a frozen lake, stark naked, with a temperature below zero and in a tearing wind, while their servants break the ice and wrap sheets round them that have been dipped in the water. They do this a dozen times or more, and the lamas dry the sheets on their own bodies. Keeping warm by will-power, so one imagines, though that's a poor sort of explanation.'"

Rutherford helped himself to more drink. "But of course, as my American friend admitted, all that had nothing much to do with longevity. It merely showed that the lamas had somber tastes in self-discipline. . . . So there we were, and probably you'll agree with me that all the evidence, so far, was less than you'd hang a dog on."

I said it was certainly inconclusive, and asked if the names "Karakal" and "Shangri-La" had meant anything to the American.

"Not a thing—I tried him with them. After I'd gone on questioning him for a time, he said: 'Frankly, I'm not keen on monasteries—indeed, I once told a fellow I met in Tibet that if I went out of my way at all, it would be to avoid them, not pay them a visit.' That chance remark of his gave me a curious idea, and I asked him when this meeting in Tibet had taken place. 'Oh, a long time ago,' he answered, 'before the War—in nineteen-eleven, I think it was.' I badgered him for further details, and he gave them, as well as he could remember. It seemed that he'd been traveling then for some American geographical society, with several colleagues, porters, and so on—in fact, a pukka expedition. Somewhere near the Kuen-Luns he met this other man, a Chinese who was being carried in a chair by native bearers. The fellow turned out to speak English quite well, and strongly recommended them to visit a certain lamasery in the neighborhood—he even offered to be the guide there. The American said they hadn't time and weren't interested, and that was that." Rutherford went on, after an interval: "I don't suggest that it means a great deal. When a man tries to remember a casual incident that happened twenty years ago, you can't build *too* much on it. But it offers an attractive speculation."

"Yes, though if a well-equipped expedition had accepted the invitation, I don't see how they could have been detained at the lamasery against their will."

"Oh, quite. And perhaps it wasn't Shangri-La at all."

We thought it over, but it seemed too hazy for argument, and I went on to ask if there had been any discoveries at Baskul.

"Baskul was hopeless, and Peshawar was worse. Nobody could tell me anything, except that the kidnaping of the aeroplane did undoubtedly take place. They weren't keen even to admit that—it's an episode they're not proud of."

"And nothing was heard of the plane afterwards?"

"Not a word or a rumor, or of its four passengers either. I verified, however, that it was capable of climbing high enough to cross the ranges. I also tried to trace that fellow Barnard, but I found his past history so mysterious that I wouldn't be at all surprised if he really were Chalmers Bryant, as Conway said. After all, Bryant's complete disappearance in the midst of the big hue and cry was rather amazing."

"Did you try to find anything about the actual kidnaper?"

"I did, but again it was hopeless. The Air Force man whom the fellow had knocked out and impersonated had since been killed, so one promising line of enquiry was closed. I even wrote to a friend of mine in America who runs an aviation school, asking if he had had any Tibetan pupils lately, but his reply was prompt and disappointing. He said he couldn't differentiate Tibetans from Chinese, and he had had about fifty of the latter—all training to fight the Japs. Not much chance there, you see. But I did make one rather quaint discovery—and which I could have made just as easily without leaving London. There was a German professor at Jena about the middle of the last century who took to globe-trotting and visited Tibet in 1887. He never came back, and there was some story about him having been drowned in fording a river. His name was Friedrich Meister."

"Good heavens—one of the names Conway mentioned!"

"Yes—though it may only have been coincidence. It doesn't prove the whole story, by any means, because the Jena fellow was born in 1845. Nothing very exciting about that."

"But it's odd," I said.

"Oh, yes, it's odd enough."

"Did you succeed in tracing any of the others?"

"No. It's a pity I hadn't a longer list to work on. I couldn't find any record of a pupil of Chopin's called Briac, though of course that doesn't prove that there wasn't one. Conway was pretty sparing with his names, when you come to think about it—out of fifty odd lamas supposed to be on the premises he only gave us one or two. Perrault and Henschell, by the way, proved equally impossible to trace."

"How about Mallinson?" I asked. "Did you try to find out what had happened to him? And that girl—the Chinese girl?"

"My dear fellow, of course I did. The awkward part was, as you perhaps gathered from the manuscript, that Conway's story ended at the moment of leaving the valley with the porters. After that he either couldn't or wouldn't tell me what happened—perhaps he might have done, mind you, if there'd been more time. I feel that we can guess at some sort of tragedy. The hardships of the journey would be perfectly appalling, apart from the risk of brigandage or even treachery among their own escorting party. Probably we shall never know exactly what did occur, but it seems tolerably certain that Mallinson never reached China. I made all sorts of enquiries, you know. First of all I tried to trace details of books, et cetera, sent in large consignments across the Tibetan frontier, but at all the likely places, such as Shanghai and Pekin, I drew complete blanks. That, of course, doesn't count for much, since the lamas would doubtless see that their methods of importation were kept secret. Then I tried at Tatsien-Fu. It's a weird place, a sort of world's-end market town, deuced difficult to get at, where the Chinese coolies from Yunnan transfer their loads of tea to the Tibetans. You can read about it in my new book when it comes out. Europeans don't often get as far. I found the people quite civil and courteous, but there was absolutely no record of Conway's party arriving at all."

"So how Conway himself reached Chung-Kiang is still unexplained?"

"The only conclusion is that he wandered there, just as he might have wandered anywhere else. Anyhow, we're back in the realm of hard facts when we get to Chung-Kiang, that's something. The nuns at the mission hospital were genuine enough, and so, for that matter, was Sieveking's excitement on the ship when Conway played that pseudo-Chopin." Rutherford paused and then added reflectively: "It's really an exercise in the balancing of probabilities, and I must say the scales don't bump very emphatically either way. Of course if you don't accept Conway's story, it means that you doubt either his veracity or his sanity—one may as well be frank."

He paused again, as if inviting a comment, and I said: "As you know, I never saw him after the War, but people said he was a good deal changed by it."

Rutherford answered: "Yes, and he was, there's no denying the fact. You can't subject a mere boy to three years of intense physical and emotional stress without tearing something to tatters. People would say, I suppose, that he came through without a scratch. But the scratches were there—on the inside."

We talked for a little time about the War and its effects on various people, and at length he went on: "But there's just one more point that I must mention—and perhaps in some ways the oddest of all. It came out during my enquiries at the mission. They all did their best for me there, as you can guess, but they couldn't recollect much, especially as they'd been so busy with a fever epidemic at the time. One of the questions I put was about the manner Conway had reached the hospital first of all—whether he had presented himself alone, or had been found ill and been taken there by some one else. They couldn't exactly remember—after all, it was a long while back—but suddenly, when I was on the point of giving up the cross-examination, one of the nuns remarked quite casually, 'I think the doctor said he was brought here by a woman.' That was all she could tell me, and as the doctor himself had left the mission, there was no confirmation to be had on the spot.

"But having got so far, I wasn't in any mood to give up. It appeared that the doctor had gone to a bigger hospital in Shanghai, so I took the trouble to get his address and call on him there. It was just after the Jap air-raiding, and things were pretty grim. I'd met the man before during my first visit to Chung-Kiang, and he was very polite, though terribly overworked—yes, terribly's the word, for, believe me, the air-raids on London by the Germans were just nothing to what the Japs did to the native parts of Shanghai. Oh, yes, he said instantly, he remembered the case of the Englishman who had lost his memory. Was it true he had been brought to the mission hospital by a woman? I asked. Oh, yes, certainly, by a woman, a Chinese woman. Did he remember anything about her? Nothing, he answered, except that she had been ill of the fever herself, and had died almost immediately. . . . Just then there was an interruption—a batch of wounded were carried in and packed on stretchers in the corridors—the wards were all full—and I didn't care to go on taking up the man's time, especially as the thudding of the guns at Woosung was a reminder that he would still have plenty to do. When he came back to me, looking quite cheerful even amidst such ghastliness, I just asked him one final question, and I dare say you can guess what it was. 'About that Chinese woman,' I said. 'Was she young?' "

Rutherford flicked his cigar as if the narration had excited him quite as much as he hoped it had me. Continuing, he said: "The little fellow looked at me solemnly for a moment, and then answered in that funny clipped English that the educated Chinese have—'Oh, no, she was most old—most old of any one I have ever seen.' "

We sat for a long time in silence, and then talked again of Conway as I remembered him, boyish and gifted and full of charm, and of the War that had altered him, and of so many mysteries of time and age and of the mind, and of the little Manchu who had been "most old," and of the strange ultimate dream of Blue Moon. "Do you think he will ever find it?" I asked.

NEIGHBOUR ROSICKY

WILLA CATHER

ONE

WHEN Doctor Burleigh told neighbour Rosicky he had a bad heart, Rosicky protested.

"So? No, I guess my heart was always pretty good. I got a little asthma, maybe. Just a awful short breath when I was pitchin' hay last summer, dat's all."

"Well now, Rosicky, if you know more about it than I do, what did you come to me for? It's your heart that makes you short of breath, I tell you. You're sixty-five years old, and you've always worked hard, and your heart's tired. You've got to be careful from now on, and you can't do heavy work any more. You've got five boys at home to do it for you."

The old farmer looked up at the Doctor with a gleam of amusement in his queer triangular-shaped eyes. His eyes were large and lively, but the lids were caught up in the middle in a curious way, so that they formed a triangle. He did not look like a sick man. His brown face was creased but not wrinkled, he had a ruddy colour in his smooth-shaven cheeks and in his lips, under his long brown moustache. His hair was thin and ragged around his ears, but very little grey. His forehead, naturally high and crossed by deep parallel lines, now ran all the way up to his pointed crown. Rosicky's face had the habit of looking interested,—suggested a contented disposition and a reflective quality that was gay rather than grave. This gave him a certain detachment, the easy manner of an onlooker and observer.

"Well, I guess you ain't got no pills fur a bad heart, Doctor Ed. I guess the only thing is fur me to git me a new one."

Doctor Burleigh swung round in his desk-chair and frowned at the old farmer. "I think if I were you I'd take a little care of the old one, Rosicky."

Rosicky shrugged. "Maybe I don't know how. I expect you mean fur me not to drink my coffee no more."

"I wouldn't, in your place. But you'll do as you choose about that. I've never yet been able to separate a Bohemian from his coffee or his pipe. I've quit trying. But the sure thing is you've got to cut out farm work. You can

feed the stock and do chores about the barn, but you can't do anything in the fields that makes you short of breath."

"How about shelling corn?"

"Of course not!"

Rosicky considered with puckered brows.

"I can't make my heart go no longer'n it wants to, can I, Doctor Ed?"

"I think it's good for five or six years yet, maybe more, if you'll take the strain off it. Sit around the house and help Mary. If I had a good wife like yours, I'd want to stay around the house."

His patient chuckled. "It ain't no place fur a man. I don't like no old man hanging round the kitchen too much. An' my wife, she's a awful hard worker her own self."

"That's it; you can help her a little. My Lord, Rosicky, you are one of the few men I know who has a family he can get some comfort out of; happy dispositions, never quarrel among themselves, and they treat you right. I want to see you live a few years and enjoy them."

"Oh, they're good kids, all right," Rosicky assented.

The Doctor wrote him a prescription and asked him how his oldest son, Rudolph, who had married in the spring, was getting on. Rudolph had struck out for himself, on rented land. "And how's Polly? I was afraid Mary mightn't like an American daughter-in-law, but it seems to be working out all right."

"Yes, she's a fine girl. Dat widder woman bring her daughters up very nice. Polly got lots of spunk, an' she got some style, too. Da's nice, for young folks to have some style." Rosicky inclined his head gallantly. His voice and his twinkly smile were an affectionate compliment to his daughter-in-law.

"It looks like a storm, and you'd better be getting home before it comes. In town in the car?" Doctor Burleigh rose.

"No, I'm in de wagon. When you got five boys, you ain't got much chance to ride round in de Ford. I ain't much for cars, noway."

"Well, it's a good road out to your place; but I don't want you bumping around in a wagon much. And never again on a hay-rake, remember!"

Rosicky placed the Doctor's fee delicately behind the desk-telephone, looking the other way, as if this were an absent-minded gesture. He put on his plush cap and his corduroy jacket with a sheepskin collar, and went out.

The Doctor picked up his stethoscope and frowned at it as if he were seriously annoyed with the instrument. He wished it had been telling tales about some other man's heart, some old man who didn't look the Doctor in the eye so knowingly, or hold out such a warm brown hand when he said good-bye. Doctor Burleigh had been a poor boy in the country before he went away to medical school; he had known Rosicky almost ever since he could remember, and he had a deep affection for Mrs. Rosicky.

Only last winter he had had such a good breakfast at Rosicky's, and that when he needed it. He had been out all night on a long, hard confinement case at Tom Marshall's,—a big rich farm where there was plenty of stock and plenty of feed and a great deal of expensive farm machinery of the newest model, and no comfort whatever. The woman had too many children and too much work, and she was no manager. When the baby was born at last, and handed over to the assisting neighbour woman, and the mother was properly attended to, Burleigh refused any breakfast in that slovenly house, and drove his buggy—the snow was too deep for a car—eight miles to Anton Rosicky's place. He didn't know another farm-house where a man could get such a warm welcome, and such good strong coffee with rich cream. No wonder the old chap didn't want to give up his coffee!

He had driven in just when the boys had come back from the barn and were washing up for breakfast. The long table, covered with a bright oil-cloth, was set out with dishes waiting for them, and the warm kitchen was full of the smell of coffee and hot biscuit and sausage. Five big handsome boys, running from twenty to twelve, all with what Burleigh called natural good manners,—they hadn't a bit of the painful self-consciousness he himself had to struggle with when he was a lad. One ran to put his horse away, another helped him off with his fur coat and hung it up, and Josephine, the youngest child and the only daughter, quickly set another place under her mother's direction.

With Mary, to feed creatures was the natural expression of affection,—her chickens, the calves, her big hungry boys. It was a rare pleasure to feed a young man whom she seldom saw and of whom she was as proud as if he belonged to her. Some country housekeepers would have stopped to spread a white cloth over the oilcloth, to change the thick cups and plates for their best china, and the wooden-handled knives for plated ones. But not Mary.

"You must take us as you find us, Doctor Ed. I'd be glad to put out my good things for you if you was expected, but I'm glad to get you any way at all."

He knew she was glad,—she threw back her head and spoke out as if she were announcing him to the whole prairie. Rosicky hadn't said anything at all; he merely smiled his twinkling smile, put some more coal on the fire, and went into his own room to pour the Doctor a little drink in a medicine glass. When they were all seated, he watched his wife's face from his end of the table and spoke to her in Czech. Then, with the instinct of politeness which seldom failed him, he turned to the Doctor and said slyly: "I was just tellin' her not to ask you no questions about Mrs. Marshall till you eat some breakfast. My wife, she's terrible fur to ask questions."

The boys laughed, and so did Mary. She watched the Doctor devour her biscuit and sausage, too much excited to eat anything herself. She drank her coffee and sat taking in everything about her visitor. She had known him when he was a poor country boy, and was boastfully proud of his success, always saying: "What do people go to Omaha for, to see a doctor, when we got the best one in the State right here?" If Mary liked people at all, she felt physical pleasure in the sight of them, personal exultation in any good fortune that came to them. Burleigh didn't know many women like that, but he knew she was like that.

When his hunger was satisfied, he did, of course, have to tell them about Mrs. Marshall, and he noticed what a friendly interest the boys took in the matter.

Rudolph, the oldest one (he was still living at home then), said: "The last time I was over there, she was lifting them big heavy milk-cans, and I knew she oughtn't to be doing it."

"Yes, Rudolph told me about that when he came home, and I said it wasn't right," Mary put in warmly. "It was all right for me to do them things up to the last, for I was terrible strong, but that woman's weakly. And do you think she'll be able to nurse it, Ed?" She sometimes forgot to give him the title she was so proud of. "And to think of your being up all night and then not able to get a decent breakfast! I don't know what's the matter with such people."

"Why, Mother," said one of the boys, "if Doctor Ed had got breakfast there, we wouldn't have him here. So you ought to be glad."

"He knows I'm glad to have him, John, any time. But I'm sorry for that poor woman, how bad she'll feel the Doctor had to go away in the cold without his breakfast."

"I wish I'd been in practice when these were getting born." The doctor looked down the row of close-clipped heads. "I missed some good breakfasts by not being."

The boys began to laugh at their mother because she flushed so red, but she stood her ground and threw up her head. "I don't care, you wouldn't have got away from this house without breakfast. No doctor ever did. I'd have had something ready fixed that Anton could warm up for you."

The boys laughed harder than ever, and exclaimed at her: "I'll bet you would!" "She would, that!"

"Father, did you get breakfast for the doctor when we were born?"

"Yes, and he used to bring me my breakfast, too, mighty nice. I was always awful hungry!" Mary admitted with a guilty laugh.

While the boys were getting the Doctor's horse, he went to the window to examine the house plants. "What do you do to your geraniums to keep them blooming all winter, Mary? I never pass this house that from the road I don't see your windows full of flowers."

She snapped off a dark red one, and a ruffled new green leaf, and put them in his buttonhole. "There, that looks better. You look too solemn for a young man, Ed. Why don't you git married? I'm worried about you. Settin' at breakfast, I looked at you real hard, and I seen you've got some grey hairs already."

"Oh, yes! They're coming. Maybe they'd come faster if I married."

"Don't talk so. You'll ruin your health eating at the hotel. I could send your wife a nice loaf of nut bread, if you only had one. I don't like to see a young man getting grey. I'll tell you something, Ed; you make some strong black tea and keep it handy in a bowl, and every morning just brush it into your hair, an' it'll keep the grey from showin' much. That's the way I do!"

Sometimes the doctor heard the gossipers in the drug-store wondering why Rosicky didn't get on faster. He was industrious, and so were his boys, but they were rather free and easy, weren't pushers, and they didn't always show good judgment. They were comfortable, and they were out of debt, but they didn't get much ahead. Maybe, Doctor Burleigh reflected, people as generous and warm-hearted and affectionate as the Rosickys never got ahead much; maybe you couldn't enjoy your life and put it into the bank, too.

TWO

When Rosicky left Doctor Burleigh's office he went into the farm-implement store to light his pipe and put on his glasses and read over the list Mary had given him. Then he went into the general merchandise place next door and stood about until the pretty girl with the plucked eyebrows, who always waited on him, was free. Those eyebrows, two thin India-ink strokes, amused him, because he remembered how they used to be. Rosicky always prolonged his shopping by a little joking; the girl knew the old fellow admired her, and she liked to chaff with him.

"Seems to me about every other week you buy ticking, Mr. Rosicky, and always the best quality," she remarked as she measured off the heavy bolt with red stripes.

"You see, my wife is always makin' goose-fedder pillows, an' de thin stuff don't hold in dem little down-fedders."

"You must have lots of pillows at your house."

"Sure. She makes quilts of dem, too. We sleeps easy. Now she's makin' a fedder quilt for my son's wife. You know Polly, that married my Rudolph. How much my bill, Miss Pearl?"

"Eight eighty-five."

"Chust make it nine, and put in some candy fur de women."

"As usual. I never did see a man buy so much candy for his wife. First thing you know, she'll be getting too fat."

"I'd like dat. I ain't much fur all dem slim women like what de style is now."

"That's one for me, I suppose, Mr. Bohunk!" Pearl sniffed and elevated her India-ink strokes.

When Rosicky went out to his wagon, it was beginning to snow,—the first snow of the season, and he was glad to see it. He rattled out of town and along the highway through a wonderfully rich stretch of country, the finest farms in the county. He admired this High Prairie, as it was called, and always liked to drive through it. His own place lay in a rougher territory, where there was some clay in the soil and it was not so productive. When he bought his land, he hadn't the money to buy on High Prairie; so he told his boys, when they grumbled, that if their land hadn't some clay in it, they wouldn't own it at all. All the same, he enjoyed looking at these fine farms, as he enjoyed looking at a prize bull.

After he had gone eight miles, he came to the graveyard, which lay just at the edge of his own hay-land. There he stopped his horses and sat still on his wagon seat, looking about at the snowfall. Over yonder on the hill he could see his own house, crouching low, with the clump of orchard behind and the windmill before, and all down the gentle hillslope the rows of pale gold cornstalks stood out against the white field. The snow was falling over the cornfield and the pasture and the hay-land, steadily, with very little wind, —a nice dry snow. The graveyard had only a light wire fence about it and was all overgrown with long red grass. The fine snow, settling into this red grass and upon the few little evergreens and the headstones, looked very pretty.

It was a nice graveyard, Rosicky reflected, sort of snug and homelike, not cramped or mournful,—a big sweep all round it. A man could lie down in the long grass and see the complete arch of the sky over him, hear the wagons go by; in summer the mowing-machine rattled right up to the wire fence. And it was so near home. Over there across the cornstalks his own roof and windmill looked so good to him that he promised himself to mind the Doctor and take care of himself. He was awful fond of his place, he admitted. He wasn't anxious to leave it. And it was a comfort to think that he would never have to go farther than the edge of his own hayfield. The snow, falling over his barnyard and the graveyard, seemed to draw things together like. And they were all old neighbours in the graveyard, most of them friends; there was nothing to feel awkward or embarrassed about. Embarrassment was the most disagreeable feeling Rosicky knew. He didn't often have it,—only with certain people whom he didn't understand at all.

Well, it was a nice snowstorm; a fine sight to see the snow falling so quietly and graciously over so much open country. On his cap and shoulders, on the horses' backs and manes, light, delicate, mysterious it fell; and with it a dry cool fragrance was released into the air. It meant rest for vegetation and men and beasts, for the ground itself; a season of long nights for sleep, leisurely breakfasts, peace by the fire. This and much more went through Rosicky's mind, but he merely told himself that winter was coming, clucked to his horses, and drove on.

When he reached home, John, the youngest boy, ran out to put away his team for him, and he met Mary coming up from the outside cellar with her apron full of carrots. They went into the house together. On the table, covered with oilcloth figured with clusters of blue grapes, a place was set, and he smelled hot coffee-cake of some kind. Anton never lunched in town; he thought that extravagant, and anyhow he didn't like the food. So Mary always had something ready for him when he got home.

After he was settled in his chair, stirring his coffee in a big cup, Mary took out of the oven a pan of *kolache* stuffed with apricots, examined them anxiously to see whether they had got too dry, put them beside his plate, and then sat down opposite him.

Rosicky asked her in Czech if she wasn't going to have any coffee.

She replied in English, as being somehow the right language for transacting business: "Now what did Doctor Ed say, Anton? You tell me just what."

"He said I was to tell you some compliments, but I forgot 'em." Rosicky's eyes twinkled.

"About you, I mean. What did he say about your asthma?"

"He says I ain't got no asthma." Rosicky took one of the little rolls in his broad brown fingers. The thickened nail of his right thumb told the story of his past.

"Well, what is the matter? And don't try to put me off."

"He don't say nothing much, only I'm a little older, and my heart ain't so good like it used to be."

Mary started and brushed her hair back from her temples with both hands as if she were a little out of her mind. From the way she glared, she might have been in a rage with him.

"He says there's something the matter with your heart? Doctor Ed says so?"

"Now don't yell at me like I was a hog in de garden, Mary. You know I always did like to hear a woman talk soft. He didn't say anything de matter wid my heart, only it ain't so young like it used to be, an' he tell me not to pitch hay or run de corn-sheller."

Mary wanted to jump up, but she sat still. She admired the way he never under any circumstances raised his voice or spoke roughly. He was city-bred, and she was country-bred; she often said she wanted her boys to have their papa's nice ways.

"You never have no pain there, do you? It's your breathing and your stomach that's been wrong. I wouldn't believe nobody but Doctor Ed about it. I guess I'll go see him myself. Didn't he give you no advice?"

"Chust to take it easy like, an' stay round de house dis winter. I guess you got some carpenter work for me to do. I kin make some new shelves for you, and I want dis long time to build a closet in de boys' room and make dem two little fellers keep dere clo'es hung up."

Rosicky drank his coffee from time to time, while he considered. His moustache was of the soft long variety and came down over his mouth like the teeth of a buggy-rake over a bundle of hay. Each time he put down his cup, he ran his blue handkerchief over his lips. When he took a drink of water, he managed very neatly with the back of his hand.

Mary sat watching him intently, trying to find any change in his face. It is hard to see anyone who has become like your own body to you. Yes, his hair had got thin, and his high forehead had deep lines running from left to right. But his neck, always clean shaved except in the busiest seasons, was not loose or baggy. It was burned a dark reddish brown, and there were deep creases in it, but it looked firm and full of blood. His cheeks had a good colour. On either side of his mouth there was a half-moon down the length of his cheek, not wrinkles, but two lines that had come there from his habitual expression. He was shorter and broader than when she married him; his back had grown broad and curved, a good deal like the shell of an old turtle, and his arms and legs were short.

He was fifteen years older than Mary, but she had hardly ever thought about it before. He was her man, and the kind of man she liked. She was rough, and he was gentle,—city-bred, as she always said. They had been shipmates on a rough voyage and had stood by each other in trying times. Life had gone well with them because, at bottom, they had the same ideas about life. They agreed, without discussion, as to what was most important and what was secondary. They didn't often exchange opinions, even in Czech,—it was as if they had thought the same thought together. A good deal had to be sacrificed and thrown overboard in a hard life like theirs, and they had never disagreed as to the things that could go. It had been a hard life, and a soft life, too. There wasn't anything brutal in the short, broad-backed man with the three-cornered eyes and the forehead that went on to the top of his skull. He was a city man, a gentle man, and though he had married a rough farm girl, he had never touched her without gentleness.

They had been at one accord not to hurry through life, not to be always skimping and saving. They saw their neighbours buy more land and feed more stock than they did, without discontent. Once when the creamery agent came to the Rosickys to persuade them to sell him their cream, he told them how much money the Fasslers, their nearest neighbours, had made on their cream last year.

"Yes," said Mary, "and look at them Fassler children! Pale, pinched little things, they look like skimmed milk. I'd rather put some colour into my children's faces than put money into the bank."

The agent shrugged and turned to Anton.

"I guess we'll do like she says," said Rosicky.

THREE

Mary very soon got into town to see Doctor Ed, and then she had a talk with her boys and set a guard over Rosicky. Even John, the youngest, had his father on his mind. If Rosicky went to throw hay down from the loft, one of the boys ran up the ladder and took the fork from him. He sometimes complained that though he was getting to be an old man, he wasn't an old woman yet.

That winter he stayed in the house in the afternoons and carpentered, or sat in the chair between the window full of plants and the wooden bench where the two pails of drinking water stood. This spot was called "Father's corner," though it was not a corner at all. He had a shelf there, where he kept his Bohemian papers and his pipes and tobacco, and his shears and needles and thread and tailor's thimble. Having been a tailor in his youth, he couldn't bear to see a woman patching at his clothes, or at the boys'. He liked tailoring, and always patched all the overalls and jackets and work shirts. Occasionally he made over a pair of pants one of the older boys had outgrown, for the little fellow.

While he sewed, he let his mind run back over his life. He had a good deal to remember, really; life in three countries. The only part of his youth he didn't like to remember was the two years he had spent in London, in Cheapside, working for a German tailor who was wretchedly poor. Those days, when he was nearly always hungry, when his clothes were dropping off him for dirt, and the sound of a strange language kept him in continual bewilderment, had left a sore spot in his mind that wouldn't bear touching.

He was twenty when he landed at Castle Garden in New York, and he had a protector who got him work in a tailor shop in Vesey Street, down near the Washington Market. He looked upon that part of his life as very happy. He became a good workman, he was industrious, and his wages were increased from time to time. He minded his own business and envied nobody's good fortune. He went to night school and learned to read English. He often did overtime work and was well paid for it, but somehow he never saved anything. He couldn't refuse a loan to a friend, and he was self-indulgent. He liked a good dinner, and a little went for beer, a little for tobacco; a good deal went to the girls. He often stood through an opera on Saturday nights; he could get standing-room for a dollar. Those were the great days of opera in New York, and it gave a fellow something to think about for the rest of the week. Rosicky had a quick ear, and a childish love of all the stage splendour; the scenery, the costumes, the ballet. He usually went with a chum, and after the performance they had beer and maybe some oysters somewhere. It was a fine life; for the first five years or so it satisfied him completely. He was never hungry or cold or dirty, and everything amused him: a fire, a dog fight, a parade, a storm, a ferry ride. He thought New York the finest, richest, friendliest city in the world.

Moreover, he had what he called a happy home life. Very near the tailor shop was a small furniture-factory, where an old Austrian, Loeffler, employed a few skilled men and made unusual furniture, most of it to order, for the rich German housewives up-town. The top floor of Loeffler's five-storey factory was a loft, where he kept his choice lumber and stored the odd pieces of furniture left on his hands. One of the young workmen he employed was a Czech, and he and Rosicky became fast friends. They persuaded Loeffler to let them have a sleeping-room in one corner of the loft. They bought good beds and bedding and had their pick of the furniture kept up there. The loft was low-pitched, but light and airy, full of windows, and good-smelling by reason of the fine lumber put up there to season. Old Loeffler used to go down to the docks and buy wood from South America and the East from the sea captains. The young men were as foolish about their house as a bridal pair. Zichec, the young cabinet-maker, devised every sort of convenience, and Rosicky kept their clothes in order. At night and on Sundays, when the quiver of machinery underneath was still, it was the quietest place in the world, and on summer nights all the sea winds blew in. Zichec often practised on his flute in the evening. They were both fond of music and went to the opera together. Rosicky thought he wanted to live like that for ever.

But as the years passed, all alike, he began to get a little restless. When spring came round, he would begin to feel fretted, and he got to drinking. He was likely to drink too much of a Saturday night. On Sunday he was languid and heavy, getting over his spree. On Monday he plunged into work again. So he never had time to figure out what ailed him, though he knew something did. When the grass turned green in Park Place, and the lilac hedge at the back of Trinity churchyard put out its blossoms, he was tormented by a longing to run away. That was why he drank too much; to get a temporary illusion of freedom and wide horizons.

Rosicky, the old Rosicky, could remember as if it were yesterday the day when the young Rosicky found out what was the matter with him. It was on a Fourth of July afternoon, and he was sitting in Park Place in the sun. The lower part of New York was empty. Wall Street, Liberty Street, Broadway, all empty. So much stone and asphalt with nothing going on, so many empty windows. The emptiness was intense, like the stillness in a great factory when the machinery stops and the belts and bands cease running. It was too great a change, it took all the strength out of one. Those blank buildings, without the stream of life pouring through them, were like empty jails. It struck young Rosicky that this was the trouble with big cities; they built you in from the earth itself, cemented you away from any contact with the ground. You lived in an unnatural world, like the fish in an aquarium, who were probably much more comfortable than they ever were in the sea.

On that very day he began to think seriously about the articles he had read in the Bohemian papers, describing prosperous Czech farming communities in the West. He believed he would like to go out there as a farm hand; it was hardly possible that he could ever have land of his own. His people had always been workmen; his father and grandfather had worked in shops. His mother's parents had lived in the country, but they rented their farm and had a hard time to get along. Nobody in his family had ever owned any land,—that belonged to a different station of life altogether. Anton's mother died when he was little, and he was sent into the country to her parents. He stayed with them until he was twelve, and formed those ties with the earth and the farm animals and growing things which are never made at all unless they are made early. After his grandfather died, he went back to live with his father and stepmother, but she was very hard on him, and his father helped him to get passage to London.

After that Fourth of July day in Park Place, the desire to return to the country never left him. To work on another man's farm would be all he asked; to see the sun rise and set and to plant things and watch them grow. He was a very simple man. He was like a tree that has not many roots, but one tap-root that goes down deep. He subscribed for a Bohemian paper printed in Chicago, then for one printed in Omaha. His mind got farther and farther west. He began to save a little money to buy his liberty. When he was thirty-five, there was a great meeting in New York of Bohemian athletic societies, and Rosicky left the tailor shop and went home with the Omaha delegates to try his fortune in another part of the world.

FOUR

Perhaps the fact that his own youth was well over before he began to have a family was one reason why Rosicky was so fond of his boys. He had almost a grandfather's indulgence for them. He had never had to worry about any of them—except, just now, a little about Rudolph.

On Saturday night the boys always piled into the Ford, took little Josephine, and went to town to the moving-picture show. One Saturday morning they were talking at the breakfast table about starting early that evening, so that they would have an hour or so to see the Christmas things in the stores before the show began. Rosicky looked down the table.

"I hope you boys ain't disappointed, but I want you to let me have de car tonight. Maybe some of you can go in with de neighbours."

Their faces fell. They worked hard all week, and they were still like children. A new jackknife or a box of candy pleased the older ones as much as the little fellow.

"If you and Mother are going to town," Frank said, "maybe you could take a couple of us along with you, anyway."

"No, I want to take de car down to Rudolph's, and let him an' Polly go in to de show. She don't git into town enough, an' I'm afraid she's gettin' lonesome, an' he can't afford no car yet."

That settled it. The boys were a good deal dashed. Their father took another piece of apple-cake and went on: "Maybe next Saturday night de two little fellers can go along wid dem."

"Oh, is Rudolph going to have the car every Saturday night?"

Rosicky did not reply at once; then he began to speak seriously: "Listen, boys; Polly ain't lookin' so good. I don't like to see nobody lookin' sad. It comes hard fur a town girl to be a farmer's wife. I don't want no trouble to start in Rudolph's family. When it starts, it ain't so easy to stop. An American girl don't git used to our ways all at once. I like to tell Polly she and

Rudolph can have the car every Saturday night till after New Year's, if it's all right with you boys."

"Sure it's all right, Papa," Mary cut in. "And it's good you thought about that. Town girls is used to more than country girls. I lay awake nights, scared she'll make Rudolph discontented with the farm."

The boys put as good a face on it as they could. They surely looked forward to their Saturday nights in town. That evening Rosicky drove the car the half-mile down to Rudolph's new, bare little house.

Polly was in a short-sleeved gingham dress, clearing away the supper dishes. She was a trim, slim little thing, with blue eyes and shingled yellow hair, and her eyebrows were reduced to a mere brush-stroke, like Miss Pearl's.

"Good evening, Mr. Rosicky. Rudolph's at the barn, I guess." She never called him father, or Mary mother. She was sensitive about having married a foreigner. She never in the world would have done it if Rudolph hadn't been such a handsome, persuasive fellow and such a gallant lover. He had graduated in her class in the high school in town, and their friendship began in the ninth grade.

Rosicky went in, though he wasn't exactly asked. "My boys ain't goin' to town tonight, an' I brought de car over fur you two to go in to de picture show."

Polly, carrying dishes to the sink, looked over her shoulder at him. "Thank you. But I'm late with my work tonight, and pretty tired. Maybe Rudolph would like to go in with you."

"Oh, I don't go to de shows! I'm too old-fashioned. You won't feel so tired after you ride in de air a ways. It's a nice clear night, an' it ain't cold. You go an' fix yourself up, Polly, an' I'll wash de dishes an' leave everything nice fur you."

Polly blushed and tossed her bob. "I couldn't let you do that, Mr. Rosicky. I wouldn't think of it."

Rosicky said nothing. He found a bib apron on a nail behind the kitchen door. He slipped it over his head and then took Polly by her two elbows and pushed her gently toward the door of her own room. "I washed up de kitchen many times for my wife, when de babies was sick or somethin'. You go an' make yourself look nice. I like you to look prettier'n any of dem town girls when you go in. De young folks must have some fun, an' I'm goin' to look out fur you, Polly."

That kind, reassuring grip on her elbows, the old man's funny bright eyes, made Polly want to drop her head on his shoulder for a second. She restrained herself, but she lingered in his grasp at the door of her room, murmuring tearfully: "You always lived in the city when you were young, didn't you? Don't you ever get lonesome out here?"

As she turned round to him, her hand fell naturally into his, and he stood holding it and smiling into her face with his peculiar, knowing, indulgent smile without a shadow of reproach in it. "Dem big cities is all right fur de rich, but dey is terrible hard fur de poor."

"I don't know. Sometimes I think I'd like to take a chance. You lived in New York, didn't you?"

"An' London. Da's bigger still. I learned my trade dere. Here's Rudolph comin', you better hurry."

"Will you tell me about London some time?"

"Maybe. Only I ain't no talker, Polly. Run an' dress yourself up."

The bedroom door closed behind her, and Rudolph came in from the outside, looking anxious. He had seen the car and was sorry any of his family should come just then. Supper hadn't been a very pleasant occasion. Halting in the doorway, he saw his father in a kitchen apron, carrying dishes to the sink. He flushed crimson and something flashed in his eye. Rosicky held up a warning finger.

"I brought de car over fur you an' Polly to go to de picture show, an' I made her let me finish here so you won't be late. You go put on a clean shirt, quick!"

"But don't the boys want the car, Father?"

"Not tonight dey don't." Rosicky fumbled under his apron and found his pants pocket. He took out a silver dollar and said in a hurried whisper: "You go an' buy dat girl some ice cream an' candy tonight, like you was courtin'. She's awful good friends wid me."

Rudolph was very short of cash, but he took the money as if it hurt him. There had been a crop failure all over the county. He had more than once been sorry he'd married this year.

In a few minutes the young people came out, looking clean and a little stiff. Rosicky hurried them off, and then he took his own time with the dishes. He scoured the pots and pans and put away the milk and swept the kitchen. He put some coal in the stove and shut off the draughts, so the place would be warm for them when they got home late at night. Then he sat down and had a pipe and listened to the clock tick.

Generally speaking, marrying an American girl was certainly a risk. A Czech should marry a Czech. It was lucky that Polly was the daughter of a poor widow woman; Rudolph was proud, and if she had a prosperous family to throw up at him, they could never make it go. Polly was one of four sisters, and they all worked; one was book-keeper in the bank, one taught music, and Polly and her younger sister had been clerks, like Miss Pearl. All four of them were musical, had pretty voices, and sang in the Methodist choir, which the eldest sister directed.

Polly missed the sociability of a store position. She missed the choir, and the company of her sisters. She didn't dislike housework, but she disliked so much of it. Rosicky was a little anxious about this pair. He was afraid Polly would grow so discontented that Rudy would quit the farm and take a factory job in Omaha. He had worked for a winter up there, two years ago, to get money to marry on. He had done very well, and they would always take him back at the stockyards. But to Rosicky that meant the end of everything for his son. To be a landless man was to be a wage-earner, a slave, all your life; to have nothing, to be nothing.

Rosicky thought he would come over and do a little carpentering for Polly after the New Year. He guessed she needed jollying. Rudolph was a serious sort of chap, serious in love and serious about his work.

Rosicky shook out his pipe and walked home across the fields. Ahead of him the lamplight shone from his kitchen windows. Suppose he were still in a tailor shop on Vesey Street, with a bunch of pale, narrow-chested sons working on machines, all coming home tired and sullen to eat supper in a kitchen that was a parlour also; with another crowded, angry family quarrelling just across the dumb-waiter shaft, and squeaking pulleys at the windows where dirty washings hung on dirty lines above a court full of old brooms and mops and ash-cans. . . .

He stopped by the windmill to look up at the frosty winter stars and draw a long breath before he went inside. That kitchen with the shining windows was dear to him; but the sleeping fields and bright stars and the noble darkness were dearer still.

FIVE

On the day before Christmas the weather set in very cold; no snow, but a bitter, biting wind that whistled and sang over the flat land and lashed one's face like fine wires. There was baking going on in the Rosicky kitchen all day, and Rosicky sat inside, making over a coat that Albert had outgrown into an overcoat for John. Mary had a big red geranium in bloom for Christmas, and a row of Jerusalem cherry trees, full of berries. It was the first year she had ever grown these; Doctor Ed brought her the seeds from Omaha when he went to some medical convention. They reminded Rosicky of plants he had seen in England; and all afternoon, as he stitched, he sat thinking about those two years in London, which his mind usually shrank from even after all this while.

He was a lad of eighteen when he dropped down into London, with no money and no connexions except the address of a cousin who was supposed to be working at a confectioner's. When he went to the pastry shop, however, he found that the cousin had gone to America. Anton tramped the streets for several days, sleeping in doorways and on the Embankment, until he was in utter despair. He knew no English, and the sound of the strange language all about him confused him. By chance he met a poor German tailor who had learned his trade in Vienna, and could speak a little Czech. This tailor, Lifschnitz, kept a repair shop in a Cheapside basement, underneath a cobbler. He didn't much need an apprentice, but he was sorry for the boy and took him in for no wages but his keep and what he could pick up. The pickings were supposed to be coppers given you when you took work home to a customer. But most of the customers called for their clothes themselves, and the coppers that came Anton's way were very few. He had, however, a place to sleep. The tailor's family lived upstairs in three rooms; a kitchen, a bedroom, where Lifschnitz and his wife and five children slept, and a living-room. Two corners of this living-room were curtained off for lodgers; in one Rosicky slept on an old horsehair sofa, with a feather quilt to wrap himself in. The other corner was rented to a wretched, dirty boy, who was studying the violin. He actually practised there. Rosicky was dirty, too. There was no way to be anything else. Mrs. Lifschnitz got the water she cooked and washed with from a pump in a brick court, four flights down. There were bugs in the place, and multitudes of fleas, though the poor woman did the best she could. Rosicky knew she often went empty to give another potato or a spoonful of dripping to the two hungry, sad-eyed boys who lodged with her. He used to think he would never get out of there, never get a clean shirt to his back again. What would he do, he wondered, when his clothes actually dropped to pieces and the worn cloth wouldn't hold patches any longer?

It was still early when the old farmer put aside his sewing and his recollections. The sky had been a dark grey all day, with not a gleam of sun, and the light failed at four o'clock. He went to shave and change his shirt while the turkey was roasting. Rudolph and Polly were coming over for supper.

After supper they sat round in the kitchen, and the younger boys were saying how sorry they were it hadn't snowed. Everybody was sorry. They wanted a deep snow that would lie long and keep the wheat warm, and leave the ground soaked when it melted.

"Yes, sir!" Rudolph broke out fiercely; "if we have another dry year like last year, there's going to be hard times in this country."

Rosicky filled his pipe. "You boys don't know what hard times is. You don't owe nobody, you got plenty to eat an' keep warm, an' plenty water to keep clean. When you got them, you can't have it very hard."

Rudolph frowned, opened and shut his big right hand, and dropped it clenched upon his knee. "I've got to have a good deal more than that, Father, or I'll quit this farming gamble. I can always make good wages railroading, or at the packing house, and be sure of my money."

"Maybe so," his father answered dryly.

Mary, who had just come in from the pantry and was wiping her hands on the roller towel, thought Rudy and his father were getting too serious. She brought her darning-basket and sat down in the middle of the group.

"I ain't much afraid of hard times, Rudy," she said heartily. "We've had a plenty, but we've always come through. Your father wouldn't never take nothing very hard, not even hard times. I got a mind to tell you a story on him. Maybe you boys can't hardly remember the year we had that terrible hot wind, that burned everything up on the Fourth of July? All the corn an' the gardens. An' that was in the days when we didn't have alfalfa yet,—I guess it wasn't invented.

"Well, that very day your father was out cultivatin' corn, and I was here in the kitchen makin' plum preserves. We had bushels of plums that year. I noticed it was terrible hot, but it's always hot in the kitchen when you're preservin', an' I was too busy with my plums to mind. Anton come in from the field about three o'clock, an' I asked him what was the matter.

" 'Nothin',' he says, 'but it's pretty hot, an' I think I won't work no more today.' He stood round for a few minutes, an' then he says: 'Ain't you near through? I want you should git up a nice supper for us tonight. It's Fourth of July.'

"I told him to git along, that I was right in the middle of preservin', but the plums would taste good on hot biscuit. 'I'm goin' to have fried chicken, too,' he says, and he went off an' killed a couple. You three oldest boys was little fellers, playin' round outside, real hot an' sweaty, an' your father took you to the horse tank down by the windmill an' took off your clothes an' put you in. Them two box-elder trees was little then, but they made shade over the tank. Then he took off all his own clothes, an' got in with you. While he was playin' in the water with you, the Methodist preacher drove into our place to say how all the neighbours was goin' to meet at the schoolhouse that night, to pray for rain. He drove right to the windmill, of course, and there was your father and you three with no clothes on. I was in the kitchen door, an' I had to laugh, for the preacher acted like he ain't never seen a naked man before. He surely was embarrassed, an' your father couldn't git to his clothes; they was all hangin' up on the windmill to let the sweat dry out of 'em. So he laid in the tank where he was, an' put one of you boys on top of him to cover him up a little, an' talked to the preacher.

"When you got through playin' in the water, he put clean clothes on you and a clean shirt on himself, an' by that time I'd begun to get supper. He says: 'It's too hot in here to eat comfortable. Let's have a picnic in the orchard. We'll eat our supper behind the mulberry hedge, under them linden trees.'

"So he carried our supper down, an' a bottle of my wild-grape wine, an' everything tasted good, I can tell you. The wind got cooler as the sun was goin' down, and it turned out pleasant, only I noticed how the leaves was curled up on the linden trees. That made me think, an' I asked your father if that hot wind all day hadn't been terrible hard on the gardens an' the corn.

" 'Corn,' he says, 'there ain't no corn.'

" 'What you talkin' about?' I said. 'Ain't we got forty acres?'

" 'We ain't got an ear,' he says, 'nor nobody else ain't got none. All the corn in this country was cooked by three o'clock today, like you'd roasted it in an oven.'

" 'You mean you won't get no crop at all?' I asked him. I couldn't believe it, after he'd worked so hard.

" 'No crop this year,' he says. 'That's why we're havin' a picnic. We might as well enjoy what we got.'

"An' that's how your father behaved, when all the neighbours was so discouraged they couldn't look you in the face. An' we enjoyed ourselves that year, poor as we was, an' our neighbours wasn't a bit better off for bein' miserable. Some of 'em grieved till they got poor digestions and couldn't relish what they did have."

The younger boys said they thought their father had the best of it. But Rudolph was thinking that, all the same, the neighbours had managed to get ahead more, in the fifteen years since that time. There must be something wrong about his father's way of doing things. He wished he knew what was going on in the back of Polly's mind. He knew she liked his father, but he knew, too, that she was afraid of something. When his mother sent over coffee-cake or prune tarts or a loaf of fresh bread, Polly seemed to regard them with a certain suspicion. When she observed to him that his brothers had nice manners, her tone implied that it was remarkable they should have. With his mother she was stiff and on her guard. Mary's hearty frankness and gusts of good humour irritated her. Polly was afraid of being unusual or conspicuous in any way, of being "ordinary," as she said!

When Mary had finished her story, Rosicky laid aside his pipe.

"You boys like me to tell you about some of dem hard times I been through in London?" Warmly encouraged, he sat rubbing his forehead along the deep creases. It was bothersome to tell a long story in English (he nearly always talked to the boys in Czech), but he wanted Polly to hear this one.

"Well, you know about dat tailor shop I worked in in London? I had one Christmas dere I ain't never forgot. Times was awful bad before Christmas; de boss ain't got much work, an' have it awful hard to pay his rent. It ain't so much fun, bein' poor in a big city like London, I'll say! All de windows is full of good t'ings to eat, an' all de pushcarts in de streets is full, an' you smell 'em all de time, an' you ain't got no money,—not a damn bit. I didn't mind de cold so much, though I didn't have no overcoat, chust a short jacket I'd outgrowed so it wouldn't meet on me, an' my hands was chapped raw. But I always had a good appetite, like you all know, an' de sight of dem pork pies in de windows was awful fur me!

"Day before Christmas was terrible foggy dat year, an' dat fog gits into your bones and makes you all damp like. Mrs. Lifschnitz didn't give us nothin' but a little bread an' drippin' for supper, because she was savin' to try for to give us a good dinner on Christmas Day. After supper de boss say I can go an' enjoy myself, so I went into de streets to listen to de Christmas singers. Dey sing old songs an' make very nice music, an' I run round after dem a good ways, till I got awful hungry. I t'ink maybe if I go home, I can sleep till morning an' forgit my belly.

"I went into my corner real quiet, and roll up in my fedder quilt. But I ain't got my head down, till I smell somet'ing good. Seem like it git stronger an' stronger, an' I can't git to sleep noway. I can't understand dat smell. Dere was a gas light in a hall across de court, dat always shine in at my window a little. I got up an' look round. I got a little wooden box in my corner fur a stool, 'cause I ain't got no chair. I picks up dat box, and under it dere is a roast goose on a platter! I can't believe my eyes. I carry it to de window where de light comes in, an' touch it and smell it to find out, an' den I taste it to be sure. I say, I will eat chust one little bite of dat goose, so I can go to sleep, and tomorrow I won't eat none at all. But I tell you, boys, when I stop, one half of dat goose was gone!"

The narrator bowed his head, and the boys shouted. But little Josephine slipped behind his chair and kissed him on the neck beneath his ear.

"Poor little Papa, I don't want him to be hungry!"

"Da's long ago, child. I ain't never been hungry since I had your mudder to cook fur me."

"Go on and tell us the rest, please," said Polly.

"Well, when I come to realize what I done, of course, I felt terrible. I felt better in de stomach, but very bad in de heart. I set on my bed wid dat platter on my knees, an' it all come to me; how hard dat poor woman save to buy dat goose, and how she get some neighbour to cook it dat got more fire, an' how she put it in my corner to keep it away from dem hungry children. Dey was a old carpet hung up to shut my corner off, an' de children wasn't allowed to go in dere. An' I know she put it in my corner because she trust me more'n she did de violin boy. I can't stand it to face her after I spoil de Christmas. So I put on my shoes and go out into de city. I tell myself I better throw myself in de river; but I guess I ain't dat kind of a boy.

"It was after twelve o'clock, an' terrible cold, an' I start out to walk about London all night. I walk along de river awhile, but dey was lots of drunks all along; men, and women too. I chust move along to keep away from de police. I git onto de Strand, an' den over to New Oxford Street, where dere was a big German restaurant on de ground floor, wid big windows all fixed up fine, an' I could see de people havin' parties inside. While I was lookin' in, two men and two ladies come out, laughin' and talkin' and feelin' happy about all dey been eatin' an' drinkin', and dey was speakin' Czech,—not like de Austrians, but like de home folks talk it.

"I guess I went crazy, an' I done what I ain't never done before nor since. I went right up to dem gay people an' begun to beg dem: 'Fellow-countrymen, for God's sake give me money enough to buy a goose!'

"Dey laugh, of course, but de ladies speak awful kind to me, an' dey take me back into de restaurant and give me hot coffee and cakes, an' make me tell all about how I happened to come to London, an' what I was doin' dere. Dey take my name and where I work down on paper, an' both of dem ladies give me ten shillings.

"De big market at Covent Garden ain't very far away, an' by dat time it was open. I go dere an' buy a big goose an' some pork pies, an' potatoes and onions, an' cakes an' oranges fur de children,—all I could carry! When I git home, everybody is still asleep. I pile all I bought on de kitchen table, an' go in an' lay down on my bed, an' I ain't waken up till I hear dat woman scream when she come out into her kitchen. My goodness, but she was surprise! She laugh an' cry at de same time, an' hug me and waken all de children. She ain't stop fur no breakfast; she git de Christmas dinner ready dat morning, and we all sit down an' eat all we can hold. I ain't never seen dat violin boy have all he can hold before.

"Two three days after dat, de two men come to hunt me up, an' dey ask my boss, and he give me a good report an' tell dem I was a steady boy all right. One of dem Bohemians was very smart an' run a Bohemian newspaper in New York, an' de odder was a rich man, in de importing business, an' dey been travelling togedder. Dey told me how t'ings was easier in New York, an' offered to pay my passage when dey was goin' home soon on a boat. My boss say to me: 'You go. You ain't got no chance here, an' I like to see you git ahead, fur you always been a good boy to my woman, and fur dat fine Christmas dinner you give us all.' An' da's how I got to New York."

That night when Rudolph and Polly, arm in arm, were running home across the fields with the bitter wind at their backs, his heart leaped for joy when she said she thought they might have his family come over for supper on New Year's Eve. "Let's get up a nice supper, and not let your mother help at all; make her be company for once."

"That would be lovely of you, Polly," he said humbly. He was a very simple, modest boy, and he, too, felt vaguely that Polly and her sisters were more experienced and worldly than his people.

SIX

The winter turned out badly for farmers. It was bitterly cold, and after the first light snows before Christmas there was no snow at all,—and no rain. March was as bitter as February. On those days when the wind fairly punished the country, Rosicky sat by his window. In the fall he and the boys had put in a big wheat planting, and now the seed had frozen in the ground. All that land would have to be ploughed up and planted over again, planted in corn. It had happened before, but he was younger then, and he never worried about what had to be. He was sure of himself and of Mary; he knew they could bear what they had to bear, that they would always pull through somehow. But he was not so sure about the young ones, and he felt troubled because Rudolph and Polly were having such a hard start.

Sitting beside his flowering window while the panes rattled and the wind blew in under the door, Rosicky gave himself to reflection as he had not done since those Sundays in the loft of the furniture-factory in New York, long ago. Then he was trying to find what he wanted in life for himself; now he was trying to find what he wanted for his boys, and why it was he so hungered to feel sure they would be here, working this very land, after he was gone.

They would have to work hard on the farm, and probably they would never do much more than make a living. But if he could think of them as staying here on the land, he wouldn't have to fear any great unkindness for them. Hardships, certainly; it was a hardship to have the wheat freeze in the ground when seed was so high; and to have to sell your stock because you had no feed. But there would be other years when everything came along right, and you caught up. And what you had was your own. You didn't have to choose between bosses and strikers, and go wrong either way. You didn't have to do with dishonest and cruel people. They were the only things in his experience he had found terrifying and horrible; the look in the eyes of a dishonest and crafty man, of a scheming and rapacious woman.

In the country, if you had a mean neighbour, you could keep off his land and make him keep off yours. But in the city, all the foulness and misery and brutality of your neighbours was part of your life. The worst things he had come upon in his journey through the world were human,—depraved and poisonous specimens of man. To this day he could recall certain terrible faces in the London streets. There were mean people everywhere, to be sure, even in their own country town here. But they weren't tempered, hardened, sharpened, like the treacherous people in cities who live by grinding or cheating or poisoning their fellow-men. He had helped to bury two of his fellow-workmen in the tailoring trade, and he was distrustful of the organized industries that see one out of the world in big cities. Here, if you were sick, you had Doctor Ed to look after you; and if you died, fat Mr. Haycock, the kindest man in the world, buried you.

It seemed to Rosicky that for good, honest boys like his, the worst they could do on the farm was better than the best they would be likely to do in the city. If he'd had a mean boy, now, one who was crooked and sharp and tried to put anything over on his brothers, then town would be the place for him. But he had no such boy. As for Rudolph, the discontented one, he would give the shirt off his back to anyone who touched his heart. What Rosicky really hoped for his boys was that they could get through the world without ever knowing much about the cruelty of human beings. "Their mother and me ain't prepared them for that," he sometimes said to himself.

These thoughts brought him back to a grateful consideration of his own case. What an escape he had had, to be sure! He, too, in his time, had had to take money for repair work from the hand of a hungry child who let it go so wistfully; because it was money due his boss. And now, in all these years, he had never had to take a cent from any one in bitter need,—never had to look at the face of a woman become like a wolf's from struggle and famine. When he thought of these things, Rosicky would put on his cap and jacket and slip down to the barn and give his work-horses a little extra oats, letting them eat it out of his hand in their slobbery fashion. It was his way of expressing what he felt, and made him chuckle with pleasure.

The spring came warm, with blue skies,—but dry, dry as a bone. The boys began ploughing up the wheat-fields to plant them over in corn. Rosicky would stand at the fence corner and watch them, and the earth was so dry it blew up in clouds of brown dust that hid the horses and the sulky plough and the driver. It was a bad outlook.

The big alfalfa field that lay between the home place and Rudolph's came up green, but Rosicky was worried because during that open windy winter a great many Russian thistle plants had blown in there and lodged. He kept asking the boys to rake them out; he was afraid their seed would root and "take the alfalfa." Rudolph said that was nonsense. The boys were working so hard planting corn, their father felt he couldn't insist about the thistles, but he set great store by that big alfalfa field. It was a feed you could depend on,—and there was some deeper reason, vague, but strong. The peculiar green of that clover woke early memories in old Rosicky, went back to something in his childhood in the old world. When he was a little boy, he had played in fields of that strong blue-green colour.

One morning, when Rudolph had gone to town in the car, leaving a work-team idle in his barn, Rosicky went over to his son's place, put the horses to the buggy-rake, and set about quietly raking up those thistles. He behaved with guilty caution, and rather enjoyed stealing a march on Doctor Ed, who was just then taking his first vacation in seven years of practice and was attending a clinic in Chicago. Rosicky got the thistles raked up, but did not stop to burn them. That would take some time, and his breath was pretty short, so he thought he had better get the horses back to the barn.

He got them into the barn and to their stalls, but the pain had come on so sharp in his chest that he didn't try to take the harness off. He started for the house, bending lower with every step. The cramp in his chest was shutting him up like a jack-knife. When he reached the windmill, he swayed and caught at the ladder. He saw Polly coming down the hill, running with the swiftness of a slim greyhound. In a flash she had her shoulder under his armpit.

"Lean on me, Father, hard! Don't be afraid. We can get to the house all right."

Somehow they did, though Rosicky became blind with pain; he could keep on his legs, but he couldn't steer his course. The next thing he was conscious of was lying on Polly's bed, and Polly bending over him wringing out bath towels in hot water and putting them on his chest. She stopped only to throw coal into the stove, and she kept the tea-kettle and the black pot going. She put these hot applications on him for nearly an hour, she told him afterwards, and all that time he was drawn up stiff and blue, with the sweat pouring off him.

As the pain gradually loosed its grip, the stiffness went out of his jaws, the black circles round his eyes disappeared, and a little of his natural colour came back. When his daughter-in-law buttoned his shirt over his chest at last, he sighed.

"Da's fine, de way I feel now, Polly. It was a awful bad spell, an' I was so sorry it all come on you like it did."

Polly was flushed and excited. "Is the pain really gone? Can I leave you long enough to telephone over to your place?"

Rosicky's eyelids fluttered. "Don't telephone, Polly. It ain't no use to scare my wife. It's nice and quiet here, an' if I ain't too much trouble to you, just let me lay still till I feel like myself. I ain't got no pain now. It's nice here."

Polly bent over him and wiped the moisture from his face. "Oh, I'm so glad it's over!" she broke out impulsively. "It just broke my heart to see you suffer so, Father."

Rosicky motioned her to sit down on the chair where the tea-kettle had been, and looked up at her with that lively affectionate gleam in his eyes. "You was awful good to me, I won't never forgit dat. I hate it to be sick on you like dis. Down at de barn I say to myself, dat young girl ain't had much experience in sickness, I don't want to scare her, an' maybe she's got a baby comin' or somet'ing."

Polly took his hand. He was looking at her so intently and affectionately and confidingly; his eyes seemed to caress her face, to regard it with pleasure. She frowned with her funny streaks of eyebrows, and then smiled back at him.

"I guess maybe there is something of that kind going to happen. But I haven't told anyone yet, not my mother or Rudolph. You'll be the first to know."

His hand pressed hers. She noticed that it was warm again. The twinkle in his yellow-brown eyes seemed to come nearer.

"I like mighty well to see dat little child, Polly," was all he said. Then he closed his eyes and lay half-smiling. But Polly sat still, thinking hard. She had a sudden feeling that nobody in the world, not her mother, not Rudolph, or anyone, really loved her as much as old Rosicky did. It perplexed her. She sat frowning and trying to puzzle it out. It was as if Rosicky had a special gift for loving people, something that was like an ear for music or an eye for colour. It was quiet, unobtrusive; it was merely there. You saw it in his eyes,—perhaps that was why they were merry. You felt it in his hands, too. After he dropped off to sleep, she sat holding his warm, broad, flexible brown hand. She had never seen another in the least like it. She wondered if it wasn't a kind of gypsy hand, it was so alive and quick and light in its communications,—very strange in a farmer. Nearly all the farmers she knew had huge lumps of fists, like mauls, or they were knotty and bony and uncomfortable-looking, with stiff fingers. But Rosicky's was like quicksilver, flexible, muscular, about the colour of a pale cigar, with deep, deep creases across the palm. It wasn't nervous, it wasn't a stupid lump; it was a warm brown human hand, with some cleverness in it, a great deal of generosity, and something else which Polly could only call "gypsy-like,"—something nimble and lively and sure, in the way that animals are.

Polly remembered that hour long afterwards; it had been like an awakening to her. It seemed to her that she had never learned so much about life from anything as from old Rosicky's hand. It brought her to herself; it communicated some direct and untranslatable message.

When she heard Rudolph coming in the car, she ran out to meet him.

"Oh, Rudy, your father's been awful sick! He raked up those thistles he's been worrying about, and afterwards he could hardly get to the house. He suffered so I was afraid he was going to die."

Rudolph jumped to the ground. "Where is he now?"

"On the bed. He's asleep. I was terribly scared, because, you know, I'm so fond of your father." She slipped her arm through his and they went into the house. That afternoon they took Rosicky home and put him to bed, though he protested that he was quite well again.

The next morning he got up and dressed and sat down to breakfast with his family. He told Mary that his coffee tasted better than usual to him, and he warned the boys not to bear any tales to Doctor Ed when he got home. After breakfast he sat down by his window to do some patching and asked Mary to thread several needles for him before she went to feed her chickens, —her eyes were better than his, and her hands steadier. He lit his pipe and took up John's overalls. Mary had been watching him anxiously all morning, and as she went out of the door with her bucket of scraps, she saw that he was smiling. He was thinking, indeed, about Polly, and how he might never have known what a tender heart she had if he hadn't got sick over there.

Girls nowadays didn't wear their heart on their sleeve. But now he knew Polly would make a fine woman after the foolishness wore off. Either a woman had that sweetness at her heart or she hadn't. You couldn't always tell by the look of them; but if they had that, everything came out right in the end.

After he had taken a few stitches, the cramp began in his chest, like yesterday. He put his pipe cautiously down on the window-sill and bent over to ease the pull. No use,—he had better try to get to his bed if he could. He rose and groped his way across the familiar floor, which was rising and falling like the deck of a ship. At the door he fell. When Mary came in, she found him lying there, and the moment she touched him she knew that he was gone.

Doctor Ed was away when Rosicky died, and for the first few weeks after he got home he was hard driven. Every day he said to himself that he must get out to see that family that had lost their father. One soft, warm moonlight night in early summer he started for the farm. His mind was on other things, and not until his road ran by the graveyard did he realize that Rosicky wasn't over there on the hill where the red lamplight shone, but here, in the moonlight. He stopped his car, shut off the engine, and sat there for a while.

A sudden hush had fallen on his soul. Everything here seemed strangely moving and significant, though signifying what, he did not know. Close by the wire fence stood Rosicky's mowing-machine, where one of the boys had been cutting hay that afternoon; his own work-horses had been going up and down there. The new-cut hay perfumed all the night air. The moonlight silvered the long, billowy grass that grew over the graves and hid the fence; the few little evergreens stood out black in it, like shadows in a pool. The sky was very blue and soft, the stars rather faint because the moon was full.

For the first time it struck Doctor Ed that this was really a beautiful graveyard. He thought of city cemeteries; acres of shrubbery and heavy stone, so arranged and lonely and unlike anything in the living world. Cities of the dead, indeed; cities of the forgotten, of the "put away." But this was open and free, this little square of long grass which the wind for ever stirred. Nothing but the sky overhead, and the many-coloured fields running on until they met that sky. The horses worked here in summer; the neighbours passed on their way to town; and over yonder, in the cornfield, Rosicky's own cattle would be eating fodder as winter came on. Nothing could be more undeathlike than this place; nothing could be more right for a man who had helped to do the work of great cities and had always longed for the open country and had got to it at last. Rosicky's life seemed to him complete and beautiful.

New York, 1928

THE VERGER

SOMERSET MAUGHAM

THERE had been a christening that afternoon at St. Peter's, Neville Square, and Albert Edward Foreman still wore his verger's gown. He kept his new one, its folds as full and stiff as though it were made not of alpaca but of perennial bronze, for funerals and weddings (St. Peter's, Neville Square, was a church much favoured by the fashionable for these ceremonies) and now he wore only his second-best. He wore it with complacence, for it was the dignified symbol of his office, and without it (when he took it off to go home) he had the disconcerting sensation of being somewhat insufficiently clad. He took pains with it; he pressed it and ironed it himself. During the sixteen years he had been verger of this church he had had a succession of such gowns, but he had never been able to throw them away when they were worn out and the complete series, neatly wrapped up in brown paper, lay in the bottom drawers of the wardrobe in his bedroom.

The verger busied himself quietly, replacing the painted wooden cover on the marble font, taking away a chair that had been brought for an infirm old lady, and waited for the vicar to have finished in the vestry so that he could tidy up in there and go home. Presently he saw him walk across the chancel, genuflect in front of the high altar and come down the aisle; but he still wore his cassock.

"What's he 'anging about for?" the verger said to himself. "Don't 'e know I want my tea?"

The vicar had been but recently appointed, a red-faced energetic man in the early forties, and Albert Edward still regretted his predecessor, a clergyman of the old school who preached leisurely sermons in a silvery voice and dined out a great deal with his more aristocratic parishioners. He liked things in church to be just so, but he never fussed; he was not like this new man who wanted to have his finger in every pie. But Albert Edward was tolerant. St. Peter's was in a very good neighbourhood and the parishioners were a very nice class of people. The new vicar had come from the East

End and he couldn't be expected to fall in all at once with the discreet ways of his fashionable congregation.

"All this 'ustle," said Albert Edward. "But give 'im time, he'll learn."

When the vicar had walked down the aisle so far that he could address the verger without raising his voice more than was becoming in a place of worship he stopped.

"Foreman, will you come into the vestry for a minute. I have something to say to you."

"Very good, sir."

The vicar waited for him to come up and they walked up the church together.

"A very nice christening, I thought, sir. Funny 'ow the baby stopped cryin' the moment you took him."

"I've noticed they very often do," said the vicar, with a little smile. "After all I've had a good deal of practice with them."

It was a source of subdued pride to him that he could nearly always quiet a whimpering infant by the manner in which he held it and he was not unconscious of the amused admiration with which mothers and nurses watched him settle the baby in the crook of his surpliced arm. The verger knew that it pleased him to be complimented on his talent.

The vicar preceded Albert Edward into the vestry. Albert Edward was a trifle surprised to find the two churchwardens there. He had not seen them come in. They gave him pleasant nods.

"Good-afternoon, my lord. Good-afternoon, sir," he said to one after the other.

They were elderly men, both of them, and they had been churchwardens almost as long as Albert Edward had been verger. They were sitting now at a handsome refectory table that the old vicar had brought many years before from Italy and the vicar sat down in the vacant chair between them. Albert Edward faced them, the table between him and them, and wondered with slight uneasiness what was the matter. He remembered still the occasion on which the organist had got into trouble and the bother they had all had to hush things up. In a church like St. Peter's, Neville Square, they couldn't afford a scandal. On the vicar's red face was a look of resolute benignity, but the others bore an expression that was slightly troubled.

"He's been naggin' them, he 'as," said the verger to himself. "He's jockeyed them into doin' something, but they don't 'alf like it. That's what it is, you mark my words."

But his thoughts did not appear on Albert Edward's clean-cut and distinguished features. He stood in a respectful but not obsequious attitude. He had been in service before he was appointed to his ecclesiastical office, but only in very good houses, and his deportment was irreproachable. Starting as a page-boy in the household of a merchant-prince, he had risen by due degrees from the position of fourth to first footman, for a year he had been single-handed butler to a widowed peeress and, till the vacancy occurred at St. Peter's, butler with two men under him in the house of a retired ambassador. He was tall, spare, grave and dignified. He looked, if not like a duke, at least like an actor of the old school who specialised in dukes' parts. He had tact, firmness and self-assurance. His character was unimpeachable.

The vicar began briskly.

"Foreman, we've got something rather unpleasant to say to you. You've been here a great many years and I think his lordship and the general agree with me that you've fulfilled the duties of your office to the satisfaction of everybody concerned."

The two churchwardens nodded.

"But a most extraordinary circumstance came to my knowledge the other day and I felt it my duty to impart it to the churchwardens. I discovered to my astonishment that you could neither read nor write."

The verger's face betrayed no sign of embarrassment.

"The last vicar knew that, sir," he replied. "He said it didn't make no difference. He always said there was a great deal too much education in the world for 'is taste."

"It's the most amazing thing I ever heard," cried the general. "Do you mean to say that you've been verger of this church for sixteen years and never learned to read or write?"

"I went into service when I was twelve, sir. The cook in the first place tried to teach me once, but I didn't seem to 'ave the knack for it, and then what with one thing and another I never seemed to 'ave the time. I've never really found the want of it. I think a lot of these young fellows waste a rare lot of time readin' when they might be doin' something useful."

"But don't you want to know the news?" said the other churchwarden. "Don't you ever want to write a letter?"

"No, me lord, I seem to manage very well without. And of late years now they've all these pictures in the papers I get to know what's goin' on pretty well. Me wife's quite a scholar and if I want to write a letter she writes it for me. It's not as if I was a bettin' man."

The two churchwardens gave the vicar a troubled glance and then looked down at the table.

"Well, Foreman, I've talked the matter over with these gentlemen and they quite agree with me that the situation is impossible. At a church like St. Peter's, Neville Square, we cannot have a verger who can neither read nor write."

Albert Edward's thin, sallow face reddened and he moved uneasily on his feet, but he made no reply.

"Understand me, Foreman, I have no complaint to make against you. You do your work quite satisfactorily; I have the highest opinion both of your character and of your capacity; but we haven't the right to take the risk of some accident that might happen owing to your lamentable ignorance. It's a matter of prudence as well as of principle."

"But couldn't you learn, Foreman?" asked the general.

"No, sir, I'm afraid I couldn't, not now. You see, I'm not as young as I

was and if I couldn't seem able to get the letters in me 'ead when I was a
nipper I don't think there's much chance of it now."

"We don't want to be harsh with you, Foreman," said the vicar. "But the
churchwardens and I have quite made up our minds. We'll give you three
months and if at the end of that time you cannot read and write I'm afraid
you'll have to go."

Albert Edward had never liked the new vicar. He'd said from the beginning that they'd made a mistake when they gave him St. Peter's. He wasn't
the type of man they wanted with a classy congregation like that. And now
he straightened himself a little. He knew his value and he wasn't going to
allow himself to be put upon.

"I'm very sorry, sir, I'm afraid it's no good. I'm too old a dog to learn
new tricks. I've lived a good many years without knowin' 'ow to read and
write, and without wishin' to praise myself, self-praise is no recommenda-
tion, I don't mind sayin' I've done my duty in that state of life in which it
'as pleased a merciful providence to place me, and if I *could* learn now I
don't know as I'd want to."

"In that case, Foreman, I'm afraid you must go."

"Yes, sir, I quite understand. I shall be 'appy to 'and in my resignation
as soon as you've found somebody to take my place."

But when Albert Edward with his usual politeness had closed the church
door behind the vicar and the two churchwardens he could not sustain the
air of unruffled dignity with which he had borne the blow inflicted upon
him and his lips quivered. He walked slowly back to the vestry and hung
up on its proper peg his verger's gown. He sighed as he thought of all the
grand funerals and smart weddings it had seen. He tidied everything up,
put on his coat, and hat in hand walked down the aisle. He locked the
church door behind him. He strolled across the square, but deep in his sad
thoughts he did not take the street that led him home, where a nice strong
cup of tea awaited him; he took the wrong turning. He walked slowly along.
His heart was heavy. He did not know what he should do with himself. He
did not fancy the notion of going back to domestic service; after being his
own master for so many years, for the vicar and churchwardens could say
what they liked, it was he that had run St. Peter's, Neville Square, he could
scarcely demean himself by accepting a situation. He had saved a tidy sum,
but not enough to live on without doing something, and life seemed to cost
more every year. He had never thought to be troubled with such questions.
The vergers of St. Peter's, like the popes of Rome, were there for life. He
had often thought of the pleasant reference the vicar would make in his
sermon at evensong the first Sunday after his death to the long and faithful
service, and the exemplary character of their late verger, Albert Edward
Foreman. He sighed deeply. Albert Edward was a non-smoker and a total
abstainer, but with a certain latitude; that is to say he liked a glass of beer
with his dinner and when he was tired he enjoyed a cigarette. It occurred
to him now that one would comfort him and since he did not carry them
he looked about him for a shop where he could buy a packet of Gold Flakes.

He did not at once see one and walked on a little. It was a long street, with all sorts of shops in it, but there was not a single one where you could buy cigarettes.

"That's strange," said Albert Edward.

To make sure he walked right up the street again. No, there was no doubt about it. He stopped and looked reflectively up and down.

"I can't be the only man as walks along this street and wants a fag," he said. "I shouldn't wonder but what a fellow might do very well with a little shop here. Tobacco and sweets, you know."

He gave a sudden start.

"That's an idea," he said. "Strange 'ow things come to you when you least expect it."

He turned, walked home, and had his tea.

"You're very silent this afternoon, Albert," his wife remarked.

"I'm thinkin'," he said.

He considered the matter from every point of view and next day he went along the street and by good luck found a little shop to let that looked as though it would exactly suit him. Twenty-four hours later he had taken it and when a month after that he left St. Peter's, Neville Square, for ever, Albert Edward Foreman set up in business as a tobacconist and newsagent. His wife said it was a dreadful come-down after being verger of St. Peter's, but he answered that you had to move with the times, the church wasn't what it was, and 'enceforward he was going to render unto Cæsar what was Cæsar's. Albert Edward did very well. He did so well that in a year or so it struck him that he might take a second shop and put a manager in. He looked for another long street that hadn't got a tobacconist in it and when he found it, and a shop to let, took it and stocked it. This was a success too. Then it occurred to him that if he could run two he could run half a dozen, so he began walking about London, and whenever he found a long street that had no tobacconist and a shop to let he took it. In the course of ten years he had acquired no less than ten shops and he was making money hand over fist. He went round to all of them himself every Monday, collected the week's takings and took them to the bank.

One morning when he was there paying in a bundle of notes and a heavy bag of silver the cashier told him that the manager would like to see him. He was shown into an office and the manager shook hands with him.

"Mr. Foreman, I wanted to have a talk to you about the money you've got on deposit with us. D'you know exactly how much it is?"

"Not within a pound or two, sir; but I've got a pretty rough idea."

"Apart from what you paid in this morning it's a little over thirty thousand pounds. That's a very large sum to have on deposit and I should have thought you'd do better to invest it."

"I wouldn't want to take no risk, sir. I know it's safe in the bank."

"You needn't have the least anxiety. We'll make you out a list of absolutely gilt-edged securities. They'll bring you in a better rate of interest than we can possibly afford to give you."

A troubled look settled on Mr. Foreman's distinguished face. "I've never 'ad anything to do with stocks and shares and I'd 'ave to leave it all in your 'ands," he said.

The manager smiled. "We'll do everything. All you'll have to do next time you come in is just to sign the transfers."

"I could do that all right," said Albert uncertainly. "But 'ow should I know what I was signin'?"

"I suppose you can read," said the manager a trifle sharply.

Mr. Foreman gave him a disarming smile.

"Well, sir, that's just it. I can't. I know it sounds funny-like, but there it is, I can't read or write, only me name, an' I only learnt to do that when I went into business."

The manager was so surprised that he jumped up from his chair.

"That's the most extraordinary thing I ever heard."

"You see, it's like this, sir, I never 'ad the opportunity until it was too late and then some'ow I wouldn't. I got obstinate-like."

The manager stared at him as though he were a prehistoric monster.

"And do you mean to say that you've built up this important business and amassed a fortune of thirty thousand pounds without being able to read or write? Good God, man, what would you be now if you had been able to?"

"I can tell you that, sir," said Mr. Foreman, a little smile on his still aristocratic features. "I'd be verger of St. Peter's, Neville Square."

JACK STILL

J. P. MARQUAND

SCOTT MATTAYE liked to tell the story best in the library at Deer Bottom Plantation, of how he saw a slender, thin-nosed man hold the destiny of a nation in his hand one July night some sixty years before. You could believe anything he had seen when he told of it in the library, because the uncouth, varied shadows of the Confederacy had never left it. There was a memory of crinoline and long-tailed coats, the memory of an era prodigious in its extremes, and the room had the marks of war.

The cold steel engravings on the wall represented landscapes as peaceful as the views on Worcester ware. He could understand why the memory of those pictures had come to him at the very instant that a polite and self-effacing civilian had presented a pocket pistol at his heart in the woods beyond Bull Run. The books were on their cracked, varnished shelves in almost the same order they had stood before the war, as old as Scott Mattaye and as wholly out of place.

"Sammy," he would say to the cook's small son, "yo' shif'less boy, raise yore candle so the gentlemen can see."

The titles on the crumbling calfskin bindings were half obliterated by dust and mold. There were forgotten works of Southern genius, unknown above the Line, surrounded by the pungent smell of decaying leather. It always seemed to Scott Mattaye that they represented what might have been, now grown as dry and sterile as the dust; he never could avoid bitterness, once he saw the books. He could feel the grip of invasion again, blundering and inexorable; and it still held his house, for the cavalry had stopped there once. The Yankee power was in that library, an uncouth alien force, stamping out the leisured cultivation of a landed gentry.

"Sammy," he would say, "hold up yore candle! . . . Yonder—there's where they cut out the paintings. You see the frames?"

Three gilt frames, just above the books, surrounded nothing but a shadowy blankness. Although they had hung barren for sixty years against the peeling wall paper, the sight of them was still startling. The smug intellectual snob-

First published in *The Saturday Evening Post*. Copyright © 1932 by the Curtis Publishing Company. Reprinted by permission of Brandt & Brandt.

bery of the place was no longer amusing, once you saw the frames, and the silence seemed to leave it.

Scott Mattaye was the one who could see it leave. When the candle flickered, the light came back, distorted, from the black windows like a flame. It was like the sweep of fire outside, when the corncribs and the barns and smokehouse had been burning. The horses on the lawn beneath the tulip trees would be pulling at their bridles. The house was full of footsteps and of nasal, ugly voices. . . . They must have been a detachment from Cooke's or Pleasonton's. They would be gawky dry-goods or ribbon clerks, who could not ride.

"Sammy," he would say, "set down that candle and fetch refreshment for the gentlemen. . . . I know what I'm saying. No Yankee cavalry would have got here, gentlemen, because at the first Bull Run we might have won the war. We had 'em whipped, I'm saying. We'd have picketed in the Washington City Capitol. I know and I believe, for I was there. I heard 'em talking."

He had heard and, once his memory started working, he could bring it back. He was young, in Stuart's cavalry again, and he had seen a nation hanging in the balance in the second-floor room of a rickety frame house the night after Bull Run was fought, and it had been as prosaic as the plantation library.

The candle guttered on the table. The empty frames were staring down, framing Scott Mattaye's belief, and his voice was shaken with it.

"It wasn't a retreat. It was a rout," he was saying. "The only time there was a rout. We had only to go."

The strength of his conviction echoed like Walt Whitman's words in a distant, mysterious cadence which was growing louder as he spoke: ". . . all the men with this coating of muck and sweat and rain, now recoiling back, pouring over the Long Bridge. . . . They drop down anywhere—on the steps of the houses, up close to the basements or fences, on the sidewalks, aside on some vacant lot. . . . Some in squads; comrades, brothers, close together —and on them, as they lay, sulkily drips the rain."

Longstreet was arguing with an officer from Johnston's staff; Federal teamsters were cutting traces at Cub Run; panic was sweeping over an improvised Union army and dark was falling. Jackson was calling for ten thousand men. . . .

"Yes, sir," Scott Mattaye was saying, "I heard them talking in the room. The door was open, and I was standing there. They didn't see me, and I heard them. I couldn't think what else to do. . . . He was a thin man in a black frock coat, thin nosed, handsome, like his statue, and it's what I say. We might have won that war. He held it in his hand like this—right there in his hand."

Human frailty and vanity and the irony of little things, working in an integration that made destiny—Scott Mattaye had seen it all. He had seen the destiny of gambler's luck that holds the balance of a war. And it started

with a gambler—it was as strange as that—a fantastic figure who had leveled
a pocket pistol at his heart.

He was asleep at Sudley Springs, Scott always said, where Stuart's cavalry
had halted after following the retreat, and sleep in war was different from
other sleep. Even when Scott Mattaye started from the depths—and he could
be conscious in a moment—the curtain of sleep would be so close behind
him that reality was blurred, mercifully, into the elements of dreaming. That
was why the beginning was always like a dream; he was sleeping on the
ground when someone gripped his shoulder.

"You, Mattaye." Though he was only half awake, he knew the voice. It
was Colonel Stuart speaking, and Scott Mattaye could have sworn the colonel
never slept. "Get up, Mattaye."

First he thought that they were in the woods on Henry House Hill, and
that he would hear the guns, but there was no sound of firing. Then he felt
the hardness of the ground and the damp. There was a smell of horses and
leather, and the dank smells of late evening. He was on the ground outside
headquarters near the ford.

"You hear me?" the colonel said. "I want you to carry a message. Come
inside."

The colonel had taken over the kitchen of a small log house. The room was
typically a poor man's; Scott Mattaye could even remember the smell of
milk pails, kerosene and bacon fat; and though half awake, he could see
unfinished timbers, an open hearth and crane, a rough-hewn trestle table
and handmade chairs. There was a lantern on the table, two pistols and a
pen and paper. Two officers with their cloaks around them were sleeping on
the floor, and a trooper from the picket was standing near the wall with an
inconspicuous man beside him in clothes which were smeared with dust.
Scott would never have noticed that man except he was a civilian and a
stranger.

"Mattaye," said the colonel, and he took off his slouch hat and laid it on
the table; and Scott remembered that his hair was neatly brushed and parted
on the side. He was magnificent there in the kitchen, already assuming the
stature of the great cavalry leader of the war. It seemed as though the drab-
ness of the place were made to set him off, the perfect background of a
picture. J. E. B. Stuart must have felt it, for he had the dramatic sense.
His blue eyes glistened; bronze lights were glowing in his beard; he tucked
his buckskin gloves into his yellow sash and pulled down his gray shell jacket.
He must have known the man by the wall was watching him, and he was
never afraid of being watched.

"Mattaye, there's some coffee on the fire—right good coffee. . . . And now,
stranger, you step forward, please, and we'll get finished. My name's Stuart
—J. E. B. Stuart—late of the United States Army, and now commanding the
First Virginia Cavalry of the Confederate States of America, and you were
taken by my picket. May I ask your name?"

The man in the dusty clothes moved into the light politely and deliberately. Though he was soiled and bedraggled, he was expensively dressed. There was a diamond on his finger and a red-stone pin in his cravat, and he wore a black-and-green embroidered vest of watered silk. Yet there was nothing vulgar; he was almost like a gentleman. His hair was half long, black and oiled; his face was ageless and impassive.

"Excuse me, suh," he said; "I've stated to you"—his voice was soft and almost toneless, and as undisturbing as a whisper—"previously that I gave myse'f up with the greatest pleasure to yore picket, suh. I had the definite and patriotic purpose of conveyin' my information to yore lines in the interest of a cause which I admire, suh, and which is so ably prosecuted by such an officer as I see before me—no flattery intended. My name is Still—Jack Still—and relieved to be in the company of a discriminatin' gentleman, an' not with them damn Yankees."

He paused and rubbed his hands together—delicate white hands, beautifully precise. The colonel sat down behind the table and tilted backward in his chair, but even in that restful attitude he did not appear relaxed.

"I place you now," he said. "A Mississippi gambler, aren't you, Mr. Still?"

"Yes, suh, to be frank," said Mr. Still. "At gentlemen's service on river steamers, peacetimes. Findin' myself in Washington City, I followed with this Yankee army as far as Centerville, helpin' these officers to divert themselves, suh. Not gentlemen, suh; all of 'em small tradesmen, most graspin' and suspicious. There would have been no misunderstandin' in the game if they could have taken losses like Southern gentlemen."

The voice of that man, Scott always said, was as soothing as a benediction, as placid as his eyes, healing frayed nerves and lulling the mind to rest.

"Chased out, eh?" Colonel Stuart said.

"Yes, suh," said Mr. Still. "Frankly, suh, there was an embarrassin' misunderstandin'. I tell you, suh, there's no such thing as honor in that damn Yankee army."

The colonel was smiling and playing with the knot of his saber.

"Killed a man, eh?" he said.

There was an instant's pause. The stranger closed his eyes and opened them, but there was no expression in his face or voice.

"Colonel," he answered, "I fail to understand."

Yet Scott Mattaye knew as sure as fate that a killer was in the room, and that the very peacefulness of Mr. Still was dangerous.

"Don't argue," the colonel said. "It's a right odd thing that parties like you should help to win a war. You're the only man across this run tonight who's seen the Yankees running, if you tell the truth, but—— Suppose I send you back. Speak up; how would you like that?"

Mr. Still sighed, and suddenly his lips curled up in a faint, slow smile.

"I'd prefer the colonel wouldn't, since he asks—always considerin' I've come here with valuable information, suh."

The colonel rose from his chair, and his spurs clinked softly as he walked across the floor. He stood looking straight at Mr. Still, and Mr. Still gazed back, enigmatic and serene.

"All right," he said; "I won't send you back, but I hope very much, mister, you're sure of everything you saw."

"You can count it right, suh," said Mr. Still. "I heard staff officers talking, and I saw the thing myself. I know when a party's busted, suh. There's nothin' between you-all and Washington City that you can call a fightin' force. The Yankee army's busted, suh. It's gone!"

"Mr. Still," the colonel said, "I've taken down your statement, and I'll send you to headquarters. It's the first time in your life you're valuable to anybody, or I miss my guess. . . . Saddle up a horse for the prisoner, Mattaye."

The man's eyes flickered, though his face was impassive.

"Prisoner, colonel?" he said. "Sholy there's no need for that. Why, here I come of my own accord, bringin' information from a Yankee staff. Sholy you don't mean to hold me prisoner and send me to headquarters? Why, colonel, it isn't nohow justice! Respectfully, I'd much prefer simply to be allowed to pass along."

"So that's it, is it?" the colonel said. "You're in trouble this side, too, are you, Mr. Still? Out of the frying pan into the fire—is that the way it is?"

"Now, suh," Mr. Still replied, "I didn't affirm such a thing, but a man like me, he has enemies, colonel. As one gentleman to another—and I come of good stock, suh—I ask leave to go my way, colonel, if you please."

The colonel turned to the table and picked up a letter.

"Mattaye," he said, "carry this and conduct this man to headquarters at Manassas. And you deliver this letter to the commanding general. You understand, Mattaye? This man has been searched, but keep an eye on him and be careful, understand? Shoot him if he tries to break away. Don't stop, don't argue. Shoot him. Still, you hear me? Mattaye, you understand?"

Stuart's eyes were on him, amiable and blue, and he spoke without malice or anger, the way he always spoke:

"Don't be afraid to kill him; you understand, Mattaye?"

Scott Mattaye stood at attention, and he felt the prisoner looking at him carefully.

"Yes, sir," said Scott Mattaye, but beneath the glance of Mr. Still he felt inadequate and young. "Yes, sir; he'll be all right."

Mr. Still straightened the pin in his cravat and smiled his faint, slow smile.

"If you insist, suh," he said. "Good night. We'll have a right nice ride."

Manassas was a good six miles away from Sudley Springs. Scott Mattaye remembered thinking that the distance seemed immense, now that he and his civilian were outside; and he still had the sense of being only half awake as they started down the road. Later, given a year of war, such an incident would have seemed like nothing, but he could not escape the unreality, then, that he should be riding with a man a half length forward to the left, whom he was told to shoot should he try to break away.

Mr. Still did not seem dangerous. His voice was sympathetic, soft and friendly.

"Trooper," he said, "I'm right ashamed to be givin' you such trouble. You must be downright tired after all this fightin'?"

"Yes," said Scott. "You keep a mite forward, please, and don't start dropping back."

"Pardon, suh," said Mr. Still. "It's the hoss. He's tired too. Trooper, let's talk sense. I'm famed for being sensible. It's why I'm livin' now. For instance, I see you fingerin' your weapon—a sight which always sets me shiverin'. Those new pistols are amazing accurate, even when a greenhorn pulls 'em. Excuse me, trooper, no offense. I'm simply demonstratin' that I won't run. I couldn't get off on this horse the colonel's loaned me. And, trooper, I've been searched. There's no more poison in me than a bunny. Will you tell me where you come from, suh?"

"Deer Bottom," said Scott Mattaye. "My people are planters there."

"Are they so?" said Mr. Still. "Of co'se, the Mattayes. I should have recollected—the very finest quality."

Scott Mattaye felt better after that. He only wondered later why Mr. Still should have recollected, or why he should have known.

They had passed the church at Sudley Springs. There were the lanterns of a field hospital beside the road, and teams were creaking past them, moving toward Manassas with the wounded. There was a slow, limping traffic all along that road, punctuated by lantern lights which flashed on sights that were like delirious thoughts—pale faces like souls in purgatory, smashed fences, blankets, haversacks.

"It must have been a mighty battle hereabouts," said Mr. Still. "It's consolin' to be riding with good blood. There's nothing like good blood. Why, trooper, a single Southern gentleman can whip a dozen Yankees. Yes, indeed, I know."

"Yes?" said Scott. "Will you kindly keep up forward, if you please?"

"Pardon," said Mr. Still. "It's just this pesky hoss. Bein' quality, you sholy know the officers at this headquarters staff where we're going. I wonder—there's a certain colonel. He resembles me a mite."

"I'm just a trooper, mister," said Scott. "I don't have truck with officers. I've never seen a one that looks like you."

"None the less," said Mr. Still, "he's yonder. Yes, he's yonder."

The night was sultry and heavy, like any July night at home, except that there was something shocked about the dark, as though a frightful thing had happened and the country where they were riding seemed to be recovering from a blow. They were riding down a rolling slope, where one could see a row of camp fires far over to the left, and the dim line of a road, and lights about an old stone house. They were crossing the battlefield in the same direction the troops had moved that morning when they had struck the Southern flank. They were riding toward the pike over an open country. The crests of fields were visible against the sky. He could see the lanterns of details still searching for the wounded, jolting, stopping and moving on; and he could hear voices across the fields above the rattling of the wagons. Except for the fires and the lanterns, there was life only upon the road. Everything

was dreaming in the night, and he could feel the dream. Outrageous memories were surrounding him, and he seemed like a ghost revisiting that place.

"Trooper," said Mr. Still, "there must be heaps of dead men here."

"Yes," said Scott, "over all those fields. First they drove us and then they broke."

"A very interestin' sight," said Mr. Still. "And where's Manassas now?"

"About three miles away," said Scott. "This here was our left."

"I understand," said Mr. Still, "you whipped 'em pretty, and why you're not still driving after is more than I can see. I wish I had been with you. I should have been, except a man like me, who's lived like me, has no place much to go."

They were out of the fields, moving through thick oak woods, when Scott Mattaye began to notice that Mr. Still kept looking back. Scott could see the white of his face turn toward him and then away. They rode at a trot past a line of wagons, and the road was clear ahead.

"Friend," said Mr. Still, "may I ride close? I want to talk in a confidential way."

"No," said Scott, "you ride up where you are."

"Very good," said Mr. Still, and he half turned in his saddle. "Then from this position I'm laying my cards on the table for a show-down, friend. They searched me back yonder, but, trooper, I've got five hundred in bills in my right boot, and it's all clear yours if you'll let me ride away. Don't stop me. Listen, friend; I've personal reasons not to go to this headquarters. There's someone there who'll know me. For private reasons, I don't pine for that."

"Why?" asked Scott. "Who's going to hurt you, mister?"

"Five hundred dollars," repeated Mr. Still. "I can pay when my luck is running bad. It's the personal disgrace. Are you listenin', friend?"

"Listen you'se'f," said Scott. "It won't help to talk to me."

"I hope it will," said Mr. Still, "for I'm simply appealing to your kindness. I can't go with you, trooper. I repeat there's a party at headquarters who will know me, and it will be embarrassin' to us both. I'm wanted in Louisiana— wanted bad by law. I came here to tell what I'd seen, but not to be held, and I can't afford to be on exhibition no way. I toss five hundred in the pot, and I ask to be let go."

Scott Mattaye could still remember, and he could feel his own breath catch again, though that man was a stranger to him always, who had come out of nothing to strike and go away. There they were riding down the road, thrown together for an instant like sticks in a whirlpool. He could almost believe that he was still asleep.

"You—what?" said Scott Mattaye.

Mr. Still turned in his saddle, an impassive, slouching shadow, and his voice was very patient:

"I'm speakin' to a gentleman, who would understand if I could explain what circumstances prevent me explainin', suh. I can only repeat, respectfully, five hundred and thanks, if you just will let me go."

Then Scott was angry. "Mister," he said, "you don't know who you're speaking to. Turn around and ride."

He should have known better, though it did not seem possible that he could be troubled on an open, traveled road. His pistol was still in his holster, but the event occurred so suddenly that he could never quite explain. Mr. Still's horse reared, and before Scott could draw a rein they both were close abreast. Then Scott felt something press against his side. Mr. Still was pointing a pocket pistol directly at his heart. The night was dark, but he could see the weapon. There was no doubt; Mr. Still was holding a pistol at his heart.

"Don't," said Mr. Still. "Trooper, don't you move or holler. Turn off yonder, right smack among those trees."

Scott turned. There was no doubting the man's voice, in spite of its softness; he would be dead if he did not turn. Then they were on a wood road in a thicket of scrub oak.

"There," said Mr. Still; "that's right and neat. Keep your horse still walking. No one's going to hold me where folks I know can stare. Yore colonel thinks he's smart, trooper, but he don't match hands with me. I keep a pocket derringer in my sleeve, and, mind you, she can speak."

Scott did not answer, and Mr. Still's voice rose a note:

"Keep yore hand off that pistol butt, unless you want to die. And get down off your horse. I'm downright sorry, trooper, but I'm going to take both these hosses and tie you to this tree."

"Suppose," said Scott; his voice was thick—"suppose I don't get down."

Though it was too dark to see, he knew that Mr. Still was smiling.

"I'm much afraid," said Mr. Still, "yo'll naturally fall off. This derringer don't look like much, but don't get passionate. Gentlemen are always so powerful rash. . . . Just swing down off that horse."

He remembered what Jeb Stuart said. Nothing could hurt a cavalryman if he had a good horse under him. He leaned to the left and shifted his weight as though preparing to dismount, at the same time gathering his reins more to the left than right. Then he let drive with his spurs at almost the same instant. Scott's mare sprang, striking Still's horse on the shoulder. There was a crack of a pistol, and Scott's left arm felt red hot, but his right was free, and he fired, in that tangle of two plunging horses, point-blank at Mr. Still.

He remembered how his pistol kicked backward in his hand. An oak branch whipped across his eyes, blinding him for an instant. Mr. Still's horse had bolted, when he saw again, and all that remained was something black on the wood road. Mr. Still was lying face downward, quiet and inert. Scott touched him with his toe, but he might as well have touched a bag of meal.

"Still!" said Scott. "You hear me, Still?"

But Mr. Still did not reply. He simply lay there, a dark spot on the road. There was a candle end in his saddlebag. The air was so still that the candle burned smoothly when Scott lighted it. Mr. Still lay in the sphere of light, elegantly listless. His pistol had dropped and lay six inches beyond the reach of his thin fingers.

"Still!" said Scott again. "You hear me?" But Mr. Still did not reply. Scott set down the candle upon a flat stone, seized Mr. Still by the shoulders and propped him against a tree. Mr. Still's face was blank and incurious; his cravat was twisted and covered with leaf mold. There was a stain on his brown coat where Scott Mattaye had shot him through the chest. Scott remembered how a deer had fallen once that he had shot. He had shot wild fowl along the tidewater; he remembered how they fell, open-eyed, incurious, exactly as Mr. Still's eyes had opened, deep, incurious, staring into the light.

"Still!" said Scott, but he doubted if the man had ever heard him.

"Four aces," said Mr. Still. "The cards are falling my way, gentlemen. . . . Sho, Henry, you'll not see me. I've sense enough for that. . . . They're runnin'. There's no mistake. The whole thing's breakin'. . . . Retreat? Why, it's a rout . . . and the cards are all my way. . . . But I won't give you trouble, Henry. I know where I belong."

Then his head dropped sideways, and Scott had the intuition that the man was dead, as clear as knowledge, although it was the first time he had ever killed a man. Scott's head was swimming and his knees were weak. His left arm was bleeding at the shoulder. He tied it with his handkerchief, using his right hand and his teeth. Then he mounted and rode slowly toward the road. He had the colonel's message to deliver, but it no longer seemed important, now that he had killed.

"Sho, Henry," Mr. Still had said, "you'll not see me." And he was right. No one would see Mr. Still again.

The road was full of life. Teams of wounded were jolting toward the junction, and supply wagons were moving to the lines. Furtive, straggling men were plodding along the road, wandering like the lost soul of Mr. Still. All the demoralization of raw troops was there; he could imagine that the whole army was blundering and groping in the night, like a monster whose brains were very small.

It was hard to tell what had happened, once he reached Manassas, for the defense works were manned, and even at that late hour the town was in confusion. The main street was packed with wagons and stretchers, and with wounded propped against the picket fences waiting for the train. In contrast, headquarters was easy enough to find, because the confusion there seemed greater. A small frame house like all the others, it was like a beehive that night. Officers and messengers kept going in and out of the door like bees, and inside there was the same concentrated, humming sound.

"Wait a minute, sonny," a sentry said. "You can't go in there."

"Message," said Scott—"message for the general."

"Sonny," said the sentry, "what do you know of generals? This place is heavin' with generals. Why, the president himself's in yonder. You git used to generals here—and they don't know what they're doing any more'n you."

Then Scott heard a voice he knew: "Scott, what are you doing here this time of night?"

An officer was standing in the doorway. It was his brother-in-law, Hugh Fleece, on General Johnston's staff.

"Message for the general, sir," Scott said. "I had an accident on the road."

"You come inside," Hugh Fleece said. "I'll see someone in just a minute. You come inside and wait."

Plain people had lived in that house until a day or two before. The traces of their humdrum life were clashing with the staccato beat of mysterious forces. He was telling Hugh Fleece what had happened, in short, broken sentences, but even while he spoke his curiosity was strong. There was a small entry with narrow stairs and a dingy run of carpet; there was a chromo on the wall—Scott could remember it—of two dead partridges beside a dish of outrageous-looking fruit, but the space was full of tobacco smoke and voices, coming from rooms to the right and left. Though there had been no violence, some inviolate, quiet attribute of that house had been erased. All the level ties of humdrum life had been broken, and one could grasp the truth of war more clearly there than on a field where a thousand men had died.

Hugh Fleece himself was like that hall. The last time Scott Mattaye had seen him, Hugh Fleece had been in white linen and a broad straw hat. His face had been broad and good-humored, but now he was in a uniform from Lichtenstein's and his face was hard, confused and lined.

"Someone will want to question you," Hugh Fleece said. "This rout report is another of these rumors. Someone will want you. Lord knows who, with everything in such a devil of a mess and no one knowing what is what. Who sent this message—Stuart? Who the devil's Stuart? You'll have to wait. The generals are dining with the president, and no one even rightly knows who is the commanding general. It is all like that up here."

Voices, orderlies, officers shouldering in and out—the place was close and stuffy and as irrational as delirium.

"You're bleeding," said Hugh. "Your sleeve's all over blood."

The mention of his bleeding made Scott faint and dizzy.

"It's just a scratch," he said. "He only grazed me. I—I wish I hadn't killed that man. It—makes me feel right sick."

"You come upstairs," Hugh Fleece said. He was helping him up the stairs. "There's a bed up in our quarters. You lie down and wait. I'll have someone to see you, if anyone will listen. . . . Were you in the fighting? . . . All right, Scott; I'll be back."

Scott should have known that Hugh Fleece would not come back. He should have known that no one would listen in the bedlam of that house.

Scott Mattaye was in a room beneath the eaves, where a lantern was burning very low. The place was strewn with overcoats and waterproof blankets, half covering a broken rocking-chair and a wide spool bed. There were religious mottoes on the wall, and he remembered one. "The Lord hears everything," it read.

Scott lay down upon the bed. He remembered that he almost fell, in a seizure of exhaustion. Then, when he closed his eyes to clear his thoughts, he saw the face of Mr. Still, just as he had seen it first—thoughtful, enigmatic and serene. It seemed to him sometimes that it was more than a memory—

that the spirit of Mr. Still was standing there beside him, lips turned upward in that slow half smile.

He must have been asleep, because, when he opened his eyes, he was confused at first. There were voices, and it seemed to him that the room was full of people, but the voices were incredible. He could not believe he heard. The lantern was so low that the room was almost dark, but he could see that a door beside the bed had opened, letting in a clear, sharp light from an adjoining chamber. It was that adjoining room, not his, that was full of men and voices.

"Risk?" someone was saying, and whoever was speaking was angry. "Has it never come under your observation that war's made up of risk?"

"And don't forget, sir," someone answered, "that I'm the one who must consider it."

"And I tell you," the first voice said more loudly, "you're stopping upstairs here and talking, with the whole war in your hand. One mite of action to-night from a military man, and not a politician, and the South will win this war. You've whipped 'em, and has there been a bona fide effort to pursue? I ask you, has there?"

"General"—it was another voice—"I beg you won't forget you're addressing, among others, the president of the Confederate States of America."

There was a pause, and Scott Mattaye was sitting bolt upright, so startled that he could not move, for he knew what had happened. The adjoining room was full of generals, and the president was there, and Scott Mattaye was in that other room, listening like a spy.

He could feel the quietness of angry men, striving to keep cool. He could feel the presence of an imponderable question, hanging above them like a cloud.

"Thank you, sir," the first voice said. "I understand politics right well, and I'm right well aware whom I'm addressing, and the dangers I run for doing it; none of which impel me to take back a word."

"General," said someone.

"Sir," the first voice answered, "I'll say my say, and then I'll leave this room. I know you rank me, Joe, but just the same I repeat you held your hand short of victory. Will there be such a chance again, gentlemen? No, never! I've heard you talking—fool's talk. You think you've got the Yankee nation whipped and that Europe will intervene, because we've driven a passel of uniformed civilians across Bull Run. Gentlemen, don't you deceive yourselves! You don't know the Yankee nation if you think that—not you, Joe, or you, Beauregard, or you, Mr. President. Yonder northward is a power twice our strength, and they're no pack of cowards.

"You give that nation time, gentlemen, and we'll be crushed as sure as we're in this stuffy room. The sole hope for a weaker power is to wage offensive war. I heard General Jackson at the hospital. He said give him ten thousand men, and he'd be in Washington City, and, gentlemen, he's right. Take Washington, and Baltimore and Maryland will come over. Seize the coal fields and threaten Philadelphia. I repeat we've got 'em in our hands tonight if we dare to take risks. Do this, and we've smashed 'em, gentlemen.

"If supplies don't come up, live off the country. There's enough to feed us. If our army's disorganized, so's theirs. There's nothing to a defeated civilian army. Give Jackson those ten thousand. Give 'em to me tonight, and I'll have Washington for you, gentlemen. Follow up, and we've won this war. Wait here, and we whip ourselves. Thank you for listening, gentlemen. It's all I've got to say."

There was another pause, a slow, long silence. Scott could hear a chair creak; feet shuffled, someone struck a match; and then silence again.

"General," someone said, chillingly polite, "perhaps you have some information you have not divulged. This Northern disorganization you take as fact I do not believe exists. This enemy moved off quietly; his left was not engaged. How do you know he's whipped? We'd admire to hear you tell us, general."

"Intuition, gentlemen," the first voice answered—"a soldier's intuition, who's seen service and read military history; the intuition that makes an officer a leader. Jackson has that intuition. Gentlemen, green troops won't hold together when they're whipped. Longstreet had that intuition when he tried to give 'em canister this afternoon. Rely on intuition when information won't come in."

"Do you think, sir," someone said, "we'll risk our army and the war on the intuition of an ex-professor of the Institute?"

"Gentlemen," the first voice answered, "I'll wish you all good night, because I do not think you will. I've spoken out of duty what I believe the truth, but this I'll add: We'll live to see T. J. Jackson the greatest general of the South. I'll be going back to the lines. Good night, Mr. President. If plain talk has offended you, I'm sorry. Good night, gentlemen."

No one answered. Scott heard footsteps and the closing of a door, and the voice was gone—always a voice to him. It was gone into the limbo of memories, for he never heard that voice again, nor knew the owner of that voice. There was the same silence, heavy, dull. He could hear the rumble of wagons outside, teamsters calling and the crack of whips.

"If you want to have a good time," someone was singing outside—"a good time——"

It was the song that Stuart's cavalry sang, but the voice seemed very distant. A chair creaked again, and someone said:

"There goes another hot-head. . . . What are we going to do?"

There was another pause; no answer.

"This is an unconfirmed report, gentlemen, that their retreat across Cub Run has degenerated into a panic, but we've only heard it from one source. Is Major Hill downstairs? Shall we call him up again?"

There was a hint of laughter, decorous and faint.

"Colonel," said someone, "will you fetch up Major Hill?"

There were footsteps again, and the closing of a door.

"If you want to have a good time." Scott could hear the voice outside singing the song again. Scott could feel himself being drawn nearer the door, for, in some strange way, the war had narrowed down to Scott Mattaye and the message in his hand.

"Here he is," said someone. . . . "Major Hill, please repeat to us what you saw again."

"I said, sir," Scott could hear a voice stuttering with suppressed excitement, "the road was blocked with abandoned artillery and wagons. No one was there. I give you my word it's not a retreat but a rout, sir. There's no resistance. There's——"

"Thank you," someone interrupted; "that will do." And there was another silence.

"May I ask who is that officer?"

"He's on my staff, Mr. President," came the answer. "One of the Hills, sir—old army. Come to think of it, he goes by the name of Crazy Hill."

The tenseness seemed to relax again into a faint hint of mirth. "Crazy Hill—why do they call him that?"

"A nickname from the academy, Mr. President, gained from his manner, but there has been no reflection on his conduct or intelligence."

"And all we have to rely on tonight is the report of Crazy Hill?"

It seemed to Scott that his blood was congealed, but he knew he could not wait. He pulled on the half-opened door, and next he was standing in a small room lighted by a lamp placed on the center of a deal table. Maps were on the table—heaps of maps and papers. There were perhaps eight men seated around this table, tired, stained officers with heavy beards and mustaches, but Scott Mattaye could never recollect the number or get their faces straight. They were all in the uniforms of generals or staff officers except one, who wore a black frock coat, setting off a slender, well-proportioned figure. His face was clean-shaven and handsome, a proud, self-conscious face. The nose was very straight; the lips were thin. Scott had seen him in the distance once, and Scott knew who he was—Jefferson Davis, president of the Confederate States of America.

"Beg pardon, sir," Scott said, and he began to stutter exactly like Crazy Hill. "I have a message for the general. I was waiting, but I thought he ought to see it, sir."

"Colonel"—a general officer, a short, peppery-looking man, half rose from his chair—"what's all this? Who let this fool in here?"

Scott flushed. He was still young enough in those days not to be awed by rank.

"I was told to wait here," he said, "in the room yonder, until someone could see me about a message I was to deliver to the general, and I've waited a right long time. I'm from Colonel Stuart, sir, with a message for General Johnston. A man from Centerville came to our picket, sir, with news the Yankees are running. There's not a fighting force between here and Washington, he said. And when I heard the gentlemen speaking—— I'm not a fool, general, if you please."

Everyone was staring at him. He saw the general's face grow red.

"Damnation!" said the general. "Have you been listening at the door? What idiot let you up here, and what's your name?"

Scott Mattaye stood up straighter, and the implication in the general's tone made him speak out plainly:

"I'm Mattaye, sir—Scott Mattaye from Deer Bottom. I was put in that next room and told to wait. It wasn't my fault the door came open, sir. If I've heard anything I should not have heard, I shall be pleased to go outside and shoot myself, sir. It's all that I can do."

He thought they were impressed by what he said, for their expressions had subtly changed.

"The Mattayes?" The president was speaking. "Of course. I know the family. He sounds like a Mattaye."

The general leaned back in his chair. "He sounds as sensible as half the nation," he said. "Wouldn't you be better pleased to keep your mouth shut, or would you rather shoot yourself?"

Then everyone was laughing, as though something in the room had snapped, bursting into strands of mirth.

Scott Mattaye had never been ashamed as he was then, for he had spoken as a gentleman, according to his best tradition. Another general officer had risen from the table—also small, with delicately formed hands—and he walked toward Scott Mattaye with quick, neat steps.

"Excuse!" he said in a slightly foreign accent. "There is General Johnston. Give him your message, please."

They had spread the message on the table, and next they were reading it over one another's shoulders.

"He's right," someone said. "They're running like a pack of hounds. Why didn't we get this before? Who kept this man waiting?"

No one answered, and even Scott Mattaye could see that the confusion of the army was in that room, with no one who could call for order.

"'Man forwarded for questioning,'" said someone, reading from the message. "Well, where is he, trooper?"

They would have been pleased to see him dead if he could have brought in Mr. Still alive.

"Man, where's your prisoner? Did you leave him with the guard?"

"He's dead," said Scott Mattaye. "I killed him."

"Killed him!" someone shouted. "Do you know what you've done? You've killed the only man who's seen the Yankees running!"

Then it seemed to Scott Mattaye that Mr. Still was there. He could have sworn that the shade of Mr. Still was standing just beside him.

"I reckon I couldn't help it," said Scott Mattaye. "It was him or me. He had a pistol on me. He tried to get away."

"Nonsense," said someone. "He had valuable information. Why should he try to get away?"

"He was wanted south, sir," Scott answered. "He was afraid that someone here would know him and I reckon he was proud. He was a gambling man."

Then, across the table, Scott saw the face of a staff colonel. He had not noticed the officer before, but now that Scott saw him, he stood out beyond all the other figures in that room. It seemed to Scott that he was looking straight into the eyes of Mr. Still, though Mr. Still was dead.

"A gambler, you said?" The officer was speaking. His eyes were deep and dark like Mr. Still's. Scott never knew his name. "Did this man say who he was?"

"He gave the name of Still, sir," Scott answered—"Jack Still."

A pale light flickered across the colonel's face, but his expression did not change.

"I see he touched you in the arm. A dark, thin man?"

"Yes, sir," said Scott, and their eyes met for an instant, and Scott could read the other's eyes as clearly as a printed page.

"Don't tell," the eyes were saying—"don't tell any more."

"Gentlemen"—the officer cleared his throat—"I knew this man. He was dangerous, and of course the trooper only did what's right. But I'll say this: I knew Jack Still. If he said the Yankees were running, you can believe that message every word, because I knew Jack Still."

"Colonel," someone asked, "he knew you were back here?"

The colonel's voice was smooth as velvet, and slow and peaceful like that other voice.

"Yes, sir," he answered, "I reckon that he knew."

Then the president was speaking, and Scott Mattaye was never sure, but sometimes he thought that the president's voice was changed:

"Gentlemen, we can't talk here all night. If the trooper will go into the next room and close the door, I should like to see him later."

Then Scott was standing in lantern light, where the closed door shut off the distinctness of the voices, which were sometimes faint and sometimes loud.

"Don't tell," the officer's eyes were saying—"don't tell any more."

His thoughts were all confusion, like the battle and the army and the sounds beyond the door. He had only heard half secrets, but the talk of armies moving was nothing to the expression on that one man's face.

"I see he touched you in the arm," the officer had said. "A dark, thin man?"

"Yes, sir." And Scott had nearly added: "About your height and build."

He had not realized what had made him stop, but he knew, now that he was alone. He had stopped from instinctive delicacy, because that colonel of the staff resembled Mr. Still. Their height and build, their eyes and voices were alike. He had not spoken of such a matter, and he would not, because no gentleman would speak.

It must have been half an hour later when he heard a tapping on the door.

"Trooper"—he knew the voice—"you may come in now."

When Scott came in, the president was standing in the room alone. The chairs were pushed back from the table, empty, but the maps and papers were still there.

"Sir?" said Scott Mattaye, but Mr. Davis was not looking at him. "Did you call me, sir?"

The president was holding a paper in his hand, and he did not appear to have heard Scott speak, for he seemed removed from everything except from his own mind. Before he answered he tore the paper once across the center, gathered the pieces and tore them once again. Then he looked at Scott Mattaye and smiled. He had a winning, pleasant smile.

"Do you know what I've torn up?" he asked, just as though he and Scott were friends.

"No, sir," Scott answered.

The president looked at him for a moment. He had level eyes; his forehead was wide and fine.

"But you can guess?" he said.

He could guess, although he did not answer, and the president seemed pleased.

"Very well, if you can guess, I'll tell you. I've torn up the orders for immediate pursuit. Some day you can tell your children that you very nearly made the army move tonight—very nearly, with the information of a gambler, backed by a man named Crazy Hill. You'll never know all the circumstances. I may be wrong, but I'm not a gambling man."

Scott Mattaye did not answer. That burst of frankness could surprise him still, for he could never explain it, except that the man was obliged to speak to someone through some reflex of emotion. He came to know that there were times when anyone must speak.

"No," said the president again, "I'm not a gambling man, Mattaye."

"Yes, sir," answered Scott, and he knew that the president was not a gambling man.

"That man—your prisoner—did he resemble anyone in this room?"

"No, sir," answered Scott; "not that I remember."

"The officer who spoke to you"—the president clasped his hands behind his back—"was moved; he was under an emotion. Was there no resemblance?"

"No, sir," answered Scott; "none that I remember."

The president had seen exactly what he had seen, and the knowledge passed wordlessly between them.

"Mattaye, I like a man who can't remember. You understand? I know you understand. There are circumstances one must not remember after they have happened. Shall we call this one? I like a man who can forget, and I should be very pleased to have you in my family."

"Your family, sir?" said Scott, and the president smiled again.

"Not as a private, Mattaye, but as an officer who can see. There were men here tonight who did not like me, and you could see. I shall be plainer later, but I repeat I've watched you, and I have the intuition that you will be very useful. I should be glad to have you in my family as an aide."

"But why, sir?" Scott asked him. "Why do you want me?"

The president stepped closer to him and lowered his voice:

"Because your prisoner was a brother of an officer in this room. You knew, and you saved the pain of making it obvious, because you are a gentleman."

The president was waiting. Scott looked down at his uniform, bleached by the sun already, and misshapen by the weather. The president was waiting and the room was hot and still. He could hear the wagons outside. "If you want to have a good time—a good time——" The echo of the song he had heard was moving through his mind. The cavalry—there were no subtleties or secrets in the cavalry. Out on the edge of the army, Jeb Stuart could say what he felt and thought, without caution, without fear. There were no rooms or voices on outpost with the cavalry. He looked at the president again, in his black frock coat—neat, precise and poised. "If you want to have a good time——"

The president was waiting.

"Is that an order, sir?" asked Scott Mattaye.

"No." The other seemed surprised. "An invitation, not an order."

"Then, sir," said Scott, "if it's no order, I'd prefer—I'm much honored, sir, but I'd rather be out with the cavalry."

There was no resentment in the cavalry, or spite, such as Scott saw for an instant before that slim man turned away. He had held the war in his hand, and had dropped it, and Scott knew why—because he was not great enough to hold a war.

"Very well," he replied. "I see I was mistaken. Go back with the cavalry."

THE SILVER MASK

HUGH WALPOLE

MISS SONIA HERRIES, coming home from a dinner-party at the Westons', heard a voice at her elbow.

'If you please—only a moment——'

She had walked from the Westons' flat because it was only three streets away, and now she was only a few steps from her door, but it was late, there was no one about and the King's Road rattle was muffled and dim.

'I am afraid I can't——' she began. It was cold, and the wind nipped her cheeks.

'If you would only——' he went on.

She turned and saw one of the handsomest young men possible. He was the handsome young man of all romantic stories, tall, dark, pale, slim, distinguished—oh! everything!—and he was wearing a shabby blue suit and shivering with the cold just as he should have been.

'I'm afraid I can't——' she repeated, beginning to move on.

'Oh, I know,' he interrupted quickly. 'Everyone says the same, and quite naturally. I should if our positions were reversed. But I *must* go on with it. I *can't* go back to my wife and baby with simply nothing. We have no fire, no food, nothing except the ceiling we are under. It is my fault, all of it. I don't want your pity, but I *have* to attack your comfort.'

He trembled. He shivered as though he were going to fall. Involuntarily she put out her hand to steady him. She touched his arm and felt it quiver under the thin sleeve.

'It's all right . . .' he murmured. 'I'm hungry . . . I can't help it.'

She had had an excellent dinner. She had drunk perhaps just enough to lead to recklessness—in any case, before she realised it, she was ushering him in, through her dark-blue painted door. A crazy thing to do! Nor was it as though she were too young to know any better, for she was fifty if she was a day and, although sturdy of body and as strong as a horse (except for a little unsteadiness of the heart), intelligent enough to be thin, neurotic and abnormal; but she was none of these.

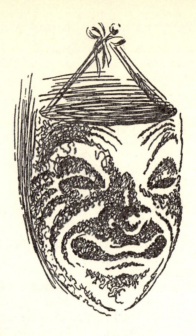

Although intelligent she suffered dreadfully from impulsive kindness. All her life she had done so. The mistakes that she had made—and there had been quite a few—had all arisen from the triumph of her heart over her brain. She knew it—how well she knew it!—and all her friends were for ever dinning it into her. When she reached her fiftieth birthday she said to herself, 'Well, now at last I'm too old to be foolish any more.' And here she was, helping an entirely unknown young man into her house at dead of night, and he in all probability the worst sort of criminal.

Very soon he was sitting on her rose-coloured sofa, eating sandwiches and drinking a whisky and soda. He seemed to be entirely overcome by the beauty of her possessions. 'If he's acting he's doing it very well,' she thought to herself. But he had taste and he had knowledge. He knew that the Utrillo was an early one, the only period of importance in that master's work, he knew that the two old men talking under a window belonged to Sickert's 'Middle Italian,' he recognised the Dobson head and the wonderful green bronze Elk of Carl Milles.

'You are an artist,' she said. 'You paint?'

'No, I am a pimp, a thief, a what you like—anything bad,' he answered fiercely. 'And now I must go,' he added, springing up from the sofa.

He seemed most certainly invigorated. She could scarcely believe that he was the same young man who only half an hour before had had to lean on her arm for support. And he was a gentleman. Of that there could be no sort of question. And he was astoundingly beautiful in the spirit of a hundred years ago, a young Byron, a young Shelley, not a young Ramón Novarro or a young Ronald Colman.

Well, it was better that he should go, and she did hope (for his own sake rather than hers) that he would not demand money and threaten a scene. After all, with her snow-white hair, firm broad chin, firm broad body, she did not look like someone who could be threatened. He had not apparently the slightest intention of threatening her. He moved towards the door.

'Oh!' he murmured with a little gasp of wonder. He had stopped before one of the loveliest things that she had—a mask in silver of a clown's face, the clown smiling, gay, joyful, not hinting at perpetual sadness as all clowns are traditionally supposed to do. It was one of the most successful efforts of the famous Sorat, greatest living master of Masks.

'Yes. Isn't that lovely?' she said. 'It was one of Sorat's earliest things, and still, I think, one of his best.'

'Silver is the right material for that clown,' he said.

'Yes, I think so too,' she agreed. She realised that she had asked him nothing about his troubles, about his poor wife and baby, about his past history. It was better perhaps like this.

'You have saved my life,' he said to her in the hall. She had in her hand a pound note.

'Well,' she answered cheerfully, 'I was a fool to risk a strange man in my house at this time of night—or so my friends would tell me. But such an old woman like me—where's the risk?'

'I could have cut your throat,' he said quite seriously.

'So you could,' she admitted. 'But with horrid consequences to yourself.'

'Oh no,' he said. 'Not in these days. The police are never able to catch anybody.'

'Well, good-night. Do take this. It can get you some warmth at least.'

He took the pound. 'Thanks,' he said carelessly. Then at the door he remarked: 'That mask. The loveliest thing I ever saw.'

When the door had closed and she went back into the sitting-room she sighed:

'What a good-looking young man!' Then she saw that her most beautiful white jade cigarette-case was gone. It had been lying on the little table by the sofa. She had seen it just before she went into the pantry to cut the sandwiches. He had stolen it. She looked everywhere. No, undoubtedly he had stolen it.

'What a good-looking young man!' she thought as she went up to bed.

Sonia Herries was a woman of her time in that outwardly she was cynical and destructive while inwardly she was a creature longing for affection and appreciation. For though she had white hair and was fifty she was outwardly active, young, could do with little sleep and less food, could dance and drink cocktails and play bridge to the end of all time. Inwardly she cared for neither cocktails nor bridge. She was above all things maternal and she had a weak heart, not only a spiritual weak heart but also a physical one. When she suffered, must take her drops, lie down and rest, she allowed no one to see her. Like all the other women of her period and manner of life she had a courage worthy of a better cause.

She was a heroine for no reason at all.

But, beyond everything else, she was maternal. Twice at least she would have married had she loved enough, but the man she had really loved had not loved her (that was twenty-five years ago), so she had pretended to despise matrimony. Had she had a child her nature would have been fulfilled; as she had not had that good fortune she had been maternal (with outward cynical indifference) to numbers of people who had made use of her, sometimes laughed at her, never deeply cared for her. She was named 'a jolly good sort,' and was always 'just outside' the real life of her friends. Her Herries relations, Rockages and Cards and Newmarks, used her to take odd places at table, to fill up spare rooms at house-parties, to make purchases for them in London, to talk to when things went wrong with them or people abused them. She was a very lonely woman.

She saw her young thief for the second time a fortnight later. She saw him because he came to her house one evening when she was dressing for dinner.

'A young man at the door,' said her maid Rose.

'A young man? Who?' But she knew.

'I don't know, Miss Sonia. He won't give his name.'

She came down and found him in the hall, the cigarette-case in his hand. He was wearing a decent suit of clothes, but he still looked hungry, haggard, desperate and incredibly handsome. She took him into the room where they had been before. He gave her the cigarette-case. 'I pawned it,' he said, his eyes on the silver mask.

'What a disgraceful thing to do!' she said. 'And what are you going to steal next?'

'My wife made some money last week,' he said. 'That will see us through for a while.'

'Do you never do any work?' she asked him.

'I paint,' he answered. 'But no one will touch my pictures. They are not modern enough.'

'You must show me some of your pictures,' she said, and realised how weak she was. It was not his good looks that gave him his power over her, but something both helpless and defiant, like a wicked child who hates his mother but is always coming to her for help.

'I have some here,' he said, went into the hall, and returned with several canvases. He displayed them. They were very bad—sugary landscapes and sentimental figures.

'They are very bad,' she said.

'I know they are. You must understand that my æsthetic taste is very fine. I appreciate only the best things in art, like your cigarette-case, that mask there, the Utrillo. But I can paint nothing but these. It is very exasperating.' He smiled at her.

'Won't you buy one?' he asked her.

'Oh, but I don't want one,' she answered. 'I should have to hide it.' She was aware that in ten minutes her guests would be here.

'Oh, do buy one.'

'No, but of course not——'

'Yes, please.' He came nearer and looked up into her broad kindly face like a beseeching child.

'Well . . . how much are they?'

'This is twenty pounds. This twenty-five——'

'But how absurd! They are not worth anything at all.'

'They may be one day. You never know with modern pictures.'

'I am quite sure about these.'

'Please buy one. That one with the cows is not so bad.'

She sat down and wrote a cheque.

'I'm a perfect fool. Take this, and understand I never want to see you again. Never! You will never be admitted. It is no use speaking to me in the street. If you bother me I shall tell the police.'

He took the cheque with quiet satisfaction, held out his hand and pressed hers a little.

'Hang that in the right light and it will not be so bad——'

'You want new boots,' she said. 'Those are terrible.'

'I shall be able to get some now,' he said and went away.

All that evening while she listened to the hard and crackling ironies of her friends she thought of the young man. She did not know his name. The only thing that she knew about him was that by his own confession he was a scoundrel and had at his mercy a poor young wife and a starving child. The picture that she formed of these three haunted her. It had been, in a way, honest of him to return the cigarette-case. Ah, but he knew, of course, that did he not return it he could never have seen her again. He had discovered at once that she was a splendid source of supply, and now that she had bought one of his wretched pictures—— Nevertheless he could not be altogether bad. No one who cared so passionately for beautiful things could be quite worthless. The way that he had gone straight to the silver mask as soon as he entered the room and gazed at it as though with his very soul! And, sitting at her dinner-table, uttering the most cynical sentiments, she was all softness as she gazed across to the wall upon whose pale surface the silver mask was hanging. There was, she thought, a certain look of the young man in that jolly shining surface. But where? The clown's cheek was fat, his mouth broad, his lips thick—and yet, and yet——

For the next few days as she went about London she looked in spite of herself at the passers-by to see whether he might not be there. One thing she soon discovered, that he was very much more handsome than anyone else whom she saw. But it was not for his handsomeness that he haunted her. It was because he wanted her to be kind to him, and because she wanted—oh, so terribly—to be kind to someone!

The silver mask, she had the fancy, was gradually changing, the rotundity thinning, some new light coming into the empty eyes. It was most certainly a beautiful thing.

Then, as unexpectedly as on the other occasions, he appeared again. One

night as she, back from a theatre, smoking one last cigarette, was preparing to
climb the stairs to bed, there was a knock on the door. Everyone of course
rang the bell—no one attempted the old-fashioned knocker shaped like an
owl that she had bought, one idle day, in an old curiosity shop. The knock
made her sure that it was he. Rose had gone to bed, so she went herself to
the door. There he was—and with him a young girl and a baby. They all
came into the sitting-room and stood awkwardly by the fire. It was at that
moment when she saw them in a group by the fire that she felt her first sharp
pang of fear. She knew suddenly how weak she was—she seemed to be turned
to water at sight of them, she, Sonia Herries, fifty years of age, independent
and strong, save for that little flutter of the heart—yes, turned to water! She
was afraid as though someone had whispered a warning in her ear.

The girl was striking, with red hair and a white face, a thin graceful little
thing. The baby, wrapped in a shawl, was soaked in sleep. She gave them
drinks and the remainder of the sandwiches that had been put there for
herself. The young man looked at her with his charming smile.

'We haven't come to cadge anything this time,' he said. 'But I wanted
you to see my wife and I wanted her to see some of your lovely things.'

'Well,' she said sharply, 'you can only stay a minute or two. It's late. I'm
off to bed. Besides, I told you not to come here again.'

'Ada made me,' he said, nodding at the girl. 'She was so anxious to see you.'

The girl never said a word but only stared sulkily in front of her.

'All right. But you must go soon. By the way, you've never told me your
name.'

'Henry Abbott, and that's Ada, and the baby's called Henry too.'

'All right. How have you been getting on since I saw you?'

'Oh, fine! Living on the fat of the land.' But he soon fell into silence and
the girl never said a word. After an intolerable pause Sonia Herries suggested
that they should go. They didn't move. Half an hour later she insisted. They
got up. But, standing by the door, Henry Abbott jerked his head towards the
writing-desk.

'Who writes your letters for you?'

'Nobody. I write them myself.'

'You ought to have somebody. Save a lot of trouble. I'll do them for you.'

'Oh no, thank you. That would never do. Well, good-night, good-night——'

'Of course I'll do them for you. And you needn't pay me anything either.
Fill up my time.'

'Nonsense . . . good-night, good-night.' She closed the door on them. She
could not sleep. She lay there thinking of him. She was moved, partly by a
maternal tenderness for them that warmed her body (the girl and the baby
had looked so helpless sitting there), partly by a shiver of apprehension that
chilled her veins. Well, she hoped that she would never see them again. Or
did she? Would she not to-morrow, as she walked down Sloane Street, stare
at everyone to see whether by chance that was he?

Three mornings later he arrived. It was a wet morning and she had decided to devote it to the settling of accounts. She was sitting there at her table when Rose showed him in.

'I've come to do your letters,' he said.

'I should think not,' she said sharply. 'Now, Henry Abbott, out you go. I've had enough——'

'Oh no, you haven't,' he said, and sat down at her desk.

She would be ashamed for ever, but half an hour later she was seated in the corner of the sofa telling him what to write. She hated to confess it to herself, but she liked to see him sitting there. He was company for her, and to whatever depths he might by now have sunk, he was most certainly a gentleman. He behaved very well that morning; he wrote an excellent hand. He seemed to know just what to say.

A week later she said, laughing, to Amy Weston: 'My dear, would you believe it? I've had to take on a secretary. A very good-looking young man— but you needn't look down your nose. You know that good-looking young men are nothing to *me*—and he does save me endless bother.'

For three weeks he behaved very well, arriving punctually, offering her no insults, doing as she suggested about everything. In the fourth week, about a quarter to one on a day, his wife arrived. On this occasion she looked astonishingly young, sixteen perhaps. She wore a simple grey cotton dress. Her red bobbed hair was strikingly vibrant about her pale face.

The young man already knew that Miss Herries was lunching alone. He had seen the table laid for one with its simple appurtenances. It seemed to be very difficult not to ask them to remain. She did, although she did not wish to. The meal was not a success. The two of them together were tiresome, for the man said little when his wife was there, and the woman said nothing at all. Also the pair of them were in a way sinister.

She sent them away after luncheon. They departed without protest. But as she walked, engaged on her shopping that afternoon, she decided that she must rid herself of them, once and for all. It was true that it had been rather agreeable having him there; his smile, his wicked humorous remarks, the suggestion that he was a kind of malevolent gamin who preyed on the world in general but spared her because he liked her—all this had attracted her—but what really alarmed her was that during all these weeks he had made no request for money, made indeed no request for anything. He must be piling up a fine account, must have some plan in his head with which one morning he would balefully startle her! For a moment there in the bright sunlight, with the purr of the traffic, the rustle of the trees about her, she saw herself in surprising colour. She was behaving with a weakness that was astonishing. Her stout, thick-set, resolute body, her cheery rosy face, her strong white hair —all these disappeared, and in their place, there almost clinging for support to the Park railings, was a timorous little old woman with frightened eyes and trembling knees. What was there to be afraid of? She had done nothing wrong. There were the police at hand. She had never been a coward before. She went home, however, with an odd impulse to leave her comfortable little house in Walpole Street and hide herself somewhere, somewhere that no one could discover.

That evening they appeared again, husband, wife and baby. She had settled herself down for a cosy evening with a book and an 'early to bed.' There came the knock on the door.

On this occasion she was most certainly firm with them. When they were gathered in a little group she got up and addressed them.

'Here is five pounds,' she said, 'and this is the end. If one of you shows his or her face inside this door again I call the police. Now go.'

The girl gave a little gasp and fell in a dead faint at her feet. It was a perfectly genuine faint. Rose was summoned. Everything possible was done.

'She has simply not had enough to eat,' said Henry Abbott. In the end (so determined and resolved was the faint) Ada Abbott was put to bed in the spare room and a doctor was summoned. After examining her he said that she needed rest and nourishment. This was perhaps the critical moment of the whole affair. Had Sonia Herries been at this crisis properly resolute and bundled the Abbott family, faint and all, into the cold unsympathising street, she might at this moment be a hale and hearty old woman enjoying bridge with her friends. It was, however, just here that her maternal temperament was too strong for her. The poor young thing lay exhausted, her eyes closed, her cheeks almost the colour of her pillow. The baby (surely the quietest baby ever known) lay in a cot beside the bed. Henry Abbott wrote letters to dictation downstairs. Once Sonia Herries, glancing up at the silver mask, was struck by the grin on the clown's face. It seemed to her now a thin sharp grin—almost derisive.

Three days after Ada Abbott's collapse there arrived her aunt and her uncle, Mr. and Mrs. Edwards. Mr. Edwards was a large red-faced man with a hearty manner and a bright waistcoat. He looked like a publican. Mrs. Edwards was a thin sharp-nosed woman with a bass voice. She was very, very thin, and wore a large old-fashioned brooch on her flat but emotional chest. They sat side by side on the sofa and explained that they had come to enquire after Ada, their favourite niece. Mrs. Edwards cried, Mr. Edwards was friendly and familiar. Unfortunately Mrs. Weston and a friend came and called just then. They did not stay very long. They were frankly amazed at the Edwards couple and deeply startled by Henry Abbott's familiarity. Sonia Herries could see that they drew the very worst conclusions.

A week later Ada Abbott was still in bed in the upstairs room. It seemed to be impossible to move her. The Edwardses were constant visitors. On one occasion they brought Mr. and Mrs. Harper and their girl Agnes. They were profusely apologetic, but Miss Herries would understand that 'with the interest they took in Ada it was impossible to stay passive.' They all crowded into the spare bedroom and gazed at the pale figure with the closed eyes sympathetically.

Then two things happened together. Rose gave notice and Mrs. Weston came and had a frank talk with her friend. She began with that most sinister opening: 'I think you ought to know, dear, what everyone is saying——' What everyone was saying was that Sonia Herries was living with a young ruffian from the streets, young enough to be her son.

'You must get rid of them all and at once,' said Mrs. Weston, 'or you won't have a friend left in London, darling.'

Left to herself, Sonia Herries did what she had not done for years, she burst into tears. What had happened to her? Not only had her will and determination gone but she felt most unwell. Her heart was bad again; she could not sleep; the house, too, was tumbling to pieces. There was dust over everything. How was she ever to replace Rose? She was living in some horrible nightmare. This dreadful handsome young man seemed to have some authority over her. Yet he did not threaten her. All he did was to smile. Nor was she in the very least in love with him. This must come to an end or she would be lost.

Two days later, at tea-time, her opportunity arrived. Mr. and Mrs. Edwards had called to see how Ada was; Ada was downstairs at last, very weak and pale. Henry Abbott was there, also the baby. Sonia Herries, although she was feeling dreadfully unwell, addressed them all with vigour. She especially addressed the sharp-nosed Mrs. Edwards.

'You must understand,' she said. 'I don't want to be unkind, but I have my own life to consider. I am a very busy woman, and this has all been forced on me. I don't want to seem brutal. I'm glad to have been of some assistance to you, but I think Mrs. Abbott is well enough to go home now—and I wish you all good-night.'

'I am sure,' said Mrs. Edwards, looking up at her from the sofa, 'that you've been kindness itself, Miss Herries. Ada recognises it, I'm sure. But to move her now would be to kill her, that's all. Any movement and she'll drop at your feet.'

'We have nowhere to go,' said Henry Abbott.

'But, Mrs. Edwards——' began Miss Herries, her anger rising.

'We have only two rooms,' said Mrs. Edwards quietly. 'I'm sorry, but just now, what with my husband coughing all night——'

'Oh, but this is monstrous!' Miss Herries cried. 'I have had enough of this. I have been generous to a degree——'

'What about my pay,' said Henry, 'for all these weeks?'

'Pay! Why, of course——' Miss Herries began. Then she stopped. She realised several things. She realised that she was alone in the house, the cook having departed that afternoon. She realised that none of them had moved. She realised that her 'things'—the Sickert, the Utrillo, the sofa—were alive with apprehension. She was fearfully frightened of their silence, their immobility. She moved towards her desk, and her heart turned, squeezed itself dry, shot through her body the most dreadful agony.

'Please,' she gasped. 'In the drawer—the little green bottle—oh, quick! Please, please!'

The last thing of which she was aware was the quiet handsome features of Henry Abbott bending over her.

When, a week later, Mrs. Weston called, the girl, Ada Abbott, opened the door to her.

'I came to enquire for Miss Herries,' she said. 'I haven't seen her about. I have telephoned several times and received no answer.'

'Miss Herries is very ill.'

'Oh, I'm so sorry. Can I not see her?'

Ada Abbott's quiet gentle tones were reassuring her. 'The doctor does not wish her to see anyone at present. May I have your address? I will let you know as soon as she is well enough.'

Mrs. Weston went away. She recounted the event. 'Poor Sonia, she's pretty bad. They seem to be looking after her. As soon as she's better we'll go and see her.'

The London life moves swiftly. Sonia Herries had never been of very great importance to anyone. Herries relations enquired. They received a very polite note assuring them that so soon as she was better——

Sonia Herries was in bed, but not in her own room. She was in the little attic bedroom but lately occupied by Rose, the maid. She lay at first in a strange apathy. She was ill. She slept and woke and slept again. Ada Abbott, sometimes Mrs. Edwards, sometimes a woman she did not know, attended to her. They were all very kind. Did she need a doctor? No, of course she did not need a doctor, they assured her. They would see that she had everything that she wanted.

Then life began to flow back into her. Why was she in this room? Where were her friends? What was this horrible food that they were bringing her? What were they doing here, these women?

She had a terrible scene with Ada Abbott. She tried to get out of bed. The girl restrained her—and easily, for all the strength seemed to have gone from her bones. She protested, she was as furious as her weakness allowed her, then she cried. She cried most bitterly. Next day she was alone and she crawled out of bed; the door was locked; she beat on it. There was no sound but her beating. Her heart was beginning again that terrible strangled throb. She crept back into bed. She lay there, weakly, feebly crying. When Ada arrived with some bread, some soup, some water, she demanded that the door should be unlocked, that she should get up, have her bath, come downstairs to her own room.

'You are not well enough,' Ada said gently.

'Of course I am well enough. When I get out I will have you put in prison for this——'

'Please don't get excited. It is so bad for your heart.'

Mrs. Edwards and Ada washed her. She had not enough to eat. She was always hungry.

Summer had come. Mrs. Weston went to Etretat. Everyone was out of town.

'What's happened to Sonia Herries?' Mabel Newmark wrote to Agatha Benson. 'I haven't seen her for ages. . . .'

But no one had time to enquire. There were so many things to do. Sonia was a good sort, but she had been nobody's business. . . .

Once Henry Abbott paid her a visit. 'I am so sorry that you are not better,' he said smiling. 'We are doing everything we can for you. It is lucky we were around when you were so ill. You had better sign these papers. Someone must look after your affairs until you are better. You will be downstairs in a week or two.'

Looking at him with wide-open terrified eyes, Sonia Herries signed the papers.

The first rains of autumn lashed the streets. In the sitting-room the gramophone was turned on. Ada and young Mr. Jackson, Maggie Trent and stout Harry Bennett were dancing. All the furniture was flung against the walls. Mr. Edwards drank his beer; Mrs. Edwards was toasting her toes before the fire.

Henry Abbott came in. He had just sold the Utrillo. His arrival was greeted with cheers.

He took the silver mask from the wall and went upstairs. He climbed to the top of the house, entered, switched on the naked light.

'Oh! Who—what——?' A voice of terror came from the bed.

'It's all right,' he said soothingly. 'Ada will be bringing your tea in a minute.'

He had a hammer and nail and hung the silver mask on the speckled, mottled wall-paper where Miss Herries could see it.

'I know you're fond of it,' he said. 'I thought you'd like it to look at.'

She made no reply. She only stared.

'You'll want something to look at,' he went on. 'You're too ill, I'm afraid, ever to leave this room again. So it'll be nice for you. Something to look at.'

He went out, gently closing the door behind him.

THE RETURN OF THE RANGERS

KENNETH ROBERTS

I

SOMEWHERE I have heard that after the first three days of fasting a man has no further desire for food, and that after thirty days he feels no discomfort whatever: that his brain is clear, his body pure, and his endurance almost unlimited. I suspect that statement in toto. I don't believe in the benefits of fasting, and ever since I tried it in the company of Major Robert Rogers on the St. Francis Expedition, I have been strongly opposed to it.

After we had seen the logs of our raft plunge over the edge of the falls, we dragged ourselves higher up the bank, dropped to the ground and lay there. Even Rogers was supine for a time—though not for long. He got to his knees. "This is no place to stay," he said. "We can't stay anywhere without a fire. We'd freeze. There'll be wood on the bank below the falls." He stood up, swaying. "That's where we go next," he said. "Come on."

We crawled after him; and it was as he said. There was wood in plenty along the shore beyond the falls, though not such wood as would build a raft. There were whole trees, hard wood for the most part, and waterlogged; windrows of twigs and branches; untold quantities of splintered pines of varying sizes, shattered by the ice-jams of previous springs.

Rogers shook his head when he had crawled over the largest of those wood-heaps. "The only thing we can do today," he told us, "is try to get warm. Maybe tomorrow we can figure out something better."

We built ourselves another fence and a roaring fire of driftwood: then stripped ourselves and dried our shredded blankets and our sorry remnants of garments. So tattered and so rotted were those wretched rags that they were next to worthless as covering, and worse than worthless as protection against cold.

Our persons, in a way, were as bad as our clothes. I was ashamed, almost, to look at Rogers and Ogden. Their scrawny bodies seemed caricatures of what they ought to be—like bodies formed by a sculptor with no knowledge of anatomy. Their muscles were stringy as those of a skun wildcat: their

From *Northwest Passage* by Kenneth Roberts. Copyright 1936, 1937 by Kenneth Roberts. Reprinted by permission of Doubleday & Company, Inc.

knees and elbows strangely knobby: their stomachs hollowed and their ribs protuberant like those of a hake that has lain for days upon a beach.

Rogers was covered with scars—red scars, blue scars, white scars. Some were bullet wounds, while others looked as though made by the claws or teeth of animals. Ogden's two bullet-holes, so recently healed, were a flaming purple, rimmed with crimson.

When the strips we called our clothes were dry, we huddled close to the fire, listening to the everlasting roar of White River Falls. The fire warmed me, and drugged by that warmth and the thunder in my ears, I neither knew how we could move from where we were, nor did I care.

II

It was a good thing for us, in a way, that we were wrecked at White River Falls. If the falls had not been there to provide us with windrows of firewood: if we had spent the night in a spot where we would have had only the fuel that we cut, we would probably have died of exhaustion and cold. Our exertions on the raft had drained us of our last reserves of strength, and it was beyond our power to drive a hatchet into a tree. As for the cold, it was so bitter that in the morning the mist from the falls had cased every branch and rock and dead leaf in a glittering envelope of ice.

We lay beside the fire until the sun had come up to take off the knife-like bite of the air.

"We'll have to eat," Rogers said. "If we don't get something in us we can't stick on the raft."

"What raft?" Ogden asked.

"We'll get a raft," Rogers said.

"I don't know how," Ogden said. "If I try to swing a hatchet, I'll cut off my legs."

"Don't worry about that," Rogers said. "I'll get the raft if you'll find the food. Listen!"

Behind us, on the dark slope of the valley, a red squirrel chirred. Far away another answered. We could hear them chipping and chapping at each other: I knew just how they looked, jerking their tails and sliding spasmodically around tree-trunks with outspread legs.

"There's the food," Rogers said. "There's only one good mouthful to a roasted red squirrel, even if he's hit in the head, but all we need is a few good mouthfuls."

"I guess we can knock down a few," Ogden said. "I don't know about getting 'em back here, if I shoot more than one. One's about all I can carry." He reached for his musket. "We better draw our loads and reload," he told me. "We can't afford to miss."

"Before you go," Rogers told us, "help me with the wood. There's only one way to get trees for a raft, and that's to burn 'em down."

We stacked piles of firewood at the base of six spruces near the water's edge: then dragged ourselves up the bank, leaving Rogers and Billy crawling from pile to pile, kindling the fires that were to fell the trees we no longer had the strength to hack down ourselves.

Ogden and I shot five squirrels during the morning, and found it difficult —not only because we couldn't hurry to a squirrel when we heard one, but because we had to wait for the squirrels to sit still: then shoot from a rest because of being unable to hold the sights steady unless we did so. Hunger cramps caught us with increasing frequency, and if a hunger cramp took hold while we were drawing a bead on a squirrel, there was nothing to do but double up and wait until it went away.

We came back, late in the morning, to find Rogers and Billy still nursing the fires at the bases of the six dry trees.

We skinned and roasted the squirrels, dividing the fifth one equally; and while we picked the meat from their mouse-like bodies, one of the trees came down with a crash.

Rogers drove us out again as soon as we had eaten. "Keep on hunting," he told us. "Shoot anything you find. I'll have these trees burned into lengths by the time you get back."

It seemed to me I couldn't drag my legs up the slope of that valley again, but somehow we did it, using our muskets as walking sticks and leaning frequently against trees. So far as I could feel, my roast squirrel had done me no good: I needed a side of mutton or a cow's hind-quarter to quiet the aching void within me. I thought bitterly of Cap Huff's idle remark about a goose being a little more than one man could eat alone, but not quite enough for two. How little Cap had known of hunger! A whole goose would no more than take the edge off my appetite.

Not far from us a partridge went out of a thicket with a thunderous roar. From the blundering sound he made among the branches, I was sure he had lit at no great distance.

"He's in a tree," I whispered to Ogden. Ordinarily, the breast of a partridge makes a toothsome preliminary to a simple meal; but as a meal itself it's not worth considering. Just now, however, this partridge seemed more desirable than anything on earth.

"Can you see him?" Ogden asked faintly.

I said I couldn't, but knew about where he was.

"Go ahead and get him," Ogden said. "I'll move off to the left and make a noise doing it, so he'll watch me. You sneak around and take him in the rear."

He lowered himself among the dead leaves and threw his arms and legs about, making feeble moaning sounds. I hoped the partridge would find such a noise impressive as I crept around the thicket and stood watching breathlessly. The trees were naked: leafless. In none of them could I see anything that looked like a bird, and I was about to call to Ogden when I saw a movement at one end of a swelling on the branch of an oak. It was the partridge, cocking an eye at Ogden's strange behavior.

I found a good rest, took careful aim and let him have it. When he scaled away from the limb on a long slant, Ogden and I stumbled as fast as we could to where he came down. It was rocky ground, clear of heavy undergrowth, and dotted with an occasional juniper bush and a thin covering of leaves; but the partridge was nowhere in sight.

"You sure he came down here?" Ogden asked.

I said I was; that he was hit hard.

"Yes, I saw him. I guess he was hit all right," Ogden agreed, "but I don't believe he came down here. We'd see him if he had. He must have gone beyond those rocks."

We went there and searched; we walked in circles, sought beneath every juniper: almost looked under every fallen leaf; but we found nothing.

"You're sure he came down at all?" Ogden asked finally.

I just nodded. The thought of losing that partridge shut off my voice completely; I was afraid that if I tried to speak, I'd sob instead.

Ogden, hollow-eyed, stared at the ground. "Guess you—guess you missed him," he said in a whisper. And then his wretched staring eyes seemed to enlarge. "Well, if that don't beat all!"

He was staring at a flat juniper that had a few brown oak leaves on it. Before my eyes the oak leaves magically altered and became a partridge—an enormous cock partridge, with ruff-feathers four inches long and a tail the size of a fan. We must have walked across him and around him twenty times.

I went down on my knees and picked him up. He was still warm—the fattest, most beautiful, angelic partridge I had ever seen. The musket ball had broken his back and left his breast untouched.

I looked up at Ogden. "I'm mighty glad you found him, Captain. Mighty glad."

"I *knew* you hit him," Ogden said. "That was a mighty pretty shot, Langdon—the best shot I ever hope to see."

III

When we returned to the falls, all six trees were down, and under each burned two fires, so to separate them into proper lengths for a raft. Rogers sat at the edge of the stream, his forehead resting on his drawn-up knees, and beside him lay Billy, asleep.

The Major looked up. He was a sight. His face and hands were black with soot: as black as Pomp Whipple's; and his eyes glared at us whitely, looking to see whether we had shot anything. I slipped the partridge's head from under my belt in back and held it up for him to see.

"Oh, by God!" he whispered. "Let's eat it before our luck changes!"

We ate the intestines first, washed and placed on a hot stone to roast. Then we had half a squirrel apiece, cut along the backbone. The partridge was more difficult to divide evenly. Having agreed that a newly-shot partridge is better raw than cooked, we seared him no more than enough to hold the meat together. Then we took off the breasts and, after considerable discussion and measuring, split them in what we agreed were equal parts. The carcass, mattering less, was quartered without argument.

Before we slept that night the twelve fires had done their work, and twelve logs lay on the bank, with nothing more to be done to them except get them into the water and fasten them together into a raft. To me, that night, the task appeared about as easy as pushing a porcupine through a musket barrel.

IV

Nowadays whenever I dream of the building of that second raft, I wake myself up by whimpering aloud, because I've been straining to move a vast log that will not budge, yet must, or death awaits me.

We drove stakes in shallow water where the bottom was soft. Then we inched a log to the bank, tumbled it to the shingle, and worried it into the stream. We couldn't roll it, because we had to leave protruding branches for binding the raft together.

In moving a log, we worked however we could: levering it with stakes: sliding it over driftwood: lying on our backs to ease our hunger cramps, and pushing with heels or shoulders, so that from head to foot we were black with soot.

When we had a log in the water, we drew it to the fixed stakes, which held it in place while we went for another log. To each one we fastened a hazel switch, so there might be something by which to seize and guide it if it broke loose; and Billy stood guard at the stakes to do what he could in case they gave way.

It was noon before we had finished our labors, lashed our muskets and other wretched belongings to the uprights, cut new paddles and woven a long rope of hazel shoots.

Rogers insisted on the rope. "We don't want this one to get away from us," he muttered over and over. "We really got to keep hold of *this* one." We thought he was right about that. We couldn't have made a third raft.

Whether it was because of the steadily increasing cold—a cold that threatened snow—or the long struggle with the logs, I cannot say; but whatever advantage we had gained from our mouthful of partridge and two mouthfuls of squirrel had now been lost. We were finished; if our lives depended on our marching a mile, we couldn't have done it.

By the time we started, poor young Billy had bad cramps and couldn't even sit upright, so we laid him on some spruce tips in the middle of the raft. With his sharp nose, his closed eyes, his mouth stretched tight over his teeth, and his dusky color, he looked tragically like a mummy without its wrappings.

We worked free of the stakes, poled ourselves slowly into midstream and sank breathless on the raft, regardless of the icy water that welled up between the logs to soak our trembling bodies. Some day, I thought, I must paint a picture of this and call it Purgatory; and then I realized such a picture would have little meaning: it couldn't show the endlessness of these journeyings—the eternal wetness and shiverings, the aching bruises to soul and body, the everlasting hunger, everlasting toil, and everlasting exhaustion.

Rogers got to his knees, and I heard him say something about falls. The word shocked me into full consciousness. "Falls?" I asked. "More falls?"

"Not bad ones," he said thickly. "Just little falls. Wattoquitchey Falls, seven miles from here. Fifty yards long. Maybe we can ride 'em."

Ogden and I struggled painfully to our feet.

"For God's sake," Ogden said, "why didn't we go there to build the raft?"

"I said 'seven miles,'" Rogers reminded him. "You couldn't march seven miles. And what about him?" He pointed at Billy. "Why, maybe I couldn't even hardly do it myself."

"Can we see these falls before we're on top of 'em?" I asked.

"See 'em?" Rogers said. "We've got to see 'em, haven't we?"

We strained our eyes downstream. A few snowflakes drifted out of the heavy sky, and from the surface of the eddying brown water rose a vapor like a faint ghost of the mist that had billowed up from White River Falls. The thought of more falls was sheerly nauseating, and I knew that if the snow came down too thickly, we might not see them until too late. . . .

Rogers broke the silence at the end of three miles. "Maybe we can ride 'em," he said again. He repeated the words in another quarter-hour. Those falls, I realized, hadn't been out of his mind all day. That was why he had insisted on making the rope of hazel switches. I wondered what would happen if we couldn't ride them; but I didn't dare ask.

V

We sighted the falls through thickening snowflakes at three o'clock, and paddled the raft over toward the left bank, so we might have opportunity to see how they looked.

At first I thought we might indeed possibly ride them, for their total drop was only about ten feet; and the quick water wasn't over fifty yards long. The closer we came, however, the more apparent it was that the raft would never get down safely unless every possible ounce of weight was removed from it. Gouts of foam shot up from the middle of the rapids, proving that the ledges beneath were sharp and dangerous; we could hardly hope to live if the raft broke up or spilled us in that turmoil.

We let the raft drop down to within a few yards of the quick water, laid one end of it against the bank and held it there with our paddles. We could see the pool at the bottom—a brown, deep pool, streaked with streamers of foam.

"I don't believe we'd better try it," Rogers said.

"Somebody's got to," Ogden said wearily. "It's the only chance we've got."

"No it isn't," Rogers said. "The best chance is for me to go down to that pool and try to catch her when she comes down."

Ogden, seized with a cramp, clutched his middle. "You can't!"

Rogers seemed not to hear him. "That's what we'll do. Take Billy ashore. Take the muskets and the rest of the stuff. I'll hold her while you do it."

Ogden hesitated.

"Captain Ogden!" Rogers said sharply. "You heard me!"

Ogden moved quickly to obey. We hurriedly collected our rusty muskets, our soaked and tattered rags of blankets, and all our other accouterments that now were rubbish; then, taking Billy by his pipestem arms, we dragged him to the bank, where he lay all asprawl, no better than a shrivelled little red corpse. At Rogers' orders we made fast the rope of hazel shoots to the stoutest of the uprights; and Ogden tested the rope while I fastened our paddles to the raft's protruding branches. The rope was firm as a cable.

"Now for God's sake!" Rogers said, "don't let go that rope till I give the signal. It'll take me some time to reach the pool, and I got to undress. When

I hold up my arm, turn her loose. Let the rope trail. If I miss the raft, maybe I can catch the rope." He fastened his own paddle beside ours and went ashore.

I joined Ogden, and together we clung to the rope. The raft plucked insistently at it, as if eager to be gone from us.

Picking up his musket, powder-horn and other belongings, Rogers went slowly from our sight into the dark woods, walking crouched over. The snow-flakes had thickened, helping to hide him from us; and I thought it likely that I'd heard his voice for the last time.

The raft seemed more and more determined to swing out into the stream and go down the falls. For fear it might pull us off our feet and drag us into the rapids, we sat in the shallows, water up to our waists, our feet wedged against rocks.

"I'll bet my way was best," Ogden muttered. "One of us ought to *tried* to ride down on it. If the Major gets a stomach cramp when he's swimming to it——" He was silent. There wasn't much more to say.

At the edge of the pool the bushes moved apart, and Rogers, a dim figure through the steadily-falling snow, could be seen peering along the shore to left and right, seeking, evidently, for a suitable position. Then he went back into the bushes, and reappeared nearer us, crawling out on a flat rock. With agonizing slowness he put down his musket, blanket, knapsack and powder-horn, and painfully undressed.

He crouched at the edge of the rock, staring up at the falls—a lonely, naked, helpless atom in that immensity of roaring white water, drifting snow-flakes, screaking forest and towering dark hills. Then he held up his arm and waved.

We let go the rope and floundered to our feet. The raft swung slowly broadside to the current and moved downstream. When it reached the quick water, it bobbed on the white riffles; flung itself forward.

It rolled and rocked. Halfway down it nosed completely under: a surge of white foam swept it from end to end. It rose again, reeling and sliding in the surges, and seemed to fling itself breathlessly to the bottom of the long slope. It plunged heavily into the swirling pool, and hung there, tilted forward, half under water. We looked to see it fall apart; but with labored slowness it came to the surface, turning gently among the clots and streaks of froth.

Rogers lowered himself from the rock. He swam arduously, with awkward jerks, as if his rump strove to rise and force his head under. He stopped once, freed his face from gouts of foam, and rolled on his side to look for the raft, which, again in the grip of the current, moved more rapidly.

He altered his course and swam spasmodically on. He found himself so close to it that he clutched for a log—clutched and missed. He kicked again; got a hand on the raft: another hand. He hung there for a time, his chin on the edge, his legs and body carried beneath the logs by the current; and I, watching him, felt my muscles quake; for I knew that no mere human, with an icy torrent plucking at his starved and weakened limbs, could cling for long to those charred tree-trunks. As if in answer to my fears, he struggled sluggishly, hitched himself along with fumbling hands, gripped one of the branches we had left as uprights on the logs, and drew himself partly from the water, so that his upper body lay upon the raft—lay so long motionless, that I thought he was sped. Then we saw that he was making futile upward movements with his knee. It caught the edge eventually, and he squirmed aboard to lie flat.

"I never thought he'd make it!" Ogden whispered; and I, shaking all over, found that my tongue and throat were dry as chips.

Now Rogers had got to his knees, and we saw him unlash a paddle from the uprights, and begin to work slowly toward shore.

VI

Driftwood from Wattoquitchey Falls warmed us and kept us alive that night; and with the first faint grayness of that miserable last day of October —miserable and yet ever-memorable—we put Billy in the middle of the raft, with our blankets under and over him, and pushed out into midstream. The snow had ceased, and had been followed by a wind so bitter that it cut and slashed us like frigid knife-blades.

There were no more falls between Wattoquitchey and Number Four: no more quick water, Rogers said—no, there was nothing but the malignant cold, which seemed determined to finish what the French and the Indians and the evil spirits of the forests and streams had tried so hard to do to us.

But on both sides the intervales grew broader: the hills retreated; and though the glacial wind could thus howl at us unrestrained, we thought it had the voice of a raging demon of the wilderness, frantic to see us at last slipping from his grasp.

Out of his streaming eyes, Rogers stared at the widening intervales. "We're going to make it," he said. "By God, I believe we're going to make it!"

It was mid-afternoon when he seized Ogden by the arm. "Look!" he cried. "Look!" He doubled over with a cramp; but thus bent he pointed awkwardly, like an actor playing the part of a hunchback. On the river bank, a hundred yards ahead, two men with axes suddenly stood.

"Why," Ogden said incredulously, "it's people again!" But I don't think Rogers could speak at all, and I know I couldn't.

The two strange, strange figures, men that weren't skeletons, men that were clothed, men that swung axes easily in ruddy strength and health— those two unbelievable men saw us, and came back along the bank, hurrying toward us.

"Don't tell 'em anything," Rogers warned us huskily as we swung the raft in toward the shore. "I'll do the talking. Don't tell anyone a damned thing till we find out all about the dirty skunk that ran off with our food!"

One of the men splashed toward us, caught our rope of hazel switches and drew us to land.

"Where's Number Four?" Rogers asked.

They just stared.

"I'm Rogers," Rogers said. "Where's Number Four?"

"Rogers!" one of the men said, and a kind of horror was in his face. "You say you're Rogers?"

"I do!"

"I've often seen you," the man said, swallowing. "It's hard to believe!" He shook his head. "We heard you was dead, Major; and I guess it's true! You was! But anyhow, you're at Number Four, Major. It's right here, and we'll help you to the fort!"

With that, slipping and splashing in excitement, they gave us the unfamiliar help of muscular arms and got us off the raft, lifted Billy to the bank, put our belongings in a heap, and made the raft fast to a stake. They gawked at the burned ends of the logs and at the alder and hazel withes that held them together, and kept staring at Rogers as if he'd been a hippogriff.

We sat down just beyond the water's edge and watched them as they made the raft fast.

"Happen to have anything to eat?" Rogers asked them, whereupon, after another look at him, they sprang up the bank and departed, running. They were back in five minutes, bringing with them a bottle a third full of rum and a piece of bread the size of my fist. "That's all we got, Major," one said. "We're out chopping wood and et the rest, but there's plenty supplies at the fort. There's turnips and fresh pork."

Rogers broke the bread in four pieces. "Why, it's bread!" he said. He gave us our portions, took a mouthful of rum, then went over and looked at Billy. He poured a little rum between his lips. When Billy opened his eyes and coughed, he gave him the bread and passed us the bottle.

That mouthful of bread moistened by rum had incredible sweetness and savor. I could feel it moving warmly inside me, as though hastening to assure my cramped and aching stomach, my thumping heart, my laboring lungs and my shivering body that their long agony was over.

"Now we'll go up to the fort," Rogers told the staring woodcutters. "Guess maybe you'd better help us a little. Leave our stuff here: then come back for it. One of you carry this Indian boy. Then we'll just lean on the two of you."

One of the men picked up Billy and carried him. The other gave Ogden and me each a shoulder, and Rogers staggered along, now and then bumping into the man who carried the Indian boy; and thus we set off for the fort, which we could see, low and square, in the middle of its dismal, snow-covered clearing—that same peaceful clearing I had idly sketched on a warm September evening less than two months ago.

There was no sentry at the gate of the fort; no one on the small parade ground on which the snow had been trodden to dirty, frozen slush. Our helpers took us across the parade to the log barrack in the center. A squat tower of hewn plank rose from its northern end. The man on whom Ogden and I leaned pulled the latch-string of the door and kicked it open. In a broad stone fireplace opposite the door a fire burned, and at either end of the room were rows of bunks. In front of the fire a blanket was spread on the floor, and around it were a dozen Provincials, rolling dice.

They looked up. One said angrily, "Keep that door shut!"

"This here's Major Rogers," one of the woodcutters said in a voice that choked with excitement.

The Provincials got slowly to their feet and faced us, stared at us and frowned with unbelief, then seemed to see something terrifying.

"Who's in command of this fort?" Rogers asked.

"We don't know his name, Major," a soldier said huskily. "We're strangers here."

"Go get him," Rogers ordered.

Three Provincials jumped together for the door at the end of the room, jostling and tripping in their haste.

Rogers walked drunkenly to a bench, and the staring soldiers fell away before him.

"Put Billy on the blanket and go back and get our muskets," Rogers told the woodcutters.

Ogden and I got to the bench with difficulty. The feel of a roof over my head and of a closed room, warmed by a fire, almost suffocated me.

The door at the end of the room burst open. A stolid-looking man in a wrinkled blue uniform peered at us, blinking. "Which?" he asked. "Which one?" He came to us. "They said Major Rogers! None of *you* are Major Rogers!"

"I'm Rogers," the Major said. "Now here: write down what I say. I can't repeat. What's your name?"

"Bellows," the officer said, "in charge of the King's stores." He clapped his hands to his pockets, looked confused, then hurried from the room. When he returned he had pencil and paper. "We didn't know——" he stammered. "We heard—where did you——"

"Get canoes," Rogers said. "Load 'em with food. Send 'em up river. Mouth of the Ammonoosuc."

"These men are Provincials," Bellows said apologetically. "They're bound home. There's only——"

"Get settlers," Rogers said. "Good canoemen. Hire 'em!"

"It's pretty bad weather," Bellows said doubtfully. "Maybe when it clears off——"

Rogers rose wavering to his feet, then straightened himself to his full height and seemed to fill the room. In a strained, hoarse voice he said: "Today! Today! Now! Can't you realize there's a hundred Rangers at the mouth of the Ammonoosuc, starving! Get men and pay 'em! Get all the settlers into the fort! Call 'em in! Drum 'em up! I'll talk to 'em! For Christ's sake, get started!"

Bellows stared at him wildly: rushed back to the door and shouted a name, adding, at the top of his lungs, "Assembly! Assembly!"

Three private soldiers tumbled into the room, one a drummer. At a gesture from Bellows he ran out on the parade ground, fumbling with his drum braces. His drum rolled and rumbled, sending chills down my spine.

To one of the other soldiers Bellows shouted, "Run to Mrs. Bellows. Get a pail of milk and a bottle of my rum."

"And some bread," Ogden said.

"All the bread she's got!" Bellows shouted.

Rogers sank down on the bench, rubbed his gaunt face with huge skeleton hands, ran his fingers through his hair. "Write an order for the food to go up river. What you got in this place?"

"Pork," Bellows said. "Fresh beef. Turnips."

"How much bread you got?"

"Not much," Bellows said. "These Provincials——"

"Provincials be damned! Let 'em go without! Put all the food you can find in those canoes, and send out for more. Send out for everything there is! Those men of mine are going to be fed, or by God I'll raid every house in the settlement!"

The drum rattled and rolled, rumbled and banged.

Bellows scribbled hastily on a sheet of paper and sent the third soldier flying from the barrack with it. There were people crowding in at the door, goggling at us.

Rogers raised his voice to be heard over the continuous rolling of the drum. "Tell me something," he said to Bellows. "Supplies of food were to meet us at the mouth of the Ammonoosuc. They were sent, weren't they?"

"Oh yes," Bellows replied, and he looked frightened. "They were in charge of Lieutenant Stephens."

"So? What did he do with 'em?"

"He brought 'em back," Bellows said. "He waited several days; then he thought you and your command must have been wiped out—and he heard firing one morning and thought it might be French and Indians, so he decided he'd better start for home."

"Listen," Rogers said, and he spoke as much to the settlers and Provincials who had crowded in through the doorway as he did to Bellows. "We finished St. Francis for you. There isn't any more St. Francis, and you can begin to move up that way and clear the land and live in peace whenever you're a mind to. But this Lieutenant Stephens who got frightened and took our food away when we were firing muskets to show him we were coming—we'll have to have a settlement with him. He isn't here, is he?"

"No," Bellows said tremulously. "He's gone back to Crown Point. You'll be going that way, too, Major, I take it?"

"No, not till afterwards," Rogers answered in a choking voice.

The crowding people stared stupidly at him as he stood before them in the firelight, unbelievably gaunt, barefooted, covered with bruises, tattered strips of strouding sagging around his legs. The shredded buckskin leggins hung loosely on his emaciated flanks; singular torn bits of garments concealed little of his ribs and bony chest: his hands were scarred, burned, sooty and pitch-stained from his labors with the raft.

"No, we'll see Lieutenant Stephens at Crown Point afterwards," Rogers said. "Now get me some beef—fat beef. I'm going back to the Ammonoosuc myself."

OLD MAN AT THE BRIDGE

ERNEST HEMINGWAY

AN OLD MAN with steel rimmed spectacles and very dusty clothes sat by the side of the road. There was a pontoon bridge across the river and carts, trucks, and men, women and children were crossing it. The mule-drawn carts staggered up the steep bank from the bridge with soldiers helping push against the spokes of the wheels. The trucks ground up and away heading out of it all and the peasants plodded along in the ankle deep dust. But the old man sat there without moving. He was too tired to go any farther.

It was my business to cross the bridge, explore the bridgehead beyond and find out to what point the enemy had advanced. I did this and returned over the bridge. There were not so many carts now and very few people on foot, but the old man was still there.

"Where do you come from?" I asked him.

"From San Carlos," he said, and smiled.

That was his native town and so it gave him pleasure to mention it and he smiled.

"I was taking care of animals," he explained.

"Oh," I said, not quite understanding.

"Yes," he said, "I stayed, you see, taking care of animals. I was the last one to leave the town of San Carlos."

He did not look like a shepherd nor a herdsman and I looked at his black dusty clothes and his gray dusty face and his steel rimmed spectacles and said, "What animals were they?"

"Various animals," he said, and shook his head. "I had to leave them."

I was watching the bridge and the African looking country of the Ebro Delta and wondering how long now it would be before we would see the enemy, and listening all the while for the first noises that would signal that ever mysterious event called contact, and the old man still sat there.

"What animals were they?" I asked.

"There were three animals altogether," he explained. "There were two goats and a cat and then there were four pairs of pigeons."

"And you had to leave them?" I asked.

"Yes. Because of the artillery. The captain told me to go because of the artillery."

"And you have no family?" I asked, watching the far end of the bridge where a few last carts were hurrying down the slope of the bank.

"No," he said, "only the animals I stated. The cat, of course, will be all right. A cat can look out for itself, but I cannot think what will become of the others."

"What politics have you?" I asked.

"I am without politics," he said. "I am seventy-six years old. I have come twelve kilometers now and I think now I can go no further."

"This is not a good place to stop," I said. "If you can make it, there are trucks up the road where it forks for Tortosa."

"I will wait a while," he said, "and then I will go. Where do the trucks go?"

"Towards Barcelona," I told him.

"I know no one in that direction," he said, "but thank you very much. Thank you again very much."

He looked at me very blankly and tiredly, then said, having to share his worry with some one, "The cat will be all right, I am sure. There is no need to be unquiet about the cat. But the others. Now what do you think about the others?"

"Why they'll probably come through it all right."

"You think so?"

"Why not," I said, watching the far bank where now there were no carts.

"But what will they do under the artillery when I was told to leave because of the artillery?"

"Did you leave the dove cage unlocked?" I asked.

"Yes."

"Then they'll fly."

"Yes, certainly they'll fly. But the others. It's better not to think about the others," he said.

"If you are rested I would go," I urged. "Get up and try to walk now."

"Thank you," he said and got to his feet, swayed from side to side and then sat down backwards in the dust.

"I was taking care of animals," he said dully, but no longer to me. "I was only taking care of animals."

There was nothing to do about him. It was Easter Sunday and the Fascists were advancing toward the Ebro. It was a gray overcast day with a low ceiling so their planes were not up. That and the fact that cats know how to look after themselves was all the good luck that old man would ever have.

THE CYPRIAN CAT

DOROTHY L. SAYERS

IT'S extraordinarily decent of you to come along and see me like this, Harringay. Believe me, I do appreciate it. It isn't every busy K.C. who'd do as much for such a hopeless sort of client. I only wish I could spin you a more workable kind of story, but honestly, I can only tell you exactly what I told Peabody. Of course, I can see he doesn't believe a word of it, and I don't blame him. He thinks I ought to be able to make up a more plausible tale than that—and I suppose I could, but where's the use? One's almost bound to fall down somewhere if one tries to swear to a lie. What I'm going to tell you is the absolute truth. I fired one shot and one shot only, and that was at the cat. It's funny that one should be hanged for shooting at a cat.

Merridew and I were always the best of friends; school and college and all that sort of thing. We didn't see very much of each other after the war, because we were living at opposite ends of the country; but we met in town from time to time and wrote occasionally and each of us knew that the other was there in the background, so to speak. Two years ago, he wrote and told me he was getting married. He was just turned forty and the girl was fifteen years younger, and he was tremendously in love. It gave me a bit of a jolt— you know how it is when your friends marry. You feel they will never be quite the same again; and I'd got used to the idea that Merridew and I were cut out to be old bachelors. But of course I congratulated him and sent him a wedding present, and I did sincerely hope he'd be happy. He was obviously over head and ears; almost dangerously so, I thought, considering all things. Though except for the difference of age it seemed suitable enough. He told me he had met her at—of all places—a rectory garden-party down in Norfolk, and that she had actually never been out of her native village. I mean, literally—not so much as a trip to the nearest town. I'm not trying to convey that she wasn't pukka, or anything like that. Her father was some queer sort of recluse—a mediævalist, or something—desperately poor. He died shortly after their marriage.

I didn't see anything of them for the first year or so. Merridew is a civil engineer, you know, and he took his wife away after the honeymoon to Liver-

pool, where he was doing something in connection with the harbour. It must
have been a big change for her from the wilds of Norfolk. I was in Birmingham, with my nose kept pretty close to the grindstone, so we only exchanged
occasional letters. His were what I can only call deliriously happy, especially
at first. Later on, he seemed a little worried about his wife's health. She was
restless; town life didn't suit her; he'd be glad when he could finish up his
Liverpool job and get her away into the country. There wasn't any doubt
about their happiness, you understand—she'd got him body and soul as they
say, and as far as I could make out it was mutual. I want to make that
perfectly clear.

Well, to cut a long story short, Merridew wrote to me at the beginning
of last month and said he was just off to a new job—a waterworks extension
scheme down in Somerset; and he asked if I could possibly cut loose and join
them there for a few weeks. He wanted to have a yarn with me, and Felice
was longing to make my acquaintance. They had got rooms at the village inn.
It was rather a remote spot, but there was fishing and scenery and so forth,
and I should be able to keep Felice company while he was working up at the
dam. I was about fed up with Birmingham, what with the heat and one thing
and another, and it looked pretty good to me, and I was due for a holiday
anyhow, so I fixed up to go. I had a bit of business to do in town, which I
calculated would take me about a week, so I said I'd go down to Little
Hexham on June 20th.

As it happened, my business in London finished itself off unexpectedly
soon, and on the sixteenth I found myself absolutely free and stuck in an
hotel with road-drills working just under the windows and a tar-spraying
machine to make things livelier. You remember what a hot month it was—
flaming June and no mistake about it. I didn't see any point in waiting, so I
sent off a wire to Merridew, packed my bag and took the train for Somerset
the same evening. I couldn't get a compartment to myself, but I found a
first-class smoker with only three seats occupied, and stowed myself thank-
fully into the fourth corner. There was a military-looking old boy, an elderly
female with a lot of bags and baskets, and a girl. I thought I should have a
nice, peaceful journey.

So I should have, if it hadn't been for the unfortunate way I'm built. It was
quite all right at first—as a matter of fact, I think I was half asleep, and I only
woke up properly at seven o'clock, when the waiter came to say that dinner
was on. The other people weren't taking it, and when I came back from the
restaurant car I found that the old boy had gone, and there were only the
two women left. I settled down in my corner again, and gradually, as we
went along, I found a horrible feeling creeping over me that there was a cat
in the compartment somewhere. I'm one of those wretched people who can't
stand cats. I don't mean just that I prefer dogs—I mean that the presence of
a cat in the same room with me makes me feel like nothing on earth. I can't
describe it, but I believe quite a lot of people are affected that way. Something
to do with electricity, or so they tell me. I've read that very often the dislike

is mutual, but it isn't so with me. The brutes seem to find me abominably fascinating—make a bee-line for my legs every time. It's a funny sort of complaint, and it doesn't make me at all popular with dear old ladies.

Anyway, I began to feel more and more awful and I realized that the old girl at the other end of the seat must have a cat in one of her innumerable baskets. I thought of asking her to put it out in the corridor, or calling the guard and having it removed, but I knew how silly it would sound and made up my mind to try and stick it. I couldn't say the animal was misbehaving itself or anything, and she looked a pleasant old lady; it wasn't her fault that I was a freak. I tried to distract my mind by looking at the girl.

She was worth looking at, too—very slim, and dark with one of those dead-white skins that make you think of magnolia blossom. She had the most astonishing eyes, too—I've never seen eyes quite like them; a very pale brown, almost amber, set wide apart and a little slanting, and they seemed to have a kind of luminosity of their own, if you get what I mean. I don't know if this sounds—I don't want you to think I was bowled over, or anything. As a matter of fact she held no sort of attraction for me, though I could imagine a different type of man going potty about her. She was just unusual, that was all. But however much I tried to think of other things I couldn't get rid of the uncomfortable feeling, and eventually I gave it up and went out into the corridor. I just mention this because it will help you to understand the rest of the story. If you can only realize how perfectly awful I feel when there's a cat about—even when it's shut up in a basket—you'll understand better how I came to buy the revolver.

Well, we got to Hexham Junction, which was the nearest station to Little Hexham, and there was old Merridew waiting on the platform. The girl was getting out too—but not the old lady with the cat, thank goodness—and I was just handing her traps out after her when he came galloping up and hailed us.

"Hullo!" he said, "why that's splendid! Have you introduced yourselves?" So I tumbled to it then that the girl was Mrs. Merridew, who'd been up to Town on a shopping expedition, and I explained to her about my change of plans and she said how jolly it was that I could come—the usual things. I noticed what an attractive low voice she had and how graceful her movements were, and I understood—though, mind you, I didn't share—Merridew's infatuation.

We got into his car—Mrs. Merridew sat in the back and I got up beside Merridew, and was very glad to feel the air and to get rid of the oppressive electric feeling I'd had in the train. He told me the place suited them wonderfully, and had given Felice an absolutely new lease on life, so to speak. He said he was very fit, too, but I thought myself that he looked rather fagged and nervy.

You'd have liked that inn, Harringay. The real, old-fashioned stuff, as quaint as you make 'em, and everything genuine—none of your Tottenham Court Road antiques. We'd all had our grub, and Mrs. Merridew said she was tired; so she went up to bed early and Merridew and I had a drink and went for a stroll round the village. It's a tiny hamlet quite at the other end of nowhere; lights out at ten, little thatched houses with pinched-up attic windows like furry ears—the place purred in its sleep. Merridew's working gang didn't sleep there, of course—they'd run up huts for them at the dams, a mile beyond the village.

The landlord was just locking up the bar when we came in—a block of a man with an absolutely expressionless face. His wife was a thin, sandy-haired woman who looked as though she was too down-trodden to open her mouth. But I found out afterwards that was a mistake, for one evening when he'd taken one or two over the eight and showed signs of wanting to make a night of it, his wife sent him off upstairs with a gesture and a look that took the heart out of him. That first night she was sitting in the porch, and hardly glanced at us as we passed her. I always thought her an uncomfortable kind of woman, but she certainly kept her house most exquisitely neat and clean.

They'd given me a noble bedroom, close under the eaves with a long, low casement window overlooking the garden. The sheets smelt of lavender, and I was between them and asleep almost before you could count ten. I was tired, you see. But later in the night I woke up. I was too hot, so took off some of the blankets and then strolled across to the window to get a breath of air. The garden was bathed in moonshine and on the lawn I could see something twisting and turning oddly. I stared a bit before I made it out to be two cats. They didn't worry me at that distance, and I watched them for a bit before I turned in again. They were rolling over one another and jumping away again and chasing their own shadows on the grass, intent on their own mysterious business—taking themselves seriously, the way cats always do. It looked like a kind of ritual dance. Then something seemed to startle them, and they scampered away.

I went back to bed, but I couldn't get to sleep again. My nerves seemed to be all on edge. I lay watching the window and listening to a kind of soft rustling noise that seemed to be going on in the big wisteria that ran along my side of the house. And then something landed with a soft thud on the sill—a great Cyprian cat.

What did you say? Well, one of those striped grey and black cats. Tabby, that's right. In my part of the country they call them Cyprus cats, or Cyprian cats. I'd never seen such a monster. It stood with its head cocked sideways, staring into the room and rubbing its ears very softly against the upright bar of the casement.

Of course, I couldn't do with that. I shooed the brute away, and it made off without a sound. Heat or no heat, I shut and fastened the window. Far out in the shrubbery I thought I heard a faint miauling; then silence. After that, I went straight off to sleep again and lay like a log till the girl came in to call me.

The next day, Merridew ran us up in his car to see the place where they were making the dam, and that was the first time I realized that Felice's nerviness had not been altogether cured. He showed us where they had diverted part of the river into a swift little stream that was to be used for working the dynamo of an electrical plant. There were a couple of planks

laid across the stream, and he wanted to take us over to show us the engine. It wasn't extraordinarily wide or dangerous, but Mrs. Merridew peremptorily refused to cross it, and got quite hysterical when he tried to insist. Eventually he and I went over and inspected the machinery by ourselves. When we got back she had recovered her temper and apologized for being so silly. Merridew abased himself, of course, and I began to feel a little *de trop*. She told me afterwards that she had once fallen into the river as a child, and been nearly drowned, and it had left her with a what d'ye call it—a complex about running water. And but for this one trifling episode, I never heard a single sharp word pass between them all the time I was there; nor, for a whole week, did I notice anything else to suggest a flaw in Mrs. Merridew's radiant health. Indeed, as the days wore on to midsummer and the heat grew more intense, her whole body seemed to glow with vitality. It was as though she was lit up from within.

Merridew was out all day and working very hard. I thought he was over-doing it and asked him if he was sleeping badly. He told me that, on the contrary, he fell asleep every night the moment his head touched the pillow, and—what was most unusual with him—had no dreams of any kind. I myself felt well enough, but the hot weather made me languid and disinclined for exertion. Mrs. Merridew took me out for long drives in the car. I would sit for hours, lulled into a half-slumber by the rush of warm air and the purring of the engine, and gazing at my driver, upright at the wheel, her eyes fixed unwaveringly upon the spinning road. We explored the whole of the country to the south and east of Little Hexham, and once or twice went as far north as Bath. Once I suggested that we should turn eastward over the bridge and run down into what looked like rather beautiful wooded country, but Mrs. Merridew didn't care for the idea; she said it was a bad road and that the scenery on that side was disappointing.

Altogether, I spent a pleasant week at Little Hexham, and if it had not been for the cats I should have been perfectly comfortable. Every night the garden seemed to be haunted by them—the Cyprian cat that I had seen the first night of my stay, and a little ginger one and a horrible stinking black Tom were especially tiresome, and one night there was a terrified white kitten that mewed for an hour on end under my window. I flung boots and books at my visitors till I was heartily weary, but they seemed determined to make the inn garden their rendezvous. The nuisance grew worse from night to night; on one occasion I counted fifteen of them, sitting on their hinder-ends in a circle, while the Cyprian cat danced her shadow-dance among them, working in and out like a weaver's shuttle. I had to keep my window shut, for the Cyprian cat evidently made a habit of climbing up by the wisteria. The door, too; for once when I had gone down to fetch something from the sitting-room, I found her on my bed, kneading the coverlet with her paws—pr'rp, pr'rp, pr'rp—with her eyes closed in a sensuous ecstasy. I beat her off, and she spat at me as she fled into the dark passage.

I asked the landlady about her, but she replied rather curtly that they kept no cat at the inn, and it is true that I never saw any of the beasts in the day-time; but one evening about dusk I caught the landlord in one of the out-houses. He had the ginger cat on his shoulder, and was feeding her with something that looked like strips of liver. I remonstrated with him for en-couraging the cats about the place and asked whether I could have a different room, explaining that the nightly caterwauling disturbed me. He half opened his slits of eyes and murmured that he would ask his wife about it; but noth-ing was done, and in fact I believe there was no other bedroom in the house.

And all this time the weather got hotter and heavier, working up for thunder, with the sky like brass and the earth like iron, and the air quivering over it so that it hurt your eyes to look at it.

All right, Harringay—I am trying to keep to the point. And I'm not con-cealing anything from you. I say that my relations with Mrs. Merridew were perfectly ordinary. Of course I saw a good deal of her, because as I explained Merridew was out all day. We went up to the dam with him in the morning and brought the car back, and naturally we had to amuse one another as best we could till the evening. She seemed quite pleased to be in my company, and I couldn't dislike her. I can't tell you what we talked about—nothing in particular. She was not a talkative woman. She would sit or lie for hours in the sunshine, hardly speaking—only stretching out her body to the light and heat. Sometimes she would spend a whole afternoon playing with a twig or a pebble, while I sat by and smoked. Restful! No. No—I shouldn't call her a restful personality, exactly. Not to me, at any rate. In the evening she would liven up and talk a little more, but she generally went up to bed early, and left Merridew and me to yarn together in the garden.

Oh! about the revolver. Yes. I bought that in Bath, when I had been at Little Hexham exactly a week. We drove over in the morning, and while Mrs. Merridew got some things for her husband, I prowled round the second-hand shops. I had intended to get an air-gun or a pea-shooter or something of that kind, when I saw this. You've seen it, of course. It's very tiny—what people in books describe as "little more than a toy", but quite deadly enough. The old boy who sold it to me didn't seem to know much about firearms. He'd taken it in pawn some time back, he told me, and there were ten rounds of ammunition with it. He made no bones about a licence or any-thing—glad enough to make a sale, no doubt, without putting difficulties in a customer's way. I told him I knew how to handle it, and mentioned by way of a joke that I meant to take a pot-shot or two at the cats. That seemed to wake him up a bit. He was a dried-up little fellow, with a scrawny grey beard and a stringy neck. He asked me where I was staying. I told him at Little Hexham.

"You better be careful, sir," he said. "They think a heap of their cats down there, and it's reckoned unlucky to kill them." And then he added something I couldn't quite catch, about a silver bullet. He was a doddering old fellow, and he seemed to have some sort of scruple about letting me take the parcel away, but I assured him that I was perfectly capable of looking after it and myself. I left him standing in the door of his shop, pulling at his beard and staring after me.

That night the thunder came. The sky had turned to lead before evening, but the dull heat was more oppressive than the sunshine. Both the Merridews seemed to be in a state of nerves—he sulky and swearing at the weather and the flies, and she wrought up to a queer kind of vivid excitement. Thunder affects some people that way. I wasn't much better, and to make things worse I got the feeling that the house was full of cats. I couldn't see them but I knew they were there, lurking behind the cupboards and flitting noiselessly about the corridors. I could scarcely sit in the parlour and I was thankful to escape to my room. Cats or no cats I had to open the window, and I sat there with my pyjama jacket unbuttoned, trying to get a breath of air. But the place was like the inside of a copper furnace. And pitch-dark. I could scarcely see from my window where the bushes ended and the lawn began. But I could hear and feel the cats. There were little scrapings in the wisteria and scufflings among the leaves, and about eleven o'clock one of them started the concert with a loud and hideous wail. Then another and another joined in—I'll swear there were fifty of them. And presently I got that foul sensation of nausea, and the flesh crawled on my bones, and I knew that one of them was slinking close to me in the darkness. I looked round quickly, and there she stood, the great Cyprian; right against my shoulder, her eyes glowing like green lamps. I yelled and struck out at her, and she snarled as she leaped out and down. I heard her thump the gravel, and the yowling burst out all over the garden with renewed vehemence. And then all in a moment there was utter silence, and in the far distance there came a flickering blue flash and then another. In the first of them I saw the far garden wall, topped along all its length with cats, like a nursery frieze. When the second flash came the wall was empty.

At two o'clock the rain came. For three hours before that I had sat there, watching the lightning as it spat across the sky and exulting in the crash of the thunder. The storm seemed to carry off all the electrical disturbance in my body; I could have shouted with excitement and relief. Then the first heavy drops fell; then a steady downpour; then a deluge. It struck the iron-baked garden with a noise like steel rods falling. The smell of the ground came up intoxicatingly, and the wind rose and flung the rain in against my face. At the other end of the passage I heard a window thrown to and fastened, but I leaned out into the tumult and let the water drench my head and shoulders. The thunder still rumbled intermittently, but with less noise and farther off, and in an occasional flash I saw the white grille of falling water drawn between me and the garden.

It was after one of these thunder-peals that I became aware of a knocking at my door. I opened it, and there was Merridew. He had a candle in his hand, and his face was terrified.

"Felice!" he said, abruptly. "She's ill. I can't wake her. For God's sake, come and give me a hand."

I hurried down the passage after him. There were two beds in his room—a great four-poster, hung with crimson damask, and a small camp bedstead drawn up near to the window. The small bed was empty, the bedclothes tossed aside; evidently he had just risen from it. In the four-poster lay Mrs. Merridew, naked, with only a sheet upon her. She was stretched flat upon her back, her long black hair in two plaits over her shoulders. Her face was waxen and shrunk, like the face of a corpse, and her pulse, when I felt it, was so faint that at first I could scarcely feel it. Her breathing was very slow and shallow and her flesh cold. I shook her, but there was no response at all. I lifted her eyelids, and noticed how the eyeballs were turned up under the upper lid, so that only the whites were visible. The touch of my finger-tip upon the sensitive ball evoked no reaction. I immediately wondered whether she took drugs.

Merridew seemed to think it necessary to make some explanation. He was babbling about the heat—she couldn't bear so much as a silk nightgown—she had suggested that he should occupy the other bed—he had slept heavily—

right through the thunder. The rain blowing in on his face had aroused him. He had got up and shut the window. Then he had called to Felice to know if she was all right—he thought the storm might have frightened her. There was no answer. He had struck a light. Her condition had alarmed him—and so on.

I told him to pull himself together and to try whether, by chafing his wife's hands and feet, we could restore the circulation. I had it firmly in my mind that she was under the influence of some opiate. We set to work, rubbing and pinching and slapping her with wet towels and shouting her name in her ear. It was like handling a dead woman, except for the very slight but perfectly regular rise and fall of her bosom, on which—with a kind of surprise that there should be any flaw on its magnolia whiteness—I noticed a large brown mole, just over the heart. To my perturbed fancy it suggested a wound and a menace. We had been hard at it for some time, with the sweat pouring off us, when we became aware of something going on outside the window—a stealthy bumping and scraping against the panes. I snatched up the candle and looked out.

On the sill, the Cyprian cat sat and clawed at the casement. Her drenched fur clung limply to her body, her eyes glared into mine, her mouth was opened in protest. She scrabbled furiously at the latch, her hind claws slipping and scratching on the woodwork. I hammered on the pane and bawled at her, and she struck back at the glass as though possessed. As I cursed her and turned away she set up a long, despairing wail.

Merridew called to me to bring back the candle and leave the brute alone. I returned to the bed, but the dismal crying went on and on incessantly. I suggested to Merridew that he should wake the landlord and get hot-water bottles and some brandy from the bar and see if a messenger could not be sent for a doctor. He departed on this errand, while I went on with my massage. It seemed to me that the pulse was growing still fainter. Then I suddenly recollected that I had a small brandy-flask in my bag. I ran out to fetch it, and as I did so the cat suddenly stopped its howling.

As I entered my own room the air blowing through the open window struck gratefully upon me. I found my bag in the dark and was rummaging for the flask among my shirts and socks when I heard a loud, triumphant mew, and turned round in time to see the Cyprian cat crouched for a moment on the sill, before it sprang in past me and out at the door. I found the flask and hastened back with it, just as Merridew and the landlord came running up the stairs.

We all went into the room together. As we did so, Mrs. Merridew stirred, sat up, and asked us what in the world was the matter.

I have seldom felt quite such a fool.

Next day the weather was cooler; the storm had cleared the air. What Merridew had said to his wife I do not know. None of us made any public allusion to the night's disturbance, and to all appearance Mrs. Merridew was in the best of health and spirits. Merridew took a day off from the waterworks, and we all went for a long drive and picnic together. We were on the best of terms with one another. Ask Merridew—he will tell you the same thing. He would not—he could not, surely—say otherwise. I can't believe, Harringay, I simply cannot believe that he could imagine or suspect me—I say, there was nothing to suspect. Nothing.

Yes—this is the important date—the 24th of June. I can't tell you any more details; there is nothing to tell. We came back and had dinner just as usual. All three of us were together all day, till bedtime. On my honour I had no private interview of any kind that day, either with him or with her. I was the first to go to bed, and I heard the others come upstairs about half an hour later. They were talking cheerfully.

It was a moonlight night. For once, no caterwauling came to trouble me. I didn't even bother to shut the window or the door. I put the revolver on the chair beside me before I lay down. Yes, it was loaded. I had no special object in putting it there, except that I meant to have a go at the cats if they started their games again.

I was desperately tired, and thought I should drop off to sleep at once, but I didn't. I must have been overtired, I suppose. I lay and looked at the moonlight. And then, about midnight, I heard what I had been half expecting: a stealthy scrabbling in the wisteria and a faint miauling sound.

I sat up in bed and reached for the revolver. I heard the "plop" as the big cat sprang up on to the window-ledge; I saw her black and silver flanks, and the outline of her round head, pricked ears and upright tail. I aimed and fired, and the beast let out one frightful cry and sprang down into the room.

I jumped out of bed. The crack of the shot had sounded terrific in the silent house, and somewhere I heard a distant voice call out. I pursued the cat into the passage, revolver in hand—with some idea of finishing it off, I suppose. And then, at the door of the Merridew's room, I saw Mrs. Merridew. She stood with one hand on each doorpost, swaying to and fro. Then she fell down at my feet. Her bare breast was all stained with blood. And as I stood staring at her, clutching the revolver, Merridew came out and found us—like that.

Well, Harringay, that's my story, exactly as I told it to Peabody. I'm afraid it won't sound very well in Court, but what can I say? The trail of blood led from my room to hers; the cat must have run that way; I *know* it was the cat I shot. I can't offer any explanation. I don't know who shot Mrs. Merridew, or why. I can't help it if the people at the inn say they never saw the Cyprian cat; Merridew saw it that other night, and I know he wouldn't lie about it. Search the house, Harringay—that's the only thing to do. Pull the place to pieces, till you find the body of the Cyprian cat. It will have my bullet in it.

THE CALL OF THE WILD

JACK LONDON

"Old longings nomadic leap,
Chafing at custom's chain;
Again from its brumal sleep
Wakens the ferine strain."

I. INTO THE PRIMITIVE

BUCK did not read the newspapers, or he would have known that trouble was brewing, not alone for himself, but for every tidewater dog, strong of muscle and with warm, long hair, from Puget Sound to San Diego. Because men, groping in the Arctic darkness, had found a yellow metal, and because steamship and transportation companies were booming the find, thousands of men were rushing into the Northland. These men wanted dogs, and the dogs they wanted were heavy dogs, with strong muscles by which to toil, and furry coats to protect them from the frost.

Buck lived at a big house in the sun-kissed Santa Clara Valley. Judge Miller's place, it was called. It stood back from the road, half hidden among the trees, through which glimpses could be caught of the wide cool veranda that ran around its four sides. The house was approached by gravelled driveways which wound about through wide-spreading lawns and under the interlacing boughs of tall poplars. At the rear things were on even a more spacious scale than at the front. There were great stables, where a dozen grooms and boys held forth, rows of vine-clad servants' cottages, an endless and orderly array of outhouses, long grape arbors, green pastures, orchards, and berry patches. Then there was the pumping plant for the artesian well, and the big cement tank where Judge Miller's boys took their morning plunge and kept cool in the hot afternoon.

And over this great demesne Buck ruled. Here he was born, and here he had lived the four years of his life. It was true, there were other dogs. There could not but be other dogs on so vast a place, but they did not count. They came and went, resided in the populous kennels, or lived obscurely in the recesses of the house after the fashion of Toots, the Japanese pug, or Ysabel,

the Mexican hairless,—strange creatures that rarely put nose out of doors or set foot to ground. On the other hand, there were the fox terriers, a score of them at least, who yelped fearful promises at Toots and Ysabel looking out of the windows at them and protected by a legion of housemaids armed with brooms and mops.

But Buck was neither house-dog nor kennel dog. The whole realm was his. He plunged into the swimming tank or went hunting with the Judge's sons; he escorted Mollie and Alice, the Judge's daughters, on long twilight or early morning rambles; on wintry nights he lay at the Judge's feet before the roaring library fire; he carried the Judge's grandsons on his back, or rolled them in the grass, and guarded their footsteps through wild adventures down to the fountain in the stable yard, and even beyond, where the paddocks were, and the berry patches. Among the terriers he stalked imperiously, and Toots and Ysabel he utterly ignored, for he was king,—king over all creeping, crawling, flying things of Judge Miller's place, humans included.

His father, Elmo, a huge St. Bernard, had been the Judge's inseparable companion, and Buck bid fair to follow in the way of his father. He was not so large,—he weighed only one hundred and forty pounds,—for his mother, Shep, had been a Scotch shepherd dog. Nevertheless, one hundred and forty pounds, to which was added the dignity that comes of good living and universal respect, enabled him to carry himself in right royal fashion. During the four years since his puppyhood he had lived the life of a sated aristocrat; he had a fine pride in himself, was ever a trifle egotistical, as country gentlemen sometimes become because of their insular situation. But he had saved himself by not becoming a mere pampered house-dog. Hunting and kindred outdoor delights had kept down the fat and hardened his muscles; and to him, as to the cold-tubbing races, the love of water had been a tonic and a health preserver.

And this was the manner of dog Buck was in the fall of 1897, when the Klondike strike dragged men from all the world into the frozen North. But Buck did not read the newspapers, and he did not know that Manuel, one of the gardener's helpers, was an undesirable acquaintance. Manuel had one besetting sin. He loved to play Chinese lottery. Also, in his gambling, he had one besetting weakness—faith in a system; and this made his damnation certain. For to play a system requires money, while the wages of a gardener's helper do not lap over the needs of a wife and numerous progeny.

The Judge was at a meeting of the Raisin Growers' Association, and the boys were busy organizing an athletic club, on the memorable night of Manuel's treachery. No one saw him and Buck go off through the orchard on what Buck imagined was merely a stroll. And with the exception of a solitary man, no one saw them arrive at the little flag station known as College Park. This man talked with Manuel, and money chinked between them.

"You might wrap up the goods before you deliver 'm," the stranger said gruffly, and Manuel doubled a piece of stout rope around Buck's neck under the collar.

"Twist it, an' you'll choke 'm plentee," said Manuel, and the stranger grunted a ready affirmative.

Buck had accepted the rope with quiet dignity. To be sure, it was an unwonted performance: but he had learned to trust in men he knew, and to give them credit for a wisdom that outreached his own. But when the ends of the rope were placed in the stranger's hands, he growled menacingly. He had merely intimated his displeasure, in his pride believing that to intimate was to command. But to his surprise the rope tightened around his neck, shutting off his breath. In quick rage he sprang at the man, who met him halfway, grappled him close by the throat, and with a deft twist threw him over on his back. Then the rope tightened mercilessly, while Buck struggled in a fury, his tongue lolling out of his mouth and his great chest panting futilely. Never in all his life had he been so vilely treated, and never in all his life had he been so angry. But his strength ebbed, his eyes glazed, and he knew nothing when the train was flagged and the two men threw him into the baggage car.

The next he knew, he was dimly aware that his tongue was hurting and that he was being jolted along in some kind of a conveyance. The hoarse shriek of a locomotive whistling a crossing told him where he was. He had travelled too often with the Judge not to know the sensation of riding in a baggage car. He opened his eyes, and into them came the unbridled anger of a kidnapped king. The man sprang for his throat, but Buck was too quick for him. His jaws closed on the hand, nor did they relax till his senses were choked out of him once more.

"Yep, has fits," the man said, hiding his mangled hand from the baggage-man, who had been attracted by the sounds of struggle. "I'm takin' 'm up for the boss to 'Frisco. A crack dog-doctor there thinks that he can cure 'm."

Concerning that night's ride, the man spoke most eloquently for himself, in a little shed back of a saloon on the San Francisco water front.

"All I get is fifty for it," he grumbled; "an' I wouldn't do it over for a thousand, cold cash."

His hand was wrapped in a bloody handkerchief, and the right trouser leg was ripped from knee to ankle.

"How much did the other mug get?" the saloon-keeper demanded.

"A hundred," was the reply. "Wouldn't take a sou less, so help me."

"That makes a hundred and fifty," the saloon-keeper calculated; "and he's worth it, or I'm a squarehead."

The kidnapper undid the bloody wrappings and looked at his lacerated hand. "If I don't get the hydrophoby—"

"It'll be because you was born to hang," laughed the saloon-keeper. "Here, lend me a hand before you pull your freight," he added.

Dazed, suffering intolerable pain from throat and tongue, with the life half throttled out of him, Buck attempted to face his tormentors. But he was thrown down and choked repeatedly, till they succeeded in filing the heavy brass collar from off his neck. Then the rope was removed, and he was flung into a cagelike crate.

There he lay for the remainder of the weary night, nursing his wrath and wounded pride. He could not understand what it all meant. What did they want with him, these strange men? Why were they keeping him pent up in this narrow crate? He did not know why, but he felt oppressed by the vague sense of impending calamity. Several times during the night he sprang to his feet when the shed door rattled open, expecting to see the Judge, or the boys at least. But each time it was the bulging face of the saloon-keeper that peered in at him by the sickly light of a tallow candle. And each time the joyful bark that trembled in Buck's throat was twisted into a savage growl.

But the saloon-keeper let him alone, and in the morning four men entered and picked up the crate. More tormentors, Buck decided, for they were evil-looking creatures, ragged and unkempt; and he stormed and raged at them through the bars. They only laughed and poked sticks at him, which he promptly assailed with his teeth till he realized that that was what they wanted. Whereupon he lay down sullenly and allowed the crate to be lifted into a wagon. Then he, and the crate in which he was imprisoned, began a passage through many hands. Clerks in the express office took charge of him; he was carted about in another wagon; a truck carried him, with an assortment of boxes and parcels, upon a ferry steamer; he was trucked off the steamer into a great railway depot, and finally he was deposited in an express car.

For two days and nights this express car was dragged along at the tail of shrieking locomotives; and for two days and nights Buck neither ate nor drank. In his anger he had met the first advances of the express messengers with growls, and they had retaliated by teasing him. When he flung himself against the bars, quivering and frothing, they laughed at him and taunted him. They growled and barked like detestable dogs, mewed, and flapped their arms and crowed. It was all very silly, he knew; but therefore the more outrage to his dignity, and his anger waxed and waxed. He did not mind the hunger so much, but the lack of water caused him severe suffering and fanned his wrath to fever-pitch. For that matter, high-strung and finely sensitive, the ill treatment had flung him into a fever, which was fed by the inflammation of his parched and swollen throat and tongue.

He was glad for one thing: the rope was off his neck. That had given them an unfair advantage; but now that it was off, he would show them. They would never get another rope around his neck. Upon that he was resolved. For two days and nights he neither ate nor drank, and during those two days and nights of torment, he accumulated a fund of wrath that boded ill for whoever first fell foul of him. His eyes turned blood-shot, and he was metamorphosed into a raging fiend. So changed was he that the Judge himself would not have recognized him; and the express messengers breathed with relief when they bundled him off the train at Seattle.

Four men gingerly carried the crate from the wagon into a small, high-walled back yard. A stout man, with a red sweater that sagged generously at the neck, came out and signed the book for the driver. That was the man, Buck divined, the next tormentor, and he hurled himself savagely against the bars. The man smiled grimly, and brought a hatchet and a club.

"You ain't going to take him out now?" the driver asked.

"Sure," the man replied, driving the hatchet into the crate for a pry.

There was an instantaneous scattering of the four men who had carried it in, and from safe perches on top the wall they prepared to watch the performance.

Buck rushed at the splintering wood, sinking his teeth into it, surging and wrestling with it. Wherever the hatchet fell on the outside, he was there on the inside, snarling and growling, as furiously anxious to get out as the man in the red sweater was calmly intent on getting him out.

"Now, you red-eyed devil," he said, when he had made an opening sufficient for the passage of Buck's body. At the same time he dropped the hatchet and shifted the club to his right hand.

And Buck was truly a red-eyed devil, as he drew himself together for the spring, hair bristling, mouth foaming, a mad glitter in his blood-shot eyes. Straight at the man he launched his one hundred and forty pounds of fury, surcharged with the pent passion of two days and nights. In mid air, just as his jaws were about to close on the man, he received a shock that checked his body and brought his teeth together with an agonizing clip. He whirled over, fetching the ground on his back and side. He had never been struck by a club in his life, and did not understand. With a snarl that was part bark and more scream he was again on his feet and launched into the air. And again the shock came and he was brought crushingly to the ground. This time he was aware that it was the club, but his madness knew no caution. A dozen times he charged, and as often the club broke the charge and smashed him down.

After a particularly fierce blow he crawled to his feet, too dazed to rush. He staggered limply about, the blood flowing from nose and mouth and ears, his beautiful coat sprayed and flecked with bloody slaver. Then the man advanced and deliberately dealt him a frightful blow on the nose. All the pain he had endured was as nothing compared with the exquisite agony of this. With a roar that was almost lionlike in its ferocity, he again hurled himself at the man. But the man, shifting the club from right to left, coolly caught him by the under jaw, at the same time wrenching downward and backward. Buck described a complete circle in the air, and half of another, then crashed to the ground on his head and chest.

For the last time he rushed. The man struck the shrewd blow he had purposely withheld for so long, and Buck crumpled up and went down, knocked utterly senseless.

"He's no slouch at dog-breakin', that's wot I say," one of the men on the wall cried enthusiastically.

"Druther break cayuses any day, and twice on Sundays," was the reply of the driver, as he climbed on the wagon and started the horses.

Buck's senses came back to him, but not his strength. He lay where he had fallen, and from there he watched the man in the red sweater.

" 'Answers to the name of Buck,' " the man soliloquized, quoting from the saloon-keeper's letter which had announced the consignment of the crate and contents. "Well, Buck, my boy," he went on in a genial voice, "we've had our little ruction, and the best thing we can do is to let it go at that. You've learned your place, and I know mine. Be a good dog and all 'll go well and the goose hang high. Be a bad dog, and I'll whale the stuffin' outa you. Understand?"

As he spoke he fearlessly patted the head he had so mercilessly pounded, and though Buck's hair involuntarily bristled at touch of the hand, he endured it without protest. When the man brought him water, he drank eagerly, and later bolted a generous meal of raw meat, chunk by chunk, from the man's hand.

He was beaten (he knew that); but he was not broken. He saw, once for all, that he stood no chance against a man with a club. He had learned the lesson, and in all his after life he never forgot it. That club was a revelation. It was his introduction to the reign of primitive law, and he met the introduction halfway. The facts of life took on a fiercer aspect; and while he faced that aspect uncowed, he faced it with all the latent cunning of his nature aroused. As the days went by, other dogs came, in crates and at the ends of ropes, some docilely, and some raging and roaring as he had come; and, one and all, he watched them pass under the dominion of the man in the red sweater. Again and again, as he looked at each brutal performance, the lesson was driven home to Buck: a man with a club was a lawgiver, a master to be obeyed, though not necessarily conciliated. Of this last Buck was never guilty, though he did see beaten dogs that fawned upon the man, and wagged their tails, and licked his hand. Also he saw one dog, that would neither conciliate nor obey, finally killed in the struggle for mastery.

Now and again men came, strangers, who talked excitedly, wheedlingly, and in all kinds of fashions to the man in the red sweater. And at such times that money passed between them the strangers took one or more of the dogs away with them. Buck wondered where they went, for they never came back; but the fear of the future was strong upon him, and he was glad each time when he was not selected.

Yet his time came, in the end, in the form of a little weazened man who spat broken English and many strange and uncouth exclamations which Buck could not understand.

"Sacredam!" he cried, when his eyes lit upon Buck. "Dat one dam bully dog! Eh? How moch?"

"Three hundred, and a present at that," was the prompt reply of the man in the red sweater. "And seein' it's government money, you ain't got no kick coming, eh, Perrault?"

Perrault grinned. Considering that the price of dogs had been boomed skyward by the unwonted demand, it was not an unfair sum for so fine an animal. The Canadian Government would be no loser, nor would its despatches travel the slower. Perrault knew dogs, and when he looked at Buck he knew that he was one in a thousand—"One in ten t'ousand," he commented mentally.

Buck saw money pass between them, and was not surprised when Curly, a good-natured Newfoundland, and he were led away by the little weazened man. That was the last he saw of the man in the red sweater, and as Curly and he looked at receding Seattle from the deck of the *Narwhal*, it was the last he saw of the warm Southland. Curly and he were taken below by Perrault and turned over to a black-faced giant called François. Perrault was a French-Canadian, and swarthy; but François was a French-Canadian half-breed, and twice as swarthy. They were a new kind of men to Buck (of which he was destined to see many more), and while he developed no affection for them, he none the less grew honestly to respect them. He speedily learned that Perrault and François were fair men, calm and impartial in administering justice, and too wise in the way of dogs to be fooled by dogs.

In the 'tween-decks of the *Narwhal*, Buck and Curly joined two other dogs. One of them was a big, snow-white fellow from Spitzbergen who had been brought away by a whaling captain, and who had later accompanied a Geological Survey into the Barrens.

He was friendly, in a treacherous sort of way, smiling into one's face the while he meditated some underhand trick, as, for instance, when he stole from Buck's food at the first meal. As Buck sprang to punish him, the lash of François's whip sang through the air, reaching the culprit first; and nothing remained to Buck but to recover the bone. That was fair of François, he decided, and the half-breed began his rise in Buck's estimation.

The other dog made no advances, nor received any; also, he did not attempt to steal from the newcomers. He was a gloomy, morose fellow, and he showed Curly plainly that all he desired was to be left alone, and further, that there would be trouble if he were not left alone. "Dave" he was called, and he ate and slept, or yawned between times, and took interest in nothing, not even when the *Narwhal* crossed Queen Charlotte Sound and rolled and pitched and bucked like a thing possessed. When Buck and Curly grew excited, half wild with fear, he raised his head as though annoyed, favored them with an incurious glance, yawned, and went to sleep again.

Day and night the ship throbbed to the tireless pulse of the propeller, and though one day was very like another, it was apparent to Buck that the weather was steadily growing colder. At last, one morning, the propeller was quiet, and the *Narwhal* was pervaded with an atmosphere of excitement. He felt it, as did the other dogs, and knew that a change was at hand. François leashed them and brought them on deck. At the first step upon the cold surface, Buck's feet sank into a white mushy something very like mud. He sprang back with a snort. More of this white stuff was falling through the air. He shook himself, but more of it fell upon him. He sniffed it curiously, then licked some up on his tongue. It bit like fire, and the next instant was gone. This puzzled him. He tried it again, with the same result. The onlookers laughed uproariously, and he felt ashamed, he knew not why, for it was his first snow.

II. THE LAW OF CLUB AND FANG

Buck's first day on the Dyea beach was like a nightmare. Every hour was filled with shock and surprise. He had been suddenly jerked from the heart of civilization and flung into the heart of things primordial. No lazy, sun-kissed life was this, with nothing to do but loaf and be bored. Here was neither peace, nor rest, nor a moment's safety. All was confusion and action, and every moment life and limb were in peril. There was imperative need to be constantly alert; for these dogs and men were not town dogs and men. They were savages, all of them, who knew no law but the law of club and fang.

He had never seen dogs fight as these wolfish creatures fought, and his first experience taught him an unforgettable lesson. It is true, it was a vicarious experience, else he would not have lived to profit by it. Curly was the victim. They were camped near the log store, where she, in her friendly way, made advances to a husky dog the size of a full-grown wolf, though not half so large as she. There was no warning, only a leap in like a flash, a metallic clip of teeth, a leap out equally swift, and Curly's face was ripped open from eye to jaw.

It was the wolf manner of fighting, to strike and leap away; but there was more to it than this. Thirty or forty huskies ran to the spot and surrounded the combatants in an intent and silent circle. Buck did not comprehend that silent intentness, nor the eager way with which they were licking their chops. Curly rushed her antagonist, who struck again and leaped aside. He met her next rush with his chest, in a peculiar fashion that tumbled her off her feet. She never regained them. This was what the onlooking huskies had waited for. They closed in upon her, snarling and yelping, and she was buried, screaming with agony, beneath the bristling mass of bodies.

So sudden was it, and so unexpected, that Buck was taken aback. He saw Spitz run out his scarlet tongue in a way he had of laughing; and he saw François, swinging an axe, spring into the mess of dogs. Three men with clubs were helping him to scatter them. It did not take long. Two minutes from the time Curly went down, the last of her assailants were clubbed off. But she lay there limp and lifeless in the bloody, trampled snow, almost literally torn to pieces, the swart half-breed standing over her and cursing horribly. The scene often came back to Buck to trouble him in his sleep. So that was the way. No fair play. Once down, that was the end of you. Well, he would see to it that he never went down. Spitz ran out his tongue and laughed again, and from that moment Buck hated him with a bitter and deathless hatred.

Before he had recovered from the shock caused by the tragic passing of Curly, he received another shock. François fastened upon him an arrangement of straps and buckles. It was a harness, such as he had seen the grooms put on the horses at home. And as he had seen horses work, so he was set to work, hauling François on a sled to the forest that fringed the valley, and returning with a load of firewood. Though his dignity was sorely hurt by thus being made a draught animal, he was too wise to rebel. He buckled down with a will and did his best, though it was all new and strange. François was stern, demanding instant obedience, and by virtue of his whip receiving instant obedience; while Dave, who was an experienced wheeler, nipped Buck's hind quarters whenever he was in error. Spitz was the leader, likewise experienced, and while he could not always get at Buck, he growled sharp reproof now and again, or cunningly threw his weight in the traces to jerk Buck into the way he should go. Buck learned easily, and under the combined tuition of his two mates and François made remarkable progress. Ere they returned to camp he knew enough to stop at "ho," to go ahead at "mush," to swing wide on the bends, and to keep clear of the wheeler when the loaded sled shot downhill at their heels.

"T'ree vair' good dogs," François told Perrault. "Dat Buck, heem pool lak hell. I tich heem queek as anyt'ing."

By afternoon, Perrault, who was in a hurry to be on the trail with his despatches, returned with two more dogs. "Billee" and "Joe" he called them, two brothers, and true huskies both. Sons of the one mother though they were, they were as different as day and night. Billee's one fault was his excessive good nature, while Joe was the very opposite, sour and introspective, with a perpetual snarl and a malignant eye. Buck received them in comradely fashion, Dave ignored them, while Spitz proceeded to thrash first one and then the other. Billee wagged his tail appeasingly, turned to run when he saw that appeasement was of no avail, and cried (still appeasingly) when Spitz's sharp teeth scored his flank. But no matter how Spitz circled, Joe whirled around on his heels to face him, mane bristling, ears laid back, lips writhing and snarling, jaws clipping together as fast as he could snap, and eyes diabolically gleaming—the incarnation of belligerent fear. So terrible was his appearance that Spitz was forced to forego disciplining him; but to cover his own discomfiture he turned upon the inoffensive and wailing Billee and drove him to the confines of the camp.

By evening Perrault secured another dog, an old husky, long and lean and gaunt, with a battle-scarred face and a single eye which flashed a warning of prowess that commanded respect. He was called Sol-leks, which means the Angry One. Like Dave, he asked nothing, gave nothing, expected nothing: and when he marched slowly and deliberately into their midst, even Spitz left him alone. He had one peculiarity which Buck was unlucky enough to discover. He did not like to be approached on his blind side. Of this offence Buck was unwittingly guilty, and the first knowledge he had of his indiscretion was when Sol-leks whirled upon him and slashed his shoulder to the bone for three inches up and down. Forever after Buck avoided his blind side, and to the last of their comradeship had no more trouble. His only apparent ambition, like Dave's, was to be left alone; though, as Buck was afterward to learn, each of them possessed one other and even more vital ambition.

That night Buck faced the great problem of sleeping. The tent, illumined by a candle, glowed warmly in the midst of the white plain; and when he, as a matter of course, entered it, both Perrault and François bombarded him with curses and cooking utensils, till he recovered from his consternation and fled ignominiously into the outer cold. A chill wind was blowing that nipped him sharply and bit with especial venom into his wounded shoulder. He lay down on the snow and attempted to sleep, but the frost soon drove him shivering to his feet. Miserable and disconsolate, he wandered about among the many tents, only to find that one place was as cold as another. Here and there savage dogs rushed upon him, but he bristled his neck-hair and snarled (for he was learning fast), and they let him go his way unmolested.

Finally an idea came to him. He would return and see how his own team mates were making out. To his astonishment, they had disappeared. Again he wandered about through the great camp, looking for them, and again he returned. Were they in the tent? No, that could not be, else he would not have been driven out. Then where could they possibly be? With drooping tail and shivering body, very forlorn indeed, he aimlessly circled the tent. Suddenly the snow gave way beneath his fore legs and he sank down. Something wriggled under his feet. He sprang back, bristling and snarling, fearful of the unseen and unknown. But a friendly little yelp reassured him, and he went back to investigate. A whiff of warm air ascended to his nostrils, and there, curled up under the snow in a snug ball, lay Billee. He whined placatingly, squirmed and wriggled to show his good will and intentions, and even ventured, as a bribe for peace, to lick Buck's face with his warm wet tongue.

Another lesson. So that was the way they did it, eh? Buck confidently selected a spot, and with much fuss and waste effort proceeded to dig a hole for himself. In a trice the heat from his body filled the confined space and he was asleep. The day had been long and arduous, and he slept soundly and comfortably, though he growled and barked and wrestled with bad dreams.

Nor did he open his eyes till roused by the noises of the waking camp. At first he did not know where he was. It had snowed during the night and he was completely buried. The snow walls pressed him on every side, and a great surge of fear swept through him—the fear of the wild thing for the trap. It was a token that he was harking back through his own life to the lives of his forbears; for he was a civilized dog, an unduly civilized dog and of his own experience knew no trap and so could not of himself fear it. The muscles of his whole body contracted spasmodically and instinctively, the hair on his neck and shoulders stood on end, and with a ferocious snarl he bounded straight up into the blinding day, the snow flying about him in a flashing cloud. Ere he landed on his feet, he saw the white camp spread out before him and knew where he was and remembered all that had passed from the time he went for a stroll with Manuel to the hole he had dug for himself the night before.

A shout from François hailed his appearance. "Wot I say?" the dog-driver cried to Perrault. "Dat Buck for sure learn queek as anyt'ing."

Perrault nodded gravely. As courier for the Canadian Government, bearing important despatches, he was anxious to secure the best dogs, and he was particularly gladdened by the possession of Buck.

Three more huskies were added to the team inside an hour, making a total of nine, and before another quarter of an hour had passed they were in harness and swinging up the trail toward the Dyea Cañon. Buck was glad to be gone, and though the work was hard he found he did not particularly despise it. He was surprised at the eagerness which animated the whole team and which was communicated to him; but still more surprising was the change wrought in Dave and Sol-leks. They were new dogs, utterly transformed by the harness. All passiveness and unconcern had dropped from them. They were alert and active, anxious that the work should go well, and fiercely irritable with whatever, by delay or confusion, retarded that work. The toil of the traces seemed the supreme expression of their being, and all that they lived for and the only thing in which they took delight.

Dave was wheeler or sled dog, pulling in front of him was Buck, then came Sol-leks; the rest of the team was strung out ahead, single file, to the leader, which position was filled by Spitz.

Buck had been purposely placed between Dave and Sol-leks so that he might receive instruction. Apt scholar that he was, they were equally apt teachers, never allowing him to linger long in error, and enforcing their teaching with their sharp teeth. Dave was fair and very wise. He never nipped Buck without cause, and he never failed to nip him when he stood in need of it. As François's whip backed him up, Buck found it to be cheaper to mend his ways than to retaliate. Once, during a brief halt, when he got tangled in the traces and delayed the start, both Dave and Sol-leks flew at him and administered a sound trouncing. The resulting tangle was even worse, but Buck took good care to keep the traces clear thereafter; and ere the day was done, so well had he mastered his work, his mates about ceased nagging him. François's whip snapped less frequently, and Perrault even honored Buck by lifting up his feet and carefully examining them.

It was a hard day's run, up the Cañon, through Sheep Camp, past the Scales and the timber line, across glaciers and snowdrifts hundreds of feet deep, and over the great Chilcoot Divide, which stands between the salt water and the fresh, and guards forbiddingly the sad and lonely North. They made good time down the chain of lakes which fills the craters of extinct volcanoes, and late that night pulled into the huge camp at the head of Lake Bennett, where thousands of gold-seekers were building boats against the breakup of the ice in the spring. Buck made his hole in the snow and slept the sleep of the exhausted just, but all too early was routed out in the cold darkness and harnessed with his mates to the sled.

That day they made forty miles, the trail being packed; but the next day, and for many days to follow, they broke their own trail, worked harder, and made poorer time. As a rule, Perrault travelled ahead of the team, packing the snow with webbed shoes to make it easier for them. François, guiding the sled at the gee-pole, sometimes exchanged places with him, but not often. Perrault was in a hurry, and he prided himself on his knowledge of ice, which knowledge was indispensable, for the fall ice was very thin, and where there was swift water, there was no ice at all.

Day after day, for days unending, Buck toiled in the traces. Always, they broke camp in the dark, and the first gray of dawn found them hitting the trail with fresh miles reeled off behind them. And always they pitched camp after dark, eating their bit of fish, and crawling to sleep into the snow. Buck was ravenous. The pound and a half of sun-dried salmon, which was his ration for each day, seemed to go nowhere. He never had enough, and suffered from perpetual hunger pangs. Yet the other dogs, because they weighed less and were born to the life, received a pound only of the fish and managed to keep in good condition.

He swiftly lost the fastidiousness which had characterized his old life. A dainty eater, he found that his mates, finishing first, robbed him of his unfinished ration. There was no defending it. While he was fighting off two or three, it was disappearing down the throats of the others. To remedy this, he ate as fast as they; and, so greatly did hunger compel him, he was not above taking what did not belong to him. He watched and learned. When he saw Pike, one of the new dogs, a clever malingerer and thief, slyly steal a slice of bacon when Perrault's back was turned, he duplicated the performance the following day, getting away with the whole chunk. A great uproar was raised, but he was unsuspected; while Dub, an awkward blunderer who was always getting caught, was punished for Buck's misdeed.

This first theft marked Buck as fit to survive in the hostile Northland environment. It marked his adaptability, his capacity to adjust himself to changing conditions, the lack of which would have meant swift and terrible death. It marked, further, the decay or going to pieces of his moral nature, a vain thing and a handicap in the ruthless struggle for existence. It was all well enough in the Southland, under the law of love and fellowship, to respect private property and personal feelings; but in the Northland, under the law of club and fang, whoso took such things into account was a fool, and in so far as he observed them he would fail to prosper.

Not that Buck reasoned it out. He was fit, that was all, and unconsciously he accommodated himself to the new mode of life. All his days, no matter what the odds, he had never run from a fight. But the club of the man in the red sweater had beaten into him a more fundamental and primitive code. Civilized, he could have died for a moral consideration, say the defence of Judge Miller's riding whip; but the completeness of his decivilization was now evidenced by his ability to flee from the defence of a moral consideration and so save his hide. He did not steal for joy of it, but because of the clamor of his stomach. He did not rob openly, but stole secretly and cunningly, out of respect for club and fang. In short, the things he did were done because it was easier to do them than not to do them.

His development (or retrogression) was rapid. His muscles became hard as iron, and he grew callous to all ordinary pain. He achieved an internal as well as external economy. He could eat anything, no matter how loathsome or indigestible; and, once eaten, the juices of his stomach extracted the last least particle of nutriment; and his blood carried it to the farthest reaches of his body, building it into the toughest and stoutest of tissues. Sight and scent became remarkably keen, while his hearing developed such acuteness that in his sleep he heard the faintest sound and knew whether it heralded peace or peril. He learned to bite the ice out with his teeth when it collected between his toes; and when he was thirsty and there was a thick scum of ice over the water hole, he would break it by rearing and striking it with stiff fore legs. His most conspicuous trait was an ability to scent the wind and forecast it a night in advance. No matter how breathless the air when he dug his nest by tree or bank, the wind that later blew inevitably found him to leeward, sheltered and snug.

And not only did he learn by experience, but instincts long dead became alive again. The domesticated generations fell from him. In vague ways he remembered back to the youth of the breed, to the time the wild dogs ranged in packs through the primeval forest and killed their meat as they ran it down. It was no task for him to learn to fight with cut and slash and the quick wolf snap. In this manner had fought forgotten ancestors. They quickened the old life within him, and the old tricks which they had stamped into the heredity of the breed were his tricks. They came to him without effort or discovery, as though they had been his always. And when, on the still cold nights, he pointed his nose at a star and howled long and wolflike, it was his ancestors, dead and dust, pointing nose at star and howling down through the centuries and through him. And his cadences were their cadences, the cadences which voiced their woe and what to them was the meaning of the stillness, and the cold, and dark.

Thus, as token of what a puppet thing life is, the ancient song surged through him and he came into his own again; and he came because men had found a yellow metal in the North, and because Manuel was a gardener's helper whose wages did not lap over the needs of his wife and divers small copies of himself.

III. THE DOMINANT PRIMORDIAL BEAST

The dominant primordial beast was strong in Buck, and under the fierce conditions of trail life it grew and grew. Yet it was a secret growth. His newborn cunning gave him poise and control. He was too busy adjusting himself to the new life to feel at ease, and not only did he not pick fights, but he avoided them whenever possible. A certain deliberateness characterized his attitude. He was not prone to rashness and precipitate action; and in the bitter hatred between him and Spitz he betrayed no impatience, shunned all offensive acts.

On the other hand, possibly because he divined in Buck a dangerous rival, Spitz never lost an opportunity of showing his teeth. He even went out of his way to bully Buck, striving constantly to start the fight which could end only in the death of one or the other.

Early in the trip this might have taken place had it not been for an unwonted accident. At the end of this day they made a bleak and miserable camp on the shore of Lake Le Barge. Driving snow, a wind that cut like a white-hot knife, and darkness, had forced them to grope for a camping place. They could hardly have fared worse. At their backs rose a perpendicular wall of rock, and Perrault and François were compelled to make their fire and spread their sleeping robes on the ice of the lake itself. The tent they had discarded at Dyea in order to travel light. A few sticks of driftwood furnished them with a fire that thawed down through the ice and left them to eat supper in the dark.

Close in under the sheltering rock Buck made his nest. So snug and warm was it, that he was loath to leave it when François distributed the fish which he had first thawed over the fire. But when Buck finished his ration and returned, he found his nest occupied. A warning snarl told him that the trespasser was Spitz. Till now Buck had avoided trouble with his enemy, but this was too much. The beast in him roared. He sprang upon Spitz with a fury which surprised them both, and Spitz particularly, for his whole experience with Buck had gone to teach him that his rival was an unusually timid dog, who managed to hold his own only because of his great weight and size.

François was surprised, too, when they shot out in a tangle from the disrupted nest and he divined the cause of the trouble. "A-a-ah!" he cried to Buck. "Gif it to heem by Gar! Gif it to heem, the dirty t'eef!"

Spitz was equally willing. He was crying with sheer rage and eagerness as he circled back and forth for a chance to spring in. Buck was no less eager, and no less cautious, as he likewise circled back and forth for the advantage. But it was then that the unexpected happened, the thing which projected their struggle for supremacy far into the future, past many a weary mile of trail and toil.

An oath from Perrault, the resounding impact of a club upon a bony frame, and a shrill yelp of pain, heralded the breaking forth of pandemonium. The camp was suddenly discovered to be alive with skulking furry forms,—starving huskies, four or five score of them, who had scented the camp from some Indian village. They had crept in while Buck and Spitz were fighting, and when the two men sprang among them with stout clubs they showed their teeth and fought back. They were crazed by the smell of the food. Perrault found one with head buried in the grub-box. His club landed heavily on the gaunt ribs, and the grub-box was capsized on the ground. On the instant a score of the famished brutes were scrambling for the bread and bacon. The clubs fell upon them unheeded. They yelped and howled under the rain of blows, but struggled none the less madly till the last crumb had been devoured.

In the meantime the astonished team-dogs had burst out of their nests only to be set upon by the fierce invaders. Never had Buck seen such dogs. It seemed as though their bones would burst through their skins. They were mere skeletons, draped loosely in draggled hides, with blazing eyes and slavered fangs. But the hunger-madness made them terrifying, irresistible. There was no opposing them. The team-dogs were swept back against the cliff at the first onset. Buck was beset by three huskies, and in a trice his head and shoulders were ripped and slashed. The din was frightful. Billee was crying as usual. Dave and Sol-leks, dripping blood from a score of wounds, were fighting bravely side by side. Joe was snapping like a demon. Once his teeth closed on the fore leg of a husky, and he crunched down through the bone. Pike, the malingerer, leaped upon the crippled animal, breaking its neck with a quick flash of teeth and a jerk. Buck got a frothing adversary by the throat, and was sprayed with blood when his teeth sank through the jugular. The warm taste of it in his mouth goaded him to greater fierceness. He flung himself upon another, and at the same time felt teeth sink into his own throat. It was Spitz, treacherously attacking from the side.

Perrault and François, having cleaned out their part of the camp, hurried to save their sled-dogs. The wild wave of famished beasts rolled back before them, and Buck shook himself free. But it was only for a moment. The two men were compelled to run back to save the grub; upon which the huskies returned to the attack on the team. Billee, terrified into bravery, sprang through the savage circle and fled away over the ice. Pike and Dub followed on his heels, with the rest of the team behind. As Buck drew himself together to spring after them, out of the tail of his eye he saw Spitz rush upon him with the evident intention of overthrowing him. Once off his feet and under that mass of huskies, there was no hope for him. But he braced himself to the shock of Spitz's charge, then joined the flight out on the lake.

Later, the nine team-dogs gathered together and sought shelter in the forest. Though unpursued, they were in a sorry plight. There was not one who was not wounded in four or five places, while some were wounded grievously. Dub was badly injured in a hind leg; Dolly, the last husky added to the team at Dyea, had a badly torn throat; Joe had lost an eye; while Billee, the goodnatured, with an ear chewed and rent to ribbons, cried and whimpered throughout the night. At daybreak they limped warily back to camp, to find the marauders gone and the two men in bad tempers. Fully half their grub supply was gone. The huskies had chewed through the sled lashings and canvas coverings. In fact, nothing, no matter how remotely eatable, had escaped them. They had eaten a pair of Perrault's moose-hide moccasins, chunks out of the leather traces, and even two feet of lash from the end of François's whip. He broke from a mournful contemplation of it to look over his wounded dogs.

"Ah, my frien's," he said softly, "mebbe it mek you mad dog, dose many bites. Mebbe all mad dog, sacredam! Wot you t'ink, eh, Perrault?"

The courier shook his head dubiously. With four hundred miles of trail still between him and Dawson, he could ill afford to have madness break out among his dogs. Two hours of cursing and exertion got the harnesses into shape, and the wound-stiffened team was under way, struggling painfully over the hardest part of the trail they had yet encountered, and for that matter, the hardest between them and Dawson.

The Thirty Mile River was wide open. Its wild water defied the frost, and it was in the eddies only and in the quiet places that the ice held at all. Six days of exhausting toil were required to cover those thirty terrible miles. And terrible they were, for every foot of them was accomplished at the risk of life to dog and man. A dozen times, Perrault, nosing the way, broke through the ice bridges, being saved by the long pole he carried, which he so held that it fell each time across the hole made by his body. But a cold snap was on, the thermometer registering fifty below zero, and each time he broke through he was compelled for very life to build a fire and dry his garments.

Nothing daunted him. It was because nothing daunted him that he had been chosen for government courier. He took all manner of risks, resolutely thrusting his little weazened face into the frost and struggling on from dim dawn to dark. He skirted the frowning shores on rim ice that bent and crackled under foot and upon which they dared not halt. Once, the sled broke through, with Dave and Buck, and they were half-frozen and all but drowned by the time they were dragged out. The usual fire was necessary to save them. They were coated solidly with ice, and the two men kept them on the run around the fire, sweating and thawing, so close that they were singed by the flames.

At another time Spitz went through, dragging the whole team after him up to Buck, who strained backward with all his strength, his fore paws on the slippery edge and the ice quivering and snapping all around. But behind him was Dave, likewise straining backward, and behind the sled was François, pulling till his tendons cracked.

Again, the rim ice broke away before and behind, and there was no escape except up the cliff. Perrault scaled it by a miracle, while François prayed for just that miracle; and with every thong and sled-lashing and the last bit of harness rove into a long rope, the dogs were hoisted, one by one, to the cliff crest. François came up last, after the sled and load. Then came the search for a place to descend, which descent was ultimately made by the aid of the rope, and night found them back on the river with a quarter of a mile to the day's credit.

By the time they made the Hootalinqua and good ice, Buck was played out. The rest of the dogs were in like condition; but Perrault, to make up lost time, pushed them late and early. The first day they covered thirty-five miles to the Big Salmon; the next day thirty-five more to the Little Salmon; the third day forty miles, which brought them well up toward the Five Fingers.

Buck's feet were not so compact and hard as the feet of the huskies. His had softened during the many generations since the day his last wild ancestor was tamed by a cave-dweller or river man. All day long he limped in agony, and camp once made, lay down like a dead dog. Hungry as he was, he would not move to receive his ration of fish, which François had to bring to him. Also, the dog-driver rubbed Buck's feet for half an hour each night after supper, and sacrificed the tops of his own moccasins to make four moccasins for Buck. This was a great relief, and Buck caused even the weazened face of Perrault to twist itself into a grin one morning, when François forgot the moccasins and Buck lay on his back, his four feet waving appealingly in the air, and refused to budge without them. Later his feet grew hard to the trail, and the worn-out foot-gear was thrown away.

At the Pelly one morning, as they were harnessing up, Dolly, who had never been conspicuous for anything, went suddenly mad. She announced her condition by a long, heart-breaking wolf howl that sent every dog bristling with fear, then sprang straight for Buck. He had never seen a dog go mad, nor did he have any reason to fear madness; yet he knew that here was horror, and fled away from it in a panic. Straight away he raced, with Dolly, panting and frothing, one leap behind; nor could she gain on him, so great was his terror, nor could he leave her, so great was her madness. He plunged through the wooded breast of the island, flew down to the lower end, crossed a back channel filled with rough ice to another island, gained a third island, curved back to the main river, and in desperation started to cross it. And all the time, though he did not look, he could hear her snarling just one leap behind. François called to him a quarter of a mile away and he doubled back, still one leap ahead, gasping painfully for air and putting all his faith in that François would save him. The dog-driver held the axe poised in his hand, and as Buck shot past him the axe crashed down upon mad Dolly's head.

Buck staggered over against the sled, exhausted, sobbing for breath, helpless. This was Spitz's opportunity. He sprang upon Buck, and twice his teeth sank into his unresisting foe and ripped and tore the flesh to the bone. Then François's lash descended, and Buck had the satisfaction of watching Spitz receive the worst whipping as yet administered to any of the team.

"One devil, dat Spitz," remarked Perrault. "Some dam day heem keel dat Buck."

"Dat Buck two devils," was François's rejoinder. "All de tam I watch dat Buck I know for sure. Lissen: some dam fine day heem get mad lak hell an' den heem chew dat Spitz all up an' spit heem out on de snow. Sure. I know."

From then on it was war between them. Spitz, as lead-dog and acknowledged master of the team, felt his supremacy threatened by this strange Southland dog. And strange Buck was to him, for of the many Southland dogs he had known, not one had shown up worthily in camp and on trail. They were all too soft, dying under the toil, the frost, and starvation. Buck was the exception. He alone endured and prospered, matching the husky in strength, savagery, and cunning. Then he was a masterful dog, and what made him dangerous was the fact that the club of the man in the red sweater had knocked all blind pluck and rashness out of his desire for mastery. He was preëminently cunning, and could bide his time with a patience that was nothing less than primitive.

It was inevitable that the clash for leadership should come. Buck wanted it. He wanted it because it was his nature, because he had been gripped tight by that nameless, incomprehensible pride of the trail and trace—that pride which holds dogs in the toil to the last gasp, which lures them to die joyfully in the harness, and breaks their hearts if they are cut out of the harness. This was the pride of Dave as wheel-dog, of Sol-leks as he pulled with all his strength; the pride that laid hold of them at break of camp, transforming them from sour and sullen brutes into straining, eager, ambitious creatures; the pride that spurred them on all day and dropped them at pitch of camp at night, letting them fall back into gloomy unrest and uncontent. This was the pride that bore up Spitz and made him thrash the sled-dogs who blundered and shirked in the traces or hid away at harness-up time in the morning. Likewise it was this pride that made him fear Buck as a possible lead-dog. And this was Buck's pride, too.

He openly threatened the other's leadership. He came between him and the shirks he should have punished. And he did it deliberately. One night there was a heavy snowfall, and in the morning Pike, the malingerer, did not appear. He was securely hidden in his nest under a foot of snow. François called him and sought him in vain. Spitz was wild with wrath. He raged through the camp, smelling and digging in every likely place, snarling so frightfully that Pike heard and shivered in his hiding-place.

But when he was at last unearthed, and Spitz flew at him to punish him, Buck flew, with equal rage, in between. So unexpected was it, and so shrewdly managed, that Spitz was hurled backward and off his feet. Pike, who had been trembling abjectly, took heart at this open mutiny, and sprang upon his overthrown leader. Buck, to whom fair-play was a forgotten code, likewise sprang upon Spitz. But François, chuckling at the incident while unswerving in the administration of justice, brought his lash down upon Buck with all his might. This failed to drive Buck from his prostrate rival, and the butt of the whip was brought into play. Half-stunned by the blow, Buck was knocked backward and the lash laid upon him again and again, while Spitz soundly punished the many times offending Pike.

In the days that followed, as Dawson grew closer and closer, Buck still continued to interfere between Spitz and the culprits; but he did it craftily, when François was not around. With the covert mutiny of Buck, a general insubordination sprang up and increased. Dave and Sol-leks were unaffected, but the rest of the team went from bad to worse. Things no longer went right. There was continual bickering and jangling. Trouble was always afoot, and at the bottom of it was Buck. He kept François busy, for the dog-driver was in constant apprehension of the life-and-death struggle between the two which he knew must take place sooner or later; and on more than one night the sounds of quarrelling and strife among the other dogs turned him out of his sleeping robe, fearful that Buck and Spitz were at it.

But the opportunity did not present itself, and they pulled into Dawson one dreary afternoon with the great fight still to come. Here were many men, and countless dogs, and Buck found them all at work. It seemed the ordained order of things that dogs should work. All day they swung up and down the main street in long teams, and in the night their jingling bells still went by. They hauled cabin logs and firewood, freighted up to the mines, and did all manner of work that horses did in the Santa Clara Valley. Here and there Buck met Southland dogs, but in the main they were the wild wolf husky breed. Every night, regularly, at nine, at twelve, at three, they lifted a nocturnal song, a weird and eerie chant, in which it was Buck's delight to join.

With the aurora borealis flaming coldly overhead, or the stars leaping in the frost dance, and the land numb and frozen under its pall of snow, this song of the huskies might have been the defiance of life, only it was pitched in minor key, with long-drawn wailings and half-sobs, and was more the pleading of life, the articulate travail of existence. It was an old song, old as the breed itself—one of the first songs of the younger world in a day when songs were sad. It was invested with the woe of unnumbered generations, this plaint by which Buck was so strangely stirred. When he moaned and sobbed, it was with the pain of living that was of old the pain of his wild fathers, and the fear and mystery of the cold and dark that was to them fear and mystery. And that he should be stirred by it marked the completeness with which he harked back through the ages of fire and roof to the raw beginnings of life in the howling ages.

Seven days from the time they pulled into Dawson, they dropped down the steep bank by the Barracks to the Yukon Trail, and pulled for Dyea and Salt Water. Perrault was carrying despatches if anything more urgent than those he had brought in; also, the travel pride had gripped him, and he purposed to make the record trip of the year. Several things favored him in this. The week's rest had recuperated the dogs and put them in thorough trim. The trail they had broken into the country was packed hard by later journeyers. And further, the police had arranged in two or three places deposits of grub for dog and man, and he was travelling light.

They made Sixty Mile, which is a fifty-mile run, on the first day; and the second day saw them booming up the Yukon well on their way to Pelly. But such splendid running was achieved not without great trouble and vexation on the part of François. The insidious revolt led by Buck had destroyed the solidarity of the team. It no longer was as one dog leaping in the traces. The encouragement Buck gave the rebels led them into all kinds of petty misdemeanors. No more was Spitz a leader greatly to be feared. The old awe departed, and they grew equal to challenging his authority. Pike robbed him of half a fish one night, and gulped it down under the protection of Buck. Another night Dub and Joe fought Spitz and made him forego the punishment they deserved. And even Billee, the good-natured, was less good-natured, and whined not half so placatingly as in former days. Buck never came near Spitz without snarling and bristling menacingly. In fact, his conduct approached that of a bully, and he was given to swaggering up and down before Spitz's very nose.

The breaking down of discipline likewise affected the dogs in their relations with one another. They quarrelled and bickered more than ever among themselves, till at times the camp was a howling bedlam. Dave and Sol-leks alone were unaltered, though they were made irritable by the unending squabbling. François swore strange barbarous oaths, and stamped the snow in futile rage, and tore his hair. His lash was always singing among the dogs, but it was of small avail. Directly his back was turned they were at it again. He backed up Spitz with his whip, while Buck backed up the remainder of the team. François knew he was behind all the trouble, and Buck knew he knew; but Buck was too clever ever again to be caught red-handed. He worked faithfully in the harness, for the toil had become a delight to him; yet it was a greater delight slyly to precipitate a fight amongst his mates and tangle the traces.

At the mouth of the Tahkeena, one night after supper, Dub turned up a snowshoe rabbit, blundered it, and missed. In a second the whole team was in full cry. A hundred yards away was a camp of the Northwest Police, with fifty dogs, huskies all, who joined the chase. The rabbit sped down the river,

THE CALL OF THE WILD

turned off into a small creek, up the frozen bed of which it held steadily. It ran lightly on the surface of the snow, while the dogs ploughed through by main strength. Buck led the pack, sixty strong, around bend after bend, but he could not gain. He lay down low to the race, whining eagerly, his splendid body flashing forward, leap by leap, in the wan white moonlight. And leap by leap, like some pale frost wraith, the snowshoe rabbit flashed on ahead.

All that stirring of old instincts which at stated periods drives men out from the sounding cities to forest and plain to kill things by chemically propelled leaden pellets, the blood lust, the joy to kill—all this was Buck's, only it was infinitely more intimate. He was ranging at the head of the pack, running the wild thing down, the living meat, to kill with his own teeth and wash his muzzle to the eyes in warm blood.

There is an ecstasy that marks the summit of life, and beyond which life cannot rise. And such is the paradox of living, this ecstasy comes when one is most alive, and it comes as a complete forgetfulness that one is alive. This ecstasy, this forgetfulness of living, comes to the artist, caught up and out of himself in a sheet of flame; it comes to the soldier, war-mad on a stricken field and refusing quarter; and it came to Buck, leading the pack, sounding the old wolf-cry, straining after the food that was alive and that fled swiftly before him through the moonlight. He was sounding the deeps of his nature, and of the parts of his nature that were deeper than he, going back into the womb of Time. He was mastered by the sheer surging of life, the tidal wave of being, the perfect joy of each separate muscle, joint, and sinew in that it was everything that was not death, that it was aglow and rampant, expressing itself in movement, flying exultantly under the stars and over the face of dead matter that did not move.

But Spitz, cold and calculating even in his supreme moods, left the pack and cut across a narrow neck of land where the creek made a long bend around. Buck did not know of this, and as he rounded the bend, the frost wraith of a rabbit still flitting before him, he saw another and larger frost wraith leap from the overhanging bank into the immediate path of the rabbit. It was Spitz. The rabbit could not turn, and as the white teeth broke its back in mid air it shrieked as loudly as a stricken man may shriek. At sound of this, the cry of Life plunging down from Life's apex in the grip of Death, the full pack at Buck's heels raised a hell's chorus of delight.

Buck did not cry out. He did not check himself, but drove in upon Spitz, shoulder to shoulder, so hard that he missed the throat. They rolled over and over in the powdery snow. Spitz gained his feet almost as though he had not been overthrown, slashing Buck down the shoulder and leaping clear. Twice his teeth clipped together, like the steel jaws of a trap, as he backed away for better footing, with lean and lifting lips that writhed and snarled.

In a flash Buck knew it. The time had come. It was to the death. As they circled about, snarling, ears laid back, keenly watchful for the advantage, the scene came to Buck with a sense of familiarity. He seemed to remember it all,—the white woods, and earth, and moonlight, and the thrill of battle. Over the whiteness and silence brooded a ghostly calm. There was not the faintest whisper of air—nothing moved, not a leaf quivered, the visible breaths of the dogs rising slowly and lingering in the frosty air. They had made short work of the snowshoe rabbit, these dogs that were ill-tamed wolves; and they were now drawn up in an expectant circle. They, too, were silent, their eyes only gleaming and their breaths drifting slowly upward. To Buck it was nothing new or strange, this scene of old time. It was as though it had always been, the wonted way of things.

Spitz was a practised fighter. From Spitzbergen through the Arctic, and across Canada and the Barrens, he had held his own with all manner of dogs and achieved to mastery over them. Bitter rage was his, but never blind rage. In passion to rend and destroy, he never forgot that his enemy was in like passion to rend and destroy. He never rushed till he was prepared to receive a rush; never attacked till he had first defended that attack.

In vain Buck strove to sink his teeth in the neck of the big white dog. Wherever his fangs struck for the softer flesh, they were countered by the fangs of Spitz. Fang clashed fang, and lips were cut and bleeding, but Buck could not penetrate his enemy's guard. Then he warmed up and enveloped Spitz in a whirlwind of rushes. Time and time again he tried for the snow-white throat, where life bubbled near to the surface, and each time and every time Spitz slashed him and got away. Then Buck took to rushing, as though for the throat, when, suddenly drawing back his head and curving in from the side, he would drive his shoulder at the shoulder of Spitz, as a ram by which to overthrow him. But instead, Buck's shoulder was slashed down each time as Spitz leaped lightly away.

Spitz was untouched, while Buck was streaming with blood and panting hard. The fight was growing desperate. And all the while the silent and wolfish circle waited to finish off whichever dog went down. As Buck grew winded, Spitz took to rushing, and he kept him staggering for footing. Once Buck went over, and the whole circle of sixty dogs started up; but he recovered himself, almost in mid air, and the circle sank down again and waited.

But Buck possessed a quality that made for greatness—imagination. He fought by instinct, but he could fight by head as well. He rushed, as though attempting the old shoulder trick, but at the last instant swept low to the snow and in. His teeth closed on Spitz's left fore leg. There was a crunch of breaking bone, and the white dog faced him on three legs. Thrice he tried to knock him over, then repeated the trick and broke the right fore leg. Despite the pain and helplessness, Spitz struggled madly to keep up. He saw the silent circle, with gleaming eyes, lolling tongues, and silvery breaths drifting upward, closing in upon him as he had seen similar circles close in upon beaten antagonists in the past. Only this time he was the one who was beaten.

There was no hope for him. Buck was inexorable. Mercy was a thing reserved for gentler climes. He manœuvred for the final rush. The circle had tightened till he could feel the breaths of the huskies on his flanks. He could see them, beyond Spitz and to either side, half crouching for the spring, their eyes fixed upon him. A pause seemed to fall. Every animal was motionless as though turned to stone. Only Spitz quivered and bristled as he staggered back and forth, snarling with horrible menace, as though to frighten off impending death. Then Buck sprang in and out; but while he was in, shoulder had at last squarely met shoulder. The dark circle became a dot on the moon-flooded snow as Spitz disappeared from view. Buck stood and looked on, the successful champion, the dominent primordial beast who had made his kill and found it good.

IV. WHO HAS WON TO MASTERSHIP

"Eh? Wot I say? I spik true w'en I say dat Buck two devils."

This was François's speech next morning when he discovered Spitz missing and Buck covered with wounds. He drew him to the fire and by its light pointed them out.

"Dat Spitz fight lak hell," said Perrault, as he surveyed the gaping rips and cuts.

"An' dat Buck fight lak two hells," was François's answer. "An' now we make good time. No more Spitz, no more trouble, sure."

While Perrault packed the camp outfit and loaded the sled, the dog-driver proceeded to harness the dogs. Buck trotted up to the place Spitz would have occupied as leader; but François, not noticing him, brought Sol-leks to the coveted position. In his judgment, Sol-leks was the best lead-dog left. Buck sprang upon Sol-leks in a fury, driving him back and standing in his place.

"Eh? eh?" François cried, slapping his thighs gleefully. "Look at dat Buck. Heem keel dat Spitz, heem t'ink to take de job."

"Go 'way, Chook!" he cried, but Buck refused to budge.

He took Buck by the scruff of the neck, and though the dog growled threateningly, dragged him to one side and replaced Sol-leks. The old dog did not like it, and showed plainly that he was afraid of Buck. François was obdurate, but when he turned his back, Buck again displaced Sol-leks, who was not at all unwilling to go.

François was angry. "Now, by Gar, I feex you!" he cried, coming back with a heavy club in his hand.

Buck remembered the man in the red sweater, and retreated slowly; nor did he attempt to charge in when Sol-leks was once more brought forward. But he circled just beyond the range of the club, snarling with bitterness and rage; and while he circled he watched the club so as to dodge it if thrown by François, for he was become wise in the ways of clubs.

The driver went about his work, and he called to Buck when he was ready to put him in his old place in front of Dave. Buck retreated two or three steps. François followed him up, whereupon he again retreated. After some time of this, François threw down the club, thinking that Buck feared a thrashing. But Buck was in open revolt. He wanted, not to escape a clubbing,

but to have the leadership. It was his by right. He had earned it, and he would not be content with less.

Perrault took a hand. Between them they ran him about for the better part of an hour. They threw clubs at him. He dodged. They cursed him, and his fathers and mothers before him, and all his seed to come after him down to the remotest generation, and every hair on his body and drop of blood in his veins; and he answered curse with snarl and kept out of their reach. He did not try to run away, but retreated around and around the camp, advertising plainly that when his desire was met, he would come in and be good.

François sat down and scratched his head. Perrault looked at his watch and swore. Time was flying, and they should have been on the trail an hour gone. François scratched his head again. He shook it and grinned sheepishly at the courier, who shrugged his shoulders in sign that they were beaten. Then François went up to where Sol-leks stood and called to Buck. Buck laughed, as dogs laugh, yet kept his distance. François unfastened Sol-leks's traces and put him back in his old place. The team stood harnessed to the sled in an unbroken line, ready for the trail. There was no place for Buck save at the front. Once more François called, and once more Buck laughed and kept away.

"T'row down de club," Perrault commanded.

François complied, whereupon Buck trotted in, laughing triumphantly, and swung around into position at the head of the team. His traces were fastened, the sled broken out, and with both men running they dashed out on to the river trail.

Highly as the dog-driver had forevalued Buck, with his two devils, he found, while the day was yet young, that he had undervalued. At a bound Buck took up the duties of leadership; and where judgment was required, and quick thinking and quick acting, he showed himself the superior even of Spitz, of whom François had never seen an equal.

But it was in giving the law and making his mates live up to it, that Buck excelled. Dave and Sol-leks did not mind the change in leadership. It was none of their business. Their business was to toil, and toil mightily, in the traces. So long as that were not interfered with, they did not care what happened. Billee, the good-natured, could lead for all they cared, so long as he kept order. The rest of the team, however, had grown unruly during the last days of Spitz, and their surprise was great now that Buck proceeded to lick them into shape.

Pike, who pulled at Buck's heels, and who never put an ounce more of his weight against the breastband than he was compelled to do, was swiftly and repeatedly shaken for loafing; and ere the first day was done he was pulling more than ever before in his life. The first night in camp, Joe, the sour one, was punished roundly—a thing that Spitz had never succeeded in doing. Buck simply smothered him by virtue of superior weight, and cut him up till he ceased snapping and began to whine for mercy.

The general tone of the team picked up immediately. It recovered its old-time solidarity, and once more the dogs leaped as one dog in the traces. At the Rink Rapids two native huskies, Teek and Koona, were added; and the celerity with which Buck broke them in took away François's breath.

"Nevaire such a dog as dat Buck!" he cried. "No, nevaire! Heem worth one t'ousan' dollair, by Gar! Eh? Wot you say, Perrault?"

And Perrault nodded. He was ahead of the record then, and gaining day by day. The trail was in excellent condition, well packed and hard, and there was no new-fallen snow with which to contend. It was not too cold. The temperature dropped to fifty below zero and remained there the whole trip. The men rode and ran by turn, and the dogs were kept on the jump, with but infrequent stoppages.

The Thirty Mile River was comparatively coated with ice, and they covered in one day going out what had taken them ten days coming in. In one run they made a sixty-mile dash from the foot of Lake Le Barge to the White Horse Rapids. Across Marsh, Tagish, and Bennett (seventy miles of lakes), they flew so fast that the man whose turn it was to run towed behind the sled at the end of a rope. And on the last night of the second week they topped White Pass and dropped down the sea slope with the lights of Skagway and of the shipping at their feet.

It was a record run. Each day for fourteen days they had averaged forty miles. For three days Perrault and François threw chests up and down the main street of Skagway and were deluged with invitations to drink, while the team was the constant centre of a worshipful crowd of dog-busters and mushers. Then three or four western bad men aspired to clean out the town, were riddled like pepper-boxes for their pains, and public interest turned to other idols. Next came official orders. François called Buck to him, threw his arms around him, wept over him. And that was the last of François and Perrault. Like other men, they passed out of Buck's life for good.

A Scotch half-breed took charge of him and his mates, and in company with a dozen other dog-teams he started back over the weary trail to Dawson. It was no light running now, nor record time, but heavy toil each day, with a heavy load behind; for this was the mail train, carrying word from the world to the men who sought gold under the shadow of the Pole.

Buck did not like it, but he bore up well to the work, taking pride in it after the manner of Dave and Sol-leks, and seeing that his mates, whether they prided in it or not, did their fair share. It was a monotonous life, operating with machine-like regularity. One day was very like another. At a certain time each morning the cooks turned out, fires were built, and breakfast was eaten. Then, while some broke camp, others harnessed the dogs, and they were under way an hour or so before the darkness fell which gave warning of dawn. At night, camp was made. Some pitched the flies, others cut firewood and pine boughs for the beds, and still others carried water or ice for the cooks. Also, the dogs were fed. To them, this was the one feature of the day, though it was good to loaf around, after the fish was eaten, for an hour or so with the other dogs, of which there were fivescore and odd. There were fierce fighters among them, but three battles with the fiercest brought Buck to mastery, so that when he bristled and showed his teeth, they got out of his way.

Best of all, perhaps, he loved to lie near the fire, hind legs crouched under him, fore legs stretched out in front, head raised, and eyes blinking dreamily at the flames. Sometimes he thought of Judge Miller's big house in the sun-kissed Santa Clara Valley, and of the cement swimming-tank, and Ysabel, the Mexican hairless, and Toots, the Japanese pug; but oftener he remembered the man in the red sweater, the death of Curly, the great fight with Spitz, and the good things he had eaten or would like to eat. He was not homesick. The Sunland was very dim and distant, and such memories had no power over him. Far more potent were the memories of his heredity that gave things he had never seen before a seeming familiarity; the instincts (which were but the memories of his ancestors become habits) which had lapsed in later days, and still later, in him, quickened and became alive again.

Sometimes as he crouched there, blinking dreamily at the flames, it seemed that the flames were of another fire, and that as he crouched by this other fire he saw another and different man from the half-breed cook before him. This other man was shorter of leg and longer of arm, with muscles that were stringy and knotty rather than rounded and swelling. The hair of this man was long and matted, and his head slanted back under it from the eyes. He uttered strange sounds, and seemed very much afraid of the darkness, into which he peered continually, clutching in his hand, which hung midway between knee and foot, a stick with a heavy stone made fast to the end. He was all but naked, a ragged and fire-scorched skin hanging part way down his back, but on his body there was much hair. In some places, across the chest and shoulders and down the outside of the arms and thighs, it was matted into almost a thick fur. He did not stand erect, but with trunk inclined forward from the hips, on legs that bent at the knees. About his body there was a peculiar springiness, or resiliency, almost catlike, and a quick alertness as of one who lived in perpetual fear of things seen and unseen.

At other times this hairy man squatted by the fire with head between his legs and slept. On such occasions his elbows were on his knees, his hands clasped above his head as though to shed rain by the hairy arms. And beyond that fire, in the circling darkness, Buck could see many gleaming coals, two by two, always two by two, which he knew to be the eyes of great beasts of prey. And he could hear the crashing of their bodies through the undergrowth, and the noises they made in the night. And dreaming there by the Yukon bank, with lazy eyes blinking at the fire, these sounds and sights of another world would make the hair to rise along his back and stand on end across his shoulders and up his neck, till he whimpered low and suppressedly, or growled softly, and the half-breed cook shouted at him, "Hey, you Buck, wake up!" Whereupon the other world would vanish and the real world come into his eyes, and he would get up and yawn and stretch as though he had been asleep.

It was a hard trip, with the mail behind them, and the heavy work wore them down. They were short of weight and in poor condition when they made Dawson, and should have had a ten days' or a week's rest at least. But in two days' time they dropped down the Yukon bank from the Barracks, loaded with letters for the outside. The dogs were tired, the drivers grumbling, and to make matters worse, it snowed every day. This meant a soft trail, greater friction on the runners, and heavier pulling for the dogs; yet the drivers were fair through it all, and did their best for the animals.

Each night the dogs were attended to first. They ate before the drivers ate, and no man sought his sleeping-robe till he had seen to the feet of the dogs he drove. Still, their strength went down. Since the beginning of the winter they had travelled eighteen hundred miles, dragging sleds the whole weary distance; and eighteen hundred miles will tell upon the life of the toughest. Buck stood it, keeping his mates up to their work and maintaining discipline, though he too was very tired. Billee cried and whimpered regularly in his sleep each night. Joe was sourer than ever, and Sol-leks was unapproachable, blind side or other side.

But it was Dave who suffered most of all. Something had gone wrong with him. He became more morose and irritable, and when camp was pitched at once made his nest, where his driver fed him. Once out of the harness and down, he did not get on his feet again till harness-up time in the morning. Sometimes, in the traces, when jerked by a sudden stoppage of the sled, or by straining to start it, he would cry out with pain. The driver examined him, but could find nothing. All the drivers became interested in his case. They talked it over at meal-time, and over their last pipes before going to bed, and one night they held a consultation. He was brought from his nest to the fire and was pressed and prodded till he cried out many times. Something was wrong inside, but they could locate no broken bones, could not make it out.

By the time Cassiar Bar was reached, he was so weak that he was falling repeatedly in the traces. The Scotch half-breed called a halt and took him out of the team, making the next dog, Sol-leks, fast to the sled. His intention was to rest Dave, letting him run free behind the sled. Sick as he was, Dave resented being taken out, grunting and growling while the traces were unfastened, and whimpering broken-heartedly when he saw Sol-leks in the position he had held and served so long. For the pride of trace and trail was his, and, sick unto death, he could not bear that another dog should do his work.

When the sled started, he floundered in the soft snow alongside the beaten trail, attacking Sol-leks with his teeth, rushing against him and trying to thrust him off into the soft snow on the other side, striving to leap inside his traces and get between him and the sled, and all the while whining and yelping and crying with grief and pain. The half-breed tried to drive him away with the whip; but he paid no heed to the stinging lash, and the man had not the heart to strike harder. Dave refused to run quietly on the trail behind the sled, where the going was easy, but continued to flounder alongside in the soft snow, where the going was most difficult, till exhausted. Then he fell, and lay where he fell, howling lugubriously as the long train of sleds churned by.

With the last remnant of his strength he managed to stagger along behind till the train made another stop, when he floundered past the sleds to his own, where he stood alongside Sol-leks. His driver lingered a moment to get a light for his pipe from the man behind. Then he returned and started his dogs. They swung out on the trail with remarkable lack of exertion, turned their heads uneasily, and stopped in surprise. The driver was surprised, too; the sled had not moved. He called his comrades to witness the sight. Dave had bitten through both of Sol-leks's traces, and was standing directly in front of the sled in his proper place.

He pleaded with his eyes to remain there. The driver was perplexed. His comrades talked of how a dog could break its heart through being denied the work that killed it, and recalled instances they had known, where dogs, too old for the toil, or injured, had died because they were cut out of the traces. Also, they held it a mercy, since Dave was to die anyway, that he should die in the traces, heart-easy and content. So he was harnessed in again, and proudly he pulled as of old, though more than once he cried out involuntarily from the bite of his inward hurt. Several times he fell down and was dragged in the traces, and once the sled ran upon him so that he limped thereafter in one of his hind legs.

But he held out till camp was reached, when his driver made a place for him by the fire. Morning found him too weak to travel. At harness-up time he tried to crawl to his driver. By convulsive efforts he got on his feet, staggered, and fell. Then he wormed his way forward slowly toward where the harnesses were being put on his mates. He would advance his fore legs and drag up his body with a sort of hitching movement, when he would advance his fore legs and hitch ahead again for a few more inches. His strength left him, and the last his mates saw of him he lay gasping in the snow and yearning toward them. But they could hear him mournfully howling till they passed out of sight behind a belt of river timber.

Here the train was halted. The Scotch half-breed slowly retraced his steps to the camp they had left. The men ceased talking. A revolver-shot rang out. The man came back hurriedly. The whips snapped, the bells tinkled merrily, the sleds churned along the trail; but Buck knew, and every dog knew, what had taken place behind the belt of river trees.

V. THE TOIL OF TRACE AND TRAIL

Thirty days from the time it left Dawson, the Salt Water Mail, with Buck and his mates at the fore, arrived at Skagway. They were in a wretched state, worn out and worn down. Buck's one hundred and forty pounds had dwindled to one hundred and fifteen. The rest of his mates, though lighter dogs, had relatively lost more weight than he. Pike, the malingerer, who, in his lifetime of deceit, had often successfully feigned a hurt leg, was now limping in earnest. Sol-leks was limping, and Dub was suffering from a wrenched shoulder blade.

They were all terribly footsore. No spring or rebound was left in them. Their feet fell heavily on the trail, jarring their bodies and doubling the fatigue of a day's travel. There was nothing the matter with them except that they were dead tired. It was not the dead tiredness that comes through brief and excessive effort, from which recovery is a matter of hours; but it was the dead tiredness that comes through the slow and prolonged strength drainage of months of toil. There was no power of recuperation left, no reserve strength to call upon. It had been all used, the last least bit of it. Every muscle, every fibre, every cell, was tired, dead tired. And there was reason for it. In less than five months they had travelled twenty-five hundred miles, during the last eighteen hundred of which they had had but five days' rest. When they arrived at Skagway, they were apparently on their last legs. They could barely keep the traces taut, and on the down grades just managed to keep out of the way of the sled.

"Mush on, poor sore feets," the driver encouraged them as they tottered down the main street of Skagway. "Dis is de las'. Den we get one long res'. Eh? For sure. One bully long res'."

The drivers confidently expected a long stopover. Themselves, they had covered twelve hundred miles with two days' rest, and in the nature of reason and common justice they deserved an interval of loafing. But so many were the men who had rushed into the Klondike, and so many were the sweethearts, wives, and kin that had not rushed in, that the congested mail was taking on Alpine proportions; also, there were official orders. Fresh batches of Hudson Bay dogs were to take the places of those worthless for the trail. The worthless ones were to be got rid of, and, since dogs count for little against dollars, they were to be sold.

Three days passed, by which time Buck and his mates found how really tired and weak they were. Then, on the morning of the fourth day, two men from the States came along and bought them, harness and all, for a song. The men addressed each other as "Hal" and "Charles." Charles was a middle-aged, lightish-colored man, with weak and watery eyes and a mustache that twisted fiercely and vigorously up, giving the lie to the limply drooping lip it concealed. Hal was a youngster of nineteen or twenty, with a big Colt's revolver and a hunting-knife strapped about him on a belt that fairly bristled with cartridges. This belt was the most salient thing about him. It advertised his callowness—a callowness sheer and unutterable. Both men were manifestly out of place, and why such as they should adventure the North is part of the mystery of things that passes understanding.

Buck heard the chaffering, saw the money pass between the man and the Government agent, and knew that the Scotch half-breed and the mail-train drivers were passing out of his life on the heels of Perrault and François and the others who had gone before. When driven with his mates to the new owners' camp, Buck saw a slipshod and slovenly affair, tent half stretched, dishes unwashed, everything in disorder; also, he saw a woman. "Mercedes" the men called her. She was Charles's wife and Hal's sister—a nice family party.

Buck watched them apprehensively as they proceeded to take down the tent and load the sled. There was a great deal of effort about their manner, but no businesslike method. The tent was rolled into an awkward bundle three times as large as it should have been. The tin dishes were packed away unwashed. Mercedes continually fluttered in the way of her men and kept up an unbroken chattering of remonstrance and advice. When they put a clothes-sack on the front of the sled, she suggested it should go on the back; and when they had it put on the back, and covered it over with a couple of other bundles, she discovered overlooked articles which could abide nowhere else but in that very sack, and they unloaded again.

Three men from a neighboring tent came out and looked on, grinning and winking at one another.

"You've got a right smart load as it is," said one of them; "and it's not me should tell you your business, but I wouldn't tote that tent along if I was you."

"Undreamed of!" cried Mercedes, throwing up her hands in dainty dismay. "However in the world could I manage without a tent?"

"It's springtime, and you won't get any more cold weather," the man replied.

She shook her head decidedly, and Charles and Hal put the last odds and ends on top the mountainous load.

"Think it'll ride?" one of the men asked.

"Why shouldn't it?" Charles demanded rather shortly.

"Oh, that's all right, that's all right," the man hastened meekly to say. "I was just a-wonderin', that is all. It seemed a mite top-heavy."

Charles turned his back and drew the lashings down as well as he could, which was not in the least well.

"An' of course the dogs can hike along all day with that contraption behind them," affirmed a second of the men.

"Certainly," said Hal, with freezing politeness, taking hold of the gee-pole with one hand and swinging his whip from the other. "Mush!" he shouted. "Mush on there!"

The dogs sprang against the breastbands, strained hard for a few moments, then relaxed. They were unable to move the sled.

"The lazy brutes, I'll show them," he cried, preparing to lash out at them with the whip.

But Mercedes interfered, crying, "Oh, Hal, you mustn't," as she caught hold of the whip and wrenched it from him. "The poor dears! Now you must promise you won't be harsh with them for the rest of the trip, or I won't go a step."

"Precious lot you know about dogs," her brother sneered; "and I wish you'd leave me alone. They're lazy, I tell you, and you've got to whip them to get anything out of them. That's their way. You ask any one. Ask one of those men."

Mercedes looked at them imploringly, untold repugnance at sight of pain written in her pretty face.

"They're weak as water, if you want to know," came the reply from one of the men. "Plum tuckered out, that's what's the matter. They need a rest."

"Rest be blanked," said Hal, with his beardless lips; and Mercedes said, "Oh!" in pain and sorrow at the oath.

But she was a clannish creature, and rushed at once to the defence of her brother. "Never mind that man," she said pointedly. "You're driving our dogs and you do what you think best with them."

Again Hal's whip fell upon the dogs. They threw themselves against the breastbands, dug their feet into the packed snow, got down low to it, and put forth all their strength. The sled held as though it were an anchor. After two efforts, they stood still, panting. The whip was whistling savagely, when once more Mercedes interfered. She dropped on her knees before Buck, with tears in her eyes, and put her arms around his neck.

"You poor, poor dears," she cried sympathetically, "why don't you pull hard?—then you wouldn't be whipped." Buck did not like her, but he was feeling too miserable to resist her, taking it as part of the day's miserable work.

One of the onlookers, who had been clenching his teeth to suppress hot speech, now spoke up:—

"It's not that I care a whoop what becomes of you, but for the dogs' sakes I just want to tell you, you can help them a mighty lot by breaking out that sled. The runners are froze fast. Throw your weight against the gee-pole, right and left, and break it out."

A third time the attempt was made, but this time, following the advice, Hal broke out the runners which had been frozen to the snow. The overloaded and unwieldly sled forged ahead, Buck and his mates struggling frantically under the rain of blows. A hundred yards ahead the path turned and sloped steeply into the main street. It would have required an experienced man to keep the top-heavy sled upright, and Hal was not such a man. As they swung on the turn the sled went over, spilling half its load through the loose lashings. The dogs never stopped. The lightened sled bounded on its side behind them. They were angry because of the ill treatment they had received and the unjust load. Buck was raging. He broke into a run, the team following his lead. Hal cried, "Whoa! whoa!" but they gave no heed. He tripped and was pulled off his feet. The capsized sled ground over him, and the dogs dashed on up the street, adding to the gayety of Skagway as they scattered the remainder of the outfit along its chief thoroughfare.

Kind-hearted citizens caught the dogs and gathered up the scattered belongings. Also, they gave advice. Half the load and twice the dogs, if they ever expected to reach Dawson, was what was said. Hal and his sister and brother-in-law listened unwillingly, pitched tent, and overhauled the outfit. Canned goods were turned out that made men laugh, for canned goods on the Long Trail is a thing to dream about. "Blankets for a hotel," quoth one of the men who laughed and helped. "Half as many is too much; get rid of them. Throw away that tent, and all those dishes—who's going to wash them, anyway? Good Lord, do you think you're travelling on a Pullman?"

And so it went, the inexorable elimination of the superfluous. Mercedes cried when her clothes-bags were dumped on the ground and article after article was thrown out. She cried in general, and she cried in particular over each discarded thing. She clasped hands about knees, rocking back and forth broken-heartedly. She averred she would not go an inch, not for a dozen Charleses. She appealed to everybody and to everything, finally wiping her eyes and proceeding to cast out even articles of apparel that were imperative necessaries. And in her zeal, when she had finished with her own, she attacked the belongings of her men and went through them like a tornado.

This accomplished, the outfit, though cut in half, was still a formidable bulk. Charles and Hal went out in the evening and bought six Outside dogs. These, added to the six of the original team, and Teek and Koona, the huskies obtained at the Rink Rapids on the record trip, brought the team up to fourteen. But the Outside dogs, though practically broken in since their landing, did not amount to much. Three were short-haired pointers, one was a Newfoundland, and the other two were mongrels of indeterminate breed. They did not seem to know anything, these newcomers. Buck and his comrades looked upon them with disgust, and though he speedily taught them their places and what not to do, he could not teach them what to do. They did not take kindly to trace and trail. With the exception of the two mongrels, they were bewildered and spirit-broken by the strange savage environment in which they found themselves and by the ill treatment they had received. The two mongrels were without spirit at all; bones were the only things breakable about them.

With the newcomers hopeless and forlorn, and the old team worn out by twenty-five hundred miles of continuous trail, the outlook was anything but bright. The two men, however, were quite cheerful. And they were proud, too. They were doing the thing in style, with fourteen dogs. They had seen other sleds depart over the Pass for Dawson, or come in from Dawson, but never had they seen a sled with so many as fourteen dogs. In the nature of Arctic travel there was a reason why fourteen dogs should not drag one sled, and that was that one sled could not carry the food for fourteen dogs. But Charles and Hal did not know this. They had worked the trip out with a pencil, so much to a dog, so many dogs, and so many days, Q. E. D. Mercedes looked over their shoulders and nodded comprehensively, it was all so very simple.

Late next morning Buck led the long team up the street. There was nothing lively about it, no snap or go in him and his fellows. They were starting dead weary. Four times he had covered the distance between Salt Water and Dawson, and the knowledge that, jaded and tired, he was facing the same trail once more, made him bitter. His heart was not in the work, nor was the heart of any dog. The Outsides were timid and frightened, the Insides without confidence in their masters.

Buck felt vaguely that there was no depending upon these two men and the woman. They did not know how to do anything, and as the days went by it became apparent that they could not learn. They were slack in all things, without order or discipline. It took them half the night to pitch a slovenly camp, and half the morning to break that camp and get the sled loaded in fashion so slovenly that for the rest of the day they were occupied in stopping and rearranging the load. Some days they did not make ten miles. On other days they were unable to get started at all. And on no day did they succeed in making more than half the distance used by the men as a basis in their dog-food computation.

It was inevitable that they should go short on dog-food. But they hastened it by overfeeding, bringing the day nearer when underfeeding would commence. The Outside dogs, whose digestions had not been trained by chronic famine to make the most of little, had voracious appetites. And when, in addition to this, the worn-out huskies pulled weakly, Hal decided that the orthodox ration was too small. He doubled it. And to cap it all, when Mercedes, with tears in her pretty eyes and a quaver in her throat, could not cajole him into giving the dogs still more, she stole from the fish-sacks and fed them slyly. But it was not food that Buck and the huskies needed, but rest. And though they were making poor time, the heavy load they dragged sapped their strength severely.

Then came the underfeeding. Hal awoke one day to the fact that his dog-food was half gone and the distance only quarter covered; further, that for love or money no additional dog-food was to be obtained. So he cut down even the orthodox ration and tried to increase the day's travel. His sister and brother-in-law seconded him; but they were frustrated by their heavy outfit and their own incompetence. It was a simple matter to give the dogs less food; but it was impossible to make the dogs travel faster, while their own inability to get under way earlier in the morning prevented them from travelling longer hours. Not only did they not know how to work dogs, but they did not know how to work themselves.

The first to go was Dub. Poor blundering thief that he was, always getting caught and punished, he had none the less been a faithful worker. His wrenched shoulder blade, untreated and unrested, went from bad to worse, till finally Hal shot him with the big Colt's revolver. It is a saying of the country that an Outside dog starves to death on the ration of the husky, so the six Outside dogs under Buck could do no less than die on half the ration of the husky. The Newfoundland went first, followed by the three short-haired pointers, the two mongrels hanging more grittily on to life, but going in the end.

By this time all the amenities and gentlenesses of the Southland had fallen away from the three people. Shorn of its glamour and romance, Arctic travel became to them a reality too harsh for their manhood and womanhood. Mercedes ceased weeping over the dogs, being too occupied with weeping over herself and with quarrelling with her husband and brother. To quarrel was the one thing they were never too weary to do. Their irritability arose out of their misery, increased with it, doubled upon it, outdistanced it. The wonderful patience of the trail which comes to men who toil hard and suffer sore, and remain sweet of speech and kindly, did not come to these two men and the woman. They had no inkling of such a patience. They were stiff and in pain; their muscles ached, their bones ached, their very hearts ached; and because of this they became sharp of speech, and hard words were first on their lips in the morning and last at night.

Charles and Hal wrangled whenever Mercedes gave them a chance. It was the cherished belief of each that he did more than his share of the work, and neither forbore to speak this belief at every opportunity. Sometimes Mercedes sided with her husband, sometimes with her brother. The result was a beautiful and unending family quarrel. Starting from a dispute as to which should chop a few sticks for the fire (a dispute which concerned only Charles and Hal), presently would be lugged in the rest of the family, fathers, mothers, uncles, cousins, people thousands of miles away, and some of them dead. That Hal's views on art, or the sort of society plays his mother's brother wrote, should have anything to do with the chopping of a few sticks of firewood, passes comprehension; nevertheless the quarrel was as likely to tend in that direction as in the direction of Charles's political prejudices. And that Charles's sister's tale-bearing tongue should be relevant to the building of a Yukon fire, was apparent only to Mercedes, who disburdened herself of copious opinions upon that topic, and incidentally upon a few other traits unpleasantly peculiar to her husband's family. In the meantime the fire remained unbuilt, the camp half pitched, and the dogs unfed.

Mercedes nursed a special grievance—the grievance of sex. She was pretty and soft, and had been chivalrously treated all her days. But the present treatment by her husband and brother was everything save chivalrous. It was her custom to be helpless. They complained. Upon which impeachment of what to her was her most essential sex prerogative, she made their lives unendurable. She no longer considered the dogs, and because she was sore and tired, she persisted in riding on the sled. She was pretty and soft, but she weighed one hundred and twenty pounds—a lusty last straw to the load dragged by the weak and starving animals. She rode for days, till they fell in the traces and the sled stood still. Charles and Hal begged her to get off and walk, pleaded with her, entreated, the while she wept and importuned Heaven with a recital of their brutality.

On one occasion they took her off the sled by main strength. They never did it again. She let her legs go limp like a spoiled child, and sat down on the trail. They went on their way, but she did not move. After they had travelled three miles they unloaded the sled, came back for her, and by main strength put her on the sled again.

In the excess of their own misery they were callous to the suffering of their animals. Hal's theory, which he practised on others, was that one must get hardened. He had started out preaching it to his sister and brother-in-law. Failing there, he hammered it into the dogs with a club. At the Five Fingers the dog-food gave out, and a toothless old squaw offered to trade them a few pounds of frozen horse-hide for the Colt's revolver that kept the big hunting-knife company at Hal's hip. A poor substitute for food was this hide, just as it had been stripped from the starved horses of the cattlemen six months back. In its frozen state it was more like strips of galvanized iron, and when a dog wrestled it into his stomach, it thawed into thin and innutritious leathery strings and into a mass of short hair, irritating and indigestible.

And through it all Buck staggered along at the head of the team as in a nightmare. He pulled when he could; when he could no longer pull, he fell down and remained down till blows from whip or club drove him to his feet again. All the stiffness and gloss had gone out of his beautiful furry coat. The hair hung down, limp and draggled, or matted with dried blood where Hal's club had bruised him. His muscles had wasted away to knotty strings, and the flesh pads had disappeared, so that each rib and every bone in his frame were outlined cleanly through the loose hide that was wrinkled in folds of emptiness. It was heartbreaking, only Buck's heart was unbreakable. The man in the red sweater had proved that.

As it was with Buck, so was it with his mates. They were perambulating skeletons. There were seven altogether, including him. In their very great misery they had become insensible to the bite of the lash or the bruise of the club. The pain of the beating was dull and distant, just as the things their eyes saw and their ears heard seemed dull and distant. They were not half living, or quarter living. They were simply so many bags of bones in which sparks of life fluttered faintly. When a halt was made, they dropped down in the traces like dead dogs, and the spark dimmed and paled and seemed to go out. And when the club or whip fell upon them, the spark fluttered feebly up, and they tottered to their feet and staggered on.

There came a day when Billee, the good-natured, fell and could not rise. Hal had traded off his revolver, so he took the axe and knocked Billee on the head as he lay in the traces, then cut the carcass out of the harness and dragged it to one side. Buck saw, and his mates saw, and they knew that this thing was very close to them. On the next day Koona went, and but five of them remained: Joe, too far gone to be malignant; Pike, crippled and limping, only half conscious and not conscious enough longer to malinger; Sol-leks, the one-eyed, still faithful to the toil of trace and trail, and mournful in that he had so little strength with which to pull; Teek, who had not travelled so far that winter and who was now beaten more than the others because he was fresher; and Buck, still at the head of the team, but no longer enforcing discipline or striving to enforce it, blind with weakness half the time and keeping the trail by the loom of it and by the dim feel of his feet.

It was beautiful spring weather, but neither dogs nor humans were aware of it. Each day the sun rose earlier and set later. It was dawn by three in the morning, and twilight lingered till nine at night. The whole long day was a blaze of sunshine. The ghostly winter silence had given way to the great spring murmur of awakening life. This murmur arose from all the land, fraught with the joy of living. It came from the things that lived and moved again, things which had been as dead and which had not moved during the long months of frost. The sap was rising in the pines. The willows and aspens were bursting out in young buds. Shrubs and vines were putting on fresh garbs of green. Crickets sang in the nights, and in the days all manner of creeping, crawling things rustled forth into the sun. Partridges and woodpeckers were booming and knocking in the forest. Squirrels were chattering, birds singing, and overhead honked the wild-fowl driving up from the south in cunning wedges that split the air.

From every hill slope came the trickle of running water, the music of unseen fountains. All things were thawing, bending, snapping. The Yukon was straining to break loose the ice that bound it down. It ate away from beneath; the sun ate from above. Air-holes formed, fissures sprang and spread apart, while thin sections of ice fell through bodily into the river. And amid all this bursting, rending, throbbing of awakening life, under the blazing sun and through the soft-sighing breezes, like wayfarers to death, staggered the two men, the woman, and the huskies.

With the dogs falling, Mercedes weeping and riding, Hal swearing innocuously, and Charles's eyes wistfully watering, they staggered into John Thornton's camp at the mouth of White River. When they halted, the dogs dropped down as though they had all been struck dead. Mercedes dried her eyes and looked at John Thornton. Charles sat down on a log to rest. He sat down very slowly and painstakingly, what of his great stiffness. Hal did the talking. John Thornton was whittling the last touches on an axe-handle he had made from a stick of birch. He whittled and listened, gave monosyllabic replies, and, when it was asked, terse advice. He knew the breed, and he gave his advice in the certainty that it would not be followed.

"They told us up above that the bottom was dropping out of the trail and that the best thing for us to do was to lay over," Hal said in response to Thornton's warning to take no more chances on the rotten ice. "They told us we couldn't make White River, and here we are." This last with a sneering ring of triumph in it.

"And they told you true," John Thornton answered. "The bottom's likely to drop out at any moment. Only fools, with the blind luck of fools, could have made it. I tell you straight, I wouldn't risk my carcass on that ice for all the gold in Alaska."

"That's because you're not a fool, I suppose," said Hal. "All the same, we'll go on to Dawson." He uncoiled his whip. "Get up there, Buck! Hi! Get up there! Mush on!"

Thornton went on whittling. It was idle, he knew, to get between a fool and his folly; while two or three fools more or less would not alter the scheme of things.

But the team did not get up at the command. It had long since passed into the stage where blows were required to rouse it. The whip flashed out, here and there, on its merciless errands. John Thornton compressed his lips. Sol-leks was the first to crawl to his feet. Teek followed. Joe came next, yelping with pain. Pike made painful efforts. Twice he fell over, when half up, and on the third attempt managed to rise. Buck made no effort. He lay quietly where he had fallen. The lash bit into him again and again, but he neither whined nor struggled. Several times Thornton started, as though to speak, but changed his mind. A moisture came into his eyes, and, as the whipping continued, he arose and walked irresolutely up and down.

This was the first time Buck had failed, in itself a sufficient reason to drive Hal into a rage. He exchanged the whip for the customary club. Buck refused to move under the rain of heavier blows which now fell upon him. Like his mates, he was barely able to get up, but, unlike them, he had made up his mind not to get up. He had a vague feeling of impending doom. This had been strong upon him when he pulled in to the bank, and it had not departed from him. What of the thin and rotten ice he had felt under his feet all day, it seemed that he sensed disaster close at hand, out there ahead on the ice where his master was trying to drive him. He refused to stir. So greatly had he suffered, and so far gone was he, that the blows did not hurt much. And as they continued to fall upon him, the spark of life within flickered and went down. It was nearly out. He felt strangely numb. As though from a great distance, he was aware that he was being beaten. The last sensations of pain left him. He no longer felt anything, though very faintly he could hear the impact of the club upon his body. But it was no longer his body, it seemed so far away.

And then, suddenly, without warning, uttering a cry that was inarticulate and more like the cry of an animal, John Thornton sprang upon the man who wielded the club. Hal was hurled backward, as though struck by a falling tree. Mercedes screamed. Charles looked on wistfully, wiped his watery eyes, but did not get up because of his stiffness.

John Thornton stood over Buck, struggling to control himself, too convulsed with rage to speak.

"If you strike that dog again, I'll kill you," he at last managed to say in a choking voice.

"It's my dog," Hal replied, wiping the blood from his mouth as he came back. "Get out of my way, or I'll fix you. I'm going to Dawson."

Thornton stood between him and Buck and evinced no intention of getting out of the way. Hal drew his long hunting-knife. Mercedes screamed, cried, laughed, and manifested the chaotic abandonment of hysteria. Thornton rapped Hal's knuckles with the axe-handle, knocking the knife to the ground. He rapped his knuckles again as he tried to pick it up. Then he stooped, picked it up himself, and with two strokes cut Buck's traces.

Hal had no fight left in him. Besides, his hands were full with his sister, or his arms, rather; while Buck was too near dead to be of further use in hauling the sled. A few minutes later they pulled out from the bank and down the river. Buck heard them go and raised his head to see. Pike was leading, Sol-leks was at the wheel, and between were Joe and Teek. They were limping and staggering. Mercedes was riding the loaded sled. Hal guided at the gee-pole, and Charles stumbled along in the rear.

As Buck watched them, Thornton knelt beside him and with rough, kindly hands searched for broken bones. By the time his search had disclosed nothing more than many bruises and a state of terrible starvation, the sled was a quarter of a mile away. Dog and man watched it crawling along over the ice. Suddenly, they saw its back end drop down, as into a rut, and the gee-pole, with Hal clinging to it, jerk into the air. Mercedes's scream came to their ears. They saw Charles turn and make one step to run back, and then a whole section of ice give way and dogs and humans disappear. A yawning hole was all that was to be seen. The bottom had dropped out of the trail.

John Thornton and Buck looked at each other.

"You poor devil," said John Thornton and Buck licked his hand.

VI. FOR THE LOVE OF A MAN

When John Thornton froze his feet in the previous December, his partners had made him comfortable and left him to get well, going on themselves up the river to get out a raft of saw-logs for Dawson. He was still limping slightly at the time he rescued Buck, but with the continued warm weather even the slight limp left him. And here, lying by the river bank through the long spring days, watching the running water, listening lazily to the songs of birds and the hum of nature, Buck slowly won back his strength.

A rest comes very good after one has travelled three thousand miles, and it must be confessed that Buck waxed lazy as his wounds healed, his muscles swelled out, and the flesh came back to cover his bones. For that matter, they were all loafing,—Buck, John Thornton, and Skeet and Nig,—waiting for the raft to come that was to carry them down to Dawson. Skeet was a little Irish setter who early made friends with Buck, who, in a dying condition, was unable to resent her first advances. She had the doctor trait which some dogs possess; and as a mother cat washes her kittens, so she washed and cleansed Buck's wounds. Regularly, each morning after he had finished his breakfast, she performed her self-appointed task, till he came to look for her ministrations as much as he did for Thornton's. Nig, equally friendly though less demonstrative, was a huge black dog, half bloodhound and half deerhound, with eyes that laughed and a boundless good nature.

To Buck's surprise these dogs manifested no jealousy toward him. They seemed to share the kindliness and largeness of John Thornton. As Buck grew stronger they enticed him into all sorts of ridiculous games, in which Thornton himself could not forbear to join; and in this fashion Buck romped through his convalescence and into a new existence. Love, genuine passionate love, was his for the first time. This he had never experienced at Judge Miller's down in the sun-kissed Santa Clara Valley. With the Judge's sons, hunting and tramping, it had been a working partnership; with the Judge's grandsons, a sort of pompous guardianship; and with the Judge himself, a stately and dignified friendship. But love that was feverish and burning, that was adoration, that was madness, it had taken John Thornton to arouse.

This man had saved his life, which was something; but, further, he was the ideal master. Other men saw to the welfare of their dogs from a sense of duty and business expediency; he saw to the welfare of his as if they were his own children, because he could not help it. And he saw further. He never forgot a kindly greeting or a cheering word, and to sit down for a long talk with them ("gas" he called it) was as much his delight as theirs. He had a way of taking Buck's head roughly between his hands, and resting his own head upon Buck's, of shaking him back and forth, the while calling him ill names that to Buck were love names. Buck knew no greater joy than that rough embrace and the sound of murmured oaths, and at each jerk back and forth it seemed that his heart would be shaken out of his body, so great was its ecstasy. And when, released, he sprang to his feet, his mouth laughing, his eyes eloquent, his throat vibrant with unuttered sound, and in that fashion remained without movement, John Thornton would reverently exclaim, "God! you can all but speak!"

Buck had a trick of love expression that was akin to hurt. He would often seize Thornton's hand in his mouth and close so fiercely that the flesh bore the impress of his teeth for some time afterward. And as Buck understood the oaths to be love words, so the man understood this feigned bite for a caress.

For the most part, however, Buck's love was expressed in adoration. While he went wild with happiness when Thornton touched him or spoke to him, he did not seek these tokens. Unlike Skeet, who was wont to shove her nose under Thornton's hand and nudge and nudge till petted, or Nig, who would stalk up and rest his great head on Thornton's knee, Buck was content to adore at a distance. He would lie by the hour, eager, alert, at Thornton's feet, looking up into his face, dwelling upon it, studying it, following with keenest interest each fleeting expression, every movement or change of feature. Or, as chance might have it, he would lie farther away, to the side or rear, watching the outlines of the man and the occasional movements of his body. And often, such was the communion in which they lived, the strength of Buck's gaze would draw John Thornton's head around, and he would return the gaze, without speech, his heart shining out of his eyes as Buck's heart shone out.

For a long time after his rescue, Buck did not like Thornton to get out of his sight. From the moment he left the tent to when he entered it again, Buck would follow at his heels. His transient masters since he had come into the Northland had bred in him a fear that no master could be permanent. He was afraid that Thornton would pass out of his life as Perrault and François and the Scotch half-breed had passed out. Even in the night, in his dreams, he was haunted by this fear. At such times he would shake off sleep and creep through the chill to the flap of the tent, where he would stand and listen to the sound of his master's breathing.

But in spite of this great love he bore John Thornton, which seemed to bespeak the soft civilizing influence, the strain of the primitive, which the Northland had aroused in him, remained alive and active. Faithfulness and devotion, things born of fire and roof, were his; yet he retained his wildness and wiliness. He was a thing of the wild, come in from the wild to sit by John Thornton's fire, rather than a dog of the soft Southland stamped with the marks of generations of civilization. Because of his very great love, he could not steal from this man, but from any other man, in any other camp, he did not hesitate an instant; while the cunning with which he stole enabled him to escape detection.

His face and body were scored by the teeth of many dogs, and he fought as fiercely as ever and more shrewdly. Skeet and Nig were too good-natured for quarrelling,—besides, they belonged to John Thornton; but the strange dog, no matter what the breed or valor, swiftly acknowledged Buck's supremacy or found himself struggling for life with a terrible antagonist. And Buck was merciless. He had learned well the law of club and fang, and he never forewent an advantage or drew back from a foe he had started on the way to Death. He had lessoned from Spitz, and from the chief fighting dogs of the police and mail, and knew there was no middle course. He must master or be mastered; while to show mercy was a weakness. Mercy did not exist in the primordial life. It was misunderstood for fear, and such misunderstandings made for death. Kill or be killed, eat or be eaten, was the law; and this mandate, down out of the depths of Time, he obeyed.

He was older than the days he had seen and the breaths he had drawn. He linked the past with the present, and the eternity behind him throbbed through him in a mighty rhythm to which he swayed as the tides and seasons swayed. He sat by John Thornton's fire, a broad-breasted dog, white-fanged and long-furred; but behind him were the shades of all manner of dogs, half-wolves and wild wolves, urgent and prompting, tasting the savor of the meat he ate, thirsting for the water he drank, scenting the wind with him, listening with him and telling him the sounds made by the wild life in the forest, dictating his moods, directing his actions, lying down to sleep with him when he lay down, and dreaming with him and beyond him and becoming themselves the stuff of his dreams.

So peremptorily did these shades beckon him, that each day mankind and the claims of mankind slipped farther from him. Deep in the forest a call was sounding, and as often as he heard this call, mysteriously thrilling and luring, he felt compelled to turn his back upon the fire and the beaten earth around it, and to plunge into the forest, and on and on, he knew not where or why; nor did he wonder where or why, the call sounding imperiously, deep in the forest. But as often as he gained the soft unbroken earth and the green shade, the love for John Thornton drew him back to the fire again.

Thornton alone held him. The rest of mankind was as nothing. Chance travellers might praise or pet him; but he was cold under it all, and from a too demonstrative man he would get up and walk away. When Thornton's partners, Hans and Pete, arrived on the long-expected raft, Buck refused to notice them till he learned they were close to Thornton; after that he tolerated them in a passive sort of way, accepting favors from them as though he favored them by accepting. They were of the same large type as Thornton, living close to the earth, thinking simply and seeing clearly; and ere they swung the raft into the big eddy by the saw-mill at Dawson, they understood Buck and his ways, and did not insist upon an intimacy such as obtained with Skeet and Nig.

For Thornton, however, his love seemed to grow and grow. He, alone among men, could put a pack upon Buck's back in the summer travelling. Nothing was too great for Buck to do, when Thornton commanded. One day (they had grub-staked themselves from the proceeds of the raft and left Dawson for the head-waters of the Tanana) the men and dogs were sitting on the crest of a cliff which fell away, straight down, to naked bed-rock three hundred feet below. John Thornton was sitting near the edge, Buck at his shoulder. A thoughtless whim seized Thornton, and he drew the attention of Hans and Pete to the experiment he had in mind. "Jump, Buck!" he commanded, sweeping his arm out and over the chasm. The next instant he was grappling with Buck on the extreme edge, while Hans and Pete were dragging them back into safety.

"It's uncanny," Pete said, after it was over and they had caught their speech.

Thornton shook his head. "No, it is splendid, and it is terrible, too. Do you know, it sometimes makes me afraid."

"I'm not hankering to be the man that lays hands on you while he's around," Pete announced conclusively, nodding his head toward Buck.

"Py Jingo!" was Hans's contribution. "Not mineself either."

It was at Circle City, ere the year was out, that Pete's apprehensions were realized. "Black" Burton, a man evil-tempered and malicious, had been picking a quarrel with a tenderfoot at the bar, when Thornton stepped good-naturedly between. Buck, as was his custom, was lying in a corner, head on paws, watching his master's every action. Burton struck out, without warning, straight from the shoulder. Thornton was sent spinning, and saved himself from falling only by clutching the rail of the bar.

Those who were looking on heard what was neither bark nor yelp, but a something which is best described as a roar, and they saw Buck's body rise up in the air as he left the floor for Burton's throat. The man saved his life by instinctively throwing out his arm, but was hurled backward to the floor with Buck on top of him. Buck loosed his teeth from the flesh of the arm and drove in again for the throat. This time the man succeeded only in partly blocking, and his throat was torn open. Then the crowd was upon Buck, and he was driven off; but while a surgeon checked the bleeding, he prowled up and down, growling furiously, attempting to rush in, and being forced back by an array of hostile clubs. A "miners' meeting," called on the spot, decided that the dog had sufficient provocation, and Buck was discharged. But his reputation was made, and from that day his name spread through every camp in Alaska.

Later on, in the fall of the year, he saved John Thornton's life in quite another fashion. The three partners were lining a long and narrow poling-boat down a bad stretch of rapids on the Forty Mile Creek. Hans and Pete moved along the bank, snubbing with a thin Manila rope from tree to tree, while Thornton remained in the boat, helping its descent by means of a pole, and shouting directions to the shore. Buck, on the bank, worried and anxious, kept abreast of the boat, his eyes never off his master.

At a particularly bad spot, where a ledge of barely submerged rocks jutted out into the river, Hans cast off the rope, and, while Thornton poled the boat out into the stream, ran down the bank with the end in his hand to snub the boat when it had cleared the ledge. This it did, and was flying down-stream in a current as swift as a millrace, when Hans checked it with the rope and checked too suddenly. The boat flirted over and snubbed in to the bank bottom up, while Thornton, flung sheer out of it, was carried down-stream toward the worst part of the rapids, a stretch of wild water in which no swimmer could live.

Buck had sprung in on the instant; and at the end of three hundred yards, amid a mad swirl of water, he overhauled Thornton. When he felt him grasp his tail, Buck headed for the bank, swimming with all his splendid strength. But the progress shoreward was slow; the progress down-stream amazingly rapid. From below came the fatal roaring where the wild current went wilder and was rent in shreds and spray by the rocks which thrust through like the teeth of an enormous comb. The suck of the water as it took the beginning of the last steep pitch was frightful, and Thornton knew that the shore was impossible. He scraped furiously over a rock, bruised across a second, and struck a third with crushing force. He clutched its slippery top with both hands, releasing Buck, and above the roar of the churning water shouted: "Go, Buck! Go!"

Buck could not hold his own, and swept on down-stream, struggling desperately, but unable to win back. When he heard Thornton's command repeated, he partly reared out of the water, throwing his head high, as though for a last look, then turned obediently toward the bank. He swam powerfully and was dragged ashore by Pete and Hans at the very point where swimming ceased to be possible and destruction began.

They knew that the time a man could cling to a slippery rock in the face of that driving current was a matter of minutes, and they ran as fast as they could up the bank to a point far above where Thornton was hanging on. They attached the line with which they had been snubbing the boat to Buck's neck and shoulders, being careful that it should neither strangle him nor impede his swimming, and launched him into the stream. He struck out boldly, but not straight enough into the stream. He discovered the mistake too late, when Thornton was abreast of him and a bare half-dozen strokes away while he was being carried helplessly past.

Hans promptly snubbed with the rope, as though Buck were a boat. The rope thus tightening on him in the sweep of the current, he was jerked under the surface, and under the surface he remained till his body struck against the bank and he was hauled out. He was half drowned, and Hans and Pete threw themselves upon him, pounding the breath into him and the water out of him. He staggered to his feet and fell down. The faint sound of Thornton's voice came to them, and though they could not make out the words of it, they knew that he was in his extremity. His master's voice acted on Buck like an electric shock. He sprang to his feet and ran up the bank ahead of the men to the point of his previous departure.

Again the rope was attached and he was launched, and again he struck out, but this time straight into the stream. He had miscalculated once, but he would not be guilty of it a second time. Hans paid out the rope, permitting no slack, while Pete kept it clear of coils. Buck held on till he was on a line straight above Thornton; then he turned, and with the speed of an express train headed down upon him. Thornton saw him coming, and, as Buck struck him like a battering ram, with the whole force of the current behind him, he reached up and closed with both arms around the shaggy neck. Hans snubbed the rope around the tree, and Buck and Thornton were jerked under the water. Strangling, suffocating, sometimes one uppermost and sometimes the other, dragging over the jagged bottom, smashing against rocks and snags, they veered in to the bank.

Thornton came to, belly downward and being violently propelled back and forth across a drift log by Hans and Pete. His first glance was for Buck, over whose limp and apparently lifeless body Nig was setting up a howl, while Skeet was licking the wet face and closed eyes. Thornton was himself bruised and battered, and he went carefully over Buck's body, when he had been brought around, finding three broken ribs.

"That settles it," he announced. "We camp right here." And camp they did, till Buck's ribs knitted and he was able to travel.

That winter, at Dawson, Buck performed another exploit, not so heroic, perhaps, but one that put his name many notches higher on the totem-pole of Alaskan fame. This exploit was particularly gratifying to the three men; for they stood in need of the outfit which it furnished, and were enabled to make a long-desired trip into the virgin East, where miners had not yet appeared. It was brought about by a conversation in the Eldorado Saloon, in which men waxed boastful of their favorite dogs. Buck, because of his record, was the target for these men, and Thornton was driven stoutly to defend him. At the end of half an hour one man stated that his dog could start a sled with five hundred pounds and walk off with it; a second bragged six hundred for his dog; and a third, seven hundred.

"Pooh! Pooh!" said John Thornton; "Buck can start a thousand pounds."

"And break it out? and walk off with it for a hundred yards?" demanded Matthewson, a Bonanza king, he of the seven hundred vaunt.

"And break it out, and walk off with it for a hundred yards," John Thornton said coolly.

"Well," Matthewson said, slowly and deliberately, so that all could hear, "I've got a thousand dollars that says he can't. And there it is." So saying, he slammed a sack of gold dust of the size of a bologna sausage down upon the bar.

Nobody spoke. Thornton's bluff, if bluff it was, had been called. He could feel a flush of warm blood creeping up his face. His tongue had tricked him. He did not know whether Buck could start a thousand pounds. Half a ton! The enormousness of it appalled him. He had great faith in Buck's strength and had often thought him capable of starting such a load; but never, as now, had he faced the possibility of it, the eyes of a dozen men fixed upon him, silent and waiting. Further, he had no thousand dollars; nor had Hans or Pete.

"I've got a sled standing outside now, with twenty fifty-pound sacks of flour on it," Matthewson went on with brutal directness; "so don't let that hinder you."

Thornton did not reply. He did not know what to say. He glanced from face to face in the absent way of a man who has lost the power of thought and is seeking somewhere to find the thing that will start it going again. The face of Jim O'Brien, a Mastodon king and old-time comrade, caught his eyes. It was as a cue to him, seeming to rouse him to do what he would never have dreamed of doing.

"Can you lend me a thousand?" he asked, almost in a whisper.

"Sure," answered O'Brien, thumping down a plethoric sack by the side of Matthewson's. "Though it's little faith I'm having, John, that the beast can do the trick."

The Eldorado emptied its occupants into the street to see the test. The tables were deserted, and the dealers and gamekeepers came forth to see the outcome of the wager and to lay odds. Several hundred men, furred and mittened, banked around the sled within easy distance. Matthewson's sled, loaded with a thousand pounds of flour, had been standing for a couple of hours, and in the intense cold (it was sixty below zero) the runners had frozen fast to the hard-packed snow. Men offered odds of two to one that Buck could not budge the sled. A quibble arose concerning the phrase "break out." O'Brien contended it was Thornton's privilege to knock the runners loose, leaving Buck to "break it out" from a dead standstill. Matthewson insisted that the phrase included breaking the runners from the frozen grip of the snow. A majority of the men who had witnessed the making of the bet decided in his favor, whereat the odds went up to three to one against Buck.

There were no takers. Not a man believed him capable of the feat. Thornton had been hurried into the wager, heavy with doubt; and now that he looked at the sled itself, the concrete fact, with the regular team of ten dogs curled up in the snow before it, the more impossible the task appeared. Matthewson waxed jubilant.

"Three to one!" he proclaimed. "I'll lay you another thousand at that figure, Thornton. What d'ye say?"

Thornton's doubt was strong in his face, but his fighting spirit was aroused —the fighting spirit that soars above odds, fails to recognize the impossible, and is deaf to all save the clamor for battle. He called Hans and Pete to him. Their sacks were slim, and with his own the three partners could rake together only two hundred dollars. In the ebb of their fortunes, this sum was their total capital; yet they laid it unhesitatingly against Matthewson's six hundred.

The team of ten dogs was unhitched, and Buck, with his own harness, was put into the sled. He had caught the contagion of the excitement, and he felt that in some way he must do a great thing for John Thornton. Murmurs

of admiration at his splendid appearance went up. He was in perfect condition, without an ounce of superfluous flesh, and the one hundred and fifty pounds that he weighed were so many pounds of grit and virility. His furry coat shone with the sheen of silk. Down the neck and across the shoulders, his mane, in repose as it was, half bristled and seemed to lift with every movement, as though excess of vigor made each particular hair alive and active. The great breast and heavy fore legs were no more than in proportion with the rest of the body, where the muscles showed in tight rolls underneath the skin. Men felt these muscles and proclaimed them hard as iron, and the odds went down to two to one.

"Gad, sir! Gad, sir!" stuttered a member of the latest dynasty, a king of the Skookum Benches. "I offer you eight hundred for him, sir, before the test, sir; eight hundred just as he stands."

Thornton shook his head and stepped over to Buck's side.

"You must stand off from him," Matthewson protested. "Free play and plenty of room."

The crowd fell silent; only could be heard the voices of the gamblers vainly offering two to one. Everybody acknowledged Buck a magnificent animal, but twenty fifty-pound sacks of flour bulked too large in their eyes for them to loosen their pouch-strings.

Thornton knelt down by Buck's side. He took his head in his two hands and rested cheek on cheek. He did not playfully shake him, as was his wont, or murmur soft love curses; but he whispered in his ear. "As you love me, Buck. As you love me," was what he whispered. Buck whined with suppressed eagerness.

The crowd was watching curiously. The affair was growing mysterious. It seemed like a conjuration. As Thornton got to his feet, Buck seized his mittened hand between his jaws, pressing in with his teeth and releasing slowly, half-reluctantly. It was the answer, in terms, not of speech, but of love. Thornton stepped well back.

"Now, Buck," he said.

Buck tightened the traces, then slacked them for a matter of several inches. It was the way he had learned.

"Gee!" Thornton's voice rang out, sharp in the tense silence.

Buck swung to the right, ending the movement in a plunge that took up the slack and with a sudden jerk arrested his one hundred and fifty pounds. The load quivered, and from under the runners arose a crisp crackling.

"Haw!" Thornton commanded.

Buck duplicated the manœuvre, this time to the left. The crackling turned into a snapping, the sled pivoting and the runners slipping and grating several inches to the side. The sled was broken out. Men were holding their breaths, intensely unconscious of the fact.

"Now, MUSH!"

Thornton's command cracked out like a pistol-shot. Buck threw himself forward, tightening the traces with a jarring lunge. His whole body was gathered compactly together in the tremendous effort, the muscles writhing and knotting like live things under the silky fur. His great chest was low to the ground, his head forward and down, while his feet were flying like mad, the claws scarring the hard-packed snow in parallel grooves. The sled swayed and trembled, half-started forward. One of his feet slipped, and one man groaned aloud. Then the sled lurched ahead in what appeared a rapid succession of jerks, though it never really came to a dead stop again . . . half an inch . . . an inch . . . two inches. . . . The jerks perceptibly diminished; as the sled gained momentum, he caught them up, till it was moving steadily along.

Men gasped and began to breathe again, unaware that for a moment they had ceased to breathe. Thornton was running behind, encouraging Buck with short, cheery words. The distance had been measured off, and as he neared the pile of firewood which marked the end of the hundred yards, a cheer began to grow and grow, which burst into a roar as he passed the firewood and halted at command. Every man was tearing himself loose, even Matthewson. Hats and mittens were flying in the air. Men were shaking hands, it did not matter with whom, and bubbling over in a general incoherent babel.

But Thornton fell on his knees beside Buck. Head was against head, and he was shaking him back and forth. Those who hurried up heard him cursing Buck, and he cursed him long and fervently, and softly and lovingly.

"Gad, sir! Gad, sir!" spluttered the Skookum Bench king. "I'll give you a
thousand for him, sir, a thousand, sir—twelve hundred, sir."

Thornton rose to his feet. His eyes were wet. The tears were streaming
frankly down his cheeks. "Sir," he said to the Skookum Bench king, "no, sir.
You can go to hell, sir. It's the best I can do for you, sir."

Buck seized Thornton's hand in his teeth. Thornton shook him back and
forth. As though animated by a common impulse, the onlookers drew back
to a respectful distance; nor were they again indiscreet enough to interrupt.

VII. THE SOUNDING OF THE CALL

When Buck earned sixteen hundred dollars in five minutes for John
Thornton, he made it possible for his master to pay off certain debts and to
journey with his partners into the East after a fabled lost mine, the history
of which was as old as the history of the country. Many men had sought it;
few had found it; and more than a few there were who had never returned
from the quest. This lost mine was steeped in tragedy and shrouded in mystery. No one knew of the first man. The oldest tradition stopped before it
got back to him. From the beginning there had been an ancient and ram-
shackle cabin. Dying men had sworn to it, and to the mine the site of which
it marked, clinching their testimony with nuggets that were unlike any
known grade of gold in the Northland.

But no living man had looted this treasure house, and the dead were dead;
wherefore John Thornton and Pete and Hans, with Buck and half a dozen
other dogs, faced into the East on an unknown trail to achieve where men
and dogs as good as themselves had failed. They sledded seventy miles up
the Yukon, swung to the left into the Stewart River, passed the Mayo and
the McQuestion, and held on until the Stewart itself became a streamlet,
threading the upstanding peaks which marked the backbone of the conti-
nent.

John Thornton asked little of man or nature. He was unafraid of the wild.
With a handful of salt and a rifle he could plunge into the wilderness and
fare wherever he pleased and as long as he pleased. Being in no haste, Indian
fashion, he hunted his dinner in the course of the day's travel; and if he failed
to find it, like the Indian, he kept on travelling, secure in the knowledge that
sooner or later he would come to it. So, on this great journey into the East,
straight meat was the bill of fare, ammunition and tools principally made
up the load on the sled, and the time-card was drawn upon the limitless
future.

To Buck it was boundless delight, this hunting, fishing, and indefinite
wandering through strange places. For weeks at a time they would hold on
steadily, day after day; and for weeks upon end they would camp, here and
there, the dogs loafing and the men burning holes through frozen muck and
gravel and washing countless pans of dirt by the heat of the fire. Sometimes
they went hungry, sometimes they feasted riotously, all according to the

abundance of game and the fortune of hunting. Summer arrived, and dogs and men packed on their backs, rafted across blue mountain lakes, and descended or ascended unknown rivers in slender boats whipsawed from the standing forest.

The months came and went, and back and forth they twisted through the uncharted vastness, where no men were and yet where men had been if the Lost Cabin were true. They went across divides in summer blizzards, shivered under the midnight sun on naked mountains between the timber line and the eternal snows, dropped into summer valleys amid swarming gnats and flies, and in the shadows of glaciers picked strawberries and flowers as ripe and fair as any the Southland could boast. In the fall of the year they penetrated a weird lake country, sad and silent, where wild-fowl had been, but where then there was no life nor sign of life—only the blowing of chill winds, the forming of ice in sheltered places, and the melancholy rippling of waves on lonely beaches.

And through another winter they wandered on the obliterated trails of men who had gone before. Once, they came upon a path blazed through the forest, an ancient path, and the Lost Cabin seemed very near. But the path began nowhere and ended nowhere, and it remained mystery, as the man who made it and the reason he made it remained mystery. Another time they chanced upon the time-graven wreckage of a hunting lodge, and amid the shreds of rotted blankets John Thornton found a long-barrelled flint-lock. He knew it for a Hudson Bay Company gun of the young days in the Northwest, when such a gun was worth its weight in beaver skins packed flat. And that was all—no hint as to the man who in an early day had reared the lodge and left the gun among the blankets.

Spring came on once more, and at the end of all their wandering they found, not the Lost Cabin, but a shallow placer in a broad valley where the gold showed like yellow butter across the bottom of the washing-pan. They sought no farther. Each day they worked earned them thousands of dollars in clean dust and nuggets, and they worked every day. The gold was sacked in moosehide bags, fifty pounds to the bag, and piled like so much firewood outside the spruce-bough lodge. Like giants they toiled, days flashing on the heels of days like dreams as they heaped the treasure up.

There was nothing for the dogs to do, save the hauling in of meat now and again that Thornton killed, and Buck spent long hours musing by the fire. The vision of the short-legged hairy man came to him more frequently, now that there was little work to be done; and often, blinking by the fire, Buck wandered with him in that other world which he remembered.

The salient thing of this other world seemed fear. When he watched the hairy man sleeping by the fire, head between his knees and hands clasped above, Buck saw that he slept restlessly, with many starts and awakenings, at which times he would peer fearfully into the darkness and fling more wood upon the fire. Did they walk by the beach of a sea, where the hairy man gathered shell-fish and ate them as he gathered, it was with eyes that roved everywhere for hidden danger and with legs prepared to run like the wind at its first appearance. Through the forest they crept noiselessly, Buck at the hairy man's heels; and they were alert and vigilant, the pair of them, ears twitching and moving and nostrils quivering, for the man heard and smelled as keenly as Buck. The hairy man could spring up into the trees and travel ahead as fast as on the ground, swinging by the arms from limb to limb, sometimes a dozen feet apart, letting go and catching, never falling, never missing his grip. In fact, he seemed as much at home among the trees as on the ground; and Buck had memories of nights of vigil spent beneath trees wherein the hairy man roosted, holding on tightly as he slept.

And closely akin to the visions of the hairy man was the call still sounding in the depths of the forest. It filled him with a great unrest and strange desires. It caused him to feel a vague, sweet gladness, and he was aware of wild yearnings and stirrings for he knew not what. Sometimes he pursued the call into the forest, looking for it as though it were a tangible thing, barking softly or defiantly, as the mood might dictate. He would thrust his nose into the cool wood moss, or into the black soil where long grasses grew, and snort with joy at the fat earth smells; or he would crouch for hours, as if in concealment, behind fungus-covered trunks of fallen trees, wide-eyed and wide-eared to all that moved and sounded about him. It might be, lying thus, that he hoped to surprise this call he could not understand. But he did not know why he did these various things. He was impelled to do them, and did not reason about them at all.

Irresistible impulses seized him. He would be lying in camp, dozing lazily in the heat of the day, when suddenly his head would lift and his ears cock up, intent and listening, and he would spring to his feet and dash away, and on and on, for hours, through the forest aisles and across the open spaces where the niggerheads bunched. He loved to run down dry watercourses, and to creep and spy upon the bird life in the woods. For a day at a time he would lie in the underbrush where he could watch the partridges drumming and strutting up and down. But especially he loved to run in the dim twilight of the summer midnights, listening to the subdued and sleepy murmurs of the forest, reading signs and sounds as man may read a book, and seeking for the mysterious something that called—called, waking or sleeping, at all times, for him to come.

One night he sprang from sleep with a start, eager-eyed, nostrils quivering and scenting, his mane bristling in recurrent waves. From the forest came the call (or one note of it, for the call was many-noted), distinct and definite as never before,—a long-drawn howl, like, yet unlike, any noise made by husky dog. And he knew it, in the old familiar way, as a sound heard before. He sprang through the sleeping camp and in swift silence dashed through the woods. As he drew closer to the cry he went more slowly, with caution in every movement, till he came to an open place among the trees, and looking out saw, erect on haunches, with nose pointed to the sky, a long, lean, timber wolf.

He had made no noise, yet it ceased from its howling and tried to sense his presence. Buck stalked into the open, half crouching, body gathered compactly together, tail straight and stiff, feet falling with unwonted care. Every movement advertised commingled threatening and overture of friendliness. It was the menacing truce that marks the meeting of wild beasts that prey. But the wolf fled at sight of him. He followed, with wild leapings, in a frenzy to overtake. He ran him into a blind channel, in the bed of the creek, where a timber jam barred the way. The wolf whirled about, pivoting on his hind legs after the fashion of Joe and of all cornered husky dogs, snarling and bristling, clipping his teeth together in a continuous and rapid succession of snaps.

Buck did not attack, but circled him about and hedged him in with friendly advances. The wolf was suspicious and afraid; for Buck made three of him in weight, while his head barely reached Buck's shoulder. Watching his chance, he darted away, and the chase was resumed. Time and again he was cornered, and the thing repeated, though he was in poor condition or Buck could not so easily have overtaken him. He would run till Buck's head was even with his flank, when he would whirl around at bay, only to dash away again at the first opportunity.

But in the end Buck's pertinacity was rewarded; for the wolf, finding that no harm was intended, finally sniffed noses with him. Then they became friendly, and played about in the nervous, half-coy way with which fierce beasts belie their fierceness. After some time of this the wolf started off at an easy lope in a manner that plainly showed he was going somewhere. He made it clear to Buck that he was to come, and they ran side by side through the sombre twilight, straight up the creek bed, into the gorge from which it issued, and across the bleak divide where it took its rise.

On the opposite slope of the watershed they came down into a level country where were great stretches of forest and many streams, and through these great stretches they ran steadily, hour after hour, the sun rising higher and the day growing warmer. Buck was wildly glad. He knew he was at last answering the call, running by the side of his wood brother toward the place from where the call surely came. Old memories were coming upon him fast, and he was stirring to them as of old he stirred to the realities of which they were the shadows. He had done this thing before, somewhere in that other and dimly remembered world, and he was doing it again, now, running free in the open, the unpacked earth underfoot, the wide sky overhead.

They stopped by a running stream to drink, and, stopping, Buck remembered John Thornton. He sat down. The wolf started on toward the place from where the call surely came, then returned to him, sniffing noses and making actions as though to encourage him. But Buck turned about and started slowly on the back track. For the better part of an hour the wild brother ran by his side, whining softly. Then he sat down, pointed his nose upward, and howled. It was a mournful howl, and as Buck held steadily on his way he heard it grow faint and fainter until it was lost in the distance.

John Thornton was eating dinner when Buck dashed into camp and sprang upon him in a frenzy of affection, overturning him, scrambling upon him, licking his face, biting his hand—"playing the general tom-fool," as John

Thornton characterized it, the while he shook Buck back and forth and cursed him lovingly.

For two days and nights Buck never left camp, never let Thornton out of his sight. He followed him about at his work, watched him while he ate, saw him into his blankets at night and out of them in the morning. But after two days the call in the forest began to sound more imperiously than ever. Buck's restlessness came back on him, and he was haunted by recollections of the wild brother, and of the smiling land beyond the divide and the run side by side through the wide forest stretches. Once again he took to wandering in the woods, but the wild brother came no more; and though he listened through long vigils, the mournful howl was never raised.

He began to sleep out at night, staying away from camp for days at a time; and once he crossed the divide at the head of the creek and went down into the land of timber and streams. There he wandered for a week, seeking vainly for fresh sign of the wild brother, killing his meat as he travelled and travelling with the long, easy lope that seems never to tire. He fished for salmon in a broad stream that emptied somewhere into the sea, and by this stream he killed a large black bear, blinded by the mosquitoes while likewise fishing, and raging through the forest helpless and terrible. Even so, it was a hard fight, and it aroused the last latent remnants of Buck's ferocity. And two days later, when he returned to his kill and found a dozen wolverenes quarrelling over the spoil, he scattered them like chaff; and those that fled left two behind who would quarrel no more.

The blood-longing became stronger than ever before. He was a killer, a thing that preyed, living on the things that lived, unaided, alone, by virtue of his own strength and prowess, surviving triumphantly in a hostile environment where only the strong survived. Because of all this he became possessed of a great pride in himself, which communicated itself like a contagion to his physical being. It advertised itself in all his movements, was apparent in the play of every muscle, spoke plainly as speech in the way he carried himself, and made his glorious furry coat if anything more glorious. But for the stray brown on his muzzle and above his eyes, and for the splash of white hair that ran midmost down his chest, he might well have been mistaken for a gigantic wolf, larger than the largest of the breed. From his St. Bernard father he had inherited size and weight, but it was his shepherd mother who had given shape to that size and weight. His muzzle was the long wolf muzzle, save that it was larger than the muzzle of any wolf; and his head, somewhat broader, was the wolf head on a massive scale.

His cunning was wolf cunning, and wild cunning; his intelligence, shepherd intelligence and St. Bernard intelligence; and all this, plus an experience gained in the fiercest of schools, made him as formidable a creature as any that roamed the wild. A carnivorous animal, living on a straight meat diet, he was in full flower, at the high tide of his life, overspilling with vigor and virility. When Thornton passed a caressing hand along his back, a snapping and crackling followed the hand, each hair discharging its pent magnetism at the contact. Every part, brain and body, nerve tissue and fibre, was keyed to the most exquisite pitch; and between all the parts there was a perfect equilibrium or adjustment. To sights and sounds and events which required action, he responded with lightning-like rapidity. Quickly as a husky dog could leap to defend from attack or to attack, he could leap twice as quickly. He saw the movement, or heard sound, and responded in less time than another dog required to compass the mere seeing or hearing. He perceived and determined and responded in the same instant. In point of fact the three actions of perceiving, determining, and responding were sequential; but so infinitesimal were the intervals of time between them that they appeared simultaneous. His muscles were surcharged with vitality, and snapped into play sharply, like steel springs. Life streamed through him in splendid flood, glad and rampant, until it seemed that it would burst him asunder in sheer ecstasy and pour forth generously over the world.

"Never was there such a dog," said John Thornton one day, as the partners watched Buck marching out of camp.

"When he was made, the mould was broke," said Pete.

"Py Jingo! I t'ink so mineself," Hans affirmed.

They saw him marching out of camp, but they did not see the instant and terrible transformation which took place as soon as he was within the secrecy of the forest. He no longer marched. At once he became a thing of the wild, stealing along softly, cat-footed, a passing shadow that appeared and disappeared among the shadows. He knew how to take advantage of every cover, to crawl on his belly like a snake, and like a snake to leap and strike. He could take a ptarmigan from its nest, kill a rabbit as it slept, and snap in mid air the little chipmunks fleeing a second too late for the trees. Fish, in open pools, were not too quick for him; nor were beaver, mending their dams, too wary. He killed to eat, not from wantonness; but he preferred to eat what he killed himself. So a lurking humor ran through his deeds, and it was his delight to steal upon the squirrels, and, when he all but had them, to let them go, chattering in mortal fear to the tree-tops.

As the fall of the year came on, the moose appeared in greater abundance, moving slowly down to meet the winter in the lower and less rigorous valleys. Buck had already dragged down a stray part-grown calf; but he wished strongly for larger and more formidable quarry, and he came upon it one day on the divide at the head of the creek. A band of twenty moose had crossed over from the land of streams and timber, and chief among them was a great bull. He was in a savage temper, and, standing over six feet from the ground, was as formidable an antagonist as even Buck could desire. Back and forth the bull tossed his great palmated antlers, branching to fourteen points and embracing seven feet within the tips. His small eyes burned with a vicious and bitter light, while he roared with fury at sight of Buck.

From the bull's side, just forward of the flank, protruded a feathered arrow-end, which accounted for his savageness. Guided by that instinct which came from the old hunting days of the primordial world, Buck proceeded to cut the bull out from the herd. It was no slight task. He would bark and dance about in front of the bull, just out of reach of the great antlers and of the terrible splay hoofs which could have stamped his life out with a single blow. Unable to turn his back on the fanged danger and go on, the bull would be driven into paroxysms of rage. At such moments he charged Buck, who retreated craftily, luring him on by a simulated inability to escape. But when he was thus separated from his fellows, two or three of the younger bulls would charge back upon Buck and enable the wounded bull to rejoin the herd.

There is a patience of the wild—dogged, tireless, persistent as life itself—that holds motionless for endless hours the spider in its web, the snake in its coils, the panther in its ambuscade; this patience belongs peculiarly to life when it hunts its living food; and it belonged to Buck as he clung to the flank of the herd, retarding its march, irritating the young bulls, worrying the cows with their half-grown calves, and driving the wounded bull mad with helpless rage. For half a day this continued. Buck multiplied himself, attacking from all sides, enveloping the herd in a whirlwind of menace, cutting out his victim as fast as it could rejoin its mates, wearing out the patience of creatures preyed upon, which is a lesser patience than that of creatures preying.

As the day wore along and the sun dropped to its bed in the northwest (the darkness had come back and the fall nights were six hours long), the young bulls retraced their steps more and more reluctantly to the aid of their beset leader. The down-coming winter was harrying them on to the lower levels, and it seemed they could never shake off this tireless creature that held them back. Besides, it was not the life of the herd, or of the young bulls, that was threatened. The life of only one member was demanded, which was a remoter interest than their lives, and in the end they were content to pay the toll.

As twilight fell the old bull stood with lowered head, watching his mates— the cows he had known, the calves he had fathered, the bulls he had mastered —as they shambled on at a rapid pace through the fading light. He could not follow, for before his nose leaped the merciless fanged terror that would not let him go. Three hundredweight more than half a ton he weighed; he had lived a long, strong life, full of fight and struggle, and at the end he faced death at the teeth of a creature whose head did not reach beyond his great knuckled knees.

From then on, night and day, Buck never left his prey, never gave it a moment's rest, never permitted it to browse the leaves of trees or the shoots of young birch and willow. Nor did he give the wounded bull opportunity to slake his burning thirst in the slender trickling streams they crossed. Often, in desperation, he burst into long stretches of flight. At such times Buck did not attempt to stay him, but loped easily at his heels, satisfied with the way the game was played, lying down when the moose stood still, attacking him fiercely when he strove to eat or drink.

The great head drooped more and more under its tree of horns, and the shambling trot grew weaker and weaker. He took to standing for long periods, with nose to the ground and dejected ears dropped limply; and Buck found more time in which to get water for himself and in which to rest. At such moments, panting with red lolling tongue and with eyes fixed upon the big bull, it appeared to Buck that a change was coming over the face of things. He could feel a new stir in the land. As the moose were coming into the land, other kinds of life were coming in. Forest and stream and air seemed palpitant with their presence. The news of it was borne in upon him, not by sight, or sound, or smell, but by some other and subtler sense. He heard nothing, saw nothing, yet knew that the land was somehow different; that through it strange things were afoot and ranging; and he resolved to investigate after he had finished the business in hand.

At last, at the end of the fourth day, he pulled the great moose down. For a day and a night he remained by the kill, eating and sleeping, turn and turn about. Then, rested, refreshed and strong, he turned his face toward camp and John Thornton. He broke into the long easy lope, and went on, hour after hour, never at loss for the tangled way, heading straight home through strange country with a certitude of direction that put man and his magnetic needle to shame.

As he held on he became more and more conscious of the new stir in the land. There was life abroad in it different from the life which had been there throughout the summer. No longer was this fact borne in upon him in some subtle, mysterious way. The birds talked of it, the squirrels chattered about it, the very breeze whispered of it. Several times he stopped and drew in the fresh morning air in great sniffs, reading a message which made him leap on with greater speed. He was oppressed with a sense of calamity happening, if it were not calamity already happened; and as he crossed the last watershed and dropped down into the valley toward camp, he proceeded with greater caution.

Three miles away he came upon a fresh trail that sent his neck hair rippling and bristling. It led straight toward camp and John Thornton. Buck hurried on, swiftly and stealthily, every nerve straining and tense, alert to the multitudinous details which told a story—all but the end. His nose gave him a varying description of the passage of the life on the heels of which he was travelling. He remarked the pregnant silence of the forest. The bird life had flitted. The squirrels were in hiding. One only he saw,—a sleek gray fellow, flattened against a gray dead limb so that he seemed a part of it, a woody excrescence upon the wood itself.

As Buck slid along with the obscureness of a gliding shadow, his nose was jerked suddenly to the side as though a positive force had gripped and pulled it. He followed the new scent into a thicket and found Nig. He was lying on his side, dead where he had dragged himself, an arrow protruding, head and feathers, from either side of his body.

A hundred yards farther on, Buck came upon one of the sled-dogs Thornton had bought in Dawson. This dog was thrashing about in a death-struggle, directly on the trail, and Buck passed around him without stopping. From the camp came the faint sound of many voices, rising and falling in a sing-song chant. Bellying forward to the edge of the clearing, he found Hans, lying on his face, feathered with arrows like a porcupine. At the same instant Buck peered out where the spruce-bough lodge had been and saw what made his hair leap straight up on his neck and shoulders. A gust of overpowering rage swept over him. He did not know that he growled, but he growled aloud with a terrible ferocity. For the last time in his life he allowed passion to usurp cunning and reason, and it was because of his great love for John Thornton that he lost his head.

The Yeehats were dancing about the wreckage of the spruce-bough lodge when they heard a fearful roaring and saw rushing upon them an animal the like of which they had never seen before. It was Buck, a live hurricane of fury, hurling himself upon them in a frenzy to destroy. He sprang at the foremost man (it was the chief of the Yeehats), ripping the throat wide open till the rent jugular spouted a fountain of blood. He did not pause to worry the victim, but ripped in passing, with the next bound tearing wide the throat of a second man. There was no withstanding him. He plunged about in their very midst, tearing, rending, destroying, in constant and terrific motion which defied the arrows they discharged at him. In fact, so inconceivably rapid were his movements, and so closely were the Indians tangled together, that they shot one another with the arrows; and one young hunter, hurling a spear at Buck in mid air, drove it through the chest of another hunter with such force that the point broke through the skin of the back and stood out beyond. Then a panic seized the Yeehats, and they fled in terror to the woods, proclaiming as they fled the advent of the Evil Spirit.

And truly Buck was the Fiend incarnate, raging at their heels and dragging them down like deer as they raced through the trees. It was a fateful day for the Yeehats. They scattered far and wide over the country, and it was not till a week later that the last of the survivors gathered together in a lower valley and counted their losses. As for Buck, wearying of the pursuit, he returned to the desolated camp. He found Pete where he had been killed in his blankets in the first moment of surprise. Thornton's desperate struggle was fresh-written on the earth, and Buck scented every detail of it down to the edge of a deep pool. By the edge, head and fore feet in the water, lay Skeet, faithful to the last. The pool itself, muddy and discolored from the sluice boxes, effectually hid what it contained, and it contained John Thornton; for Buck followed his trace into the water, from which no trace led away.

All day Buck brooded by the pool or roamed restlessly about the camp. Death, as a cessation of movement, as a passing out and away from the lives of the living, he knew, and he knew John Thornton was dead. It left a great void in him, somewhat akin to hunger, but a void which ached and ached, and which food could not fill. At times, when he paused to contemplate the carcasses of the Yeehats, he forgot the pain of it; and at such times he was aware of a great pride in himself,—a pride greater than any he had yet experienced. He had killed man, the noblest game of all, and he had killed in the face of the law of club and fang. He sniffed the bodies curiously. They had died so easily. It was harder to kill a husky dog than them. They were no match at all, were it not for their arrows and spears and clubs. Thenceforward he would be unafraid of them except when they bore in their hands their arrows, spears, and clubs.

Night came on, and a full moon rose high over the trees into the sky, lighting the land till it lay bathed in ghostly day. And with the coming of the night, brooding and mourning by the pool, Buck became alive to a stirring of the new life in the forest other than that which the Yeehats had made. He stood up, listening and scenting. From far away drifted a faint, sharp yelp, followed by a chorus of similar sharp yelps. As the moments passed the yelps grew closer and louder. Again Buck knew them as things heard in that other world which persisted in his memory. He walked to the centre of the open space and listened. It was the call, the many-noted call, sounding more luringly and compelling than ever before. And as never before, he was ready to obey. John Thornton was dead. The last tie was broken. Man and the claims of man no longer bound him.

Hunting their living meat, as the Yeehats were hunting it, on the flanks of the migrating moose, the wolf pack had at last crossed over from the land of streams and timber and invaded Buck's valley. Into the clearing where the moonlight streamed, they poured in a silvery flood; and in the centre of the clearing stood Buck, motionless as a statue, waiting their coming. They were awed, so still and large he stood, and a moment's pause fell, till the boldest one leaped straight for him. Like a flash Buck struck, breaking the neck. Then he stood, without movement, as before, the stricken wolf rolling in agony behind him. Three others tried it in sharp succession; and one after the other they drew back, streaming blood from slashed throats or shoulders.

This was sufficient to fling the whole pack forward, pell-mell, crowded together, blocked and confused by its eagerness to pull down the prey. Buck's marvellous quickness and agility stood him in good stead. Pivoting on his hind legs, and snapping and gashing, he was everywhere at once, presenting a front which was apparently unbroken so swiftly did he whirl and guard from side to side. But to prevent them from getting behind him, he was forced back, down past the pool and into the creek bed, till he brought up against a high gravel bank. He worked along to a right angle in the bank which the men had made in the course of mining, and in this angle he came to bay, protected on three sides and with nothing to do but face the front.

And so well did he face it, that at the end of half an hour the wolves drew back discomfited. The tongues of all were out and lolling, the white fangs showing cruelly white in the moonlight. Some were lying down with heads raised and ears pricked forward; others stood on their feet, watching him; and still others were lapping water from the pool. One wolf, long and lean and gray, advanced cautiously, in a friendly manner, and Buck recognized the wild brother with whom he had run for a night and a day. He was whining softly, and, as Buck whined, they touched noses.

Then an old wolf, gaunt and battle-scarred, came forward. Buck writhed his lips into the preliminary of a snarl, but sniffed noses with him. Whereupon the old wolf sat down, pointed nose at the moon, and broke out the long wolf howl. The others sat down and howled. And now the call came to

Buck in unmistakable accents. He, too, sat down and howled. This over, he came out of his angle and the pack crowded around him, sniffing in half-friendly, half-savage manner. The leaders lifted the yelp of the pack and sprang away into the woods. The wolves swung in behind, yelping in chorus. And Buck ran with them, side by side with the wild brother, yelping as he ran.

And here may well end the story of Buck. The years were not many when the Yeehats noted a change in the breed of timber wolves; for some were seen with splashes of brown on head and muzzle, and with a rift of white centring down the chest. But more remarkable than this, the Yeehats tell of a Ghost Dog that runs at the head of the pack. They are afraid of this Ghost Dog, for it has cunning greater than they, stealing from their camps in fierce winters, robbing their traps, slaying their dogs, and defying their bravest hunters.

Nay, the tale grows worse. Hunters there are who fail to return to the camp, and hunters there have been whom their tribesmen found with throats slashed cruelly open and with wolf prints about them in the snow greater than the prints of any wolf. Each fall, when the Yeehats follow the movement of the moose, there is a certain valley which they never enter. And women there are who become sad when the word goes over the fire of how the Evil Spirit came to select that valley for an abiding-place.

In the summers there is one visitor, however, to that valley, of which the Yeehats do not know. It is a great, gloriously coated wolf, like, and yet unlike, all other wolves. He crosses alone from the smiling timber land and comes down into an open space among the trees. Here a yellow stream flows from rotted moosehide sacks and sinks into the ground, with long grasses growing through it and vegetable mould overrunning it and hiding its yellow from the sun; and here he muses for a time, howling once, long and mournfully, ere he departs.

But he is not always alone. When the long winter nights come on and the wolves follow their meat into the lower valleys, he may be seen running at the head of the pack through the pale moonlight or glimmering borealis, leaping gigantic above his fellows, his great throat a-bellow as he sings a song of the younger world, which is the song of the pack.

THE JUKEBOX AND THE KALLIKAKS

THEIR real name was Callinan, not Kallikak; but on Misery Road, titles are apt to wander, and Misery Road itself had once been Missouri Road.

The Callinan name had survived five years of the Road, four babies, and innumerable clashes between Pa and the Town Board of Larkspur. But when the fifth baby had no more discretion than to turn out to be twins, the chairman of the Board rose in his wrath and, with unintentional permanence, rechristened the entire family.

The crux of the matter was that twins were going to mean a double ration of milk. Double rations of milk came out of the Welfare Fund, and the Welfare Fund came out of the pockets of the taxpayers, while Misery Road infants caroused like baby bacchanals.

Sorely tried on this occasion, the chairman of the Board pounded both fists on the table and gave tongue. "Callinans!" he roared. "Kallikaks is what they are. Next thing you know, we'll have the Jukes on relief here, too!"

As he had majored in sociology in college and had studied the two notorious families, he felt the witticism was both apt and distinguished, and his temper improved noticeably. Most of Larkspur, however, had never heard of either Jukes or Kallikaks, so it was the name that lingered in their minds rather than the chairman's educational background, and in a short time it was more or less accepted that the Kallikaks lived on Misery Road. The point was negligible, since neither Pa nor Ma could read or write, and in any case they were involved in their own name calling, the twins being boys and the Kallikaks having got used to girls, as evidenced by Amanda, Sarah, Dolly, and Hester.

The new babies lay in a packing box, bursting with health and that excellent Larkspur milk which must have tasted so deliciously of taxpayers, and they beamed at their parents.

"We've gotta call 'em something," Ma pointed out reasonably, leaning over the infant nest, her hair coming down, Hester sociably in her arms, and Amanda clutching a fistful of skirt.

"Mark," said Pa, inspired to sudden firmness. "And this un's Jeb."

His wife looked at him with open admiration. "Mark 'n' Jeb," she repeated approvingly. "Mark's eyes is slantier and Jeb's nose points higher, and that'll do to tell 'em apart."

In the eighteen years following the twins' arrival, these were the only factors that remained unchanged. Mark's eyes continued to slant and Jeb's nose to tilt, while the twins themselves grew strong and tall, dark-haired and dark-eyed, with their mother's unplanned charm, their father's aimlessness, and a sturdy love for each other, like twin birches.

Time, not content with turning sprouts into saplings, had further outraged the Town Board by producing more Kallikaks, in the endearing shapes of Ella-Lou, Jeremiah, Caroline, and the baby, Tad, who had been something of a surprise. However, the ranks had been reduced by Amanda's marriage and by the departure of Sarah to the city, where she worked off her ambitions in a department store and sometimes cried at night for Misery Road.

Baby Tad slept in the packing box that had cuddled his kinfolk, and the only change in the house was caused by the acquisition of a massive gasoline lamp, promoted by one of Pa's more intricate trades and presented to his wife on the occasion of their tenth anniversary. The lamp was regarded as dangerous, and it was never used, but it had pink roses and blue forget-me-nots on its bulging milk-white curves, and it received a great deal of respect. Mark and Jeb particularly yearned over it, as it had come into their lives when they were five years old, that age of delicate impressions, and their father had spun them a dream tale of a golden-haired, flower-eyed princess who apparently always traveled around in a perfect welter of roses and forget-me-nots.

The twins lived in a home that was full of drafts and affection, and they shared with their family a passion for all lovely sounds, whether originating from a red-winged blackbird or Pa's guitar. The latter they were occasionally allowed to play, but not often, since it had been handed down from Pa's own father and had been heard humming to itself nights in a melancholy and romantic way.

Rich in each other's company, they were no more concerned with the world outside than was the whippoorwill that sang witlessly in the swamp.

It is written (and documented) that even a whippoorwill is susceptible and that love can be a sword. Between Jeb and Mark, there fell the shadow of Corinne.

They saw her first on one of those glimmery days in midspring when the sun is as warm and soft as a kitten's paw and the sky is as blue as an angel's eyes. Misery Road and the path along Cover-Me-Up Creek were latticed with hawthorn bloom, the wild crabapple trees were putting out pink and creamy buds, and the grass along the roadside was golden green, sprinkled with dandelions and all drunk with dew.

It was, in fact, a day so outlandishly beautiful that it put both Jeb and Mark in mind of the gasoline lamp and the fairy-tale princess, but Jeb only remarked comfortably that it was real nice out, and Mark said it would be hot come midday. Neither of them spoke of the princess, but they jumped the creek, circled a ring of birch trees, stepped out into a flower-caught meadow, and there she was.

Mark, who had been whistling, swallowed his closing notes and nearly choked on that spasm of the heart which is caused by beauty. Jeb, with no whistling to stop, stopped breathing.

Her hair was as bright as the sun, her eyes were fringed gentians, and her mouth was a redbird's wing. She was wearing a green dress that clung to her in curves that were like the curves of a cloud, and her little feet were in bright-green slippers with heels so magically high that they looked absurd in the tangle of meadowsweet and cuckoo-flowers.

A little sighing wind ran over the tall grass and counted all the clover tops. It blew a lock of hair across the vision's face, and when she put up her hand to push it back, two bright bracelets, as real gold as dandelions, jangled music on her wrist.

Jeb and Mark stared, and she gave them an encouraging smile. "Ain't you two never seen a girl before?" she inquired.

Jeb turned bright pink. "I'm s-sorry," he said, stumbling over three syllables he had known since extreme youth, having been a scrupulous baby. "We didn't expect to find no one here."

She shrugged. "Meadow's free, so far as I know. What's your names?"

"Jeb," said Jeb shyly.

"Mark," said Mark.

"Mine's Corinne." They weren't the kind of young men she was used to, but they were real cute and much more interesting than all this meadow and sky. "Corinne Porter," she added, becoming autobiographical.

Mark said, "We're Kallikaks."

"Come again?"

"Kallikak. It was somethin' else once, but we don't rightly remember what." Mark had always had an easier tongue than Jeb. "Corinne's a real pretty name."

She smiled again, this time just for Mark. Something moved in Jeb's heart, emerald-eyed and unlovable. It took a great deal of beauty from the day, but none from Corinne.

Mark was smiling back. "Where'd you come from, Corinne? I ain't never seen you in these parts before."

"We're just looking around. We ain't settled on staying." It seemed an unnecessary detail to add that her father had left the last town by request, three orthodox jumps ahead of the sheriff. These abrupt changes of climate were occasionally advisable. "We took a house up there aways," she said coolly, jerking her thumb vaguely northward.

The twins nodded. That would be the old house at Cat's Corner, which had been abandoned years ago. It had holes in its roof, where the stars shone through, and squirrels, field mice and people were continually moving their families in and out.

A long silence fell, and Corinne began to suspect that the meadow and

the sky were not much duller than the twins. Still, their masculine admiration was very gratifying, and she gave them her smile again, causing the whole meadow to glitter and spin. "Ma'll raise hell if I don't get home," she remarked, turned in a whirl of skirts and left them.

They watched her go, yearning to be the ground under her little feet but not knowing how to attain this useful ambition. When a twist in the landscape swallowed her up, they sighed, deep-hearted, and set their own feet on the path toward home.

There was a difference in their silence now. It was no longer companionable.

When Jeb awoke at midnight, it was to a feeling of emptiness. This was not caused by an appreciable void in the Kallikak house, since Pa and Ma were in the bed, Tad was nesting in the packing box, Dolly, Hester, Ella-Lou and Caroline were clustered like dahlia petals in the lean-to, and Jeremiah and a visiting dog named Sam were lying across Jeb's legs. There was not so much an absence of life as a superfluity of it, but to Jeb there was one sleep-wrapped breathing too few.

He slid out from under Jeremiah and Sam, dragged on Pa's shirt and his own trousers, and took another look at the spot where Mark should have been sleeping. There was only pale moonlight, and a finger of it stole up the wall and pointed out that something else was missing.

Pa's guitar.

Jeb caught his breath, torn between the perfidiousness of the crime and the wish that he had thought of it first, and then he plunged out into the night, heading furiously for Cat's Corner.

Arrived there, he slowed down and listened. Dimly there came to his ears the faintest humming, as of orchestral bees dipping into honey pots. This was Mark's prelude to song, and in better moments, one of Jeb's favorite noises.

This was not one of his better moments. He went around the side of the decayed old house, and there was Mark, cradling the guitar. Corinne was nowhere in sight.

"That's Pa's guitar," said Jeb accusingly, ignoring the real issue and taking the unethical path of moral rectitude, which would indicate that love is not as ennobling as some people think.

Mark, recovering from the sight of his brother stalking out of the moonlight, said with dignity, "Pa lended it to me."

"He never," said Jeb with conviction.

"He would if I'd asked him."

"He wouldn't," said Jeb.

The fact that Jeb was right gave him an unfair advantage in this exchange of thoughts. Mark gazed at him hostilely for a moment, then suddenly swept his fingers across the strings of the guitar. It was a beautiful chord, but love, noble or not, is stronger than musical appreciation.

Jeb snatched the guitar from him and hurled it into a bed of nettles.

War was thus openly declared. Mark's fist caught Jeb high on the cheek-bone; Jeb drove his elbow into Mark's ribs. Mark gave a grunt and went backwards, and they rolled together on the cold, wet grass, wrestling, biting and kicking.

When a heavy hand landed on them, they were too busy to pay attention, and it was not until they were jerked sharply apart that they stopped fighting long enough to discover a large, red-faced man glowering down on them.

There was nobody else it could be but Corinne's pa. Jeb blushed and Mark paled, nicely balancing between them the classic reactions of affected hearts. Their host gave no indication of sharing any such tender emotions. "Start talking," he invited grimly. "What you doing prowling around in the middle of the night, interfering with decent folks' sleep?"

Jeb and Mark got to their feet with as much dignity as they could manage. Mark walked over to the nettle patch and retrieved the guitar. "We're real sorry we woke you up, Mr. Porter," he said. This was a hard man to warm to, but he was Corinne's father and entitled to courtesy. "I just came to play this here for your daughter, and maybe sing a little."

It had the ring of truth in it. Porter was aware that Corinne had a very persuasive influence on young men, although he never remembered such a downy pair as this. He gave a short bark of laughter. "You sure come calling on the wrong girl!"

"Ain't Corinne your daughter?"

"She's mine, all right. But she ain't the moonlight-and-guitar type of a dame. Corinne's strictly a jukebox girl."

"A what?"

"A jukebox girl. Cripes, you know what a jukebox is!"

They shook their heads, and he stared at them, finding a certain morbid fascination in such ignorance. "It's like a big red icebox," he said finally. "You put in a nickel, and the music comes out. Folks dance to it, and Corinne's real crazy about dancing. There was a jukebox near where we stayed in Tipton, and she mighty near got engaged to a guy who took her dancing there."

"Tipton," said Jeb, sorting out the one relevant fact. Tipton was a long way off, but if it had a jukebox, he would go and see this thing his princess loved. He shot a quick look at Mark, and his heart sank. Clear as daylight, Mark was thinking the same thing.

Porter suddenly remembered his interrupted sleep. "You two come lally-gagging around here again," he said briskly, "I'll knock your ears off." He turned back toward the house, added "Beat it!" over his shoulder, and would have slammed the door behind him except that there had been no doors at Cat's Corner in ten years.

The twins stood still for a moment where he had left them. Then Jeb drew in his breath, forgetting their feud. "Mark," he said anxiously, "you really believe they's such a thing as red iceboxes with music in 'em?"

For a moment, the old family love nearly rose up and smothered the new love for Corinne. Then the thought of her, hair all glittery and mouth like wild strawberries, hardened Mark's heart. "You keep on y'r side of the fence, Jeb Kallikak," he said, "and I'll keep on mine."

The next morning, Jeb and Mark, having hastily absorbed breakfasts of mush and drippings, departed in opposite directions.

Their elaborate precautions, taken to conceal the fact that each was hitch-hiking to Tipton, were completely nullified by the discovery that there was only one jukebox in that unprogressive town. This was lodged in the shadowy confines of a small bar and grill (E. Affelt, Proprietor), and Mark was already there when Jeb arrived, panting.

Mark eyed his brother coldly and without any sign of recognition. E. Affelt, troubled by a strong sense of ditto marks, looked at them anxiously and rubbed the back of his head in a gesture so habitual it had given him a bald spot. "You brothers?" he said finally, having worked it out.

They scowled at him, and Mark said, "I ain't here to discuss who's kin to who. You got a jukebox?"

Their host admitted he had and inquired brightly, "You want to see it?" He was not feeling bright, but he had to start somewhere. The twins nodded, and he led them to the back of his establishment. There, among the tables and chairs, pushed against a wall and flanked by a potted palm that was unwell, stood the jukebox.

They gazed at it in silent awe. Not only was it red, as Mr. Porter had promised, but it was gold and green, too, and there were lights shining out richly through a glass porthole, and scrawly gilt letters danced across its front. It was as big as an emperor's throne and more gorgeous than a sunset.

"Want to hear it play?" said Mr. Affelt. They nodded respectfully and he held out his hand, palm up. "Takes a nickel, you know."

They did know, because Corinne's father had told them. Jeb's ears turned pink. Mark dug deep into his pockets in the absolutely unfounded hope that some furtive hen might have laid a nest egg there.

"Broke," said Mr. Affelt, who was good at symptoms. "Well, I'll loan you a nickel, and you can wash some glasses to make it up to me." He dipped into his pocket, produced the needed sum, and fed it delicately to the jukebox. A deep sigh swelled up from its interior.

"Does that," said Mr. Affelt. "It's getting pretty old."

The sigh gave way to a rumbling, the rumbling to a hiccup. And then— loud and clear and fierce and fine and free—a burst of music swept the room in a vast wave of sound. The dead palm fronds stirred under the breeze, and the beer glasses jostled one another.

"Cheerful, ain't it?" said Mr. Affelt.

This was like saying that the streets of heaven were nice and bright.

Jeb and Mark, their mouths ajar with wonder, listened raptly from the first blast of inhaling woodwinds down to the last glutted sob of the trombone. The jukebox coughed, the final ineffable rag of sound wavered away. There was silence.

Jeb and Mark sighed together. First the gasoline lamp. Then Corinne. And now this.

Jeb gave Mr. Affelt a velvety look and said, "That was beautiful." This surprised Mr. Affelt, who had said hard words in his day about the jukebox. "Make it do it again," said Jeb.

"That's two nickels you owe me," the proprietor warned, touched by their wonder, but not that touched. He pushed another coin into the slot. The music surged up again, and a cowboy tenor lamented hoarsely under a Texas moon, came to a bad end and sang posthumous regrets with admirable vitality.

When it finished, the twins turned to their host in double trustfulness. Mr. Affelt shook a bewildered head, found three more nickels in his pocket, and lined them up on a table. "That's two bits' worth of washing up you owe me," he said sternly, "and when you finish those three nickels, that's all you get. I got ears same as anybody else, and that thing squawks at me all night. Can't stand it in the daytime, too."

He paddled off to the bar, muttering. Three songs later, dazzled and drunk with sound, his guests found him there and accepted their dish towels meekly, putting such a high, dreamy gloss on each glass that Mr. Affelt cordially invited them to come again.

Jeb shook his head. "We live out Larkspur way."

Mr. Affelt leaned over the bar and stared at him incredulously. "Mean to say you come all that distance just to hear an old broken-down jukebox?"

"It's what Corinne likes," Jeb said simply. "I had to know what my girl likes."

"*My* girl," Mark warned. There was a moment's silence, then he added casually, "'Course, I don't know why I can't learn to play and sing them dance tunes just as good as a jukebox. If that's what Corinne likes," he said virtuously, "that's what she ought to have."

"I c'n sing, too," said Jeb desperately.

"Ho!" said Mark. "Like a foghorn you c'n sing. Like a old bullfrog on a lily pad. Who'd listen to you?"

"I'll tell Pa if you take his guitar."

"No you won't," said Mark with simple faith. "You won't never tell."

There was no answer to that. Jeb spun on his heel and headed for the door. When he finally got back to Larkspur, via two trucks and a tired delivery cart, he found that Mark had arrived ahead of him, first even in the matter of transportation, and was already telling Caroline, Jeremiah and Tad of the wonder he had seen.

Naturally, they understood perfectly well that it was a fairy tale, but they warmly appreciated his inventing such a splendid thing.

Next evening Pa was sitting up with a sick deck of cards, and when Mark took the guitar down off the wall, Ma merely said, "Lovey, that's Pa's," in mild reproof. She then went back to helping Baby Tad wash the dog Sam with an old bar of laundry soap. Baby Tad must have been a throwback of some sort; no other member of the family had ever felt this warm attachment to soap.

"I know, Ma," said Mark politely, and soft-stepped out the door, hoping to get to Cat's Corner before Jeb did. Actually, he caught him up at Endwise Hollow, and they concluded their pilgrimage together with their silence a wall between them.

Corinne was sitting on the front stoop, her chin in her hands and a scowl drawing her eyebrows together.

"Corinne," said Mark, just breathing her name.

She turned, straightened her back and rearranged her legs. They were good-looking young men, all right; she wondered if they had the price of a beer between them, decided they didn't, and sighed.

Jeb felt the answering twist in his heart like a knife. "What's the trouble, Corinne?"

She frowned at her little green slippers, their sharp heels digging into the grass. "I'm good and sick of this place," said Corinne crossly. "Sometimes I get so bored I could scream."

Mark pulled the guitar up close to his heart and drew a deep breath. The tunes he'd heard on the jukebox had been caged in his head since yesterday, and he knew he could coax them out of the strings. "I'll sing for you, Corinne," he said.

Jeb swallowed hard. It wasn't true that he was an old bullfrog on a lily pad. Maybe he couldn't keep a tune, but he was very sincere.

Corinne said, "Who wants to sit and listen to songs?"

"It's a special one," Mark said wistfully. "I learned it off a jukebox."

She gave him her sudden interest. "What do you know about jukeboxes?"

"They're just like heaven," said Mark promptly, in the tones of a man who had studied jukeboxes since childhood.

Corinne gazed at him speculatively. She wouldn't have picked Mark for the jukebox type, but it was a very deceiving world. Anyway, there must be something jingling in his pockets, because jukeboxes needed nickels. "You like to dance, Mark?" she asked, melting appreciably. "You go for bright lights and lots of noise?"

"I like anything you like, Corinne."

Jeb, listening, clenched his fists. It wasn't fair. He had seen the jukebox too and loved it with all his heart. It wasn't fair for Mark to woo her with what Jeb had seen. "Corinne," he said.

She turned to him.

"I'll take you dancin', Corinne," he said eagerly. "I'll take you to places where they's a hundred jukeboxes. You'll be wearin' gold slippers and you'll dance on red velvet." Not for a moment did he doubt his ability to give her this or anything else. "You be my girl, Corinne, and you c'n have whatever in the world you ask for."

Mark said, "Where'll you get the money, Jeb Kallikak?"

Precisely this thought had passed through Corinne's mind. In her experience, which was extensive, she had found that the bigger they talked, the less they had. It began to look as if Mark was more her type. She turned toward him and away from Jeb.

Mark reached out his hand to her.

His intention had been to help her up from the stoop, a most innocent and reverent gesture. Jeb, however, in a fevered and quite inaccurate flash of intuition, instantly visioned his brother pulling Corinne into his arms. His imagination then catapulted him toward their inevitable kiss. It was not to be borne.

For the second time in eighteen years, Jeb struck his brother.

Mark hit back. Corinne screamed.

There was an explosion from the house like a Roman candle, and Corinne's father burst out the door, madder than a scalded cat and spitting oaths. "Them two back again!" howled Mr. Porter apoplectically. "Hell on wheels, Corinne, I thought you'd at least been bit by a sheriff!"

He yanked the twins apart. "Git!" he said. "Git the blazes out of here!"

"Pa!" said Corinne, suddenly realizing that the shortage of young men was about to become even more acute.

"Shut your mouth!" said Porter furiously.

"I won't shut my mouth!" said Corinne. She could be twice as furious, and besides, she was a female. "It's your own fault we're stuck out here halfway to nowhere. Don't you start knocking my boy friends around!"

"I'm sick of finding 'em fighting all over the yard," Porter said bitterly.

"Some yard!" said his daughter. "Anyway, it only happens because there's two of them and they get mad at each other."

"Well, then, choose one," Porter growled. "Choose one, and tell the other to git out."

Corinne bit her lip and looked at the twins. They were pleasing to look at, and she would have much preferred to keep them both, but she knew her father could be pushed just so far.

Mark stepped forward. "You're my girl, Corinne," he said. "Don't you forget it."

Jeb said, "You're mine."

There was a distant rumble as of thunder. That was Corinne's father warming up again. Corinne offered up a brisk prayer for inspiration. It came, and a pussy-cat smile curved the corners of her mouth. "I know what to do," she announced with satisfaction.

The thunder receded. "About time," said Porter.

Corinne turned to Jeb and Mark, who had given up breathing. She eyed them quite affectionately. At least, if she was going to be denied fifty percent of her suitors, she was not going to be denied adequate compensation. "Whichever one of you gives me the nicest present," said Corinne in a voice like clear water, "that's whose girl I'll be."

They stared at her. Porter gave a short laugh. "Bet they can't scratch up a plugged nickel between the two of 'em!"

The pussy-cat smile stayed in place. "Don't be silly, Pa," said Corinne purely. "They can earn it, can't they? I'll give them a whole week." She jangled the bracelets on her arm. "In a week, I should think, a man could earn enough for a pretty nice present."

Her father looked at her with real respect. She touched his arm. "Come on, Pa. You leave 'em alone now." She turned back to the twins for a moment, spinning on her spike heels. "Remember, you've got a whole week," she said, and left them.

Jeb sighed heavily.

Mark dug his fists into pockets that always seemed to be empty and scowled. "You keep out of my way is all."

Jeb nodded, feeling the cold breeze of solitude. Always before, they'd made their plans together. He and Mark were walking different roads now, for sure, and it was like having a year when the Lord had left out the summer.

It was quite impossible to conceal Corinne's ultimatum from the Kallikak family. Jeremiah and Caroline tracked Mark to old Mrs. Peters' garden the next day, confirmed with their own eyes a rumor that their brother was weeding the pansy bed and rushed home to report the revolutionary tidings.

Pa Kallikak was sincerely shocked. He didn't like to hear such things about a son of his, and he wandered uneasily over to Mrs. Peters' house and leaned over the fence. "Earnin' money, son?" he inquired. "What you plannin' to buy?"

Mark didn't want to call Pa nosy, but he sure was persistent, and if he didn't get an answer now, he'd put Ma on the problem. "I'm buyin' a gift for Corinne," Mark said reluctantly.

Pa nodded. "We figured you was sweet on that girl. What's happened to Jeb?"

"I ain't seen him."

Pa said sadly, "You two boys ain't livin' in the same pod together no more."

"I guess not," said Mark. After a moment, Pa's question caught up with him, and he said sharply, "Ain't you seen him neither? Ain't he workin' somewheres?"

"Carrie and Jeremiah says no."

That settled it. You couldn't hide a beetle in a hedgehog nest without Carrie and Jeremiah knowing. Mark frowned and jerked at a weed.

Pa looked at him with honest concern. "You'll burn yourself out in the prime of y'r youth," said Pa warningly and ambled off, shaking his head.

Mark sat back on his heels. After Mrs. Peters' garden, there was the doctor's driveway and then Miss Hill's rock garden. But when he got through, Mark was heading for the Elite Jewelry Store, and there he would put his money down on a ring with a stone in it that had lights like the stars over Larkspur in wintertime. By the end of the week, he'd have earned enough money to own it, and then he could march up to Corinne and put it on her finger, and she'd never think of Jeb again.

Mark pulled up a pansy by mistake and had to stuff it back into the damp ground extremely fast. It was fretting about Jeb that got him doing things like that, he thought crossly. Because if Jeb wasn't out earning money in Larkspur, what was he up to?

Jeb got home that night an hour after sundown, and he looked as cheerful as a bee in clover.

Mark was in a mixed mood. He had made his down payment on the ring but on the other hand, Miss Hill's idea of planting a rock garden was to try each rock in twenty different places, and she wanted him back tomorrow. He regarded his twin's briskness without enthusiasm. "Where you been all day?"

"Out," said Jeb.

"Out where?"

"Just out."

It was a most unsatisfactory conversation and carried no useful clues whatever. "You ain't been workin'," Mark accused. "I been workin' like a horse."

"Who says I ain't been workin'?" said Jeb mildly.

"No one in Larkspur's seen you all day, and Carrie and Jeremiah hunted all over."

"Larkspur ain't the whole world," Jeb remarked.

He seemed maddeningly pleased with himself, and Mark gave him a hard look. "I s'pose you went out in the woods and shot a squirrel," he said caustically. "Goin' to give it to Corinne so's she can make herself a fur coat, I guess."

A faraway look came into Jeb's eyes. "What I got f'r Corinne," he said softly, "is gonna be so beautiful—" He broke off, looked at his twin with forgiving pity and walked on into the house.

Mark kicked a puffball, exploding it, started to kick a juniper bush and just missed Carrie, who was crouched down behind it. He dragged her out and held her up at arm's length, but her pigtails stuck out so charmingly and she looked so docile that he put her down. "Allus creepin' around behind things," he grunted, his mind already on other matters.

"I was very int'rested," said Carrie with dignity. "Mark, when you and Jeb give Corinne her presents, kin I come 'n' watch? I and Jeremiah?"

He remembered the jewelry-store ring with all the fires leaping in it, and a great wave of cheerfulness swept over him. "Whole world c'n come and watch for all I care," Mark said generously. "The whole world and all his kinfolk."

It was not perhaps the whole world that turned out for Corinne's gift day, but it was certainly all the Kallikaks.

They arrived in battalions, Carrie and Jeremiah first, since they were always first at important occasions and their family recognized and respected their rights. Once this priority was established, Dolly, Hester, Ella-Lou, Tad and the dog Sam put in their appearance and ranged themselves neatly in the Cat's Corner yard.

Corinne, who had been waiting with considerable impatience to see how her investment was going to work out, regarded her uninvited guests with very negative enthusiasm. They stared back, steadfast and admiring, weakhearted wherever beauty was concerned.

The arrival of Pa and Ma Kallikak rounded out the audience. Pa identified Corinne by the simple process of deducting her from his own family, and he gave her a very courtly bow of sincere welcome. Ma said, "Where's your folks, lovey?" smiling because Corinne was so pretty.

Corinne shrugged.

"You mean they ain't comin'?" Ma shook her head in real distress, feeling that only a matter of grave urgency could have kept the Porters away. Kallikaks assembled by instinct. When Baby Tad fell down the woodchuck hole that time, there were eight rescuers to pull him out and comfort his wails, not counting the woodchuck who had taken a slightly different attitude.

Pa gave his wife a gentle punch with his elbow. "Here's Mark," he said proudly. He had every reason to be proud. Mark was as brushed and neat as a member of the Town Board, and he was carrying a package that was very small but beautifully wrapped in tissue paper and shiny ribbon.

The package seemed to be about a good size for a jeweler's box. Corinne touched her lips hopefully with the tip of her pink tongue.

Pa said, "Where's Jeb, boy? Ain't seen him all day."

"Ain't he here?" Mark looked uneasy. "We'd better wait."

"I'll open your package first," said Corinne, holding out her hand.

Mark shook his head. There wasn't any satisfaction unless she opened it when Jeb was there. "I don't want—" he began, and broke off.

Jeb was coming, running down the road. He was empty-handed.

"Where you been?" said Mark.

"Where's my present?" said Corinne.

"Down the road." Jeb looked as pleased with himself as a rooster that's just crowed the sun out of bed. "I'll bring it up, Corinne, soon's you've opened Mark's." He nodded toward the package in his twin's hand.

It wasn't like Jeb to be so almighty sure of himself. Mark clutched the ring a little more tightly. "Let's see yours first."

"Can't," said Jeb sunnily. "It ain't wrapped, so it ain't fair for me to show mine first."

"What's that got to do with it?"

Corinne gave a small sputter of impatience. They were capable of standing there arguing until the stars came out. There was a flutter of skirt, a quick grab like a pigeon going after a kernel of corn, and Mark's package changed hands. "It's mine," said Corinne, forestalling any further argument. "I can open it when I want to."

Mark scowled, and she took a second out from opening the gift to give him a smile that turned his heart to butter. He decided it didn't matter which she opened first; his would be the best, anyway. Only he wished she wouldn't rip off the paper. The man at the shop had done the wrapping with great tenderness, and it ought to be unfolded slowly, like a bud that was fixing to be a blossom.

The little blue velvet box surrendered itself to Corinne's hands, and she snatched off the lid. The ring winked up at the sky like a dewdrop, like a star, like a tiny baby icicle with the sun shining through it. A little tinkle of wonder ran up and down the line of Kallikaks.

Corinne caught her breath. "Gee, Mark, it's really something," she said and slipped it on, stretching her hand out to admire it, the way women have done ever since Eve first put her finger through a sunbeam.

Mark looked pleased and modest, cast a quick, triumphant look at Jeb and got the shock of a lifetime. Jeb's face completely failed in its duty to register defeat. "It's real pretty, Mark," Jeb said kindly. "Too bad it just ain't pretty enough."

Corinne looked up from the glitter on her hand. "What's yours, Jeb?" she demanded. "Hurry up and show me." Things were going a lot better than she had expected; maybe she would get a necklace, too.

"I'll show you," Jeb assured her. "Just stay where you are." He turned and left them, walking with his shoulders swinging.

Mark watched him go, wild with curiosity to know what had made his twin so cocksure.

He had only a minute to wait.

Jeb came back up the road, leading a battered old horse with a straw hat falling over its brow and long ears waving through. Behind the horse, a tipsy-looking wagon lurched and grumbled. Mark got one good look at what was in the wagon, and then his mouth fell wide open.

Big and red and shiny and beautiful, a jukebox rode in state to the Porters' door. Like a king, like an emperor.

"Jehoshaphat!" said Pa. A shiver of delight ran over the Kallikak kids, the way wind runs over a wheat field.

Mark felt his heart sink like a bird falling out of the sky. The jukebox was a gift beyond all mortal dreams. He had lost Corinne. He looked at Jeb hopelessly and said, "How'd you get it?"

"It's Mr. Affelt's," Jeb told him proudly. "He's buyin' a new one, and he said I c'd have this if I'd work it out at his place. All I gotta do is hitchhike to Tipton every day, and by the end of the summer everything's evened up." No shadow crossed his face at the thought of a lost season of blossom. He looked adoringly at Corinne. "It's worth it," he said.

They all turned to gaze respectfully at the recipient of this magnificent, this priceless gift. Mark's heart ached all the way through.

Corinne stood staring back at them. Her face was a vivid shade of pink, and she seemed to be struggling for words. Speechlessness was something the Kallikaks could appreciate under the circumstances.

And then she exploded.

"You silly fool, Jeb Kallikak!" She threw the words at him, almost screaming. "What's the use of a jukebox in a place where they ain't even any electricity to play it with!"

It took her two steps to get to Mark. She put her arms up around his neck, and the ring on her hand shone like a diamond. "I love my ring, Mark honey," Corinne said.

The landscape froze for a long moment in time. There was Mark, the girl he had won wrapped around his neck. There was a row of Kallikaks, holding their breaths.

Very slowly, Mark undid Corinne's fingers. He said, "You c'n keep the ring, Corinne."

She looked up at him, puzzled. "Of course I can keep the ring, Mark. I'm your girl now, like I promised."

"You ain't no girl of mine," said Mark Kallikak hoarsely.

"What do you mean?" she asked in amazement.

Mark told her in terms that were exact and scornful. "No woman who ain't got the sense to know that a jukebox is the most beautiful present in the world," said Mark, "is goin' to spend her days hangin' around my neck."

"But, Mark! It's not my fault Jeb's such a dumb ox he forgot about not having electricity around here. It's not my fault—"

"I didn't forget," said Jeb miserably. "I just figgered it didn't matter."

"It don't matter," said Mark.

Corinne blazed out resentfully. "What good's a jukebox you can't play?"

All the Kallikaks turned grave eyes on her, pondering the incomprehensible question. The gasoline lamp with the roses and forget-me-nots had never been lighted. You didn't have to wash in Cover-Me-Up Creek to appreciate its wonderful wetness. You didn't have to eat the apples off a tree just because you had stared at its baby blossoms against a blue sky.

The Kallikak court stood in judgment. Corinne was beautiful and the jukebox was beautiful and they were, both of them, dumb. But deep down in the heart of the jukebox, there was music. And deep down in the heart of Corinne, there was just Corinne.

"C'mon, Jebby," said Mark.

"Where to?" said Jeb heavily. And then, all at once, he felt a whole lot warmer. It was a long time since Mark had called him Jebby.

"Home," Mark told him. "We're goin' to move that jukebox in alongside the lamp, and you 'n' me is goin' to Tipton and work for Mr. Affelt together. That way, it'll only take half the summer. And anyway," he said, "some things is worth workin' for."

Pa Kallikak, trailing his sons home in the gathering twilight, considered this statement with some anxiety. It might be true, but he just hoped he would never get himself in a position where he would have to find out.

THE STRANGE RIDE OF
MORROWBIE JUKES

RUDYARD KIPLING

Alive or dead—there is no other way.
—NATIVE PROVERB

THERE is no invention about this tale. Jukes by accident stumbled upon a village that is well known to exist, though he is the only Englishman who has been there. A somewhat similar institution used to flourish on the outskirts of Calcutta, and there is a story that if you go into the heart of Bikanir, which is in the heart of the Great Indian Desert, you shall come across not a village but a town where the Dead who did not die but may not live have established their headquarters. And, since it is perfectly true that in the same Desert is a wonderful city where all the rich money-lenders retreat after they have made their fortunes (fortunes so vast that the owners cannot trust even the strong hand of the Government to protect them, but take refuge in the waterless sands), and drive sumptuous C-spring barouches, and buy beautiful girls and decorate their palaces with gold and ivory and Minton tiles and mother-o'-pearl, I do not see why Jukes's tale should not be true. He is a Civil Engineer, with a head for plans and distances and things of that kind, and he certainly would not take the trouble to invent imaginary traps. He could earn more by doing his legitimate work. He never varies the tale in the telling, and grows very hot and indignant when he thinks of the disrespectful treatment he received. He wrote this quite straightforwardly at first, but he has touched it up in places and introduced Moral Reflections: thus:—

In the beginning it all arose from a slight attack of fever. My work necessitated my being in camp for some months between Pakpattan and Mubarakpur—a desolate sandy stretch of country as every one who has had the misfortune to go there may know. My coolies were neither more nor less exasperating than other gangs, and my work demanded sufficient attention to keep me from moping, had I been inclined to so unmanly a weakness.

On the 23rd December 1884, I felt a little feverish. There was a full moon at the time, and, in consequence, every dog near my tent was baying it. The brutes assembled in twos and threes and drove me frantic. A few days previously I had shot one loud-mouthed singer and suspended his carcass *in terrorem* about fifty yards from my tent-door, but his friends fell upon, fought for, and ultimately devoured the body: and, as it seemed to me, sang their hymns of thanksgiving afterwards with renewed energy.

The light-headedness which accompanies fever acts differently on different men. My irritation gave way, after a short time, to a fixed determination to slaughter one huge black and white beast who had been foremost in song and first in flight throughout the evening. Thanks to a shaking hand and a giddy head I had already missed him twice with both barrels of my shotgun, when it struck me that my best plan would be to ride him down in the open and finish him off with a hog-spear. This, of course, was merely the semi-delirious notion of a fever-patient; but I remember that it struck me at the time as being eminently practical and feasible.

I therefore ordered my groom to saddle Pornic and bring him round quietly to the rear of my tent. When the pony was ready, I stood at his head prepared to mount and dash out as soon as the dog should again lift up his voice. Pornic, by the way, had not been out of his pickets for a couple of days; the night air was crisp and chilly; and I was armed with a specially long and sharp pair of persuaders with which I had been rousing a sluggish cob that afternoon. You will easily believe, then, that when he was let go he went quickly. In one moment, for the brute bolted as straight as a die, the tent was left far behind, and we were flying over the smooth sandy soil at racing speed. In another we had passed the wretched dog, and I had almost forgotten why it was that I had taken horse and hog-spear.

The delirium of fever and the excitement of rapid motion through the air must have taken away the remnant of my senses. I have a faint recollection of standing upright in my stirrups, and of brandishing my hog-spear at the great white Moon that looked down so calmly on my mad gallop; and of shouting challenges to the camelthorn bushes as they whizzed past. Once or twice, I believe, I swayed forward on Pornic's neck, and literally hung on by my spurs—as the marks next morning showed.

The wretched beast went forward like a thing possessed, over what seemed to be a limitless expanse of moonlit sand. Next, I remember, the ground rose suddenly in front of us, and as we topped the ascent I saw the waters of the Sutlej shining like a silver bar below. Then Pornic blundered heavily on his nose, and we rolled together down some unseen slope.

I must have lost consciousness, for when I recovered I was lying on my stomach in a heap of soft white sand, and the dawn was beginning to break dimly over the edge of the slope down which I had fallen. As the light grew stronger I saw I was at the bottom of a horseshoe-shaped crater of sand, opening on one side directly on to the shoals of the Sutlej. My fever had altogether left me, and, with the exception of a slight dizziness in the head, I felt no bad effects from the fall over night.

Pornic, who was standing a few yards away, was naturally a good deal exhausted, but had not hurt himself in the least. His saddle, a favourite polo one, was much knocked about, and had been twisted under his belly. It took me some time to put him to rights, and in the meantime I had ample opportunities of observing the spot into which I had so foolishly dropped.

At the risk of being considered tedious, I must describe it at length; inasmuch as an accurate mental picture of its peculiarities will be of material assistance in enabling the reader to understand what follows.

Imagine then, as I have said before, a horseshoe-shaped crater of sand with steeply-graded sand walls about thirty-five feet high. (The slope, I fancy, must have been about 65°.) This crater enclosed a level piece of ground about fifty yards long by thirty at its broadest part, with a rude well in the centre. Round the bottom of the crater, about three feet from the level of the ground proper, ran a series of eighty-three semicircular, ovoid, square, and multilateral holes, all about three feet at the mouth. Each hole on inspection showed that it was carefully shored internally with drift-wood and bamboos, and over the mouth a wooden drip-board projected, like the peak of a jockey's cap, for two feet. No sign of life was visible in these tunnels, but a most sickening stench pervaded the entire amphitheatre—a stench fouler than any which my wanderings in Indian villages have introduced me to.

Having remounted Pornic, who was as anxious as I to get back to camp, I rode round the base of the horseshoe to find some place whence an exit would be practicable. The inhabitants, whoever they might be, had not thought fit to put in an appearance, so I was left to my own devices. My first attempt to 'rush' Pornic up the steep sand-banks showed me that I had fallen into a trap exactly on the same model as that which the ant-lion sets for its prey. At each step the shifting sand poured down from above in tons, and rattled on the drip-boards of the holes like small shot. A couple of ineffectual charges sent us both rolling down to the bottom, half choked with the torrents of sand; and I was constrained to turn my attention to the river-bank.

Here everything seemed easy enough. The sand hills ran down to the river edge, it is true, but there were plenty of shoals and shallows across which I could gallop Pornic, and find my way back to *terra firma* by turning sharply to the right or the left. As I led Pornic over the sands I was startled by the faint pop of a rifle across the river; and at the same moment a bullet dropped with a sharp '*whit*' close to Pornic's head.

There was no mistaking the nature of the missile—a regulation Martini-Henry 'picket.' About five hundred yards away a country-boat was anchored in midstream; and a jet of smoke drifting away from its bows in the still morning air showed me whence the delicate attention had come. Was ever a respectable gentleman in such an *impasse*? The treacherous sand slope allowed no escape from a spot which I had visited most involuntarily, and a promenade on the river frontage was the signal for a bombardment from some insane native in a boat. I'm afraid that I lost my temper very much indeed.

Another bullet reminded me that I had better save my breath to cool my porridge; and I retreated hastily up the sands and back to the horseshoe, where I saw that the noise of the rifle had drawn sixty-five human beings from the badger-holes which I had up till that point supposed to be untenanted. I found myself in the midst of a crowd of spectators—about forty men, twenty women, and one child who could not have been more than five years old. They were all scantily clothed in that salmon coloured cloth which one associates with Hindu mendicants, and, at first sight, gave me the impression of a band of loathsome *fakirs*. The filth and repulsiveness of the assembly were beyond all description, and I shuddered to think what their life in the badger-holes must be.

Even in these days, when local self-government has destroyed the greater part of a native's respect for a Sahib, I have been accustomed to a certain amount of civility from my inferiors, and on approaching the crowd naturally expected that there would be some recognition of my presence. As a matter of fact there was; but it was by no means what I had looked for.

The ragged crew actually laughed at me—such laughter I hope I may never hear again. They cackled, yelled, whistled, and howled as I walked into their midst; some of them literally throwing themselves down on the ground in convulsions of unholy mirth. In a moment I had let go Pornic's head, and, irritated beyond expression at the morning's adventure, commenced cuffing those nearest to me with all the force I could. The wretches dropped under my blows like nine-pins, and the laughter gave place to wails for mercy; while those yet untouched clasped me round the knees, imploring me in all sorts of uncouth tongues to spare them.

In the tumult, and just when I was feeling very much ashamed of myself for having thus easily given way to my temper, a thin, high voice murmured in English from behind my shoulder: 'Sahib! Sahib! Do you not know me? Sahib, it is Gunga Dass, the telegraph-master.'

I spun round quickly and faced the speaker.

Gunga Dass (I have, of course, no hesitation in mentioning the man's real name) I had known four years before as a Deccanee Brahmin lent by the Punjab Government to one of the Khalsia States. He was in charge of a branch telegraph-office there, and when I had last met him was a jovial, full-stomached, portly Government servant with a marvellous capacity for making bad puns in English—a peculiarity which made me remember him long after I had forgotten his services to me in his official capacity. It is seldom that a Hindu makes English puns.

Now, however, the man was changed beyond all recognition. Caste-mark, stomach, slate-coloured continuations, and unctuous speech were all gone. I looked at a withered skeleton, turbanless and almost naked, with long matted hair and deep-set codfish-eyes. But for a crescent-shaped scar on the left cheek—the result of an accident for which I was responsible— I should never have known him. But it was indubitably Gunga Dass, and— for this I was thankful—an English-speaking native who might at least tell me the meaning of all that I had gone through that day.

The crowd retreated to some distance as I turned towards the miserable figure, and ordered him to show me some method of escaping from the crater. He held a freshly-plucked crow in his hand, and in reply to my question climbed slowly on a platform of sand which ran in front of the holes, and commenced lighting a fire there in silence. Dried bents, sand-poppies, and drift-wood burn quickly; and I derived much consolation from the fact that he lit them with an ordinary sulphur match. When they were in a bright glow, and the crow was neatly spitted in front thereof, Gunga Dass began without a word of preamble:—

'There are only two kinds of men, Sar. The alive and the dead. When you are dead you are dead, but when you are alive you live.' (Here the crow demanded his attention for an instant as it twirled before the fire in danger of being burnt to a cinder.) 'If you die at home and do not die when you come to the ghât to be burnt you come here.'

The nature of the reeking village was made plain now, and all that I had known or read of the grotesque and the horrible paled before the fact just communicated by the ex-Brahmin. Sixteen years ago, when I first landed in Bombay, I had been told by a wandering Armenian of the existence, somewhere in India, of a place to which such Hindus as had the misfortune to recover from trance or catalepsy were conveyed and kept, and I recollect laughing heartily at what I was then pleased to consider a traveller's tale. Sitting at the bottom of the sand-trap, the memory of Watson's Hotel, with its swinging punkahs, white-robed servants and the sallow-faced Armenian, rose up in my mind as vividly as a photograph, and I burst into a loud fit of laughter. The contrast was too absurd!

Gunga Dass, as he bent over the unclean bird, watched me curiously. Hindus seldom laugh, and his surroundings were not such as to move him that way. He removed the crow solemnly from the wooden spit and as solemnly devoured it. Then he continued his story, which I give in his own words:—

'In epidemics of the cholera you are carried to be burnt almost before you are dead. When you come to the riverside the cold air, perhaps, makes you alive, and then, if you are only little alive, mud is put on your nose and mouth and you die conclusively. If you are rather more alive, more mud is put; but if you are too lively they let you go and take you away. I was too lively, and made protestation with anger against the indignities that they endeavoured to press upon me. In those days I was Brahmin and proud man. Now I am dead man and eat'—here he eyed the well-gnawed breast bone with the first sign of emotion that I had seen in him since we met—'crows, and—other things. They took me from my sheets when they saw that I was too lively and gave me medicines for one week, and I survived successfully. Then they sent me by rail from my place to Okara Station, with a man to take care of me; and at Okara Station we met two other men, and they conducted us three on camels, in the night, from Okara Station to this place, and they propelled me from the top to the bottom, and the other two succeeded, and I have been here ever since two and a half years. Once I was Brahmin and proud man, and now I eat crows.'

'There is no way of getting out?'

'None of what kind at all. When I first came I made experiments frequently and all the others also, but we have always succumbed to the sand which is precipitated upon our heads.'

'But surely,' I broke in at this point, 'the river-front is open, and it is worth while dodging the bullets; while at night——'

I had already matured a rough plan of escape which a natural instinct of selfishness forbade me sharing with Gunga Dass. He, however, divined my unspoken thought almost as soon as it was formed; and, to my intense astonishment, gave vent to a long low chuckle of derision—the laughter, be it understood, of a superior or at least of an equal.

'You will not'—he had dropped the Sir after his first sentence—'make any escape that way. But you can try. I have tried. Once only.'

The sensation of nameless terror which I had in vain attempted to strive against, overmastered me completely. My long fast—it was now close upon ten o'clock, and I had eaten nothing since tiffin on the previous day—combined with the violent agitation of the ride had exhausted me, and I verily believe that, for a few minutes, I acted as one mad. I hurled myself against the sand-slope. I ran round the base of the crater, blaspheming and praying by turns. I crawled out among the sedges of the river-front, only to be driven back each time in an agony of nervous dread by the rifle-bullets which cut up the sand round me—for I dared not face the death of a mad dog among that hideous crowd—and so fell, spent and raving, at the curb of the well. No one had taken the slightest notice of an exhibition which makes me blush hotly even when I think of it now.

Two or three men trod on my panting body as they drew water, but they were evidently used to this sort of thing, and had no time to waste upon me. Gunga Dass, indeed, when he had banked the embers of his fire with sand, was at some pains to throw half a cupful of fetid water over my head, an attention for which I could have fallen on my knees and thanked him, but he was laughing all the while in the same mirthless, wheezy key that greeted me on my first attempt to force the shoals. And so, in a half-fainting state, I lay till noon. Then, being only a man after all, I felt hungry, and said as much to Gunga Dass, whom I had begun to regard as my natural protector. Following the impulse of the outer world when dealing with natives, I put my hand into my pocket and drew out four annas. The absurdity of the gift struck me at once, and I was about to replace the money.

Gunga Dass, however, cried: 'Give me the money, all you have, or I will get help, and we will kill you!'

A Briton's first impulse, I believe, is to guard the contents of his pockets; but a moment's thought showed me of the folly of differing with the one man who had it in his power to make me comfortable; and with whose help it was possible that I might eventually escape from the crater. I gave him all the money in my possession, Rs. 9-8-5—nine rupees, eight annas, and five pie—for I always keep small change as *bakshish* when I am in camp. Gunga

Dass clutched the coins, and hid them at once in his ragged loin-cloth, looking round to assure himself that no one had observed us.

'Now I will give you something to eat,' said he.

What pleasure my money could have given him I am unable to say; but inasmuch as it did please him I was not sorry that I had parted with it so readily, for I had no doubt that he would have had me killed if I had refused. One does not protest against the doings of a den of wild beasts; and my companions were lower than any beasts. While I eat what Gunga Dass had provided, a coarse *chapatti* and a cupful of the foul well-water, the people showed not the faintest sign of curiosity—that curiosity which is so rampant, as a rule, in an Indian village.

I could even fancy that they despised me. At all events they treated me with the most chilling indifference, and Gunga Dass was nearly as bad. I plied him with questions about the terrible village, and received extremely unsatisfactory answers. So far as I could gather, it had been in existence from time immemorial—whence I concluded that it was at least a century old—and during that time no one had ever been known to escape from it. [I had to control myself here with both hands, lest the blind terror should lay hold of me a second time and drive me raving round the crater.] Gunga Dass took a malicious pleasure in emphasising this point and in watching me wince. Nothing that I could do would induce him to tell me who the mysterious 'They' were.

'It is so ordered,' he would reply, 'and I do not yet know any one who has disobeyed the orders.'

'Only wait till my servant finds that I am missing,' I retorted, 'and I promise you that this place shall be cleared off the face of the earth, and I'll give you a lesson in civility, too, my friend.'

'Your servants would be torn in pieces before they came near this place; and, besides, you are dead, my dear friend. It is not your fault, of course, but none the less you are dead *and* buried.'

At irregular intervals supplies of food, I was told, were dropped down from the land side into the amphitheatre, and the inhabitants fought for them like wild beasts. When a man felt his death coming on he retreated to his lair and died there. The body was sometimes dragged out of the hole and thrown on to the sand, or allowed to rot where it lay.

The phrase 'thrown on to the sand' caught my attention, and I asked Gunga Dass whether this sort of thing was not likely to breed a pestilence.

'That,' said he, with another of his wheezy chuckles, 'you may see for yourself subsequently. You will have much time to make observations.'

Whereat, to his great delight, I winced once more and hastily continued the conversation: 'And how do you live here from day to day? What do you do?' The question elicited exactly the same answer as before—coupled with the information that 'this place is like your European heaven; there is neither marrying nor giving in marriage.'

Gunga Dass had been educated at a Mission School, and, as he himself admitted, had he only changed his religion 'like a wise man,' might have avoided the living grave which was now his portion. But as long as I was with him I fancy he was happy.

Here was a Sahib, a representative of the dominant race, helpless as a child and completely at the mercy of his native neighbours. In a deliberate lazy way he set himself to torture me as a schoolboy would devote a rapturous half-hour to watching the agonies of an impaled beetle, or as a ferret in a blind burrow might glue himself comfortably to the neck of a rabbit. The burden of his conversation was that there was no escape 'of no kind whatever,' and that I should stay here till I died and was 'thrown on to the sand.' If it were possible to forejudge the conversation of the Damned on the advent of a new soul in their abode, I should say that they would speak as Gunga Dass did to me throughout that long afternoon. I was powerless to protest or answer; all my energies being devoted to a struggle against the inexplicable terror that threatened to overwhelm me again and again. I can compare the feeling to nothing except the struggle of a man against the overpowering nausea of the Channel passage—only my agony was of the spirit and infinitely more terrible.

As the day wore on, the inhabitants began to appear in full strength to catch the rays of the afternoon sun, which were now sloping in at the mouth of the crater. They assembled by little knots, and talked among themselves without even throwing a glance in my direction. About four o'clock, so far as I could judge, Gunga Dass rose and dived into his lair for a moment, emerging with a live crow in his hands. The wretched bird was in a most draggled and deplorable condition, but seemed to be in no way afraid of its master. Advancing cautiously to the river-front, Gunga Dass stepped from tussock to tussock until he had reached a smooth patch of sand directly in the line of the boat's fire. The occupants of the boat took no notice. Here he stopped, and, with a couple of dexterous turns of the wrist, pegged the bird on its back with outstretched wings. As was only natural, the crow began to shriek at once and beat the air with its claws. In a few seconds the clamour had attracted the attention of a bevy of wild crows on a shoal a few hundred yards away, where they were discussing something that looked like a corpse. Half a dozen crows flew over at once to see what was going on, and also, as it proved, to attack the pinioned bird. Gunga Dass, who had lain down on a tussock, motioned to me to be quiet, though I fancy this was a needless precaution. In a moment, and before I could see how it happened, a wild crow, who had grappled with the shrieking and helpless bird, was entangled in the latter's claws, swiftly disengaged by Gunga Dass, and pegged down beside its companion in adversity. Curiosity, it seemed, overpowered the rest of the flock, and almost before Gunga Dass and I had time to withdraw to the tussock, two more captives were struggling in the upturned claws of the decoys. So the chase—if I can give it so dignified a name—continued until Gunga Dass had captured seven crows. Five of them he throttled at once, reserving two for further operations another day. I was a good deal impressed by this, to me, novel method of securing food, and complimented Gunga Dass on his skill.

'It is nothing to do,' said he. 'To-morrow you must do it for me. You are stronger than I am.'

This calm assumption of superiority upset me not a little, and I answered peremptorily: 'Indeed, you old ruffian? What do you think I have given you money for?'

'Very well,' was the unmoved reply. 'Perhaps not to-morrow, nor the day after, nor subsequently; but in the end, and for many years, you will catch crows and eat crows, and you will thank your European God that you have crows to catch and eat.'

I could have cheerfully strangled him for this; but judged it best under the circumstances to smother my resentment. An hour later I was eating one of the crows; and, as Gunga Dass had said, thanking my God that I had a crow to eat. Never as long as I live shall I forget that evening meal. The whole population were squatting on the hard sand platform opposite their dens, huddled over tiny fires of refuse and dried rushes. Death, having once laid his hand upon these men and forborne to strike, seemed to stand aloof from them now; for most of our company were old men, bent and worn and twisted with years, and women aged to all appearance as the Fates themselves. They sat together in knots and talked—God only knows what they found to discuss—in low equable tones, curiously in contrast to the strident babble with which natives are accustomed to make day hideous. Now and then an access of that sudden fury which had possessed me in the morning would lay hold on a man or woman; and with yells and imprecations the sufferer would attack the steep slope until, baffled and bleeding, he fell back on the platform incapable of moving a limb. The others would never even raise their eyes when this happened, as men too well aware of the futility of their fellows' attempts and wearied with their useless repetition. I saw four such outbursts in the course of that evening.

Gunga Dass took an eminently business-like view of my situation, and while we were dining—I can afford to laugh at the recollection now, but it was painful enough at the time—propounded the terms of which he would consent to 'do' for me. My nine rupees eight annas, he argued, at the rate of three annas a day, would provide me with food for fifty-one days, or about seven weeks; that is to say, he would be willing to cater for me for that length of time. At the end of it I was to look after myself. For a further considera- tion—videlicet my boots—he would be willing to allow me to occupy the den next to his own, and would supply me with as much dried grass for bedding as he could spare.

'Very well, Gunga Dass,' I replied; 'to the first terms I cheerfully agree, but, as there is nothing on earth to prevent my killing you as you sit here and taking everything that you have' (I thought of the two invaluable crows at the time), 'I flatly refuse to give you my boots and shall take whichever den I please.'

The stroke was a bold one, and I was glad when I saw that it had suc- ceeded. Gunga Dass changed his tone immediately, and disavowed all inten- tion of asking for my boots. At the time it did not strike me as at all strange that I, a Civil Engineer, a man of thirteen years' standing in the Service, and, I trust, an average Englishman, should thus calmly threaten murder and violence against the man who had, for a consideration it is true, taken me under his wing. I had left the world, it seemed, for centuries. I was as certain then as I am now of my own existence, that in the accursed settlement there was no law save that of the strongest; that the living dead men had thrown behind them every canon of the world which had cast them out; and that I had to depend for my own life on my strength and vigilance alone. The crew of the ill-fated *Mignonette* are the only men who would understand my frame of mind. 'At present,' I argued to myself, 'I am strong and a match for six of these wretches. It is imperatively necessary that I should, for my own sake, keep both health and strength until the hour of my release comes—if it ever does.'

Fortified with these resolutions, I ate and drank as much as I could, and made Gunga Dass understand that I intended to be his master, and that the least sign of insubordination on his part would be visited with the only punishment I had it in my power to inflict—sudden and violent death. Shortly after this I went to bed. That is to say, Gunga Dass gave me a double arm-ful of dried bents which I thrust down the mouth of the lair to the right of his, and followed myself, feet foremost; the hole running about nine feet into the sand with a slight downward inclination, and being neatly shored with timbers. From my den, which faced the river-front, I was able to watch the waters of the Sutlej flowing past under the light of a young moon and compose myself to sleep as best I might.

The horrors of that night I shall never forget. My den was nearly as nar-row as a coffin, and the sides had been worn smooth and greasy by the contact of innumerable naked bodies, added to which it smelt abominably. Sleep was altogether out of the question to one in my excited frame of mind. As the night wore on, it seemed that the entire amphitheatre was filled with legions of unclean devils that, trooping up from the shoals below, mocked the unfortunates in their lairs.

Personally I am not of an imaginative temperament—very few Engineers are—but on that occasion I was as completely prostrated with nervous terror as any woman. After half an hour or so, however, I was able once more to calmly review my chances of escape. Any exit by the steep sand walls was, of course, impracticable. I had been thoroughly convinced of this some time before. It was possible, just possible, that I might, in the uncertain moon-light, safely run the gauntlet of the rifle shots. The place was so full of terror for me that I was prepared to undergo any risk in leaving it. Imagine my delight, then, when after creeping stealthily to the river-front I found that the infernal boat was not there. My freedom lay before me in the next few steps!

By walking out to the first shallow pool that lay at the foot of the project-ing left horn of the horseshoe, I could wade across, turn the flank of the crater, and make my way inland. Without a moment's hesitation I marched briskly past the tussocks where Gunga Dass had snared the crows, and out

in the direction of the smooth white sand beyond. My first step from the
tufts of dried grass showed me how utterly futile was any hope of escape; for,
as I put my foot down, I felt an indescribable drawing, sucking motion of the
sand below. Another moment and my leg was swallowed up nearly to the
knee. In the moonlight the whole surface of the sand seemed to be shaken
with devilish delight at my disappointment. I struggled clear, sweating with
terror and exertion, back to the tussocks behind me and fell on my face.

My only means of escape from the semicircle was protected with a quicksand!

How long I lay I have not the faintest idea; but I was roused at the last
by the malevolent chuckle of Gunga Dass at my ear. 'I would advise you,
Protector of the Poor' (the ruffian was speaking English) 'to return to your
house. It is unhealthy to lie down here. Moreover, when the boat returns,
you will most certainly be rifled at.' He stood over me in the dim light of
the dawn, chuckling and laughing to himself. Suppressing my first impulse
to catch the man by the neck and throw him on to the quicksand, I rose
sullenly and followed him to the platform below the burrows.

Suddenly, and futilely as I thought while I spoke, I asked: 'Gunga Dass,
what is the good of the boat if I can't get out *anyhow*?' I recollect that even
in my deepest trouble I had been speculating vaguely on the waste of ammunition in guarding an already well protected foreshore.

Gunga Dass laughed again and made answer: 'They have the boat only
in daytime. It is for the reason that *there is a way*. I hope we shall have the
pleasure of your company for much longer time. It is a pleasant spot when
you have been here some years and catch roast crow long enough.'

I staggered, numbed and helpless, towards the fetid burrow allotted to me, and fell asleep. An hour or so later I was awakened by a piercing scream —the shrill, high-pitched scream of a horse in pain. Those who have once heard that will never forget the sound. I found some little difficulty in scrambling out of the burrow. When I was in the open, I saw Pornic, my poor old Pornic, lying dead on the sandy soil. How they had killed him I cannot guess. Gunga Dass explained that horse was better than crow, and 'greatest good of greatest number is political maxim. We are now Republic, Mister Jukes, and you are entitled to a fair share of the beast. If you like, we will pass a vote of thanks. Shall I propose?'

Yes, we were a Republic indeed! A Republic of wild beasts penned at the bottom of a pit, to eat and fight and sleep till we died. I attempted no protest of any kind, but sat down and stared at the hideous sight in front of me. In less time almost than it takes me to write this, Pornic's body was divided, in some unclean way or other; the men and women had dragged the fragments on to the platform and were preparing their morning meal. Gunga Dass cooked mine. The almost irresistible impulse to fly at the sand walls until I was wearied laid hold of me afresh, and I had to struggle against it with all my might. Gunga Dass was offensively jocular till I told him that if he addressed another remark of any kind whatever to me I should strangle him where he sat. This silenced him till silence became insupportable, and I bade him say something.

'You will live here till you die like the other Feringhi,' he said coolly, watching me over the fragment of gristle that he was gnawing.

'What other Sahib, you swine? Speak at once, and don't stop to tell me a lie.'

'He is over there,' answered Gunga Dass, pointing to a burrow-mouth about four doors to the left of my own. 'You can see for yourself. He died in the burrow as you will die, and I will die, and as all these men and women and the one child will also die.'

'For pity's sake tell me all you know about him. Who was he? When did he come, and when did he die?'

This appeal was a weak step on my part. Gunga Dass only leered and replied: 'I will not—unless you give me something first.'

Then I recollected where I was, and struck the man between the eyes, partially stunning him. He stepped down from the platform at once, and, cringing and fawning and weeping and attempting to embrace my feet, led me round to the burrow which he had indicated.

'I know nothing whatever about the gentleman. Your God be my witness that I do not. He was as anxious to escape as you were, and he was shot from the boat, though we all did all things to prevent him from attempting. He was shot here.' Gunga Dass laid his hand on his lean stomach and bowed to the earth.

'Well, and what then? Go on!'

'And then—and then, Your Honour, we carried him into his house and gave him water, and put wet cloths on the wound, and he laid down in his house and gave up the ghost.'

'In how long? In how long?'

'About half an hour, after he received his wound. I call Vishn to witness,' yelled the wretched man, 'that I did everything for him. Everything which was possible, that I did!'

He threw himself down on the ground and clasped my ankles. But I had my doubts about Gunga Dass's benevolence, and kicked him off as he lay protesting.

'I believe you robbed him of everything he had. But I can find out in a minute or two. How long was the Sahib here?'

'Nearly a year and a half. I think he must have gone mad. But hear me swear, Protector of the Poor! Won't Your Honour hear me swear that I never touched an article that belonged to him? What is Your Worship going to do?'

I had taken Gunga Dass by the waist and had hauled him on to the platform opposite the deserted burrow. As I did so I thought of my wretched fellow-prisoner's unspeakable misery among all these horrors for eighteen months, and the final agony of dying like a rat in a hole, with a bullet wound in the stomach. Gunga Dass fancied I was going to kill him and howled pitifully. The rest of the population, in the plethora that follows a full flesh meal, watched us without stirring.

'Go inside, Gunga Dass,' said I, 'and fetch it out.'

I was feeling sick and faint with horror now. Gunga Dass nearly rolled off the platform and howled aloud.

'But I am Brahmin, Sahib—a high-caste Brahmin. By your soul, by your father's soul, do not make me do this thing!'

'Brahmin or no Brahmin, by my soul and my father's soul, in you go!' I said, and, seizing him by the shoulders, I crammed his head into the mouth of the burrow, kicked the rest of him in, and, sitting down, covered my face with my hands.

At the end of a few minutes I heard a rustle and a creak; then Gunga Dass in a sobbing, choking whisper speaking to himself; then a soft thud— and I uncovered my eyes.

The dry sand had turned the corpse entrusted to its keeping into a yellow-brown mummy. I told Gunga Dass to stand off while I examined it. The body—clad in an olive-green hunting-suit much stained and worn, with leather pads on the shoulders—was that of a man between thirty and forty, above middle height, with light, sandy hair, long moustache, and a rough unkempt beard. The left canine of the upper jaw was missing, and a portion of the lobe of the right ear was gone. On the second finger of the left hand was a ring—a shield-shaped bloodstone set in gold, with a monogram that might have been either 'B. K.' or 'B. L.' On the third finger of the right hand was a silver ring in the shape of a coiled cobra, much worn and tarnished. Gunga Dass deposited a handful of trifles he had picked out of the burrow at my feet, and, covering the face of the body with my handkerchief,

I turned to examine these. I give the full list in the hope that it may lead to the identification of the unfortunate man:—

1. Bowl of a briarwood pipe, serrated at the edge; much worn and blackened; bound with string at the screw.

2. Two patent-lever keys; wards of both broken.

3. Tortoise-shell-handled penknife, silver or nickel, name-plate, marked with monogram 'B. K.'

4. Envelope, postmark undecipherable, bearing a Victorian stamp, addressed to 'Miss Mon——' (rest illegible)—'ham'—'nt.'

5. Imitation crocodile-skin notebook with pencil. First forty-five pages blank; four and a half illegible; fifteen others filled with private memoranda relating chiefly to three persons—a Mrs. L. Singleton, abbreviated several times to 'Lot Single,' 'Mrs. S. May,' and 'Garmison,' referred to in places as 'Jerry' or 'Jack.'

6. Handle of small-sized hunting-knife. Blade snapped short. Buck's horn, diamond-cut, with swivel and ring on the butt; fragment of cotton cord attached.

It must not be supposed that I inventoried all these things on the spot as fully as I have here written them down. The notebook first attracted my attention, and I put it in my pocket with a view to studying it later on. The rest of the articles I conveyed to my burrow for safety's sake, and there, being a methodical man, I inventoried them. I then returned to the corpse and ordered Gunga Dass to help me to carry it out to the river-front. While we were engaged in this, the exploded shell of an old brown cartridge dropped out of one of the pockets and rolled at my feet. Gunga Dass had not seen it; and I fell to thinking that a man does not carry exploded cartridge-cases, especially 'browns,' which will not bear loading twice, about with him when shooting. In other words, that cartridge-case had been fired inside the crater. Consequently there must be a gun somewhere. I was on the verge of asking Gunga Dass, but checked myself, knowing that he would lie. We laid the body down on the edge of the quicksand by the tussocks. It was my intention to push it out and let it be swallowed up—the only possible mode of burial that I could think of. I ordered Gunga Dass to go away.

Then I gingerly put the corpse out on the quicksand. In doing so, it was lying face downward, I tore the frail and rotten khaki shooting-coat open, disclosing a hideous cavity in the back. I have already told you that the dry sand had, as it were, mummified the body. A moment's glance showed that the gaping hole had been caused by a gunshot wound; the gun must have been fired with the muzzle almost touching the back. The shooting-coat, being intact, had been drawn over the body after death, which must have been instantaneous. The secret of the poor wretch's death was plain to me in a flash. Some one of the crater, presumably Gunga Dass, must have shot him with his own gun—the gun that fitted the brown cartridges. He had never attempted to escape in the face of the rifle-fire from the boat.

I pushed the corpse out hastily, and saw it sink from sight literally in a few seconds. I shuddered as I watched. In a dazed, half-conscious way I turned to peruse the notebook. A stained and discoloured slip of paper had been inserted between the binding and the back, and dropped out as I opened the pages. This is what it contained: 'Four out from crow-clump; three left; nine out; two right; three back; two left; fourteen out; two left; seven out; one left; nine back; two right; six back; four right; seven back.' The paper had been burnt and charred at the edges. What it meant I could not understand. I sat down on the dried bents turning it over and over between my fingers, until I was aware of Gunga Dass standing immediately behind me with glowing eyes and outstretched hands.

'Have you got it?' he panted. 'Will you not let me look at it also? I swear that I will return it.'

'Got what? Return what?' I asked.

'That which you have in your hands. It will help us both.' He stretched out his long, bird-like talons, trembling with eagerness.

'I could never find it,' he continued. 'He had secreted it about his person. Therefore I shot him, but nevertheless I was unable to obtain it.'

Gunga Dass had quite forgotten his little fiction about the rifle-bullet. I heard him calmly. Morality is blunted by consorting with the Dead who are alive.

'What on earth are you raving about? What is it you want me to give you?'

'The piece of paper in the notebook. It will help us both. Oh, you fool! You fool! Can you not see what it will do for us? We shall escape!'

His voice rose almost to a scream, and he danced with excitement before me. I own I was moved at the chance of getting away.

'Do you mean to say that this slip of paper will help us? What does it mean?'

'Read it aloud! Read it aloud! I beg and I pray to you to read it aloud.'

I did so. Gunga Dass listened delightedly, and drew an irregular line in the sand with his fingers.

'See now! It was the length of his gun-barrels without the stock. I have those barrels. Four gun-barrels out from the place where I caught crows. Straight out do you mind me? Then three left. Ah! Now well I remember how that man worked it out night after night. Then nine out, and so on. Out is always straight before you across the quicksand to the North. He told me so before I killed him.'

'But if you knew all this why didn't you get out before?'

'I did *not* know it. He told me that he was working it out a year and a half ago, and how he was working it out night after night when the boat had gone away, and he could get out near the quicksand safely. Then he said that we would get away together. But I was afraid that he would leave me behind one night when he had worked it all out, and so I shot him. Besides, it is not advisable that the men who once get in here should escape. Only I, and *I* am a Brahmin.'

The hope of escape had brought Gunga Dass's caste back to him. He stood up, walked about and gesticulated violently. Eventually I managed to make him talk soberly, and he told me how this Englishman had spent six months

night after night in exploring, inch by inch, the passage across the quicksand; how he had declared it to be simplicity itself up to within about twenty
yards of the river-bank after turning the flank of the left horn of the horseshoe. This much he had evidently not completed when Gunga Dass shot
him with his own gun.

In my frenzy of delight at the possibilities of escape I recollect shaking
hands wildly with Gunga Dass, after we had decided that we were to make
an attempt to get away that very night. It was weary work waiting throughout
the afternoon.

About ten o'clock, as far as I could judge, when the Moon had just risen
above the lip of the crater, Gunga Dass made a move for his burrow to bring
out the gun-barrels whereby to measure our path. All the other wretched
inhabitants had retired to their lairs long ago. The guardian boat drifted
down-stream some hours before, and we were utterly alone by the crow-
clump. Gunga Dass, while carrying the gun-barrels, let slip the piece of paper which was to be our guide. I stooped down hastily to recover it, and,
as I did so, I was aware that the creature was aiming a violent blow at the
back of my head with the gun-barrels. It was too late to turn round. I must
have received the blow somewhere on the nape of my neck, for I fell senseless at the edge of the quicksand.

When I recovered consciousness, the Moon was going down, and I was
sensible of intolerable pain in the back of my head. Gunga Dass had disappeared and my mouth was full of blood. I lay down again and prayed that
I might die without more ado. Then the unreasoning fury which I have before mentioned laid hold upon me, and I staggered inland towards the walls
of the crater. It seemed that some one was calling to me in a whisper—
'Sahib! Sahib! Sahib!' exactly as my bearer used to call me in the mornings.
I fancied that I was delirious until a handful of sand fell at my feet. Then
I looked up and saw a head peering down into the amphitheatre—the head
of Dunnoo, my dog-boy, who attended to my collies. As soon as he had
attracted my attention, he held up his hand and showed a rope. I motioned,
staggering to and fro the while, that he should throw it down. It was a
couple of leather punkah-ropes knotted together, with a loop at one end. I
slipped the loop over my head and under my arms; heard Dunnoo urge something forward; was conscious that I was being dragged, face downward, up
the steep sand-slope, and the next instant found myself choked and half-
fainting on the sand hills overlooking the crater. Dunnoo, with his face ashy
gray in the moonlight, implored me not to stay but to get back to my tent
at once.

It seems that he had tracked Pornic's footprints fourteen miles across the
sands to the crater; had returned and told my servants, who flatly refused
to meddle with any one, white or black, once fallen into the hideous Village
of the Dead; whereupon Dunnoo had taken one of my ponies and a couple
of punkah ropes, returned to the crater, and hauled me out as I have
described.

SHE WENT BY GENTLY

PAUL VINCENT CARROLL

IT WAS close on three when the knock came in the night. She was out
of bed on the instant in her old flannelette nightgown, with her silver-
gray hair tossed down her back. The night-light was flickering quietly
as, in the shadows by the elm tree outside, she discerned Manahan's un-
shaven face under the battered hat.

"The pains is bad on the girl," came his voice. "I think maybe it's surely
her time."

"Go before me fast and have plenty of hot water," she answered. "I'll
be at your heels with Frank."

She heard his foot in the night hurrying off as she drew on her heavy dress
over the nightgown. Himself stirred and put his beard irascibly outside the
blankets.

"You'll go none," he snapped. "A slut like that, that gets her child outside of priest and law. Four miles uphill on a mountain road and the mists
swarmin'."

"I'll go," she said quietly, and crossing, she ruffled Frank's unruly hair
on the little camp bed. "Be risin', Frank, and let you carry the lantern for
me to Manahan's."

"If there was just a drop o' tay before we'd start, ma," he protested
sleepily.

"There's no time, son."

"A grand pass we've come to, in this country," grumbled himself. "En-
couragin' the huzzies and the sluts to be shameless. I'd let her suffer. A
good bellyful o' sufferin' would keep her from doin' it again."

He moved coughingly into the deep warm hollow she had vacated in the
bed. The strictures of his uncharitable piety followed her into the silver
and ebony of the mountainy night. She went gently . . . her feet almost
noiseless. There was an inward grace in her that spilt out and over her physical lineaments, lending them a strange litheness and beauty of movement.
Frank was a little ahead of her, swinging the storm lantern. He was munch-

ing a currant scone plastered with butter. His sturdy little legs took the steep
sharp-pebbled incline with careless grace. Now and again, he mannishly
kicked a stone from his path and whistled in the dark.

"Careful now, Frank, in case you'd slip over the bank in the dark," she
admonished.

"Och, ma," he protested, "the way you talk! You'd think I wasn't grew
up. It makes little of a fella."

She smiled and watched him lovingly in the silver dark. He was her
youngest. The others had all followed the swallows into the mighty world.
Martin was in America, Annie in England, Matthew in Glasgow, Paddy in
the Navy, Mary Kate a nursemaid in Canada, Michael was at rest somewhere in Italy. His C.O. had said in a letter that he had died well. If that
meant that he had had the priest in his last hours, then God be praised,
for he was her wayward one. She preferred him dying full of grace to dying
full of glory. . . . But Frank was still with her. He had her eyes and gen-

tleness and the winning tilt of the head. It would be good to have him to close her weary eyes at the end of all . . .

They had now crossed the cockeyed little bridge over a dashing tawny stream and the mountains came near her and about her like mighty elephants gathered in a mystic circle for some high purpose. Everywhere in the vast silvery empire of the dark there was the deep silence of the eternal, except for the rebellious chattering of the mountain streams racing with madcap abandon to the lough below. They were the *enfants terribles* of the mighty house, keeping it awake and uneasy. Now and again a cottage lifted a sleepy eye out of its feathery thatch, smiled at her knowingly and slumbered again. All of them knew her . . . knew of her heroism, her quiet skilled hands, her chiding, coaxing voice in the moments of peril. . . . In each of them she had been the leading actress in the great primitive drama of birth.

The climb was now gruelling and Frank took her arm pantingly. The lantern threw its yellow ray merrily ahead. All would be well.

She ruffled his hair playfully, and smiled secretively under the black mask of the night.

At a mischievous bend on the mountain path, the Manahan cottage suddenly jumped out of the mist like a sheep dog and welcomed them with a blaze of wild, flowering creepers. Inside, the middle-aged labourer was bending over a dark deep chimney nook. A turf fire burned underneath on the floor. From a sooty hook far up, a rude chain hung down and supported a large pot of boiling water. She nodded approvingly and donning her overalls moved away in the direction of the highly-pitched cries from an inner room.

"If there's anythin' else I can do . . ." he called, half-shyly, after her.

"Keep a saucepan of gruel thin and hot," she answered. "And put the bottle of olive oil on the hob in case we'd need it. Play about, Frank, and behave yourself till I call you."

She went smilingly to the bed and looked down at the flushed tearful face, the big bloodshot eyes and the glossy tossed hair of the girl. No more than eighteen, she thought, but a well-developed little lass with a full luscious mouth and firm shapely breasts. Jim Cleary who skipped to England in time had had a conquest worth his while. . . . The little rebel, caught in the ruthless trap of Nature, grabbed her hands beseechingly, held on to them hysterically and yelled.

"Oh, Maura, ma'am, please, please, please . . ." she sobbed.

Maura chaffed her hands, soothed her gently, clacked her tongue admonishingly and pretended to be very disappointed at her behaviour.

"Now, now, now, Sadie," she reproved her. "A fine soldier *you* are! When I was here at *your* comin', your mother, God rest her, bit her lip hard and said no word at all. Come on now, and be your mother's daughter."

"Ah, sure how could I be like me poor dead mother, and me like this, and all agin me?" sobbed Sadie.

"Am *I* agin ye, child?" soothed Maura, "and I after walkin' four miles of darkness to be with you!"

The tears came now but silently, as Maura's skilful hands warmed to her work . . .

Frank remained in the kitchen at a loss until suddenly the door opened and a large nanny goat sailed in with perfect equanimity and balefully contemplated this stranger on home ground. Frank looked askance at her full-length beard and her formidable pair of horns, but this was of small consequence to the goat which advanced on Frank and in the wink of an eye had whipped his handkerchief out of his top pocket and stuffed it in her mouth. Frank's protest brought an assurance from Manahan who was stooped over the fire bringing the gruel to the boil.

"She'll not touch you," he said without turning his head.

"But she has me handkerchief," protested Frank.

"Ah, sure isn't she only playing with you!" returned Manahan heedlessly.

But by this time the goat had consumed the handkerchief with terrific relish, and was about to make a direct attack on the sleeve of his jersey. Frank dashed for the door with the goat after him. In the little yard he dived behind the water barrel that caught the rain-water from the roof. The goat snuffed past him in the darkness, and Frank hastily retraced his steps to the kitchen and barred the door.

He was just in time to see his mother put a generous spoonful of butter into a bowl of thin steaming gruel.

"Go in and feed this to your daughter, and coax her to take it," she directed Manahan. "She's quiet and aisy now and all will be well." He obeyed her shyly and without a word.

"You must be a big grown-up fella tonight and help your ma, Frank," she said.

"Anythin' you say, ma," he answered. "What is it?"

The baby had come forth without a cry. It was limp and devoid of any sign of life. She carried it quickly but calmly to the open peat fire, as close to the grimy chain as the heat would allow. It was naked and upside down. Frank, under her calm directions, held it firmly by its miniature ankles.

"Be a good son now and don't let it fall," she warned him, and plastering her own hands with the warm olive oil, she started to work methodically on the tiny body. Up, down and across the little chest, lungs and buttocks went the skilful fingers rhythmically until the newborn skin glistened like a silver-wrought piece of gossamer. The long minutes went by heavily. The oil lamp flickered and went out, leaving the dancing rays and shadows of the fire to light this crude drama with its eternal theme. Five minutes, seven, ten . . . without fruit or the promise of fruit. . . . But the moving fingers went on with rhythmic ruthlessness, searching for the spark that must surely be hidden there in a fold of the descending darkness. Frank's face was flushed, his eyes gathered up with the pain of exertion, his breath coming in spasms. On his mother's forehead beads of sweat gathered, rivuletted down the gray gentle face and flowed on to the newborn body to be ruthlessly merged in the hot oily waves of her massaging.

Then suddenly, as the tension had reached almost to the unbearable, a thin, highly-pitched cry came from the tiny spume-filled lips. She seized the baby, pushed Frank from her, turned it upright, grabbed a chipped, handle-less cup of cold water and even as the fluttering life hesitated on the minia-ture features for one solitary second to receive its divine passport and the symbol of its eternal heritage, she poured a little of the water on the tiny skull and said, "I baptise you, in the Name of the Father and of the Son and of the Holy Ghost."

She wrapped the little corpse in the remnant of a torn sheet, without tear or trace of any sentiment, placed it in a drawer she took from the crazy wardrobe, and having made the Sign of the Cross over it gave it no further attention.

When she saw that the bowl was almost empty of gruel, she chased Manahan out with a gesture and settled the little mother comfortably. She was adjusting her wet, tearstained hair over her pillow when suddenly she felt Sadie's arms tightly about her neck. Her big eyes were quiet now and the pain and the travail were gone, but the tears came rushing from them again as Maura kissed and soothed her.

"I wish I had me mother," she sobbed. "Maura, ma'am, I'm goin' to be a good girl from now on."

"You have never been a bad one, darlin'," coaxed Maura, tucking the faded bedclothes into her back. "A wee bit foolish maybe, but the world and the years will learn ye. Sleep now and I'll see you tonight."

She re-donned her old black cloak in the kitchen.

"I'll tell Maloney to bring you up a white box," she said to Manahan. "It will save you the journey down."

On the mountain path she went noiselessly, with Frank a little ahead, carrying the extinguished lantern. The dawn greeted her from the heights with far-flung banners of amber and amethyst. The heights themselves ceased from their eternal brooding for a brief moment of time and gave her a series of benign obeisances. The racing rivulets tossed her name from one to the other on the Lord's commendation. The sun himself, new-risen and generous, sent a very special ray of light that caught up her tossed hair and rolled it in priceless silver.

"Why do men lie prone in their beds," she murmured, "and the great glory of God washin' the hills with holy fire?"

Shamus Dunne was taking in his two nanny goats for the milking as she passed his cottage.

"The blessin' o' God light on ye, woman," he said, touching his wind-swept hat.

"And on yourself too, Shamus," she answered. "How is the little fella now?"

"Ah, sure isn't he over a stone weight already. Ah, woman-oh, wasn't it the near thing that night? Ah, sure only for yourself, wasn't me whole world lost?"

"Arrah, men always think the worst at such times," she answered smilingly.

"Sure, there was never any great fear of the worst that night! Herself, within, is much too good a soldier for that!"

Frank had now discovered a salmon tin and was kicking it vigorously before him. She took out her rosary at the bend where the path dips perilously between two ageless boulders, and as she trudged along, she began counting the beads effortlessly. There on the heights at dawn, caught between the gold and the deepening blue of day, she might have been a pilgrim out of a Europe that has long since vanished, or maybe a Ruth garnering the lost and discredited straws of the age-old Christian thought.

Frank had now lobbed his salmon tin on the lofty fork of a tree, and when she caught up with him, he took her arm undemonstratively. Himself would be up now, she thought, with his braces hanging, and maybe a hole in his sock that she had overlooked. He wouldn't be able to find the soap and the towel even if they were both staring at him, and of course if he blew the fire, even with a thousand breaths, it would never light for him. . . . But no matter now. Thanks be to God, there was an egg left in the cracked bowl that would do his breakfast. If the little white pullet in the barn laid in the old butter box, Frank would have one, too, with the help o' God. . . . When the cock himself laid an egg, Glory be, *she'd* get one all to herself!

They crossed the rickety bridge, as the dawn was losing its virgin colour. Frank saw a squirrel and rushed ahead of her. She paused for a moment and contemplated the restless waters. They took to her like a rich tawny wine poured out of some capacious barrel by some high ruthless hand who had suddenly discovered the futility of all riches. A May blossom rushed under the incongruous arch and emerged to get caught between a moss-covered stone and a jagged piece of rock. There was a turmoil and pain for a moment, and then it freed itself and rushed on. She wondered if it was the little soul she had lately saved, rushing on in a virgin panic to the eternal waters. . . . Maybe it was. . . . Maybe she was just an imaginative old fool. . . . Ah, sure what harm anyway to be guessing at infinite mysteries, and she so small on a mountain road?

Himself met her in the stone-floored kitchen. Indeed, yes, he was trailing his braces, and the sulky fire was just giving a last gasp before expiring.

"I suppose you saved the slut's bastard," he commented acidly.

She bent on her knees to blow the fire aflame again.

"I saved him," she answered, and a flame leaped suddenly upwards and made a sweet and unforgettable picture of her face.

TALE OF MY AUNT JENEPHER'S WOOING

DONN BYRNE

I

I DON'T suppose that one family ever held two more outwardly dissimilar people than my uncle Valentine and my aunt Jenepher. My uncle Valentine is a vast violent man, his shoulders spreading like a sail, and bearded from belly to eyes. That great fan-shaped ruddy beard, very like Samson's, covers—ladies of quality have told me—one of the handsomest faces in the United Kingdom, but ladies of quality have a way of overrating the lovers of their youth. My uncle Valentine's entry into a room illustrates that actuary's phrase, riot and civil commotion. My uncle Valentine never speaks, he bellows. There are three great sounds that have dignity—thunder, the crash of the sea against rocks, and the conversational tones of my uncle Valentine.

My aunt Jenepher, though not a small woman, is tiny beside that immense red presence. My uncle Valentine is second of the immense family my grandfather had, and of which there are left only he and my uncle Cosimo and my aunt Jenepher. My aunt Jenepher is the youngest, and it would seem that out of a gallant and handsome line (whose beauty has not descended to this generation, more pity!) she was the masterpiece. You would never have taken her for a woman in her middle thirties, so girlish was her figure, so lissom it was, so like a young eager tree. There is no blacker, more silken hair in all Ireland than is on my aunt Jenepher's head. Her brow and nose are noble, but not that cold Phidian nobility of statues. Her mouth is among the prettiest mouths in the world and always smiling, either the open smile of merriment or the soft smile of reflection. Her head is balanced like a flower on its stalk, like a soft dignified flower on its graceful stalk. The lashes of my aunt Jenepher's eyes are like the petals of a flower. It is impossible for unhappiness, black unhappiness, to exist where my aunt Jenepher is. When my aunt Jenepher enters a room, you feel that windows are thrown open in the springtime. When my aunt Jenepher speaks in her sweet contralto, you feel you have never known the full values of human speech before, so soft, so vibrant that deep voice is.

My uncle Valentine has an eye like a hawk, to use the country expression.

There is nothing he cannot see, from the look of guilt in your eye to the defect in the horse you are trying to sell him, no matter how cleverly concealed. There will be one shrewd look, and you will be treated to an apocryphal genealogy of your family in no generation of which is the issue legitimate, but always interesting. There is a belief in Ireland that my uncle Valentine can see around a corner, to use another country phrase.

To watch Aunt Jenepher walk about that old house of ours, the gardens and lawns, you would not know she has not two eyes as good as any other person's. When one has walked in the dark since ever so little, one develops a sense of direction and of obstacles. This is a very good explanation. There is also another, quoting Saint Luke: "He shall give His angels charge over thee, to help thee: and in their hands they shall bear thee up, lest at any time thou dash thy foot against a stone." You can take your choice. Myself I prefer the latter one. About Destiny Bay she went without any help, if you except that gold-headed ebony stick she carried that had once been the sainted Bishop Berkeley's. Every flower in the garden she knew: the violets and daffodils of spring, the roses of summer, the great hedges of lupins, with their heavy honey odour; and where the hives of the bees were she was at home. That ancient mysterious commonwealth had a kinship with her.

"There is no honey in Ireland like our honey," the old gardener used to say: "and do you know why, young fellow, your Honour? Because the bees like working for your aunt, Miss Jenepher."

The feathered quality of the ferns and the glossiness of the flowers he ascribed to her presence. "For what do flowers grow on?" he would ask. " 'Tis not th' excellence of soil, but the kindliness of the people. For God's sake," he would call out to my aunt, "will your Ladyship leave them dahlias be. You have the heart crossways in me."

"Have you any flowers for luncheon, Duncan?"

"I can spare none," he would say grimly. But he would turn up five minutes later with bunches. "—and let your Ladyship not be bothering me again."

She always says she never misses her sight, does my aunt Jenepher. She pities us, because this sight of ours interrupts our other senses and we cannot get the true value of the lark's song, or of the thrush's or the linnet's or the blackbird's rhapsody, or the song the wind makes among the heather, or the scent of the heather itself, the soft intoxicating Celtic scent.

That may be. But, my God! Not to have eyes for the sweet heads of the two-year-olds in the paddock, for the glossy pack racing up the five-furlong course to the post! Not to see the huge Atlantic break in rosettes, in fountains, in clouds of foam on the cliffs of Destiny Bay! The unnamable beauty of the evening star by the small crescent moon! The mountains with their purple regal coats! The daffodils that sway like young girls dancing! How can one believe in God, if one has not eyes?

"There is only one thing I cannot imagine, Kerry. Flowers and mountains, horses, men and girls, I can imagine. But one thing is a mystery to me."

"What is that, Aunt Jenepher?"

"Clear water."

"Water!" said my uncle Valentine in a voice of horror, for my uncle Valentine is none of your blue ribbon men. "Water be damned!"

II

After a while in electric New York; or in soft unchanging London; or on the golden strands of the Caribbean; or in Venice singing with beauty; or in that Monegasque gambling den, where sooner or later all good Irishmen are to be found, it is good for body and soul to wander back to Destiny Bay. It is an Ulster cranny. Around the thirty square miles or so of the district the mountains spread like a horseshoe, and in front of it are the cliffs and strand facing the Atlantic like an armed man. No railroad comes within ten miles of my people's house, for there is nothing to develop there. Here and there are great fertile fields where grows barley, or flax. Here are great stretches of bogland, where the red-billed moor hen and the snipe, and the invisible whistling otter are sole tenantry. Those of the peasants who speak Erse speak the beautiful tongue of Bishop Bedell's Bible. Those who speak English speak the tongue of Cromwell, the simple powerful phrasing of the solemn oath and covenant. They are all planter folk, barring ourselves. The only other family there of high standing—I speak of those mentioned in "The Nobility and Gentry"—are the Pascoes, Cornish soldiering people who came over and were granted lands. The name Destiny Bay has a peculiar derivation. The Erse name was Port Fale, but my grandfather, Sir Alick MacFarlane, a most dogmatic man, had it changed. Some whirlwind of Irish politics decided him to erase everything Irish from his manor. He had the local schoolmaster come to him.

"What does Port Fale mean?"

"The bay of the cliff, Sir Alick."

"Isn't there a word 'Fale', destiny?" asked my grandfather. "How about Lia Fale, the Stone of Destiny?"

"It isn't the same word, Sir Alick."

My grandfather bristled. I am told that one of the supplementary wonders of the world was to see my grandfather bristling.

"Are you contradicting me?" he asked the poor little man. And so our home and the district about it came to be known as Destiny Bay.

The only place in the United Kingdom where the gypsies ever intermarry with householders is at Destiny Bay. So that between the Scottish, and Irish, and Cornish and gypsy blood we are a violent restless folk. The people of Donegal call us the "Paganachs", or pagans, and the dwellers in Derry speak of us as the mountainy people. But of course that is nothing to what we call these good law-abiding folk. It is certain that the Most Reverend the Lord Primate of all Ireland mentions us specially in his prayers, but this was due to an incident concerning a narrow-minded vicar who objected to having his church used for a main of cockfighting. It isn't very interesting and you can read about it elsewhere. His sister published a pamphlet entitled "The Martyrdom of the Reverend Timothy White."

Always Destiny Bay was a good place to return to. The hawthorn trees heavy with moss, the shrubs near the cliffs, flying like sphinxes landward, because of the weight of the Atlantic storms, the crying of the curlew and the peewit, the vast sailing moon—all these were things not to be duplicated elsewhere. Always there would be my aunt Jenepher with her gracious beautiful presence and her understanding, and my uncle Valentine, who is the easiest man in the world to borrow money from. Always there was something of interest in Destiny: a London Prize Ring fight between a gypsy and a local man; a horse race for ten pounds a side; or there would be great news, as of Molly MacGuigan, the barber's daughter, having gone to America with the Hibernian Players and been hailed as a second Bernhardt; or how Johnny Malone had won the accordion playing championship of the world at Crystal Palace, London.

I had come back from Denmark, whither I had gone as honorary secretary to the Head of the Irish Agricultural Commission, investigating why the melancholy Danes were cutting us out of the English butter market. Just hard work on their part.

"I'm glad you're home, Kerry," my uncle Valentine greeted me. "I'm back from Dublin myself. I'm gey glad you're home."

"What's wrong, sir?"

"Your aunt Jenepher's dying."

I was terrified, for there was something in the dejection of that great violent man that was like a battleship of the line striking her colours. I sped to my aunt Jenepher. I found her sitting by the fire in the Tower room.

"Is that you, Kerry, long lad?"

"What's amiss, Aunt Jenepher?"

She was thinner, paler than usual, but nothing about her, it seemed to me, betokened dying. I told my uncle so after dinner.

"It's just a foolish idea of yours, Uncle Valentine."

"I tell you the woman's dying."

"She's not dying."

"The woman's dying."

"But she's not, Uncle Valentine!"

"She's dying," insisted my uncle Valentine, "but she'll die happy," said he.

He told me that she, who had loved the garden so much, loved the bees, loved the wind from the heather mountains, would go out no longer, but remained about the great rambling house.

"You know how she loved to walk down the yew lane, even in winter weather."

I said I did. I could never think of the dignity and beauty of our long alley of golden yews without seeing the beauty and dignity of my aunt Jenepher, and her walking between them in the last warmth of the setting sun.

"What's come on her, Uncle Valentine?"

"Somebody has bought the Pascoe house and is doing it up to live there.

Who it is I don't know, but an American of some kind, I think, and it's broken your aunt Jenepher's heart."

There was a romance in my aunt Jenepher's life that had to do with the Pascoes. The last of them, Digory, and she had been betrothed. Digory had been terribly wild and had spent the last of the family money, racing unluckily, and it was at my aunt Jenepher's suggestion he had gone East to make a new fortune. I think the six months before he went and while he was engaged to my aunt Jenepher were the worthiest and happiest of his life. He was a tall handsome fellow, with dark passionate eyes. He set sail for the Malay States, to work on a rubber plantation, but at Marseilles he disembarked, waiting over between boats, and went to Monte Carlo on the chance of recouping fortune there instead of in the East.

"While he was there," said my uncle Valentine, "he had the devil's own hard luck, and as often happens he took a dislike to a man playing at the same table who was always winning. You go a little crazy in a gambling place, Kerry my boy; and the thought came to Digory that this man was the cause of his bad luck.

"This man was a fat tubby little fellow, who had made a fortune in groceries, and was now lording it on the Riviera. There was nothing this man wanted to be taken for more than a great gentleman. Digory, as you've seen from his picture, looked like a king. He had the manners of a grand duke, too, had Digory. Only for the cruel strain in the lad he'd have been a great fellow.

"Digory gets it into his head that if this man could be induced to leave the tables his luck would turn. So he bumps into the grocer man. 'You've struck me!' says Digory. 'I'm sorry,' says the grocer. 'Sorry be damned!' says Digory. 'My friends will wait on you.'

"So he sends Sir Alastair Baird and Roaring Johnny McLaughlin around to the poor grocery fellow. There weren't two finer men in Ireland than Baird and Johnny. Nobility was oozing from them. They told him Major Digory Pascoe wanted satisfaction for the insult. And the grocer fellow, mind you, afraid not to be thought a gentleman, consented. Baird told me the sweat was pouring from him.

"Digory said: 'So much the better. If I kill this fellow my luck'll change.' Digory was superstitious. I've never seen a better shot with a duelling pistol than Digory. 'Twas he killed Captain Kelly at Boulogne. Begad, Kerry, Digory was nearly a teetotaller for fear it would spoil his aim.

"So they met the next morning back of Monte. The grocer's knees were knocking, and he had to tie a handkerchief around the butt of the pistol on account of the wetness of his hand. Roaring Johnny said it was the funniest thing he had ever seen in his life. My bold Digory was cool as be-damned, for it wasn't his first nor his fifth time out, so—"

"I don't want to hear about it, Uncle Valentine. I think it's scandalous for a gentleman to kill an inoffensive beggar for a whim."

My uncle Valentine gave that vast laugh of him, that is like thunder.

"Begad, no!" he said. "The grocer killed Digory."

III

My uncle Valentine was a bad liar, because he was not practised in the art. This is not to be ascribed to virtue but to arrogance. Where the meaner sort of person had to double like a hare, he stood like the Irish wolf dog. In the matter of the death of Digory he could not tell the truth, so in putting off an explanation of Digory's end through floods by land or sea, the Act of God or the King's enemies, he fell into a worse lie. He kept Digory alive for the present. At Christmas and at Easter we wrote letters from Digory, addressed from the Malay States, or Borneo, or Cochin-China, telling how his health was, his prospects, and of the hard luck from simooms and hurricanes and tornadoes which was retarding his progress. My uncle Valentine would vanish into his study and coming back with an armful of letters tied with ribbons of various shades, from one of them he would select a pleasant sentiment, which even to my inexperienced ears sounded hardly masculine. We posted them in Dublin or Belfast in time to get to Destiny Bay for Christmas morning or the Saturday before Easter.

"My dear Jenepher," my uncle Valentine would read aloud. "This is trusting you are in the excellent health which I enjoy, and for which God be thanked." And then would follow a dissertation on the simoom or on rubber, which we had bodily taken from the excellent encyclopedia of Mr. Britannica's. "To-night when the stars are in full glory in God's heaven, and when I should be revelling in the jewellery of the universe my thoughts are with you and my Ulster home. O Head of dark locks!" We had changed "auburn" to "dark." And concluded: "Yours very sincerely, Digory Pascoe." Damned good! we thought it.

"Thank you, Valentine, and thank you, dear Kerry, for reading it," my aunt Jenepher would say.

"We'll be losing you some of these days, Jenepher. But we won't let you go for a long time yet. Hey, Kerry?"

"Dear Valentine! Dear Kerry!"

But afterwards my uncle Valentine would wipe his forehead and say:

"Begad, boy, we'll have to send Digory home some of these days and drown him on the voyage. That'll make a good elegant end."

But for twelve years, Digory managed to evade his "good, elegant end", until it seemed, according to my uncle Valentine, that my aunt Jenepher was near hers.

"Go down," said my uncle Valentine, "to the Widow McGinty's hotel, and bring up what I left there. 'Tis something I got in Dublin."

"Have you brought something else home?"

"Mind your own business and do what I tell you!"

There was always a sporting element about what my uncle Valentine brought home. Once it was a large brown bear he had purchased from a gypsy. " 'Twill keep away burglars," said my uncle Valentine, as though any poor Godforsaken burglar would trust himself to the hellhounds of Destiny Bay. He chained it in a corner of the stables, and fed it with honey and turnips and an occasional bottle of whiskey. One morning the bear escaped and cleaned up the Croppy Boy bar of patrons and attendants, and getting most riotously drunk it made straight for the police barracks, where it clawed the tunic and trousers off a constable and was proceeding to embrace the sergeant when a bullet put an end to its career. It became over-Hibernicised, poor Bruin! And once my uncle Valentine, playing picquet with the Duc de Corey, that peer of the old Holy Roman Empire, brought home the most prized ducal possession. The duke was of an extremely religious disposition as well as having a passion for cards, and so had his coffin made, a beautiful mahogany affair, silver-mounted. He loved picquet to distraction, but he was no match for my uncle Valentine.

"Put this in the drawing-room," my uncle Valentine told the astonished servants. "We'll use it as a cellarette." And only the prospect of tears from my aunt Jenepher restored his last home to the poor old duke.

So that I didn't know what to expect at the Widow McGinty's hotel.

"Did Sir Valentine MacFarlane leave anything here?"

"He left a gentleman, Master Kerry, the nicest-spoken gentleman I ever did see, a poodle dog, and three cases o' German wine. The wine and the dog I'm sending up, and here's the gentleman."

He was a tall swarthy man, with something of the gypsy in his appearance. A fine-looking, brave man. A man you would trust your life to.

"Your uncle Valentine," he told me, "asked me to come up and stay a while here. Your uncle Valentine," he smiled, "is a very cogent man."

"He is," I agreed. "But forgetful. He omitted to tell me your name."

"My name is Patrick Herne," he said. "But your uncle Valentine asked me to go under another name, the name of Digory Pascoe."

"Great God!" I said to myself.

"Your uncle explained he had a sister who is blind and not well, and that there was a boy-and-girl attachment between your aunt and this Pascoe. If this deception can help the unfortunate lady I am only too glad."

"You are very kind," I uttered savagely. And then my heart misgave me, for looking at the man I found he *was* very kind. And looking more closely still I found him intensely like the old picture of Digory my aunt had. Many years older, naturally, but uncannily like Digory.

"You aren't Digory Pascoe? Are you?"

"No," he said. "I'm not. I'm just Patrick Herne."

IV

I told my uncle Valentine that the whole scheme was outrageous. And moreover, my aunt Jenepher would know at once that it wasn't Digory Pascoe.

"My dear Kerry," my uncle Valentine patronised, "when you've seen as much of the world as I have, you'll be surprised how easily women are fooled."

"That may be, but how are you going to explain—"

"Explain?" roared my uncle Valentine. "Didn't I find him? Haven't I done my share? It's up to you to explain him," he said. "Aren't you the world's champion explainer? Didn't I hear you explain successfully to the Colonel of the Welsh Borderers that your twenty-year-old blind hunter was a slip of a colt and would one day win the Grand National for him? You could explain the horns and tail off the devil himself."

There was no need for much explanation, for the man Patrick Herne had better brains than either of us, which is not saying a lot, God knows. Besides, my aunt Jenepher asked for no explanation at all. With his immense kindness there was great dignity to Herne. It was a pleasure to me to sit by him and my aunt Jenepher and hear him talk of the East Indies where he undoubtedly had been. He made you feel the explosive sunshine of the places, the brown Cingalese and men of Java and Borneo, the flowers that had strange dramatic colouring, the yellow priests with shaven heads, the stately elephants, the gongs of the temples. He knew so much about animals that it enchanted us, my uncle Valentine and me, to listen to him. We, who had been bred to dogs and horses and our quarry the fox, knew the authentic note when he spoke of the elephant and tiger and the spotted pard, and the little sun bear of Borneo, that is not bigger than a big dog, and has the pathetic quality of a child.

"I had a bear myself once," said my uncle Valentine, "that got to taking a drop too much, and one day—" and he would proceed to relate the scandalous episode of the constable's trousers.

It seemed to us that we had known this man all our living days, so much at home with him we were. He came with us to races, he came to fairs. He stepped into the rugged, somehow florid life of Destiny Bay as though he belonged there. A smaller man would have been swamped by it. I have never seen anything in life or on the stage like his grave courtesy. He was as much with my aunt Jenepher as possible, and it was he who enticed her out into the gardens and woods again, saying he had forgotten this and that. I liked to see them together, wandering through the garden or down the alley of yews, he so big, so rugged, so handsome in his way, so gravely courteous; she so lovely, such beauty shining from darling soul through sweet perfect body, and her low laughter coming like music at some story of Herne's, or her face attuned to wonder at some recital of foreign parts. He had a manner of giving his arm that I doubt if even my uncle Valentine, great gentleman though he was, could equal.

My aunt Jenepher had two great talents, though she was very shy about them. She was a wonderful pianist, though of, I suppose, a low order of playing. I mean this: anything she had ever heard she could play through and of course she could not read and so naturally there was an immensity of music unknown to her. My uncle Valentine used, three or four times a year, to get a man from Dublin to come and play new famous compositions, and so wonderful was Aunt Jenepher's memory that she could always remember them. Myself I'd rather hear her play the searching folk music of Ulster, or pipe music such as she could imitate wonderfully, than anything else. I suppose people will laugh at me, just as I myself smile at an unknowledgeable man on a horse, or handling a boat. But there— As though Patrick Herne were as close to her as myself or my uncle Valentine, my aunt Jenepher went to the great piano and played: I can remember nights when we sat in the drawing-room of Destiny Bay in formal broadcloth and linen, while my aunt Jenepher played. It is a great square room, with heavy furniture and paintings of MacFarlanes, with wax candles and lamps, and through the door-like windows which my uncle Valentine had put in, the golden August moon rose high over Creetyre Point, and a very faint chiming of the sea seemed to keep time with my aunt Jenepher playing.

It struck me, and I nearly had to laugh aloud, that my uncle Valentine was a very puzzled man. Before he had brought Patrick Herne to the house, he had imagined for himself a picture of my aunt Jenepher dying, wasting away as the ladies in the early part of the reign of good Queen Victoria wasted, of a romantic but quite sanitary disease. They grew frailer every day, while the lover of their youth stood by, a strong silent figure suffering visibly. They drew a last romantic breath, the broken-hearted family bowed in grief, the strong silent figure went into exile, to shoot rhinoceros in Mashonaland, or to visit the Dalai Lama in Tibet. That is what rhinoceros and the Dalai Lama are for.

And here was my aunt Jenepher, in the best of health, playing my uncle Valentine's favourite, in fact his only opera, "The Bohemian Girl", her exquisite white hands flitting like butterflies over the keys. There were lines of wonder in my uncle's red forehead. There was a look of wonder about his immense red beard.

I have said my aunt Jenepher had two talents: the other was a trifle grotesque, and of which she was very much ashamed, but which had a quaint vital beauty. My aunt Jenepher was the best whistler I have ever heard, as I have previously said.

There is supposed to be something unladylike in this performance, and there is a country proverb that directs you to beat the devil out of a woman caught in the act. But I challenge you to find anything but beauty in my aunt Jenepher's whistling. You might be passing by our house and lands and hear the sweet high trill of a country song distilling itself in the clear air, each grace note, each shake, clear and crystal as dewdrops falling from the whitethorn branches, so that if you were a country person you would say: "Is it the fairies are in it, I wonder, and they on the march this day of spring? Or is it some foreign melodious bird that Sir Valentine is after buying for his delectation? Begor, I'll have the least taste of a squint!" And looking over the privet hedge you would see a very lovely Irish gentlewoman, seated on an old stone bench, her head lifted to the distant mountains, her sweet eyebrows raised, her exquisite hands resting on an antique gold-mounted ebony cane, sending through her lips in notes sweet as the blackbird's some old

melody like "The Coolin." But if you wished to hear that you had better not
pry, for the song would vanish as all secret lovely things vanish when you
pry, like the little shoe-making leprechaun or the young of the otter, or the
kingfisher that is the blue bird of poets.

There was magic in her whistling. I have often seen my uncle Valentine
when the black mood was on him, standing with his hand thrust into his
immense mane of red beard, aloof, terrible. Then my aunt Jenepher would
enter the room, and there would begin to float in the air the strains of jig or
hornpipe, "The Swallowtail Coat", or "The Green Fields of America", so
cogent, so airy, so gay, but you could not help noticing it. She would pay no
attention to my uncle Valentine, but go about the room, and sooner or later
you would hear the tap-tap of my uncle Valentine's foot upon the floor, and
then a rhythmic sound as of a drum beating softly. My uncle Valentine was
dancing. But my aunt Jenepher affected never to notice it. She went about
her offices and later on out of the room, evidently as unhearing as she was
unseeing.

She had the habit of playing the accompaniment to her whistling upon
the piano. Nobody had ever heard her at this, I think, but my uncle Valentine and myself and others of the family, until one night we came in with
the man, Patrick Herne. Her face flooded with a soft ruddy colour that was
like the deeper sort of rose, but she went on playing and whistling.

One day my uncle Valentine and I came into the garden before lunch—
Herne had gone off somewhere for the morning, and down near the beehives
was my aunt Jenepher. She was whistling but there was no particular set
tune to it. It was a clear wild trilling sound like a bird's. Indeed I remember seeing the blackbirds hopping baffledly near the netted strawberry beds,
stopping and putting their heads on one side in critical admiration.

"There you are!" said my uncle Valentine tragically. "That's done it." And
he sat down on one of the stone benches.

"What, sir?" said I.

"Did you hear that?" said he.

"I did," said I. "It's only my aunt Jenepher whistling."

"It's only—" he jeered. "It's only— You may be the white-headed boy of
the old ducks at Trinity," he told me with great contempt, "but to me, and
fundamentally," he said, "you're only an ignorant, mountainy mick!"

V

The re-building, re-furbishing, re-decoration of the Pascoe home bothered
my uncle fearfully. "It's deeper than old friendship," he said, "for we have
been here since Ireland was first discovered by our great ancestor, the Egyp-
tian Parthelon. The Pascoes have only been here since Oliver Cromwell's
time, and though they were but newcomers, yet our people got used to
them. Nearly three hundred years we've been side by side. They were a fine
Cornish family.

"I'm cursed if I know what sort are coming here at all," he said. "It was in London the sale was arranged, so the lawyers tell me.

"Myself," he told Patrick Herne, "am a great one for old faces, old ties. Yourself, Mr. Herne, are the first one I've taken to for a long time. I've a great mind," he said, "to go travelling again so as to avoid these new people."

"They mayn't be bad, Sir Valentine," said our butler, James Carabine.

"They'll never be like the Pascoes, a strange roaring race," said my uncle Valentine. And he began to tell the history of the Pascoes. There was great-grandfather Pascoe who had come from India with a fortune, so immense, so fat a man that he had to be assisted up from his chair every time he sat down. He would be served by none but Indian servants, and as the poor devils died off like flies in Ireland he was always sending for more. There was a field near Pascoe Manor called "The Indian Burial Ground." There was also a corner called the "Indian Queen's" where slept two bronze beauties, for great-grandfather Pascoe had not been so respectable as he might have been. There was also "Pirate Pascoe" who had privateered against the French in the Bonaparte wars. He had one mental failing: he believed every vessel on the sea was French, so he stripped and gutted Yankee clippers, honest Hollanders, an occasional British boat, everything that came his way. He was hanged on Tower Hill. They were all a wild race. Digory's father had had a fancy woman from among the gypsies and a child by her before he married Digory's mother.

"She was not his fancy woman, please your Honour, Sir Valentine," said Carabine. "She was his lawful wedded wife."

James Carabine was himself half gypsy and half Irish. He had soldiered with my uncle Valentine in the war against the Boers and earned the Maltese Cross "For Valour" for saving my uncle Valentine's—his officer's—life at Spion Kop. So that James Carabine was more a friend to the house than a servant, and privileged to speak at all times.

"What do you mean, James Carabine?"

"Alick Pascoe, please your Honour, married this woman in the Romany way, across the Romany fire, with Romany witnesses. It was valid in the eyes of the Romany people and valid in the eyes of God."

My uncle Valentine thought for a while.

"What became of her, Carabine?" I asked.

"One day she left, Master Kerry, whether it was on account of ill treatment from Pascoe, or the weight of four walls and a roof, I cannot tell. But she tucked her child under her arm and went down the road with her head high, for she was a princess of Romany. Where she went after, it is beyond me to tell,—to the fertile fields of Alabama, or the lowlands of Holland, or to Grim Tartary, as they call it. Or they may be dead itself. I've heard it denied," said James Carabine, "that gypsies die, but that I know to be untrue, though they die hard."

"That marriage, James Carabine, might be valid in the eyes of God," decided my uncle, "but it would not be valid with the Ulster King-at-Arms."

"Och, him!" said Carabine.

"Nor it wouldn't be valid with me," said my uncle, "who am High Sheriff of the County of Tyrconnell, and a Justice of the King's Peace."

"Then it wouldn't be valid at all," said Carabine.

"You seem to put a great deal of value on birth and breeding," said Patrick Herne.

"I do, sir," said my uncle Valentine, "and so do you, for you're the most sensible man I ever met. Would you take an ordinary horse without any particular blood in him, and run him for the Derby race?"

"I would not," said Herne.

"Would you enter an unbred dog for the Waterloo Cup?"

"I would not."

"There you are," said my uncle Valentine.

"But, Uncle Valentine," I ventured, "from the poorest and most obscure people great men arise. Even in our own day and certainly in all times good and just and powerful men arise from nothing."

"Seemingly, Kerry," said my uncle Valentine, "but these beacons of justice and power are nothing but units of great families lost by marriage on the distaff side, by poverty in which there is nothing ignoble, by this circumstance and that, and when the opportunity arrives, through staying-power and courage, which are the attributes of nobility, these men succeed, proving illustrious blood."

"Uncle Valentine," I laughed, "I suppose you believe that in the Kingdom of Heaven there are nothing but old families."

"Who else could there be, Kerry?" asked my uncle Valentine.

For our own family, my uncle Valentine placed it far above the Plantagenets and Capets, "for we are descended from Par-the-lon," he said, "who was the first invader of Ireland, and who came from Egypt, as the Annals of the Four Masters prove. This Par-the-lon," he continued, "was a younger son of the King of Egypt of his time, as is shown by documentary evidence in the British Museum. And this king was descended from Nimrod, son of Cash, son of Ham, son of Noah. It was from Nimrod," said my uncle Valentine, "that we got our fine seat in the saddle and our taste for the fox.

"The genealogy of Noah you can look up in your Bible, and you'll find him directly descended from Adam and Eve, so that you might say that we Mac-Farlanes of Destiny Bay are personally created by God!"

I wish you could have seen my uncle Valentine as he pronounced this, his great glossy red beard on his immense broad chest, his fine head raised. He was like some ancient ruddy majestic Assyrian king.

"But, Uncle Valentine," I suggested, "every one is personally created by God. Johnny the Gander down in the village, and Mollie McGinty that keeps the hotel, and the travelling tinkers, and—"

My uncle Valentine brought his vast fist down on the table so that the plates jumped from their mats, and the portraits on the walls rattled and the candles scattered their wax.

"I will have no atheism talked in this house," thundered my uncle Valentine.

VI

I never saw a person who loved the country around Destiny Bay more than Patrick Herne did. The heather, the rowan trees, the little streams, the thunder of the sea's artillery against the cliffs, its galloping cavalry entranced him. He had the faculty of silence which is a gift direct from Heaven.

"I suppose I'll soon have to be going," he said wistfully to me one day. "Your aunt Jenepher's well now, and—I have enjoyed myself here."

"Where are you going?" I asked.

"I don't know," he said. "I had a place settled before I came here, but now it's gone wrong. It's a bad thing to be this way: to have no occupation and plenty of money, and no place to go."

"Then why don't you stay with us?" I asked. "Soon I'll have a wandering fit and my uncle Valentine will get lonely. And the hunting here is good. Small as it is, there isn't a better pack of foxhounds in Ireland than my uncle Valentine's. We love to have you. My uncle Valentine feels at home with you, and you're all right."

"I'm not 'all right'," said Patrick Herne. "I was once a clown in a circus."

He smiled at my astonishment. "Yes," he said, "a clown with a powdered face, and red paint at the tip of his nose."

"Oh, that's difficult," I said.

"It is," he understood me.

I was afraid of a faint tinge of I won't say contempt but of patronage coming into my uncle Valentine's feeling for Herne. My uncle Valentine comes from a feudal stock, in a place where feudalism existed a hundred years longer than in any other spot in Europe, and where as yet we are but half-civilised. My uncle Valentine was more accustomed to govern people than to philosophise, so one can hardly blame this old-world gentleman for not accepting one who had been a clown with a painted nose as his equal. This is a reprehensible viewpoint in modern days, I know. I will admit freely that the beadle is the equal of the bishop and the foot soldier of the field marshal; but then, I will admit anything, loathing arguments.

"You weren't always a clown?" I asked.

"No," said Herne, digging in his pockets for his pipe. "I was an animal trainer, lions and tigers."

"By God! That's a man's job."

"It requires some skill," said Herne, "and a great deal of sympathy, and a tremendous faith in the presence of God.

"Oh, I like Destiny Bay," he burst out, "I hate to go. The sea and the bonny mountains and the purple bogs, and the gypsies, coming and going, the Lovells and the Lees and the Hernes—"

"You're a gypsy, Patrick Herne," I discovered.

"Only half," he said, "the other half—"

"Is Pascoe, by God!" I roared, for now I saw whence the resemblance to

Digory came. "You're by Digory Pascoe's father out of the Romany girl, the Romany wife, I mean—I'm sorry, Patrick Herne."

"Wife or girl, does it matter," laughed Herne, "now I'm here?"

I thought I had made enough discoveries for one day, but in the afternoon, talking to my aunt Jenepher in the garden, she broke suddenly into the discussion we were having with this question:—

"Kerry, who is this man you and Valentine have told me was Digory Pascoe?"

There are occasions when lying is of no use.

"How did you know?"

"You might deceive a person with face or hand, Kerry, but you can never deceive with a voice. A voice is the vibrations of a person's being, and, dear

Kerry," she put her hand up to where my shoulder was, "Digory Pascoe has been dead these many years."

"And you let us write those letters?"

"It was such a kind sweet thing of you and brother Valentine to do, and I was afraid to tell you I knew. You were both such dears."

"Why aren't you afraid now, Aunt Jenepher?"

But she gave no reason.

"Tell me about this man, Kerry."

"I can't tell you much, Aunt Jenepher. But I like him. I think he is a fine man, a courageous man, and a kind man."

"I know that, Kerry," she said. "I know all that. I can stand beside a person and know him. His virtues and defects, Kerry, they come to me like soft music, or like little jarring sounds. I like this man. I like his silence, Kerry. One would never be afraid while that man is about."

"He's all right," I agreed, "Patrick Herne is."

"It's strange, Kerry," my aunt Jenepher went on, "to get the sense that a person is thinking the same as you're thinking. Often I stand here in the alley of yews when the sun is going down, and the little chill of evening is on the land, and the flowers give their last sigh before closing for the night, and the scent of heather is in the air—I know that God is walking along the cliffs of Destiny, and, Kerry, that man knows it too. Though we say nothing, yet we each know it, and each knows the other knows it."

"Myself," I said lightly, "I have a weakness for the moonlight and a touch of courting," and I kissed her when she blushed.

But I was worried and puzzled, so much that my uncle Valentine noticed it when he came.

"There you are," he said, "with a face on you as long as a fool's funeral! What's wrong with you?"

"I was just thinking."

"You flatter yourself," said my uncle Valentine.

VII

My uncle Valentine was himself worried that night. I could see it in the depth of the wrinkles on his brow; in his lack of attention to the trout Patrick Herne and I had caught that day; in this little detail and that. Sooner or later, I knew, he would acquaint us with what was bothering him, for he was not a man to keep things in long.

"Did you ever," he asked suddenly, "did you ever hear me talk about a horse?"

James Carabine stood still in his tracks, and Patrick Herne smiled. My aunt Jenepher looked up.

"Never, sir," I answered. "Indeed, I might say I never knew the word pass your lips."

"It was Limerick Pride," said my uncle. And then I knew it was serious.

Limerick Pride, by Sarsfield out of Haughty Lady, seventeen years before, was my uncle Valentine's property, and from colt to six-year-old had won everything before it in Ireland. The Leopardstown Gold Cup, the Irish Derby, the Irish Two Thousand Guineas. Indeed, Limerick Pride was so good that for the Baldoyle Vase, he was handicapped at the prohibitive weight of nine stone four pounds. As a hurdler he took everything before him. And then my uncle Valentine had a week of dreadful losses at the Sheridan Club, and sold out his own personal possessions. Limerick Pride went to the States, where he was a complete failure, so much so that he passed from owner to owner and at last came down to work in a cab. Thence some one rescued him, and all trace was lost of him. To part with him all but broke my uncle's heart, and the story of his later misfortunes nearly drove the red baronet crazy. But spend how much money he cared not, he could never find Limerick Pride again.

"The loss of Limerick Pride and the death of your dear father, Kerry, were the two great trials of my life," I've heard my uncle Valentine say. "If it hadn't been a matter of honour, Kerry, I'd have shot the horse with my own hands before parting with him, and letting him into the hands of strangers."

"Do you remember Limerick Pride, James Carabine?"

"Do I remember my mother, your Honour?" answered Carabine.

"Limerick Pride was a horse of mine that I was very attached to," explained my uncle Valentine to Patrick Herne. "He was a great horse with the heart of a lion and some of the best blood in the world. He was by Sarsfield out of Haughty Lady, who was himself by Simple Soldier out of Jessamy Bride, who was by Simplicity out of Simonette, who was by Covenanter out of Quaker Lady—"

"Covenanter," broke in Carabine, "was by Game Cove out of Aunt Dorothy, and Game Cove was by Irish Gamester out of Covessa."

"Covessa herself," said my uncle Valentine, "was by Covert Coat out of Dogaressa."

"Best blood in Ireland," muttered Carabine, "and for horses or sportsmen that means the world."

"The last time I saw that horse was fifteen years ago, as a six-year-old, in Vine's auction rooms in Dublin."

We were all silent, knowing how much he took the parting to heart.

"Until I saw him to-day," he said, "with two other horses in Pascoe's ten-acre."

"Go to hell!" called Carabine in excitement. "It's a damned lie!"

" 'Tis not a lie. James Carabine, would you know that horse?"

"Would I know Limerick Pride, Sir Valentine? Would I know him in the dark! And moreover, hadn't he got the queerest marking I ever saw on a horse? He was pure chestnut but for a white left ear."

"You'll find him in Pascoe's ten-acre," said my uncle. "The fellow that's bought the place from you," he winked violently at Patrick Herne—my aunt Jenepher and I took an immediate interest in our plates—"this man, whoever he is, and you say you don't know, has sent up a collection of cattle would do your heart good to see. Jerseys and Royal Dexters. There are a couple of hunters I like, three harness horses, my old darling Limerick Pride, and a trick mule.

"And a trick mule," shouted my uncle Valentine. I could see Carabine shudder. "What do you think of a fellow would have a trick mule?"

"I have a low opinion," said Carabine.

"I'm going over to London by the midnight train to Dublin," said my uncle Valentine, "and find out from the head lawyers who has bought the place. And I'm going to make him sell me my horse Limerick Pride."

"He might give him to you," suggested Patrick Herne.

"Give away Limerick Pride!" laughed my uncle. "The man would have to be crazy, and moreover, do you think I'd accept a present from the sort of man who would have a trick mule?"

"I don't suppose you would," said Herne.

"But sell him he will," said my uncle Valentine grimly, "for if he doesn't, he might as well settle in Hell as in Destiny Bay."

It was late that night after my uncle Valentine had left that Patrick Herne told me he was going too, the very next day.

"Where to, in God's name?"

"I think I'll put in a while in Africa."

"But why?"

"Oh, I suppose it's the gypsy wandering instinct," he laughed. "By the way, you can bring Limerick Pride across and put him in the paddock. He's a present from me to your uncle."

"Are you—"

"Yes," he said, "I'm the beggar with the trick mule. It's an old pal of mine. We worked together for years."

"But you're not going to leave Pascoe Manor?"

"It's just what I'm going to do, Kerry, my lad. I'll send up a steward from Dublin, and come back now and then. You might use the hunters for me, and if you don't mind keep an eye on Caligula the mule. He's not a bad sort."

"My uncle Valentine will be very put out at your going, Patrick Herne," I said.

"I'm going now so as to avoid arguments. I hate them as much as you do, Kerry."

"There'll be somebody 'll be heart-broken at your going, Patrick Herne. I don't suppose I should tell you, but there it is."

"You don't," said Herne slowly, "mean your aunt Jenepher?"

"I do."

"Are you sure of that? Are you quite sure, Kerry?"

"Utterly sure."

"Then I'll stay," said Patrick Herne.

VIII

I said: "All that's very fine. There's nothing I like better myself than to have a thing out. But why waste these splendid azure days in argument? The sun and the sea will not wait until you have all argued and settled, and had first principles discussed. I know my uncle Valentine. There's nothing he'd like better than to see you and my aunt Jenepher married. But—he'll spend the winter evenings arguing about it. He'll hold up the whole course of Irish politics until he has you knighted. He may even have a private bill introduced into Parliament about the Romany marriage. You don't know my uncle Valentine. This will be meat and drink to him.

"My dear Patrick Herne, go and get a license and be married here. Clear out of the way till he comes back. Take Aunt Jenepher to the Mediterranean with you, and by the time you come back, Pascoe Manor will be ready, and my uncle Valentine will be like a lamb. He'll be ten days in London. He won't stir out of the card room at White's until he's cleaned the place up. There will be old friends at the Service Clubs. Do it now."

So well did I argue and so expeditiously did I put everything through that I had them before the parson in our small Tudor church, before either of them really knew what was happening. Our church is a sweet old church, thick-builded, as it must be near the sea, and grey, and here and there yellow with stonewort. The light comes into it gently and glimmers on the brasses of the MacFarlanes who are dead and gone, and one always feels there is an angel about, a grey-bearded drowsy Georgian angel who takes snuff. The martins and the swallows build their nests in the eaves and the wild bees nest in the graveyard, and my uncle Valentine will not have them ousted, for he is lord of the manor. Without, in the graveyard in spring, are bluebells and primroses, and in summer are woodbine and wild roses. And the huddled mounds do not make you think of Death, but of old folk or children sleeping, so peaceful it is.

"It was ordained," said our padre, "for the mutual society, help and comfort, that the one ought to have of the other, both in prosperity and adversity. Into which holy estate these two persons present—"

I was standing behind so that I could not see my aunt Jenepher's face, but I could her small black hat, her costume of heather tweed, her beautiful small brown shoes, and from her left wrist hung Bishop Berkeley's cane, and in her hand was a great bunch of heather, that Carabine had searched the mountains for the evening before, a royal purple bunch with strands of white heather. And beside her was Herne, big and fine, like some powerful, well-blooded, great-hearted horse, and finer praise than that there is not in this world. I was thinking to myself what a fine recruit we had taken for Clan McFarlane.

" 'Wilt thou have this woman to be thy wedded wife, to live together after God's ordinance—' "

It was nice, a peaceful wedding. Behind us in the body of the church were Carabine, and Duncan the gardener, and the whole household of Destiny Bay, and a swarthy band of gypsies who all loved my aunt Jenepher and who had come to see her married. For best man I had pressed into service my cousin Jenico from Spanish Men's Rest, and as bridesmaid we had Eleanor Pendleton, pretty Nelly Pendleton, with her burning auburn hair. A fine gathering, and a lovely, a peaceful day.

"'. . . Wilt thou obey him in sickness and in health, and forsaking all other, keep thee only unto him, so long as ye both shall live?'" And my aunt Jenepher answered: "I will."

"'Who giveth this woman to be married to this man?'" asked the padre.

I was thinking of the letter I would have to write to my uncle Valentine that afternoon, and picking phrases for it: "My dear uncle Valentine: I know you will be delighted to hear—" when my cousin Jenico brought his heel sharply into my cannon bone.

"'Who giveth this woman to be married to this man?'"

"I give this woman—" I said, and I noticed a look of anxiety in the parson's eyes. Behind us in the church was the heavy thump of feet. I looked over my shoulder, and I saw the big presence, still wrapped in the huge travelling coat, and the immense copper-coloured beard. And then a hand caught me by the shoulder, and sent me spinning down the chancel until I bumped into the baptismal font.

"Stand aside, you pup," I heard, and, "I give this woman to be married to this man," roared my uncle Valentine.

THROUGH THE VEIL

A. CONAN DOYLE

HE WAS a great shock-headed, freckle-faced Borderer, the lineal descendant of a cattle-thieving clan in Liddesdale. In spite of his ancestry he was as solid and sober a citizen as one would wish to see, a town councillor of Melrose, an elder of the Church, and the chairman of the local branch of the Young Men's Christian Association. Brown was his name—and you saw it printed up as "Brown and Handiside" over the great grocery stores in the High Street. His wife, Maggie Brown, was an Armstrong before her marriage, and came from an old farming stock in the wilds of Teviothead. She was small, swarthy, and dark-eyed, with a strangely nervous temperament for a Scotch woman. No greater contrast could be found than the big, tawny man and the dark little woman, but both were of the soil as far back as any memory could extend.

One day—it was the first anniversary of their wedding—they had driven over together to see the excavations of the Roman Fort at Newstead. It was not a particularly picturesque spot. From the northern bank of the Tweed, just where the river forms a loop, there extends a gentle slope of arable land. Across it run the trenches of the excavators, with here and there an exposure of old stonework to show the foundations of the ancient walls. It had been a huge place, for the camp was fifty acres in extent, and the fort fifteen. However, it was all made easy for them since Mr. Brown knew the farmer to whom the land belonged. Under his guidance they spent a long summer evening inspecting the trenches, the pits, the ramparts and all the strange variety of objects which were awaiting to be transported to the Edinburgh Museum of Antiquities. The buckle of a woman's belt had been dug up that very day, and the farmer was discoursing upon it when his eyes fell upon Mrs. Brown's face.

"Your good leddy's tired," said he. "Maybe you'd best rest a wee before we gang further."

Brown looked at his wife. She was certainly very pale, and her dark eyes were bright and wild.

"What is it, Maggie? I've wearied you. I'm thinkin' it's time we went back."

"No, no, John, let us go on. It's wonderful! It's like a dreamland place. It all seems so close and so near to me. How long were the Romans here, Mr. Cunningham?"

"A fair time, mam. If you saw the kitchen midden-pits you would guess it took a long time to fill them."

"And why did they leave?"

"Well, mam, by all accounts they left because they had to. The folk round could thole them no longer, so they just up and burned the fort aboot their lugs. You can see the fire marks on the stanes."

The woman gave a quick little shudder. "A wild night—a fearsome night," said she. "The sky must have been red that night—and these grey stones, they may have been red also."

"Aye, I think they were red," said her husband. "It's a queer thing, Maggie, and it may be your words that have done it; but I seem to see that business aboot as clear as ever I saw anything in my life. The light shone on the water."

"Aye, the light shone on the water. And the smoke gripped you by the throat. And all the savages were yelling."

The old farmer began to laugh. "The leddy will be writin' a story aboot the old fort," said he. "I've shown many a one ower it, but I never heard it put so clear afore. Some folk have the gift."

They had strolled along the edge of the foss, and a pit yawned upon the right of them.

"That pit was fourteen foot deep," said the farmer. "What d'ye think we dug oot from the bottom o't? Weel, it was just the skeleton of a man wi' a spear by his side. I'm thinkin' he was grippin' it when he died. Now, how cam' a man wi' a spear doon a hole fourteen foot deep. He wasna' buried there, for they aye burned their dead. What make ye o' that, mam?"

"He sprang doon to get clear of the savages," said the woman.

"Weel, it's likely enough, and a' the professors from Edinburgh couldna gie a better reason. I wish you were aye here, mam, to answer a' oor deeficulties sae readily. Now, here's the altar that we foond last week. There's an inscreeption. They tell me it's Latin, and it means that the men o' this fort give thanks to God for their safety."

They examined the old worn stone. There was a large, deeply cut "VV" upon the top of it.

"What does 'VV' stand for?" asked Brown.

"Naebody kens," the guide answered.

"*Valeria Victrix*," said the lady softly. Her face was paler than ever, her eyes far away, as one who peers down the dim aisles of over-arching centuries.

"What's that?" asked her husband sharply.

She started as one who wakes from sleep. "What were we talking about?" she asked.

"About this 'VV' upon the stone."

"No doubt it was just the name of the Legion which put the altar up."

"Aye, but you gave some special name."

"Did I? How absurd! How should I ken what the name was?"

"You said something—'*Victrix*,' I think."

"I suppose I was guessing. It gives me the queerest feeling, this place, as if I were not myself, but someone else."

"Aye, it's an uncanny place," said her husband, looking round with an expression almost of fear in his bold grey eyes. "I feel it mysel'. I think we'll just be wishin' you good evenin', Mr. Cunningham, and get back to Melrose before the dark sets in."

Neither of them could shake off the strange impression which had been left upon them by their visit to the excavations. It was as if some miasma had risen from those damp trenches and passed into their blood. All the evening they were silent and thoughtful, but such remarks as they did make showed that the same subject was in the mind of each. Brown had a restless night, in which he dreamed a strange, connected dream, so vivid that he woke sweating and shivering like a frightened horse. He tried to convey it all to his wife as they sat together at breakfast in the morning.

"It was the clearest thing, Maggie," said he. "Nothing that has ever come to me in my waking life has been more clear than that. I feel as if these hands were sticky with blood."

"Tell me of it—tell me slow," said she.

"When it began, I was oot on a braeside. I was laying flat on the ground. It was rough, and there were clumps of heather. All round me was just darkness, but I could hear the rustle and the breathin' of men. There seemed a great multitude on every side of me, but I could see no one. There was a low chink of steel sometimes, and then a number of voices would whisper, 'Hush!' I had a ragged club in my hand, and it had spikes o' iron near the end of it. My heart was beatin' quickly, and I felt that a moment of great danger and excitement was at hand. Once I dropped my club, and again from all round me the voices in the darkness cried, 'Hush!' I put oot my hand, and it touched the foot of another man lying in front of me. There was someone at my very elbow on either side. But they said nothin'.

"Then we all began to move. The whole braeside seemed to be crawlin' downwards. There was a river at the bottom and a high-arched wooden bridge. Beyond the bridge were many lights—torches on a wall. The creepin' men all flowed towards the bridge. There had been no sound of any kind, just a velvet stillness. And then there was a cry in the darkness, the cry of a man who had been stabbed suddenly to the hairt. That one cry swelled out for a moment, and then the roar of a thoosand furious voices. I was runnin'. Everyone was runnin'. A bright red light shone out, and the river was a scarlet streak. I could see my companions now. They were more like devils than men, wild figures clad in skins, with their hair and beards streamin'. They were all mad with rage, jumpin' as they ran, their mouths open, their arms wavin', the red light beatin' on their faces. I ran, too, and yelled out curses like the rest. Then I heard a great cracklin' of wood, and I knew that the palisades were doon. There was a loud whistlin' in my ears, and I was aware that arrows were flying past me. I got to the bottom of a dyke, and I saw a hand stretched doon from above. I took it, and was dragged to the top. We looked doon, and there were silver men beneath us holdin' up their spears. Some of our folk sprang on to the spears. Then we others followed, and we killed the soldiers before they could draw the spears oot again. They shouted loud in some foreign tongue, but no mercy was shown them. We went ower them like a wave, and trampled them doon into the mud, for they were few, and there was no end to our numbers.

"I found myself among buildings, and one of them was on fire. I saw the flames spoutin' through the roof. I ran on, and then I was alone among the buildings. Someone ran across in front o' me. It was a woman. I caught her by the arm, and I took her chin and turned her face so as the light of the fire would strike it. Whom think you that it was, Maggie?"

His wife moistened her dry lips. "It was I," she said.

He looked at her in surprise. "That's a good guess," said he. "Yes, it was just you. Not merely like you, you understand. It was you—you yourself. I saw the same soul in your frightened eyes. You looked white and bonnie and wonderful in the firelight. I had just one thought in my head—to get you awa' with me; to keep you all to mysel' in my own home somewhere beyond the hills. You clawed at my face with your nails. I heaved you over my shoulder, and I tried to find a way oot of the light of the burning hoose and back into the darkness.

"Then came the thing that I mind best of all. You're ill, Maggie. Shall I stop? My God! you have the very look on your face that you had last night in my dream. You screamed. He came runnin' in the firelight. His head was bare; his hair was black and curled; he had a naked sword in his hand, short and broad, little more than a dagger. He stabbed at me, but he tripped and fell. I held you with one hand, and with the other——"

His wife had sprung to her feet with writhing features.

"Marcus!" she cried. "My beautiful Marcus! Oh, you brute! you brute! you brute!" There was a clatter of tea-cups as she fell forward senseless upon the table.

They never talk about that strange, isolated incident in their married life. For an instant the curtain of the past had swung aside, and some strange glimpse of a forgotten life had come to them. But it closed down, never to open again. They live their narrow round—he in his shop, she in her household—and yet new and wider horizons have vaguely formed themselves around them since that summer evening by the crumbling Roman fort.

THE THREE STRANGERS

THOMAS HARDY

AMONG the few features of agricultural England which retain an appearance but little modified by the lapse of centuries may be reckoned the high, grassy and furzy downs, coombs, or ewe-leases, as they are indifferently called, that fill a large area of certain counties in the south and southwest. If any mark of human occupation is met with hereon, it usually takes the form of the solitary cottage of some shepherd.

Fifty years ago such a lonely cottage stood on such a down, and may possibly be standing there now. In spite of its loneliness, however, the spot, by actual measurement, was not more than five miles from a county-town. Yet that affected it little. Five miles of irregular upland, during the long inimical seasons, with their sleets, snows, rains, and mists, afford withdrawing space enough to isolate a Timon or a Nebuchadnezzar; much less, in fair weather, to please that less repellent tribe, the poets, philosophers, artists, and others who "conceive and meditate of pleasant things."

Some old earthen camp or barrow, some clump of trees, at least some starved fragment of ancient hedge is usually taken advantage of in the erection of these forlorn dwellings. But, in the present case, such a kind of shelter had been disregarded. Higher Crowstairs, as the house was called, stood quite detached and undefended. The only reason for its precise situation seemed to be the crossing of two footpaths at right angles hard by, which may have crossed there and thus for a good five hundred years. Hence the house was exposed to the elements on all sides. But, though the wind up here blew unmistakably when it did blow, and the rain hit hard whenever it fell, the various weathers of the winter season were not quite so formidable on the coomb as they were imagined to be by dwellers on low ground. The raw rimes were not so pernicious as in the hollows, and the frosts were scarcely so severe. When the shepherd and his family who tenanted the house were pitied for their sufferings from the exposure, they said that upon the whole they were less inconvenienced by "wuzzes and flames" (hoarses

From *Wessex Tales* by Thomas Hardy. Reprinted by permission of the Trustees of the Hardy Estate, Macmillan & Co., Ltd., and the Macmillan Company of Canada, Ltd.

and phlegms) than when they had lived by the stream of a snug neighboring valley.

The night of March 28, 182—, was precisely one of the nights that were wont to call forth these expressions of commiseration. The level rainstorm smote walls, slopes, and hedges like the cloth-yard shafts of Senlac and Crecy. Such sheep and outdoor animals as had no shelter stood with their buttocks to the winds; while the tails of little birds trying to roost on some scraggy thorn were blown inside-out like umbrellas. The gable-end of the cottage was stained with wet, and the eavesdroppings flapped against the wall. Yet never was commiseration for the shepherd more misplaced. For that cheerful rustic was entertaining a large party in glorification of the christening of his second girl.

The guests had arrived before the rain began to fall, and they were all now assembled in the chief or living room of the dwelling. A glance into the apartment at eight o'clock on this eventful evening would have resulted in the opinion that it was as cosy and comfortable a nook as could be wished for in boisterous weather. The calling of its inhabitant was proclaimed by a number of highly polished sheep crooks without stems that were hung orna-mentally over the fireplace, the curl of each shining crook varying from the antiquated type engraved in the patriarchal pictures of old family Bibles to the most approved fashion of the last local sheep-fair. The room was lighted by half a dozen candles having wicks only a trifle smaller than the grease which enveloped them, in candlesticks that were never used but at high-days, holy-days, and family feasts. The lights were scattered about the room, two of them standing on the chimney piece. This position of candles was in itself significant. Candles on the chimney piece always meant a party.

On the hearth, in front of a back-brand to give substance, blazed a fire of thorns, that crackled "like the laughter of the fool."

Nineteen persons were gathered here. Of these, five women, wearing gowns of various bright hues, sat in chairs along the wall; girls shy and not shy filled the window-bench; four men, including Charley Jake the hedge-car-penter, Elijah New the parish-clerk, and John Pitcher, a neighboring dairy-man, the shepherd's father-in-law, lolled in the settle; a young man and maid, who were blushing over tentative *pourparlers* on a life companion-ship, sat beneath the corner-cupboard; and an elderly engaged man of fifty or upward moved restlessly about from spots where his betrothed was not to the spot where she was. Enjoyment was pretty general, and so much the more prevailed in being unhampered by conventional restrictions. Absolute confidence in each other's good opinion begat perfect ease, while the finishing stroke of manner, amounting to a truly princely serenity, was lent to the majority by the absence of any expression or trait denoting that they wished to get on in the world, enlarge their minds, or do any eclipsing thing what-ever—which nowadays so generally nips the bloom and *bonhomie* of all except the two extremes of the social scale.

Shepherd Fennel had married well, his wife being a dairyman's daughter from a vale at a distance, who brought fifty guineas in her pocket—and kept

them there, till they should be required for ministering to the needs of a
coming family. This frugal woman had been somewhat exercised as to the
character that should be given to the gathering. A sit-still party had its ad-
vantages; but an undisturbed position of ease in chairs and settles was apt to
lead on the men to such an unconscionable deal of toping that they would
sometimes fairly drink the house dry. A dancing-party was the alternative;
but this, while avoiding the foregoing objection on the score of good drink,
had a counterbalancing disadvantage in the matter of good victuals, the
ravenous appetites engendered by the exercise causing immense havoc in the
buttery. Shepherdess Fennel fell back upon the intermediate plan of mingling short dances with short periods of talk and singing, so as to hinder
any ungovernable rage in either. But this scheme was entirely confined to her
own gentle mind: the shepherd himself was in the mood to exhibit the most
reckless phases of hospitality.

The fiddler was a boy of those parts, about twelve years of age, who had a
wonderful dexterity in jigs and reels, though his fingers were so small and
short as to necessitate a constant shifting for the high notes, from which he
scrambled back to the first position with sounds not of unmixed purity of
tone. At seven the shrill tweedle-dee of this youngster had begun, accompanied by a booming ground-bass from Elijah New, the parish-clerk, who
had thoughtfully brought with him his favorite musical instrument, the serpent. Dancing was instantaneous, Mrs. Fennel privately enjoining the players
on no account to let the dance exceed the length of a quarter of an hour.

But Elijah and the boy, in the excitement of their position, quite forgot
the injunction. Moreover, Oliver Giles, a man of seventeen, one of the
dancers, who was enamored of his partner, a fair girl of thirty-three rolling
years, had recklessly handed a new crown-piece to the musicians, as a bribe
to keep going as long as they had muscle and wind. Mrs. Fennel, seeing
the steam begin to generate on the countenances of her guests, crossed over
and touched the fiddler's elbow and put her hand on the serpent's mouth.
But they took no notice, and fearing she might lose her character of genial
hostess if she were to interfere too markedly, she retired and sat down helpless. And so the dance whizzed on with cumulative fury, the performers
moving in their planet-like courses, direct and retrograde, from apogee to
perigee, till the hand of the well-kicked clock at the bottom of the room had
traveled over the circumference of an hour.

While these cheerful events were in course of enactment within Fennel's
pastoral dwelling, an incident having considerable bearing on the party had
occurred in the gloomy night without. Mrs. Fennel's concern about the growing fierceness of the dance corresponded in point of time with the ascent of a
human figure to the solitary hill of Higher Crowstairs from the direction of
the distant town. This personage strode on through the rain without a pause,
following the little-worn path which, further on in its course, skirted the
shepherd's cottage.

It was nearly the time of full moon, and on this account, though the sky
was lined with a uniform sheet of dripping cloud, ordinary objects out of

doors were readily visible. The sad, wan light revealed the lonely pedestrian
to be a man of supple frame; his gait suggested that he had somewhat passed
the period of perfect and instinctive agility, though not so far as to be otherwise than rapid of motion when occasion required. At a rough guess, he might
have been about forty years of age. He appeared tall, but a recruiting sergeant, or other person accustomed to the judging of men's heights by the eye,
would have discerned that this was chiefly owing to his gauntness, and that
he was not more than five-feet-eight or nine.

Notwithstanding the regularity of his tread, there was caution in it, as in
that of one who mentally feels his way; and despite the fact that it was not a
black coat nor a dark garment of any sort that he wore, there was something
about him which suggested that he naturally belonged to the black-coated
tribes of men. His clothes were of fustian, and his boots hobnailed, yet in
his progress he showed not the mud-accustomed bearing of hobnailed and
fustianed peasantry.

By the time that he had arrived abreast of the shepherd's premises the rain
came down, or rather came along, with yet more determined violence. The
outskirts of the little settlement partially broke the force of wind and rain,
and this induced him to stand still. The most salient of the shepherd's
domestic erections was an empty sty at the forward corner of his hedgeless

garden, for in these latitudes the principle of masking the homelier features of your establishment by a conventional frontage was unknown. The traveler's eye was attracted to this small building by the pallid shine of the wet slates that covered it. He turned aside, and, finding it empty, stood under the pent-roof for shelter.

While he stood, the boom of the serpent within the adjacent house, and the lesser strains of the fiddler, reached the spot as an accompaniment to the surging hiss of the flying rain on the sod, its louder beating on the cabbage-leaves of the garden, on the eight or ten beehives just discernible by the path, and its dripping from the eaves into a row of buckets and pans that had been placed under the walls of the cottage. For at Higher Crow-stairs, as at all such elevated domiciles, the grand difficulty of housekeeping was an insufficiency of water; and a casual rainfall was utilized by turning out, as catchers, every utensil that the house contained. Some queer stories might be told of the contrivances for economy in suds and dishwaters that are absolutely necessitated in upland habitations during the droughts of summer. But at this season there were no such exigencies; a mere acceptance of what the skies bestowed was sufficient for an abundant store.

At last the notes of the serpent ceased and the house was silent. This cessation of activity aroused the solitary pedestrian from the reverie into which he had elapsed, and, emerging from the shed, with an apparently new intention, he walked up the path to the house-door. Arrived here, his first act was to kneel down on a large stone beside the row of vessels, and to drink a copious draught from one of them. Having quenched his thirst, he rose and lifted his hand to knock, but paused with his eye upon the panel. Since the dark surface of the wood revealed absolutely nothing, it was evident that he must be mentally looking through the door, as if he wished to measure thereby all the possibilities that a house of this sort might include, and how they might bear upon the question of his entry.

In his indecision he turned and surveyed the scene around. Not a soul was anywhere visible. The garden path stretched downward from his feet, gleaming like the track of a snail; the roof of the little well (mostly dry), the well-cover, the top rail of the garden-gate, were varnished with the same dull liquid glaze; while, far away in the vale, a faint whiteness of more than usual extent showed that the rivers were high in the meads. Beyond all this winked a few bleared lamplights through the beating drops—lights that denoted the situation of the county-town from which he had appeared to come. The absence of all notes of life in that direction seemed to clinch his intentions, and he knocked at the door.

Within, a desultory chat had taken the place of movement and musical sound. The hedge-carpenter was suggesting a song to the company, which nobody just then was inclined to undertake, so that the knock afforded a not unwelcome diversion.

"Walk in!" said the shepherd, promptly.

The latch clicked upward, and out of the night our pedestrian appeared upon the door-mat. The shepherd arose, snuffed two of the nearest candles, and turned to look at him.

Their light disclosed that the stranger was dark in complexion and not unprepossessing as to feature. His hat, which for a moment he did not remove, hung low over his eyes, without concealing that they were large, open, and determined, moving with a flash rather than a glance round the room. He seemed pleased with his survey, and, baring his shaggy head, said, in a rich, deep voice: "The rain is so heavy, friends, that I ask leave to come in and rest awhile."

"To be sure, Stranger," said the shepherd. "And faith, you've been lucky in choosing your time, for we are having a bit of a fling for a glad cause— though, to be sure, a man could hardly wish that glad cause to happen more than once a year."

"Nor less," spoke up a woman. "For 'tis best to get your family over and done with, as soon as you can, so as to be all the earlier out of the fag o't."

"And what may be this glad cause?" asked the stranger.

"A birth and christening," said the shepherd.

The stranger hoped his host might not be made unhappy either by too many or too few of such episodes and, being invited by a gesture to a pull at the mug, he readily acquiesced. His manner, which, before entering, had been so dubious, was now altogether that of a careless and candid man.

"Late to be traipsing athwart this coomb—hey?" said the engaged man of fifty.

"Late it is, Master, as you say.—I'll take a seat in the chimney corner, if you hve nothing to urge against it, Ma'am; for I am a little moist on the side that was next the rain."

Mrs. Shepherd Fennel assented, and made room for the self-invited comer, who, having got completely inside the chimney corner, stretched out his legs and arms with the expansiveness of a person quite at home.

"Yes, I am rather cracked in the vamp," he said freely, seeing that the eyes of the shepherd's wife fell upon his boots, "and I am not well fitted either. I have had some rough times lately, and have been forced to pick up what I can get in the way of wearing, but I must find a suit better fit for working-days when I reach home."

"One of hereabouts?" she inquired.

"Not quite that—further up the country."

"I thought so. And so be I; and by your tongue you come from my neighborhood."

"But you would hardly have heard of me," he said quickly. "My time would be long before yours, Ma'am, you see."

This testimony to the youthfulness of his hostess had the effect of stopping her cross-examination.

"There is only one thing more wanted to make me happy," continued the newcomer, "and that is a little baccy, which I am sorry to say I am out of."

"I'll fill your pipe," said the shepherd.

"I must ask you to lend me a pipe likewise."

"A smoker, and no pipe about 'ee?"

"I have dropped it somewhere on the road."

The shepherd filled and handed him a new clay pipe, saying, as he did so, "Hand me your baccy-box—I'll fill that too, now I am about it."

The man went through the movement of searching his pockets.

"Lost that too?" said his entertainer, with some surprise.

"I am afraid so," said the man with some confusion. "Give it to me in a screw of paper." Lighting his pipe at the candle with a suction that drew the whole flame into the bowl, he resettled himself in the corner and bent his looks upon the faint steam from his damp legs, as if he wished to say no more.

Meanwhile the general body of guests had been taking little notice of this visitor by reason of an absorbing discussion in which they were engaged with the band about a tune for the next dance. The matter being settled, they were about to stand up when an interruption came in the shape of another knock at the door.

At sound of the same the man in the chimney corner took up the poker and began stirring the brands as if doing it thoroughly were the one aim of his existence; and a second time the shepherd said, "Walk in!" In a moment another man stood upon the straw-woven door-mat. He too was a stranger.

This individual was one of a type radically different from the first. There was more of the commonplace in his manner, and a certain jovial cosmopolitanism sat upon his features. He was several years older than the first arrival, his hair being slightly frosted, his eyebrows bristly, and his whiskers cut back from his cheeks. His face was rather full and flabby, and yet it was not altogether a face without power. A few grog-blossoms marked the neighborhood of his nose. He flung back his long drab greatcoat, revealing that beneath it he wore a suit of cinder-gray shade throughout, large heavy seals, of some metal or other that would take a polish, dangling from his fob as his only personal ornament. Shaking the water drops from his low-crowned glazed hat, he said, "I must ask for a few minutes' shelter, comrades, or I shall be wetted to my skin before I get to Casterbridge."

"Make yourself at home, Master," said the shepherd, perhaps a trifle less heartily than on the first occasion. Not that Fennel had the least tinge of niggardliness in his composition; but the room was far from large, spare chairs were not numerous, and damp companions were not altogether desirable at close quarters for the women and girls in their bright-colored gowns.

However, the second comer, after taking off his greatcoat, and hanging his hat on a nail in one of the ceiling-beams as if he had been specially invited to put it there, advanced and sat down at the table. This had been pushed so closely into the chimney corner, to give all available room to the dancers, that its inner edge grazed the elbow of the man who had ensconced himself by the fire; and thus the two strangers were brought into close companionship. They nodded to each other by way of breaking the ice of unacquaintance, and the first stranger handed his neighbor the family mug—a huge vessel of brown ware, having its upper edge worn away like a threshold by the rub of whole generations of thirsty lips that had gone the way of all flesh, and bearing the following inscription burnt upon its rotund side in yellow letters:

THERE IS NO FUN
UNTiL i CUM.

The other man, nothing loth, raised the mug to his lips, and drank on, and on, and on—till a curious blueness overspread the countenance of the shepherd's wife, who had regarded with no little surprise the first stranger's free offer to the second of what did not belong to him to dispense.

"I knew it!" said the toper to the shepherd with much satisfaction. "When I walked up your garden before coming in, and saw the hives all of a row, I said to myself, 'Where there's bees there's honey, and where there's honey there's mead.' But mead of such a truly comfortable sort as this I really didn't expect to meet in my older days." He took yet another pull at the mug, till it assumed an ominous elevation.

"Glad you enjoy it!" said the shepherd warmly.

"It is goodish mead," assented Mrs. Fennel, with an absence of enthusiasm which seemed to say that it was possible to buy praise for one's cellar at too heavy a price. "It is trouble enough to make—and really I hardly think we shall make any more. For honey sells well, and we ourselves can make shift with a drop o' small mead and metheglin for common use from the comb-washings."

"Oh, but you'll never have the heart!" reproachfully cried the stranger in cinder-gray, after taking up the mug a third time and setting it down empty. "I love mead, when 'tis old like this, as I love to go to church o' Sundays, or to relieve the needy any day of the week."

"Ha, ha, ha!" said the man in the chimney corner, who, in spite of the taciturnity induced by the pipe of tobacco, could not or would not refrain from this slight testimony to his comrade's humor.

Now the old mead of those days, brewed of the purest first-year or maiden honey, four pounds to the gallon—with its due complement of white of eggs, cinnamon, ginger, cloves, mace, rosemary, yeast, and processes of working, bottling, and cellaring—tasted remarkably strong; but it did not taste so strong as it actually was. Hence, presently, the stranger in cinder-gray at the table, moved by its creeping influence, unbuttoned his waistcoat, threw himself back in his chair, spread his legs, and made his presence felt in various ways.

"Well, well, as I say," he resumed, "I am going to Casterbridge, and to Casterbridge I must go. I should have been almost there by this time; but the rain drove me into your dwelling, and I'm not sorry for it."

"You don't live in Casterbridge?" said the shepherd.

"Not as yet; though I shortly mean to move there."

"Going to set up in trade, perhaps?"

"No, no," said the shepherd's wife. "It is easy to see that the gentleman is rich, and don't want to work at anything."

The cinder-gray stranger paused, as if to consider whether he would accept that definition of himself. He presently rejected it by answering, "Rich is not quite the word for me, Dame. I do work, and I must work. And even if I only get to Casterbridge by midnight I must begin work there at eight tomorrow morning. Yes, het or wet, blow or snow, famine or sword, my day's work tomorrow must be done."

"Poor man! Then, in spite o' seeming, you be worse off than we," replied the shepherd's wife.

"'Tis the nature of my trade, men and maidens. 'Tis the nature of my trade more than my poverty. . . . But really and truly I must up and off, or I shan't get a lodging in the town." However, the speaker did not move, and directly added, "There's time for one more draught of friendship before I go; and I'd perform it at once if the mug were not dry."

"Here's a mug o' small," said Mrs. Fennel. "Small, we call it, though to be sure 'tis only the first wash o' the combs."

"No," said the stranger, disdainfully. "I won't spoil your first kindness by partaking o' your second."

"Certainly not," broke in Fennel. "We don't increase and multiply every day, and I'll fill the mug again." He went away to the dark place under the stairs where the barrel stood. The shepherdess followed him.

"Why should you do this?" she said, reproachfully, as soon as they were alone. "He's emptied it once, though it held enough for ten people; and now he's not contented wi' the small, but must needs call for more o' the strong! And a stranger unbeknown to any of us. For my part, I don't like the look o' the man at all."

"But he's in the house, my honey; and 'tis a wet night, and a christening. Daze it, what's a cup of mead more or less? There'll be plenty more next bee-burning."

"Very well—this time, then," she answered, looking wistfully at the barrel. "But what is the man's calling, and where is he one of, that he should come in and join us like this?"

"I don't know. I'll ask him again."

The catastrophe of having the mug drained dry at one pull by the stranger in cinder-gray was effectually guarded against this time by Mrs. Fennel. She poured out his allowance in a small cup, keeping the large one at a discreet distance from him. When he had tossed off his portion the shepherd renewed his inquiry about the stranger's occupation.

The latter did not immediately reply, and the man in the chimney corner, with sudden demonstrativeness, said, "Anybody may know my trade—I'm a wheelwright."

"A very good trade for these parts," said the shepherd.

"And anybody may know mine—if they've the sense to find it out," said the stranger in cinder-gray.

"You may generally tell what a man is by his claws," observed the hedge-carpenter, looking at his own hands. "My fingers be as full of thorns as an old pincushion is of pins."

The hands of the man in the chimney corner instinctively sought the shade, and he gazed into the fire as he resumed his pipe. The man at the table took up the hedge-carpenter's remark, and added smartly, "True; but the oddity of my trade is that, instead of setting a mark upon me, it sets a mark upon my customers."

No observation being offered by anybody in elucidation of this enigma, the shepherd's wife once more called for a song. The same obstacles presented themselves as at the former time—one had no voice, another had forgotten the first verse. The stranger at the table, whose soul had now risen to a good working temperature, relieved the difficulty by exclaiming that, to start the company, he would sing himself. Thrusting one thumb into the armhole of his waistcoat, he waved the other hand in the air, and, with an extemporizing gaze at the shining sheep-crooks above the mantelpiece, began:

> *O my trade it is the rarest one,*
> > *Simple shepherds all—*
> *My trade is a sight to see;*
> *For my customers I tie, and take them up on high,*
> *And waft 'em to a far countree!*

The room was silent when he had finished the verse—with one exception, that of the man in the chimney corner, who at the singer's word, "Chorus!" joined him in a deep bass voice of musical relish:

> *And waft 'em to a far countree!*

Oliver Giles, John Pitcher the dairyman, the parish-clerk, the engaged man of fifty, the row of young women against the wall, seemed lost in thought not of the gayest kind. The shepherd looked meditatively on the ground, the shepherdess gazed keenly at the singer, and with some suspicion; she was doubting whether this stranger were merely singing an old song from recollection, or was composing one there and then for the occasion. All were as perplexed at the obscure revelation as the guests at Belshazzar's Feast, except the man in the chimney corner, who quietly said, "Second verse, stranger," and smoked on.

The singer thoroughly moistened himself from his lips inward, and went on with the next stanza as requested:

> *My tools are but common ones,*
> > *Simple shepherds all—*
> *My tools are no sight to see:*
> *A little hempen string, and a post whereon to swing,*
> *Are implements enough for me!*

Shepherd Fennel glanced round. There was no longer any doubt that the stranger was answering his question rhythmically. The guests one and all started back with suppressed exclamations. The young woman engaged to the man of fifty fainted halfway, and would have proceeded, but finding him wanting in alacrity for catching her she sat down trembling.

"Oh, he's the—!" whispered the people in the background, mentioning the name of an ominous public officer. "He's come to do it! 'Tis to be at Caster-bridge jail tomorrow—the man for sheep-stealing—the poor clockmaker we heard of, who used to live away at Shottsford and had no work to do—Timothy Summers, whose family were astarving, and so he went out of Shottsford by the highroad, and took a sheep in open daylight, defying the farmer and the farmer's wife and the farmer's lad, and every man jack among 'em. He" (and they nodded toward the stranger of the deadly trade) "is come from up the country to do it because there's not enough to do in his own county-town, and he's got the place here, now our own country-man's dead; he's going to live in the same cottage under the prison wall."

The stranger in cinder-gray took no notice of this whispered string of observations, but again wetted his lips. Seeing that his friend in the chimney corner was the only one who reciprocated his joviality in any way, he held out his cup toward that appreciative comrade, who also held out his own. They clinked together, the eyes of the rest of the room hanging upon the singer's actions. He parted his lips for the third verse; but at that moment another knock was audible upon the door. This time the knock was faint and hesitating.

The company seemed scared; the shepherd looked with consternation to-ward the entrance, and it was with some effort that he resisted his alarmed wife's deprecatory glance, and uttered for the third time the welcoming words, "Walk in!"

The door was gently opened, and another man stood upon the mat. He, like those who had preceded him, was a stranger. This time it was a short, small personage, of fair complexion, and dressed in a decent suit of dark clothes.

"Can you tell me the way to—?" he began: when, gazing round the room to observe the nature of the company among whom he had fallen, his eyes lighted on the stranger in cinder-gray. It was just at the instant when the latter, who had thrown his mind into his song with such a will that he scarcely heeded the interruption, silenced all whispers and inquiries by bursting into his third verse:

> *Tomorrow is my working day,*
> > *Simple shepherds all—*
> *Tomorrow is a working day for me:*
> *For the farmer's sheep is slain, and the lad who did it ta'en,*
> *And on his soul may God ha' merc-y!*

The stranger in the chimney corner, waving cups with the singer so heartily that his mead splashed over on the hearth, repeated in his bass voice as before:

> *And on his soul may God ha' merc-y!*

All this time the third stranger had been standing in the doorway. Finding now that he did not come forward or go on speaking, the guests particularly regarded him. They noticed to their surprise that he stood before them, the picture of abject terror—his knees trembling, his hand shaking so violently that the door-latch by which he supported himself rattled audibly: his white lips were parted, and his eyes fixed on the merry officer of justice in the middle of the room. A moment more and he had turned, closed the door, and fled.

"What a man can it be?" said the shepherd.

The rest, between the awfulness of their late discovery and the odd conduct of this third visitor, looked as if they knew not what to think, and said nothing. Instinctively they withdrew further and further from the grim gentleman in their midst, whom some of them seemed to take for the Prince of Darkness himself, till they formed a remote circle, an empty space of floor being left between them and him—

> . . . circulas, cujus centrum diabolus.

The room was so silent—though there were more than twenty people in it—that nothing could be heard but the patter of the rain against the window-shutters, accompanied by the occasional hiss of a stray drop that fell down the chimney into the fire, and the steady puffing of the man in the corner, who had now resumed his pipe of long clay.

The stillness was unexpectedly broken. The distant sound of a gun reverberated through the air—apparently from the direction of the county-town.

"Be jiggered!" cried the stranger who had sung the song, jumping up.

"What does that mean?" asked several.

"A prisoner escaped from the jail—that's what it means."

All listened. The sound was repeated, and none of them spoke but the man in the chimney corner, who said quietly, "I've often been told that in this county they fire a gun at such times; but I never heard it till now."

"I wonder if it is *my* man?" murmured the personage in cinder-gray.

"Surely it is!" said the shepherd involuntarily. "And surely we've zeed him! That little man who looked in at the door by now, and quivered like a leaf when he zeed ye and heard your song!"

"His teeth chattered, and the breath went out of his body," said the dairyman.

"And his heart seemed to sink within him like a stone," said Oliver Giles.

"And he bolted as if he'd been shot at," said the hedge-carpenter.

"True—his teeth chattered, and his heart seemed to sink; and he bolted as if he'd been shot at," slowly summed up the man in the chimney corner.

"I didn't notice it," remarked the hangman.

"We were all awondering what made him run off in such a fright," faltered one of the women against the wall, "and now 'tis explained!"

The firing of the alarm-gun went on at intervals, low and sullenly, and their suspicions became a certainty. The sinister gentleman in cinder-gray roused himself. "Is there a constable here?" he asked, in thick tones. "If so, let him step forward."

The engaged man of fifty stepped quavering out from the wall, his betrothed beginning to sob on the back of the chair.

"You are a sworn constable?"

"I be, Sir."

"Then pursue the criminal at once, with assistance, and bring him back here. He can't have gone far."

"I will, Sir, I will—when I've got my staff. I'll go home and get it, and come sharp here, and start in a body."

"Staff!—never mind your staff; the man'll be gone!"

"But I can't do nothing without my staff—can I, William, and John, and Charles Jake? No; for there's the king's royal crown apainted on en in yaller and gold, and the lion and the unicorn, so as when I raise en up and hit my prisoner, 'tis made a lawful blow thereby. I wouldn't 'tempt to take up a man without my staff—no, not I. If I hadn't the law to gie me courage, why, instead o' my taking up him he might take up me!"

"Now, I'm a king's man myself, and can give you authority enough for this," said the formidable officer in gray. "Now then, all of ye, be ready. Have ye any lanterns?"

"Yes—have ye any lanterns?—I demand it!" said the constable.

"And the rest of you able-bodied—"

"Able-bodied men—yes—the rest of ye!" said the constable.

"Have you some good stout staves and pitchforks—"

"Staves and pitchforks—in the name o' the law! And take 'em in yer hands and go in quest, and do as we in authority tell ye!"

Thus aroused, the men prepared to give chase. The evidence was, indeed, though circumstantial, so convincing, that but little argument was needed to show the shepherd's guests that after what they had seen it would look very much like connivance if they did not instantly pursue the unhappy third stranger, who could not as yet have gone more than a few hundred yards over such uneven country.

A shepherd is always well provided with lanterns; and, lighting these hastily, and with hurdle-staves in their hands, they poured out of the door, taking a direction along the crest of the hill, away from the town, the rain having fortunately a little abated.

Disturbed by the noise, or possibly by unpleasant dreams of her baptism, the child who had been christened began to cry heartbrokenly in the room overhead. These notes of grief came down through the chinks of the floor to the ears of the women below, who jumped up one by one, and seemed glad of the excuse to ascend and comfort the baby, for the incidents of the last half-hour greatly oppressed them. Thus in the space of two or three minutes the room on the ground-floor was deserted quite.

But it was not for long. Hardly had the sound of footsteps died away when a man returned round the corner of the house from the direction the pursuers had taken. Peeping in at the door and seeing nobody there, he entered leisurely. It was the stranger of the chimney corner, who had gone out with the rest. The motive of his return was shown by his helping himself to a cut piece of skimmer-cake that lay on a ledge beside where he had sat, and which he had apparently forgotten to take with him. He also poured out half a cup more mead from the quantity that remained, ravenously eating and drinking these as he stood. He had not finished when another figure came in just as quietly—his friend in cinder-gray.

"Oh—you here?" said the latter, smiling. "I thought you had gone to help in the capture." And this speaker also revealed the object of his return by looking solicitously round for the fascinating mug of old mead.

"And I thought you had gone," said the other, continuing his skimmer-cake with some effort.

"Well, on second thoughts, I felt there were enough without me," said the first confidentially, "and such a night as it is, too. Besides, 'tis the business o' the Government to take care of its criminals—not mine."

"True; so it is. And I felt as you did, that there were enough without me."

"I don't want to break my limbs running over the humps and hollows of this wild country."

"Nor I neither, between you and me."

"These shepherd-people are used to it—simple-minded souls, you know, stirred up to anything in a moment. They'll have him ready for me before the morning, and no trouble to me at all."

"They'll have him, and we shall have saved ourselves all labor in the matter."

"True, true. Well, my way is to Casterbridge; and 'tis as much as my legs will do to take me that far. Going the same way?"

"No, I am sorry to say! I have to get home over there" (he nodded indefinitely to the right), "and I feel as you do, that it is quite enough for my legs to do before bedtime."

The other had by this time finished the mead in the mug, after which, shaking hands heartily at the door, and wishing each other well, they went their several ways.

In the meantime the company of pursuers had reached the end of the hog's-back elevation which dominated this part of the down. They had decided on no particular plan of action; and, finding that the man of the baleful trade was no longer in their company, they seemed quite unable to form any such plan now. They descended in all directions down the hill, and straightway several of the party fell into the snare set by Nature for all misguided midnight ramblers over this part of the cretaceous formation. The "lanchets," or flint slopes, which belted the escarpment at intervals of a dozen yards, took the less cautious ones unawares, and losing their footing on the rubbly steep they slid sharply downward, the lanterns rolling from their hands to the bottom, and there lying on their sides till the horn was scorched through.

When they had again gathered themselves together, the shepherd, as the man who knew the country best, took the lead, and guided them round these treacherous inclines. The lanterns, which seemed rather to dazzle their eyes and warn the fugitive than to assist them in the exploration, were extinguished, due silence was observed; and in this more rational order they plunged into the vale. It was a grassy, briery, moist defile, affording some shelter to any person who had sought it; but the party perambulated it in vain, and ascended on the other side. Here they wandered apart, and after an interval closed together again to report progress. At the second time of closing in they found themselves near a lonely ash, the single tree on this part of the coomb, probably sown there by a passing bird some fifty years before. And here, standing a little to one side of the trunk, as motionless as the trunk itself appeared the man they were in quest of, his outline being well defined against the sky beyond. The band noiselessly drew up and faced him.

"Your money or your life!" said the constable sternly to the still figure.

"No, no," whispered John Pitcher. " 'Tisn't our side ought to say that. That's the doctrine of vagabonds like him, and we be on the side of the law."

"Well, well," replied the constable, impatiently; "I must say something, mustn't I? and if you had all the weight o' this undertaking upon your mind, perhaps you'd say the wrong thing, too!—Prisoner at the bar, surrender in the name of the Father—the Crown, I mane!"

The man under the tree seemed now to notice them for the first time, and, giving them no opportunity whatever for exhibiting their courage, he strolled slowly toward them. He was, indeed, the little man, the third stranger; but his trepidation had in a great measure gone.

"Well, travelers," he said, "did I hear you speak to me?"

"You did; you've got to come and be our prisoner at once!" said the constable. "We arrest 'ee on the charge of not biding in Casterbridge jail in a decent proper manner to be hung tomorrow morning. Neighbors, do your duty, and seize the culpet!"

On hearing the charge, the man seemed enlightened, and, saying not another word, resigned himself with preternatural civility to the search-party, who, with their staves in their hands, surrounded him on all sides, and marched him back toward the shepherd's cottage.

It was eleven o'clock by the time they arrived. The light shining from the open door, a sound of men's voices within, proclaimed to them as they approached the house that some new events had arisen in their absence. On entering they discovered the shepherd's living-room to be invaded by two officers from Casterbridge jail, and a well-known magistrate who lived at the nearest country-seat, intelligence of the escape having become generally circulated.

"Gentlemen," said the constable, "I have brought back your man—not without risk and danger; but every one must do his duty! He is inside this circle of able-bodied persons, who have lent me useful aid, considering their ignorance of Crown work.—Men, bring forward your prisoner!" And the third stranger was led to the light.

"Who is this?" said one of the officials.

"The man," said the constable.

"Certainly not," said the turnkey; and the first corroborated his statement.

"But how can it be otherwise?" asked the constable. "Or why was he so terrified at sight o' the singing instrument of the law who sat there?" Here he related the strange behavior of the third stranger on entering the house during the hangman's song.

"Can't understand it," said the officer coolly. "All I know is that it is not the condemned man. He's quite a different character from this one; a gaunt-ish fellow, with dark hair and eyes, rather good-looking, and with a musical bass voice that if you heard it once you'd never mistake as long as you lived."

"Why, souls—'twas the man in the chimney corner!"

"Hey—what?" said the magistrate, coming forward after inquiring particulars from the shepherd in the background. "Haven't you got the man after all?"

"Well, Sir," said the constable, "he's the man we were in search of, that's true; and yet he's not the man we were in search of. For the man we were in search of was not the man we wanted, Sir, if you understand my everyday way; for 'twas the man in the chimney corner!"

"A pretty kettle of fish altogether!" said the magistrate. "You had better start for the other man at once."

The prisoner now spoke for the first time. The mention of the man in the chimney corner seemed to have moved him as nothing else could do. "Sir," he said, stepping forward to the magistrate, "take no more trouble about me. The time is come when I may as well speak. I have done nothing; my crime is that the condemned man is my brother. Early this afternoon I left home at Shottsford to tramp it all the way to Casterbridge jail to bid him farewell. I was benighted, and called here to rest and ask the way. When I opened the door I saw before me the very man, my brother, that I thought to see in the condemned cell at Casterbridge. He was in this chimney corner; and jammed close to him, so that he could not have got out if he had tried, was the executioner who'd come to take his life, singing a song about it and not knowing that it was his victim who was close by, joining in to save appearances. My brother looked a glance of agony at me, and I know he meant, 'Don't reveal what you see; my life depends on it.' I was so terror-struck that I could hardly stand, and, not knowing what I did, I turned and hurried away."

The narrator's manner and tone had the stamp of truth, and his story made a great impression on all around. "And do you know where your brother is at the present time?" asked the magistrate.

"I do not. I have never seen him since I closed this door."

"I can testify to that, for we've been between ye ever since," said the constable.

"Where does he think to fly to?—what is his occupation?"

"He's a watch-and-clock-maker, Sir."

"'A said 'a was a wheelwright—a wicked rogue," said the constable.

"The wheels of clocks and watches he meant, no doubt," said Shepherd Fennel. "I thought his hands were palish for's trade."

"Well, it appears to me that nothing can be gained by retaining this poor man in custody," said the magistrate; "your business lies with the other, un-questionably."

And so the little man was released off-hand; but he looked nothing the less sad on that account, it being beyond the power of magistrate or constable to raze out the written troubles in his brain, for they concerned another whom he regarded with more solicitude than himself. When this was done, and the man had gone his way, the night was found to be so far advanced that it was deemed useless to renew the search before the next morning.

Next day, accordingly, the quest for the clever sheep-stealer became general and keen, to all appearance at least. But the intended punishment was cruelly disproportioned to the transgression, and the sympathy of a great many country-folk in that district was strongly on the side of the fugitive. Moreover, his marvelous coolness and daring in hob-and-nobbing with the hangman, under the unprecedented circumstances of the shepherd's party, won their admiration. So that it may be questioned if all those who ostensibly made themselves so busy in exploring woods and fields and lanes were quite so thorough when it came to the private examination of their own lofts and outhouses. Stories were afloat of a mysterious figure being occasionally seen in some old overgrown trackway or other, remote from turnpike roads, but when a search was instituted in any of these suspected quarters nobody was found. Thus the days and weeks passed without tidings.

In brief, the bass-voiced man of the chimney corner was never recaptured. Some said that he went across the sea, others that he did not, but buried himself in the depths of a populous city. At any rate, the gentleman in cinder-gray never did his morning's work at Casterbridge, nor met anywhere at all, for business purposes, the genial comrade with whom he had passed an hour of relaxation in the lonely house on the coomb.

The grass has long been green on the graves of Shepherd Fennel and his frugal wife; the guests who made up the christening party have mainly fol-lowed their entertainers to the tomb; the baby in whose honor they all had met is a matron in the sere and yellow leaf. But the arrival of the three strangers at the shepherd's that night, and the details connected therewith, is a story as well-known as ever in the country about Higher Crowstairs.

THE OLD MAN

HOLLOWAY HORN

1931

MARTIN THOMPSON was not a desirable character. He possessed a clever, plausible tongue, and for years past had lived, with no little success, on his wits. He had promoted doubtful boxing competitions and still more doubtful sweepstakes. He had been a professional backer, in which capacity he had defrauded the bookies; again, a bookmaker who had swindled his "clients." There was more cunning than imagination in his outlook, but, within his limits, he possessed a certain distorted ability.

He was known to his intimates as Knocker Thompson, and as such had a surprisingly wide reputation. In outward appearance he was a gentleman, for long experience had taught him to avoid the flashy and distinctive in dress. Indeed, his quiet taste had often proved a valuable business asset.

Naturally, his fortunes varied, but he was usually more or less in funds. As Knocker sometimes said in his more genial moments: "For every mug that dies there's ten others born."

Funds were rather low, however, on the evening when he met the old man. Knocker had spent the early part of the evening with two acquaintances in a hotel near Leicester Square. It was a business meeting, and relations had been a little strained; opinions had been freely expressed which indicated a complete lack of confidence in Knocker, and an unmistakable atmosphere had resulted. Not that he *resented* the opinions in the least, but at that juncture he *needed* the unquestioned trust of the two men.

He was not in the best of humours, therefore, as he turned into Whitcomb Street on his way to Charing Cross. The normal plainness of his features was deepened by a scowl, and the general result startled the few people who glanced at him.

But at eight o'clock in the evening, Whitcomb Street is not a crowded thoroughfare, and there was no one near them when the old man spoke to him. He was standing in a passage near the Pall Mall end, and Knocker could not see him clearly.

"Hullo, Knocker!" he said.

Reprinted by permission of the author and Christy & Moore, Ltd.

Thompson swung round.

In the darkness he made out the dim figure, the most conspicuous feature of which was a long, white beard.

"Hullo!" returned Thompson, suspiciously, for as far as he knew he did not number among his acquaintances an old man with a white beard.

"It's cold . . ." said the old man.

"What d'you want?" asked Thompson curtly. "Who are you?"

"I am an old man, Knocker."

"Look here, what's the game? I don't know you . . ."

"No. But I know you."

"If that's all you've got to say . . ." said Knocker uneasily.

"It is nearly all. Will you buy a paper? It is not an ordinary paper, I assure you."

"How do you mean . . . not an ordinary paper?"

"It is to-morrow night's *Echo*," said the old man calmly.

"You're loopy, old chap, that's what's wrong with you. Look here, things aren't too brisk, but here's half a dollar . . . and better luck!" For all his lack of principle, Knocker had the crude generosity of those who live precariously.

"Luck!" The old man laughed with a quietness that jarred on Knocker's nerves. In some queer way it seemed to run up and down his spine.

"Look here!" he said again, conscious of some strange, unreal quality in the old, dimly-seen figure in the passage. "What's the blinking game?"

"It is the oldest game in the world, Knocker."

"Not so free with my name . . . if you don't mind."

"Are you ashamed of it?"

"No," said Knocker stoutly. "What do you want? I've got no time to waste with the likes of you."

"Then go . . . Knocker."

"What do you *want?*" Knocker insisted, strangely uneasy.

"Nothing. Won't you take the paper? There is no other like it in the world. Nor will there be—for twenty-four hours."

"I don't suppose there *are* many of to-morrow's papers on sale . . . yet," said Knocker with a grin.

"It contains to-morrow's winners," said the old man, in the same casual manner.

"I don't think!" retorted Knocker.

"There it is; you may read for yourself."

From the darkness a paper was thrust at Knocker, whose unwilling fingers closed on it. A laugh came from somewhere in the recesses in the passage, and Knocker was alone.

He was suddenly and uncomfortably aware of his beating heart, but gripped himself and walked on until he came to a lighted shop front where he glanced at the paper.

"Thursday, July 29, 1926 . . ." he read.

He thought a moment.

It was Wednesday . . . he was positive it was Wednesday. He took out his diary. It was Wednesday, the twenty-eighth day of July—the last day of the Kempton Park meeting. He had no doubt on the point, none whatever.

With a strange feeling he glanced at the paper again. July 29, 1926. He turned to the back page almost instinctively—the page with the racing results. Gatwick. . . .

That day's meeting was at Kempton Park. To-morrow was the first day of the Gatwick meeting, and there, staring at him, were the five winners. He passed his hand across his forehead; it was damp with cold perspiration.

"There's a trick somewhere," he muttered to himself, and carefully re-examined the date of the paper. It was printed on each page . . . clear and unaltered. He scrutinised the unit figure of the year, but the "six" had not been tampered with.

He glanced hurriedly at the front page. There was a flaring headline about the Coal Strike . . . that wasn't twenty-*five*. With professional care he ex-amined the racing results. Inkerman had won the first race . . . Inkerman—and Knocker had made up his mind to back Paper Clip with more money than he could afford to lose. Paper Clip was merely an also-ran. He noticed that people who passed were glancing at him curiously. Hurriedly he pushed the paper into an inner pocket and walked on.

Never had Knocker so needed a drink. He entered a snug little "pub" near Charing Cross and was thankful to find the saloon bar nearly deserted. Forti-fied with his drink he turned again to the paper. Inkerman had come home at 6 to 1. He made certain hurried but satisfactory calculations. Salmon House had won the second; he had expected that, but not at such a price . . . 7 to 4 on. Shallot—Shallot of all horses!—had romped away with the third, the big race. Seven lengths . . . at 100 to 8! Knocker licked his dry lips. There was no fake about the paper in his hand. He knew the horses that were running at Gatwick the following day and the results were there before him. The fourth and fifth winners were at short prices; but Inkerman and Shallot were enough . . .

It was too late to get into touch with any of the bookmakers that evening, and in any case it would not be advisable to put money on before the day of the race. The better way would be to go to Gatwick in the morning and wire the bets from the course.

He had another drink . . . and another.

Gradually, in the genial atmosphere of the saloon bar, his uneasiness left him. The affair ceased to appear uncanny and grotesque, and became a part of the casual happenings of the day. Into Knocker's slightly fuddled brain came the memory of a film he had once seen which had made a big impres-sion on him at the time. There was an Eastern magician in the film, with a white beard, a long, white beard just like the one belonging to the old man. The magician had done the most extraordinary things . . . on the screen.

But whatever the explanation, Knocker was satisfied it was not a fake. The old chap had not asked for any money; indeed, he had not even taken the half-crown that Knocker had offered him. And as Knocker knew, you always collected the dibs—or attempted to—if you were running a fake.

He thought pleasantly of what he would do in the ring at Gatwick the following day. He was in rather low water, but he could put his hands on just about enough to make the bookies sit up. And with a second winner at 100 to 8!

He had still another drink and stood the barman one too.

"D'you know anything for to-morrow?" The man behind the bar knew Thompson quite well by sight and reputation.

Knocker hesitated.

"Yes," he said. "Sure thing. Salmon House in the second race. Price'll be a bit short, but it's a snip."

"Thanks very much; I'll have a bit on meself."

Ultimately he left the saloon bar. He was a little shaky; his doctor had warned him not to drink, but surely on such a night . . .

The following morning he went to Gatwick. It was a meeting he liked, and usually he was very lucky there. But that day it was not merely a question of luck. There was a streak of caution in his bets on the first race, but he flung caution to the wind after Inkerman had come in a comfortable winner —*and at* 6 *to* 1. The horse and the price! He had no doubts left. Salmon House won the second, a hot favourite at 7 to 4 on.

In the big race most of the punters left Shallot alone. The horse had little form, and there was no racing reason why anyone should back him. He was among what the bookies call "the Rags." But Knocker cared nothing for "form" that day. He spread his money judiciously. Twenty here, twenty there. Not until ten minutes before the race did he wire any money to the West End offices, but some of the biggest men in the game opened their eyes when his wires came through. He was out to win a fortune. And he won.

As the horses entered the straight one of them was lengths ahead of the field. It carried the flashing yellow and blue of Shallot's owner. The groan that went up from the punters around him was satisfactory, but there was no thrill in the race for him; he had been certain that Shallot would win. There was no objection . . . and he proceeded to collect.

His pockets were bulging with notes, but his winnings were as nothing compared with the harvest he would reap from the big men in the West End. He ordered a bottle of champagne, and with a silent grin drank the health of the old man with the beard before he sent for the taxi that would take him back to the station. There was no train for half-an-hour, and, when at last it started, his carriage had filled with racing men, among whom were several he knew. The wiser race-goers rarely wait until the end of a meeting.

Knocker was usually very expansive after a good day, but that afternoon he took no part in the conversation, with the exception of an occasional grunt when a remark was made to him. Try as he would he could not keep his thoughts away from the old man. It was the memory of the laugh that remained with him most vividly. He could still feel that queer sensation down his spine. . . .

On a sudden impulse he took out the paper, which was still in his pocket.

He had no real interest in news, as such, for racing absorbed the whole of his very limited imagination. As far as he could tell from a casual inspection it was a very ordinary sort of paper. He made up his mind to get another in town and compare the two in order to see if the old man had spoken the truth. Not that it mattered very much, he assured himself.

Suddenly his incurious glance was held. A paragraph in the stop-press column had caught his eye. An exclamation burst from him.

"Death in race-train," the paragraph was headed. Knocker's heart was pumping, but he read on mechanically: "Mr. Martin Thompson, a well-known racing man, died this afternoon as he was returning from Gatwick."

He got no further; the paper fell from his limp fingers on to the floor of the carriage.

"Look at Knocker," someone said. "He's ill . . ."

He was breathing heavily and with difficulty.

"Stop . . . stop the train," he gasped, and strove to rise and lurch towards the communication cord.

"Steady on, Knocker," one of them said, and grasped his arm. "You sit down, old chap . . . mustn't pull that darned thing . . ."

He sat down . . . or rather collapsed into the seat. His head fell forward. They forced whisky between his lips, but it was of no avail.

"He's dead," came the awestruck voice of the man who held him.

No one noticed the paper on the floor. In the general upset it had been kicked under the seat, and it is not possible to say what became of it. Perhaps it was swept up by the cleaners at Waterloo.

Perhaps . . .

No one knows.

THE ROLLICKING GOD

NUNNALLY JOHNSON

HERE and now, before the high bar of public opinion, I charge Marshall Mount of the New York Sphere and Smack Riley of the Grays with having cost the Grays the pennant last year.

You know Mount, of course. You've been pestered undoubtedly with quotations from his column, In My Humble Opinion, which appears on the Sphere's sporting page each morning.

"Did you see what Marshall Mount said about Benny Leonard—how he said Benny is the Saint-Saëns of the ring?" Or, as likely as not, you quote him yourself. "What do you think of Marshall Mount's calling Hank Gowdy the Schopenhauer of the diamond?" Stuff like that.

And as for Smack, who doesn't know him and his big bat?

These, then, are the facts, the evidence:

It was in April, during the first home series at the Stadium, that I met Mount, a tall, lanky, frowzy young fellow, shambling a little and with no taste whatever in neckties. He slid into a working-press seat at my side. At first, never having seen him before, I took him to be just another actor, one with more nerve than usual. He had a kind of embarrassed air, and as he sat down he dropped a couple of new books which, I suppose, he'd brought along to read during the more exciting parts of the game. When he leaned over to pick them up he dropped three pencils out of his pocket, and while picking up the pencils he dropped a notebook, three letters, a pocket comb, two moth balls and a baby's nursing bottle. He was that kind of bird.

"You ought to tie all those things to you with strings," I said, "or else carry a postman's satchel."

"I don't know," he replied doubtfully, weighing the suggestions. "They never dropped out before. At least, not so many of them at once. Have you got a cigarette?"

There's no man living can call me a tightwad, so I gave him one. Then it occurred to me, after witnessing his search through every pocket and the nursing bottle, that he needed a match. He thanked me, lit the cigarette and produced a score book.

The game that day was, as I said next morning in the Ledger, a wow. It seesawed for a while, and then in the end good old Smack Riley ambled up to the pan, leaned on one of Coveleskie's fast ones, and sweet COOKIE!— into the Harlem River, or nearly. It was the Smacker's first homer of the season at the Stadium.

I've learned pretty well to control myself in crises like this, for if we baseball writers aren't calm, who will be? But this fellow on my left, this Mount, sprang to his feet, spilling his books, his pencils and three new and theretofore undiscovered moth balls, and let out a roar:

"Beautiful!"

Honestly, I just looked at him.

"What did you say?" I asked.

"I say he's beautiful, positively beautiful!"

"If you mean Smack"—and any man in the Ledger office will tell you whether I can be sarcastic or not—"then you ought to wait and see Nick Altrock."

He looked actually impatient—and me the dean of sporting writers!

"His swing," he explained; "the way he threw his body into that terrific effort. It was just a flash, the fraction of a second of it; but it was rhythm, grace, beauty. It reminded me, truly, of Walter Pater—just for that instant."

As my friends will tell you, I am a plain man, a baseball reporter with no frills. What this bird was talking about I did not know. Smack had hit a home run. The game belonged to the Grays. What else was going on, I, speaking personally, could not see.

"Beautiful!" he repeated. "I never had any idea that a baseball player could crystallize so much of authentic glory in one movement."

"What are you, anyway," I demanded—"one of these poets?"

"Oh, excuse me," he replied hastily—we were getting our stuff together to climb out. "My name is Mount. I'm from the Sphere. I'm going to cover the Grays for a while." Then he added, as though to himself, "All season, I hope. I'd like to see that fellow again. It was marvelous, that swing."

"Well," I said amiably, for after all he was one of us baseball reporters, "as long as they don't come three at a time it's jake with me."

As he climbed up the stairs to the runway his left garter broke and dragged on the ground behind him.

I may as well add right here that as the season went along I found out that that fellow found all that beauty he was talking about in strikes as well as home runs. One day I remember he wrote:

"There is a strength in one of Riley's swings, even when he misses the ball, that holds all the coördination of which the human body is capable. In this ball player's mighty failures there is a lesson for our young playwrights, a lesson that Eugene O'Neill has already learned. We believe that we had rather see Smack Riley strike out than any other player make a hit. Life is not so much what one gains as what one tries for."

Right then and there he ought to have been hanged.

The next morning after that meeting I looked up his story. Well, I clipped it out. I was going to save it for the Smithsonian Institution. It was what one might easily call a jewel. What he had said at the Stadium about Smack Riley's beauty was just a suggestion of what he had to say in his story about it. Grace, ease, coördinated effort, rhythm, beauty—all that was in a baseball story. Furthermore, in that same story there were two mentions of George Bernard Shaw, one each of Rudolph Valentino, Lord Dunsany, Man o' War, Professor Copeland of Harvard, and seven of Eugene O'Neill. He included also three actresses, two books and five plays. The only way you could tell it was a baseball story was the box score at the end; and, honestly, when I looked I half expected to find a cast of characters. As I said, I was going to save it, but a week later I threw it away. All his stories turned out to be like that.

That afternoon I went to Harry Kelly of the Blade.

"Who is this Mount?" I said. "And what theater does he think today's game is being played in?"

Harry wasn't sure. Mount had come from Rutgers, he said, had lived south of Washington Square and had written two one-act plays, the kind that are produced by companies that are just a lot of æsthetes together, giving everything for art, gratis. He'd been on the Sphere two years. First he was rewriting, but they'd had to take him off that. Every story he wrote, whether it was about a five-legged calf in Lima, Ohio, or a fire on the Brooklyn water front, contained at least one reference to Ethel Barrymore's speaking voice, one to the Russian ballet and two to Jeritza. Subsequently they'd had to lift him out of the financial department after he'd included an essay on the art of Bozo Snyder, the burlesque comedian, in a story purporting to tell the fall of the French franc.

"Well," I said, "it looks to me as though he were going to be just as great a loss here."

The way I figured it was that those that knew Saint-Saëns and Schopenhauer didn't know Benny Leonard and Hank Gowdy, and those that knew Benny and Hank didn't care who Saint-Saëns and Schopenhauer were.

I went back to my seat. Down the rail, just next to the Grays' dugout, was Mount. Hanging on the rail, listening to him and all attention, was Smack Riley. They talked until the Grays went out to the field for the first inning.

"Some story you had this morning," I said when Mount came over. Honestly, I couldn't go any further than that.

"Oh!" He seemed surprised. "Glad you liked it." His eyes followed Smack, loping out to right. "That man," he said, "is a genuine artist."

"Smack Riley!" I exclaimed. "Get out! Smack Riley never drew a line in his life!"

He didn't have a word to say to that, of course, for I had him dead to rights. I'd known Smack from the day he reached the Grays' training camp five years before, and if he was an artist then I'm a dry-point etcher.

II

Personally speaking, I'll admit I never saw anything in the way of baseball reporting in my life like that stuff Mount shot over last season. That first day's story was just a hint of what was coming. In August he started that column of his, In My Humble Opinion, on the sporting page of the Sphere. Evidently he had permission to write about anything on this earth; but mostly, I imagine, he was expected to write about sports. Pretty soon it began to look like a serial appreciation of Smack Riley the artist, Smack Riley the æsthete, Smack Riley the Walter Pater of the diamond.

He wrote as if baseball had just been invented. All kinds of art and artistry that everybody had always overlooked, Mount found and wrote about —the way Ty Cobb, whom I usually call the Georgia Peach, started for first; the way Tris Speaker played the outfield; the way George Sisler took a high one. Eugene O'Neills of the diamond, Lord Dunsanys of the diamond, Wedekinds of the diamond, Wagners—Richard—of the diamond. And once when he didn't approve of a fellow he wrote that he was the Harold Bell Wright of the diamond, which seemed to be the only thing he could think of to call O'Hara. Next day he came to the Stadium in a nervous sweat.

"Do you suppose," he worried, "that O'Hara will be insulted at what I wrote? I did it, I'm afraid, a little hastily."

I assured him that Tad O'Hara had probably never heard of but three Wrights in his life—one being an old-time second baseman and the two others the aviators.

I read his stuff every day. Practically everything in it was over my head, but—well, it was a curiosity. I'd be the last person in the world to say anything against æsthetics. To a certain extent it is all right, none better, and nobody is a heartier supporter of the arts than I; but when it came to saying, over and over again, how beautiful Smack Riley was when he struck out— well——

The two soon got to be prime buddies, and when the team took the road in May the acquaintanceship took up so much of Smack's time that our three-year-old poker foursome, consisting of Harry Kelly, Matthews, the second-string catcher, Smack and me, was broken up. Smack was out, always, with something very important to talk over, in whispers, with Marshall Mount. They talked all the way to St. Louis that trip, and I'd never have guessed that Smack knew that many words.

They were that way throughout the season. It was art that brought them together. In Washington, Mount took Smack to the Corcoran Art Gallery, in Chicago, to the Chicago Museum. But as long as the old mace, as I called it, whanged away at the ball with as much success as it did, neither I nor Hall Miller, the manager, cared. Artist or no artist, the big bum was hitting 'em straight and hard, day after day, and what a home-run record he was piling up!

The sporting writers were, of course, giving a good third of their space to him; but what was funny, one of the highbrow weeklies ran a story about him. Mr. Smack Riley, it was called. By Marshall Mount, of course. It was the same stuff—form, rhythm, grace, force, coördination, beauty.

I got to calling Mount Smack's Boswell. Being literary too, he got it right off, and smiled. But Smack wouldn't take any kidding. "This Mount is a artist," he declared; "a artist of the first water."

We tried a little ragging, but Smack was for busting somebody on the ear.

"Well," I said, "speaking personally, I think you're off your nut." I told him right out, the big bum!

I was sure of it a few days later when I caught him reading Primal Grace by a fellow with a name not less than Greek. His face got red.

"If you say anything about this, you big bum," he said, "I'll knock you for a row of stumps." I came right back at him.

"I'm not going to say anything about it, you big bum," I said; "but don't think your threats have anything to do with it, you big bum."

He didn't say anything else, but I didn't want any hard feelings.

"Look here, Smack," I said, "we've been pretty good friends. Let's don't let art come between us. Now what's all this racket?"

Smack laid Primal Grace down.

"Mapes," he said, "I reckon the gang is a little sore; but look, Mount's right about this thing. There is an art to baseball. It's got all the qualities of epict drama. Some day people are going to see it and they're going to put up statues to baseball players in museums and things, like the old Greeks put them up to discus players and javerin throwers.

"Mapes," he said, "I've seen the handwriting on the wall. I'm going to get one of them statues. I'm going to get the first one. I'm going to be the first artist of the game, the first native American athaletic artist. I'm giving all my thoughts——"

All of Smack's thoughts!

"—all my thoughts to it." He fished into his pocket. "Look here." He handed me some manuscript paper. "See that? That's a part I'm going to play in a show."

I looked at it. It was labeled, Gods Athirst, a Masque. A cast of characters, gods, maidens, and Smack's part, Arno, a Rollicking God. I couldn't help it. I've got no more control over my face than the next fellow. I laughed. The peace negotiations fell through.

"Gimme"—Smack was snarling—"gimme that manuscript! What could anybody expect from a boob like you? What d'you know about art, or anything else for that matter? I got a good mind to soak you."

"Go ahead, you big bum," I retorted, but he didn't.

III

By the time the pennant race was in what I called its last stages, Smack was an acknowledged artist. That is, other artists were acknowledging him. To give Mount no more than his due, he certainly sold Smack to the highbrow crowd.

Once they had him down in Greenwich Village to speak on The Human Body—As it is and as it Should Be. Greenwich Village! And to art students! Personally speaking, the English language means nothing to me. I'm not its protector. It can get in trouble and stay in trouble for all I care. But truly, it's wicked to do things to it that Smack does. It tears my heart out. I'm that sympathetic when Smack gets hold of five words in close succession. For when he gets through with them you couldn't get twenty pfennigs for them, even in the Balkan States, where they need languages so much.

But Smack got away with it. "Gorgeously naïve" was the way Mount described it the next day, and "the simple truth of an authentic artist" was what Smack had to say on human grace and rhythm.

Somebody took motion pictures of him. He posed in a tiger skin for a magazine on physical culture. And another magazine, so fine that up to that time it had run nothing but art photographs of Mary Pickford, Billie Burke and Irene Castle, published a full-page mood study of our bucko. A mood study!

And then he made his appearance as Arno a Rollicking God in Gods Athirst at the Artists' Playhouse, down in the Village. The Grays had reached town a few days before from the final swing around the circuit. Leading by four games and with the gang playing championship ball every minute, the old gonfalon, as I sometimes call it, seemed sewed up. Smack, the big bum, was whanging away in great shape, with the old home runs clicking every four or five days and plenty of singles between. It looked pretty rosy for the Grays when the Gulls hit town for that last series of six games. Four games behind the Grays, the Gulls did not look like a very serious menace.

I went early that night to the Artists' Playhouse. Anybody who knows where I rank in artistic circles will be able to tell you whether I got an invitation or not. It was very exclusive, the door man told me, and not even J. P. Morgan himself could get in without an invitation. So that meant, of course, that I had to slip him a simoleon.

The Artists' Playhouse was a dump if ever there was one. If you can imagine a theater different from the Hippodrome in every respect, bar none, you know what the Artists' Playhouse looked like. Mount was already there, down front, talking to a couple of bloods wearing orange ties. I took a back seat, where I wouldn't be seen and thrown out on charges of cleanliness. The place filled up. The audience consisted of frowzy men and frowzier women, all smoking cigarettes, and I do not exaggerate when I say that two of them had on horn-rimmed spectacles.

After a while, without any preliminaries, the lights went out. The foot-lights, following some hesitation, opened their eyes. The curtain went up, revealing, the program said, "At the Foot of the Mountain of the Gods," but I regarded this as a gross exaggeration. On the other hand, I do not know how to describe this scenery other than to say that I have never seen anything like it anywhere, and I have seen almost everything.

Low music first, and then a few girls suffering pitifully from malnutrition and down, apparently, to their last garment, tripped lightly out and hoofed it a bit. They ran hither and thither, being cunning, roguish, playful and what not, and in this festive fashion consumed about five minutes. Then, suddenly, they all prostrated themselves toward the left rear entrance. Some-body blew a bugle. A drum rolled. Then Henry Dudley Riley—by the pro-gram—entered.

He entered slowly, taking long steps, being stealthy, just like a milk wagon. He was next to naked, but composed. He looked around slowly at first and then began to rollick. He waved his arms, and one of them was so unfortunate as to catch a lightly clad maiden under the chin, lifting her off her feet. She sat down heavily, with an astonished look on her face. I laughed, but nobody else did. Smack didn't notice; he was very intent on his rollicking.

He paused occasionally to raise a clenched fist at the chandelier and swear, by pantomime, a mighty oath to the gods athirst, but mostly he played tag with the gals. I confess here and now that I do not know much about dancing. Frisco, Pat Rooney, Eddie Leonard, Harry Greb—they're about my speed. But without looking it up in the books, I'm willing to risk a small sum, say, ten simoleons, that Smack Riley did everything wrong that it is possible to do on two feet except to fall into the orchestra. I couldn't have laughed more heartily if I'd just seen an umpire shot.

The highbrows, though, were enthralled. They must have been ready to believe anything they read in the Sphere, for the only way Smack could have been worse would have been by wearing a fire bucket on each foot. He'd knocked down half the scenery before he was through, and there wasn't a girl on the stage that didn't have the fear of God in her eyes as she heard the galumph-galumph of Smack Riley's bare Number 12's pounding play-fully along behind her.

Then it ended. Arno backed into what was left of the scenery, stepped on a rope, tripped and dived into the wings. Speaking personally, I hoped he'd been knocked unconscious, for I, at any rate, still had some pride in the good old masculine sex. He didn't come out again, even to acknowledge the applause, which was good and loud. They called him bravo. And the next time I saw Smack he had his shirt and pants on and was thanking the au-dience individually, as he made his way to the door, for their kind ap-preciation.

I listened in, eavesdropped on some of the talk: "Primitive genius . . .

astounding sense of grace . . . liquid movements . . . crude brilliance . . .
a sparkle of greatness ever present . . . a reserve strength."

IV

It was a great day for baseball when the Grays and Gulls took the field.
The Stadium was packed. Forty thousand people if there was a bat boy—
and there was a bat boy. The Grays, fighting sportsmen every one of them,
smelled the World Series receipts; and the Gulls, just as true disciples of all
that is highest and finest in sport, were also thinking about the jack that
might be theirs. Both teams were keyed up, snappy, and the crowd soon
showed that it was prepared to roar its lungs out.

I looked for Smack. He was at the rail talking to Marshall Mount again,
and somehow the sight depressed me, gave me a feeling that all was not
well. Of course I had no reason for believing that the exhibition of the night
before had cured the Smacker, but I did, at bottom, have some hope that it
had.

Presently he pried himself loose from Mount and, with the rest of the
Grays, went out for fielding practice. It was then I saw that something was
indeed wrong, and as near as I could figure it, the Smacker was still dizzy with
art. For at the first fungo he exhibited some strange and, to me, incomprehensible didos. He started for the ball with long, stealthy strides, his arms
swaying rhythmically with the swing of his body—and his body swung
wickedly. It was a curious galumph and it served to bring him where the
ball came down exactly forty-five seconds after the ball was down.

One of the boys in the press box chuckled.

"Who does that bum think he is, Gertrude Hoffman?" The open bleachers threw back its head and bayed at the sun. "Nick Altrock's got nothing
on that bird!" Everybody had noticed it; but only Mount and I, it seemed,
had an inkling of the explanation; and Mount, the fathead, appeared anything but dissatisfied.

The second fungo he could have taken in his tracks. Instead, he chose
to run gracefully around in a circle, swinging his arms most beautifully, and
the ball nearly landed on his bean. The bleachers roared. Good old Smack
Riley was being funny for them! Good old Smack!

It might have been Greek, all right, but it wasn't baseball.

Then the game started. Rush worked for the Grays and Rocker hurled
for the Gulls, and for five innings they put up what I would call a corking
pitchers' battle. It was three up, three down, with only now and then a fluky
bingle getting a man on one of the hassocks. And during that time the owner
of the splendid body in the right field was given no opportunity to do anything with it. At bat he got one hit, a single, and was left on first. It was
not until the first half of the sixth that anything happened for the records.

Hoban, first up for the Gulls, beat out a bunt. Then he stole second.
Darber sent a slow roller to short and Hoban made third on the out. This

wasn't so good, but time would tell, as I have said so many times. And then Heinie Schmidt raised a fly to right, directly at old reliable Smack Riley.

Everything else being even, I would have breathed a sigh of relief, but nothing else was even. I wanted to close my eyes, but I didn't. Maybe—perhaps—there was a chance that the big bum's eye would be working and his mean right arm prepared for the shot to the plate if Hoban tried to score after the catch, but——

I watched Smack, together with forty thousand others, while he moved stealthily backward and forward, waving his arms to the tempo of the Humoresque, under that falling ball. Hoban was holding third by a toe, ready to dash for the plate if anything happened.

And then Smack caught it—caught it somewhere around his left shoulder blade. Not a graceful catch, perhaps, but it would do. And in the same second a roar swept the stands. Hoban had started for the plate—a desperate chance for a run that might mean the game.

Then Smack whipped back his arm, his eye on the plate and the speeding Hoban. He took a long, slow step, and at that instant I realized that it wasn't Smack out there, but Arno the Rollicking God. His hand went back nearly to the ground. He hopped once or twice like a shot putter, and finally, with a sinuous movement, he got rid of the ball toward the plate. By the time it reached the catcher, Hoban had crossed the plate, gone to the dugout and written a post card to his cousin in Duluth, Minnesota.

There was what I would call pandemonium, mostly in the form of boos for the Smacker; but he appeared undisturbed, his art still intact. Three seats to my left Mount spoke:

"That pose was astoundingly like the Discus Thrower, don't you think? Just a flash, a haunting touch of beauty."

That one tally looked as big as seven, for it ended all scoring for the time being. It was again one-two-three in the sixth and the seventh, with Rush pitching first-rate ball. In fact one run began to look as though it were all that was going to be necessary.

But in the eighth the Grays snapped out of it. Rush, whose last recorded hit occurred the year Tris Speaker got his first gray hair, socked one into left field and it was good for a single. Harrigan grounded out to first, Rush taking second. Then Rocker skyrocketed, walking Massey and Hedges on eight straight balls.

Boom! The roar started. The break was here and the crowd realized it. The Grays were swarming out of their dugout, crouching on the grass, barking across the swell of the infield at the runners. There was a tightening among the Gulls. The infielders leaned a little farther forward. The drive was coming and they were ready to meet it.

The formless surge of sound, rolling in mass volume over the field, began to settle into a steady thump-thump, a pounding of feet, as forty thousand people caught the thrill.

And then the Smacker crawled out of the trench, caught up three bats and started for the plate. The bases full and the king up! Forgotten was that slow throw home. This was the minute! This was drama—epic drama!

Smack Riley swung his clubs slowly while Rocker and Dowden conferred. Then he tossed two of them aside and stepped into the batter's box. He dug his cleats in the dirt, got a toe hold, waved his wagon tongue. Dowden, his mask adjusted, squatted, and Rocker tried his first, a curve over the outside, low.

Wow!

The Smacker had larruped it down the third-base line for a mile, into the bleachers—foul by inches. Rocker had nearly fainted. And when he saw Harry Lannigan, the Gulls' manager waving to him from the dugout that his bath was ready, he smiled a happy smile. He did not even wait to see who was coming from the bull pen to relieve him.

A smallish figure had separated himself from the warmers-up down by the exit gate and was coming slowly across the field. Smack, accustomed to such changes, leaned carelessly on his bat, resting his rhythm for a few seconds. He might well have been an actor posing in a hired dress suit. The smallish figure neared the diamond, and the Smacker, noting it for the first time, straightened up suddenly.

"Mulligan," bawled the announcer, "now pitching for the Gulls!"

A newcomer to the league, Mulligan was small, terrifically ugly, red-haired and gnarled in appearance, and he chewed on the world's largest cud of tobacco. He sauntered into this breach coolly. And with the bases full, Smack Riley at the bat, forty thousand people storming and a pennant not far in the future—it was what I would refer to as a tight pinch.

But it was the Smacker, and not Mulligan, who seemed dumfounded. His eyes were frozen on the little pitcher, now tossing a practice ball to Dowden. And Mulligan's ruddy face was worth a look or two as it shifted shapes regularly with the grinding of his tobacco. The Smacker was paralyzed. Nor did he move until Tim Hurley, the umpire at the plate, called him.

"This ain't no hotel lobby," he said.

The Banzai of Bingle, as I called him once, momentarily regained life. With a nervous jerk he stepped forward and swung his bat tentatively. But it died down slowly, and the forty thousand pounded, pounded, pounded, roaring—roaring for blood. Then Mulligan began to wind up.

I myself, a veteran of the press box, the dean of sporting writers, have never seen anything like that wind-up, and, as I say, I have seen pretty nearly everything. But Mulligan! He involved himself in a chaos of arms and legs that showed no signs whatever of solution. His right arm swung three times and then plunged squarely through.

He slapped himself in the face with his left foot. He laid his thorax on the pitcher's plate. He revolved his head four times, strangled himself with his elbows, bit the back of his right knee, got both feet off the ground at the same time, remained stationary in the air, and finally, at the height of the maneuver, exuded the ball, it emerging, strangely enough, from his Adam's apple.

It was a strike. The Smacker did not even lift his bat from his shoulder, though the ball split the plate. He was paralyzed again; and if he'd been only a little more lifelike he might have passed for a statue—Athlete Dumfounded.

Mulligan got the ball back and the same thing happened again. This time the ball appeared from the small of his back, but, wherever it came from, it proved to be another strike all the same.

The Stadium stood up, boomed its call to the four ends of Harlem.

The Smacker stood oblivious of his demise. His glazed eyes remained on Mulligan and, as he watched, the red-haired pitcher shifted the tumor of plug cut from the right side of his head to the left. The shape of his whole superstructure was altered. Whereas there had been a goiter on the right side, there was then a wen on the left. It was astounding—and terrible. And then there was a sudden higher roar. The Smacker had crumpled to the ground in a swoon.

V

Readers, the rest is eyewitness stuff corroborated by the records and explainable by psychology.

You don't remember who finished second in the league last year, for nobody ever remembers who finished second; but I'll tell you. It was the Grays.

There was another inning to this game I've described, to be sure, and five other games to be played, but this is one of those things stranger and more tragic than fiction. I could have made this the final game of the season, and it the deciding game, too, but these are facts.

When they took the heart out of Smack Riley they took the heart out of the Grays, and after that they played with all the skill of nine Bulgars. But as I said, I'm only a plain man, just a reporter, and not a dramatic critic, as Mount is now, or even a psychologist, so I can account for what happened only by what I saw and heard.

I was present when Smack was brought back to life. I saw the baffled and tortured look in his eyes, the look which remained there throughout the series. I was present when he uttered his first words on regaining consciousness, the only words that he ever uttered on the subject. They were poignant sounds, rising from the soul of a tormented Arno.

"That," he said slowly, thoughtfully, shuddering again at the very thought, "was the most unæsthetic thing I ever seen."

I witnessed also his pitiful trips to the plate, a broken man, with scarcely life enough to lift his bat, and his doleful trips back to the bench. And I was there at the end of the sixth game—the sixth game the Grays had lost in succession, and the pennant gone—when the first original thought the Smacker ever had came into his head with dazzling clearness. It was prompted by a remark from Harrison, the center fielder.

"Well, Smack," he said, "it's all over, and you'll not get that superheterodyne radio set you said you was, the first day of the season, outa the series money."

The Smacker rose suddenly. A gleam of understanding came into his eyes, the first, I suppose, in years. He crawled out of the dugout, selected a bat carefully and then straightened up. His arm went back, less like Arno than anything he'd done in weeks, and in a flash a long black bat whirred through the air straight at the press box.

"There's too damned much æsthetics going on round here!"

The bat reached Mount, but the words didn't. It caught him on the ear, and now he is the only dramatic critic in New York with a cauliflower ear.

And these, readers, are the facts, the evidence on which I accuse Marshall Mount of the Sphere and Smack Riley of the Grays.

WAS IT A DREAM?

GUY DE MAUPASSANT

I HAD loved her madly!

"Why does one love? Why does one love? How queer it is to see only one being in the world, to have only one thought in one's mind, only one desire in the heart, and only one name on the lips—a name which comes up continually, rising, like the water in a spring, from the depths of the soul to the lips, a name which one repeats over and over again, which one whispers ceaselessly, everywhere, like a prayer.

"I am going to tell you our story, for love only has one, which is always the same. I met her and loved her; that is all. And for a whole year I have lived on her tenderness, on her caresses, in her arms, in her dresses, on her words, so completely wrapped up, bound, and absorbed in everything which came from her, that I no longer cared whether it was day or night, or whether I was dead or alive, on this old earth of ours.

"And then she died. How? I do not know; I no longer know anything. But one evening she came home wet, for it was raining heavily, and the next day she coughed, and she coughed for about a week, and took to her bed. What happened I do not remember now, but doctors came, wrote, and went away. Medicines were brought, and some women made her drink them. Her hands were hot, her forehead was burning, and her eyes bright and sad. When I spoke to her, she answered me, but I do not remember what we said. I have forgotten everything, everything, everything! She died, and I very well remember her slight, feeble sigh. The nurse said: 'Ah!' and I understood, I understood!

"I knew nothing more, nothing. I saw a priest, who said: 'Your mistress?' and it seemed to me as if he were insulting her. As she was dead, nobody had the right to say that any longer, and I turned him out. Another came who was very kind and tender, and I shed tears when he spoke to me about her.

"They consulted me about the funeral, but I do not remember anything that they said, though I recollected the coffin, and the sound of the hammer when they nailed her down in it. Oh! God, God!

"She was buried! Buried! She! In that hole! Some people came—female friends. I made my escape and ran away. I ran, and then walked through the streets, went home, and the next day started on a journey.

"Yesterday I returned to Paris, and when I saw my room again—our room, our bed, our furniture, everything that remains of the life of a human being after death—I was seized by such a violent attack of fresh grief, that I felt like opening the window and throwing myself out into the street. I could not remain any longer among these things, between these walls which had inclosed and sheltered her, which retained a thousand atoms of her, of her skin and of her breath, in their imperceptible crevices. I took up my hat to make my escape, and just as I reached the door, I passed the large glass in the hall, which she had put there so that she might look at herself every day from head to foot as she went out, to see if her toilette looked well, and was correct and pretty, from her little boots to her bonnet.

"I stopped short in front of that looking-glass in which she had so often been reflected—so often, so often, that it must have retained her reflection. I was standing there, trembling, with my eyes fixed on the glass—on that flat, profound, empty glass—which had contained her entirely, and had possessed her as much as I, as my passionate looks had. I felt as if I loved that glass. I touched it; it was cold. Oh! the recollection! sorrowful mirror, burning mirror, horrible mirror, to make men suffer such torments! Happy is the man whose heart forgets everything that it has contained, everything that has passed before it, everything that has looked at itself in it, or has been reflected in its affection, in its love! How I suffer!

"I went out without knowing it, without wishing it, and toward the cemetery. I found her simple grave, a white marble cross, with these few words:

"'She loved, was loved, and died.'

"She is there, below, decayed! How horrible! I sobbed with my forehead on the ground, and I stopped there for a long time, a long time. Then I saw that it was getting dark, and a strange, mad wish, the wish of a despairing lover, seized me. I wished to pass the night, the last night, in weeping on her grave. But I should be seen and driven out. How was I to manage? I was cunning, and got up and began to roam about in that city of the dead. I walked and walked. How small this city is, in comparison with the other, the city in which we live. And yet, how much more numerous the dead are than the living. We want high houses, wide streets, and much room for the four generations who see the daylight at the same time, drink water from the spring, and wine from the vines, and eat bread from the plains.

"And for all the generations of the dead, for all that ladder of humanity that has descended down to us, there is scarcely anything, scarcely anything! The earth takes them back, and oblivion effaces them. Adieu!

"At the end of the cemetery, I suddenly perceived that I was in its oldest part, where those who had been dead a long time are mingling with the soil, where the crosses themselves are decayed, where possibly newcomers will be

put to-morrow. It is full of untended roses, of strong and dark cypress-trees, a sad and beautiful garden, nourished on human flesh.

"I was alone, perfectly alone. So I crouched in a green tree and hid myself there completely amid the thick and somber branches. I waited, clinging to the stem, like a shipwrecked man does to a plank.

"When it was quite dark, I left my refuge and began to walk softly, slowly, inaudibly, through that ground full of dead people. I wandered about for a long time, but could not find her tomb again. I went on with extended arms, knocking against the tombs with my hands, my feet, my knees, my chest, even with my head, without being able to find her. I groped about like a blind man finding his way, I felt the stones, the crosses, the iron railings, the metal wreaths, and the wreaths of faded flowers! I read the names with my fingers, by passing them over the letters. What a night! What a night! I could not find her again!

"There was no moon. What a night! I was frightened, horribly frightened in these narrow paths, between two rows of graves. Graves! graves! graves! nothing but graves! On my right, on my left, in front of me, around me, everywhere there were graves! I sat down on one of them, for I could not walk any longer, my knees were so weak. I could hear my heart beat! And I heard something else as well. What? A confused, nameless noise. Was the noise in my head, in the impenetrable night, or beneath the mysterious earth, the earth sown with human corpses? I looked all around me, but I cannot say how long I remained there; I was paralyzed with terror, cold with fright, ready to shout out, ready to die.

"Suddenly, it seemed to me that the slab of marble on which I was sitting, was moving. Certainly it was moving, as if it were being raised. With a bound, I sprang on to the neighboring tomb, and I saw, yes, I distinctly saw the stone which I had just quitted rise upright. Then the dead person appeared, a naked skeleton, pushing the stone back with its bent back. I saw it quite clearly, although the night was so dark. On the cross I could read:

" 'Here lies Jacques Olivant, who died at the age of fifty-one. He loved his family, was kind and honorable, and died in the grace of the Lord.'

"The dead man also read what was inscribed on his tombstone; then he picked up a stone off the path, a little, pointed stone, and began to scrape the letters carefully. He slowly effaced them, and with the hollows of his eyes he looked at the places where they had been engraved. Then with the tip of the bone that had been his forefinger, he wrote in luminous letters, like those lines which boys trace on walls with the tip of a lucifer match:

" 'Here reposes Jacques Olivant, who died at the age of fifty-one. He hastened his father's death by his unkindness, as he wished to inherit his fortune, he tortured his wife, tormented his children, deceived his neighbors, robbed everyone he could, and died wretched.'

"When he had finished writing, the dead man stood motionless, looking at his work. On turning round I saw that all the graves were open, that all the dead bodies had emerged from them, and that all had effaced the lies inscribed on the gravestones by their relations, substituting the truth instead. And I saw that all had been the tormentors of their neighbors— malicious, dishonest, hypocrites, liars, rogues, calumniators, envious; that they had stolen, deceived, performed every disgraceful, every abominable action, these good fathers, these faithful wives, these devoted sons, these chaste daughters, these honest tradesmen, these men and women who were called irreproachable. They were all writing at the same time, on the threshold of their eternal abode, the truth, the terrible and the holy truth of which everybody was ignorant, or pretended to be ignorant, while they were alive.

"I thought that *she* also must have written something on her tombstone, and now running without any fear among the half-open coffins, among the corpses and skeletons, I went toward her, sure that I should find her immediately. I recognized her at once, without seeing her face, which was covered by the winding-sheet, and on the marble cross, where shortly before I had read:

" '*She loved, was loved, and died.*'

I now saw:

" '*Having gone out in the rain one day, in order to deceive her lover, she caught cold and died.*'

"It appears that they found me at daybreak, lying on the grave unconscious."

THE LADY

CONRAD RICHTER

I WOULD never believe that my father had run away with the money. Oh, I knew well enough what the people of Moro were saying: that no one really knew anything about us but Judge Sessions and he had known only my mother; that my father was too fancy a dresser to be an honest "commission boy"; that he used to pay attention to a questionable woman, Mrs. Consuelo Blount, who less than a month before had left the country, and that they were probably together somewhere in Colorado right now.

It was a barefaced lie, I told anyone who spoke it in my hearing. I said he had gone to Mrs. Blount only to learn Spanish, which he needed at the commission house. I said many other things to his credit, and not a word of the two bad things I knew he had really done, one of them being with another woman while my mother lay in her last illness back in Missouri, and the other, his unwillingness to bring her West when they found she had lung fever. She had wanted to come. The malady ran in the family. Her cousin Albert had been expected to die with it, but he had gone to New Mexico territory, where he studied law, had married into a wealthy Spanish family, and was now a judge for three or four counties, riding or driving the circuit as well as anybody.

I can still hear my mother tell my father that if she got away from the steamy air of the Missouri, she believed she would be well and could be up and get his meals again. But he had breathed the air of the Missouri all his life, he told her, and it hadn't hurt him. Only after her death did he quit the other woman, give up the house, and hunt up my mother's cousin in New Mexico, which was as far as the railroad ran then. He said he did it for me, to save me from the weak lungs of my family, but I rather thought it remorse. He wanted to get a little virtue from doing at last the thing he had so bitterly failed to do before.

However, many men fail their wives without failing their employers. My father wasn't the sort to do both. I have his photograph now, on the thick shiny brown cardboard they used then, with a zigzag curlycue for a line at the bottom, the whole thing yellow with age. It's hard to believe that he was only twenty-nine years old. He looks forty, a fine figure of a man with a soft brown mustache and white hands which in Missouri never did much more than toil on the white pages of ledgers. He carried himself straight in his well-cut clothes, and his eyes looked out at you steadily. Never, I felt, would he have abandoned me in a place like Moro, a thousand miles from Missouri, and if some woman could have made him do such a thing, as they say women can, it wasn't in him to have gone off with so little fuss, as if he'd be seeing me the next day or the one after that and knowing all the time that he was deserting me for good. He didn't even raise the whip or look back as he drove off in one of the rigs from Caldwell's Livery Stable. I followed him on foot over the acequia madre to the Quintana ranch lane and stood by one of the adobe gateposts watching his dust till buckboard and white-footed bay horse were lost in the blurred horizon.

Only one thing troubled me, and I tried not to think of it. Why hadn't he let me go along? He was driving, he said, to the vicinity of the Greenhorn Mountains, which the Mexicans call La Sierra, a range that reaches its back two and a half miles into the blue sky. Most of the year it's topped with snow. I was crazy to go with him and had begged him to take me. He had the room and packed nothing more than a sack or two of oats that I could see. But he said, no, he couldn't and wouldn't tell why.

Later on we knew that old Boreas Luna had sent two of his Mexicans down to the commission house for cash to buy another flock of sheep, that Mr. Kidd hadn't trusted the money to them, and so had sent it special with my father, in gold eagles and a few silver dollars, all done up in tight rolls of newspaper wrapped in sacking, sewed compactly, and hidden at the bottom of the oats. There were different accounts of the amount going around. Some said six thousand and some swore it was eleven, but all agreed it was what the commission house owed old Boreas for his wool clip, less what stood against his name on the company books.

About every day after that I went down to see if my father had come back. It was a long walk and no shade after leaving the cottonwoods of Old Town. Except for the several blocks of business district near the depot, the buildings of New Town were spread over a large area of desert, where they stood exposed to the brassy New Mexican sun. Two years before this when the railroad had come to the territory, everybody thought it would run through Old Town. But the railroad people were too smart for that. They weren't building the railroad to develop the country, Mr. Younger at the commission house said, but to make money. The land at Old Town was watered by acequias and owned by old Mexican families who would have profited. So the engineers ran the railroad where they could get land for little or nothing. They set the station right out on the desert and tacked the sign MORO on it. This was going to be the town now, they said, and they sold plots of cheap desert land at fancy prices.

On my way I passed Caldwell's Livery Stable. It wasn't much of a stable then, just a low adobe building big enough for an office and bunk room pegged around the walls for harness. Most of the rigs were kept outside and the horses in a corral, where they stood listless in the heat of summer and snow of winter. A long way off I could see that the bay with white feet wasn't there. That didn't prove anything, I told myself stoutly. My father and his horse might both be down at the commission house.

The sign on the commission house read: KIDD & Co., *Forwarding and Commission Merchants*. The buildings stood by the railroad track so freight cars could load and unload in the huge man-made caves. The largest held the offices, among other things, and the first thing I looked for was my father's desk with the rickety pine case of pigeonholes above it, the top ones much higher than I could reach. As a rule, ledgers and daybooks lay open together with bills and bills of lading, all held down by lumps-of-ore paperweights, and the pigeonholes were stuffed with yellow sheets. But now pigeonholes, desk, and stool all had a bare emptiness that gave me suddenly a sick feeling. Men were coming and going, but none of them turned out to be the one I hoped to see, and I went on to where I used to find him sometimes, in the dark warehouse aisles smelling of tea and green coffee, of dyes from the bales of ginghams and calicos, of rope and saddles, of boots and sides of leather, of bacon and lard, of the cold metallic smell of hardware, the good sharp scent of tobacco, and the strong chemical odor of sheep-dip.

He wasn't there, nor on the great splintery platforms where freight wagons and pack trains were loaded, so I went to the feed warehouse, which I liked best. Here were walls of flour piled in sacks and barrels, and bins of corn, barley and oats and chop, the latter of which always smelled good enough to eat. Only the feedhouse men were there, and I went on to the last of the warehouses and the only ill-smelling one. More than once had I seen it piled to the roof with rotting hides and greasy fleeces. It was the custom then to send the latter out to the scouring mills, of which Moro had three, and when the wool came back it was light and fluffy. Often had I jumped into the huge bins and rolled around in the soft drifts, but today I only looked into the dark hot cavern and then went back to the office to try to find out when my father was coming.

The men had always been very friendly. Now they hardly let on that I was there. Only Mr. Kidd would actually look at me. He was a thick, bald-headed man with black mustache and eyebrows, and when he caught sight of me his dark eyes would flash and he'd bark low and short to one of the men. This man would speak to Mr. Younger. Neither would look my way, but I knew it was about me they had spoken. After a while Mr. Younger would come over to me.

He was a small man like Mr. Kidd but slight and wiry. I learned there that you could never go on names, because Mr. Kidd was old and Mr. Younger even older.

"How are you today, Jud?" he'd say, and his hard-bitten face would give me a smile.

"Is he back?" I'd ask, quick hope from his cheerfulness rising in me.

At that Mr. Younger's eyes would turn a bleak blue while his face kept on smiling.

"Not yet. At least not so far as I know," he'd say as if to make my father's absence less final and to hold out a hope of him still coming, although all of them knew then that old Boreas had sent word he had seen neither the money nor my father.

I'd stand for a little while, digesting the disappointment and getting hold of myself.

"Could you use a boy today?" I'd ask him.

"Not right today," he'd say thoughtfully and no hint that they wouldn't hire or trust the son of a man who ran off with eleven thousand dollars, just regret that there was no opening, and the door left open for tomorrow.

So I'd hang around another minute trying to think of something else to say, but the mind of a boy doesn't work very well under circumstances like that, and the sixty seconds of a minute are mighty long when you've transacted your business, shot your bolt for the day, and you knew they were waiting for you to go. After all, there was another day. My father might come home tomorrow or even tonight. The commission house never closed. Day and night it was open to freighters, who kept arriving at all hours.

I don't know how long this might have gone on if one morning I hadn't come in and found a new man working at my father's desk. The sight of someone there sent my hopes soaring at first, but when I saw it was not my father, it shook me. I knew then, despite what Mr. Younger implied, they never expected to see my father back, and for a long time I didn't go in again.

II

My father and I had rooms in what had once been a fine house on the plaza. People still called it La Casa Nuñoz after the original owner although the adobe was badly washed and all the rooms facing the street had become shops and a Mexican restaurant. Like most native buildings, it had but one story. To the rear and facing the south was a large patio like a hotel courtyard with a gallery running partway around it. There were in the patio: a well, a massive cottonwood, and by day a swarm of children, together with a parrot in a woven willow cage. The parrot belonged to the Padillas.

We weren't burdened with furniture, just a hard Mexican bed, a chair, and my father's brassbound trunk in one room; a wood cookstove, pine table, chair, small bench, a few dishes, and water bucket in the other. Most times we dined here on eggs from local ranchers and on bacon, crackers, coffee, dried fruit, and pickles my father got wholesale at the commission house. The smells of La Sena drifted constantly in our rooms, but we never ate there. On special occasions my father took me to the Railroad House in the new town.

At first when my father didn't return, I lay awake half the night wondering what would become of me. Hailing from Missouri, my father thought himself superior to the Mexicans and sometimes had embarrassed me by showing it in front of them. Lying there in bed, I could imagine them talking among themselves with satisfaction of the just fate that had befallen the Anglo boy whose father had run off with Señor Kidd's gold.

How little I knew of Mexicans then, of their natural sympathies and pity for someone whose father or brother had come afoul the law! I found that instead of hating me, the native women and girls gave me soft pitying or bright admiring glances from their dark eyes as I passed. Both Señora Padilla and Señora José García fed me tortillas. But it was another of Spanish blood who was my deliverer and ministering angel.

This was the lady called Doña Ellen, the wife of my mother's cousin, Albert Sessions. A native-born New Mexican, she was the daughter of a Mexican mother and English father. Of course, I knew that New Mexico was a territory of the United States and its natives were citizens of our country, and yet to me it was as if Cousin Albert had married someone foreign as from Guatemala or Brazil. Cousin Albert always spoke to me on the street, but his wife had never recognized or spoken to me, perhaps because I so assiduously avoided her.

This very day I had seen her around town in her fancy buggy with space under the sides of the seat for the rubber-tired, brass-rimmed wheels to turn with a flourish. The buggy had yellow spokes, brass lamps on either side of the patent-leather dashboard, and a matching yellow cloth top that could be thrown back as in convertible cars today. The buggy top was generally up to shield Doña Ellen from the New Mexican sun. I had just passed the lumber yard in New Town headed for home when I heard a rig overtake me and saw its wheels stop beside me in the deep floury dust. When I looked up, there were the stylish undercut buggy with the yellow top and the lady herself holding the tan reins.

"Good afternoon, Jud. You are Jud, aren't you?" she asked brightly. "You're the very one I hoped to see. Won't you get in with me and I'll drive you back to Old Town."

To my surprise, her accent was English rather than Spanish. The stylish slant of her sailor straw and the genteel softness of her driving gloves were certainly non-Mexican, her hair, a golden Anglo color against her blue eyes. But never would I get in beside her at that moment. There flashed through my mind the tale they told of her Spanish temper and her wild English love for horses. They said she was a girl away at convent school when a mozo had put a spade bit on her favorite riding horse and after long and cruel training taught him to bow low. When the girl came home from school, he had proudly showed her horse off to her, but one look at the maimed and bleeding mouth, and she had struck the mozo down with the heavy end of her crop. The story was that she had killed him.

When I asked my father he said he didn't know if it was true or not, but I must remember she was a Johnson y Campo, that the Johnson y Campo sheep ranch took in a great Spanish grant beyond the Prietas. For generations her people had had the power of life and death over their peons, especially here in the Arriba country, and a fine horse to them meant more than a peon.

When I held off from the buggy, I expected her to drive away with English abruptness and dismissal, but she was all feminine Mexican wile now.

"Don't you want to ride with me, Jud?" she asked, wrinkling her eyebrows at me in that playful Spanish gesture of hurt, a characteristic I was to see in her a thousand times afterward, a trick of expression almost childlike, she who was anything but a child. At the same time that she spoke to me so lightly, there was something indefinably sad about her. I suspect now it was only the faint inconsolable melancholy of her Latin blood. But at the time it seemed like something else, as if some secret past grief sucked the joy of life from her. I remembered how quick the Mexicans said she was to violent anger and complete forgiveness, and I think that is what quieted my fear and stitched a bond between us, this secret sorrow of hers like mine and her complete forgiveness of me for the crime of which my father was accused.

There was something else I didn't recognize at first, in fact not for weeks afterward, but which I learned to observe and know so well. This was her complex femininity. She could be very capable, determined, willful, also satiric and funny at times. All this on occasion could vanish and an appealing helplessness come into her blue eyes and even into the way she sat or stood, so that others, and especially men, could not forbear rescuing her, throwing themselves into her cause, bringing to pass what she wished, indeed doing it with masculine pleasure and great satisfaction to themselves.

Today she seemed to me innocent as beautiful, what she asked so reasonable, even tolerant, that before I knew it I was stumbling around the wheels and climbing up on the cushions which in most buggies were hard black leather but which here were of soft rose cloth, and we were off down the road with a feeling that no automobile can give me today, of flowing animal limbs and muscles, of a bright tan harness with silver trimmings and a silver whip socket engraved with a name in script that I couldn't read. Everyone, I noticed, looked up with lively interest to see us go by as almost no one looks at a car today. I saw with pride that she drove her favorite horse I had heard so much about, the fastest in the territory and her great pet. I remembered my father saying that when he asked her how many children she had, she had told him two, both boys, one nine and one seven years old. My father learned later that she had given birth to only one child, my cousin Willy, whom I had never met, and that by her seven-year-old boy she must have meant this horse called Critter, who had been named by her father half in jest before he died.

Presently we stopped in front of the large shabby Casa Nuñoz. Here she cut the horse to my side so she could alight.

"Will you hold him for me?" she asked. "Critter hates to be tied. If we were out on the mesa, I'd let him stand, but he's so curious. He likes to move here and there and examine everything, and I don't want him wandering around town with a buggy."

Never had I held a horse, and I felt sure this one she called Critter knew it. He was dark, not black, middle, or red bay, the latter of which the Mexicans call colorado. Rather he was a shade called oscura, which is sometimes only a dirty color but in Critter was a peculiar shade of brown. For the first time I was close enough to see faint inner black markings like on certain furs rich ladies wear. He was not stylish like they, however. There was no check rein and now that he had stopped he rather lounged. I had seen much more handsome and spirited horses and wondered why a lady like Mrs. Sessions with such a fancy buggy liked him well enough to consider him one of her boys.

Today I was to get an inkling of the reason. As I took his bridle I saw him examine me quietly, almost benignly, from the great round world of his eye, in which I could make out a curious image of myself and of the Casa Nuñoz behind me. He saw my fear of him, I'm sure. I also like to think that he saw the confused loneliness of an insecure and half-starved boy. This may be pure imagination on my part. Be that as it may, after a minute or two I was no longer afraid but absorbed in watching him. He had apparently accepted me and turned his attention to his surroundings. I could have sworn that he surveyed intelligently and in turn the church, the bell towers, the Sisters' school next to it, the bandstand in the center of the little park, and La Casa Nuñoz closer at hand. From time to time he would turn his attention to things that passed, horses, riders, vehicles, drivers, foot travelers, children, and even a yellow butterfly. His ears constantly worked back and forward like pointers of mental acquisitiveness. I had the curious feeling that he observed and speculated on the large goiter of Mrs. Montoya as she crossed the plaza and the purpose of Xavier Sandoval and his carpenters as they trimmed and planed several new vigas for the church under the great cottonwood that stood over the entrance.

Mrs. Sessions stayed in the house a long time. I saw young Gus Padilla run out and come back with old Ezequiel Salazar, the owner of Casa Nuñoz. Then the boy reappeared and with importance took hold of Critter's bridle.

"Doña Ellen wants to see you inside," he informed me.

I went, somewhat puzzled and reluctant. In my father's and my rooms I found a little group of people including old Ezequiel, Mrs. García, Mrs. Padilla, and a number of their children, all at a respectful distance from Mrs. Sessions, who in some unexplained way made our kitchen seem rude and barbarous, unfit to hold such a lady as she.

"Jud, we've been holding a little junta about you," she said almost gaily.

I stood startled and awkward, not knowing what to make of it, but convinced that whatever the purpose it was not good. Mrs. Sessions went on.

"The judge and I don't like you living here by yourself. It's not well for a young boy and we're afraid you don't get enough to eat. How would you like to come over to my house and stay till your father gets back?"

"I don't think I would like it," I said quickly.

"He would like it fine, Doña Ellen," Mrs. García informed in Spanish, and old Ezequiel added solemnly that what I said should be considered as from an ignorant boy who didn't know what he was saying, that in truth I would be overjoyed to live there.

"No, I want to stay here!" I stammered, retreating toward the door, but the stout form of Mrs. Padilla blocked my way.

"He is in reality very unhappy and lonely here, Doña Ellen," she declared.

"How can he expect to live here alone?" that old villain Ezequiel added. "Since his father left him, he never sent him a peso to pay for these rooms. To make ends meet I should rent them to Abundio Sais, who asked me about them."

"It isn't good for him to be so much alone, Doña," Mrs. García spoke up. "In your house he would have Epifania and Manuel for company now, and later on when you came to town he would have your son. It is no small thing to have a cousin to play with and speak with and read and spell the English language with."

"I'm a bad reader and speller," I protested.

Old Ezequiel waved his hand.

"You mustn't be deceived by his tricks, Doña Ellen. His father could read and write very well or never could he have been a trusted clerk and messenger of the commission house. Like father, like son," he added, after which his black eyes gazed triumphantly at me as if he had given me the black name I deserved for opposing my eviction from the premises.

"That's enough!" Cousin Albert's wife reproved sharply, and I thought I saw her eyes blaze at him for a moment. Then to me as if it was all decided: "Manuel will come for your trunk and other things. Now let's go over to the house and I'll show you where you will sleep."

She took my arm. I felt the strong pressure of her hand and that there was no further use to try to escape or rebel. Before I knew it we were out on the plaza, where she left Critter looking curiously after her while we went on foot near by to a street called La Placita, one of the spokes radiating from the square.

The white Sessions house, known as the Johnson y Campo house, looked large and imposing to me. The front door was locked, but Cousin Albert's wife didn't give up and go around to another door. She pulled the fancy bellrope and stood her ground till it was opened by a flurried Mexican woman whom she called Epifania. Doña Ellen waited. I expected a scene, at least a reprimand from the Spanish temper, but there was just a silent moment between them. Then we entered.

I found myself in an immense dim hall, wide as a parlor and twice as long, with mysterious doors on either side, one of which was open, revealing ghostly shapes of sheets over indeterminate pieces of furniture. Mrs. Sessions showed me that new and astonishing institution she called the bathroom, a frightening place with a great white tin tub on a high platform as if on a throne, after which she took me to a much nicer room with a white iron bed, the figure of Christ on the cross on a wall, and soft washed Navajo rugs on the floor. This was Willy's room, she told me, and would be mine until they moved in, when another bed would be put in for me.

"You are all right now, Jud," she promised me. "Friends of your father will look after you till he gets back."

Her references to my father and his friends, and that he would be back, warmed me like wine and bathed all the strange objects around me. But after she had gone something went out of the house. It seemed foreign. Even its air smelled like incense. Unseen presences with a strong Spanish will and flavor seemed to come out of hiding to cast their influence in the air, presences much more native and alien than Cousin Albert's wife and, I felt, not so favorably disposed toward me.

After going to bed I remembered what my father had said of the Johnson y Campo family, its power over life and death of its peons, and the story of Doña Ellen and the mozo who had incurred her displeasure. The act, they said, had occurred more than ten years ago some twenty miles distant on the other side of the Prietas, and yet I could imagine the poor Mexican struck down and lying senseless outside my window. There came to me the peculiar memory of the lady's hands today as they had held the reins and as one of them had taken my arm. Once later on I heard her say amusedly that her hands didn't match the rest of her, that they were too large, that driving and especially holding back fast horses from her youth had developed them abnormally. I could see nothing large about them. All I felt tonight was a certain indefinable power and mastery in them. I was glad that she and Cousin Albert planned to stay out on the ranch until fall. By that time, I was sure that my father would be back.

III

Next morning with the New Mexican sun shining in my window and lying brightly across the kitchen floor during breakfast, the house seemed like a different place, and the world, too. Not only then but after I sallied forth from the house, I found my status in Old Town had changed.

Old Ezequiel, with drooping eye, crooked stick, and the picture of avarice and chicanery, stopped me on the plaza to talk to me with deference in front of everyone. Lawyer Beasley, whose house stood next door to my Cousin Albert's—they had married sisters—acknowledged my existence by inclining his head curtly but unmistakably to me when he passed. And the Old Town boys talked to me of my absent father with new and evident respect.

"Your papa will be back soon now," Goyo Sánchez, whose full name was Gregorio, promised me. "His cousin the judge will see that he goes free."

"For a while he may go to jail, but it will not be so bad," Pas Ramírez assured. "My Uncle Ángel is in the penitentiary at Santa Fe for six years. They let him come home for weddings and funerals."

"Yes, and you'll have Señor Kidd's eleven thousand pesos besides"—this from Lino García, whose full name was Rosalino. He was financially minded, delivering barrels of water from the river to residents of New Town who had no wells as yet.

I answered angrily that my father had never taken the money, but they looked at me with instant dismay and disappointment. I saw that I was losing caste, that I must not object to my rank as embezzler's son if I wanted to swim with them in the river, rope milk cows pastured in the Big Bosque, and ride barebacked, often naked, some of the broken-down horses grazing there. At Epifania's orders, I went back to the house for midday dinner and found a great dish of frijoles, hot with chile that burned all the way down. When she asked how I liked them I could only say "Muy bueno" with tears running down my cheeks. Epifania thought I cried because of my hunger and her kindness in supplying it. She kept filling my plate. I couldn't stop her, and all the way back to the Big Bosque my insides were on fire.

But it was the first day my stomach had been filled since my father left, and late that afternoon coming back for supper, with the late sun slanting through the cottonwoods and time standing still as it does in New Mexico, with the stillness unbroken save for the drawn-out call of the mourning dove, I felt that life was sweet again, and the one who had saved me was Cousin Albert's lady, who had put me under her ægis and the protection of the powerful Johnson y Campo name. As I turned up La Placita from the plaza, the walls of her and Cousin Albert's house ahead of me glistened white in the sun like a citadel of peace and security which could not easily be broken.

In this I found that I was mistaken.

My first inkling came the second week the judge moved back to town. He had come alone at first, called by the September term of court. He slept in the Old Town house during the week, returning to the ranch for the weekend. Any uneasiness I felt for his coming soon vanished. He had me call him Cousin Albert like my mother used to do, and treated me kindly, almost as a son, a slender delicate man with a white skin and unusual heavy black beard. This together with his deep voice and powerful phrases never ceased to surprise me in one so frail. Sheets still hung over the furniture in the parlor, and tonight as usual he sat in the wide hall by the hanging brass lamp which he had pulled down to read the Denver paper that had come on the evening train. In the shadows on a settee, I lay content just to be near this one remaining link to my mother. Presently the hand bell on the end of the long cord that ran to the rear of the house tinkled, and the judge rose with the paper still in his hands and went to the door himself.

"Oh, good evening, Amado. Come in," he said heartily, and I saw a durably dressed Mexican with strong, brown, almost Oriental face and eyes. I knew him as Sheriff Martínez. There were two Martínez brothers in Moro. It was the custom for Amado to run for sheriff on the Republican ticket and Francisco on the Democratic. Whichever won appointed his brother as first deputy, and a Martínez had been sheriff for Moro County since most men could remember. Usually it was Amado. At his silence tonight and the grave way he entered, I saw Cousin Albert's heartiness dissipate.

"Is anything the matter?" he asked.

"You haven't heard from the ranch?"

"You mean our ranch?" Cousin Albert seemed surprised. "Sit down, Amado."

But both men remained standing.

"You remember last year, Judge, when Señor Beasley drove his herd through Ojo Canyon? I don't mean that Señor Beasley was there himself. But his foreman said his patrón told him it was too far to drive around on the public road through Canyon del Norte. The cattle would lose weight. His patrón said his wife was a Johnson y Campo herself, a sister of Doña Ellen, and that Jeffcoat could come through. Riders and buckboards came through all the time and they were never stopped. Now Señor Beasley knows very well how narrow Ojo Canyon is. I didn't see for myself what the cattle did to your señora's garden, but I heard. Also what Doña Ellen thought of that garden. Your señora and Jeffcoat had very hard words. She warned him never to come over your private road with a herd again."

"Yes, yes, of course," the judge said impatiently as if to urge him on.

"Well, Jeffcoat's men came through again this morning. He had a herd of fat steers Señor Beasley wanted to ship before the early price dropped. So he took Ojo Canyon like the other time. There was Doña Ellen's new garden and rosebushes and a new fence around them. Jeffcoat did not stop."

"We mustn't blame Jeffcoat. This is Beasley's doings," Cousin Albert said angrily.

"Perhaps," the sheriff spoke under his breath with dry Spanish malice, "perhaps it is a pity that Señor Beasley wasn't there instead of Jeffcoat."

The judge looked sober. "You mean someone was hurt."

"About as bad as a man can be hurt," the sheriff said gravely. "From all reports, there was only one shot. I saw for myself that it was a very good shot. The bullet found the forehead."

· The judge stood almost like a statue.

"Did his men say who did it?"

The sheriff avoided his eyes. "Who knows? A herd of cattle makes much dust. It is hard to see. But all could hear the rifle speak. It came, they said, from the portal of your house."

"How long was the shot?"

"From all accounts," the sheriff repeated, looking away, "it was a long shot and a very good one."

Cousin Albert was silent for a while as if wrestling with something grave.

"Well, I expect you to do whatever is right and necessary, Amado."

"Gracias á Dios, I don't have to do anything. Don Carlos came in tonight. He said it was him who fired the shot."

"Charley! Why didn't he come here to see me?"

"He told me he thought you wouldn't like to leave him out on bail on a murder charge. So I left him with Choppo and came right over."

"Thank you, Amado." I could see that Cousin Albert was much affected. He folded his paper and laid it on the table. Then he took his large cream-colored hat from the rack.

"I'll walk along back with you and talk to him," he said. "Meantime, you better send for Tom."

For a long time after they had gone, and later in my bed, I lay going over what was said and the pictures created in my mind. There had been something incomplete about the story, something that passed between the two men that puzzled me, something not so much spoken as left unsaid but which each understood. I wondered how Charley could have done such a violent thing. They said that he had once been a good enough shot with the rifle, trained by his English father, but of late the only things he was known to do were drink whisky and drive fast horses.

He was still more blond than Doña Ellen. We boys called him the Englishman, not only from his light hair and florid cheeks but because of his eccentricities and curious British nature. He was one of the reasons we went to New Town on Saturday evenings. Then the Englishman could be found in town drinking at the Antlers Bar. Punctually at eight o'clock he would come out, unknot the hitching-rope, get in his buggy, and race his fast horse up and down the two blocks of business street. On the way back he was invariably halted and fined for exceeding the speed limit. With evident satisfaction he would pay the fine and go back to the bar, while the spectators collected for the event would reluctantly scatter.

Next morning when I got up Cousin Albert was already gone, but Pas and Goyo were waiting for me outside the back door. They informed me that the Englishman's horse was in our stable, and we spent the greater part of the morning standing around him talking in suppressed excitement. It was the same bahío with black mane and tail we had seen the Englishman race last Saturday night. It gave me a curious feeling to see him standing there so calmly, shoving his nose into the hay and energetically chewing, unaware that his master was locked up for murder only a few blocks away.

"It is his horse," Pas said at length. "But it is not he, they say, that killed the Anglo."

"Who was he, then?" I asked, eager to hear the family name cleared.

"It was not a he, but a she," Pas declared mysteriously.

For a moment I didn't know what he meant. Then I saw Manuel bearing down upon us. Doña Ellen always referred to him as a mozo, which meant "boy," but he was some fifty years old, a short heavy man like so many Mexicans his age, with a powerful torso and tremendous face now distorted with rage.

"What lie is this, you son-of-a-goat!" he roared and tried to get his huge hands on Pas. Those hands, it was said, could rope the wildest running horse in a corral and bring him to a stop without snubbing-post or saddle horn. If they had got hold of Pas, there was no telling what they might have done, but Pas was too quick for him and dodged out in the alley, where we presently joined him.

"Now let's go down to the jail," Pas said daringly. "We will ask the Englishman himself who fired the shot that killed Señor Jeffcoat."

All the way down the alley what he had said earlier pierced me. Exactly what did he mean that it had not been a he but a she that had done it? It came back to plague me now that Sheriff Martínez had not used the word "man" as the expert with the rifle who had fired the shot, but "person." I remembered the story about Doña Ellen as a girl. A whole procession of uneasy thoughts troubled me as we stood outside the jail under a small window which Pas and Goyo informed me opened into the Englishman's cell. Although Pas called loudly and brazenly, no face appeared at the bars and no voice answered.

It was late noon when I came back up the alley to find Doña Ellen's buggy outside the stable and her pet horse, Critter, in the next box stall to her brother's bahío. An empty carriage that had evidently been filled with baggage and criadas from the ranch stood in the driveway while its horses out in the alley chewed corn from nose bags before starting back to the Prietas.

Manuel scowled at me.

"You better make steps for the house. If you are wise you will say nothing from that young liar of a he goat," he warned me.

The rite of dinner at such a time I would have gladly avoided, but Manuel herded me ahead of him toward the back door with all the energy of a loader who slaps his thighs and cries "Hu-cha!" while driving sheep onto the cattle cars. Not wishing to be a sheep, I ran around to the front door.

The house seemed another place when I entered it. Moving slowly down the hall, I saw that the sheets had been taken from the familiar shapes in the long parlor, disclosing wholly unfamiliar furnishings. There were twin scarlet sofas with rolled ends, chairs in red-and-gold brocade that looked like Mexico, a tall object with filigree brass legs rising to marble shelves and crowned with a painted china lamp. Broad walnut frames inlaid with gold on the wall held only the tiniest of pictures. Another frame enclosed a wreath and one a bunch of withered flowers, mementos of some funeral.

The doors to the other rooms opening on the wide hall were open now and I saw across the way a second parlor, not so long as the other, but with a couch, an organ, a blue fireplace, a globe on a stand, and a lacy nest of artificial flowers hanging from the ceiling. As I went on I had glimpses into other high-ceiling rooms, furnished with heavy and ornate brass beds, canopies, marble-top bureaus, dressers, and tables, engravings on the walls, china lamps in various sizes, Brussels carpet on the floor. Most every room had in addition to the bed a couch or lounge of some kind. I had never seen such a lot of them in a single house. A stranger would suppose the Johnson y Campos the laziest and sleepiest of families.

I stopped before reaching the dining-room, but Doña Ellen must have seen my head pass outside the window, else she heard the front door. She came out in the hall looking even more delicate and blue-eyed than I remembered.

"Hello, Jud! Where have you been?" she greeted, as if I and not she was the one who needed comforting. "We've had to start. Come in."

She took my cold hand in her warm one and drew me into the dining-room, where dinner stood on the massive table affixed to the floor, flanked by long polished benches of enormous pine planking on either side.

"This is Willy," she said, leading me where a dark-haired, delicate-looking boy sat in front of a scarcely touched plate. "Your place, Jud, is right beside him. I hope you two will be friends. You're cousins, you know, and blood is thicker than water."

Once I was settled long enough to recover myself and observe what was going on around me, I saw Cousin Albert at the head of the table looking kindly and approvingly at me. His wife didn't take her seat where I expected, but sat opposite Willy and me. I soon found that she needed no formal position at the doña's head of the table to hold court, but could take care of herself wherever she was.

Before I came she had evidently been telling the judge and Willy of some incident. Now I listened to her, a little surprised to find it amusing. She finished, turned to me, asked me questions about myself, confided to me one or two intimate things about the ranch, then wove the four of us into her conversation. Her flow of talk was fluent, Spanish in character but spoken in English for my benefit and managed with both English and Spanish skill. It was impossible not to listen and watch, too. She seemed to make light of their unspoken affliction.

I found this a characteristic I was to see much of, her manner of disregarding trouble and danger by making fun of them both. It was this, I think, together with her playful feminine wile and Latin melancholy, as if deep inside of her she knew her serious fate all the time, that made men want to deliver her from the dangers she so confidently disdained and the trouble she so rashly courted.

At first, sitting there at the table, I wondered if shooting and death had actually occurred. Then with dinner done, it was as if the pleasant interlude, like an act in a play, was over. Faint sadness settled on her face. Gravity returned to Cousin Albert. When I glanced at Willy his dark eyes looked back at me wordlessly. What the look meant I had no idea, but I felt that I liked him and that we would get along.

There was no telephone in the house those days to inform your friends that you had come to town, but news traveled about as fast then as now, particularly upon an event like this when your friends were expected to rally around and offer support and encouragement. It was something of a revelation to see the house bright and almost gay that evening, with wine in glasses taken from a rack of four marble shelves along the wall. The Ignacio Bacas and the Felipe Chávezes, who spoke mostly Spanish, came, and the Wilmots and the Kidds, who spoke mostly English. These were sheep people or those who did business with them.

Others arriving later included Tom Dold, the family lawyer since Cousin Albert had sat on the bench. A bachelor like Mr. Younger, he reminded me of him also in his fund of good humor, but was portlier, had a more courteous gentlemanly air and slower Alabama or Mississippi speech. Not a word so far that I heard in English was spoken of Ellen's brother languishing in jail, but Mr. Dold's stories and confident manner spoke continuously saying, have no fear, everything in Moro County is under control.

When Willy and I were sent to bed, his mother excused herself from the company and came back to see that he was properly covered in his new quarters. Late September nights can be cool in Moro. He occupied my late bed which had been his, and I was in another narrower one placed in the room since last night. His mother tucked him in and kissed him good night. Then she came over and did the same to me.

No one had kissed me since my mother had done it several years before. I remembered Cousin Albert's wife's hands as brisk and masterful, but when she pressed the covers around my neck and shoulders I thought I had never felt a touch more gentle and soft. That such hands could have the stain of blood on them seemed to me unthinkable. I felt myself relax, grateful that for tonight at least sleep would solve all problems, including that of making any more talk to Willy this first night of our acquaintance when tragedy and constraint lay so heavy on us both.

"Buenas noches, Jud," she said, using the Spanish to me as she had to Willy, as if to intimate that I would have to learn more of the language now.

"Good night, Doña Ellen," I said.

"Call me Cousin Ellen," she corrected, and waited.

"Good night, Cousin Ellen," I replied dutifully.

She looked down at me in warm approval, but even as she smiled I imagined I saw deep inconsolable shadows in her eyes.

IV

The Moro County courthouse stood a little way off the plaza at the corner of Audiencia Street and what was then called New Town Road. Today the building looks very old and ordinary, as if always used for mercantile purposes. But those days I thought it imposing, a kind of family government house since Cousin Albert held the highest office in it and ruled over it like a king in his rude palace.

More than once I had ventured into its dim tunnels and gazed on doors painted with such mysterious and important names as TREASURER, ASSESSOR, COUNTY CLERK, COMMISSIONERS, and their Spanish equivalents. The most important and exciting doors to me were marked COURTROOM and JUDGE'S CHAMBERS. The latter I had not entered, but since they were the legal offices of Cousin Albert, the door had given me a warm and proud feeling.

Now, after what had happened on the ranch, the aspect of the whole building changed. I found myself avoiding it whenever possible. Something dark, unfriendly, almost frightening had come over it and the jail where Ellen's brother, Charley, awaited trial. I knew it couldn't be Charley or his fate. He meant little or nothing to me. No, it must be something else. I remembered what Pas had hinted at. That must be the secret of my shock, an implication so incredible and terrible that I didn't dare think of it openly.

From the beginning I looked to see if anyone else might know and feel as I did. Willy came under my scrutiny first. He was a quiet boy with pale skin and a shock of heavy black Mexican hair. Although his face could light up like the sun coming out on a patch of sunflowers, there were times when he looked at me with something inexpressible in his dark eyes. I watched Cousin Albert, too, but his grave face and eyes, his gallant black beard and slender arched back told me nothing.

I waited for Willy's grandmother to come in from the ranch for the trial. They called her Mama Grande instead of the usual Abuelita. She would know, I felt, for she had been there when it happened. If she hadn't seen it herself, she surely would have demanded every detail from those who did. A short, stout native woman with a swarthy face, she had the blackest of eyes. Those eyes gave the impression of having looked on many unpleasant things, the butchery of sheep, torture by Indians, the stabbing and shooting-down of men in cold blood, and other wickedness common in this raw land. She had a tongue that ran on rapidly in Spanish like many of her kind, but her face and black eyes to me remained unreadable.

When Ellen's sister, Doña Ana, came over from next door to see her mother, I thought I caught a glimpse of fear in her face, but I felt it might have been for her husband. Even before coming to my cousin's house to live I had heard how since their marriage Lawyer Beasley had dominated and restrained her, taking over her inheritance, keeping her on a strict allowance, laying down her expenses for the house, naming the prices she must pay even for such small things as eggs and chile, trimming the wages of the native servants until she had to put up with some of the poorest.

Epifania had once told me how Doña Ana had looked as a girl.

"Ah, you should see those two girls together when they are little. About the same size. Only a year or more between them. But such a difference! Doña Ana morena. How you say in English?—dark. Not ugly dark. We Mexicans think dark very pretty. Dark skin, black hair, black eyes, and lively as a kitten. And Doña Ellen with white skin and hair of gold like her father. You wouldn't believe they come from the same mother."

Now I found Doña Ana older-looking than Ellen, worn-faced and somber-eyed. It was strange to see her and think that before her marriage she had been beautiful and gay. Today she seemed apprehensive, to have no will or decision of her own.

"Snell thinks I should," several times she defended herself. "I'll see what Snell thinks," she said when Ellen urged them to dinner.

She grew visibly nervous when Ellen asked if she wouldn't sit with her and her mother at the trial.

"I'm not sure what Snell wants," was all she would say.

I suspected she was here today without his permission. More than once her daughter, Felicitas, said they had better go. Doña Ana hung on as if she feared to stay but hated more to leave, as if since this shooting had come between them she didn't know when she would see her mother and sister again. From the start, Felicitas refused to sit down. I thought her the prettiest girl I had ever seen, a little younger than I, with an English skin, hazel eyes, and golden hair. I felt that this was how Ellen must have looked when she was young, but Felicitas would have little to do with her Aunt Ellen now, regarding her with an attitude I was sure came from her father. Indeed she treated us all with veiled hostile coolness, as if we had shown ourselves the bitter enemy and persecutor of her parent. Only on Willy once or twice when he wasn't looking did I see her glance soften.

My eyes searched the faces of others, too—of Tom Dold and Dr. George Gammel, who were most often at the house, as well as the Wilmots, the Rodeys, and the Kidds. But they told me nothing. As for the native friends who came, their faces were impossible for an Anglo to read.

Meanwhile the trial was approaching and Willy and I were told we would have to attend. I suspect it was the idea of Tom Dold, who defended Charley, that we boys sitting with Ellen and her mother would arouse the sympathy of the jury. The most that it aroused in me was the belief that my unspoken fears might be brought out in our presence. All the time that Willy and I had to sit there, with witness after witness being questioned, with every sentence translated by the court interpreter from Spanish to English or the other way around, with recesses and irksome delays, with Cousin Albert sitting watchfully on the bench, and people, including many cattlemen from out of the county, crowding the room to the doors and windows, I remembered what Pas Ramírez had hinted and waited for it to raise its ugly head in the courtroom.

The witness I disliked more than any other was Lawyer Beasley.

"That's my Uncle Snell and he hates us," Willy had whispered the first day. "When Grandfather died, he wanted us to let him take over and manage the ranch. But only Tía Ana would sign."

I remembered the first time I had seen the name. My father had brought home a copy of the *Moro Sentinel* and in it was his advertisement:

J. SNELL BEASLEY, attorney at law
Legal Advice and Counsel. Collections Made.
Loans Arranged. Deeds. Mortgages.
All Instruments of Writing
Promptly Attended to.

My father said he was the shrewdest and richest lawyer in the county and told me stories to prove it. One, I recall, was how he had collected a note for the Silverio Garcías. A Baca County cattleman owed the Garcías twenty thousand dollars. For years he refused to pay. Beasley told the Garcías he would collect it in or out of court, but his fee would be half of the amount, and the Garcías finally signed a paper promising him ten thousand dollars. Then Beasley settled the debt quickly for eleven thousand. His share was ten thousand, the Garcías' only one.

Another time, my father said, Beasley was engaged by a cattleman named Lassen to defend him for the murder of a Mexican sheepherder. There was no doubt of his acquittal among the cattlemen in Baca County, but Beasley had fixed a juror to hold out for conviction, or so everyone openly said. This hung the jury, and a new trial was ordered, when Lassen was acquitted. The first time Beasley took Lassen's cattle as his fee, the second time his ranch, and this was the ranch whose foreman, Jeffcoat, had been shot in Ojo Canyon.

And now here Lawyer Beasley was in court before me. Of all the Jeffcoat sympathizers, many of them from Baca County, he was the most dangerous to reckon with. A short thick man with a red mottled face, he sat directly behind the prosecuting attorney and often leaned forward to speak to him. When at last he was put on the stand as owner of the cattle, he let loose long blasts of answers and testimony on his wife's right to send their cattle through Ojo Canyon that, I felt, shook Charley's defense to its foundations.

But no word did he breathe of the specter that lay on my heart, and when I looked up and saw Cousin Albert sitting unaffected on the bench, the faces of the jurors as before, the procedure of the court unchanged, and other witnesses being called as if nothing had happened, I had the same feeling as the night when Cousin Albert and Sheriff Martínez had talked, as if all were playing a part.

My chief hope was from something Tom Dold had said.

"Don't worry about Charley, Ellen. Every man we let on the jury has something to do with the sheep business. Or else with somebody who does. Most of them have Spanish blood besides."

But I knew that Snell Beasley was not playing a part. I think he must have expected a hung jury, for the last day he let Doña Ana make the show of attending her brother's trial. The jury was out scarcely an hour when they came in with a verdict of not guilty. Freed now, the prisoner pushed to his mother and Ellen in the crowd. Doña Ana was so carried away by the excitement that she, too, made her way to their side.

It was a pretty scene, Charley hugged and kissed by his mother and sisters while the sheepmen stood around watching with enjoyment and approval. In her emotion, Doña Ana looked years younger, and I was struck by the contrast the two sisters made today, Ellen with her white English skin and golden hair, and Ana dark and glowing.

Then suddenly the red face of Lawyer Beasley appeared. The excitement seemed to go out of Ana. Her face aged visibly as her husband took her arm and they moved away.

I saw soberness and pity on many faces, but it didn't bother me. My relief was too great, not so much that Charley was freed but that court and jury had recognized no other who could have fired the shot. I went home in peace. At supper Ellen said we had stood by loyally, that already we had missed so much school it wouldn't hurt us to miss a little more and so she was taking us out for a week's holiday to the ranch. It seemed then that God was back in his heaven and all was right with the world.

There was a celebration at the house that evening, with dozens of guests, including the family of Apolonio Sena, who had testified in Charley's behalf. Next morning Charley went back to the ranch, taking his mother with him. I think the idea was to get him away from the saloons while the cattlemen were still in town.

We made ready to leave early the same afternoon. It was a cloudless fall day, of which there are so many in the Southwest. Manuel brought Critter and the yellow-top buggy around to the front of the house. The horse, which had hardly been out of his stall during the trial, was impatient to be off. As a rule with three in the buggy the driver, who must sit on the adjoining knees of the other two, would be the lightest in weight. But it was plain that Critter would be too much for a boy today, and I had to take Willy on my lap.

"It will make you strong, holding up each other," Ellen said lightly while Critter chafed to go.

Just the way she spoke to him as she took the lines gave me complete confidence which did not waver though we turned the corner of Iglesia Street on two wheels and went down what is now Center Avenue with a cloud of dust behind us.

It was exciting to ride with her again, her light talk and fun, her feminine presence very near to me, her superb mastery of horse and the desert spaces. Pleasure in my new life swam about me. Once we had forded the river and were up on the escarpment with the broad mesa stretching before us, washing up to the Prietas like a wave foaming with dried bunch grass, I could hardly wait for the hunting that she promised us. Looking ahead, the Prietas were like a long wall of dark sand sprinkled with moss, but the sand, Willy informed me, was rock and the green moss cedars and pines where mule deer and mountain lion could be found.

Halfway across the mesa we overtook a group of horsemen, evidently cattlemen returning to Baca County from the trial. They looked around and saw us coming but did not get out of our way. Ellen had to turn Critter aside on the level mesa to pass.

"Hu-cha! Hucha!" one of them sent up the sheepman's cry derisively after us.

"Don't look back!" Ellen cautioned us, careful, I thought, neither to increase or slacken Critter's pace, but presently the same voice yelled again. I couldn't understand what it said, but I think Ellen did because when I looked at her something in her face and shoulders had changed.

I heard hoofbeats coming after us, and that was when I learned the congenital truth about Critter, that he could never let another horse around him, and at such a time not even Ellen could hold him. Now as the hoofbeats came closer, he answered with a burst of speed that left the other quickly behind. Ellen tried to curb him. I still retain a vivid picture of her in my mind, her gloved hands sawing on the tan lines, her slight body half lifted to its feet.

"You fool!" she cried, exasperated. "They'll think we're running away."

She could do nothing with him until sounds of pursuit behind us had ceased. Then she slowed him down and furiously turned him around. The horsemen were now a mile or two in the rear, and she drove slowly back until close to them. Here in the trail she waited for them to come.

Willy and I were silent. What he thought I had no means of knowing, but when I glanced at Ellen the transformation in her astonished me. I am much older now and experience has taught me never to be surprised at the presence of fire and flint wanting only provocation to show themselves in the softest and slightest of girls and women, especially those with a blond or red coloring. But then it was a revelation to me to see with what hard relish she faced the oncoming riders. Her feminine trusting and helpless way with men had vanished and been replaced with something else, still feminine but without pity and boding no good for anyone, herself included.

Critter stood perfectly quiet while the riders came, as if his honor was not involved so long as he faced them. They gave the yellow-top buggy a wide berth, turning far aside as Ellen had before. None of them offered to molest us or even speak to her, but when they were by and Ellen passed them again, they let out a series of shrill derisive Texas yells. This time she did not stop. We drove on toward the mountains, and nothing more was said about it, but the incident made a strong impression on me.

If I thought Ellen a lady in town, she was still more so out here. Over the years I always thought her to be at her best among the natives. They seemed to infect her with a special charm. Hardly had we approached the scattered cluster of adobe buildings when Johnson y Campo Mexicans surrounded the buggy. They didn't run or swarm. They appeared to be already there to celebrate, as if they knew we were coming and could wait for us. Time meant nothing to them, and now this was the moment they had all looked forward to. The men pulled off their unwieldy hats with surprising respect and grace. The swarthy women smiled. The black eyes of the children, who were miniature replicas of their elders, shone at their patrona. Even men who looked to me like rascals and thieves asked with gentle courtesy of the health and well-being of Ellen and Willy, whom they called Guillo. I was introduced as Willy's cousin, and my well-being became instantly their consuming interest and concern.

But never for a moment could I treat them as Ellen and Willy did. There was, I soon found, a great art in it, a precise stage between superiority and warm interest which I never could attain. Other Mexican ricos I had seen in town showed no such manner. Indeed, some of them treated the poor of their own race with rude and brutal contempt, and I wondered if Ellen's secret might not have been inherited from her father. For the first time I had a glimpse of him. In the long adobe horse stables, in a place called the tackroom, among the bridles, saddles, collars, and pieces of harness on the wall were tacked up photographs of Johnson y Campo horses, often with a rider or driver. Sometimes it was Ellen or Charley but usually their father, whom I found to my surprise had been a one-armed man of presence and intensity.

Where I felt him most was in the house, in what they called the gunroom, with New Mexican grizzly skins on the floor and on the wall deer, elk, and antelope heads and a considerable rack of pistols and rifles, all interstudded with photographs, some of them framed, of Ellen's father standing with his foot on a prostrate bear or mountain lion or sighting his rifle, the barrel supported by the stump of his left arm.

The second day at the ranch Ellen took us on the promised hunting trip. She drove me in the buckboard along a pair of wheel tracks that wound for miles through the cedars and then out to a lonely expanse of plain. Willy rode his blue pony, the one they called a grullo. Up near a round treeless mountain, which his mother said was an extinct volcano, she pointed out distant motionless or slowly moving objects which I couldn't make out at first but which gradually took shape for me as small brown living creatures as they moved curiously toward us and then white as they alternately turned and ran.

They still seemed in entire safety from us when Ellen suddenly stopped the horse, passed the lines to me, drew a rifle from beneath the seat, stood up in the buckboard, and fired. The lunge of the horse threw her back into the seat, but not too quickly to keep me from seeing one of the inquisitive brown-and-white wraiths drop to the range while the others fled. When we reached it, I found a beautiful small deerlike creature lying on the grass with blood running from its mouth and from a well-directed hole in its graceful head.

It seemed incredible to me that destruction had occurred so accurately and at such a great distance. I had always wanted a rifle of my own to knock over prairie dogs rearing by their sandy burrows, and I didn't understand at first why Ellen's splendid shooting should bother me. Turning, I saw Willy a few yards away sitting motionless on his pony staring at the dead antelope.

Still in the saddle, he held his mother's unquiet horse while she had me help her lift the game to the back of the buckboard, where the bleeding head was left hanging over the edge. Then we drove back to the ranch house. It was very strange. Our hunting had been successful. This was exactly what we wanted, what we had come out to the ranch for, and yet some inexplicable shadow for me had fallen over the sunlit plain.

V

We stayed at the ranch for nearly two weeks, school or no school, and if it was a bit long for me, it was short for Willy and his mother. Just how the news that Ellen was home traveled over the wide uninhabited region, I don't know, but the Piños came visiting from Embudo Canyon and the Xavier Oteros from what they called the Red Lake region. Tom Dold and Doc Gammel journeyed out from town for both weekends along with Cousin Albert, and evenings were lively with late dinners, wine, and cards, the days with horses, hunting, and game.

I was glad to get away, especially from the game dinners and the dead antelope and deer hanging in a row in the cold dry air out of reach of the dogs and sun. Town had become somehow peaceful and civilized in my mind, and when we drove back through Ojo Canyon to the East Mesa I felt escape from something, I didn't know quite what. Even the air seemed free again, and it gave me a wonderful feeling to see Moro lying far below us, hardly distinguishable at this distance except for the wisp of black smoke hanging above it from the invisible railroad.

Town seemed even better as we drove into Audiencia Street and the plaza. Then we came to the white house on La Placita and saw workmen laying brick between the two houses.

"What in the world are they doing?" Ellen asked Chepa and Epifania, who rushed out when they saw us.

They seemed agitated and confused.

"It is to be a wall, señora," Chepa said.

"What in heaven for?"

"Señora! Doña Ana and Felicitas daren't come over any more! Not even Suplicante! They must stay over there and we must stay over here. As long as we live."

"It is to be a high wall, señora," Epifania said. "Seven feet up and from street to alley, Suplicante told us."

Ellen did not ask who had ordered this. We all knew. She said nothing for the moment, but as we went into the house I caught a glimpse of her face, and her cheeks and eyes were frightening.

"I didn't tell you," Cousin Albert said when he came home from the courthouse, "because I didn't want to spoil your holiday. It would have upset you more than it's worth. It may turn out to be not too bad. Snell is having his revenge now. He's working off his temper. In fact, it might turn out to be a good thing."

I often thought later on how tragically wrong he was. Perhaps he knew it even then. He may have been trying to put the best possible face on a blight that would be evident to everyone in Moro and for miles around. Certainly I was only a boy and saw it. Could it be that nothing dared be said outright about Ellen at the trial; that it was not the Western code to accuse a lady so darkly? But now, without breaking the code, without saying a word, Beasley was giving notice that he didn't feel her a fit associate for his wife and children, who were her own sister, niece, and nephew.

What Ellen thought I do not know. More than once while the men were at work on the wall, and especially when her brother-in-law came out to look it over, I saw her eyes like agates and that familiar, hard, curiously smaller look on her face like a tightly nailed but attractive box.

It was gone and in its place a kind of gay desperation when friends called.

"Do you know you take your life in your hands to come? We're in quarantine and under siege, you know," she'd greet guests in the playful way they all knew so well. Her dinners were too late in the evening for Willy and me. We ate our supper much earlier, but in our room we could hear her poke fun at her brother-in-law and his wall.

"It's a pity you can't see it by daylight. You know how Snell is. He won't hire Anglo bricklayers. They cost too much. No, he hires Abundio Sais and his brother, Ascensión, who never laid anything but dobes. Now, we all know that dobes take no mortar, so Abundio forgets the mortar for one brick and Ascensión forgets the mortar for another, and the next round Abundio has to put on abundio mortar and Ascensión has to give his brick more ascension, and that's the way it goes, more abundio and ascension, till the wall looks like the stripes of a zebra."

After the laughter, her voice came again, mockingly.

"But Albert's going to talk to Snell. Perhaps he'll graciously let us cover up our side with adobe. Then it will be easier to abide it."

Of course, we knew that she would never have Cousin Albert ask Snell and that, no matter what was done to the wall, never could she abide it. Most every evening since we came back she either had guests at the house or was a guest in some other. But days were a trial to her. Many an afternoon we came home from school and found Critter hitched up in front of the house, with Ellen at the door, hatted and coated to take us for a ride.

Once the buggy wheels rolled clear of town, you could feel her other self return, her old self, the one I liked best. We drove all the roads and lanes through the irrigated small ranches along the river, and the more populated roads through the native villages of Yrisarri and Gutierreztown. But mostly Ellen took the wheel tracks that crossed and crisscrossed, wheeled and looped, on the mesa. There were two mesas, one across the river, another across the railroad. Here the range rolled and dipped and curled and was cut by all sorts of dry watercourses so that the trails skirted the edge of deep draws, and where you could look across wide cañadas.

It wasn't only to get away from town that she went, I think, but to be driving Critter. There was a certain relationship between Ellen and her horse that only those who ride or drive horses can understand today. It may be that he was a link to her dead father, as Dr. Gammel once claimed, but the brute was close to her in his own right, much closer than I, for example, a silent companion on the empty desolate spaces, one who never failed her, and much stronger than any of us so that when he obeyed and did her will, she drew from his strength as well as from her own.

But at dusk when we got back to the house, the wall was always there, not an idle rumor that could be lived down and forgotten, rather a monument pointing as long as it stood. Words you could reply to and criminal charges could be refuted in court, but how would you answer or disprove an evil brick wall? Every day when town and ranch folk went by, there it was to see and remember, reviving the dark whispers.

I think it was when she couldn't stand the wall any more that she would drive to the ranch, and that was why during the holidays we went to Rancho Antiguo. But she always gave other reasons for going.

"Wouldn't you like a white Christmas?" she asked as we walked home from midnight Mass. "The only snow this year is up in La Sierra. How would you like to run up and see the Pereas?"

She made it sound so easy, as if it were only an hour's drive, but I knew the Greenhorns, which she called La Sierra, were forty miles away and the ranch of the Pereas must be farther. The morning we left, Moro was still in shadow but far to the north the sun was already red on the snowy summits. Critter kept up his incredible trot all the way except now and then on the grades when he slipped back into a running walk.

"He's resting when he does that," Willy informed me. "It's the Indian shuffle."

I had never seen anyone received as Ellen was at Rancho Antiguo, like someone of royal family. I suspected the Pereas seldom saw visitors up here near the Colorado border, but next day guests came from Trinidad and they treated her the same. The men surrounded her, drawing out her talk and laughter. The women did the unheard-of Spanish act of listening, and children watched her in a kind of wondering worship.

Long after Willy and I went to bed in a huge room with others younger than we were, we could hear her laugh next door in the old sala, a particular kind of laugh I seldom hear today except among women and girls of Spanish blood or among those who learned it from them, a series of quick, tiny, almost incoherent explosions, tumbling out all at once like mixed-up notes of music, without rhyme or reason, very virgencita, contagious, and delightful to hear.

But if Ellen was looked up to at the Pereas', Critter was not. The Perea family was noted for raising white sheep and black horses. Any colt of another color was promptly sold, and they had no use for Critter's oscuro shade. "It's the color of the dirt," they said. Also, their horses were their chattels, not their friends. They reined them high and trained them to walk and prance in style. Critter's lounging ways, the low posture of his head, and his indifference to showing spirit to order invited their contempt.

Moreover, Critter declined to graze away with the other horses, but hung around close to the ranch house, cropping what grass he could find. He seemed concerned about us in this strange place. The first time Willy went to the excusado, or water closet, the grand like of which there was nothing outside at the Johnson y Campo ranch, he did not come out for a long time. Critter kept grazing closer. Finally he ambled up, pushed the door open with his nose, stuck his head in, and looked around. It was, Ellen said afterward, as if he wanted to see what this place was and what Willy was doing in it. This excited the Pereas' huge amusement and their remarks nettled Ellen.

"Why are you such a baby?" she scolded Critter. "You won't stay with the other horses. You have to hang around me like a spoiled child around its mother."

Whether he understood her, I have no notion. He looked back at her calmly, then went on grazing, but Ellen was plainly impatient with him. So he couldn't follow us when we went to the mountains, she had him put in a corral. We saw him looking after us as we drove away to scenery more beautiful than I knew existed. The crowning point of the trip was a grassy trail through a high valley called Canyon de Espíritu Santo, or Holy Ghost Canyon, where the blue firs and red-boled pines drooped with moss and a crystal cold river rushed down from a snowy peak at the head of the canyon.

We came back elated from our trip, but the first thing we heard as we neared the ranch was Critter whinnying at us from where he stood with his head over the corral fence.

Early next morning I felt a hand shake me under the heavy blankets spun from native fleeces. It was Ellen saying that we must go. Sleepily Willy begged to stay another day.

"No, it's impossible," his mother said. "We could be snowed in for weeks up here."

When we sat up we saw through the dim window what looked like fine bits of gray wool slowly falling to the ground as I had often seen them shaken to the floor of the hide building at the commission house. The ground already lay covered, and when we left we could see our tracks deep in the white road. We could also see the Pereas standing on the portal waving after us, while far above and behind them on the mountainsides gusts of white swirled over the firs and pines.

We ourselves didn't feel the force of the wind till we left the shelter of the mountains. Coming to the mouth of the canyon, we could see in front of us the white particles driven almost horizontally from the northwest. Critter saw them, too. His ears pricked, and when the wind reached him, tossing his mane, he answered with doubled speed.

Willy laughed. "He doesn't like it, Mama."

"I hope it stings him," his mother said. "He's been a very temperamental boy."

At first it was pleasant enough racing through the snow, but after an hour or two it had grown much colder and the snow was thicker and finer, a solid white curtain closing us in. The rolling foothills that had been so pleasant when we came through them a few days before were blotted out and the road with them.

"How do we know where we are?" Willy wondered.

I guessed that Ellen knew no more than we did, but she answered at once. "San Antonio knows."

"He might have forgotten us here in the Arriba country," Willy pointed out.

"No," she promised confidently, "I told Father Goshard I'd get a new robe for San Antonio, the best China silk and a gold hem. If we get lost up here in the snow, San Antonio knows he'd never get it."

I gazed at Ellen curiously. Sometimes when the Spanish came out in her, she surprised me.

The cold by now was intense. We huddled under what blankets we had, the rubber shield of the buggy buttoned up tight from dash to top with the reins passing through a slit. The isinglass peekholes were almost constantly blinded with snow except when a jolt from the wheels or our hands would clear them. But when we looked out, all we could see was the brown furry shape of Critter, a tiny moving island in the midst of a white wilderness with neither sky above nor solid ground beneath.

Only once did I see anything besides Critter and his frozen breath. That was when we passed close to a landmark strange to me, a lone butte like a giant idol with a tree growing out of its head. I could remember passing no such object on the way up. For a moment the butte stood there revealed, then fresh waves of white blotted it out. But it couldn't blot out a terrible conviction from my mind. For the last hours Ellen had made no attempt to guide Critter, letting him choose his own way in the barren waste. Now I knew that he must be lost. More than once his trot dragged to a walk and we could feel the snow pushing against the buggy box. Sometimes he frightened us by stopping altogether. Peering out, we watched him rub one side of his head, then the other against the ends of the shafts. Ellen said she thought he was rubbing the icicles from his eyes, a remark which sobered me. After this he went on, but sooner or later, I felt, the snow must stop him and bury us in its depths.

The day dragged, growing no lighter. It seemed a week since we had left the Pereas and even since we ate the lunch they had packed for us. Suddenly

Ellen startled us by her cry. Looking out of the peephole, I saw what appeared to be a wide gray streak in the snow. It ran at right angles to our course and disappeared into the blizzard.

"You wonderful thing!" she screamed. I thought at first she called to this mysterious outline on the white earth. Then I realized it had been to Critter. "It's the Baca road!" she told us. "He never took the road to town. He's brought us down behind the Prietas straight for the ranch."

As if recognition of the familiar landmark raised his spirits also, the brown furry shape, almost black now with sweat, stepped up his pace. Down here there seemed to be less snow. We learned afterward that it had started to fall much later at the ranch. We reached places where the wind had left our trail almost bare, and here Critter let himself go. He had been dragging a heavy buggy with three people through snow and often drifts for hours. By all accounts he should have been worn out, brought to one of those violent trembling spells that in a Western horse means exhaustion and death. But now his legs fairly flew. The stable and alfalfa ahead seemed to tap new energies in his being. I had never seen a horse lay himself so close to the ground, as if to spare every inch of up-and-down motion.

There was great excitement at the ranch when we arrived. They hadn't known we had ever left town. Mama Grande, aroused by the commotion, called demandingly from the portal that we come in at once. But Ellen refused to go until she saw Critter cared for. He steamed in the frosty air like a railroad engine on a zero morning. When I climbed stiffly to the ground I saw that not a hair on his body but was laid, curled, twisted with sweat and wind.

Fidel came running to take over the unhitching and lead him to his stall. The hay that we thought he had run for lay plentiful in his manger, but now that he had reached it, there was no effort to touch it. He stood with hoofs somewhat far apart, head down, his ice-and-snow-rimmed eyes paying attention to none of us, as if what he wanted most in the world was just to stand there and never move. This was how he stayed while Fidel and Teofilo rubbed him down.

All this time Mama Grande, bundled up in a great woolen rebozo, stood in the entry chattering angrily, bombarding Ellen with questions, calling God's wrath down on the Pereas for letting us go, while swarthy faces nodded intently behind her. Once Fidel spoke in support of her. His strong brown weathered face was grave.

"Dios was with you, Doña Ellen," he said. "The snow drifts worse on the Moro road. Deep as a house sometimes. Had Critter gone that way, never maybe would you have got through."

It was late in the evening when he brought word to the house.

"It is well now. Critter has started to eat."

VI

The blizzard did something to Ellen. I never knew exactly what. Perhaps it was Critter that did it. Perhaps it had been the close call of death, not so much on her as on Willy. As she drove us back to town I felt her definitely changed from the person who had driven us to Rancho Antiguo. At home, confronted by the wall, I was aware of bitter emotions working in her again, but once inside of the house she seemed to master and hide them. In the days that followed I noticed that she avoided the wall, staying in parts of the house where it couldn't be seen, sewing with her own fingers the promised robe for San Antonio and taking it to church several times to measure and fit.

The second week she called Willy.

"I want you to go over to your Tía Ana for me. Say I hope they can come to dinner Saturday evening. It will be just family, theirs and ours. Of course, I expect Uncle Snell and Felicitas. Say I hope Felicitas can stay up for the evening."

I could feel Willy's slow surprise.

"Do you think they'll come?"

"Well, we know they've come before. After all, Ana is my sister and Felicitas your blood cousin. We love them and I'm sure they love us."

Willy stared at his mother. This was a new Ellen, one I had never seen before, and evidently Willy hadn't either.

"But do you think he'll let her?"

"He should—if we think of him with charity and kindness. Charity and kindness can do wonders, Father Goshard says, even to Snell Beasley. You and Jud must treat him with love, Willy, when you see him."

"How do you mean?" Willy looked dismayed.

"Talk and act toward him like nothing had happened, as if he never sent his herd up Ojo Canyon. If we treat him with love, then perhaps everything will be all right."

Once we were outside, Willy made a face to me, a face of wonder and things unspoken as only those of Latin blood can. Reluctantly he took his way toward the forbidden wall and then behind it, keeping me close beside him. I could see that he was uneasy. When Felicitas sprang out at us in the patio, he fairly jumped.

"Willy Sessions! You better get out of here!" she threatened.

Willy seemed relieved if anything by the encounter.

"I don't need to get out," he stammered. "Mama says we love you and you love us and everything is going to be all right."

The girl stared at him. She moved up and planted herself directly in front of him.

"What did you say, Willy?"

"Felicitas!" Willy implored her. "Do me the favor. Go and tell your mother for Mama. Tell her that we love you and you love us and she wants you over for dinner Saturday night. Uncle Snell, too."

"You better go, Willy Sessions, before Papa comes home and hears you."

"Felicitas!" Willy begged. "Do me the favor. Just tell your mama for Mama. Tell her—"

Felicitas put her fingers over her ears.

"I don't hear you," she chanted. "I don't hear you. I didn't hear a word you said."

Willy looked at me. His face was haggard. He considered his aunt's brick house like a prisoner the gibbet.

"Come along in, Jud!" he begged. "Whatever you do, stand by me. Don't run off."

I could see that he was afraid. Slowly he pushed open the side door and went in with me close behind. There looking at us, as frightened as we, stood his aunt. I think she had been watching from the window.

"Tía Ana!" Willy cried, grateful to see her, and stammered out his mother's invitation.

He spoke incoherently. I could hardly understand him, but she must have, for she startled us by bursting into tears. She hugged him and cried over him, then pushed him aside and looked quickly out of the window.

"Now you better go, Willy. Tell your mother a thousand thanks. Tell her I have a day to think about. I'm afraid that we can't come next Saturday. Maybe not the next either. But one of these Saturdays God will smile and it will be all right. Then we will come and I will let her know."

When Cousin Albert came home, Ellen told him. Cousin Albert nodded. I noticed that he looked at her gravely, as if this was a strange Ellen, she who used to make light and poke fun at such things. But if he had judicial reservations, he kept them to himself. After all, she was the child of several races, with long lines of conflicting ancestors rising in her from the past for a moment or two before falling back into the rich and ancient blood stream. To me, an Anglo boy from Missouri without a drop of the blood of the conquerors or of the English gentry in his veins, Ellen seemed still more of that mysterious creature, a lady, with all the contradictions and complexities of her sex.

What puzzled and almost awed me was the stretch of peace and content in the house that followed Ellen's offer of love. Even the icy heart of winter seemed mellowed by some unknown beneficent influence. I had never seen a gentler January in Moro, with temperate days and a great balminess to the air. The snowfall of some weeks ago had long since melted. The moisture had soaked into the ground, where next spring, everyone agreed, it would produce abundant grass on the range. Despite frost at night, both banks were fringed all winter with green along the river, and the laguna in the Big Bosque had the placidity of September. I could sit there on an old cottonwood log of a late January or early February day and, warmed by the sun, imagine it almost summer with the tule growing luxuriantly around it, with redwing blackbirds riding the bent cattails and some rare waterfowl swimming from the depths of the green reeds.

But the Beasleys never sent word about the dinner. Ellen kept Saturday evenings open for them, and when they did not come Willy and I would stay up to eat with her. Cousin Albert was at court in San Ysidro County. On this certain Saturday night, I remember, we were to have a sopapillas for dessert, a sweet hollow puff fried like a doughnut, of which I was very fond. I never got enough of them. We were still at the mutton when we became aware of excitement in the kitchen. I had heard Ellen warn Epifania several times against loud kitchen talk while we were at the dinner table. Now her cheeks flushed slightly as it kept up, but she said nothing. Then the kitchen door opened and Teofilo from the ranch burst into the dining-room.

"Dios nos ayuda, patrona!" he groaned. "God help us, mistress!" and fell down on his knees by the side of Ellen's chair.

I had never seen anything like this, a grown man such as Teofilo acting like a grief-stricken child to a mother younger than he. But it was apparent from Ellen's and Willy's faces, as well as from those of Epifania and Chepa looking in from the kitchen door, that all was perfectly regular.

"What is it, Teo?" Ellen asked. "Is it Doña Sofía!"

"No, gracias á Dios."

"Is it Don Carlos?"

He ducked his head lower as if a sensitive spot had been touched.

"He is the one, patrona."

"Is he living?"

"Thanks to God, when I left. But the holes in him are deep and he lost much blood."

"Blood!" Something hard and ugly had come into Ellen's voice. We all felt it, including Teofilo. Before saying more, he got to his feet as if what he was about to tell would be blasphemy from his knees.

Once on his feet, the story came out swiftly and with such passionate hissing of sibilants and rolling of r's that it was difficult for me to follow. But I understood enough—how Charley had started that afternoon for town on his regular Saturday-night spree. At the mesa end of the canyon he had met two men on horseback. He didn't know their names but thought he had seen them before and that they hailed from Baca County. They had stopped him and asked if he was Charley Johnson y Campo. Yes, he said, he was. They asked, was he the one who had sworn in court he had shot and killed Frank Jeffcoat. Yes, Charley said, he guessed he had. Then they pulled their revolvers and fired on him and galloped off. Charley himself told all this an hour later to the sheepherder who discovered him and who had run to the ranch with the news. When Fidel and others got there, they found their patrón still in the buggy. Except for jumping a few feet to one side, his well-trained horse hadn't moved.

When I looked at Ellen, the new gentleness of the last weeks had wholly vanished. Her blue eyes were almost black.

"Run for Dr. Gammel. Send him to the ranch. Tell him to hurry."

"The doctor is already gone, patrona," Teofilo said. "I stopped at his house first. Doña Sofía said that is the way I must do it."

"Then you can help Manuel harness Critter. I will drive out myself as soon as I change my clothes."

Before she could get away, Fidel arrived from the ranch with another smoking horse and the word that Charley was dead. He had met the doctor on the mesa and told him, but the good señor doctor said he was the coroner and had to go anyhow. Besides, Doña Sofía would probably need him. But he was relieved he would not have to push his horse now. He would stay at the ranch till tomorrow.

Epifania and Chepa acted like stricken nuns, and Manuel was a subdued mountain of flesh. Even Fidel, one of the most competent and self-reliant Mexicans I ever knew, was much affected. But if Ellen mourned, it was in secret. Her cool English blood seemed to disengage itself from the warm Spanish blood and take charge. She dispatched Manuel for Amado Martínez. The door to the second parlor was shut while she talked to the sheriff. All I heard was his promise to send a telegram to Cousin Albert when he left.

Ellen drove Willy and me to the ranch. Once we had left town, she seemed more Spanish than English. The cry of grief with which she and Mama Grande greeted each other sounded almost foreign to me, as did the velorio del defunto a night or two later in the big house, with the natives coming in and sitting on benches around the white walls, the songs of death and sorrow, murder and revenge, and the supper served with the inevitable café and vino. All the time the corpse lay in a coffin of pine boards made by the ranch carpenter and covered with black cloth, his blond hair and English features looking out of place here amid the foreign talk and songs and dark faces.

Willy was my whispering informant, telling me who everyone was. The singer was called the rezador, paid to sing and paid to stop. The glum-looking man on the end of his bench was Noé Vigil, whose jokes and pranks were told all over the sheep range. The woman by the coffin was old Josefina, so ancient that she addressed Willy's grandmother as niña, "child." The one next to her they called the Chicken Woman because she had come to work at the ranch house with a chicken under her arm, saying it had laid her an egg when she had nothing to eat and she wouldn't stay if the chicken couldn't. Mama Grande had had the chicken secretly done away with, for how could she keep a chicken in the house?—and the woman had searched for it all day and then cried all night.

Services for Uncle Charley were held in the ranch chapel, with Father Goshard and priests from Salado and Tajique in charge. Only the family and important family friends could get into the chapel. It was a chilly gray day. There was no heat except from the candles, and it felt cold as a cave, but not so cold as outside, where more than a hundred Mexicans from the ranch and surrounding region stood in the bitter wind listening to what sounds of the Mass came through the open door before the holy words were caught up and dissipated into the soundless void.

Services were delayed, waiting for Doña Ana. Not till they had given her up and Father Goshard was at the altar did she come with Beasley. I thought he tried to keep her to the rear, but she slipped up to the front between Ellen and Mama Grande, where she held a hand of each. That was also the way they stood at the grave, while Beasley waited expressionless just behind her. I was next to him and had full opportunity to inspect the man and measure him, to see the dark blood in his temples and the thick immovable way he stood.

It was an unforgettable scene. A desert graveyard is to me one of the loneliest sights in the world, an expression of man's transience and unimportance on earth, and the Rancho Zelandia cemetery was no exception. The few stone markers had been visibly mended after being twice knocked down by the herd. Wooden crosses, split and broken by hoofs, had been bound by twine. This, with the empty tinsel that Mexicans like to heap on their graves, gave the place a shabby and pitiful air. To me our little group of humans standing there by the open grave looked helpless and insignificant, mere grains of dust against the vast spaces beyond.

How anyone could harbor hate at a time like this, I didn't understand. A short distance from the open grave was the patch of unsanctified desert waste where two or three men slept unblessed and unmarked. Here could be seen the still partially fresh mound of Frank Jeffcoat. His grave and Charley's were not a hundred yards apart. They stood out like unhealed scars from the rest of the landscape, and I wondered how many more lives would be dragged down into the dark and silent earth before it was over.

Willy and I stayed until the last shovelful of dry New Mexican soil was thrown on the coffin. When we turned away, all we could see of Uncle Snell and Aunt Ana was a buggy vanishing up Ojo Canyon.

VII

There was difficulty finding the men who had shot and killed Charley. No one had seen two strangers on horseback in the vicinity that day, not even the herder who had first found the wounded man.

But a week later Apolonio Sena, a sheep rancher who had testified for Charley's character at the trial, was shot and killed on his ranch, and this time the men who had done it were recognized and named. They were Grover Reid and Earl Paulson of the Muleshoes in Baca County. Most everyone, I think, felt at once that these were the same men who had done the earlier killing. First there had been two of them, as Charley had said. Then the shooting of Frank Jeffcoat was involved in both cases. Both were outspoken "Jeffcoats," a term we had begun to call cattlemen and their sympathizers. It became a recognized word in Moro and was used in testimony during the trial.

At first most of us were not too excited over the fate of the Apolonio Sena killers. Then we grew aware that there might be more to their trial than we thought. No evidence had turned up to name and try the murderers of Charley, but there was plenty against those of the second victim and if they were the same men in both cases, it didn't matter too much for which crime they were convicted. The important thing was that they be tried and, if guilty, punished. In fact, by the time it came around, the trial of Reid and Paulson became perhaps the most important and significant to take place in the county, not so much for the crime named in the case but because it stood for the more sensational murder never officially mentioned in the trial, that of Charley Johnson y Campo.

The first time I became conscious of possible ugly complications ahead was before the two men had been arrested.

"I hope those two Jeffcoats cleared out for Old Mexico," Tom Dold said to Cousin Albert.

It sounded strange to me from him. I expected Cousin Albert to reply that, no matter who they murdered, the two men should be caught and tried. To my surprise, he turned to Tom with that certain expression on his face which meant, this is in confidence, but you are more right than you know.

"If I wasn't an official sworn to recognize the legal processes," he confided in a low voice, "I'd be tempted to send a friend to suggest that they get out of the country before those processes catch up to them and us all."

Now what made him say that, I wondered, and especially the words "us all"? Whatever his thoughts, I'm sure he said nothing of them to Ellen. She had been hard hit by Charley's murder. She might have made light of Charley in life, become impatient with him as a rancher and been annoyed by his heavy drinking, but his tragedy after his ordeal in court on behalf of her garden, if of nothing more, had affected her harder than I had supposed possible. This was brought home to me when we were back in the house at Moro. Cousin Albert had returned to court in San Ysidro County. That evening Tom Dold, the Kidds, and others were in the sala.

"Well, Paulson and Reid were brought in today," Tom mentioned. "The first thing they wanted was their lawyer."

I saw the quick lift of Ellen's head.

"I should think no decent lawyer in Moro County would be anxious to defend them."

"I'm afraid they hadn't much trouble. They didn't have to go very far."

We all knew whom he meant.

"I'm not surprised," Ellen said bitterly. "I hope you will volunteer your services to help prosecute them."

"My services wouldn't be very welcome, Ellen."

"Well, I shan't rest till both of them are convicted and hung," she answered, and her vehemence surprised me. When I glanced at Willy, his face, usually sallow enough, looked pale.

"The Jeffcoats are saying," Tom went on, "that since Charley was freed by the court, Reid and Paulson should be freed also."

"But Charley didn't go free," Ellen declared swiftly. "He's dead, and that should be the fate of these men, too."

She said it with such passion and devotion to her murdered brother that I felt strong sympathy for her and her cause. Indeed, I thought her admirable as she sat there, faithful, with high principles that refused to give, and yet very attractive, too. When the motion was brought by Beasley that Cousin Albert disqualify himself from sitting in the case because of the linking of the two killings in the public mind, I silently applauded her quiet relentlessness that, I'm sure, left him no other course than to insist upon hearing the case himself.

"To abandon the bench in this case would be deserting your mother," I once heard him tell Willy. "She'd think it public admission that I thought these two Jeffcoats had cause to do what they did."

I thought it fine on Ellen's part to bear such an influence on the court for right and justice. Not till the Grand Jury had returned an indictment, the two men had been arraigned, and threatening Jeffcoats from several counties had begun rallying in their defense did I realize what lay ahead of us—another ugly and interminable trial, vindictiveness and more vindictiveness. I saw that the one on whom the brunt of it would fall was not Ellen so much as Cousin Albert, who had had little or nothing to do with it but must stand up for her interest, bringing in if possible a verdict she would regard as just, and then endure the storm that must break on him.

That evening I watched him in the wide hall, the brass reading-lamp pulled down, the Denver paper in his hands. He looked slight, a small-boned, sensitive-skinned man, and yet there was visible in the way he sat there, in his slender back and the cut and projection of his beard, a doughtiness that made me feel good to have some of the same blood as his flowing in my veins.

The trial was set for the fall term of court. For some time I had noticed that Willy was not himself. In the morning when he first sat up in bed, his face looked dead white against the heavy black bang that inevitably came down over his forehead. Ellen had Dr. Gammel examine him and leave twisted white papers containing an ugly-tasting powder.

All spring while the peaches and apricots were in delicate bloom against the raw brown land, when cottonwoods were budding and the major domo had his men cleaning out the acequia madre, Willy's complaint grew no better. The clanking of our windmill in the steady southwest wind seemed to make him nervous, and when we came upon men standing or squatting together on the sunny side of buildings and corral walls, he would give them a wide berth as if against any mention of the coming trial and guilts involved. The courthouse he avoided as the pesthouse. When Cousin Albert was in town and Ellen sent the boy to his father on an errand, Willy would ask me to go instead.

"I'll do something for you, Jud," he would say.

There were only two places around Moro that drew him. One was the stable. Here with the strong scent of horses, with Critter's calm presence and the deep sound of his molars grinding hay and corn, Willy would spend hours, talking of horses, sheep, and the ranch, addressing his remarks to Manuel or to me, if I'd listen, getting into the box stall, running his hand over Critter's neck and legs, brushing out his mane and tail. Critter suffered him to do anything, crawl between his legs, lift a foreleg to look at a hoof, or all four legs one after the other, practice leaping up to his bare back, or lead him around the stall by the forelock.

The other place Willy haunted was the Big Bosque. He would bridle Critter. Then he and I would ride him bareback across the river through the unplanted grove of ancient cottonwoods. Here the town disappeared. All we could see were sky and the wide land, the craggy trunks and the rise to the mesa beyond. The grass was already greening up in wet places, and far ahead a violet haze spread over the ground. When you came closer you found it was endless patches of early pink loco in bloom.

Now as I look back I think that Willy felt things ahead that I didn't. He wasn't trying to forget so much as to recapture while there was still time. For this he was given an exceptional summer. Everyone said they had never seen the range greener. When school was finished for another term and we had moved back to the ranch, he cleaved to his saddle like an ax bit to the handle. With Critter and Cousin Albert's buggy team in the stable, there had been no room in town for his pony. Now he made up for it, and I had to ride with him.

There's a blessed amnesia about life in the saddle, especially in the West, that is more like survival in the Elysian Fields than oblivion. Willy had never felt, I think, what I had in the big house in the canyon. To him it was home, the Casa Grande, the house of many rooms. Whenever in the past there had been need of a new room, the Campos had simply laid out more dobe bricks to dry and added the walls they wanted. There were now some twenty-six or -seven rooms, one entering the other or into some small hall, and all built around a central patio shaded by two narrow-leaved mountain cottonwoods. Willy knew every room like the back of his hand. He had been born in one. In the patio he had watched troupes of entertainers and rope dancers from Old Mexico.

But now, I think, sharpened by shock in his own lifetime, Willy had begun to feel the emanation of things long past, dark ancient influences in the house, perhaps shadows cast by the future. We never spoke of them. All I knew was that when we went out of the house, he seemed to feel better, as I did, and that once lifted to our ponies' backs we had freed ourselves for a time from the presence of evil or its power to harm us. Even the patches of cemetery with Frank Jeffcoat's and Charley's graves became at once harmless, something beneath us, to be left far behind. Riding out, we were prisoners suddenly escaped to the unfettered world of land and sky. Before, behind, and beneath us swept the open range, fenceless, seemingly without border or end. This was the older, more joyous world where the Creator and the mark of His hand were still to be seen and felt. We breathed air never before tasted by a human being. We watered our horses in ponds unnamed and unknown except by the tule, wild waterfowl, and the wandering herder. To come on these or on some bright wild garden of range flowers carpeting the ground, blossoms that probably had never before been seen by the human eye and probably would not again, gave us a feeling of the largesse of God and of receiving favors directly from His hand.

Mexican workers, perhaps of necessity, are great ones to rise early. In Old Town I knew them to be up drinking their coffee and getting ready to go about their work when most Anglos were still asleep. Out on the ranch, lights twinkled in the jacals when all remained dark. With the day coming alive, the natives were ready to live and have a part in it. Willy and I seldom saw the sunrise. Our beds were too snug. The hour we liked best was just before sundown, when the glare of the desert day is gone. Then the soft red sunlight lies on the western slopes of the grassy swells and buttes and the violet light from distant mountains begins to reach out to you and beyond.

Often we loitered in some distant spot so we could ride home through it without talking, just living, our minds closed to civilized things such as courts and houses, open only to the delicious awareness of a more pagan and primitive existence. We watched the evening rite of distant horses, mere specks, grazing peacefully while night came down over them. All the time we were aware of the vistas, the land running on and on. The plains birds, the horned larks and the longspurs, were audible symbols of this endlessness. Almost never could we see them at this hour, only hear their wild plaintive notes that seemed to come out of the air from no apparent direction.

June was the perfect month at our altitude. As the calendar turned to July, the priceless rains came, especially such rains as used to fall then. Mornings as a rule were brilliant and clear. Gradually after lunch giant thunderheads would build up, Himalayan cloud peaks that could be seen for sixty or eighty miles. Promptly at four o'clock every day the heavenly irrigation would be turned on. Mama Grande used to say that you could set your clock by it. The long mountain thunder rolled along the Prietas so that for minutes, or so it seemed, we heard the continuous reverberations of a single clap. Sometimes it would rain gently all night. Sometimes it would be over for the day in an hour or two, in either case leaving a drenched and fragrant world.

This is the scent more than any other that takes me back to Willy, the penetrating pungence of wet cedars. The smell of the sun on dry cedars is something entirely different. Through both wet and dry cedars Willy and I rode unreckoned miles, the familiar deep body sounds of our loping horses in our ears, the moisture from the occasional loud sneezes pleasantly cooling our faces.

Willy hated, I know, to see the summer days go by and especially in the cedars. They grew in a belt two to five miles wide and unnumbered miles long at the foot of the Prietas, a rolling, sometimes almost level country of riders' delight. The open range is nearly always the same, the cedar country different, filled with constantly changing scenes. On the open range the rider is conspicuous for miles. In the cedars he is hidden, swallowed up in an endless succession of glades and parks like small clear green lakes of grass where

for the distance of a few yards or rods the cedars and pinyons for some unknown reason refuse to grow.

I remember two or three spots Willy showed me that the Mexicans said
were evil. They looked to me like any other, patches of grama grass swarming with blue or black seed heads, surrounded by clumps of the dwarf trees.

"Once in the past a very bad thing happened here," Willy told me in a low
voice.

"What kind of bad thing?"

"Blood. See, even our ponies know it."

It was true that they didn't like to stop and graze here as they did other
places. Willy and I would stay as long as we dared, tasting the sensation of
chill. Suddenly, as if some unknown thing was about to burst out of the de-
formed cedars, we would look at each other, dig our heels into our ponies'
sides, and gallop off, heading for the open range where as far as we could see
lay the calm peace of the wide spaces.

There was one thing, we were to learn, that we couldn't gallop away from
so easily. This was the trial to come, the contest between good and evil, or
was it between evil and evil? Anyhow, it lay directly ahead, coming nearer
and still nearer each time the sun rose.

VIII

When we left the ranch in September, the coming trial had already taken
over the town. Crossing the mesa, we could see numerous black dots on the
public road north of us, indicating an unusual number of rigs and riders
converging on Moro. Fall's Wagon Yard near the river looked full, we noticed, as we drove by, and we found the plaza and even some of the narrow
streets of Old Town choked with horses and unhitched teams.

It was all the more significant since this was roundup time on the cattle
ranches. Of course, some of the visitors were sheepmen intent on seeing judgment overtake their enemy who had shot down two of their fellow ranchers
in cold blood. But most of them were cowmen who hated sheep. Their badge
was plain enough to us. The sheepmen might look wild and rough, but it was
more the wild roughness of an old fleece long worn on the seat of an armchair. I think most of the cowmen knew Judge Sessions' wife or at least her
yellow-top buggy. I noticed that those in the street gazed belligerently at us
as we drove by.

"Pay no attention, muchachos," Ellen said, "looks don't kill. We won't
perish."

"They carry guns," Willy reminded.

"Yes, you can tell the devil by his hoofs and horns and the cowman by his
spurs and pistols."

Even in the sanctuary of the big white house on La Placita I could feel
the tension in the town. In this high dry climate of New Mexico, sultriness
is almost unknown. Yet here it was in Moro, an oppression that did not

pass like a storm in a matter of hours but hung black over the mesa for days, gathering force and fervor until it should finally break and discharge its burden on those beneath.

Ellen must have felt it as I did, but reveled in it. This was the Spanish in her, responding to crowds, emotion, and suspense. Anyone could see now that the trial concerned more than justice to Apolonio Sena. The house had never been so filled since I knew it. First Mama Grande came in for the duration. Then ranching friends of the family visited while attending the trial, the Pereas from La Sierra, and others I had never seen before. The front part of the house buzzed and bombilated with them, and a constant hum came from the rear. Fidel had brought Piedad, a maid, along with Mama Grande, and Teofilo had driven a ranch wagon to town with Mama Grande's tremendous leather brassbound trunk and the carcasses of several sheep for the table.

This time Willy and I were not required to go to the trial, but hardly a detail was spared our young ears. News from the courtroom reached our kitchen and stable as quickly and sometimes quicker than it did the two parlors. At dinner and supper the long cloth-covered plank table in the dining-room supported a lively discussion of the trial in general and the last session in detail and particular. At the head of the table, on her rawhide-seated chair overlaid with a scarlet cushion to raise her a little, Ellen reigned over her court, never letting it get out of hand, injecting lightness and wit when it became too serious, bringing it back to proper decorum when it grew too lively, delivering the crowning comment on the person or thing under discussion.

"There are two places," she would say, "where, no matter how dull, we must listen and never interrupt or ask questions or argue. One is in church." Everyone would laugh at Father Goshard if he was there. "The other is in court," and then the laughter would be at Cousin Albert.

"I am old, yes," she would sometimes sigh. She looked to be in her twenties at such a time and yet I knew she must be ten years older to have had Willy. "But, praise to God, Señora Vargas" (naming an aged crone) "is older than I."

Not all of her comments were light.

"That child of double adultery," I heard her say once, a phrase which made my hair stand on end.

To my surprise, the name of the lawyer who defended the murderers was never mentioned. But a great deal was said about el culebrón, "the large snake," and it took me some time to realize that this was their name for Snell Beasley, and then I understood the scorn, contempt, and sometimes hissing with which the word was spoken.

Cousin Albert would say little or nothing about the case. At times he inserted a few calming sentences, often in English, which in itself had the effect of dignity and restraint.

"Ask me a month from now," he'd say when appealed to for some opinion bearing on the trial. "Today I'm just a piece of furniture pulled up to Ellen's table. I don't hear and I don't speak."

He spoke Spanish well enough but with a Missouri accent like mine. Neither of us could ever hope to equal Willy, who, raised in the language, had only to let the Spanish flow out of him like his breath, belying his three-quarters Anglo blood. His pronunciation of words like "guarniciones," almost like a guttural clearing of the throat, ever excited my admiration.

The only time Willy and I had to attend the trial was when Cousin Albert sentenced the killers. A verdict of first-degree murder had been brought in by the sheepman jury, a great victory for the prosecution. Only Willy and his father didn't seem to share in the triumph, not even when the verdict was upheld and appeal for a new trial denied. As far as Cousin Albert was concerned, it seemed unfortunate because, of all the participants, he had had the hardest time, hearing the endless testimony and arguments, ruling on allegations, statements, and motions for dismissal, silencing the angry demonstration of the Jeffcoats from time to time, and keeping the case generally in hand. Now at the sentencing he looked very formidable, his black beard and stern eyes frightening me a little from the bench as he gazed at the two prisoners standing in the box.

"Grover Reid and Earl Paulson, like other citizens of this territory you enjoyed the privileges of life, liberty, and the pursuit of happiness. You watched the grass green in the spring and the young calves leap. But you were unsatisfied, and cruelly and forever deprived a fellow citizen of the said life and pursuit of happiness, one Apolonio Diego Luis Felipe Sena. You are now remanded to the custody of Sheriff Martínez to be returned to your cells, and on Friday, February twentieth, you will be taken to the jail yard and duly hanged by the neck until dead."

The words and the way he spoke them sent a chill along my spine. He turned and glanced down into the packed court. I fancied he was looking at me, but immediately knew his eyes were on Ellen near by. For a moment something passed between them. His look seemed to say he had vindicated her trust in him and delivered the murderers not only of Apolonio Sena but also probably of her brother to their proper end. Then I thought he looked suddenly tired as he turned away.

"Well, thank the Lord they'll get theirs," I said to Willy in Spanish as we went out.

He didn't answer, and when we reached the bright New Mexican winter sunlight I saw that he kept his face away.

Ellen had wanted to give a supper party that evening in celebration, but Cousin Albert overruled it. He said it would look unseemly and if she held it he wouldn't attend. It was the first time I heard him take such a firm stand in opposition to her and I thought the ordeal of the trial had steeled him. To my surprise, she did not mock or disregard him.

"Whatever you think, Albert," she said.

From this time on I thought I detected a change in their relationship. Up to now Cousin Albert had been the one to come to her.

"Are you all right?" his solicitude had seemed to say. "Can I do anything for you?"

He used to stand waiting a long time just to see her come out of her room or into the sala. Now it was she who came to him. Was he all right? Could she or Epifania do anything for him? And when there was nothing else, she would set herself to entertain and amuse him, to put him in a happier mood. Usually she would act out her story, talk like some person we all knew, intersperse her chatter with amusing exclamations like "Carambambamba!" which was a burlesquing of "caramba" and much like saying "phooey" or "fiddle-faddle." She had such charm with it, Latin ways of playfully crinkling her young face that no one could resist and Cousin Albert didn't try. He would sit in his chair watching her, listening to her mocking voice, his face faintly warmed by the picture he saw and the contradictions and laughter he heard. But when he left or she turned away, I noticed that the grave melancholy returned.

I thought at first that her increased affection for him was gratitude, payment in her kind for his justice in avenging Charley, but later I was not so sure. I knew that some cattlemen were still in the town and heard that they had made threats against us.

"You can't stop the bull from bellowing," Ellen said.

But one night after the sentence, men on horseback came riding up La Placita in the early hours of the morning, shot out the plate-glass windows of both front parlors, and rode out again, yelling and shooting into the air. It took several days to get fresh glass shipped by train from Pueblo, and this time Ellen did not say "Carambambamba!" She gave Willy and me strict orders to stay off the street except on our way to and from school. Mama Grande grew alarmed and would let Ellen go nowhere on foot. Only Cousin Albert went his usual way, marching his doughty figure twice daily to his court chambers.

All the time the hanging grew closer. Since early fall Willy had had a cold. Romadizo, or hay fever, some would call it today, but you didn't get hay fever in the middle of winter, not until late February or early March when the foothill sabinos sent their powdery pollen on the breeze. Soon Willy grew untalkative even to me. At night he sweated like a colt that had eaten loco weed, and I helped him change to a dry sleeping-garment the night after Manuel told us that the two godless savages had been finally hung, after refusing to kneel with the executioner and preacher when the latter prayed for them.

Now I expected the full fury of the cattlemen to be directed against us. For several nights Willy and I lay listening for the quiet of our Old Town street to be broken. Nothing happened. The hangman's victims were duly buried in the Protestant cemetery. The last cattlemen who had stayed for the execution, we were told, drifted back to their ranches in Baca and San Ysidro counties.

"It's all over now, gracias á Dios," Mama Grande said and went home to the ranch.

But I wasn't so sure. Once Tom Dold came to see Ellen when Cousin Albert wasn't at home. I noticed they were closeted behind closed doors. What they talked about I didn't know. Twice a day she seemed to grow restless until Cousin Albert would return from the courthouse. Long before his usual hour she began looking for him, extraordinary in someone so self-contained and active as she.

"Did you see my sewing?" she would ask if caught in the act, or else her prayerbook, which surprised me, for only on occasion I saw her sew and almost never found her with her prayerbook.

Term of court at Moro was over now. Next on the calendar was the spring term in Baca County. No railroad had then reached Porvenir, and to get there from Moro meant a three days' journey by buggy. Some earlier judges in the territory had ridden the circuit horseback and many stories were told about them. But more roads, such as they were, had come into use today and Cousin Albert made his rounds with Dan and Choppo in his black pole buggy.

"Will you do me a favor, Albert?" Ellen asked him at the dining-table one day.

"Gladly, if I can," he told her.

"Ask Judge Otero to take over Baca this spring."

He looked startled.

"Judge Otero? But how could I do that?"

"You could say you were indisposed." And when he looked pained, "You must be very tired. You've had a long and difficult ordeal."

"I am a little tired, yes," he admitted, "but not indisposed."

"It's the same thing. Wouldn't you do it for me?" she begged. Her face and eyes were so soft and helpless upon him I didn't see how he could resist.

Cousin Albert looked profoundly disturbed.

"I would do anything for you, Ellen, anything within reason. This, I'm afraid, is impossible. Judge Otero and many others would think me afraid."

It was the word "afraid" that suddenly betrayed to me what she was driving at, revealed as by a blinding light the specter that haunted the back of Ellen's mind. For a moment I could see the wild uninhabited region he must traverse on his way to Baca County, the lonely canyons he must pass through, the remote mesas to be crossed and dry stream beds to be threaded, where the sudden sound of thunder echoing among the barren cliffs and hills might not be heard by another human ear and where a trail might lie for days abandoned except to wild things and stray cattle.

For about a week I didn't hear Ellen bring up the matter again.

"Will you take Willy with you, Albert?" she suddenly begged him the day before he left.

"Willy?" He drew back. "Ellen, you ask the most impractical things."

"Why is it impractical? A change often helps a cold. You know how miserable he's been." She saw him hesitate and pushed her advantage. A very torrent of Spanish words and a woman's reasoning ensued. Now when I

glance back I think I can read her thought, her realization that it was she who had got him into the position from which there was no retreat, and this was her last resort to protect him. Her intuition told her that not even the most hardened of men would fire on a buggy if it contained a young boy. Her religious faith was small and her theology smaller, but it may be she believed that if like Abraham she would offer her son as a sacrifice, Dios would not take the life of one so innocent and unsinful.

"I cannot do it, Ellen," Cousin Albert declared. "If I did—"

"This time I will not let you go," Ellen interrupted. "If you won't take him, you must take me!"

I knew then, by her emotion, and Cousin Albert knew too, that she meant it. I knew also that if there was one thing a man hated, it was to hide behind a woman's petticoats. He considered a long time and his face was pale, but in the end he agreed reluctantly to her demand.

Willy's eyes lighted when his mother told him, and the first color in some weeks came to his face. He looked half cured already and pleaded that I be permitted to go along. No, that would put too big a burden on his father, Ellen told him, and, besides, surely he wanted me to stay and look after her?

He did not protest too much then. You could see he was wild with excitement over the chance to be with his father, to be free from school and out in the range country he loved. There would be mountains and canyons he had never laid eyes on. But, most of all, he would be away from Moro, would leave the hanging and the two fresh graves behind him.

Court in Baca County was to open Monday morning. Willy and his father left the previous Wednesday in the black buggy. Manuel brought it around in front of the house in the morning. A scattering of local people came to wish the judge well and see him off. Among them was George Atkins, the druggist, with his camera and tripod.

I have an enlarged print of the scene he snapped on the plate that day. It hangs framed and faded on my wall. Beyond the buggy and horses you can see some of the curious witnesses and anxious well-wishers. A few Mexican women have black rebozos over their heads, and some of the men wear boots over their trousers, not the fancy short dress boots worn today but the long, rough, genuine Western boot that reached to the knee.

Of course, the center of attraction in the photograph is Dan and Choppo, the blood bays, a matched pair except for Choppo's white nose. Both horses' heads are high. The blinders flap wide of their eyes. Their harness looks heavy and coarse compared to the tan harness that Ellen used on Critter. In the picture Dan has one front foot raised, pawing to go. In the buggy holding the reins sits Cousin Albert, his back slender and straight, his black beard covering the black strings of the tie he generally wore, his hat not the ten-gallon one of today but the Western hat worn then with a narrow brim and a high crown. Beside him sits Willy looking happier than any photographer before had been able to snap him.

I am not on the picture, having stood behind George Atkins to watch him pop in and out of the black cloth, and there is only a trace of Ellen's skirt on the photograph. But I have a vivid memory of her standing just inside the gate, her face colorless, her white fingers fluttering, her eyes straining after the buggy until it turned and vanished into the plaza.

IX

There are a few small things we know now about Cousin Albert's and Willy's journey on the circuit. It is one of the most famous cases in New Mexican personal history. People still talk about it. But we knew almost nothing then.

With the others gone, Ellen left for the ranch in the morning. She did not ask me along. Of course, I had my school, but she seemed to have forgotten me. The day before, she had been restless, almost feverish. This morning she was calmer. Her travelers had been on their way a full day now. She had done what she could to prevent Cousin Albert from going. Failing in that, she had sent Willy to insure his safety on the way.

A week later when she came back from the ranch, she seemed like her old self. The period of suspense was over. Cousin Albert's trip to Baca County took only three days at most. He must have arrived long since and everything was all right.

I suppose I looked a little forlorn.

"Pobrecito!" she said. "I shouldn't have left you alone in the house. You suffer like me with Willy away."

That evening at dinner she tried to make up for her neglect.

"You missed the trip with Willy. Now I must tell you some things you missed. The country is nothing much. But the people make up for it. The first night you would have stayed with the Romeros. There is Cosme. He doesn't count. The all-important are his four sisters. They are the priceless ones. What one says, the others must say, too. Everything is said four times. It is like an echo. It runs all around the room. Oye, oye, oye, oye. Callete, callete, callete, callete. Listen, listen, listen, listen. Silence, silence, silence, silence. It's true. It's true. It's true. It's true. If one of them forgets to say it, the others look at her in horror. She has failed to support her sisters. She's committed treason. It's like intimating her sister is a liar."

Her description of the Romeros was delicious. It made me laugh.

"And then San Mateo," she went on. "Have you ever spent the night in an Indian pueblo? No, I'm sure, not a boy from Missouri. Well, you would be an honored guest. You would be the cousin of Albert, el Juez Sessions. Carasco, the governor, is our friend. Your Indian bed is very hard, just a rug on the floor, and the room is shut up so tight you can't breathe. And you think you hear strange primitive things during the night, but maybe to hear them you must have Indian blood in you like I do."

She was at her best regaling me with Cousin Albert's third stopping-place, almost at the end of his journey.

"The Banburys are the English ones. They raise sheep and wolfhounds, almost as many hounds as sheep and still bigger. When you sit at dinner, there's a tremendous dog like a lean and hungry lobo sitting on each side of you, watching you eat, and very hungry. You think you better be quick getting the food to your mouth or it will be snatched away. You are in a dobe house with a dobe floor five thousand miles from London, and yet everything is English, the talk, the jokes, the table. They even have an English sheepherder, a wonderful old man with a beard like Moses. Queen Victoria is his saint. He was born on the same day, and to him she's the empress of heaven as well as of India. Even their dress is English. One time my father and I came just at dinner. A Lady Somebody or other was at the table in a low-cut evening dress. When she stood up I found she had tucked it into a man's riding-britches."

It was curious to hear Ellen gibe at the ways of the Banburys as if the English were an incomprehensible race when all the time you knew that her own father had been British to his toes. But that was one of her most delightful characteristics, making fun of her own blood, whether English or Spanish, exaggerating incidents and conversation, spicing her talk with liveliness and charm. Tonight I felt flattered that she did it entirely for me.

I fancied at dinner that all the while Ellen chattered and laughed, Chepa served us with a cruel face. Ellen noticed it at last.

"Chepa. What is it?" she asked.

"Nothing, patrona," the servant said.

Ellen's eyes grew thoughtful.

"There is something."

"Nothing, nothing, patrona," Chepa blurted and hurried out into the kitchen.

I saw now that Ellen had sobered, the familiar melancholy shadow fallen across her face.

"Will you go down to the courthouse for me, Jud? See if Amado is still there. Tell him I would like to see him. Right away."

It was necessary to go to several restaurants before finding the sheriff. I thought he looked at me gravely and that he exchanged an uneasy look with the deputy who sat across the table. When finally he arrived at the house, his brother was with him. It was not a good sign.

Ellen received them in the wide hall.

"Have you heard from the judge, Amado?" she asked at once.

"No, señora, not yet," the sheriff said.

"Well, have you heard anything about him?"

"No, señora, nothing definite. There is not time." He said it very elaborately, almost profoundly, too profoundly for the meager information conveyed. It was, I thought, also faintly distant, as if already there was a slight change in position or relationship between them.

"Everyone is so strange," Ellen declared. "First Chepa and now you. I am sure you know something, a rumor perhaps. What have you heard?"

The two brothers exchanged masked glances.

"We have a visitor from Baca County, señora, that is all."

"Who is that?"

"Señor Haddon, the deputy sheriff."

"Well, tell me! What did he come for? What did he have to say?"

"He just brought news that the judge was late, señora."

"Well, how late? Did he finally get there?"

"We don't know, señora. He told us there is no emergency. Court is being postponed till the judge comes. They have a small calendar and plenty of time. No harm is done."

"But where is the judge? Why didn't he get there? Why don't you go out with your men and see where he is?"

"Señor Haddon just got here this afternoon, señora. There has not been time. If you wish, we will go over the trail in the morning. But I am sure it is not necessary, señora. The judge is probably there by this time. Maybe he got sick or his team broke down. You must not worry. If anything had happened, we would have heard about it and Señor Haddon would have found out about it on the way."

The sheriff and his party left in the morning, but learned nothing, except that Cousin Albert had never reached Porvenir. The story of the judge's delay, his unknown whereabouts, and finally his complete disappearance became the chief topic in Moro and the rest of the territory as well. Mama Grande heard of it at the ranch and sent Fidel for particulars. A succession of friends called at the house to ask for news and pay their sympathy. Tom Dold and Dr. Gammel were the faithful ones. Every day they were with Ellen at one time or another. Now that the initial bad news was broken, the Martínez brothers called regularly to report whenever they were in town.

It seemed incredible to me that posses of keen and experienced men from two counties could search the trail and find nothing. They learned that the judge and Willy had spent the first night with the Romeros and the second at the San Mateo pueblo. Next morning an Indian boy shepherd with a small flock of sheep and goats had seen the judge and Willy drive by some eight or ten miles west of the pueblo. The judge had waved to him. Apparently this boy was the last to have laid eyes on either one. They had never reached the Banburys', and none of the Banbury shepherds had seen a trace of them. It was as if they had been swallowed up by the earth itself.

Of all the mysteries that ever gripped the territory, this, I think, has puzzled many of us the most. There had been tragic disappearances in New Mexico before, and a number have happened since, unsolved cases of men and women who set out on a journey through the sparsely settled country never to be seen or heard of again. But most of these concerned obscure people. This had happened to a United States judge on official rounds of duty and to his eleven-year-old son, and yet nothing more could apparently be done about it than if the victims had been nameless emigrants from a passing wagon train.

It was hard on me, but Ellen was the one on whom everything centered. The suspense day after day and night after night must have been very great. Afternoons and evenings she had to receive callers and hear their questions together with the recitation of all the wild stories and rumors going the rounds. One account was that the judge, Willy, and the two horses had been shot and buried along with the burned and dismantled buggy in the sand, and that unless the winds someday might unearth them, their remains would never be found. Another was that Willy had been spared and taken to the lonely highlands of Old Mexico, where he was given to a remote Mexican family to raise so that in time he would no longer remember his mother and father or his New Mexican home. A third story was that Cousin Albert had fled with another woman and taken Willy forcibly along, and that he had died of homesickness and sorrow, to be buried in California.

What turned out worse than the ugly rumors as time went on were the clues that aroused hope only to be proved false. Some claimed they had seen a white boy among the Navajos north of Gallup and that it had been Willy. Some swore the judge had been recognized alive and well, in Denver or El Paso or some other place, that he had seemed dazed as if bereft of his memory. Cousin Albert's horses, Choppo and Dan, were said to have been seen and identified in the hands of strangers, and his pole buggy as well.

Through it all Ellen bore up splendidly, her cheeks a little feverish, her eyes too brilliant perhaps. Sometimes I thought that she bore up too well, that she almost enjoyed the excitement, the attention, the stream of visitors, especially the constant consolation of Tom Dold and Dr. Gammel. She must feel some responsibility, I thought. And yet, here she was, affected certainly but going on almost as before, still the lady, in the last extremity untouchable, the possessor of some quality difficult to name. You could see and hear it and yet never know exactly what it was except that in sorrow, as in pleasure, she was just a little beyond reach, not wholly duty-bound, answerable only to herself.

Then I learned that I was mistaken. The word came that the county authorities had given up the search. Amado Martínez himself broke the bad news one sunny afternoon. He had evidently braced himself for the task, and had asked Mr. Kidd, as a friend of Ellen's, to come along.

"We have done all we can, señora," the sheriff said. "I can't ask the men to keep on looking forever. The country is too big and we have found nothing. Now we must stop."

"That doesn't mean they won't be found sometime, Ellen," Mr. Kidd added kindly. "Why don't you go away for a while? To Denver or St. Louis or some new place where you can forget. Try not to think of Albert and Willy. I'm sure they would want it that way."

This time Ellen didn't go to the door with them when they left. She sat in her chair, very pale. Her face had a transparent quality sometimes seen in the cheeks of the dead, of flesh very transient and about to vanish.

"God forgive me," I heard her say in Spanish, "that I've never been able to cry."

I don't think she knew I was there, or cared. Ever since the dinner when the bad news had come, she had been strange to me, almost ignored me. I grew to suspect that she begrudged my being alive and well, sleeping in Willy's room and going to his school while he had suffered this unspeakable calamity.

But now she turned and saw me. Something in her eyes seized on me. I thought afterward that what caught her was my kinship to Cousin Albert and Willy, that I was blood of their blood, the closest living thing to either of them she had left.

"Never let anyone stop you, Jud, from doing what you think you should do," she told me passionately. "Had I followed my senses, I would have gone with Albert, no matter how much he hated to hide behind my skirts. If he wouldn't have taken me in his buggy, I could have gone in my own. It might have shamed him. He might have taken some wild out-of-the-way trail where no one would see him. But I could have taken that trail, too. Then if anything would have happened, I'd have been with him. If the Jeffcoats jumped him, I'd have been there to talk them out of it. If in the end they killed him, they would have had to kill me, too."

At her words the old admiration, affection, and loyalty for her flooded up in me, and more than once during the night when I remembered what she said, warm tears rose to my young eyes.

X

When the authorities gave up, that was when Ellen said she herself would start looking for Cousin Albert and Willy. Tom Dold and Dr. Gammel protested, and Mr. Kidd, when he heard about it, was much disturbed. With Mrs. Kidd he came to the house to advise and urge against it. Ellen heard them all quietly.

"No one will hurt a woman," she said. "Besides, I am taking Fidel and Teofilo along. And Jud," she added with a glance at me. "If he is not afraid."

"Few of us were afraid, Ellen, that they would dare touch the judge and Willy!" Mr. Kidd reminded.

"Albert never carried a gun," she answered. "I am going armed." Something in her eyes and the way she said it brought up the old uncertainties about her in my mind.

We left for the ranch next morning. Mama Grande heard the plan with her expressionless black eyes.

"If it will help you to go, you must go," she said to Ellen. "But why take another boy into that bad country? What can he do?"

"Jud is Willy's cousin," she reminded. "He missed the first trip. Now he can see where Willy went."

That's what Ellen said, but I felt she had another and deeper reason for taking me, one rather of fate and of meetness. Whatever happened to Cousin Albert she was willing to have happen to her, and what happened to Willy I was not above having happen to me.

We left the ranch in a brilliant sunrise which back in Missouri would have meant rain but here betokened nothing but another Southwestern day. Ellen and I drove in her familiar yellow-top buggy, an object that would betray her identity wherever we went and as far as the moving object could be seen. Critter was in the shafts. Fidel and Teofilo followed in the light wagon. Fidel used it at times to service the sheepherders. Now it was packed to the sheet with provisions, utensils, and bedding, also several saddles. Spare horses and Willy's blue pony, Mono, were on behind.

It was good to look around and see the wagon following us, and especially the presence of Fidel and Teo, the latter the ablest of sheepherders, a good cook and substitute caporal. Both men had inherited the best qualities of both the Spaniard and Indian. I never knew them to be tired. Their eyes, black, sharp, shrewd, fearless, missed nothing. They were, I felt, the ablest of companions in this rough and dangerous country they knew so well. Neither wore guns as the cowboys did, but I was aware that Ellen had had them put firearms in the wagon. Her own light rifle protruded from under the buggy seat on the floor between us.

Ellen said she meant to follow Cousin Albert's route as faithfully as she knew how. Late that afternoon we passed through Cienega Canyon and stayed with the Romeros. The four sisters greeted Ellen like a cousin, a rich, important, and respected cousin toward whom they felt fervid sympathy. Ah, true enough, it was just three—or was it four?—weeks ago that the judge had stopped with them, and Guillermo. Never had they seen His Honor looking more handsome or Guillermo happier. Who then would have supposed that this unknown and terrible evil was waiting for them beyond?

Not until I heard them did I remember what Ellen had told me, how they all repeated what the other said. The air was filled with ojalá, ojalá, ojalá, ojalá, and que lástima, que lástima, que lástima, que lástima and ah dolor, ah dolor, ah dolor, ah dolor till my head swam in the ranch house sala and I escaped to Fidel and Teo by their fire near the corrals, where they were surrounded admiringly by the Romero ranch help. Here men were in control and the talk in keeping with the serious mission.

I was glad to get away in the morning and I think Ellen was, too.

"I hoped they'd remember something important Albert had said," Ellen told me. "Some word about home or that he had changed his plans. But they could tell us nothing. Nothing but por Dios, por Dios, por Dios, por Dios, and es verdad, es verdad, es verdad, es verdad."

She mimicked them to perfection, but there was no fun in it today, only a frightening quality I could not quite name. It was in her eyes, too, as she kept looking ahead. We had left the plains now for higher ground. This beautiful Indian country, I knew, must have been one of the last things Willy and Cousin Albert had seen. But there was little pleasure for us in the cinnamon boles of the giant pines, the patches of sun and shadow, the clear spring-fed mountain streams so precious in a dry land. Then we went down into a deep red rock canyon where we found the irrigated fields and adobe houses of San Mateo pueblo. Here Willy and Cousin Albert had spent their last known night.

The short, stout pueblo governor, Carasco, a striking figure in iron-gray hair against a rich copper face and a bright red headband, welcomed us with dignity. Nothing could be hurried. Certain rites of respect and hospitality had to be carried out as if all were well. That evening in his own house, watched by the black eyes of his wife and others, he talked to Ellen about Cousin Albert. He spoke Spanish with a curious Indian accent, hard for me to understand.

I had the impression that he chose his words carefully.

"Who knows what happened to my friend, the white alcalde and his son? There are devils that rise out of the ground. They float through the air and hover over their prey. Sometimes they even ride horses and lie in wait," he added significantly, watching her closely to see if she caught what he was saying.

"Yes, I understand, Carasco," Ellen said.

His beady eyes gazed on her with satisfaction. Then he went on.

"They say the alcalde and his son stay with us at San Mateo and then are never seen again except by an Indian boy of the pueblo. It makes it look bad for the Indian. But the Indians are not devils without reason, señora. Neither the San Mateos nor the Navajos. And if they want to be devils, it would hardly be to their friend Alberto, but to those who run their cattle over Indian lands, who take the Indian grass and treat him like dirt when he asks them to go back to their own country."

His short thick figure mounted on a black horse, he rode out beside the buggy next morning. Some three or four miles west of the pueblo, he pointed out where the Indian sheepherder boy had seen Cousin Albert's black buggy pass. We were out of the pines now, in a broad semi-arid country of low cedars. The wind was blowing, the fine sand already rising. The gray air and dust-shrouded sky gave everything a look of desolation.

"This is the place, Fidel," Ellen said. "From here on."

I knew what Ellen meant. I could feel it myself, a forsaken quality that reminded me of the wind-swept cemetery at Rancho Zelandia. But here there was more than human graves abandoned to the barren waste. Something else could be felt, a wildness far back in time and the human heart, so that the friendly pueblo Indian waving from his horse where we had left him seemed like the last outpost of civilization behind us.

Presently Ellen stopped Critter and motioned Fidel to drive abreast. They conferred, and from here on either Fidel or Teo went on foot ahead of the buggy, eyes keenly examining the trail and ground adjoining. Sometimes one would leap on a saddled horse and ride him to the right or left to investigate some peculiar landmark or shape of sand. The broken hills were so dry they could support only scattered cedars, but twice we came to wide draws or cañadas where flats of green grass—and once, grazing cattle—testified to the presence of water. The cattle testified also to something else. We were now in the country of the Jeffcoats. The hair at the back of my neck stirred. But whatever Ellen and the two Mexicans felt was not confided to me.

I saw that our slow careful pace would leave us far short of any habitation that night. Toward late afternoon we came to the malpai. We saw it a long way off, a black ridge of broken blocks of lava reaching across the face of the land. On one side the winds had created a region of sand and sand dunes several miles deep and running as far as the eye could see. Nothing but salt bushes and blue sage grew here. This was where Fidel and Teo showed the greatest interest, examining the ground minutely, tramping and riding far to investigate when I could see nothing unusual. With the malpai still before us, we camped in a draw where a slender rivulet of water ran clear as crystal from the ugly black rock. That night, so far as I could tell, Ellen slept calmly in her sugan. Whenever I roused, which was often, I saw that one of the Mexicans remained awake, either sitting by the fire, staring into it in a manner of the sheepherder, or standing off in the shadows listening. One time it would be Fidel, another time Teo. I never found out when they changed.

The men confided little to me. They spoke guardedly even to Ellen, but that we stayed there for several days told volumes. Where the long arm of malpai finally ended and the trail ran around it was the place where Fidel and Teo spent the most time, going over it minutely, examining every yard of trailside, digging into hundreds of dunes and spreading the sand out on the ground. In the end they found nothing.

More than once I grew tired and rode my pony off into the rugged country, hoping to find a clue to the missing travelers in some hidden draw or rincón, yet fearing to catch a glimpse of a Jeffcoat rider watching like an Indian from one of the ridges. But I saw no one and nothing, only the immense dry broken earth, the endless sand and the black landmark of malpai which made it impossible for me to get lost. Beyond lay a wilderness of arroyos, buttes, and mesas, and standing up over them, Gorezón, a natural monument like a giant head and shoulders of a desert tribal god which Willy must have seen from the buggy.

It seemed impossible for any place to be so empty of life, so devoid of human traces. Suddenly I would see a small cloud of dust moving toward me from far away. The feeling that a rider, a human being on a horse, was at last peopling the solitude and coming toward me rose uncontrollably in my breast. Then the small cloud of dust would veer and I could see it was only the wind, after which everything was more lonely and desolate than before. Sometimes, sitting motionless on my horse, I would hear a sound like someone coming, perhaps Willy or Cousin Albert, I thought, riding through the salt bushes behind me. I would whirl and nothing would be there, but in a moment a gust of wind would reach me and I knew it was again only the mocking invisible air.

On the side hills, in the small canyons the sand was eternally blowing, drifting like gray snow close to the earth. When at last I'd ride back to the malpai I'd see where the tracks of the horses, including my own, had already filled up and looked like the rest of the bleak landscape so that the spot where another person and I had spoken together, a place touched with human presence and emotion, had become no more than the rest of the deadened landscape.

Each day at the malpai I thought Ellen's face grew more weary and baffled. Not even the two nights we stayed at the Banburys' were able to soften it, the friendliness of the wolfhounds, the English hospitality, the majesty of the old Lancastershire shepherd, as Ellen had said, like a vision of Moses in his white beard and hair. This was the first time, I think, that she ever admitted to herself the possibility that the enigma, like many others she knew, might never be solved, Cousin Albert and Willy never found, their fate swallowed up like the riddle of the Sphinx in the well-kept secrets of this aloof and silent land.

XI

It was strange to come back to Moro without Cousin Albert and Willy, without a trace of them, to know no more about them than before. The town seemed an empty shell today. When we came to La Placita, Ellen stood for a moment at the door as if she couldn't bear entering the dead house. Then she gave a little movement as if she must somehow go through with it, and went in.

What gave me the strangest feeling was passing the courthouse. Cousin Albert had always seemed such a prominent and indispensable figure. It seemed impossible that the county could get along without him. Now already a new man, Judge Saxton, had been appointed from Washington and was at this moment in Porvenir sitting at the spring term of Baca County court where Cousin Albert was to have been.

The worst was to think of Cousin Albert and Willy gone, perhaps done away with, their bodies hidden in some unmarked grave, and then to see Snell Beasley going about his business unaffected, more alive and prosperous than ever. His political power, they said, had risen with Cousin Albert out of the way. Judge Saxton, we knew, was Beasley's friend and had been appointed through his influence. I watched Beasley pass the house on his way to his office in the morning, short, thick, vigorous, and I wondered at the animal sources of such vitality, as I had once wondered in the cedars at the Herculean powers of a sheep-killing bear.

Even Tom Dold, I thought, seemed impressed by Beasley's growing importance. He told Ellen that her brother-in-law had taken a younger man into his office, George Steffy, a lawyer from Baca County. Apparently it gave Beasley more time for outside activities. More than once I saw him drive out in a new rubber-tired topless buggy, the kind we called a runabout. He seemed to be cogitating, scheming as he drove, a heavy figure that caused the springs to sag on the driver's side.

But I think Ellen was unprepared as I was for the news Tom brought her from Beasley one evening at dinner. Carefully, I noticed, he wove Snell Beasley's name into the table talk until Ellen flushed.

"Tom, it seems each time you come you have something good to say about Snell. Perhaps I should be interested in my brother-in-law, but I am not. Please, let's not talk about Snell Beasley."

Tom looked grave.

"This time I've been asked to speak for him, Ellen. He wants me to argue the case in his behalf."

"Argue what case?"

"Your willingness to sell Critter."

Ellen went white.

"I wouldn't dream of parting with Critter, Tom. And if I did, hardly would I put him at the mercy of that brute."

"I was only interested," Tom went on gravely, "in the possible mending of relations between you two. It might also change things between you and your sister."

I could see that Ellen was angry.

"I am not interested in any change of relations between Snell Beasley and me, Tom. Between Ana and me, yes. But I don't see that giving him Critter would help that."

Through the rest of dinner I saw that Ellen looked at him with intense questioning eyes. What she thought she did not tell me, but I suspect she kept learning, as I had, the bitter truth that Cousin Albert was indeed gone, that another power reigned and even Tom was ready to bow before it. The king was dead, long live the king. The phrase ran through my head that night. I had never quite understood it before.

But if Beasley was king now, at least he couldn't have Critter. It was a small thing, I knew, beside the loss of Willy and Cousin Albert. Nevertheless, it gave me satisfaction. We still had the fastest horse in the territory, or so I thought. I wasn't so sure of it when we heard that Beasley had bought a racing horse in Texas and was bringing him home to use in the shafts of his runabout.

I asked Manuel about it the day the horse was led down the alley to the stable next door, followed by a small crowd. Manuel regarded me with black unreadable eyes.

"Pretty fine-looking nag. Hardly six years old. About ten hundred pounds. I can chin fifteen hands, but I couldn't chin him. Looks fast. Arabian blood, Goyo told me. Day after tomorrow, he says, they take him down and exercise him on the track."

The Moro track was an open piece of dry sandy land on the other side of the railroad. There was a half-mile circular course and a straightaway on one side for quarter racing. I went there on Saturday afternoon and was surprised to see that a few other persons had gathered. One prominent man of town arrived in his own rig to watch. Beasley's new horse was already there, and my heart sank as I saw him on the track. He was a thoroughbred, a little longer and rangier than Critter, a chestnut and more handsome, with a lighter, almost blond mane and tail. Moreover, he was younger than Critter, just coming into his power, while Critter was soon to pass the peak of his prime, if already he hadn't done so. Looking at him, I could well believe what they said about his Arabian blood. His speed was impressive, and there was a professional look about him in the sulky with Goyo on the seat, his legs spread. Several men I knew held their watches on him and afterward spoke jovially to Beasley, who had stood alone, his thick neck thrust forward, watching the performance.

There was a great deal of talk in Moro about the new horse that month, occasional brief accounts in the *Optic* of small races in which Beasley's horse left the others far behind. The *Optic* called him the Racer. Most Anglos referred to him as the Arabian, the Mexicans as El Arabe. Beasley challenged any horse in the territory, and this was freely quoted in talk and print. But if Ellen saw or heard of it, she ignored it. The only time she referred to it was when, nettled by her silence to the challenge, I blurted out that people thought she was afraid of running Critter.

I knew then by the instant brilliance of her eyes that I had struck fire.

"You haven't been down to the track, Jud?"

I kept silent. She gazed at me with that Spanish look of feminine hurt. Then she went on.

"Jud, when a member of Mama Grande's people died, they believed in mourning. A black cloth was put up at the door to tell people that those in the house were in sorrow so no one going by would laugh too loud or carry on unseemly. The native people respected it. Most of the men took off their hats when they passed. If the person who died was near and dear to us, the black cloth was kept up till it literally wore to pieces or blew away. Sometimes it was up for two years."

She stopped and watched me to see how I was taking it. Then she went on.

"The Anglos, when they came, had other customs. Now, I am part Anglo. I'm of the newer generation. I hate mourning. I refuse to put it on when I don't know what happened to Albert and Willy, where they are, whether they are living or dead. But that doesn't mean I race horses or even talk about racing them. I hoped that since Willy and Albert were your cousins, you'd feel the same way, that you wouldn't go near the track. People may see you and think that I sent you to spy on Snell's new horse. We know this is untrue, but they don't. The truth is that even if Albert and Willy were still here, I wouldn't race Critter. Critter isn't a racehorse. He's my buggy horse. He's devoted to me and I'm devoted to him. Long before Albert and Willy left us, people urged me to put him on the track. But I never have and I never will. I think this should be made more emphatic. The next time Tom comes to the house, I'll ask him to inform Snell and who ever else is necessary."

From the way Lawyer Beasley went by the next time I saw him, I suspected that Tom had told him. He had a look on his face that might be described as curdled amusement. He seemed to take Ellen's refusal as a kind of joke, as if he were saying to himself, so you think you won't race with me? It was curious to see an emotion like that working in the thick flesh and face of the man. He seemed to balance his heavy form with a certain triumph as if he felt she was afraid and that everyone else knew it, too, which gave him the title by point of rules.

But I didn't know Snell Beasley very well then, nor the extremes of cunning to which his ambition went, that he never would be satisfied with victory by forfeit, that his amusement and sense of triumph came rather from something else he was working out in his mind.

It was true that Ellen had put on no mourning. On the other hand, she had certainly given no parties since Cousin Albert had left, and when she went to another house for the evening it was only for a quiet dinner with friends. Mostly she busied herself with the ranch, was out with Mama Grande half the time. Once when Dr. Gammel called and found her away, he told me it was a good thing she had the sheep business to throw herself into. It took her mind off her tragedy.

Inevitably, when she was in town, she drove out for a ride in the afternoon. Often she took me along, and I could feel the good it did her when we got away from the lonely house and still more when we reached the end of town. Here were scenes with which Cousin Albert or Willy had been less actively associated and from which they did not keep leaping into her mind.

Also, I think it helped her just to go, to keep moving, to have the wheels turning and Critter bearing her on.

This afternoon she was not at the house when I came home. I went out to the stable. Critter's box stall was empty. Manuel told me she had left two hours before, that she said something about driving north to the Saturnino Montoyas'. As we talked we saw Goyo take the Beasley horse down the alley from the stable next door.

"Now where is he going in the runabout this time of day?" Manuel rumbled, moving to the door and looking after. "It's late for his patrón to drive anyplace."

Something in what he said or the way he said it aroused my curiosity, and I followed. As I went down the alley I fancied an air of expectancy in Old Town. A few more people than usual were out in the plaza, most of them moving down toward Audiencia Street. They glanced at me curiously, I thought, as I came after, some with amusement, some with anticipation in the dark eyes. I found the racehorse and runabout had stopped in front of Beasley's office. A little group gathered around them. As I approached, Beasley himself came out. I couldn't hear his careful orders to Goyo, who started driving the racehorse away. Beasley looked around, pleased, at the crowd. Tom Dold and Frank Gomez, the county treasurer, were across the street in front of the courthouse.

"If she won't race that fast horse of hers on the track, we'll have to do it on her own ground," he called.

I learned afterward that Beasley himself had seen Ellen drive north on New Town Road. It was the same road my father had taken to the Greenhorns and Ellen to the Pereas'. But all I was aware of at the time was people moving down Audiencia Street. I followed, giving no sign of recognition to Tom Dold, and I noticed that he gave none to me.

A few spectators already waited on New Town Road when we reached it, and the number increased as the news got abroad. The hack that customarily met the train came with some citizens from New Town. They piled out, hailing friends in the crowd. A spirited air pervaded most of the spectators, Anglos and Mexicans alike. But uneasiness, I thought, could be felt among the sheep people, and this was my own feeling.

Far up the road I could see Goyo driving slowly north. Not a sign of another horse or rig as far as my eyes could reach. Maybe she won't come, I said to myself hopefully, surprised at my reluctance to have the match finally come off, I who had earlier urged her to arrange it. Finally, far up the road toward the Montoyas' I thought I saw a puff of dust rising.

Before I could be sure, Lino García came along with his old crowbait and water cart loaded with barrels and boys. They stopped and Pas Ramírez sent a García boy back among the empty barrels to make room for me on the seat. Then we drove north on the road to see what we could see. The dust now included a dot, and my eyes strained on the speck, hoping it might be only a light wagon or saddle horse of some rancher.

Pas Ramírez was the first to identify it.

"It's her—la doña," he said, adding the latter out of respect to me.

I couldn't be sure, but as we went on and the speck came toward us, my eyes finally made out the yellow-top buggy. I knew the horse must be Critter, probably trotting a little faster on the way home. Alone in the seat would be Ellen, unsuspecting what lay ahead. As she approached we saw Goyo, still traveling toward her, look over his shoulder several times as if measuring the distance back to Old Town. He drew the racer to a walk as the yellow-top buggy came close.

Hardly had the two rigs passed when Goyo swung the chestnut around. It seemed Beasley had given him wise and wily instructions, for he waited until the buggy must have been a hundred yards in front. Then we thought we saw him shake the reins and the racehorse started to come from behind. We were not close enough to see, but I could imagine Critter's ears pricking at the sound of hoofs overtaking him and Ellen tightening the reins to hold him, which I knew well she could never do. All we definitely saw was Goyo pulling out to the left to go around, and then the two horses side by side and neither one passing, by which we knew they had started to run.

"Mira! Here they come!" Pas Ramírez yelled, and we all stood up.

Those were the days of no fences. The road lay across the prairie and was wide as you chose to make it. My mind was taken up, as always when I came in contact with Beasley, with the astute craftiness of the schemer. Here was a natural racecourse, a straightaway for miles, as were so many Western roads, with Old Town, including its audience of inhabitants, as the finish. Looking at the horses from in front, we had no idea how fast they were already coming. Only in the nick of time did Lino recognize our danger. Never, in my opinion, would either of the two horses have stopped for us. Lino got his cart off the road just as they went by. I had a glimpse of Critter, the bit between his teeth, that stubborn forward look to his head and neck, and of Ellen looking helpless and exasperated in the buggy, sawing vainly on the lines to hold him, while half a length behind him the racehorse tore on, eyes glazing, his mane and tail streaming, Goyo half raised from the seat, the whip in his hand.

Once they were by, all we could see were the two rigs through a cloud of dust. Although Lino whipped his crowbait and sent him galloping behind them, none of us could tell for sure which was ahead, only that they were still on opposite sides of the road as they reached Old Town. By the time we got there, they were far beyond. I had a glimpse of Tom Dold and the county treasurer looking thoughtful and of Beasley turning away darkly toward his office while the Mexicans chattered in great animation and the sheepmen looked solidly pleased.

We learned afterward that never for a moment had Goyo been able to get around the yellow-top buggy, that at the outskirts of town Ellen was almost a length ahead, and that when they reached where the crowd stood the thickest, Critter was still going like such a torrent she daren't think of turning up Audiencia Street but kept him on New Town Road. He was halfway to the railroad tracks before she could stop him. The water cart took me part

of the distance. I got out and ran the rest on foot. When I reached the buggy, Ellen, white and shaken, was driving Critter slowly back, his coat laid from neck and shoulders halfway to his rump with sweat.

"You devil!" she was saying angrily to him when she stopped to let me in.

"He was wonderful," I told her.

"He's a stubborn, vain, unprincipled brute!" she answered. "I could kill him with good grace."

We saw a black knot of people up around Audiencia Street waiting for her to drive back, but to my disappointment she turned up Alameda Street to the plaza to avoid them. I protested.

"They saw Critter come in ahead and that's enough," she insisted. "They shouldn't have seen that much. There was no occasion for a race at this time and no decency in it. They should know it."

XII

Despite Ellen's anger over the race, it did her good, I think. Her victory over Beasley softened, if faintly, some of her bitterness against him. She felt more resigned. By the time fall came around, it seemed that the agitation over Cousin Albert's and Willy's disappearance had begun to blow over.

Then word arrived that a sheepherder in a remote corner of Baca County had seen a cowboy from the Bar B ranch riding Dan, one of Cousin Albert's horses. Salomón Baca, owner of the sheep, had taken his herder to town to swear out an affidavit. A few nights later the herder's flock was scattered and trampled by horses and the herder himself killed. A warrant had been issued for the cowboy and Beasley had been engaged to defend him.

Now things were all stirred up again. The incident, with many versions and details, was on everyone's lips, reviving the earlier tragedy that had mothered it. Hardly had all this happened when word came that a body had been discovered. That evening Amado Martínez called at the house and was closeted with Ellen. They wouldn't let me in the room. When the sheriff left, he patted my shoulder. Ellen had come out more composed than I expected.

"I have news for you, Jud. They've found your father," she said.

It's always been very much of a riddle to me the way things happen, the pattern in which they appear. We expect one thing, foresee a certain conclusion, but something unforeseen often comes about. It's as if the mind or power making the moves on life's chessboard plays the game on a scale and with a code that we can never comprehend. Try as we might to take in all the facts and sift the probabilities, what eventually turns out is often something that none of us expected. Here had been the tragic disappearance of one of the most prominent persons in the territory and his son, a mystery which many had tried to solve. It was generally supposed they had been buried in the desolate wastes, and now a body was found. But instead of it being one of the missing pair, it was the body of my father, whose disappearance by this time had been almost forgotten except by me and I had stoutly believed him still alive.

When Ellen told me, my face must have gone white, for she led me to one of the couches and put her arm around me. She told me quietly all the sheriff had said to her. The body had been found in a high canyon in the Greenhorn Mountains, where it had lain covered by snow most of the year. Apparently he had been taken there alive, murdered, and the money stolen. They were bringing the body back to Moro now.

"Don't worry. Your father will have Christian burial in the Protestant cemetery. I'll see Reverend Crandall myself in the morning."

We found next day that the sheriff hadn't told everything, that much of the body had been preyed on by birds and vermin and only the pair of heavy trousers had kept the flesh intact below. They wouldn't let me see it, but I think Ellen had and it must have made a shocking impression on her. All the while the minister read the burial service over the tightly closed pine coffin, her mind, I think, was not on the ravages of wild creatures and the elements on the body inside of it, but on the bodies of Cousin Albert and Willy, still unfound.

There were those who said that Ellen Sessions had refused to wear mourning for her husband and son but had put it on for the father of her cousin by marriage. This was unadulterated nonsense. My father's death and burial had only brought home to her the shocking realities of Willy's and Cousin Albert's disappearance. Now she felt she had no other way than to accept them as dead and all it implied. She wore no mourning at my father's funeral. The day afterward she took the train to Denver to buy materials, and, when she came back, called the dressmakers in.

She looked older, thinner, and if anything more beautiful in black the morning she asked me to stay home from school. Her face, I thought, was like marble.

"I want to call on Mr. Beasley," she told me. She had never called him that before. "I haven't discussed the matter with Tom or anyone, but I feel I would like to have a witness. You're the only son I have now, Jud, and I wish you would go along." Just the way she looked at me, I felt a dependence that made me more of a man.

Never have I fancied lawyers' offices very much in general or Snell Beasley's in particular. Much would I have given to get out of going with her that morning. I put on my best gray suit and new black stockings as if dressing for church or the scaffold, and Ellen, when I saw her, did not reassure me. She seemed calm enough, as if going to church, but there was with it a certain sad and bitter dedication which I have seen some women assume in religious services but which Ellen had never before affected.

To my surprise, Manuel was waiting with Critter and the buggy outside.

We could have easily walked the short distance to the plaza, then crossed
it to Audiencia Street and down half a block to Burro Alley and the dusty
brick building across the street from the courthouse.

More than once had Ellen instructed Willy and me how, when we were
with her, to leap out first and help her down from the buggy. I tried to do
that now, especially since there were men in front of the courthouse watching. I'm sure I didn't know what I was doing, but Ellen gravely accepted my
help. Then, without knocking, she went into the office and I followed.

My first impression was the strong stale scent of tobacco and tobacco ashes
and the stronger reek of cuspidors. I saw George Steffy look up in surprise
and a little fright, I thought, from his desk piled with books and papers,
while behind him through the parted doors which did not open on hinges
as other doors I knew but were drawn apart, I had a glimpse of a deeper
and more dangerous region. This Ellen at once entered, not stopping at Mr.
Steffy's desk to inquire as I supposed she would.

There was nothing for me to do except push after. I found we were in a large room with shelves. One whole wall was lined with yellow leather books, and on the other hung framed pictures of men and of horses, of the Beasley house, of the courthouse, and even of the corner of Burro Alley and Audiencia Street with Beasley standing in front of his brick office. There were chairs and a green bag on the floor, and in the corner the largest desk I ever saw, a great flat-top piled still more with documents and books than George Steffy's, and behind the desk the thick form and powerful face of Willy's Uncle Snell. His face wasn't lifted. It was only the eyes that peered up, almost squinted, as if to say, who is this?—the fierce large eye and the smaller drooping one which I had heard referred to as "his little bitty eye." I don't know which one frightened me the most.

Hearing something, I turned and saw George Steffy hastily take his hat and leave, closing both doors carefully behind him. I had the feeling that Beasley would dress him down properly afterward for not stopping us, but now that he was cornered and had no way to escape except with ignominy, he faced us and I felt that in the last analysis it was not he who was cornered but we who had foolishly entered his den and put ourselves at his mercy.

Even Ellen seemed aware of this. She seated herself on the edge of a chair with a rawhide seat which looked dirty to me, and regarded him for a few moments.

"I've come to you in peace, Snell, to ask a favor."

She said it humbly, almost abased, but I saw it didn't appease her brother-in-law. At her words a tongue of red fire seemed to leap up and enliven the cavern of his fierce eye for a moment while his little bitty eye gave no clue. She went on.

"I want to ask if you will speak to your clients for me. I mean the cattlemen in Baca County. I beg of them to tell me something. Oh, I don't want to know who was involved in this terrible thing or any detail of what happened. All I ask of them is to let me know where the bodies of Willy and Albert may be found so I can bring them to Moro, have them decently buried and the Christian service read over them."

It seemed a small and deserving request to me, but I noticed no answering pity or sympathy in his eyes.

"And you feel my cattlemen clients should be able to tell you that?" he asked in a tone which I didn't recognize then but which I do now as that of a powerful lawyer leading a witness into a trap where he would presently destroy him.

"I do," Ellen answered.

"Perhaps you feel that I myself might be able to tell you?"

"God forbid," Ellen said so low I could scarcely hear her.

"What do you mean by that?"

"Just God forbid," she repeated.

To my dismay, an expression of righteous indignation gripped him at her reply. The lower part of his face twitched, and I had the feeling that deeper forces were inexplicably stirring and rising from unknown pits inside of him.

"You say you come in peace and then insult and vilify me by your aspersions." He spoke in a surprisingly calm and controlled voice. "First, let me point out that there is not the slightest proof that your boy and husband are dead as you assume, let alone murdered and hidden in the wilderness as you insinuate. Secondly, you assume that the perpetrators of such a gross and hideous crime are my own clients who could tell you where the bodies are, if they wished, and that this makes me either a dupe ignorant of the true nature of my clients or a confederate equally guilty with them of murder. Thirdly, you set up this imaginary set of circumstances and accusations and forget that if these grossly improbable things were true it would still be you and your husband who by persecution of other human beings set in motion acts against God and man that brought the final culmination to pass."

If he had stopped there, I thought he might have had something, but his flush of triumph carried him on. His little bitty eye twinkled like a dark star.

"Finally, you seem to have overlooked or won't admit the report I have heard from a number of sources, and which from association and relationship with you I must respect, that Albert has long been growing weary of your efforts to dominate and influence his judicial acts, so that finally he had no other course than to knowingly and willfully abandon you to your fate."

Ellen rose to her feet.

"That's a lie, Snell, and you know it."

He sat looking at her with satisfaction that was positively evil.

" 'The truth is mighty and will prevail,' " he quoted. " 'The mills of God grind slowly but they grind exceedingly small.' For a long time you have been riding high. You have done what you liked and been above the law. You have influenced and manipulated the law in the cases of others, causing in the end the ruin of your brother, your husband and son. You have even tried to interfere with the personal life of your sister and her household. But now reality has caught up to you and you will have to face justice and reformed conditions. No longer are you able to dictate to the bench."

Ellen's cheeks were flat white.

"Are you going to get me the information I asked, Snell, so Albert's and Willy's bodies can be brought home and decently buried?"

He gazed at her with baneful delight.

"I have told you that I know nothing, that my clients know nothing. Now I will add that, on the contrary, did my clients know something and had they given me the information in the priestly confidence that exists between an honorable lawyer and his client, I could and would tell you nothing, and the courts would sustain me. No, not even if the bodies of Albert and Willy were buried as you say, their remains to be dug up by coyotes and other scavengers of the wild and never to be found or seen by humankind again."

He was a devil, the very devil himself, I thought. For a little while Ellen stood shocked and trembling. Then she took my arm and we left. Critter and the yellow-top buggy were waiting. I helped her in. We drove off. She said no word to me on the way home, not until she reached the door of the house.

"I hoped it could be done without further bloodshed, Jud, but now I see he must be dealt with as the dog he is."

"Cousin Ellen, don't!" I begged, following her into the house, where she stopped and turned.

"What, Jud?" she asked quietly.

"I don't know," I stammered, unwilling to put my fear into words that could trouble us both.

Her eyes probed mine.

"I'm glad you came along, Jud. It's sometimes better to know that life may be a more serious and inescapable thing than you think when you are young. Then you feel the world is good and troubles can always be avoided. But when you grow older you find that they hem you in, first on one side and then on the other, and finally you get to a point where you can no longer live honorably, when the dead cry out for justice but nobody will administer it and you've got to attend to it yourself."

I didn't know fully what she meant, but I knew enough. As she disappeared behind the door, I had a moment's glimpse of her room, the carved bureau and wardrobe, the Brussels carpet on the floor, the polished French brass bed. There were lacy things hanging from the ceiling, and a painted fragile china lamp on a stand. All was very feminine except for one jarring note. In the far corner beside the bed I had the glimpse of an object from the ranch. Only the barrel was visible above the elaborate bedcover, but it was enough. I knew that ever since Charley had been shot, she had kept a pearl-handled revolver lying on the marble-top table at the head of her bed. Now I was aware that on our return from her search of the malpai she must have brought her light rifle to town, and I wondered how she had managed it in the buggy so that I didn't see it.

Ellen didn't appear for lunch or dinner that day. This was most unusual. Not even on the day the news came about Cousin Albert and Willy had she taken to her room. I hoped that Dr. Gammel or Tom Dold or some of her other friends might come this evening, but no one called.

"How is she?" I asked Chepa when she brought out the tray that evening.

"You can see for yourself," Chepa said, showing me the food almost untouched.

"Shouldn't I go for Dr. Gammel?"

"For what? She is not sick. She is not in bed. She just walks the room. She is like a leona. I heard where you were today, but what did she do?"

"It was Señor Beasley who did it," I said.

"Ah, him!" Chepa nodded grimly and went out in the kitchen.

That evening I lay on a settee in the wide hall near the door to her room. Twice I heard the scratching of a pen. The cutting strokes made me uneasy. Later when all was silent, I heard the door open.

"Jud, what are you doing there?"

"I guess I lay down and fell asleep."

"Well, go to your bed," she ordered me.

I did with reluctance as she told. There was something about my room this evening that gave me an unpleasant feeling. I looked out of the window. Then I knew what it was. Light shone in the Beasley home next door, especially in the room opposite Ellen's bedroom. I could see just the top of the window. Before the wall had been put up Willy and I had often watched his Uncle Snell sitting in this room, which served as an office at home. Invariably he was at his desk under the light of a green-shaded oil lamp. The same colored light came from the top of the window tonight. Standing on the bed, I could peer over the wall and see him sitting at the desk now, going over a pile of papers.

Ellen's room was next to mine. From the absence of light falling on our side of the wall, I could tell that it was in darkness. And yet from time to time I thought I heard her moving about. Then I couldn't lie still, but had to stand up on my hard Mexican bed and stare at the black target of Beasley sitting at his desk by the green-shaded lamp. I would stand a long time, rigid, waiting, listening, until from sheer weariness I would lie down again.

Once when I pushed back the covers and stood up, the light from Beasley's window was gone. The brick house was dark, the windows dim and silent. When I lay down, I could see far over the roof next door the stars shining steadily in the velvety dark-blue territorial sky. Gratefully I closed my eyes and let sleep overtake me.

XIII

I seldom saw Ellen now until noon. She stayed in the seclusion of her room. What she did in there all the morning was a mystery that I felt could be fathomed only by other ladies and their maids. Chepa went in from time to time with hot water, breakfast and other things. Sometimes I would hear talking, but it was mostly in Chepa's voice or that of Epifania, who went in, too. When Ellen dressed and came out at last, I was always a little shocked at what I saw. This was not the Ellen I knew. She looked as if she hadn't slept, as if she had had a battle most of the night.

Nights were bad for me, too. I thought what a relief it would be to leave the tragic white house and its brick companion next door. I asked why we didn't go to the ranch. Out there I felt I could sleep untroubled by every stir and creaking. It would be pure bliss to crumple up on my stomach at night and let the world go, knowing it would take care of itself till morning. But she wouldn't leave. Something would come into her face.

"No, Jud, I can't. Not yet," she would say.

Several times when I heard Chepa or Epifania going in or out or when Dr. Gammel came, I tried to post myself where I would get a glimpse inside. I wanted to see if the rifle was still there, but never was I quick enough.

Tom and the doctor called most every day. I know Tom Dold asked her to marry him, and I felt that the doctor had always wanted her. But she was impatient with them both.

"What do you have in your blood that other men don't have?" she asked me once, and I learned that she was thinking of Cousin Albert. "Why do some men talk too much? It's a woman's art and right. A man should sit quietly and let a woman do the talking. He should be warmed and refreshed by it. And if the woman is in no mood to talk, he should be sympathetic and silent. But I must listen to Tom Dold reciting all the petty doings of the court, especially of Snell Beasley, and all the stories going the rounds. Half of them he's told me before. Then I must be bored stiff listening to the doctor talk about the mistakes of Moses and the sins of the church and the morality of being an atheist or agnostic and all the sayings of Robert Ingersoll. You know I'm no saint myself or too strong a believer, but I can't swallow the righteousness of the ungodly and the wickedness of the good."

The third of the faithful trio who came to see her was Father Goshard, the big gaunt Belgian, who could often be seen with a small Mexican girl in each hand in front of the church and rectory on the plaza. He liked young people and usually asked me to stay in the sala when he called. Ellen seldom treated him with the pious reverence showed him by most of her people. The first time I heard them together I feared he would be offended, but soon I saw that he took delight in her attitude toward him as an equal and in her quick readiness to give her opinion on the most sacred of matters.

I remember once after they had disputed back and forth for an hour, Ellen turned to me.

"It's not in me to let any man get the upper hand of me, Jud, not even my saintly and dogmatic spiritual father."

That, I reflected, was a fair statement of Ellen.

"I agree with the French woman, Father, on your silly story about Eve," she said at another time. "Not temptation but gluttony must have been the first sin. I think you'd agree, too, if you priests were women with a babe guzzling and gorging at your breast."

It shocked me a little, but the priest only laughed that day. He seemed heartily to enjoy her unpredictable contradictions. But he did not laugh now at her acrimonious thrusts at God and man, and especially not at her bitterness over the impunity of Snell Beasley.

"Why should he still be alive after what happened to Albert and Willy?" she asked once.

" 'Vengeance is mine, saith the Lord.' "

"Then why are there public trials and executions?" she said quickly. "Why not let it all to God?"

"There is the duty of serving the established courts of law and order," the priest said. "And there is taking the law into our own hands, serving the baser passions in our own breasts."

"I fight," Ellen said in a low voice. "But it goes hard and takes very long."

" 'My yoke is easy and my burden is light!' " the priest quoted. "You are young. There is still peace and happiness for you."

"If you refer to another marriage sometime, Father, it could never be even if I wished it," she said. "I'll never really know if Albert is dead."

The old priest watched her from the deep eyes in his gaunt face.

"Why don't you submit to the will of God, child?" he asked. "Where and by what means Judge Sessions and Willy came to leave this life, we don't know. But the fact of their departure is evident to all. It's better to accept it and have Masses said for your son's soul."

"Sometimes it's best not to admit too much to one's self, Father," Ellen answered. "So long as there's hope, there's less evil in the world and in the heart."

I think the priest caught that.

"You put your faith not in God, child, but in rumors," he chided. "I hear these rumors, too. Somebody has seen the judge or Willy in California or Wyoming or Old Mexico—mostly in Old Mexico. They are living or kept there now against their will. It takes money to investigate these rumors. I hear someone is always traveling far for you at your expense."

"What is money beside the lives of those you love?" she asked.

"There are many rumors in the world and little truth in any of them, child. Their only vitality is in the hope they arouse. When they prove false, there is bitter disappointment and renewal of hatred."

"That's true, Father," Ellen admitted. "But if someone tells me he has seen Albert or Willy alive, I can't sit idly by and do nothing. They may need me. And I can't sit idly by when my own brother-in-law defends the man seen with one of Albert's horses and who murdered the sheepherder who testified to it."

"Have no fear, child," the priest said, "God will not defend the wicked. The courts will never acquit him."

That's what we all thought, and it was a shock even to me when word came from Baca County that the cowboy had been freed. The Baca County jury, we heard, had been putty in Beasley's hands. I hoped for his own safety that he would be detained at court in Baca County a long time. But at noon the second day after the news, Manuel told me that the racehorse was back in the stable.

Most of the stables of Old Town were of one-story adobe. Even ours, although larger than most, was of a single floor, with a large carriage room and another for hay and feed and a still smaller one with harness on the wall and a bunk for Manuel. The Beasley stable was different, of brick like the house and of a shape like stables of rich men in Missouri, with gables and a fancy roof rising to a kind of central pinnacle topped with a weathervane where an iron arrow swung in the wind.

I was standing in the alley looking gloomily at the brick house and wondering how it would all end when I saw a hand beckon me from the stable. Walking closer, I saw it again. The doors were open. Beasley's runabout and sulky were both there, the shafts up against the wall, the racer in his stall, but Goyo was out somewhere. I wondered what I had seen. Then Felicitas stepped out from behind the steps as I went in.

"What do you want?" she demanded.

"I don't want anything," I told her.

"You'll catch it, coming over here."

"What did you call me for, then?"

"I never called you."

"Maybe not out loud, but your hand did."

"It did not."

"Then you must have the St. Vitus dance or something."

"I don't have St. Vitus dance, but you'll have it if my father catches you."

"Maybe he won't be up and around long to catch me," I told her enigmatically.

We fought for a good while, but she didn't tell me to go. The longer I stayed, the surer I was she had beckoned me. When her small brother, Jackie, came in and surprised us, she surprised me by calling me Goyo and making sure Jackie understood by pointing to me.

"Goyo! Goyo!" she said.

"Goyo," little Jackie said too, peering at me doubtfully, and I marveled at the inherited cunning in the girl, protecting herself by preparing his brain if he should repeat anything of my presence to his father.

"Goyo goes by-by now," I said mockingly and turned to leave.

"Wait," she said, swiftly coming after me to the door where she took a small bunch of flowers from under her apron. I don't know the English name, but we called them maritas in Spanish. She held them out to me.

"For Willy," she said in a low voice.

"Willy's dead," I said harshly.

"I know," she told me.

For a moment I considered taking the flowers from her hand and throwing them on the manure pile, but in the end I took them to Ellen, saying they were for Willy from Felicitas. I refrained from adding what she had said about Willy being dead. For the first time in days I saw Ellen's face soften. She poured water herself from her bedroom pitcher and set the flowers in a vase on the marble-top table in her room.

XIV

It was Felicitas's flowers, I believe, that for a time staved off the inevitable, touched a spot in Ellen that neither Tom nor the doctor or priest had been able to reach. Before the maritas wilted, she dried them and tied the golden-brown bunch with white ribbon. They were the only flowers she had to stand for Willy's death, and they made a bond now between her and Felicitas. But they made, if anything, no more than an uneasy truce between her and Felicitas's father, I felt, and that it would never last.

Gracias á Dios, Chepa used to say, that we mortals never know what is ahead for us. Now I have heard Mexicans speak otherwise, especially old sheepherders who had spent their lives reading the sky and range. They insist that the future is written down for us, every whit, that there are always signs. Fidel, the wisest man on the ranch, used to answer, yes, of course, it is all written down, but who can read the handwriting of el Dios? As for signs, who knows for sure what they mean until he can look back and see what they portended by the things that came to pass?

What was destined to happen those years is all to be found today in dusty files. First came the heavy winter snowfall that turned the range the following summer into a garden for those sheep that hadn't been smothered by the snow. Then, like the lean years in Egypt after the fat years, came the great drought. For some twenty months no snow or rain worthy of the name fell.

But the worst was not yet, not until after the national elections. I remember going to the depot for Ellen to get the latest returns. Cleveland, if elected, had promised to put wool on the free list. What happened is history, but the interpretation is something else. I have heard it argued endlessly pro and con, depending on which side of the political fence you stood. Some claimed it was the free wool that brought the panic of '93, others that it was the drought. All I know is that wool dropped to seven cents a pound, in some cases to five, that sheep sold for a dollar apiece, and that such a time of ruin, desolation, and wretchedness ensued over the territory as I never saw before or since.

The only good I knew it to do was to bring an end to Ellen's mourning over what had happened to Willy and Cousin Albert.

"Thank God they are not living now!" more than once she told me.

It troubled me to think that it took a terrible means as this to bring a change in her, to restore her active old-time self. Energies that had lain dormant or been dammed up in her so long began to be released again in their natural channels. I remember her especially the following spring on the ranch which by now had become a ghastly place. The great Johnson y Campo lamb crop, once a rich source of income, had turned into a cruel liability. As they were born, lambs had to be killed to save their mothers. If we didn't, the milkless ewes would walk off and leave them to starve anyway. But Ellen was the patrona again, and I can still hear her voice heartening the discouraged lambers, the range around them desolate with dust and dead sheep under a pitiless sky.

The lambing was scarcely over when Mama Grande died. Fidel showed me the ground at the bottom of the grave still damp from the snows of two winters before, but from there on up the brown Southwestern soil was dry as dust.

"She knew better days. These were hard for her to take," Ellen told me. "She is better off out of this kind of world!"

But if Mama Grande was better off, Ellen wasn't. Just the sight of Beasley, when he arrived, brought up all I had heard of him lately—that there was no holding him, that these were times ripe for him and his kind. He was making himself a great fortune, perhaps the largest in the territory, calling notes, foreclosing, buying ranches for little or nothing. The days of the panic were only harvest time to him. I remembered what Father Goshard had said, that no man had great influence unless God gave him the power, and it sorely tested my faith in religion and goodness that God could favor and support such a man as J. Snell Beasley.

He came to the ranch alone driving his racehorse, which he ordered Teofilo to put up, almost as if he himself were the patrón. He met Ellen coolly and without pretense of regret at the death of his children's abuelita.

"Your sister hasn't been too well," he said. "I thought it best if she and the children were spared the ordeal of the funeral and also finding the ranch in such a state."

It was almost as if he had said a state of ruin and decay.

"I'm sorry for Ana's sake that she didn't come. All of us have only one mother," Ellen said.

He gave that cool look of his, a little out of focus, a little amused, a little terrifying, hinting without words or details of things still to come. I watched him at the funeral and afterward, not mingling with the mourners but striding about, putting his nose here and there, asking sharp questions of the peons, inspecting the ranch buildings, finally ordering his horse and buggy and driving off with goodbyes to no one.

"He is one I am glad to see go," Teofilo told me. "He makes my stomach to curl. He looks and he looks, but he tells nobody what he sees."

"They say he has the evil eye," an old man said. "Now which is it, the big eye that stares at you like a steer, or the little eye that squints at you like a bull?"

"I do not know about things like the evil eye," Fidel answered. "All I know is sorrow that our old doña is gone. Now our young doña stands alone against him and Doña Ana."

In the days that followed I saw, or thought I saw, that Tom Dold was worried too. I knew that Ellen was hard hit. She had spent thousands trying to solve the mystery of Cousin Albert and Willy, hoping to find their bodies. Some of this had gone to unscrupulous characters who preyed on her. Most of it she had borrowed. Now for some time banks and private lenders had been calling in their notes. Money was hard to get. Ellen was forced to sell thousands of sheep to the packing houses, and the pitifully small price per head was quickly swallowed up in interest and running expenses. I had hoped that Mama Grande's death might leave enough to pay Ellen's debts. I had heard stories of fortunes in gold and silver that Mexican ricos, afraid to trust banks, kept buried under their houses. But if Mama Grande had any secret hoard, we never knew of it. All she left was her share in the ranch, evenly divided between her two surviving daughters, and this brought not a dollar to Ellen.

It was singular to see Ellen unworried. The worse her situation, the more her debtors hounded her, the more it seemed to mend the deep wounds of her unsolved tragedy, to help her believe that perhaps Willy's and Albert's deaths were for the best after all. Almost never, except late at night, could she be found in her room. She and Critter were inseparable again. She drove him and her yellow-top buggy everywhere, to the ranch to manage what she had left, to her creditors to appease and stave them off, to her old Mexican family friends to borrow a little so she might hold on until better times returned.

It all agreed with her. Activity was her nature. I never saw her looking better. There were no visible signs of debts or difficulty. If anyone looked worried, it was Tom Dold or Mr. Kidd or the doctor or myself. When Mr. Kidd offered me a job at the commission house, I jumped at the chance. It meant I could contribute a little toward our expenses of living, although I knew I never dare mention this to Ellen. As it was, she felt plainly hurt when I told her.

"You're only a boy, Jud. You should be in school."

"I'm fifteen," I told her. "Lots of boys go to work at twelve."

"Is it that you miss Willy? Are you too alone in the house?"

I nodded. She was silent a long time and I knew of what she was thinking.

"Very well. Then I give my consent. But you must never leave me, Jud. Remember, this house is yours as long as you live."

It was like a breath of fresh air and a new life to leave the gloomy old white casa for the commission house, if only in the daytime. Young as I was, I became a member of the commission-house clan. I found it a big jolly family, free from tragedy, and very much alive, patronizing the same restaurant, dance hall, and livery stable, taking the same train to Trinidad on holidays, playing tricks on one another and especially on me, the newest member. We had a mandolin-and-guitar club, and one evening a week those off duty got together in Mr. Younger's office to practice the latest Eastern songs and pieces.

And yet through all my daily life in this hive of commerce, through the scent of sheep-dip and hides and of horses and mules from the loading platforms; through the sounds of business, banter, and the scratch of ledger pens; through the gray-brown dust of sandstorms and the white dust of unloading flour, I couldn't shut out the ugly day-by-day reports from the panic-ridden range, the sad things that were happening to others and which inevitably must engulf Ellen and the old Johnson y Campo name. The tragic part was that men still had to fight for their existence when times at last had begun to improve. The cycle had turned. Rain was already falling on the range, new grass appearing. Wool and lamb prices had steadied. The worst was over and most ranchers had begun to breathe hopefully again.

That was when Beasley played his hand. All through the months of drought and panic when expenses were heartbreaking and income nonexistent or trifling, he let Ellen struggle with Rancho Zelandia. But once the hardest times were over and promise of recovery and profit began to appear, then in the name of his half-owner wife he entered suit, filing a bill in equity, citing mismanagement, neglect, and non-payment of interest and principal on Ellen's notes which he had bought up in his wife's name, demanding an accounting, a receivership, and public sale of the ranch's real and personal property.

He entered the suit swiftly and without warning while court was still in session, and Judge Saxton put it through at the end of the term. Tom Dold struggled manfully, but he was no match for the weight of debt and charges which were true of many ranchers in these days. Moreover, Ellen refused to testify on any allegation that would make out her sister a liar.

"That's Snell, not Ana, speaking," was all she would say. Even if Judge Saxton had not owed his appointment to Beasley's influence, he would have had little choice in the matter. The case was heard without jury. Beasley's law partner, George Steffy, was named as receiver and the ranch and stock put on the block. Few except Ellen dared offend Beasley by bidding, and Ellen had neither cash nor collateral left to do it, nor wealthy friends to come to her assistance. The famous old Johnson y Campo ranch and stock, including the Grant, were bought by Beasley for less than fifty thousand, none of which would be divided with Ellen. Her share was to be paid to her sister on Ellen's unpaid debts.

I heard of the final blow at the commission house one afternoon. The same day Pas Ramírez, now a loader, cornered me against a car of outgoing wool.

"It is too bad, but she will fix him now?" he said.

"I don't know what you mean, Pas," I told him.

"Oh, you know, but you don't like to say it right out. You think it might be used in court against her. Don't worry, amigo. I would say nothing."

"I'm still not sure what you mean. If you mean what I think you do, you are dead wrong."

"No, you are the one who is wrong, amigo," he told me. "I know she has waited a long time. Years ago the wolf howled for his due. But the Anglo in her waited, thinking the foolish Anglo thought that if you pet him the wolf will turn into a dog. Sometimes the Spanish and Indian also wait a long time. But they know the wolf will always be a wolf. They wait for the best time to suit their purpose, and in the end they move. Now she has no other way. He has everything and she has nothing. She will not let him take the ranch, the only thing she has left. She will fix him now like she fixed Frank Jeffcoat long ago."

I went home hating to face Ellen that evening, but she wasn't at the house. The Wilmots had taken her home to dinner after the sheriff's sale. Chepa said she had sent word that it would be late when she came in. During the evening Dr. Gammel called and I told him where she was. Knowing he would be with her made me feel a little better. I didn't hear her when she came, and her door was closed when I went to the commission house in the morning.

But Chepa and Epifania told me enough. Their faces were dark and bitter.

"You know, Señor Jud?" they asked. They had added the "señor" only since I worked at the commission house.

"Yes, I know," I told them gloomily.

"She dare touch nothing on the ranch, only a few little things that he will say belong to her. Ay de mí! Did you ever hear of such a thing! What will become of her now?"

"I don't know," I told them, eating breakfast as fast as I could.

"There is a message for you," Chepa said. "She told me last night when she came in. She must go out to the ranch tomorrow. It is the last time. You must go with her."

I winced at that. It was like Ellen. Not, could I get off from work, but I must take off and go along. That day when I asked Mr. Kidd for leave, he gave me a look from under his black eyebrows and ordered me into his office. This was the mysterious, exclusive, unattainable room I had long wanted to see, but I scarcely looked around at it today.

"You know that this is the end of her and the ranch?" he asked.

"I'm afraid it is, sir."

"What is she going to do? How does she expect to live?"

"I don't know, sir."

"I suppose you think I should have given her a hand?"

"I didn't think about it, sir."

"Have you ever looked in our books?"

"Just my own ledger, sir."

"Well, if you had, you'd have found that we carried her for some nineteen thousand dollars. I could have sold the debt to Beasley long ago at twenty cents on the dollar. I didn't then, although it looked at the time like we'd never get a penny. You know that, don't you?"

"I don't know, sir."

Mr. Kidd looked at me. His eyes and eyebrows were both very dark. I knew she could expect no more help from that quarter.

"You don't know? What do you mean?"

"I don't know what I mean, sir."

"I think I know. It's no use, Jud. It's too late."

I had no idea what he meant. He sat for a long time staring away from me. The only thing in his line of vision was the painting of a naked and voluptuous woman half covered by a rare old Navajo blanket on the wall. He went on.

"You mean she's always been a lady."

"Yes, sir," I said, but that wasn't exactly what I meant.

"Jud, do you know what a lady is?"

"Yes, sir. I think I do."

"I don't think you do. A lady is a woman of great charm or position or both who because of it has never had to do anything for herself but has always had somebody to do it for her. Did you ever think of that before?"

"No, sir."

"Well, it's time you understood some of these things. Ellen was a Johnson y Campo. If there was a Campo who had more than she had, I never heard of it. She was born to the purple, to the ranch, to the family name, and money. There was always something or somebody to take care of her. When she was young, it was her father. When Frank Jeffcoat ruined her garden and one of them shot him, she had her brother Charley to fall back on. When Charley was tried, she had Albert to free him and to convict his murderers when they came to trial for another crime. Now Albert and Charley are gone. Her father and mother are gone. The ranch and her money are gone. She needs someone more than ever, somebody to take up her cause, solve her problems, and take care of her. There she is, attractive, beautiful, worldly. Tom Dold is a gentleman, but he's not your Cousin Albert by a long shot, and George Gammel drinks too much most of the time. There's nobody left to come to her rescue any more."

I kept thinking about it on the way to the ranch next morning with Ellen. The mesa had never looked more beautiful, the air like wine, the Prietas crystal clear, and the ranch headquarters, when we came to it, like the capitol of some small empire. It had rained during the night and the Johnson y Campo range looked fresh and green. It was the only time I recall that I would have preferred a sandstorm. With the sky gray, the sun a dull red ball, and dust flying, the ranch wouldn't have been so hard to give up.

Today it was an ordeal. I had never seen Fidel's face so grave as when he came to take Critter. Even the Casa Grande looked more desirable now that it was no longer Ellen's.

As we came up on the portal, one of the doors opened and Snell Beasley, thick, active, all business, appeared.

"You can come in," he said curtly, and I looked to see how Ellen liked being invited into her own house. She gave no sign, entering the familiar sala almost as a visitor, seating herself presently in the chair Beasley indicated, as if this house was not part of her, as if she hadn't been born in one room and spent much of her life in the others.

"I had hoped Ana would be here," she said quietly.

"No," Beasley answered. Then as if something in her remark had nettled him, he went on sharply: "Before we get to the few things you may claim, I want to tell you that I might have claimed a good deal more. We could have taken everything you have, the house in town and your horse and buggy."

All she said was a low "Thank you."

"No," he said heavily, "we don't want your house now or your horse. He's getting up in years. I have a better one. Now shall we get down to business?"

All through the scenes that followed I marveled at Ellen. How could she go through in a couple of hours what would normally take days to dispose of? How could she give up all this so calmly? What was going on in her head? Was she really the one she had been acting the role of lately, the gentlewoman courteously agreeing, accepting, taking with good grace her humiliation? Or could she be waiting like Pas implied, letting Beasley do his worst, seeing how far he would go, which would give her final violent act all the more reason and sympathy? Without some planned solution in her mind, I felt she couldn't control herself like this.

In the end she had me carry some small things to the buggy. She asked her brother-in-law to deliver the rest with Teofilo or Fidel.

"Now we must go, Jud," she said.

First she drove around the ranch headquarters, the lambing pens, the chapel, then to the edge of the cedars where Willy and I used to ride. She was taking a last look at everything.

"Look," she said once, "I don't need to touch a line. He knows where to go."

It was true. Critter seemed to know. He went to the cemetery and beyond it to a spot where the whole Grant could be seen spread out before us with the Greenhorn Mountains a white crown to the north.

"I think Critter wants to see it himself," Ellen said. Then to the horse, "Now that's enough. He'll think we're stealing something. Sooner or later we've got to go home."

When we returned to headquarters, the Mexicans, who had been watching, were waiting for us. It was a scene like I had witnessed before but not with today's implications. I saw again that, charming as she could be with her own kind, she was at her best with those below her, with children, servants, peons, those who looked up to her, Mexicans or Anglos. Then something transformed her and she burned with a purity and simplicity that is difficult to set down. No actress could have matched her. She stepped down from the buggy to shake every hand, had a word in Spanish for each, an act that caused many of them, especially older men and women, to break down and fall on their knees, kissing her hand or skirt, pouring out their memories of her father and mother and Don Carlos.

What Beasley must have thought if he watched from the window, I have no idea. But as we drove up through the canyon I bled for her. I began to see more clearly what Mr. Kidd had said, that always she had had this great ranch behind her, someone to espouse her cause and solve her problems. What had she left now? To whom could she go any more? All she had were a house in town, an old horse, and a young stripling like me.

As for Critter, he seemed weary as I. Once we had left the steeper downslope where the buggy rolled of its own volition, I noticed that he dragged. It was true he had already traveled from town to ranch that day, but there had been a time when twenty miles would scarcely have laid a hair on him.

I mentioned something of this to Ellen.

"He's older," she said. "But not old. He's still younger than Willy. They were born almost on the same day two years apart."

Just the way she said it made me glance at her. She sat there on the faded cushions of her yellow-top buggy, erect, well dressed as always, her suit coat and skirt of the best English material, her little green hat with the feather jaunty, her driving gloves open at the wrist and flaring in the genteel manner.

"He's older," I insisted. "We're all older."

"He says you're older, boy," she said.

At the sound, Critter broke at once into a faster pace, but presently slowed again to his old trot. We were well on the mesa when I glanced back and saw another rig behind us, just emerging from the cedars at the mouth of the canyon. Farther out on the mesa I looked again. It was still there, almost the same distance behind us as before. Whoever it was showed no disposition to close the gap between. But when we reached the pile of rocks blackened on one side from fires of generations of leñeros, I thought the rig was definitely nearer and that the horse looked like Beasley's.

Ellen never looked back at all. We passed the region of rolling lomas, crossed the big cañada and the Prieta Wash, and were on the almost level part of the mesa when I thought I heard a steel shoe strike a stone. Glancing again, I saw the rig closer behind us now and coming fast. It was definitely the runabout and the racer with Beasley himself driving. I'm sure Critter heard the sound, too. His ears had pricked and his pace increased. Ellen heard it now and looked over her shoulder.

Afterward she told Tom and me that her first impulse had been to turn Critter directly off the road to the north. She guessed at once, as did I, that Beasley had chosen the spot to race, that he was unsatisfied with taking the ranch and sheep, that now with the town just ahead of us in plain view across the river he intended to beat her horse and take the only laurels she had left. For a moment, she told us, she hesitated to humiliate Critter, make him show the white feather, and by the time she had made up her mind it was too late. Critter had definitely accepted the challenge.

I had been in races behind Critter before and have been in others since, but there was something about this one that troubled me from the start. Even the mesa, the sight of Moro lying spread out on the river plain below, and the low Tecoletenos Mountains far on the horizon had a different look and feel today. But it was Critter who moved me the most, no longer the pet but the old servitor unwilling to admit his years.

Some men mellow as they age, leave the fires of manhood behind them and handle better than in their youth. Critter was none of these. Ellen knew it, I'm sure. I had seen her half stand at the lines before, but never her shoes so planted on the foot iron, her body weight and strength thrown against the bit. I still don't know, was it her long aversion to race Critter or her woman's intuition to try to save him from his first defeat? Either way, there was no stopping him today more than any other time. This she soon found out. He had the will to go, and there was nothing to do but let him have his way.

I did feel that Critter had the advantage of the road. The racer would have to take the rougher ground beside it. Critter's mane and tail were streaming and yet as we went on something in him fell short. I remembered his old effortlessness, when without the benefit of trying he seemed to fly like the road-runner, half on the ground, half in the air. Today he seemed to run as fast as he ever did, but the magic of easy power was lacking. I could feel the undercurrents of exertion, striving, and strain.

Slowly but steadily the racer pulled up beside him. When he was younger, the near approach of the other horse would have been the signal for Critter to let loose a burst of speed that would have left his rival far behind. Now it was apparent that Critter had already given his best. I had a glimpse of Beasley squatting forward on his light runabout seat, his arms outstretched. As he came abreast he threw us a curious cool, almost impassive look, then flicked his whip and the chestnut started pulling ahead.

"Help me, Jud!" Ellen suddenly panted.

She was having trouble with the right-hand line, I noticed, and the moment I took hold of it with her, I knew why she had called me. Critter was pulling hard toward his rival. I used both hands but without effect. Despite our three arms, there was no holding him. We might as well be pulling on a locomotive. Never had he let a horse around him, and he wouldn't now. I fancied I saw the wild look in his eye toward his rival. Then with a furious swerve that carried us with him like matchsticks he threw himself against the chestnut and all was lost in a crashing of buggies and bodies and horses upturned with their legs in the air.

They said afterward that a dozen people in Moro watched the race, that it was especially visible from the depot and the commission house, where men quickly climbed to the roof to see the outcome. In almost no time riders and rigs were hurrying to ford the river and reach the scene. What had happened they couldn't tell from town, but they knew it was bad. What they found was a boy with a broken arm, a woman with a scarred and bleeding face, one horse still on the ground, the other standing quietly by in broken shafts, his only sign of disaster the brown dirt smeared on his sweated hide. That was the racer, but his driver lay under the overturned runabout, and when strong hands righted it, he still lay unmoving.

Ellen waited till Dr. Gammel finished with him.

"Look at Critter!" then she begged him, which he did.

"He's done for. The broken shaft hooked him. He looks like he hit barb wire. I doubt if he's got any blood left. The kindest thing you can do for him is let me shoot him and put him out of his misery."

Such a look of blinding anger came into Ellen's eyes that I thought the doctor quailed.

"I would shoot you first, George!" she told him, and sent to town for Manuel.

We stayed until Manuel came and for some time afterward, until Critter was on his unsteady feet. Then we drove down with Tom Dold in his buggy. People on Audiencia Street and the plaza watched silently as we drove by. When we reached La Placita, a little group stood in front of the Beasley house.

"I must go to Ana first," Ellen said.

I followed with my bandaged arm. Tom Dold and the doctor helped her up the steps. She did not knock. One of them opened the door for her and she went in. I had a glimpse of Ana surrounded by Beasley's friends and their wives. What would happen now I had no notion. But when Ana looked up and saw Ellen, it was as if no one but they were in the room. A strange nameless cry rose from each of them, and the two sisters ran into each other's arms.

I watched them for a long moment. Tears flowed from them both. It was the first time I had seen Ellen cry. The pair kept embracing, comforting, chattering to each other, as only the Spanish can. It was strange that at a time like this I should remember what Mr. Kidd had said, that Ellen's deliverers were all gone, that there was no one left to rescue a lady any more, and yet here she was, delivered in the arms of her only sister, the widow of probably the richest man in the territory.

I wish it were possible to add that Willy and Cousin Albert came back. For years I kept saying to myself, it can't end like this—they will surely turn up someday. But they never did. Their bodies were never found. Only the whispering wind knows where they lie, for those unknown men involved in it must be dead today. Now, looking back over sixty years, I feel this may be the reason why the unsolved mystery remains to many of us the most haunting of earlier happenings in the annals of New Mexico.